FAVORITE
FAIRY TALES

THE CHILDHOOD CHOICE
OF REPRESENTATIVE
MEN AND WOMEN

ILLUSTRATED
BY
PETER NEWELL

NEW YORK AND LONDON
HARPER & BROTHERS PUBLISHERS
MCMVII

CONTENTS

iii

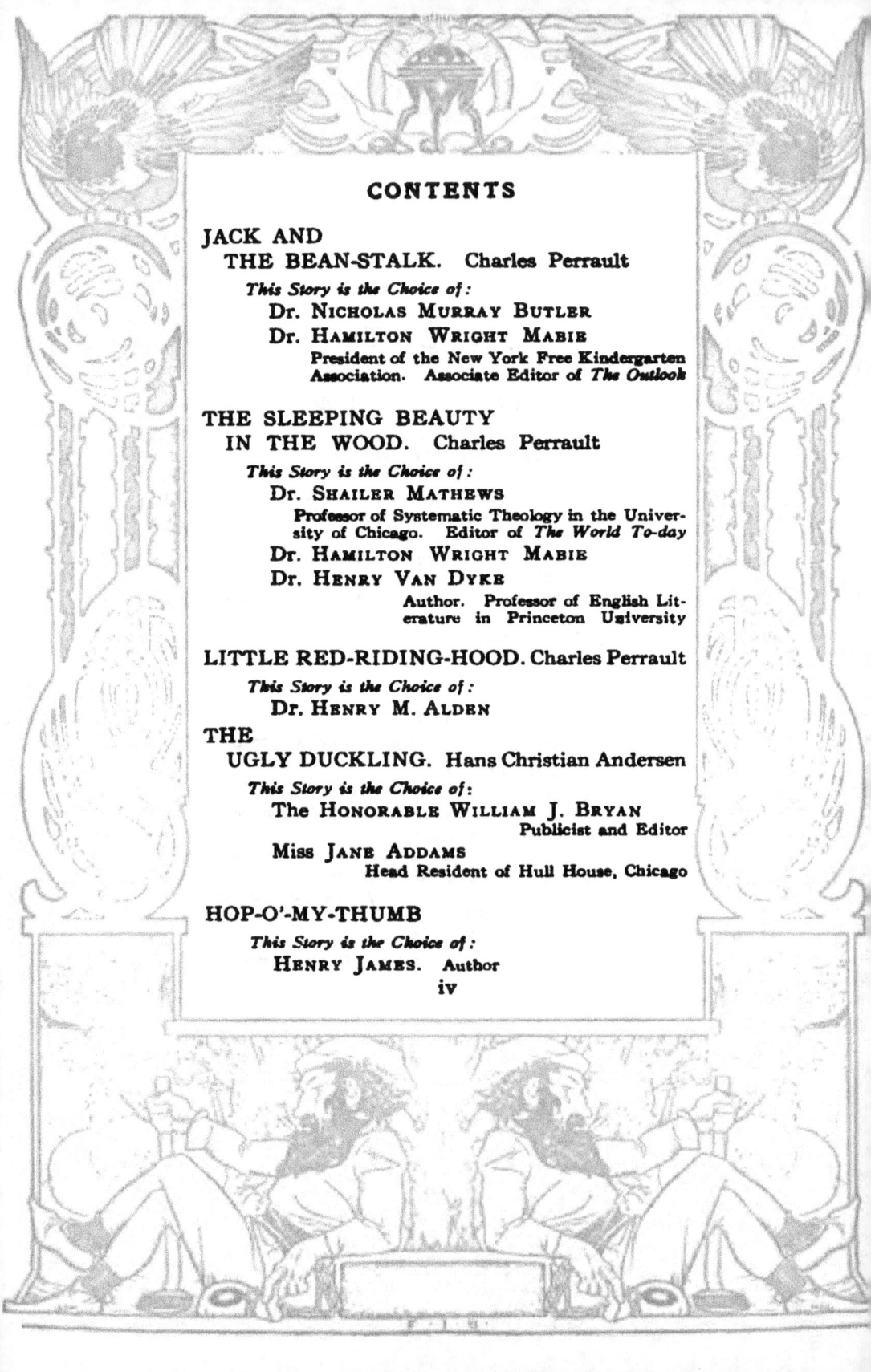

CONTENTS

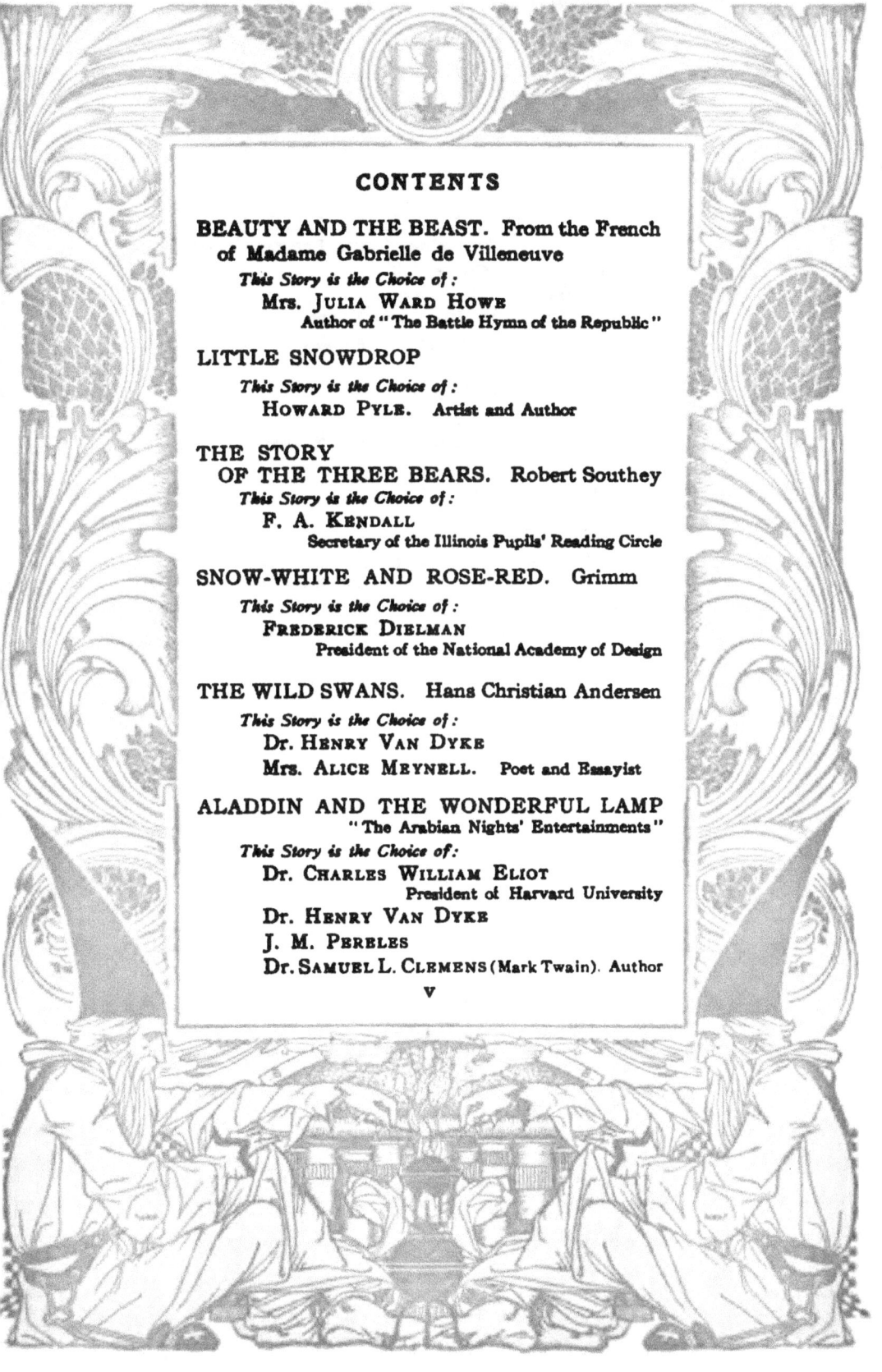

CONTENTS

v

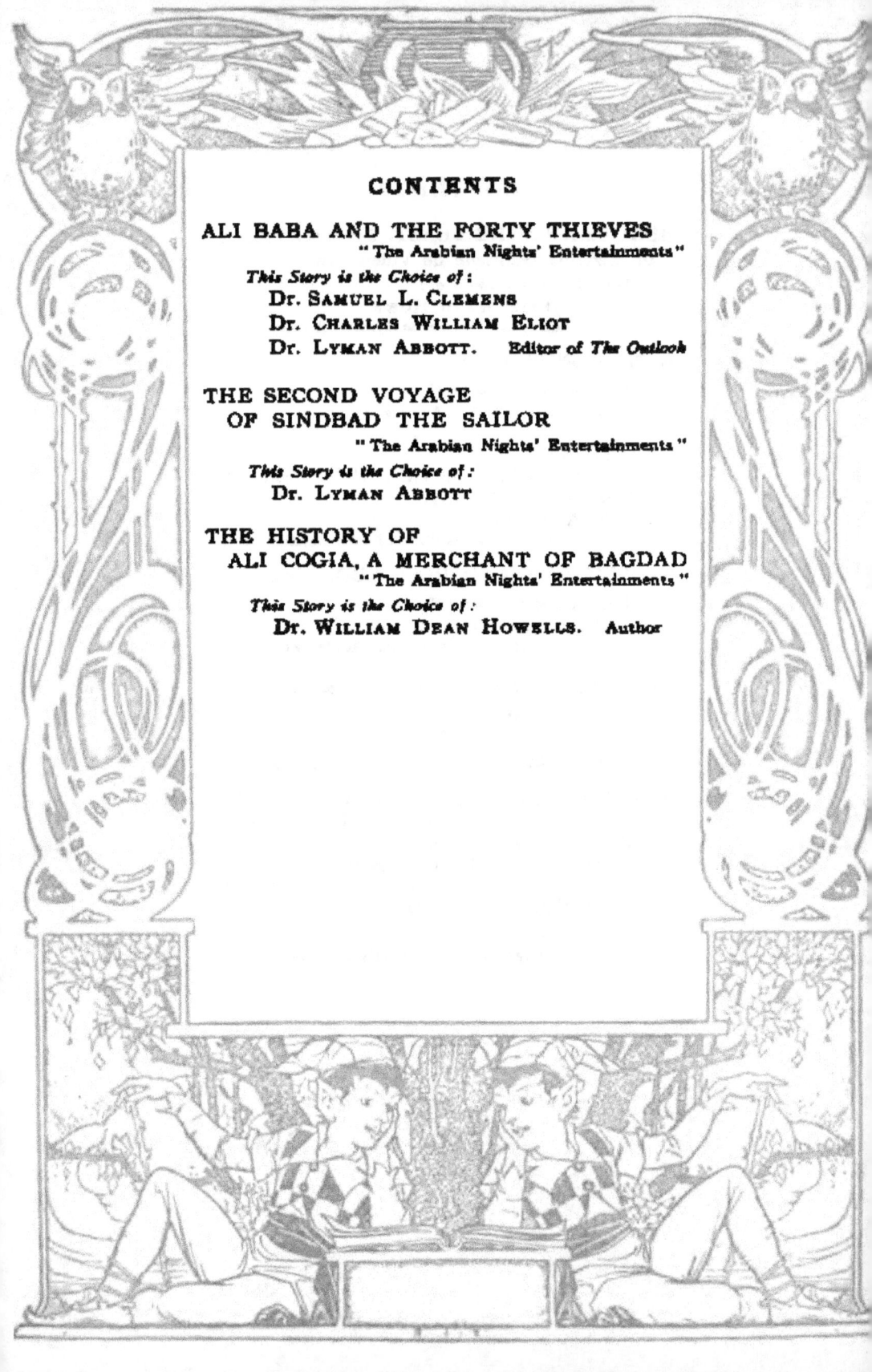

CONTENTS

ILLUSTRATIONS

vii

ILLUSTRATIONS

Decorative borders by
Francis I. Bennett

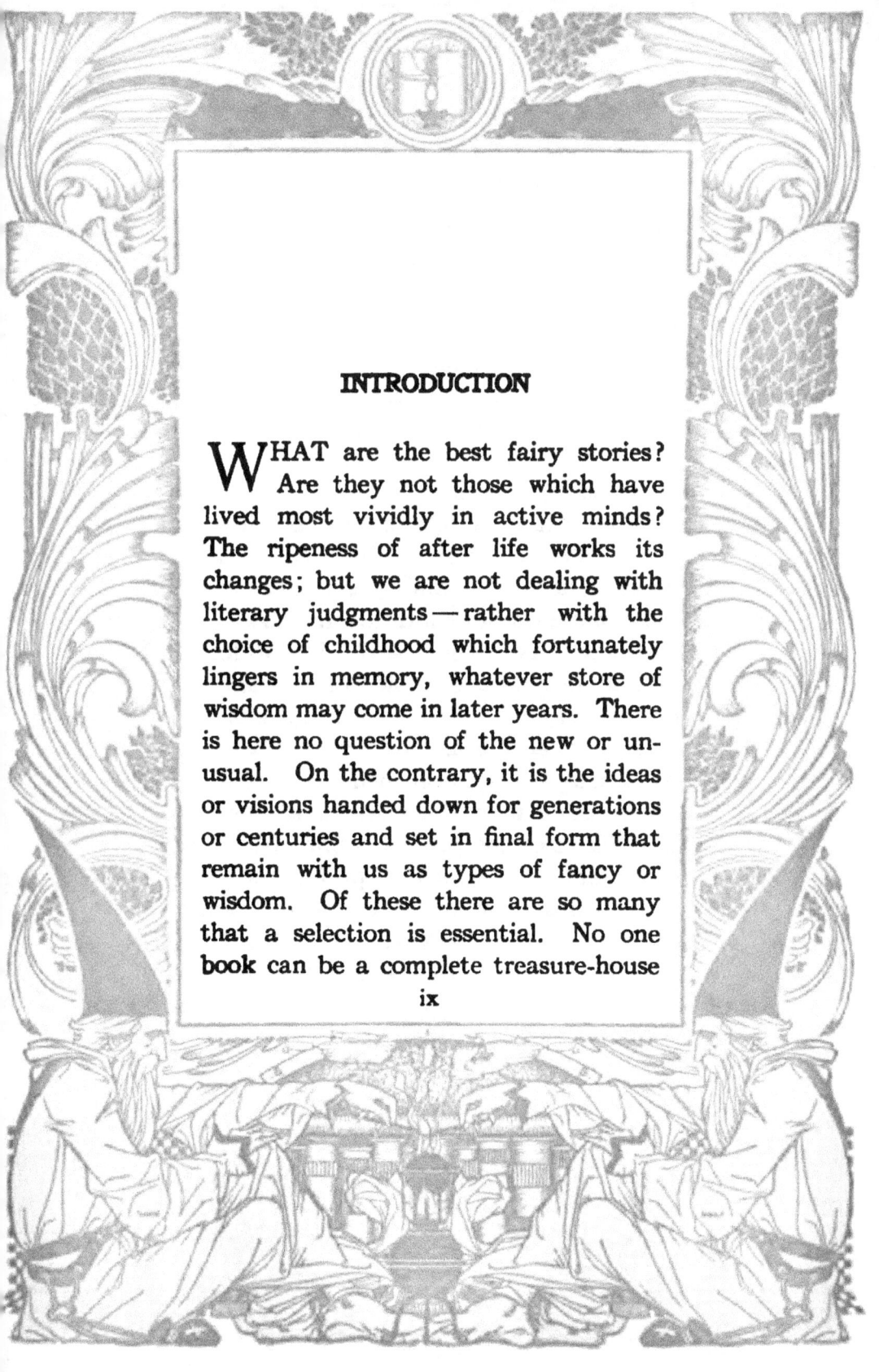

INTRODUCTION

WHAT are the best fairy stories?
Are they not those which have
lived most vividly in active minds?
The ripeness of after life works its
changes; but we are not dealing with
literary judgments — rather with the
choice of childhood which fortunately
lingers in memory, whatever store of
wisdom may come in later years. There
is here no question of the new or un-
usual. On the contrary, it is the ideas
or visions handed down for generations
or centuries and set in final form that
remain with us as types of fancy or
wisdom. Of these there are so many
that a selection is essential. No one
book can be a complete treasure-house

ix

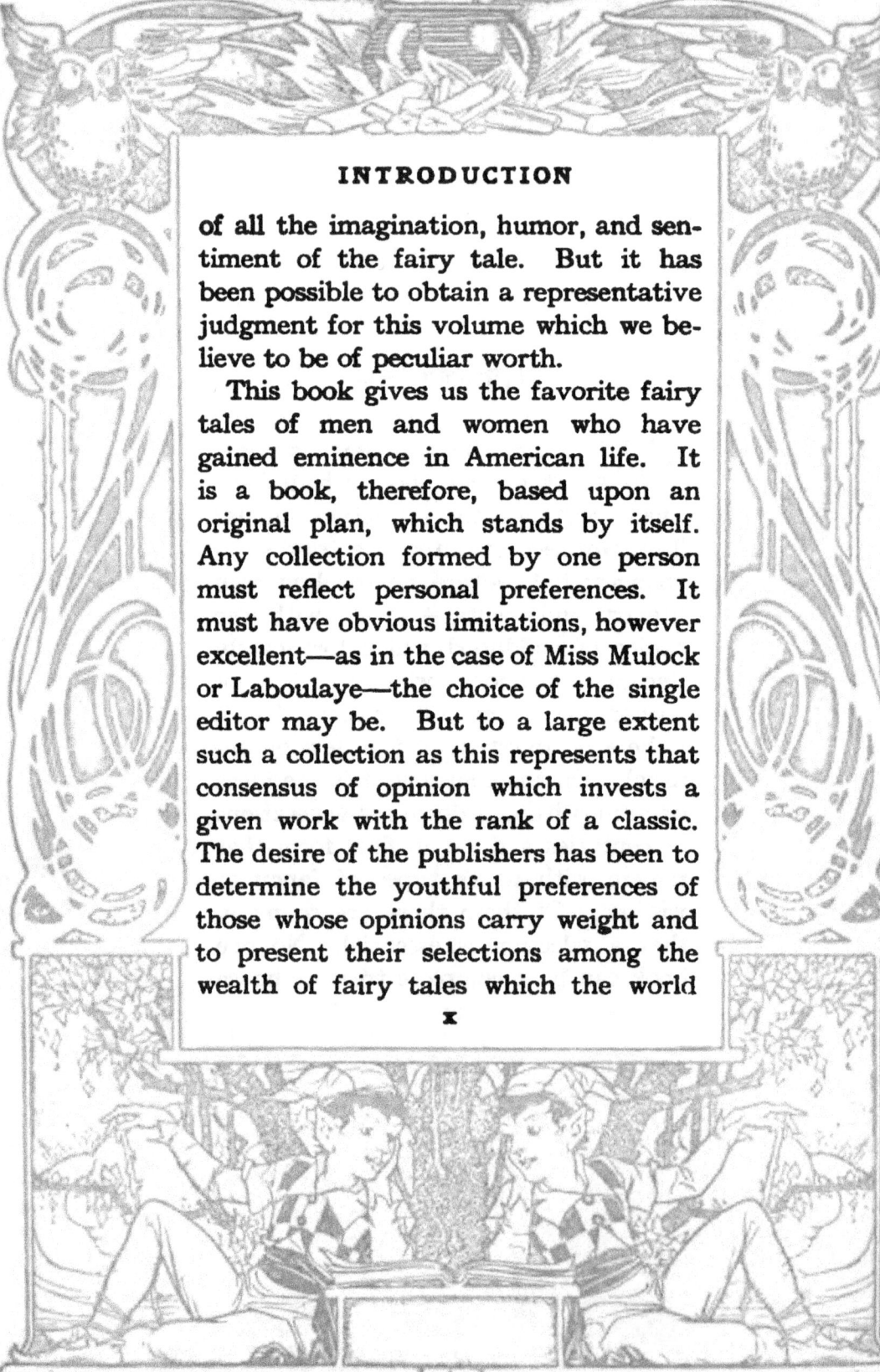

INTRODUCTION

of all the imagination, humor, and sentiment of the fairy tale. But it has been possible to obtain a representative judgment for this volume which we believe to be of peculiar worth.

This book gives us the favorite fairy tales of men and women who have gained eminence in American life. It is a book, therefore, based upon an original plan, which stands by itself. Any collection formed by one person must reflect personal preferences. It must have obvious limitations, however excellent—as in the case of Miss Mulock or Laboulaye—the choice of the single editor may be. But to a large extent such a collection as this represents that consensus of opinion which invests a given work with the rank of a classic. The desire of the publishers has been to determine the youthful preferences of those whose opinions carry weight and to present their selections among the wealth of fairy tales which the world

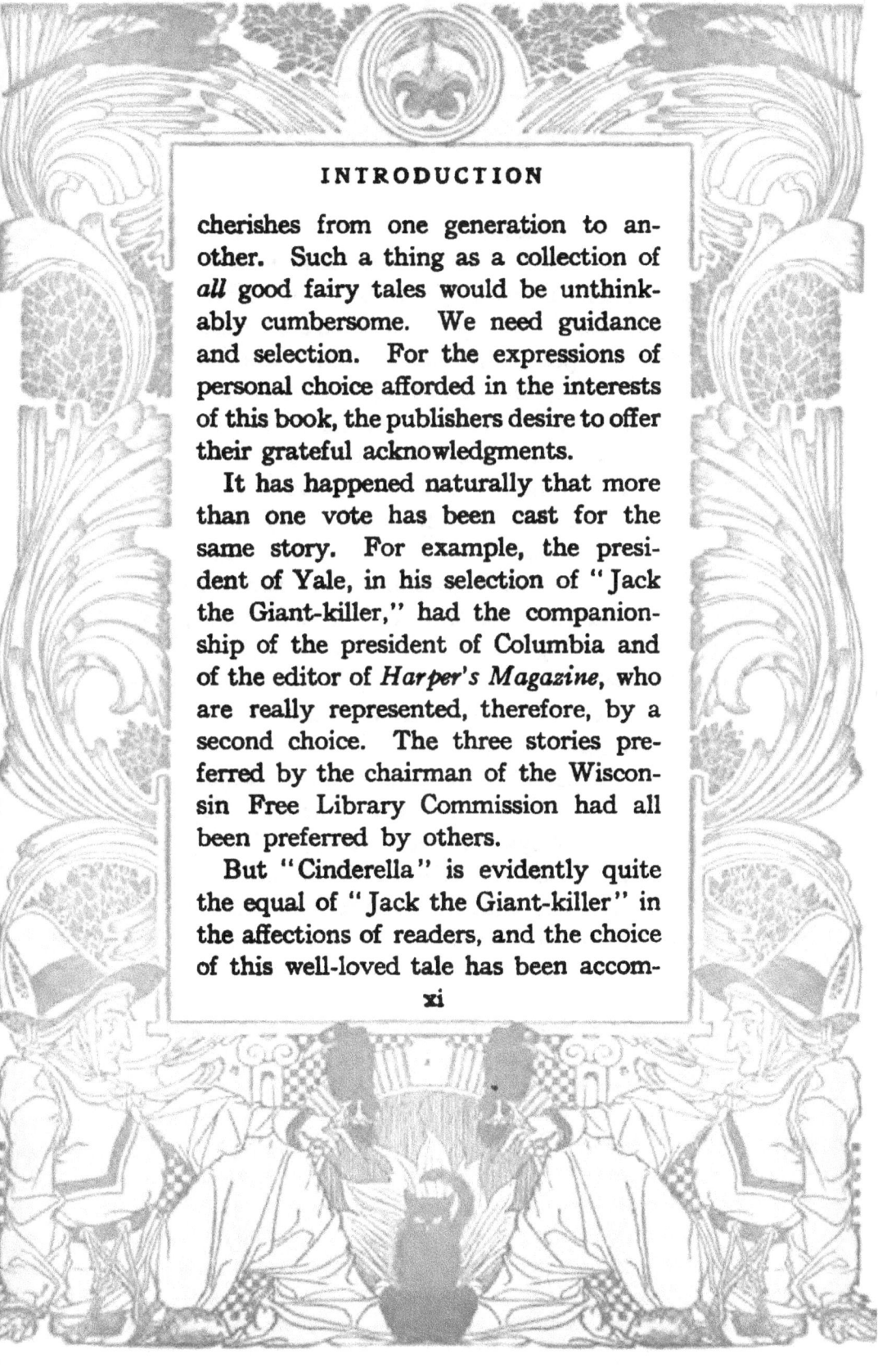

INTRODUCTION

cherishes from one generation to another. Such a thing as a collection of *all* good fairy tales would be unthinkably cumbersome. We need guidance and selection. For the expressions of personal choice afforded in the interests of this book, the publishers desire to offer their grateful acknowledgments.

It has happened naturally that more than one vote has been cast for the same story. For example, the president of Yale, in his selection of "Jack the Giant-killer," had the companionship of the president of Columbia and of the editor of *Harper's Magazine*, who are really represented, therefore, by a second choice. The three stories preferred by the chairman of the Wisconsin Free Library Commission had all been preferred by others.

But "Cinderella" is evidently quite the equal of "Jack the Giant-killer" in the affections of readers, and the choice of this well-loved tale has been accom-

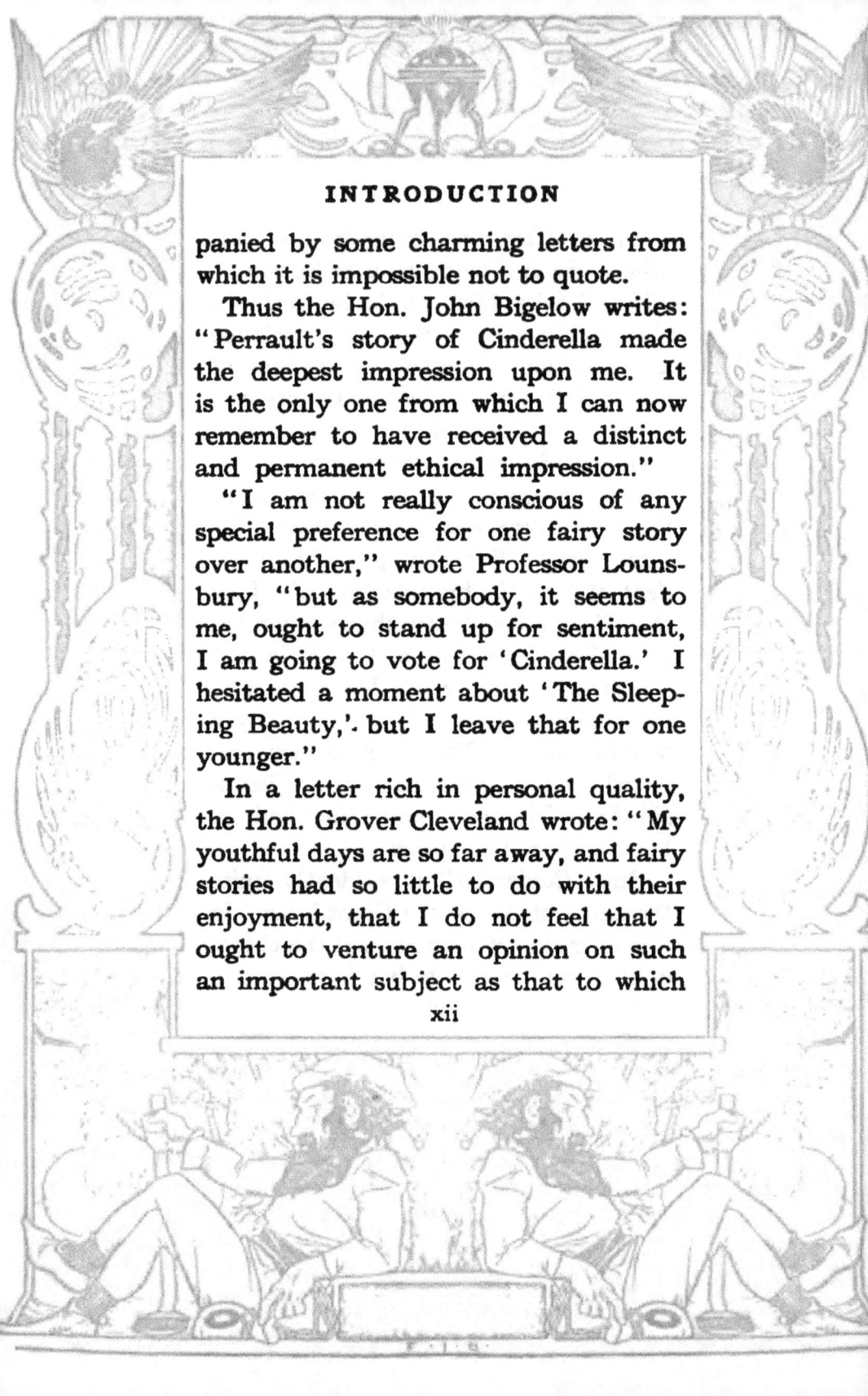

INTRODUCTION

panied by some charming letters from which it is impossible not to quote.

Thus the Hon. John Bigelow writes: "Perrault's story of Cinderella made the deepest impression upon me. It is the only one from which I can now remember to have received a distinct and permanent ethical impression."

"I am not really conscious of any special preference for one fairy story over another," wrote Professor Lounsbury, "but as somebody, it seems to me, ought to stand up for sentiment, I am going to vote for 'Cinderella.' I hesitated a moment about 'The Sleeping Beauty,' but I leave that for one younger."

In a letter rich in personal quality, the Hon. Grover Cleveland wrote: "My youthful days are so far away, and fairy stories had so little to do with their enjoyment, that I do not feel that I ought to venture an opinion on such an important subject as that to which

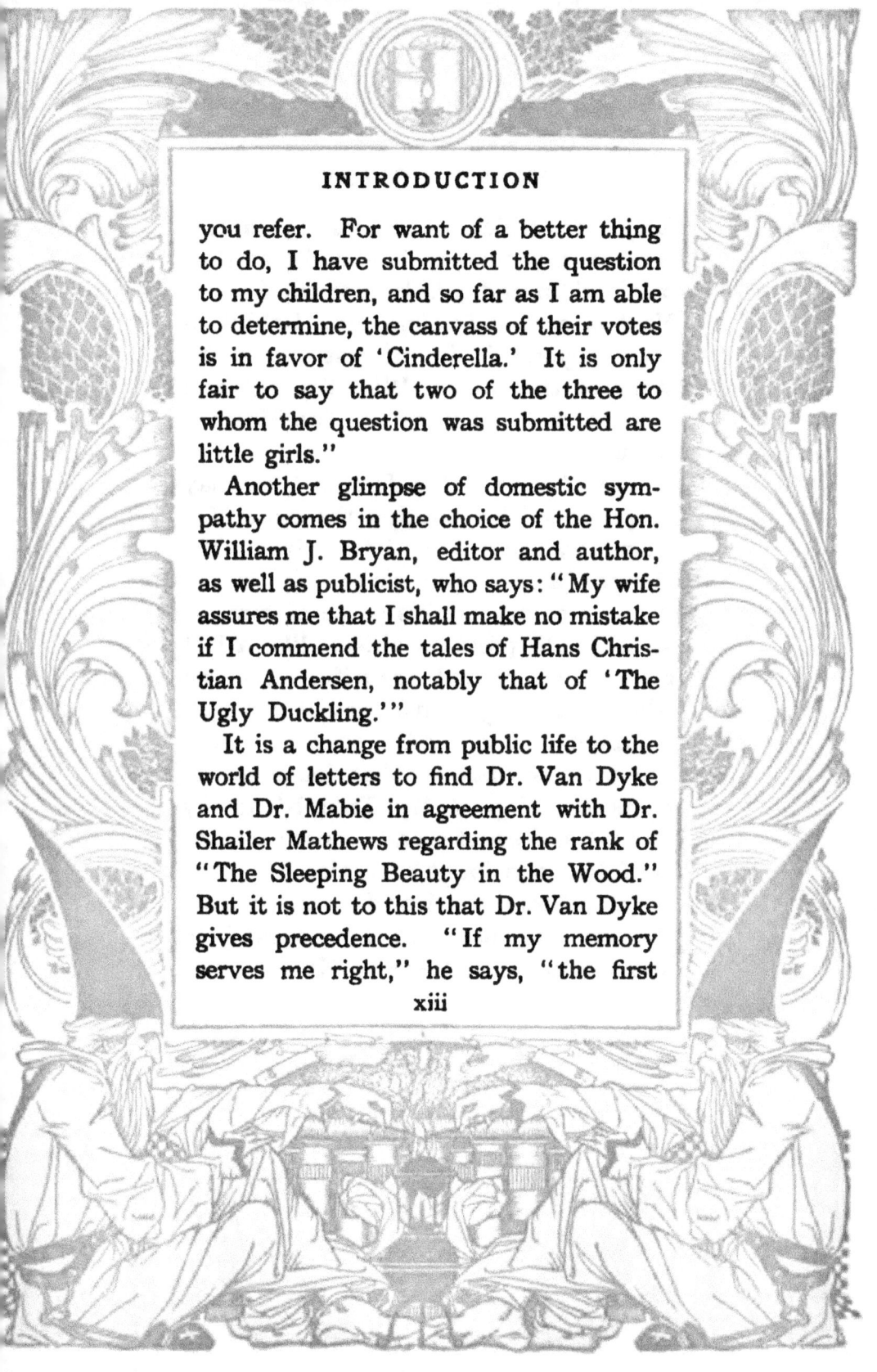

you refer. For want of a better thing to do, I have submitted the question to my children, and so far as I am able to determine, the canvass of their votes is in favor of 'Cinderella.' It is only fair to say that two of the three to whom the question was submitted are little girls."

Another glimpse of domestic sympathy comes in the choice of the Hon. William J. Bryan, editor and author, as well as publicist, who says: "My wife assures me that I shall make no mistake if I commend the tales of Hans Christian Andersen, notably that of 'The Ugly Duckling.'"

It is a change from public life to the world of letters to find Dr. Van Dyke and Dr. Mabie in agreement with Dr. Shailer Mathews regarding the rank of "The Sleeping Beauty in the Wood." But it is not to this that Dr. Van Dyke gives precedence. "If my memory serves me right," he says, "the first

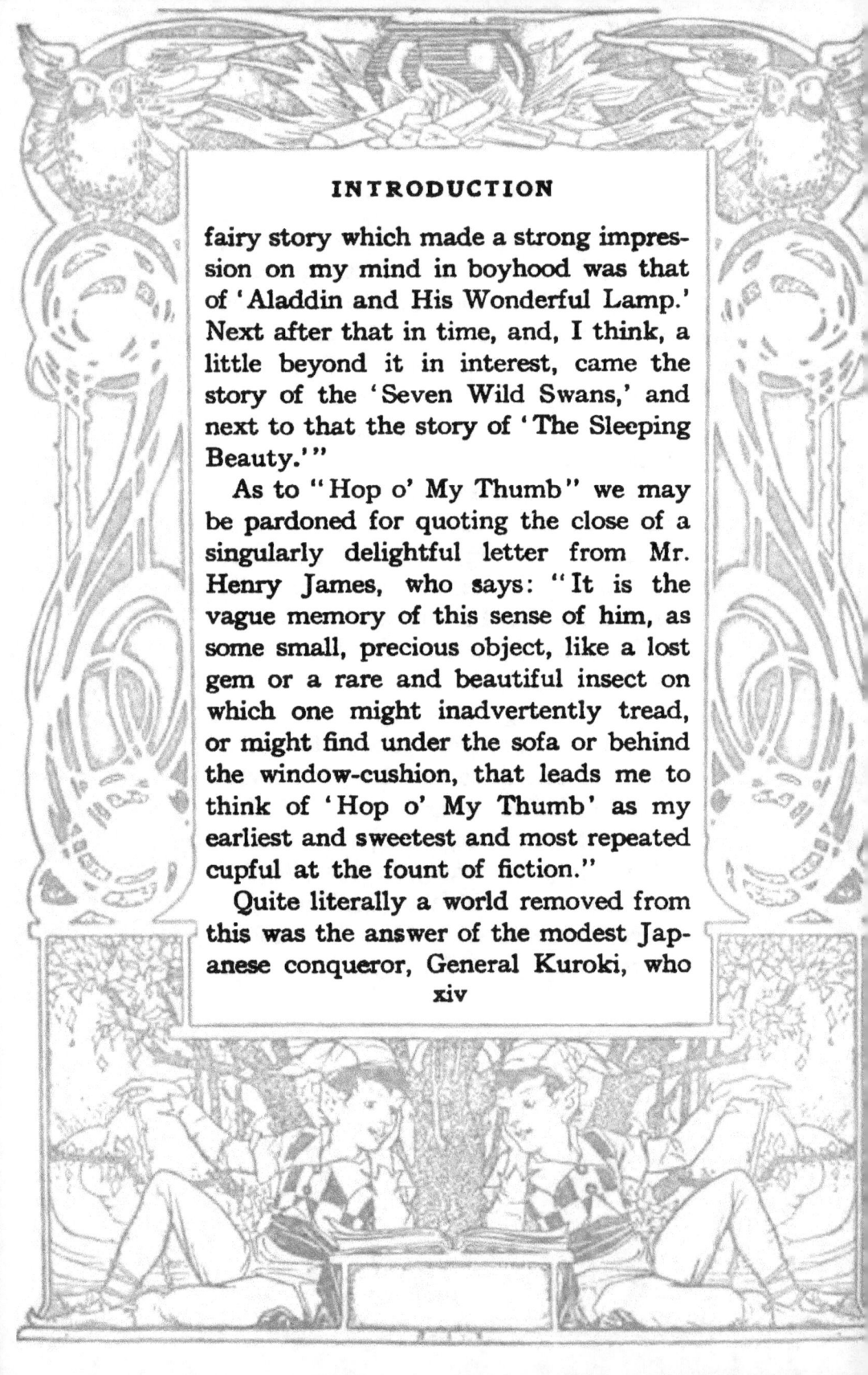

INTRODUCTION

fairy story which made a strong impression on my mind in boyhood was that of 'Aladdin and His Wonderful Lamp.' Next after that in time, and, I think, a little beyond it in interest, came the story of the 'Seven Wild Swans,' and next to that the story of 'The Sleeping Beauty.'"

As to "Hop o' My Thumb" we may be pardoned for quoting the close of a singularly delightful letter from Mr. Henry James, who says: "It is the vague memory of this sense of him, as some small, precious object, like a lost gem or a rare and beautiful insect on which one might inadvertently tread, or might find under the sofa or behind the window-cushion, that leads me to think of 'Hop o' My Thumb' as my earliest and sweetest and most repeated cupful at the fount of fiction."

Quite literally a world removed from this was the answer of the modest Japanese conqueror, General Kuroki, who

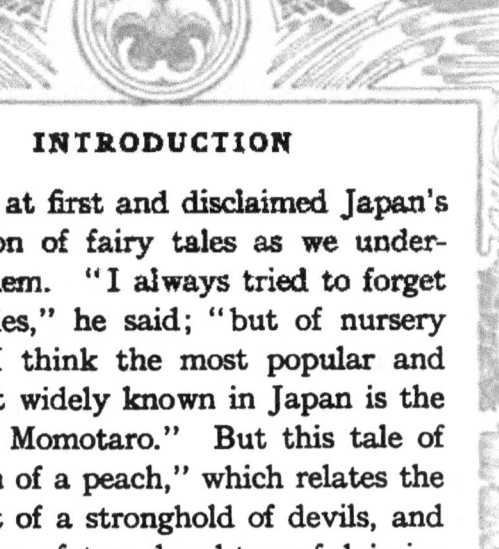

INTRODUCTION

laughed at first and disclaimed Japan's possession of fairy tales as we understand them. "I always tried to forget fairy tales," he said; "but of nursery stories I think the most popular and the most widely known in Japan is the story of Momotaro." But this tale of the "son of a peach," which relates the conquest of a stronghold of devils, and the rescue of two daughters of daimios does not come within the scope of this volume.

A broader choice than those which have been quoted is afforded by Mrs. Elizabeth Stuart Phelps Ward, who writes: "As a child I was a great reader and lover (and a small creator) of fairy tales. But of them all the only ones which come readily to my mind are Hans Christian Andersen's." Equally comprehensive is the answer of Mrs. Georgia A. Kendrick, the lady principal of Vassar College: "Grimm's tales stand to me for the best of that kind of lore."

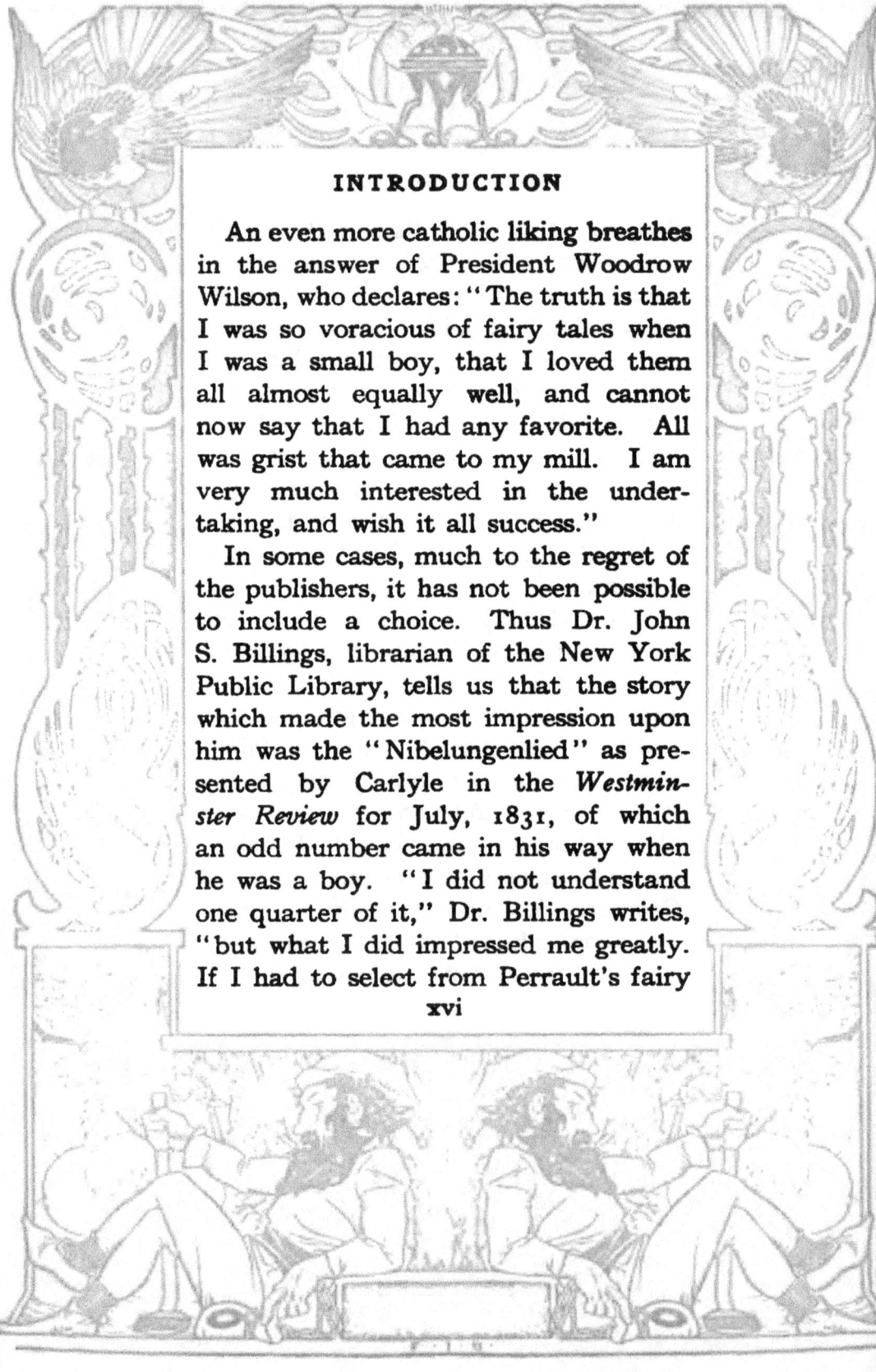

INTRODUCTION

An even more catholic liking breathes in the answer of President Woodrow Wilson, who declares: "The truth is that I was so voracious of fairy tales when I was a small boy, that I loved them all almost equally well, and cannot now say that I had any favorite. All was grist that came to my mill. I am very much interested in the undertaking, and wish it all success."

In some cases, much to the regret of the publishers, it has not been possible to include a choice. Thus Dr. John S. Billings, librarian of the New York Public Library, tells us that the story which made the most impression upon him was the "Nibelungenlied" as presented by Carlyle in the *Westminster Review* for July, 1831, of which an odd number came in his way when he was a boy. "I did not understand one quarter of it," Dr. Billings writes, "but what I did impressed me greatly. If I had to select from Perrault's fairy

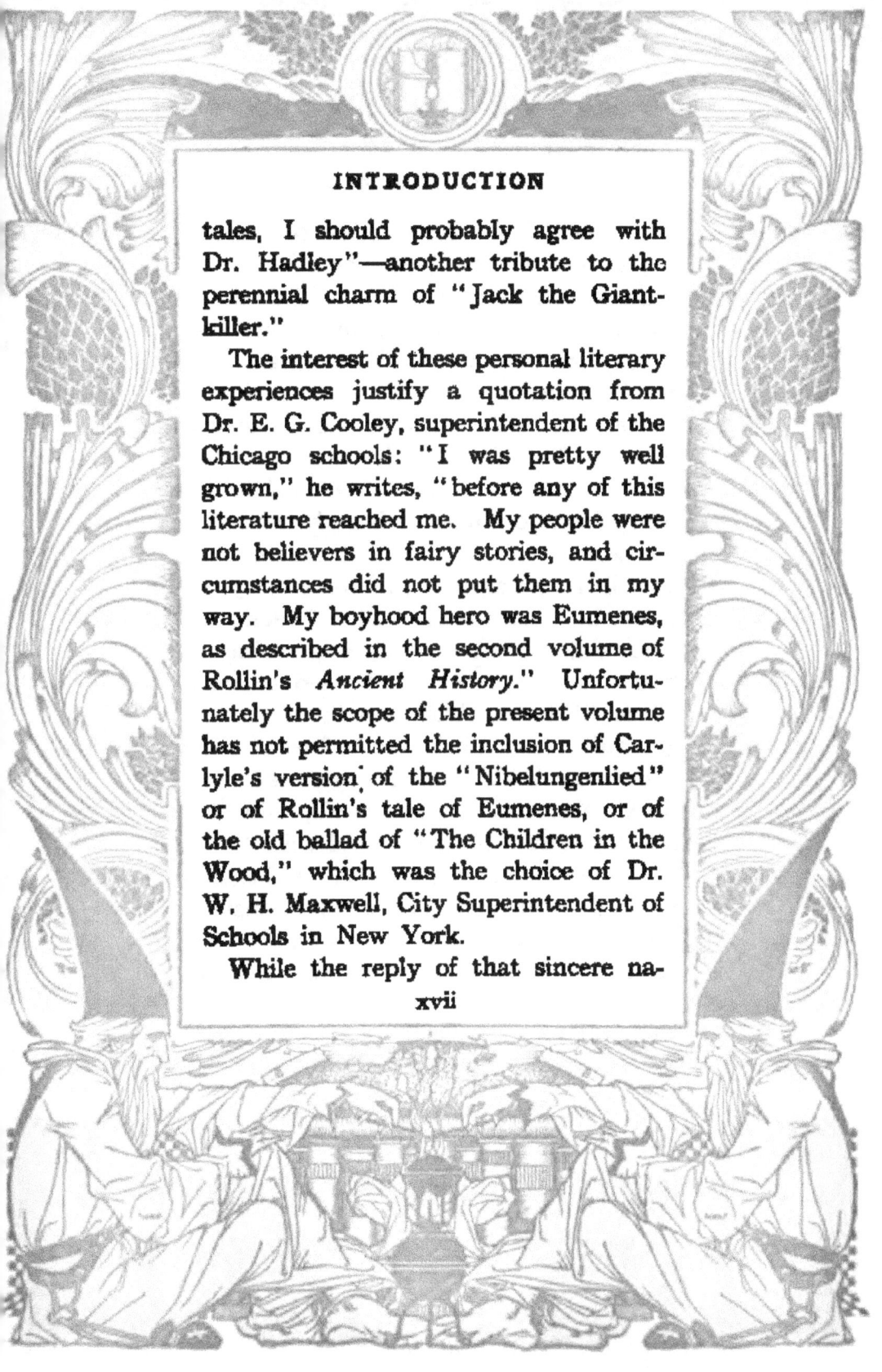

INTRODUCTION

tales, I should probably agree with
Dr. Hadley"—another tribute to the
perennial charm of "Jack the Giant-
killer."

The interest of these personal literary
experiences justify a quotation from
Dr. E. G. Cooley, superintendent of the
Chicago schools: "I was pretty well
grown," he writes, "before any of this
literature reached me. My people were
not believers in fairy stories, and cir-
cumstances did not put them in my
way. My boyhood hero was Eumenes,
as described in the second volume of
Rollin's *Ancient History.*" Unfortu-
nately the scope of the present volume
has not permitted the inclusion of Carlyle's version of the "Nibelungenlied"
or of Rollin's tale of Eumenes, or of
the old ballad of "The Children in the
Wood," which was the choice of Dr.
W. H. Maxwell, City Superintendent of
Schools in New York.

While the reply of that sincere na-

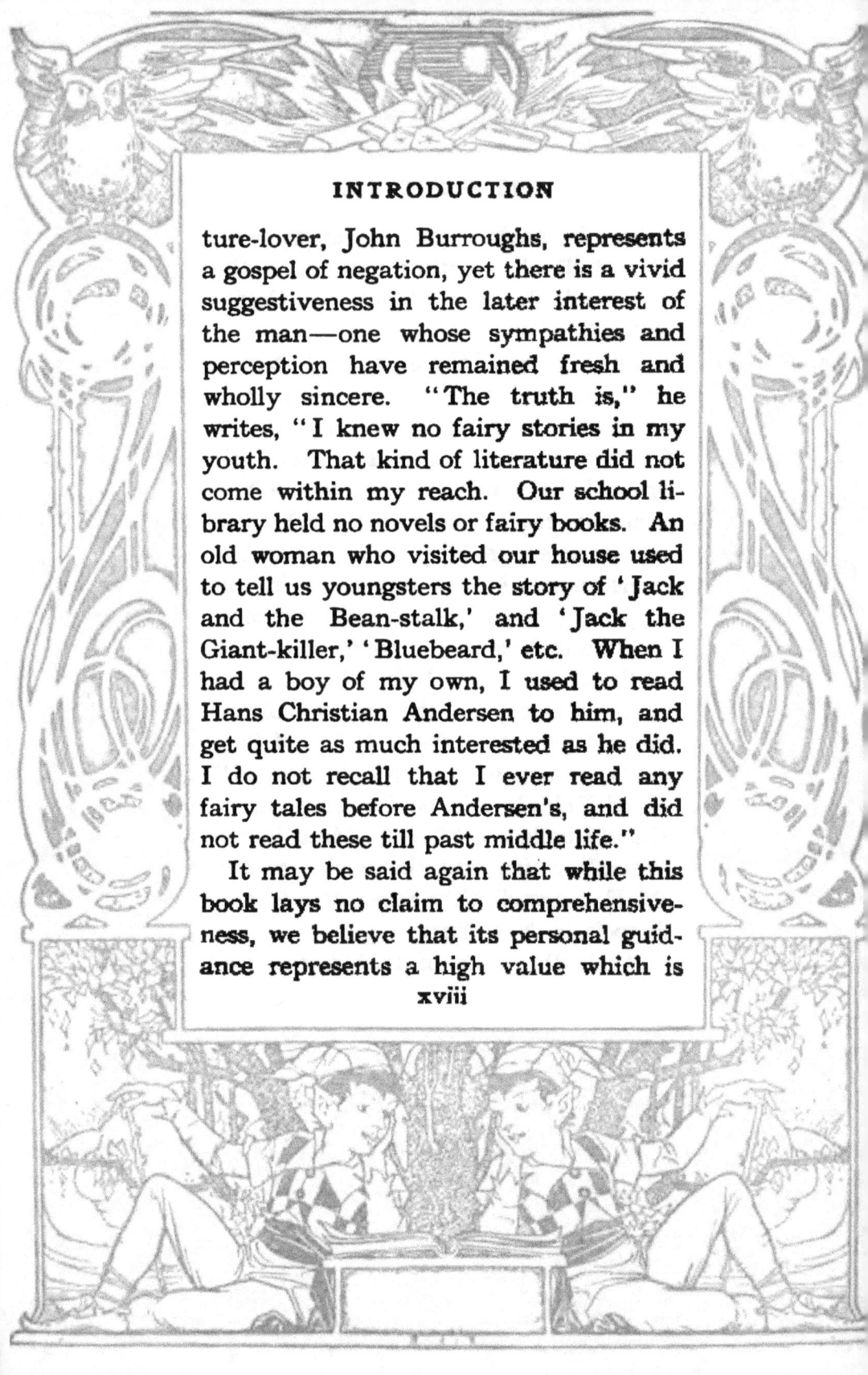

INTRODUCTION

ture-lover, John Burroughs, represents
a gospel of negation, yet there is a vivid
suggestiveness in the later interest of
the man—one whose sympathies and
perception have remained fresh and
wholly sincere. "The truth is," he
writes, "I knew no fairy stories in my
youth. That kind of literature did not
come within my reach. Our school library held no novels or fairy books. An
old woman who visited our house used
to tell us youngsters the story of 'Jack
and the Bean-stalk,' and 'Jack the
Giant-killer,' 'Bluebeard,' etc. When I
had a boy of my own, I used to read
Hans Christian Andersen to him, and
get quite as much interested as he did.
I do not recall that I ever read any
fairy tales before Andersen's, and did
not read these till past middle life."

It may be said again that while this
book lays no claim to comprehensive-
ness, we believe that its personal guidance represents a high value which is

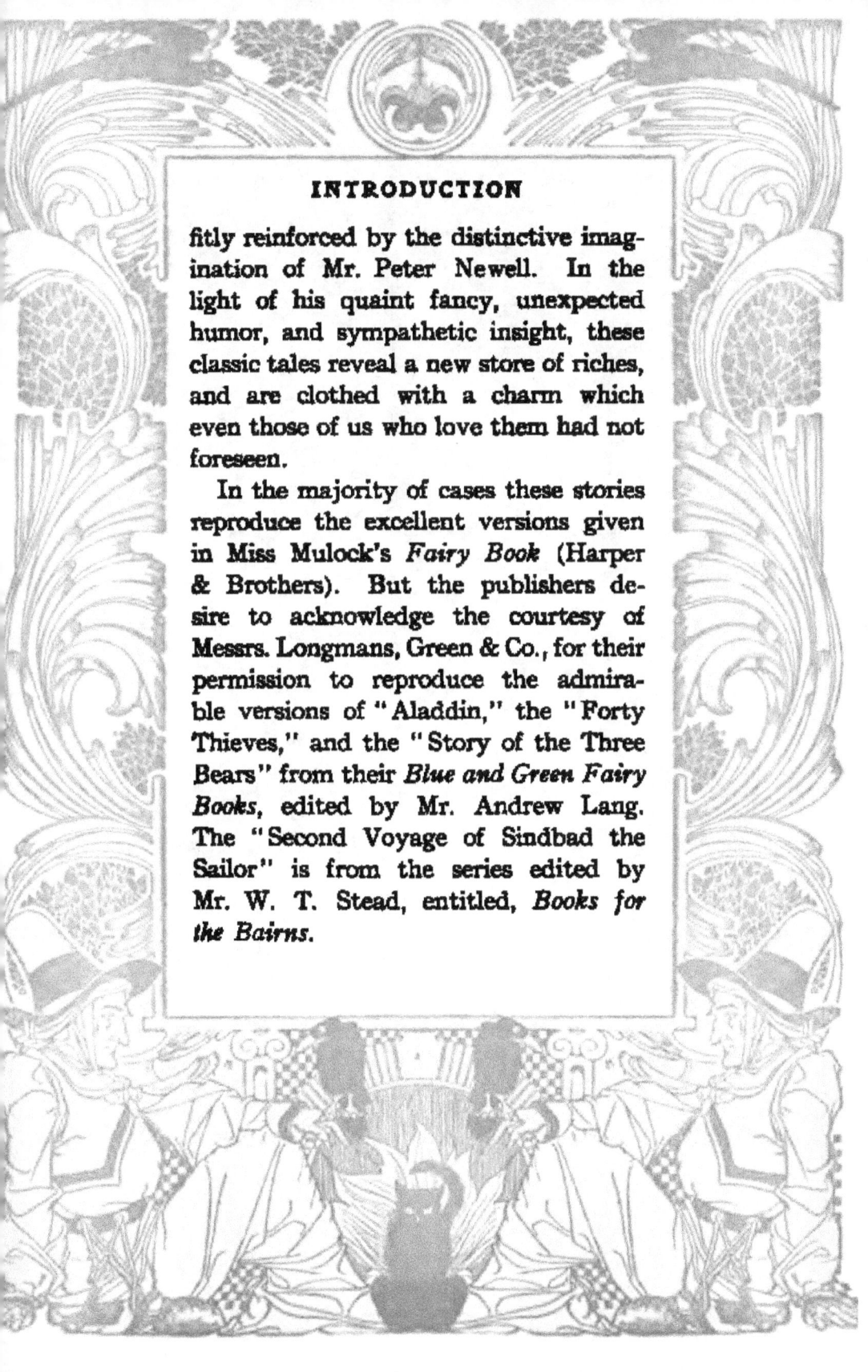

INTRODUCTION

fitly reinforced by the distinctive imagination of Mr. Peter Newell. In the light of his quaint fancy, unexpected humor, and sympathetic insight, these classic tales reveal a new store of riches, and are clothed with a charm which even those of us who love them had not foreseen.

In the majority of cases these stories reproduce the excellent versions given in Miss Mulock's *Fairy Book* (Harper & Brothers). But the publishers desire to acknowledge the courtesy of Messrs. Longmans, Green & Co., for their permission to reproduce the admirable versions of "Aladdin," the "Forty Thieves," and the "Story of the Three Bears" from their *Blue and Green Fairy Books*, edited by Mr. Andrew Lang. The "Second Voyage of Sindbad the Sailor" is from the series edited by Mr. W. T. Stead, entitled, *Books for the Bairns*.

[See p. 209

"Can't you render me some assistance?"

FAVORITE FAIRY TALES

sieges, and the means to conquer or surprise a foe. He was above the common sports of children, but hardly any one could equal him at wrestling; or, if he met with a match for himself in strength, his skill and address always made him the victor.

In those days there lived on St. Michael's Mount, of Cornwall, which rises out of the sea at some distance from the main-land, a huge giant. He was eighteen feet high and three yards round, and his fierce and savage looks were the terror of all his neighbors. He dwelt in a gloomy cavern on the very top of the mountain, and used to wade over to the main-land in search of his prey. When he came near, the people left their houses; and after he had glutted his appetite upon their cattle he would throw half a dozen oxen upon his back, and tie three times as many sheep and hogs round his waist, and so march back to his own abode.

"I will broil you for my breakfast"

I will wait for the presence.

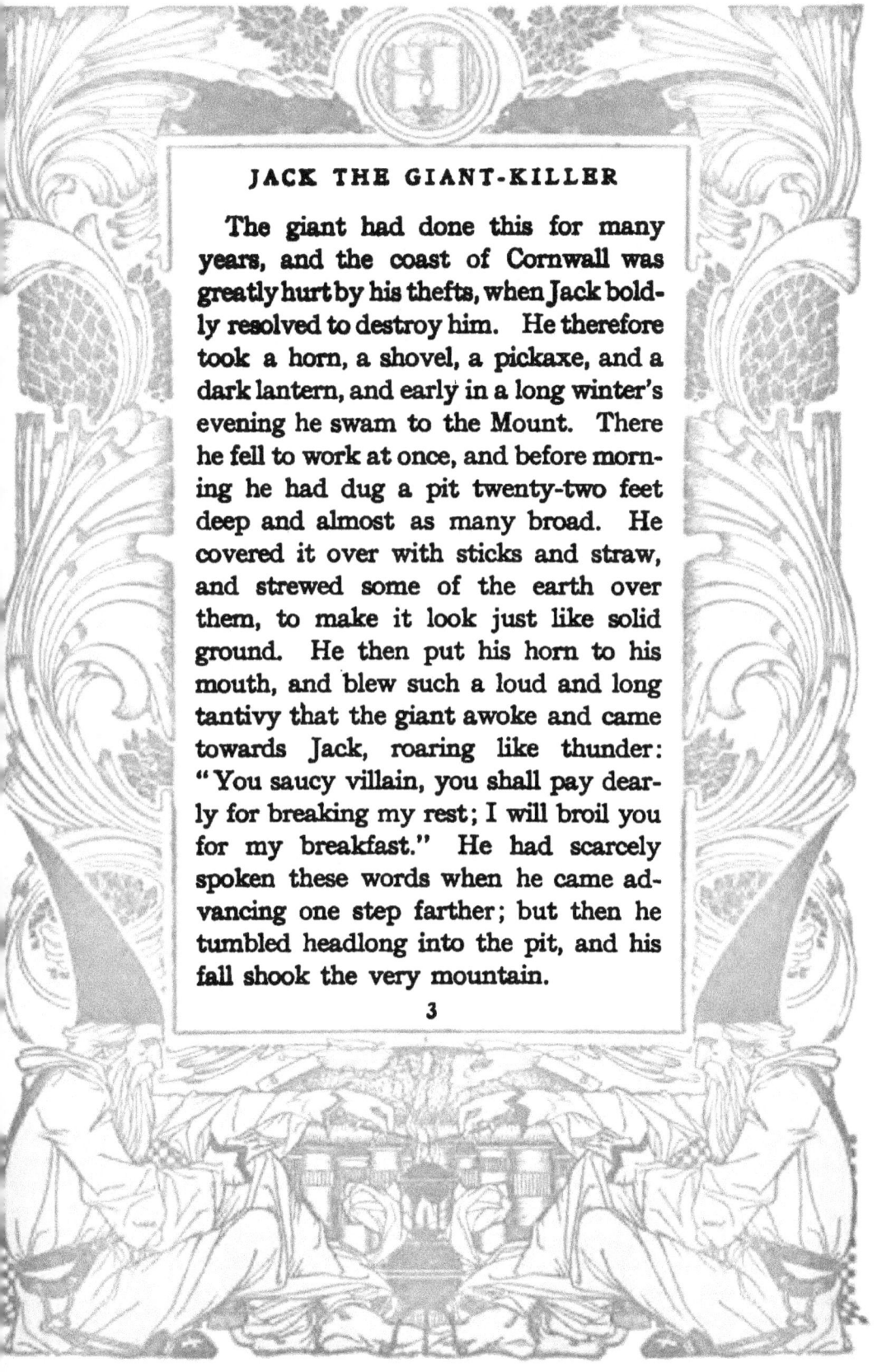

The giant had done this for many years, and the coast of Cornwall was greatly hurt by his thefts, when Jack boldly resolved to destroy him. He therefore took a horn, a shovel, a pickaxe, and a dark lantern, and early in a long winter's evening he swam to the Mount. There he fell to work at once, and before morning he had dug a pit twenty-two feet deep and almost as many broad. He covered it over with sticks and straw, and strewed some of the earth over them, to make it look just like solid ground. He then put his horn to his mouth, and blew such a loud and long tantivy that the giant awoke and came towards Jack, roaring like thunder: "You saucy villain, you shall pay dearly for breaking my rest; I will broil you for my breakfast." He had scarcely spoken these words when he came advancing one step farther; but then he tumbled headlong into the pit, and his fall shook the very mountain.

FAVORITE FAIRY TALES

over with the skulls and bones of men and women. The giant took him into a large room, where lay the hearts and limbs of persons who had been lately killed; and he told Jack, with a horrid grin, that men's hearts, eaten with pepper and vinegar, were his nicest food, and, also, that he thought he should make a dainty meal on his heart. When he had said this he locked Jack up in that room, while he went to fetch another giant, who lived in the same wood, to enjoy a dinner off Jack's flesh with him. While he was away, Jack heard dreadful shrieks, groans, and cries from many parts of the castle; and soon after he heard a mournful voice repeat these lines:

> "Haste, valiant stranger, haste away,
> Lest you become the giant's prey.
> On his return he'll bring another,
> Still more savage than his brother;
> A horrid, cruel monster who,
> Before he kills, will torture you.
> Oh, valiant stranger! haste away,
> Or you'll become these giants' prey."

This warning was so shocking to poor Jack that he was ready to go mad. He ran to the window and saw the two giants coming along arm in arm. This window was right over the gates of the castle. "Now," thought Jack, "either my death or freedom is at hand."

There were two strong cords in the room. Jack made a large noose with a slip-knot at the ends of both these, and, as the giants were coming through the gates, he threw the ropes over their heads. He then made the other ends fast to a beam in the ceiling, and pulled with all his might, till he had almost strangled them. When he saw that they were both black in the face, and had not the least strength left, he drew his sword and slid down the ropes; he then killed the giants, and thus saved himself from a cruel death. Jack next took a great bunch of keys from the pocket of Blunderbore, and went into the castle again. He made a strict search

7

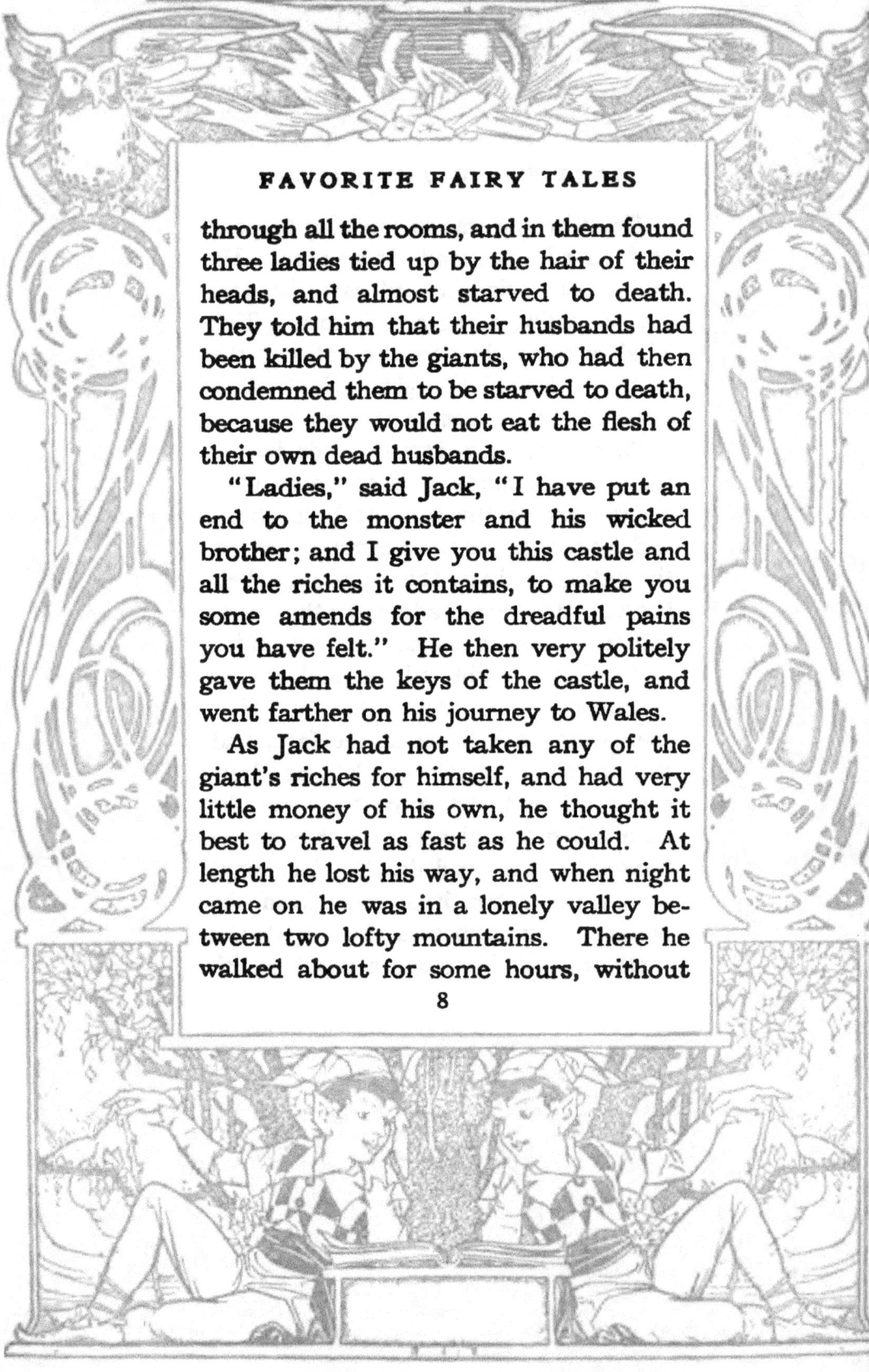

through all the rooms, and in them found three ladies tied up by the hair of their heads, and almost starved to death. They told him that their husbands had been killed by the giants, who had then condemned them to be starved to death, because they would not eat the flesh of their own dead husbands.

"Ladies," said Jack, "I have put an end to the monster and his wicked brother; and I give you this castle and all the riches it contains, to make you some amends for the dreadful pains you have felt." He then very politely gave them the keys of the castle, and went farther on his journey to Wales.

As Jack had not taken any of the giant's riches for himself, and had very little money of his own, he thought it best to travel as fast as he could. At length he lost his way, and when night came on he was in a lonely valley between two lofty mountains. There he walked about for some hours, without

8

seeing any dwelling-place, so he thought himself very lucky at last in finding a large and handsome house. He went up to it boldly, and knocked loudly at the gate; when, to his great terror and surprise, there came forth a monstrous giant with two heads. He spoke to Jack very civilly, for he was a Welsh giant, and all the mischief he did was by private and secret malice, under the show of friendship and kindness.

Jack told him that he was a traveller who had lost his way, on which the huge monster made him welcome, and led him into a room where there was a good bed in which to pass the night. Jack took off his clothes quickly; but though he was so weary he could not go to sleep. Soon after this he heard the giant walking backward and forward in the next room, and saying to himself:

"Though here you lodge with me this night,
　You shall not see the morning light;
　My club shall dash your brains out quite.'

FAVORITE FAIRY TALES

"Say you so?" thought Jack. "Are these your tricks upon travellers? But I hope to prove as cunning as you." Then, getting out of bed, he groped about the room, and at last found a large, thick billet of wood; he laid it in his own place in the bed, and hid himself in a dark corner of the room. In the middle of the night the giant came with his great club, and struck many heavy blows on the bed, in the very place where Jack had laid the billet, and then he went back to his own room, thinking he had broken all his bones. Early in the morning Jack put a bold face upon the matter, and walked into the giant's room to thank him for his lodging.

The giant started when he saw him, and he began to stammer out: "Oh, dear me! is it you? Pray how did you sleep last night? Did you hear or see anything in the dead of the night?"

"Nothing worth speaking of," said Jack, carelessly; "a rat, I believe, gave

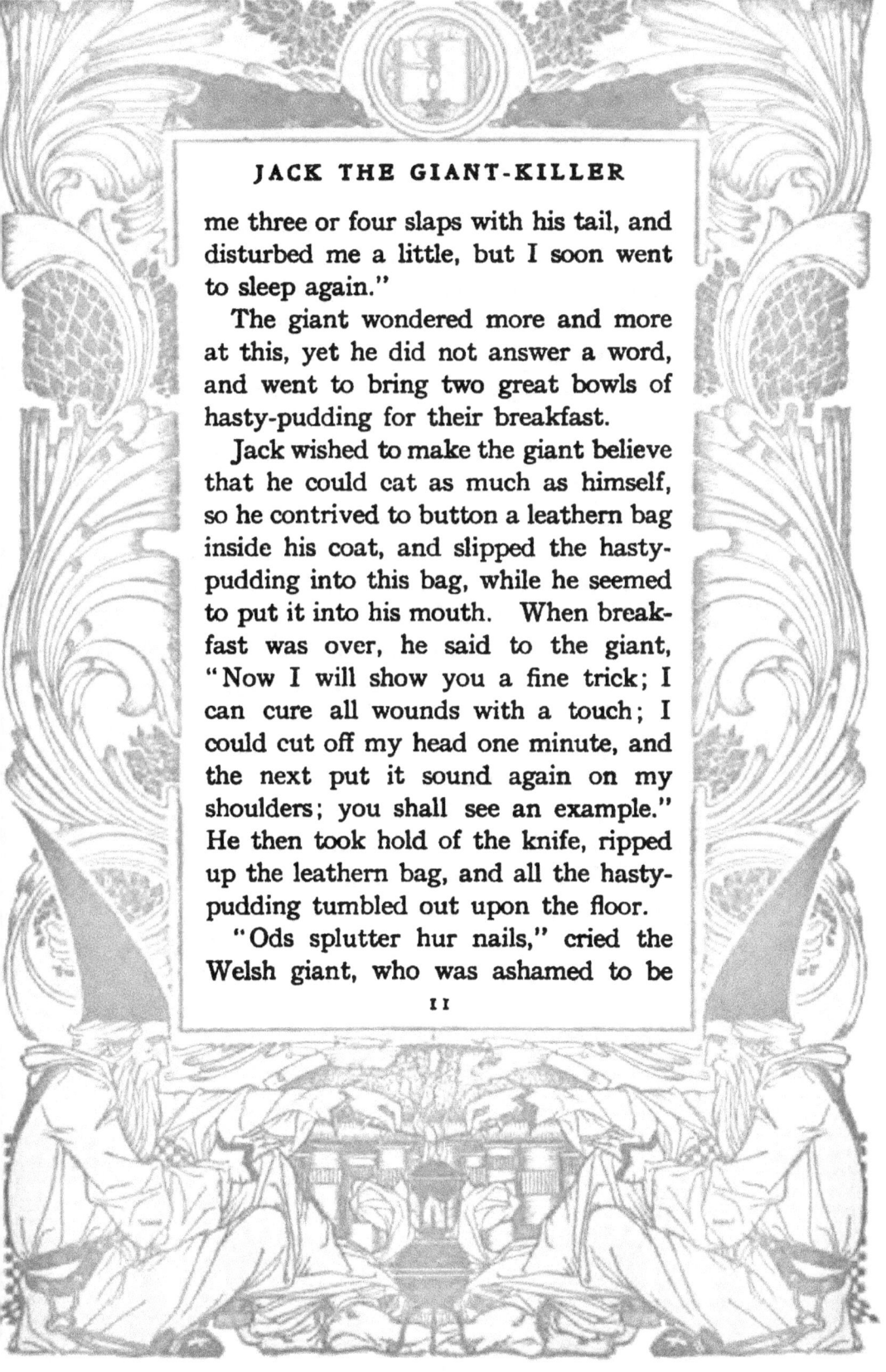

me three or four slaps with his tail, and disturbed me a little, but I soon went to sleep again."

The giant wondered more and more at this, yet he did not answer a word, and went to bring two great bowls of hasty-pudding for their breakfast.

Jack wished to make the giant believe that he could eat as much as himself, so he contrived to button a leathern bag inside his coat, and slipped the hasty-pudding into this bag, while he seemed to put it into his mouth. When breakfast was over, he said to the giant, "Now I will show you a fine trick; I can cure all wounds with a touch; I could cut off my head one minute, and the next put it sound again on my shoulders; you shall see an example." He then took hold of the knife, ripped up the leathern bag, and all the hasty-pudding tumbled out upon the floor.

"Ods splutter hur nails," cried the Welsh giant, who was ashamed to be

11

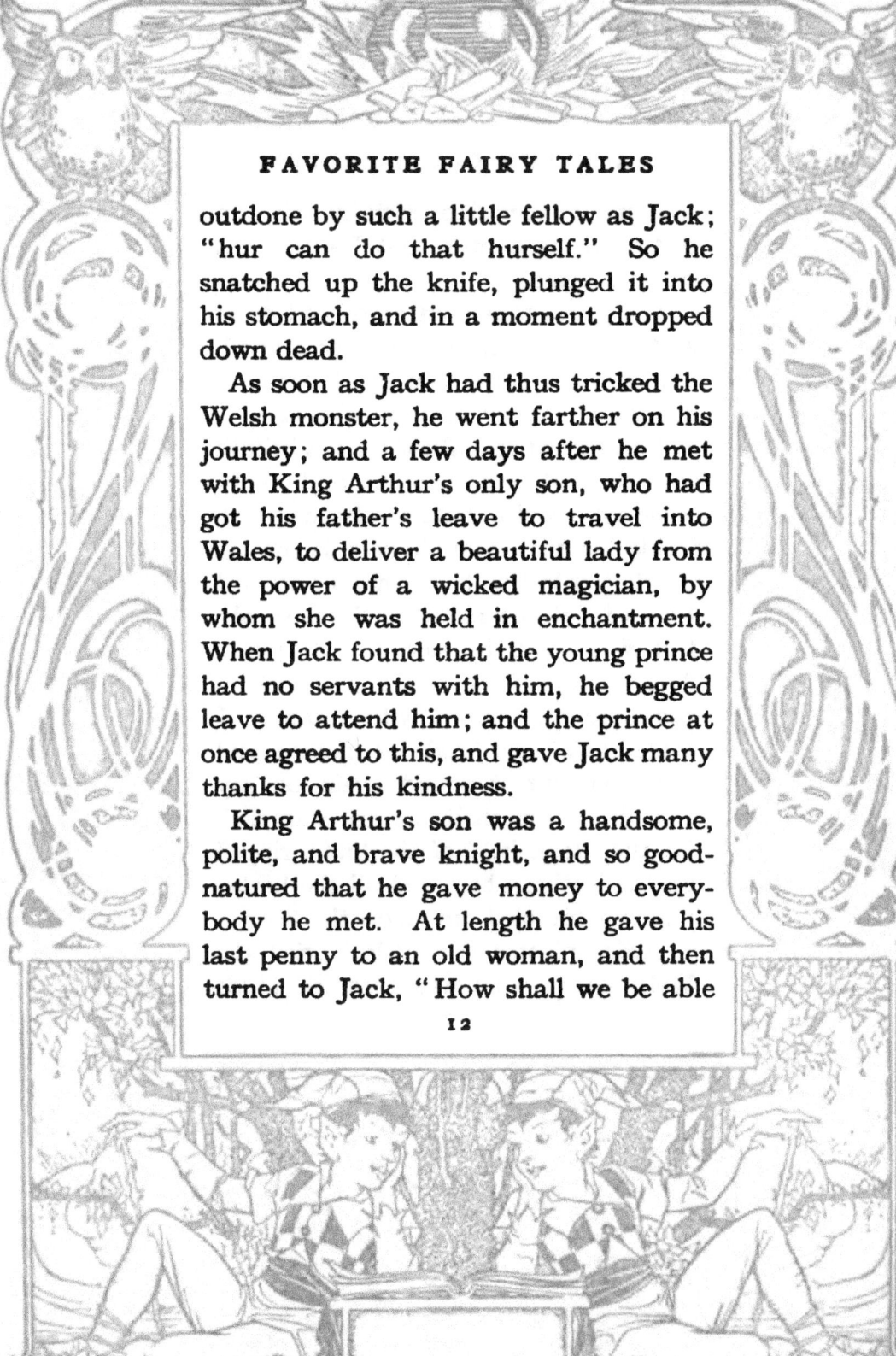

outdone by such a little fellow as Jack; "hur can do that hurself." So he snatched up the knife, plunged it into his stomach, and in a moment dropped down dead.

As soon as Jack had thus tricked the Welsh monster, he went farther on his journey; and a few days after he met with King Arthur's only son, who had got his father's leave to travel into Wales, to deliver a beautiful lady from the power of a wicked magician, by whom she was held in enchantment. When Jack found that the young prince had no servants with him, he begged leave to attend him; and the prince at once agreed to this, and gave Jack many thanks for his kindness.

King Arthur's son was a handsome, polite, and brave knight, and so good-natured that he gave money to everybody he met. At length he gave his last penny to an old woman, and then turned to Jack, "How shall we be able

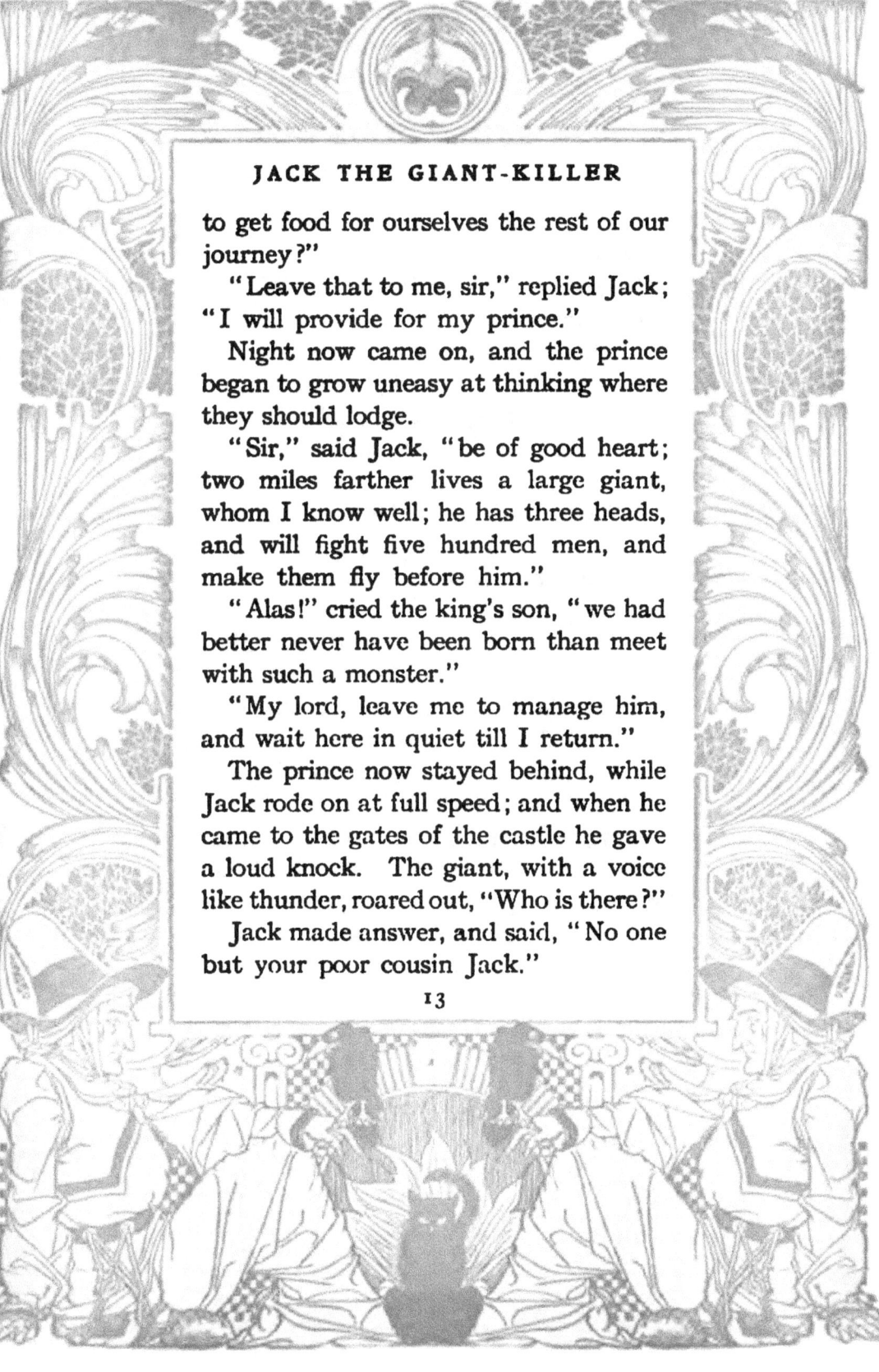

to get food for ourselves the rest of our journey?"

"Leave that to me, sir," replied Jack; "I will provide for my prince."

Night now came on, and the prince began to grow uneasy at thinking where they should lodge.

"Sir," said Jack, "be of good heart; two miles farther lives a large giant, whom I know well; he has three heads, and will fight five hundred men, and make them fly before him."

"Alas!" cried the king's son, "we had better never have been born than meet with such a monster."

"My lord, leave me to manage him, and wait here in quiet till I return."

The prince now stayed behind, while Jack rode on at full speed; and when he came to the gates of the castle he gave a loud knock. The giant, with a voice like thunder, roared out, "Who is there?"

Jack made answer, and said, "No one but your poor cousin Jack."

"Well," said the giant, "what news, Cousin Jack?"

"Dear uncle," said Jack, "I have heavy news."

"Pooh!" said the giant, "what heavy news can come to me? I am a giant with three heads, and can fight five hundred men, and make them fly before me."

"Alas!" said Jack, "here's the king's son coming with two thousand men to kill you, and to destroy the castle and all that you have."

"Oh, Cousin Jack," said the giant, "this is heavy news indeed! But I have a large cellar underground, where I will hide myself, and you shall lock, bolt, and bar me in, and keep the keys till the king's son is gone."

Now, when Jack had barred the giant fast in the vault, he went back and fetched the prince to the castle; they both made themselves merry with the wine and other dainties that were in the

14

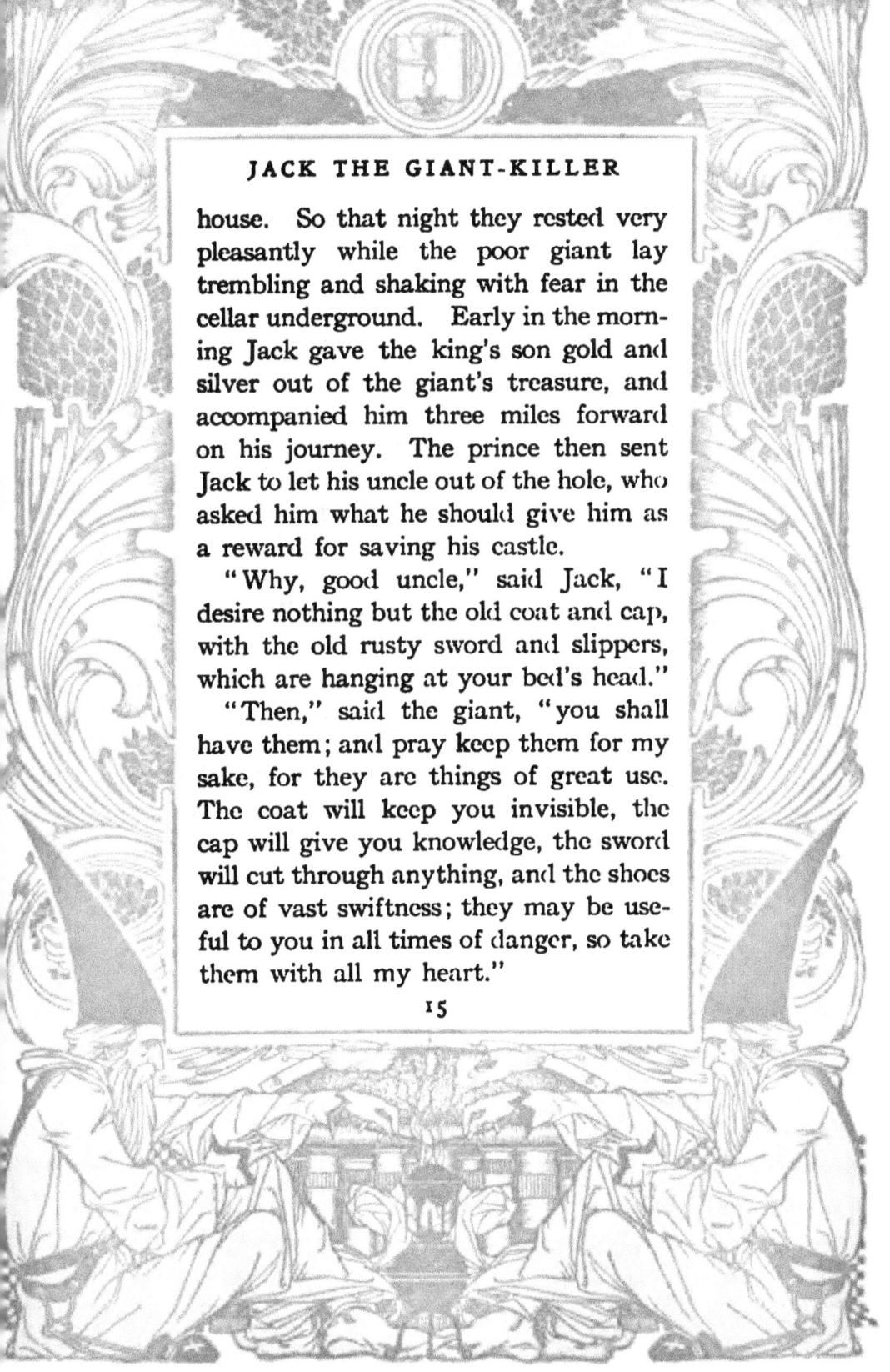

house. So that night they rested very pleasantly while the poor giant lay trembling and shaking with fear in the cellar underground. Early in the morning Jack gave the king's son gold and silver out of the giant's treasure, and accompanied him three miles forward on his journey. The prince then sent Jack to let his uncle out of the hole, who asked him what he should give him as a reward for saving his castle.

"Why, good uncle," said Jack, "I desire nothing but the old coat and cap, with the old rusty sword and slippers, which are hanging at your bed's head."

"Then," said the giant, "you shall have them; and pray keep them for my sake, for they are things of great use. The coat will keep you invisible, the cap will give you knowledge, the sword will cut through anything, and the shoes are of vast swiftness; they may be useful to you in all times of danger, so take them with all my heart."

15

Jack gave many thanks to the giant, and then set off to the prince. When he had come up to the king's son, they soon arrived at the dwelling of the beautiful lady, who was under the power of a wicked magician. She received the prince very politely and made a noble feast for him; when it was ended, she rose, and, wiping her mouth with a fine handkerchief, said, "My lord, you must submit to the custom of my palace; to-morrow morning I command you to tell me on whom I bestow this handkerchief, or lose your head." She then left the room.

The young prince went to bed very mournful, but Jack put on his cap of knowledge, which told him that the lady was forced, by the power of enchantment, to meet the wicked magician every night in the middle of the forest. Jack now put on his coat of darkness and his shoes of swiftness and was there before her. When the lady came

16

she gave the handkerchief to the magician. Jack, with his sword of sharpness, at one blow cut off his head; the enchantment was then ended in a moment, and the lady was restored to her former virtue and goodness. She was married to the prince on the next day, and soon after went back, with her royal husband and a great company, to the court of King Arthur, where they were received with loud and joyful welcomes; and the valiant hero Jack, for the many great exploits he had done for the good of his country, was made one of the Knights of the Round Table.

As Jack had been so lucky in all his adventures, he resolved not to be idle for the future, but still to do what services he could for the honor of the king and the nation. He therefore humbly begged his majesty to furnish him with a horse and money, that he might travel in search of new and strange exploits. "For," said he to the king, "there are many giants yet living in the remote parts of Wales, to the great terror and distress of your majesty's subjects; therefore, if it please you, sire, to favor me in my design, I will soon rid your kingdom of these giants and monsters in human shape."

Now when the king heard this offer, and began to think of the cruel deeds of these blood-thirsty giants and savage monsters, he gave Jack everything proper for such a journey. After this, Jack took leave of the king, the prince, and all the knights, and set off, taking with him his cap of knowledge, his sword of sharpness, his shoes of swiftness, and his invisible coat, the better to perform the great exploits that might fall in his way. He went along over hills and mountains, and on the third day he came to a wide forest. He had hardly entered it when on a sudden he heard dreadful shrieks and cries, and, forcing his way through the trees, saw a mon-

18

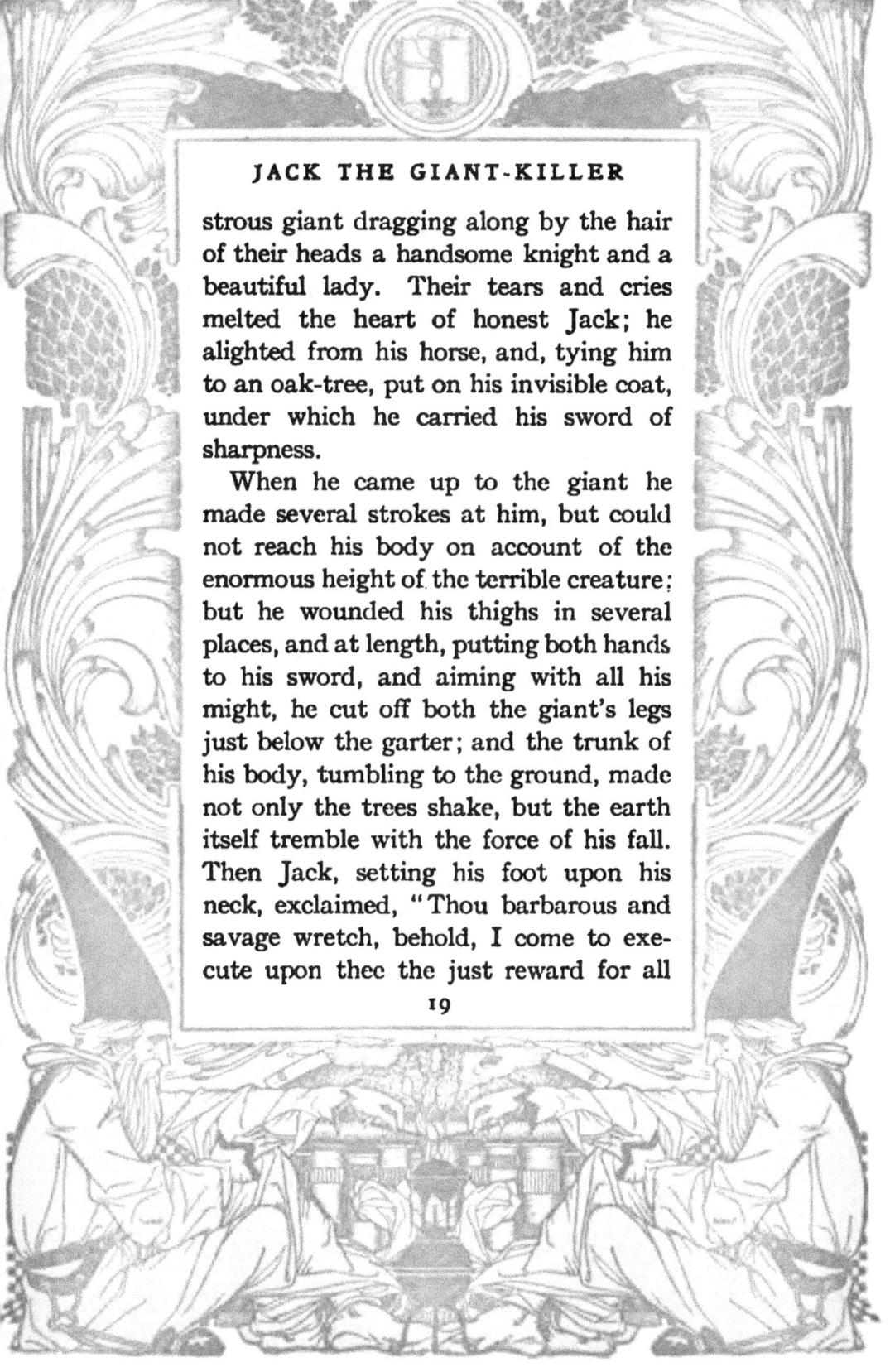

strous giant dragging along by the hair of their heads a handsome knight and a beautiful lady. Their tears and cries melted the heart of honest Jack; he alighted from his horse, and, tying him to an oak-tree, put on his invisible coat, under which he carried his sword of sharpness.

When he came up to the giant he made several strokes at him, but could not reach his body on account of the enormous height of the terrible creature; but he wounded his thighs in several places, and at length, putting both hands to his sword, and aiming with all his might, he cut off both the giant's legs just below the garter; and the trunk of his body, tumbling to the ground, made not only the trees shake, but the earth itself tremble with the force of his fall. Then Jack, setting his foot upon his neck, exclaimed, "Thou barbarous and savage wretch, behold, I come to execute upon thee the just reward for all

thy crimes," and instantly plunged his sword into the giant's body. The huge monster gave a groan, and yielded up his life into the hands of the victorious Jack the Giant-killer, while the noble knight and the virtuous lady were both joyful spectators of his sudden death. They not only returned Jack hearty thanks for their deliverance, but also invited him to their house, to refresh himself after his dreadful encounter, as likewise to receive a reward for his good services.

"No," said Jack, "I cannot be at ease till I find out the den that was the monster's habitation."

The knight, on hearing this, grew very sorrowful, and replied: "Noble stranger, it is too much to run a second hazard: this monster lived in a den under yonder mountain, with a brother of his, more fierce and cruel than himself; therefore, if you should go thither, and perish in the attempt, it would be a heart-break-

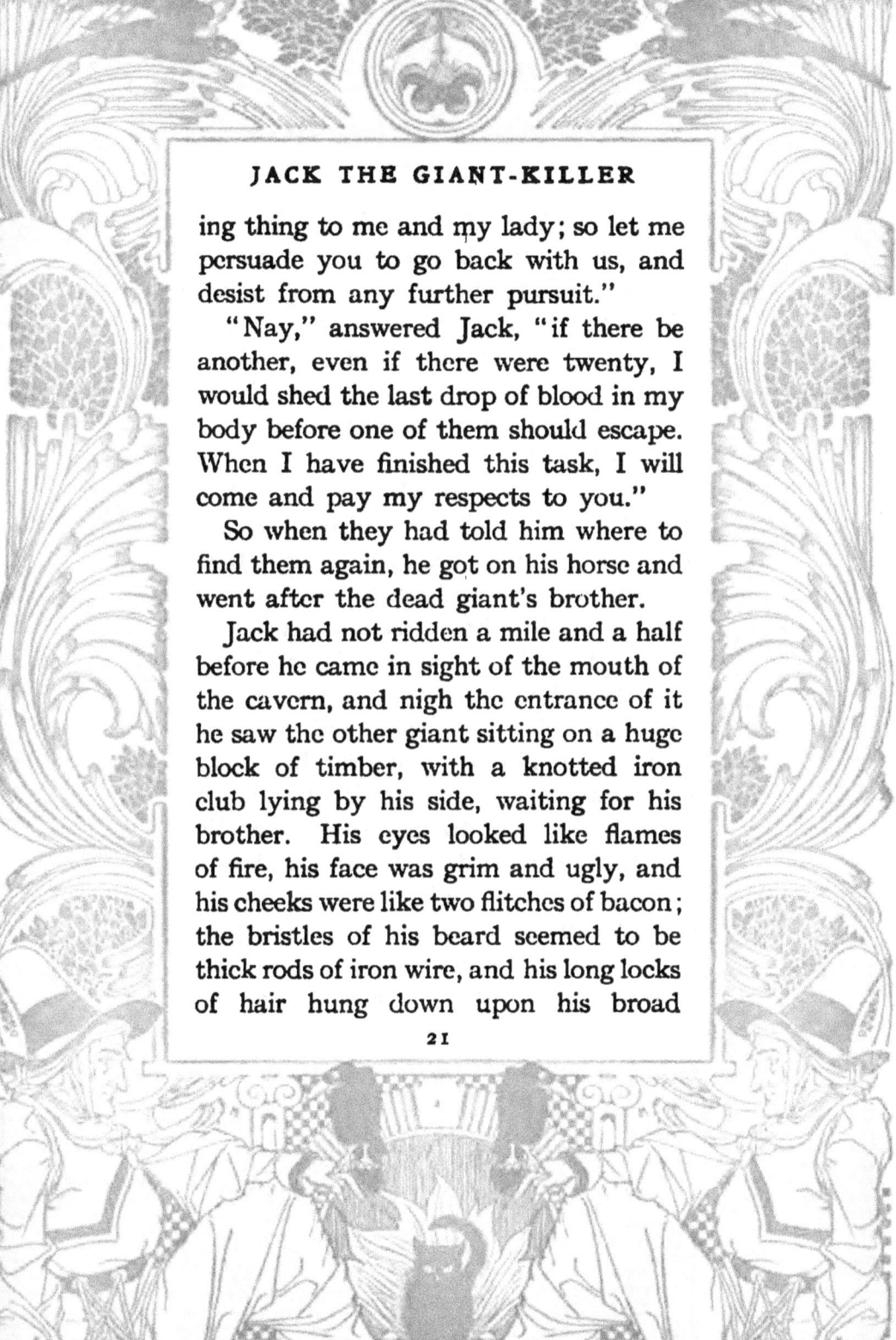

ing thing to me and my lady; so let me persuade you to go back with us, and desist from any further pursuit."

"Nay," answered Jack, "if there be another, even if there were twenty, I would shed the last drop of blood in my body before one of them should escape. When I have finished this task, I will come and pay my respects to you."

So when they had told him where to find them again, he got on his horse and went after the dead giant's brother.

Jack had not ridden a mile and a half before he came in sight of the mouth of the cavern, and nigh the entrance of it he saw the other giant sitting on a huge block of timber, with a knotted iron club lying by his side, waiting for his brother. His eyes looked like flames of fire, his face was grim and ugly, and his cheeks were like two flitches of bacon; the bristles of his beard seemed to be thick rods of iron wire, and his long locks of hair hung down upon his broad

21

shoulders like curling snakes. Jack got down from his horse and turned him into a thicket; then he put on his coat of darkness and drew a little nearer to behold this figure, and said, softly, "Oh, monster! are you there? It will not be long before I shall take you fast by the beard."

The giant all this while could not see him, by reason of his invisible coat, so Jack came quite close to him, and struck a blow at his head with his sword of sharpness; but he missed his aim, and only cut off his nose, which made him roar like loud claps of thunder. He rolled his glaring eyes round on every side, but could not see who had given him the blow; so he took up his iron club, and began to lay about him like one that was mad with pain and fury.

"Nay," said Jack, "if this be the case, I will kill you at once. So saying, he slipped nimbly behind him, and jumping upon the block of timber, as

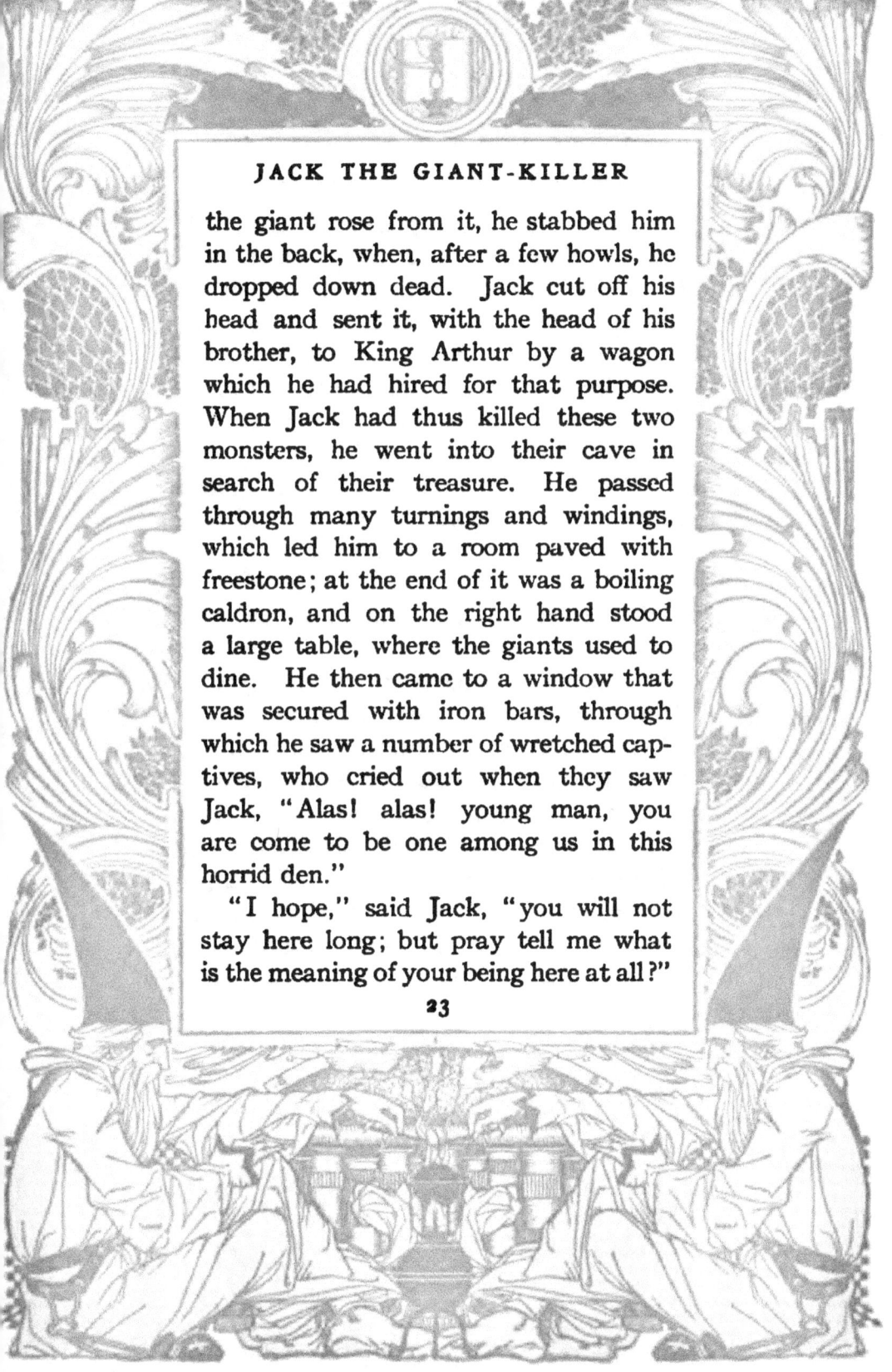

the giant rose from it, he stabbed him in the back, when, after a few howls, he dropped down dead. Jack cut off his head and sent it, with the head of his brother, to King Arthur by a wagon which he had hired for that purpose. When Jack had thus killed these two monsters, he went into their cave in search of their treasure. He passed through many turnings and windings, which led him to a room paved with freestone; at the end of it was a boiling caldron, and on the right hand stood a large table, where the giants used to dine. He then came to a window that was secured with iron bars, through which he saw a number of wretched captives, who cried out when they saw Jack, "Alas! alas! young man, you are come to be one among us in this horrid den."

"I hope," said Jack, "you will not stay here long; but pray tell me what is the meaning of your being here at all?"

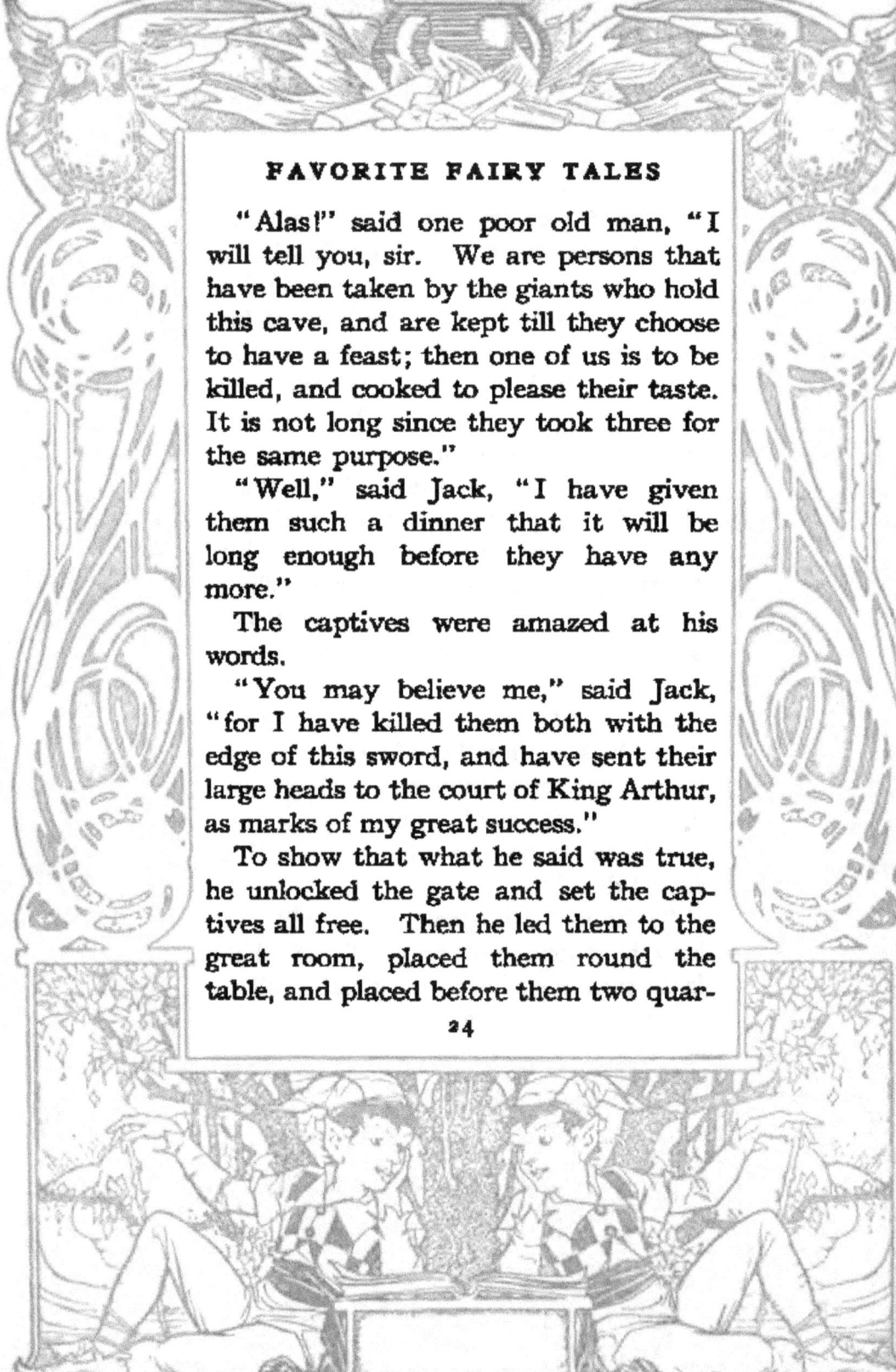

"Alas!" said one poor old man, "I will tell you, sir. We are persons that have been taken by the giants who hold this cave, and are kept till they choose to have a feast; then one of us is to be killed, and cooked to please their taste. It is not long since they took three for the same purpose."

"Well," said Jack, "I have given them such a dinner that it will be long enough before they have any more."

The captives were amazed at his words.

"You may believe me," said Jack, "for I have killed them both with the edge of this sword, and have sent their large heads to the court of King Arthur, as marks of my great success."

To show that what he said was true, he unlocked the gate and set the captives all free. Then he led them to the great room, placed them round the table, and placed before them two quar-

ters of beef, with bread and wine, upon
which they feasted their fill. When
supper was over they searched the
giant's coffers, and Jack divided among
them all the treasures. The next morning they set off to their homes, and Jack
to the knight's house, whom he had left
with his lady not long before.

He was received with the greatest joy
by the thankful knight and his lady,
who, in honor of Jack's exploits, gave
a grand feast, to which all the nobles
and gentry were invited. When the
company were assembled, the knight
declared to them the great actions of
Jack, and gave him, as a mark of re-
spect, a fine ring, on which was engraved the picture of the giant dragging
the knight and the lady by the hair,
with this motto round it:

"Behold in dire distress were we,
　　Under a giant's fierce command;
But gained our lives and liberty
　　From valiant Jack's victorious hand."

3

25

Among the guests then present were
five aged gentlemen, who were fathers
to some of those captives who had been
freed by Jack from the dungeon of the
giants. As soon as they heard that he
was the person who had done such won-
ders, they pressed round him with tears
of joy, to return him thanks for the happiness he had caused them. After this
the bowl went round, and every one
drank the health and long life of the
gallant hero. Mirth increased, and the
hall was filled with peals of laughter.

But, on a sudden, a herald, pale and
breathless, rushed into the midst of the
company, and told them that Thundel,
a savage giant with two heads, had heard
of the death of his two kinsmen, and was
come to take his revenge on Jack, and
that he was now within a mile of the
house, the people flying before him like
chaff before the wind. At this news the
very boldest of the guests trembled;
but Jack drew his sword, and said: "Let

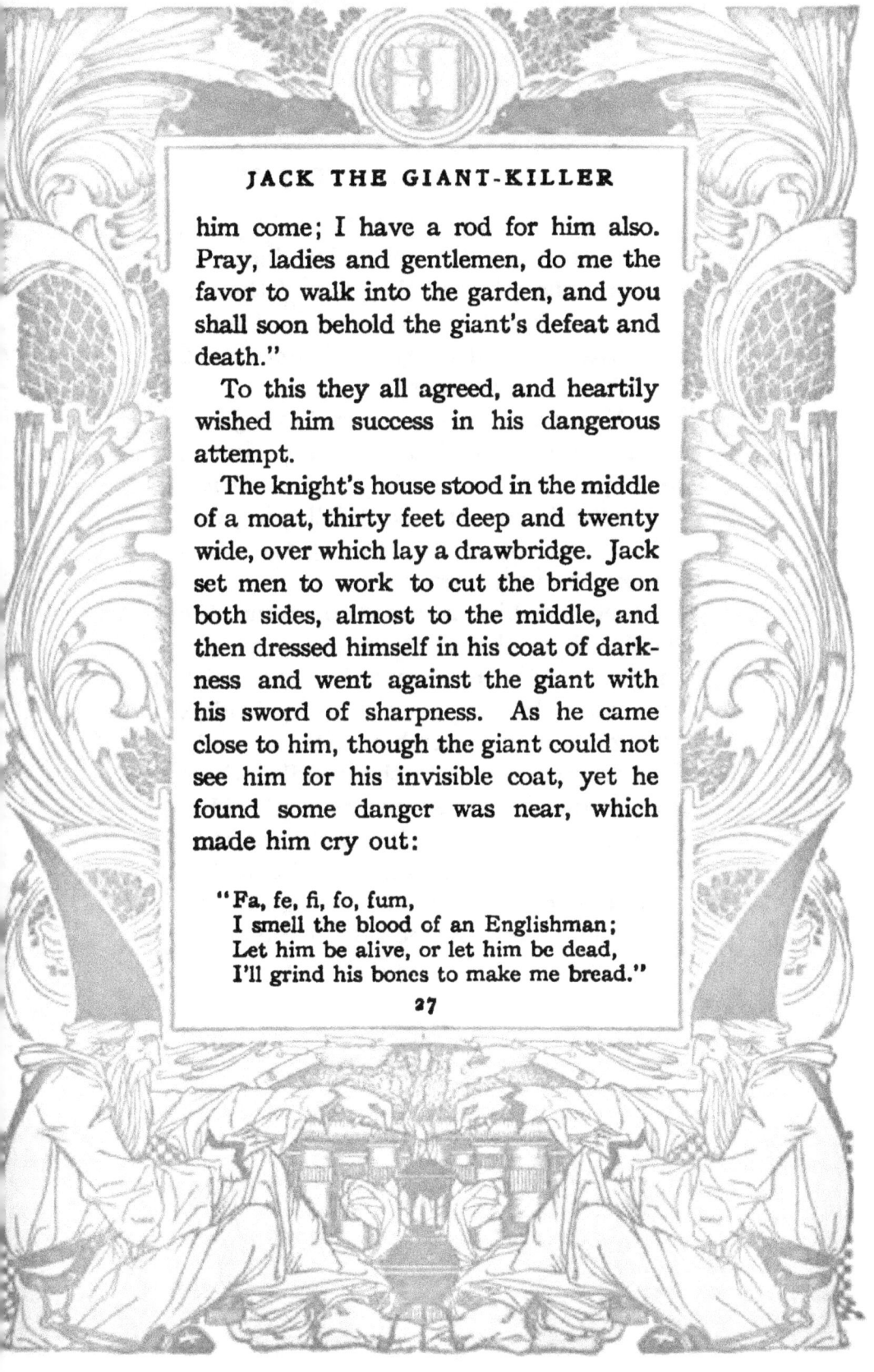

him come; I have a rod for him also. Pray, ladies and gentlemen, do me the favor to walk into the garden, and you shall soon behold the giant's defeat and death."

To this they all agreed, and heartily wished him success in his dangerous attempt.

The knight's house stood in the middle of a moat, thirty feet deep and twenty wide, over which lay a drawbridge. Jack set men to work to cut the bridge on both sides, almost to the middle, and then dressed himself in his coat of darkness and went against the giant with his sword of sharpness. As he came close to him, though the giant could not see him for his invisible coat, yet he found some danger was near, which made him cry out:

"Fa, fe, fi, fo, fum,
I smell the blood of an Englishman;
Let him be alive, or let him be dead,
I'll grind his bones to make me bread."

27

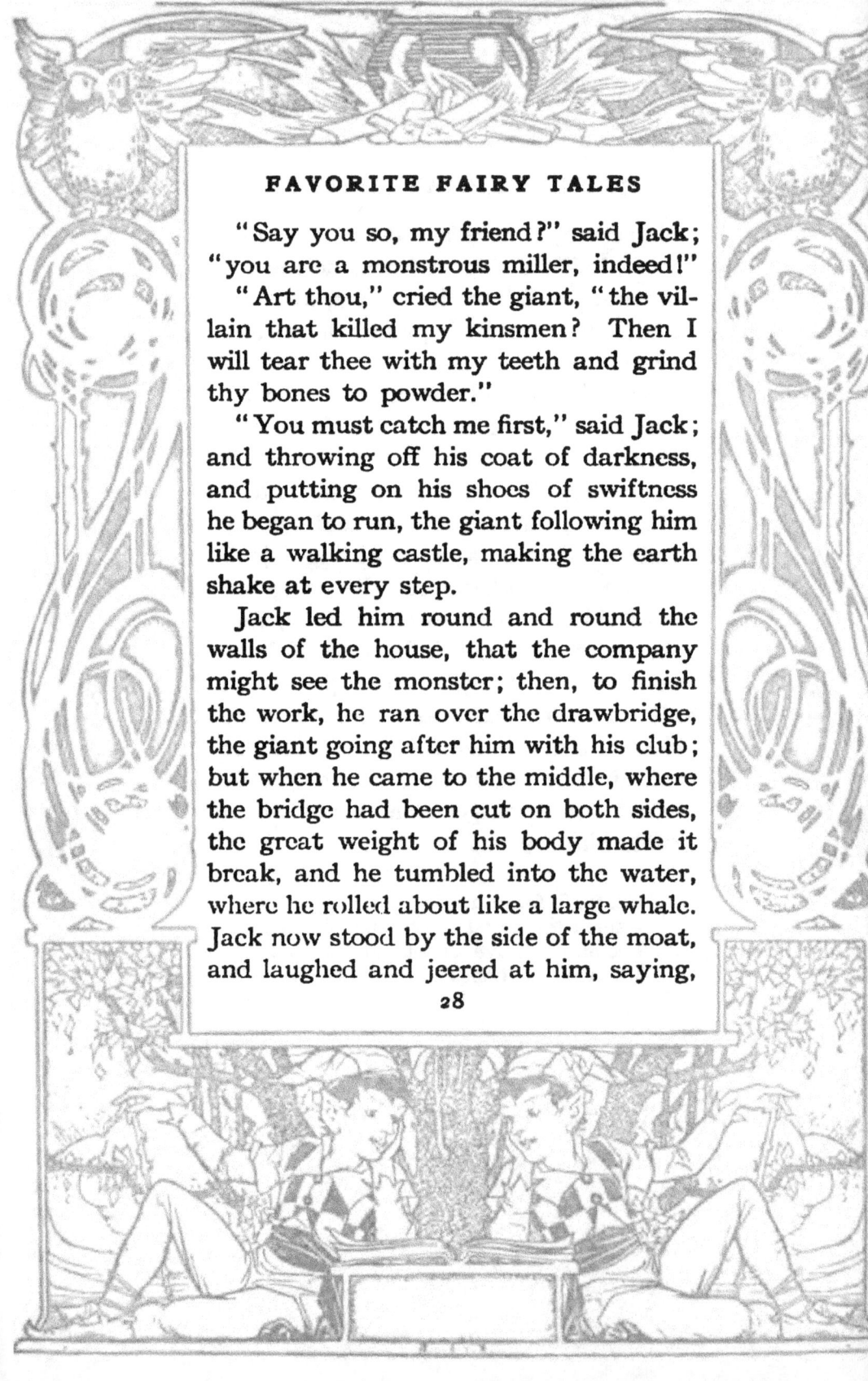

"Say you so, my friend?" said Jack; "you are a monstrous miller, indeed!"

"Art thou," cried the giant, "the villain that killed my kinsmen? Then I will tear thee with my teeth and grind thy bones to powder."

"You must catch me first," said Jack; and throwing off his coat of darkness, and putting on his shoes of swiftness he began to run, the giant following him like a walking castle, making the earth shake at every step.

Jack led him round and round the walls of the house, that the company might see the monster; then, to finish the work, he ran over the drawbridge, the giant going after him with his club; but when he came to the middle, where the bridge had been cut on both sides, the great weight of his body made it break, and he tumbled into the water, where he rolled about like a large whale. Jack now stood by the side of the moat, and laughed and jeered at him, saying,

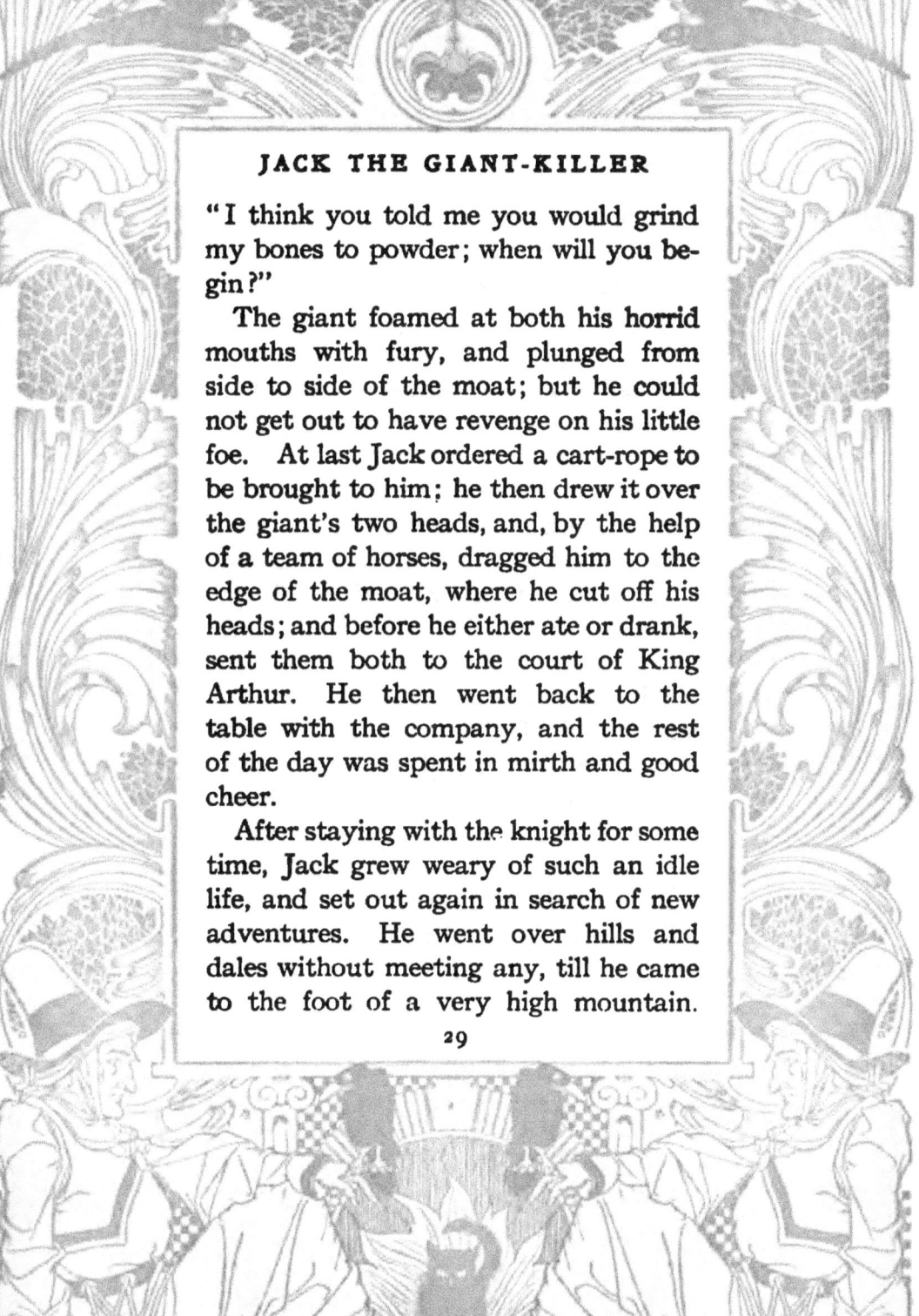

"I think you told me you would grind my bones to powder; when will you begin?"

The giant foamed at both his horrid mouths with fury, and plunged from side to side of the moat; but he could not get out to have revenge on his little foe. At last Jack ordered a cart-rope to be brought to him; he then drew it over the giant's two heads, and, by the help of a team of horses, dragged him to the edge of the moat, where he cut off his heads; and before he either ate or drank, sent them both to the court of King Arthur. He then went back to the table with the company, and the rest of the day was spent in mirth and good cheer.

After staying with the knight for some time, Jack grew weary of such an idle life, and set out again in search of new adventures. He went over hills and dales without meeting any, till he came to the foot of a very high mountain.

Here he knocked at the door of a small and lonely house, and an old man, with a head as white as snow, let him in.

"Good father," said Jack, "can you lodge a traveller who has lost his way?"

"Yes," said the hermit, "I can, if you will accept such fare as my poor house affords."

Jack entered, and the old man set before him some bread and fruit for his supper. When Jack had eaten as much as he chose, the hermit said: "My son, I know you are the famous conqueror of giants; now, at the top of this mountain is an enchanted castle, kept by a giant named Galligantus, who, by the help of a vile magician, gets many knights into his castle, where he changes them into the shape of beasts. Above all, I lament the hard fate of a duke's daughter, whom they seized as she was walking in her father's garden, and brought hither through the air in a chariot drawn by two fiery dragons, and

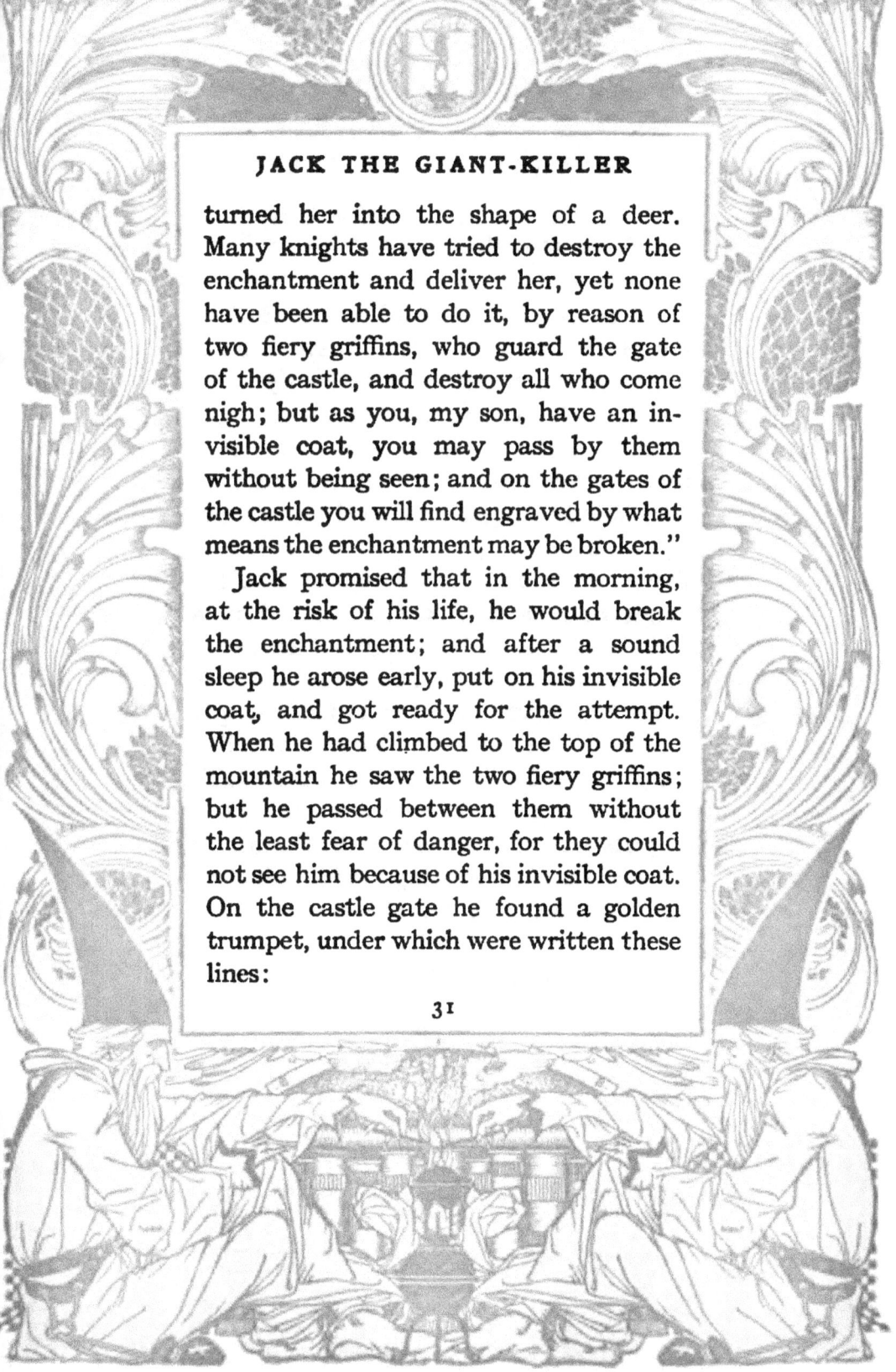

turned her into the shape of a deer.
Many knights have tried to destroy the
enchantment and deliver her, yet none
have been able to do it, by reason of
two fiery griffins, who guard the gate
of the castle, and destroy all who come
nigh; but as you, my son, have an invisible coat, you may pass by them
without being seen; and on the gates of
the castle you will find engraved by what
means the enchantment may be broken."

Jack promised that in the morning,
at the risk of his life, he would break
the enchantment; and after a sound
sleep he arose early, put on his invisible
coat, and got ready for the attempt.
When he had climbed to the top of the
mountain he saw the two fiery griffins;
but he passed between them without
the least fear of danger, for they could
not see him because of his invisible coat.
On the castle gate he found a golden
trumpet, under which were written these
lines:

31

"Whoever can this trumpet blow,
Shall cause the giant's overthrow."

As soon as Jack had read this he
seized the trumpet and blew a shrill
blast, which made the gates fly open
and the very castle itself tremble. The
giant and the conjuror now knew that
their wicked course was at an end, and
they stood biting their thumbs and shaking with fear. Jack, with his sword of
sharpness, soon killed the giant, and the
magician was then carried away by a
whirlwind. All the knights and beautiful ladies, who had been changed into
birds and beasts, returned to their proper
shapes. The castle vanished away like
smoke, and the head of the giant Galligantus was sent to King Arthur. The
knights and ladies rested that night at
the old man's hermitage, and the next
day they set out for the court. Jack
then went up to the king, and gave his
majesty an account of all his fierce

32

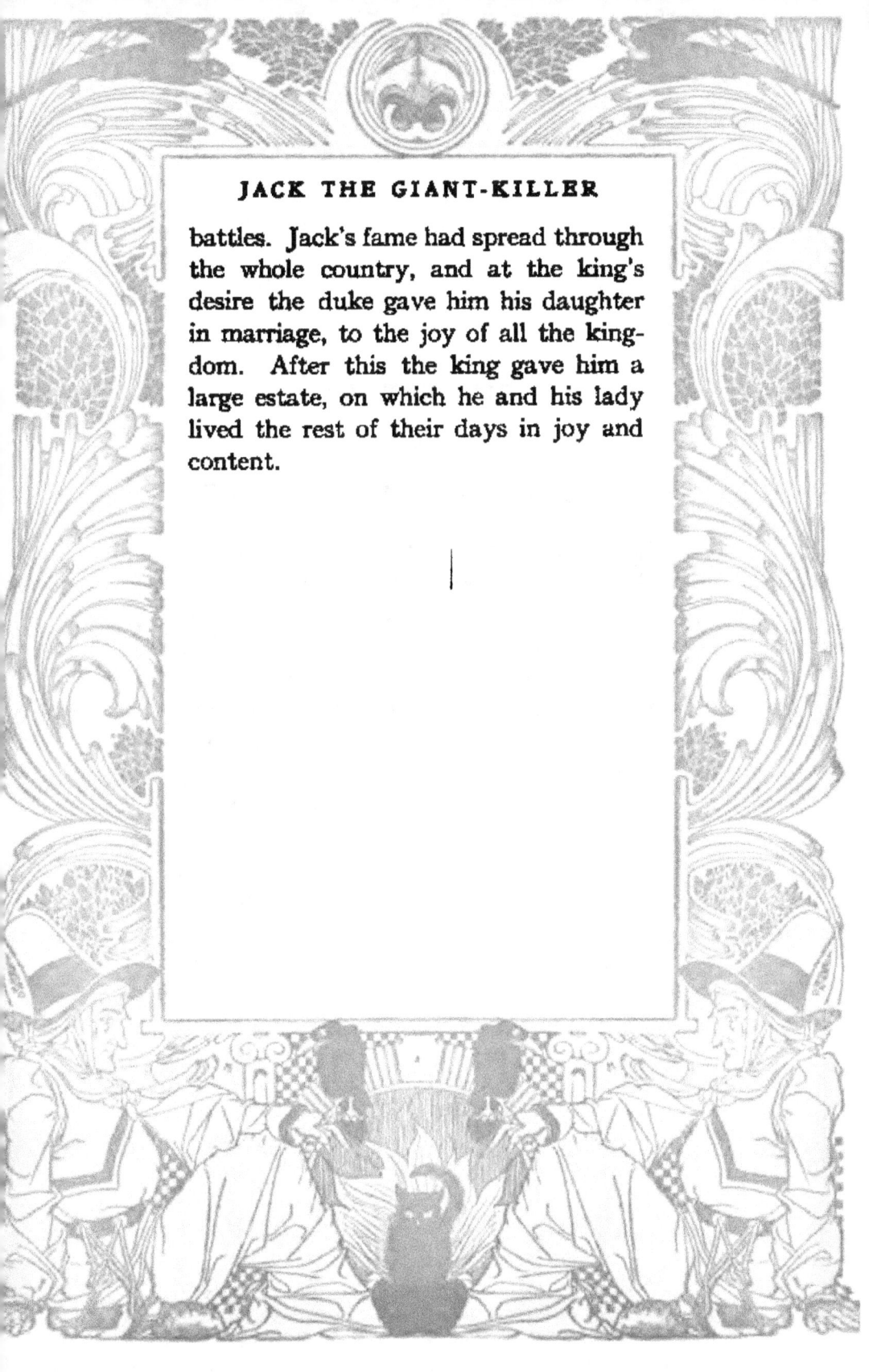

JACK THE GIANT-KILLER

battles. Jack's fame had spread through the whole country, and at the king's desire the duke gave him his daughter in marriage, to the joy of all the kingdom. After this the king gave him a large estate, on which he and his lady lived the rest of their days in joy and content.

CINDERELLA

OR

THE LITTLE GLASS SLIPPER

THERE was once an honest gentleman who took for his second wife a lady, the proudest and most disagreeable in the whole country. She had two daughters exactly like herself in all things. He also had one little girl, who resembled her dead mother, the best woman in all the world. Scarcely had the second marriage taken place than the step-mother became jealous of the good qualities of the little girl, who was so great a contrast to her own two daughters. She gave her all the menial occupations of the house: com-

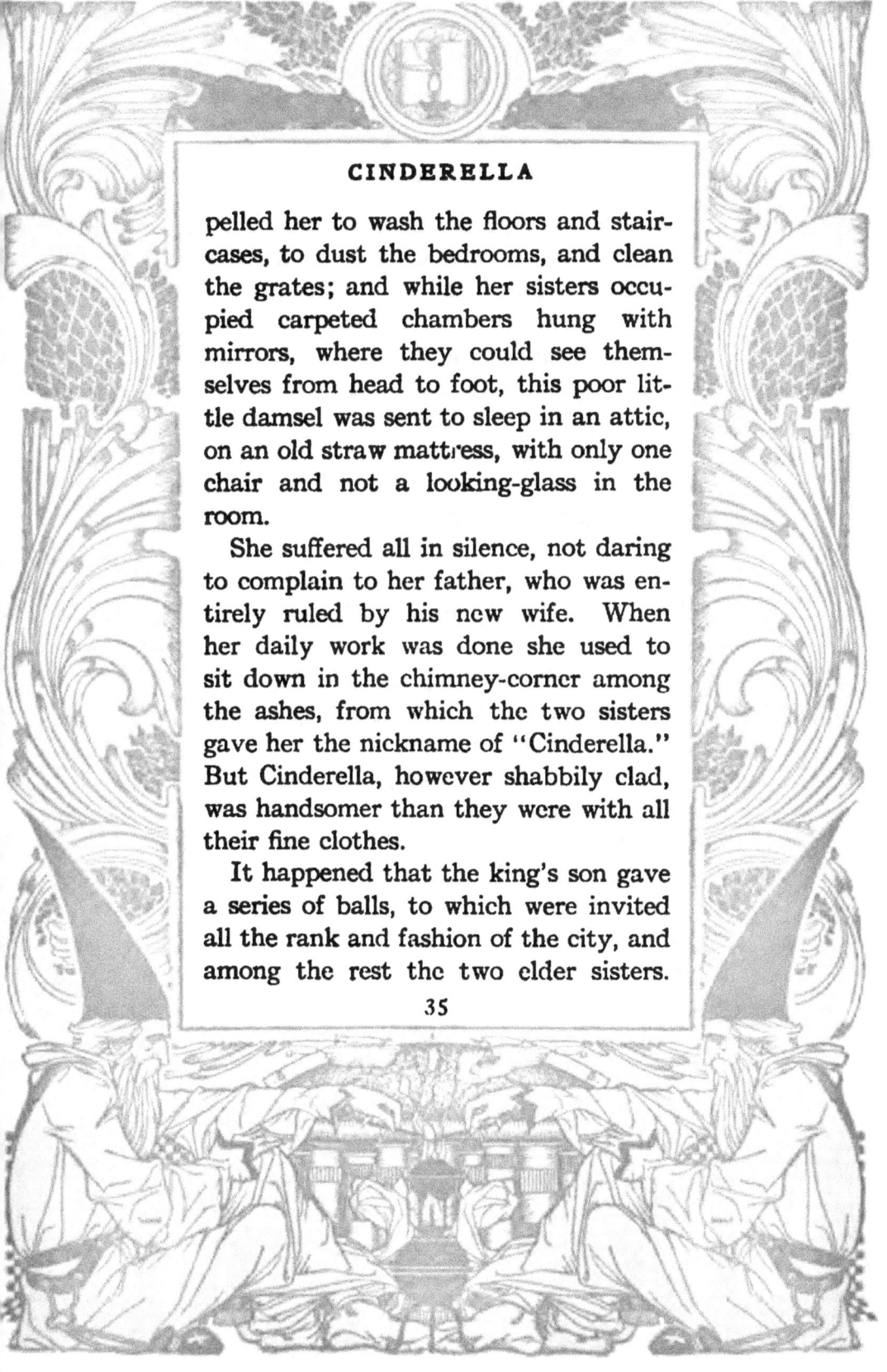

pelled her to wash the floors and stair-
cases, to dust the bedrooms, and clean
the grates; and while her sisters occupied carpeted chambers hung with
mirrors, where they could see themselves from head to foot, this poor little damsel was sent to sleep in an attic,
on an old straw mattress, with only one
chair and not a looking-glass in the
room.

She suffered all in silence, not daring
to complain to her father, who was entirely ruled by his new wife. When
her daily work was done she used to
sit down in the chimney-corner among
the ashes, from which the two sisters
gave her the nickname of "Cinderella."
But Cinderella, however shabbily clad,
was handsomer than they were with all
their fine clothes.

It happened that the king's son gave
a series of balls, to which were invited
all the rank and fashion of the city, and
among the rest the two elder sisters.

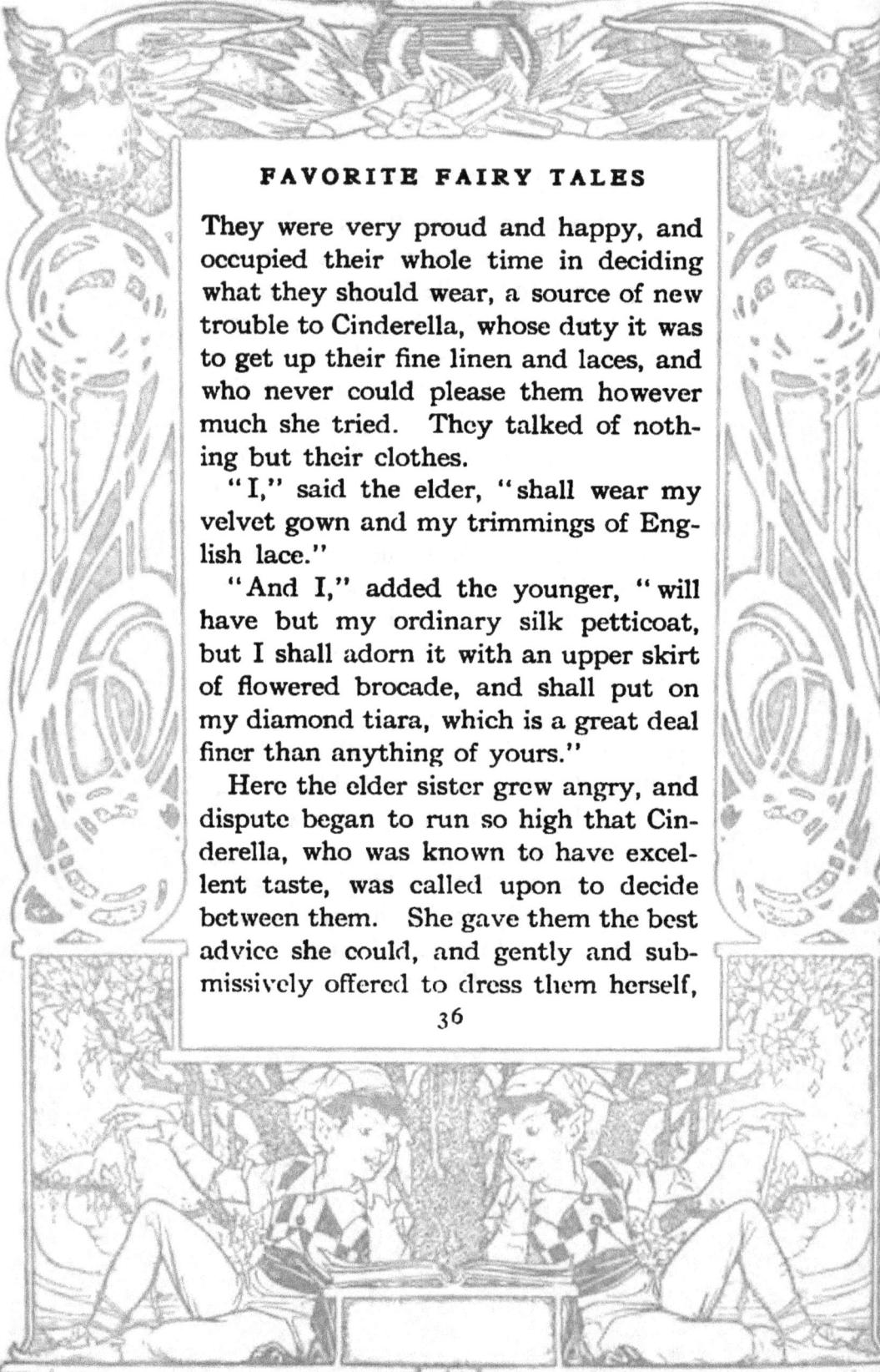

They were very proud and happy, and occupied their whole time in deciding what they should wear, a source of new trouble to Cinderella, whose duty it was to get up their fine linen and laces, and who never could please them however much she tried. They talked of nothing but their clothes.

"I," said the elder, "shall wear my velvet gown and my trimmings of English lace."

"And I," added the younger, "will have but my ordinary silk petticoat, but I shall adorn it with an upper skirt of flowered brocade, and shall put on my diamond tiara, which is a great deal finer than anything of yours."

Here the elder sister grew angry, and dispute began to run so high that Cinderella, who was known to have excellent taste, was called upon to decide between them. She gave them the best advice she could, and gently and submissively offered to dress them herself,

and especially to arrange their hair,
an accomplishment in which she ex-
celled many a noted coiffeur. The important evening came, and she exercised
all her skill to adorn the two young
ladies. While she was combing out the
elder's hair, this ill-natured girl said,
sharply, "Cinderella, do you not wish
you were going to the ball?"

"Ah, madam" (they obliged her always to say madam), "you are only
mocking me; it is not my fortune to
have any such pleasure."

"You are right; people would only
laugh to see a little cinder-wench at a
ball."

Any other than Cinderella would have
dressed the hair all awry, but she was
good, and dressed it perfectly even and
smooth, and as prettily as she could.

The sisters had scarcely eaten for two
days, and had broken a dozen stay-laces
a day, in trying to make themselves
slender; but to-night they broke a dozen

37

more, and lost their tempers over and over again before they had completed their toilet. When at last the happy moment arrived, Cinderella followed them to the coach; after it had whirled them away, she sat down by the kitchen fire and cried.

Immediately her godmother, who was a fairy, appeared beside her. "What are you crying for, my little maid?"

"Oh, I wish — I wish —" Her sobs stopped her.

"You wish to go to the ball; isn't it so?"

Cinderella nodded.

"Well, then, be a good girl and you shall go. First run into the garden and fetch me the largest pumpkin you can find."

Cinderella did not comprehend what this had to do with her going to the ball, but, being obedient and obliging, she went. Her godmother took the pumpkin, and, having scooped out all

38

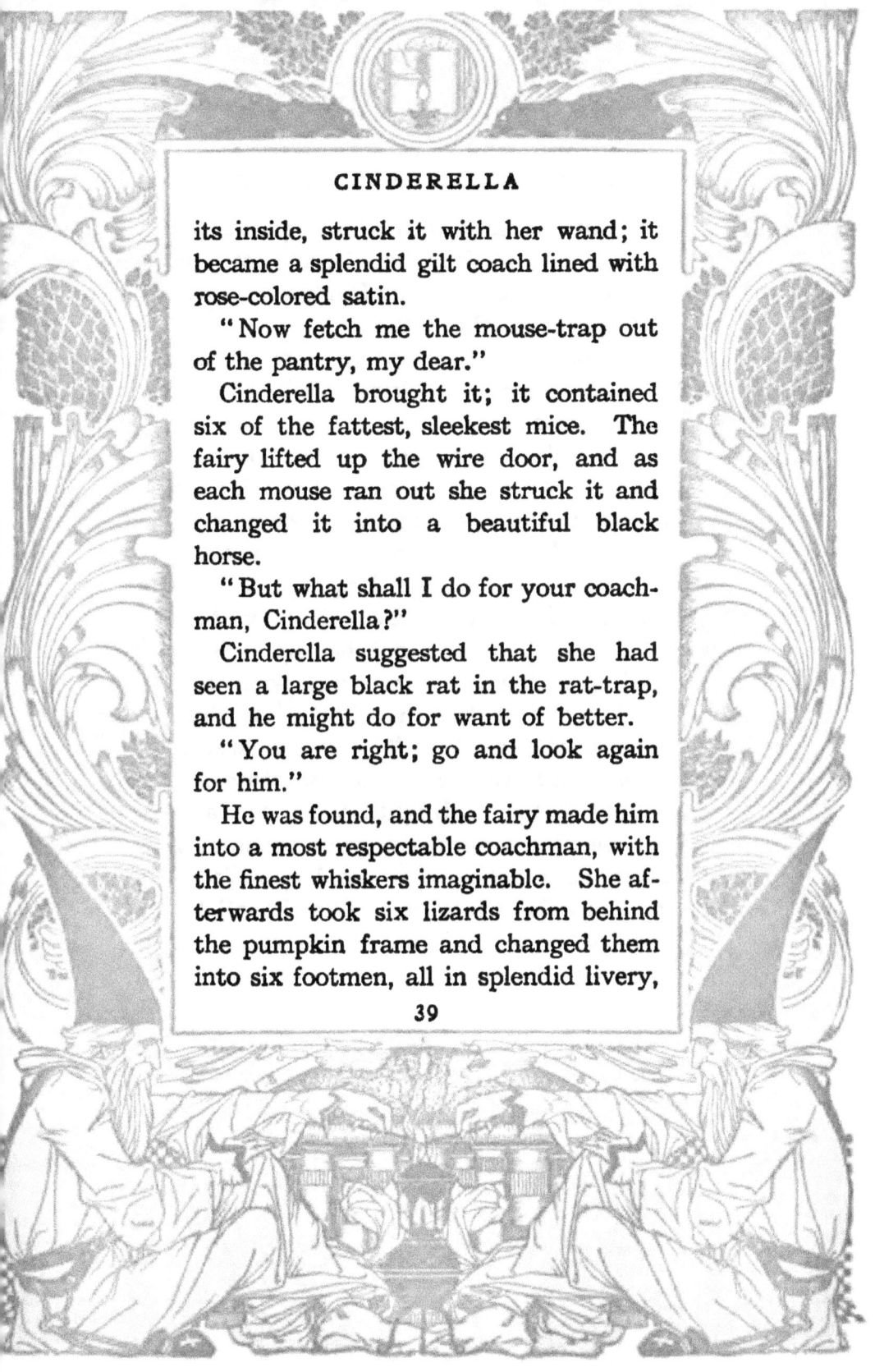

its inside, struck it with her wand; it became a splendid gilt coach lined with rose-colored satin.

"Now fetch me the mouse-trap out of the pantry, my dear."

Cinderella brought it; it contained six of the fattest, sleekest mice. The fairy lifted up the wire door, and as each mouse ran out she struck it and changed it into a beautiful black horse.

"But what shall I do for your coachman, Cinderella?"

Cinderella suggested that she had seen a large black rat in the rat-trap, and he might do for want of better.

"You are right; go and look again for him."

He was found, and the fairy made him into a most respectable coachman, with the finest whiskers imaginable. She afterwards took six lizards from behind the pumpkin frame and changed them into six footmen, all in splendid livery,

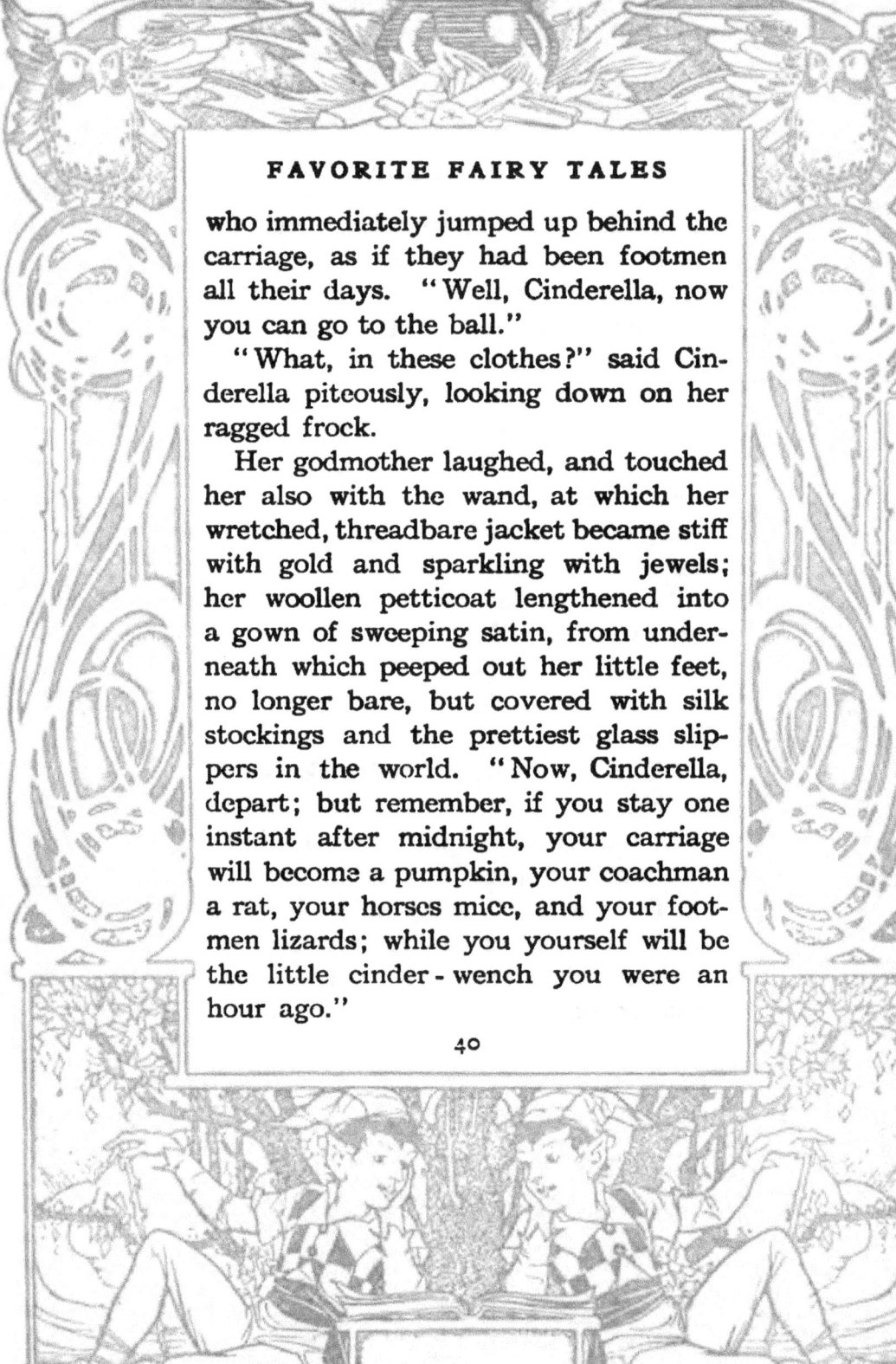

who immediately jumped up behind the carriage, as if they had been footmen all their days. "Well, Cinderella, now you can go to the ball."

"What, in these clothes?" said Cinderella piteously, looking down on her ragged frock.

Her godmother laughed, and touched her also with the wand, at which her wretched, threadbare jacket became stiff with gold and sparkling with jewels; her woollen petticoat lengthened into a gown of sweeping satin, from underneath which peeped out her little feet, no longer bare, but covered with silk stockings and the prettiest glass slippers in the world. "Now, Cinderella, depart; but remember, if you stay one instant after midnight, your carriage will become a pumpkin, your coachman a rat, your horses mice, and your footmen lizards; while you yourself will be the little cinder-wench you were an hour ago."

CINDERELLA

Cinderella promised without fear, her heart was so full of joy.

Arrived at the palace, the king's son, whom some one, probably the fairy, had told to await the coming of an un-invited princess whom nobody knew, was standing at the entrance ready to receive her. He offered her his hand, and led her with the utmost courtesy through the assembled guests, who stood aside to let her pass, whispering to one another, "Oh, how beautiful she is!" It might have turned the head of any one but poor Cinderella, who was so used to be despised that she took it all as if it were something happening in a dream.

Her triumph was complete; even the old king said to the queen, that never since her majesty's young days had he seen so charming and elegant a person. All the court ladies scanned her eagerly, clothes and all, determining to have theirs made next day of exactly the same pattern. The king's son himself led her out to dance, and she danced so gracefully that he admired her more and more. Indeed, at supper, which was fortunately early, his admiration quite took away his appetite. For Cinderella herself, with an involuntary shyness she sought out her sisters, placed herself beside them, and offered them all sorts of civil attentions, which, coming as they supposed from a stranger, and so magnificent a lady, almost overwhelmed them with delight.

While she was talking with them she heard the clock strike a quarter to twelve, and making a courteous adieu to the royal family, she re-entered her carriage, escorted tenderly by the king's son, and arrived in safety at her own door. There she found her godmother, who smiled approval, and of whom she begged permission to go to a second ball, the following night, to which the queen had earnestly invited her.

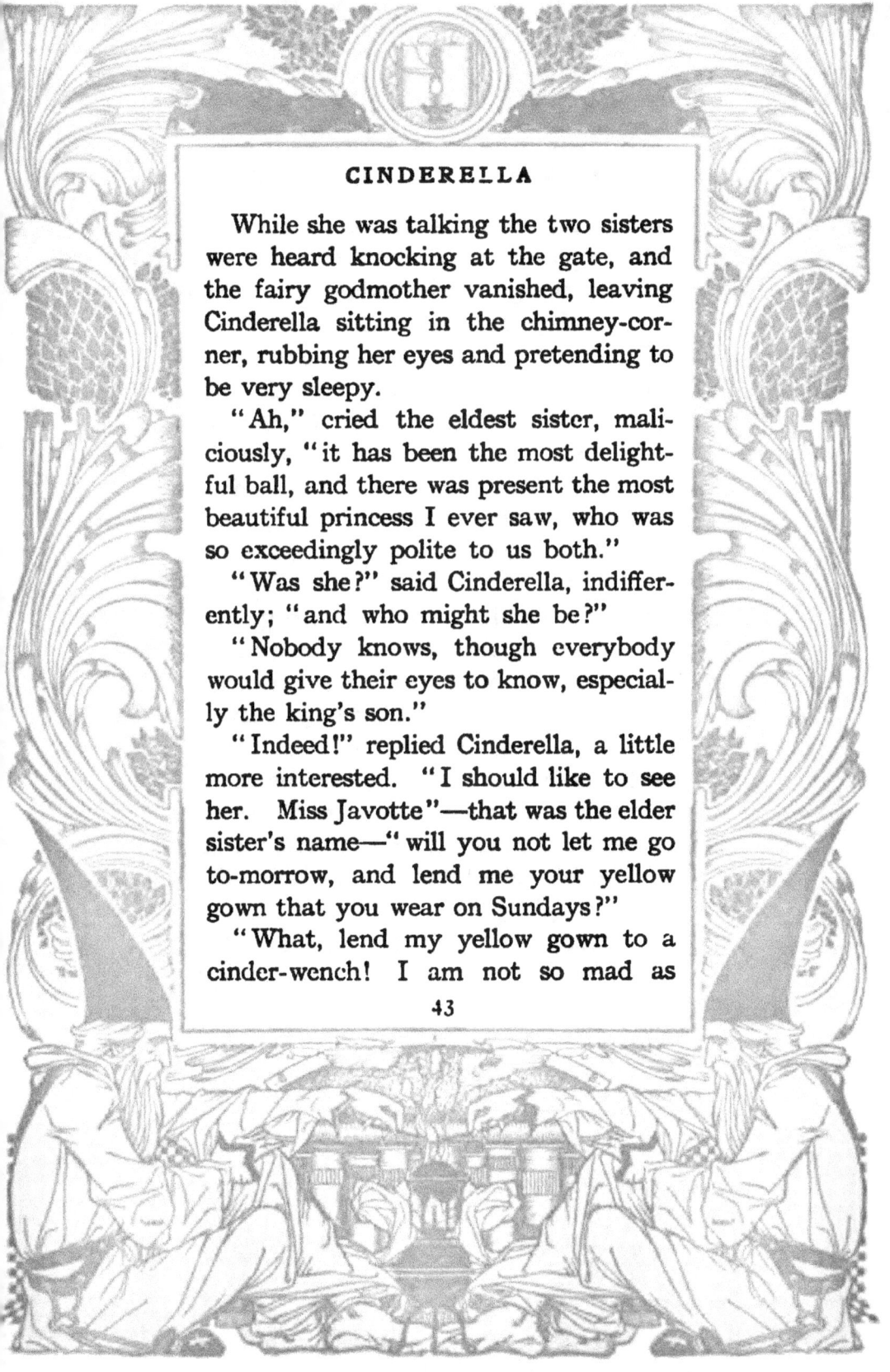

CINDERELLA

While she was talking the two sisters were heard knocking at the gate, and the fairy godmother vanished, leaving Cinderella sitting in the chimney-corner, rubbing her eyes and pretending to be very sleepy.

"Ah," cried the eldest sister, maliciously, "it has been the most delightful ball, and there was present the most beautiful princess I ever saw, who was so exceedingly polite to us both."

"Was she?" said Cinderella, indifferently; "and who might she be?"

"Nobody knows, though everybody would give their eyes to know, especially the king's son."

"Indeed!" replied Cinderella, a little more interested. "I should like to see her. Miss Javotte"—that was the elder sister's name—"will you not let me go to-morrow, and lend me your yellow gown that you wear on Sundays?"

"What, lend my yellow gown to a cinder-wench! I am not so mad as

43

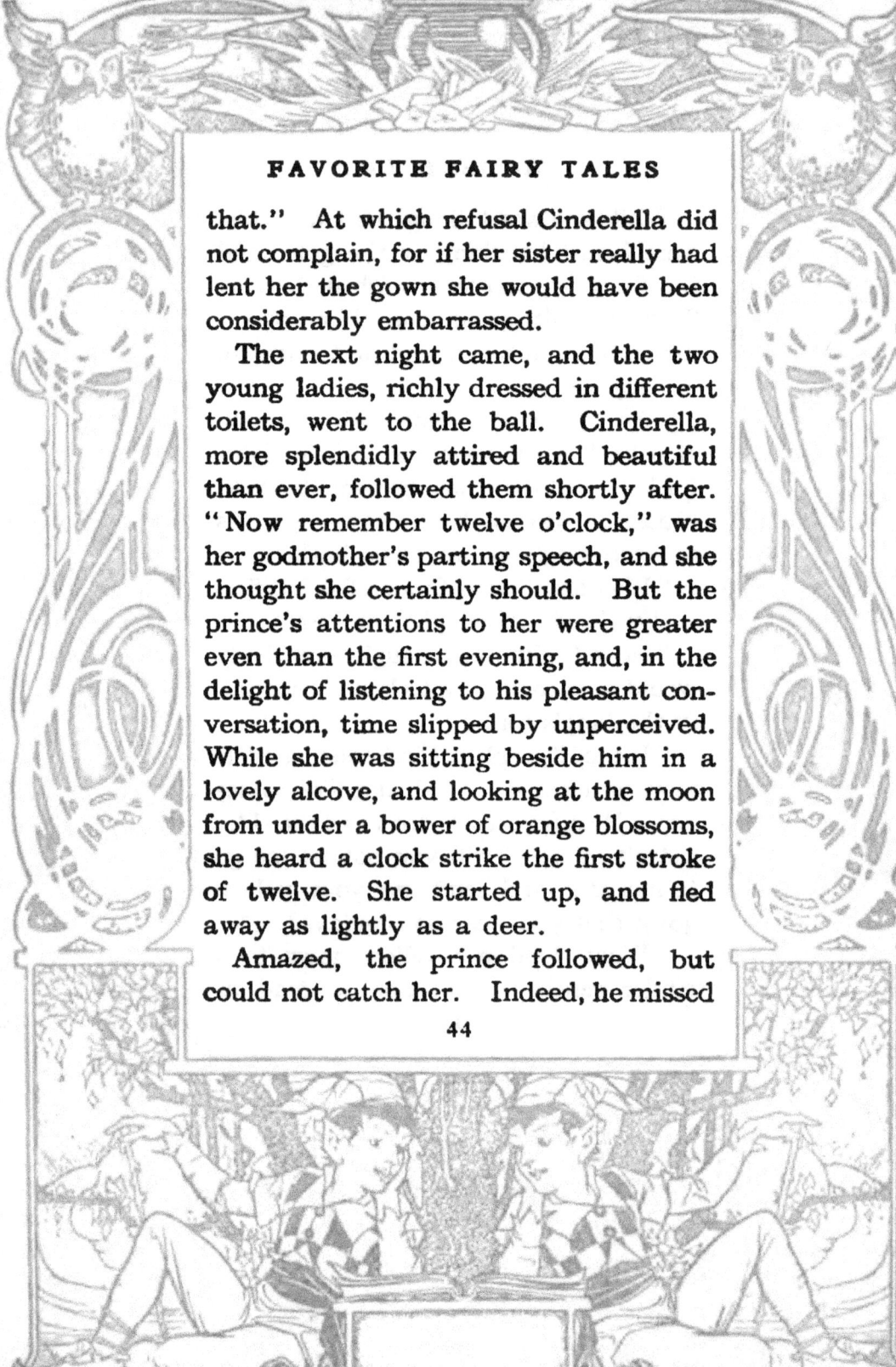

that." At which refusal Cinderella did
not complain, for if her sister really had
lent her the gown she would have been
considerably embarrassed.

The next night came, and the two
young ladies, richly dressed in different
toilets, went to the ball. Cinderella,
more splendidly attired and beautiful
than ever, followed them shortly after.
"Now remember twelve o'clock," was
her godmother's parting speech, and she
thought she certainly should. But the
prince's attentions to her were greater
even than the first evening, and, in the
delight of listening to his pleasant conversation, time slipped by unperceived.
While she was sitting beside him in a
lovely alcove, and looking at the moon
from under a bower of orange blossoms,
she heard a clock strike the first stroke
of twelve. She started up, and fled
away as lightly as a deer.

Amazed, the prince followed, but
could not catch her. Indeed, he missed

his lovely princess altogether, and only saw running out of the palace doors a little dirty lass whom he had never beheld before, and of whom he certainly would never have taken the least notice. Cinderella arrived at home breathless and weary, ragged and cold, without carriage or footmen or coachman, the only remnant of her past magnificence being one of her little glass slippers—the other she had dropped in the ballroom as she ran away.

When the two sisters returned they were full of this strange adventure: how the beautiful lady had appeared at the ball more beautiful than ever, and enchanted every one who looked at her; and how as the clock was striking twelve she had suddenly risen up and fled through the ballroom, disappearing no one knew how or where, and dropping one of her glass slippers behind her in her flight. How the king's son had remained inconsolable until he chanced to pick up the little glass slipper, which he carried away in his pocket, and was seen to take it out continually, and look at it affectionately, with the air of a man very much in love; in fact, from his behavior during the remainder of the evening, all the court and royal family were convinced that he had become desperately enamoured of the wearer of the little glass slipper.

Cinderella listened in silence, turning her face to the kitchen fire, and perhaps it was that which made her look so rosy, but nobody ever noticed or admired her at home, so it did not signify, and next morning she went to her weary work again just as before.

A few days after, the whole city was attracted by the sight of a herald going round with a little glass slipper in his hand, publishing, with a flourish of trumpets, that the king's son ordered this to be fitted on the foot of every lady in the kingdom, and that he wished

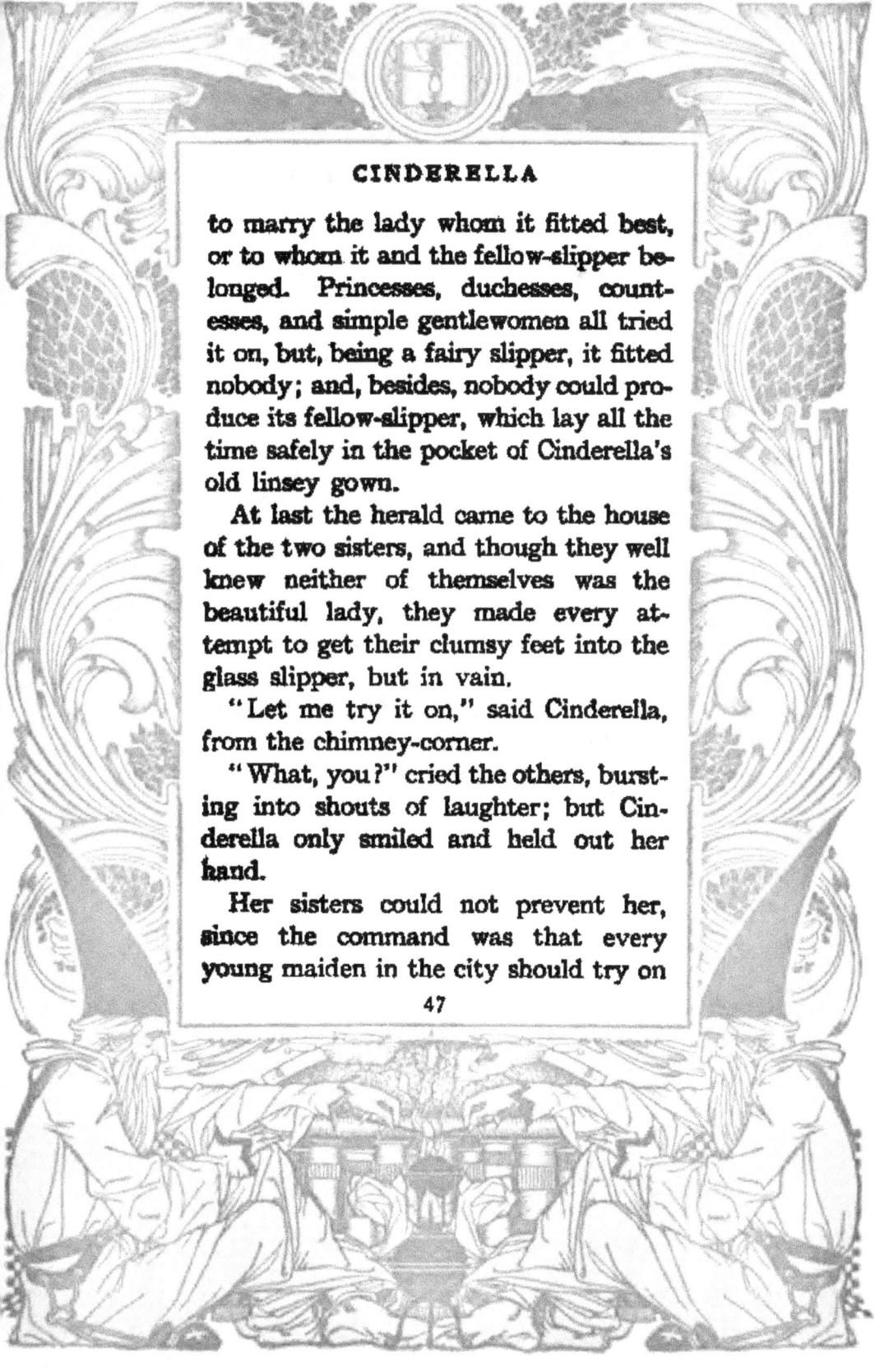

to marry the lady whom it fitted best, or to whom it and the fellow-slipper belonged. Princesses, duchesses, countesses, and simple gentlewomen all tried it on, but, being a fairy slipper, it fitted nobody; and, besides, nobody could produce its fellow-slipper, which lay all the time safely in the pocket of Cinderella's old linsey gown.

At last the herald came to the house of the two sisters, and though they well knew neither of themselves was the beautiful lady, they made every attempt to get their clumsy feet into the glass slipper, but in vain.

"Let me try it on," said Cinderella, from the chimney-corner.

"What, you?" cried the others, bursting into shouts of laughter; but Cinderella only smiled and held out her hand.

Her sisters could not prevent her, since the command was that every young maiden in the city should try on

47

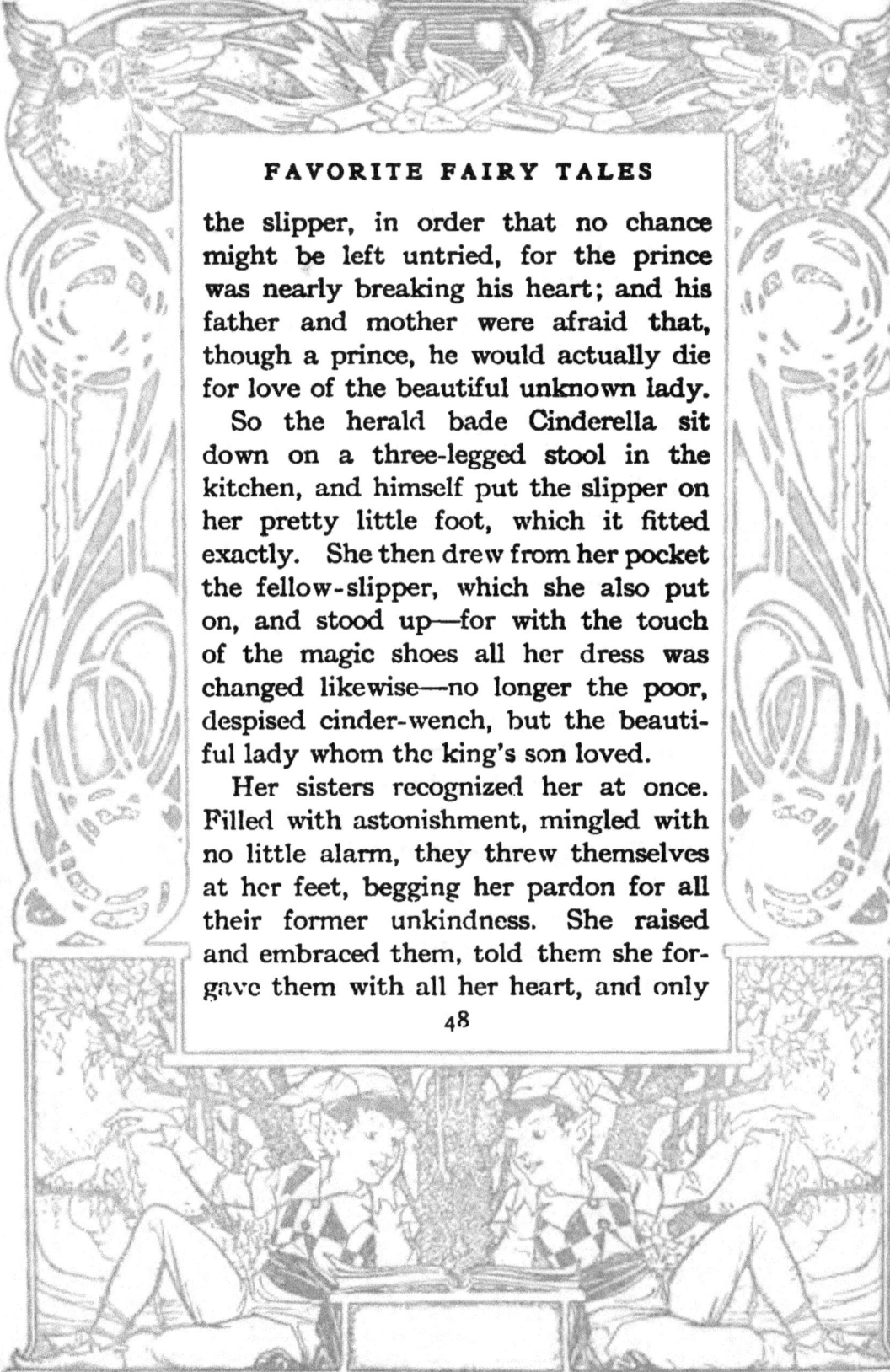

the slipper, in order that no chance might be left untried, for the prince was nearly breaking his heart; and his father and mother were afraid that, though a prince, he would actually die for love of the beautiful unknown lady.

So the herald bade Cinderella sit down on a three-legged stool in the kitchen, and himself put the slipper on her pretty little foot, which it fitted exactly. She then drew from her pocket the fellow-slipper, which she also put on, and stood up—for with the touch of the magic shoes all her dress was changed likewise—no longer the poor, despised cinder-wench, but the beautiful lady whom the king's son loved.

Her sisters recognized her at once. Filled with astonishment, mingled with no little alarm, they threw themselves at her feet, begging her pardon for all their former unkindness. She raised and embraced them, told them she forgave them with all her heart, and only

The slipper fitted exactly

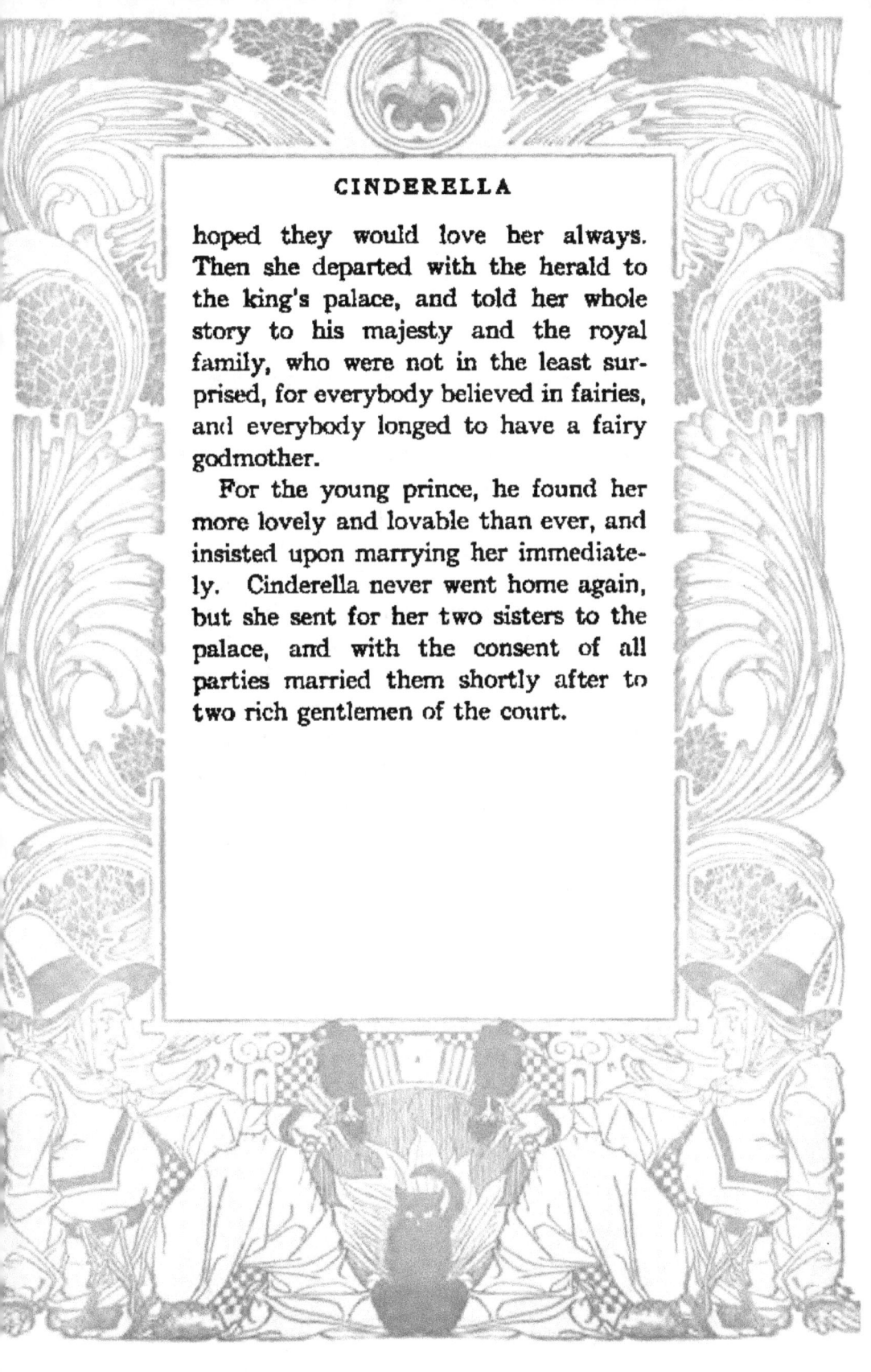

hoped they would love her always.
Then she departed with the herald to
the king's palace, and told her whole
story to his majesty and the royal
family, who were not in the least surprised, for everybody believed in fairies,
and everybody longed to have a fairy
godmother.

For the young prince, he found her
more lovely and lovable than ever, and
insisted upon marrying her immediately. Cinderella never went home again,
but she sent for her two sisters to the
palace, and with the consent of all
parties married them shortly after to
two rich gentlemen of the court.

JACK AND THE BEAN-STALK

IN the days of King Alfred there lived a poor woman whose cottage was in a remote country village many miles from London. She had been a widow some years, and had an only child named Jack, whom she indulged so much that he never paid the least attention to anything she said, but was indolent, careless, and extravagant. His follies were not owing to a bad disposition, but to his mother's foolish partiality. By degrees he spent all that she had — scarcely anything remained, but a cow.

One day, for the first time in her life, she reproached him: "Cruel, cruel boy! you have at last brought me to beggary.

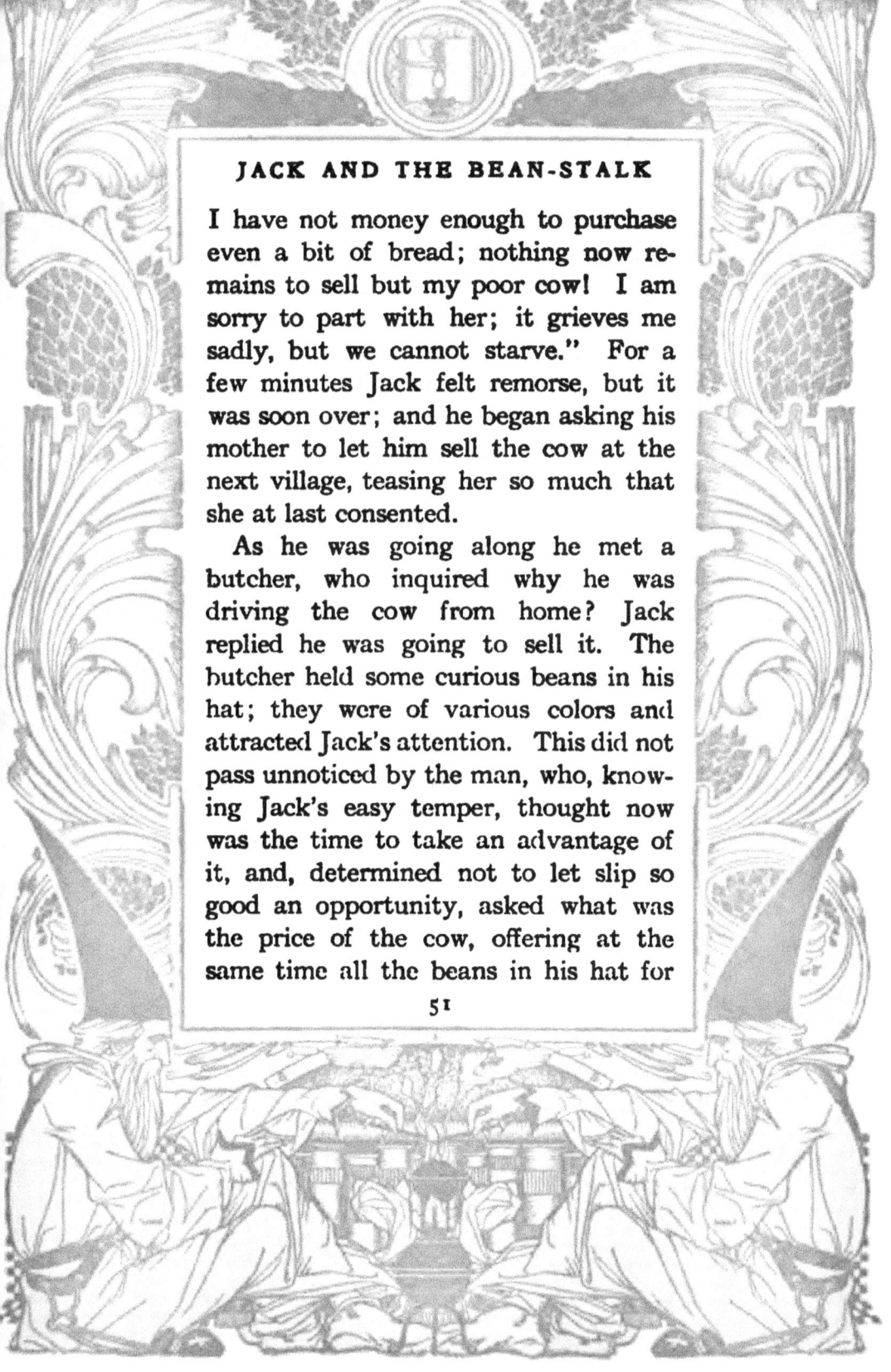

I have not money enough to purchase even a bit of bread; nothing now remains to sell but my poor cow! I am sorry to part with her; it grieves me sadly, but we cannot starve." For a few minutes Jack felt remorse, but it was soon over; and he began asking his mother to let him sell the cow at the next village, teasing her so much that she at last consented.

As he was going along he met a butcher, who inquired why he was driving the cow from home? Jack replied he was going to sell it. The butcher held some curious beans in his hat; they were of various colors and attracted Jack's attention. This did not pass unnoticed by the man, who, knowing Jack's easy temper, thought now was the time to take an advantage of it, and, determined not to let slip so good an opportunity, asked what was the price of the cow, offering at the same time all the beans in his hat for

her. The silly boy could not conceal the pleasure he felt at what he supposed so great an offer; the bargain was struck instantly, and the cow exchanged for a few paltry beans. Jack made the best of his way home, calling aloud to his mother before he reached the door, thinking to surprise her.

When she saw the beans and heard Jack's account, her patience quite forsook her; she tossed the beans out of the window, where they fell on the garden-bed below. Then she threw her apron over her head and cried bitterly. Jack attempted to console her, but in vain, and, not having anything to eat, they both went supperless to bed. Jack awoke early in the morning, and, seeing something uncommon darkening the window of his bedchamber, ran down-stairs into the garden, where he found some of the beans had taken root and sprung up surprisingly; the stalks were of an immense thickness, and had

twined together until they formed a
ladder like a chain, and so high that
the top appeared to be lost in the
clouds. Jack was an adventurous lad;
he determined to climb up to the top,
and ran to tell his mother, not doubt-
ing but that she would be as much
pleased as he was. She declared he
should not go, said it would break her
heart if he did—entreated and threatened, but all in vain. Jack set out, and
after climbing for some hours reached
the top of the bean-stalk quite exhausted. Looking around, he found himself
in a strange country; it appeared to be
a barren desert — not a tree, shrub,
house, or living creature was to be seen;
here and there were scattered fragments
of stone; and at unequal distances small
heaps of earth were loosely thrown together.

Jack seated himself pensively upon
a block of stone and thought of his
mother; he reflected with sorrow upon

his disobedience in climbing the bean-
stalk against her will, and concluded
that he must die of hunger. However,
he walked on, hoping to see a house
where he might beg something to eat
and drink. He did not find it; but he
saw at a distance a beautiful lady, walking all alone. She was elegantly clad
and carried a white wand, at the top
of which sat a peacock of pure gold.

Jack, who was a gallant fellow, went
straight up to her, when, with a be-
witching smile, she asked him how he
came there. He told her all about the
bean-stalk. The lady answered him by
a question, "Do you remember your
father, young man?"

"No, madam; but I am sure there is
some mystery about him, for when I
name him to my mother she always
begins to weep, and will tell me nothing."

"She dare not," replied the lady,
"but I can and will. For know, young

54

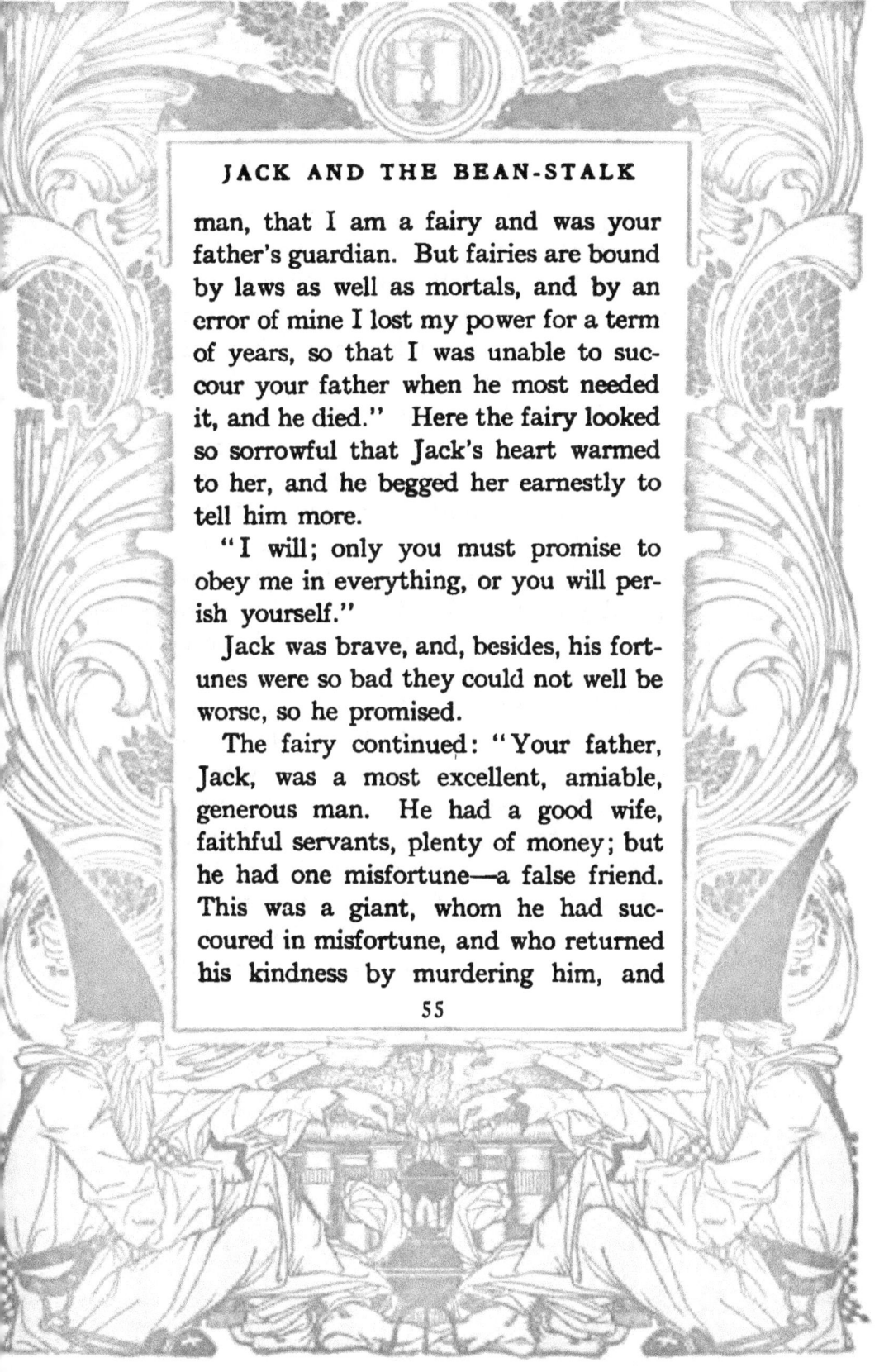

man, that I am a fairy and was your father's guardian. But fairies are bound by laws as well as mortals, and by an error of mine I lost my power for a term of years, so that I was unable to succour your father when he most needed it, and he died." Here the fairy looked so sorrowful that Jack's heart warmed to her, and he begged her earnestly to tell him more.

"I will; only you must promise to obey me in everything, or you will perish yourself."

Jack was brave, and, besides, his fortunes were so bad they could not well be worse, so he promised.

The fairy continued: "Your father, Jack, was a most excellent, amiable, generous man. He had a good wife, faithful servants, plenty of money; but he had one misfortune—a false friend. This was a giant, whom he had succoured in misfortune, and who returned his kindness by murdering him, and

55

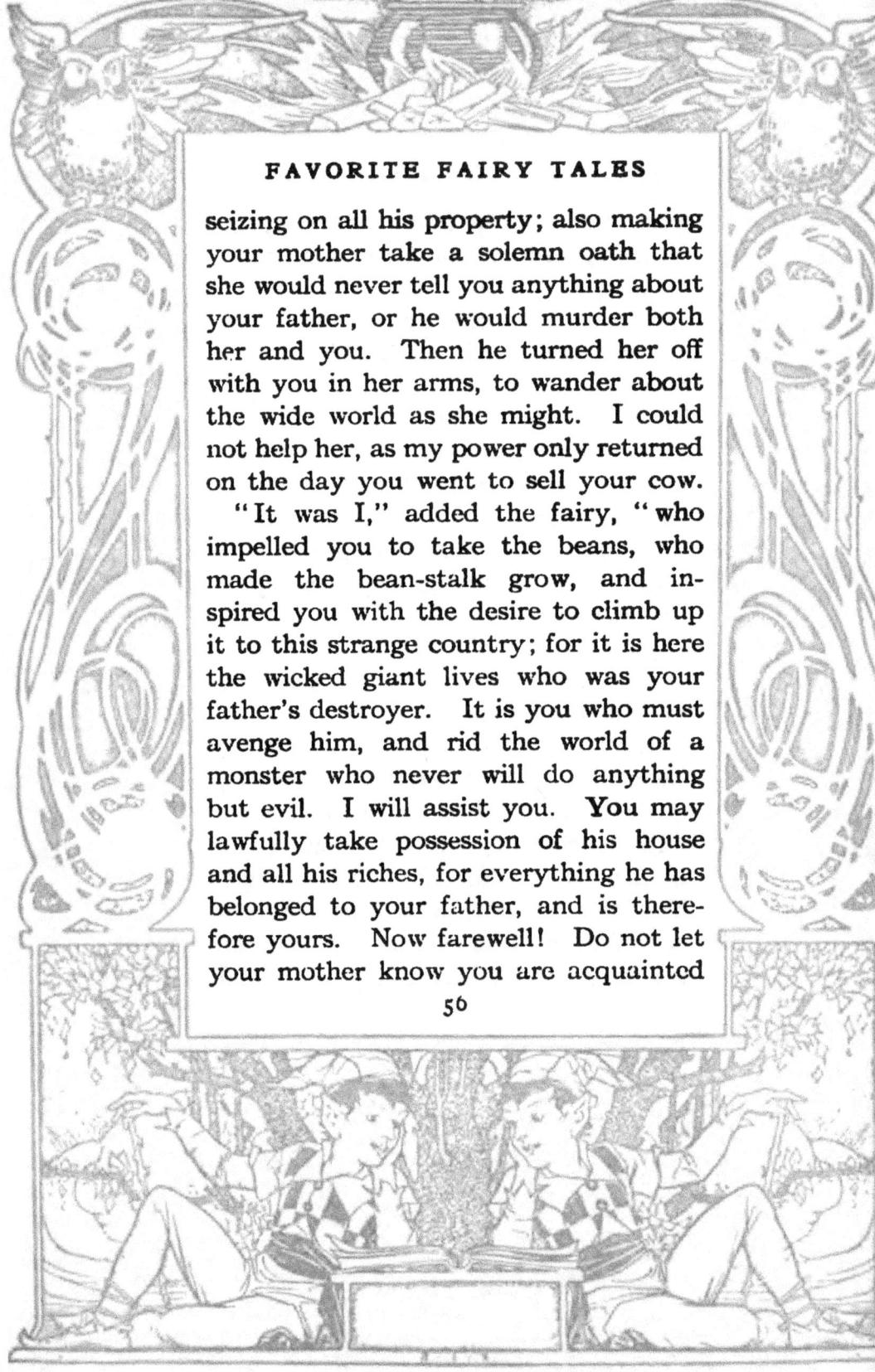

seizing on all his property; also making your mother take a solemn oath that she would never tell you anything about your father, or he would murder both her and you. Then he turned her off with you in her arms, to wander about the wide world as she might. I could not help her, as my power only returned on the day you went to sell your cow.

"It was I," added the fairy, "who impelled you to take the beans, who made the bean-stalk grow, and inspired you with the desire to climb up it to this strange country; for it is here the wicked giant lives who was your father's destroyer. It is you who must avenge him, and rid the world of a monster who never will do anything but evil. I will assist you. You may lawfully take possession of his house and all his riches, for everything he has belonged to your father, and is therefore yours. Now farewell! Do not let your mother know you are acquainted

56

with your father's history. This is my command, and if you disobey me you will suffer for it. Now go."

Jack asked where he was to go.

"Along the direct road till you see the house where the giant lives. You must then act according to your own just judgment, and I will guide you if any difficulty arises. Farewell!"

She bestowed on the youth a benignant smile, and vanished.

Jack pursued his journey. He walked on till after sunset, when to his great joy, he espied a large mansion. A plain-looking woman was at the door; he accosted her, begging she would give him a morsel of bread and a night's lodging. She expressed the greatest surprise, and said it was quite uncommon to see a human being near their house; for it was well known that her husband was a powerful giant, who would never eat anything but human flesh, if he could possibly get it; that he would walk fifty

miles to procure it, usually being out the whole day for that purpose.

This account greatly terrified Jack, but still he hoped to elude the giant, and therefore he again entreated the woman to take him in for one night only, and hide him where she thought proper. She at last suffered herself to be persuaded, for she was of a compassionate and generous disposition, and took him into the house. First they entered a fine large hall magnificently furnished; they then passed through several spacious rooms in the same style of grandeur; but all appeared forsaken and desolate. A long gallery came next; it was very dark—just light enough to show that, instead of a wall on one side, there was a grating of iron which parted off a dismal dungeon, from whence issued the groans of those victims whom the cruel giant reserved in confinement for his own voracious appetite.

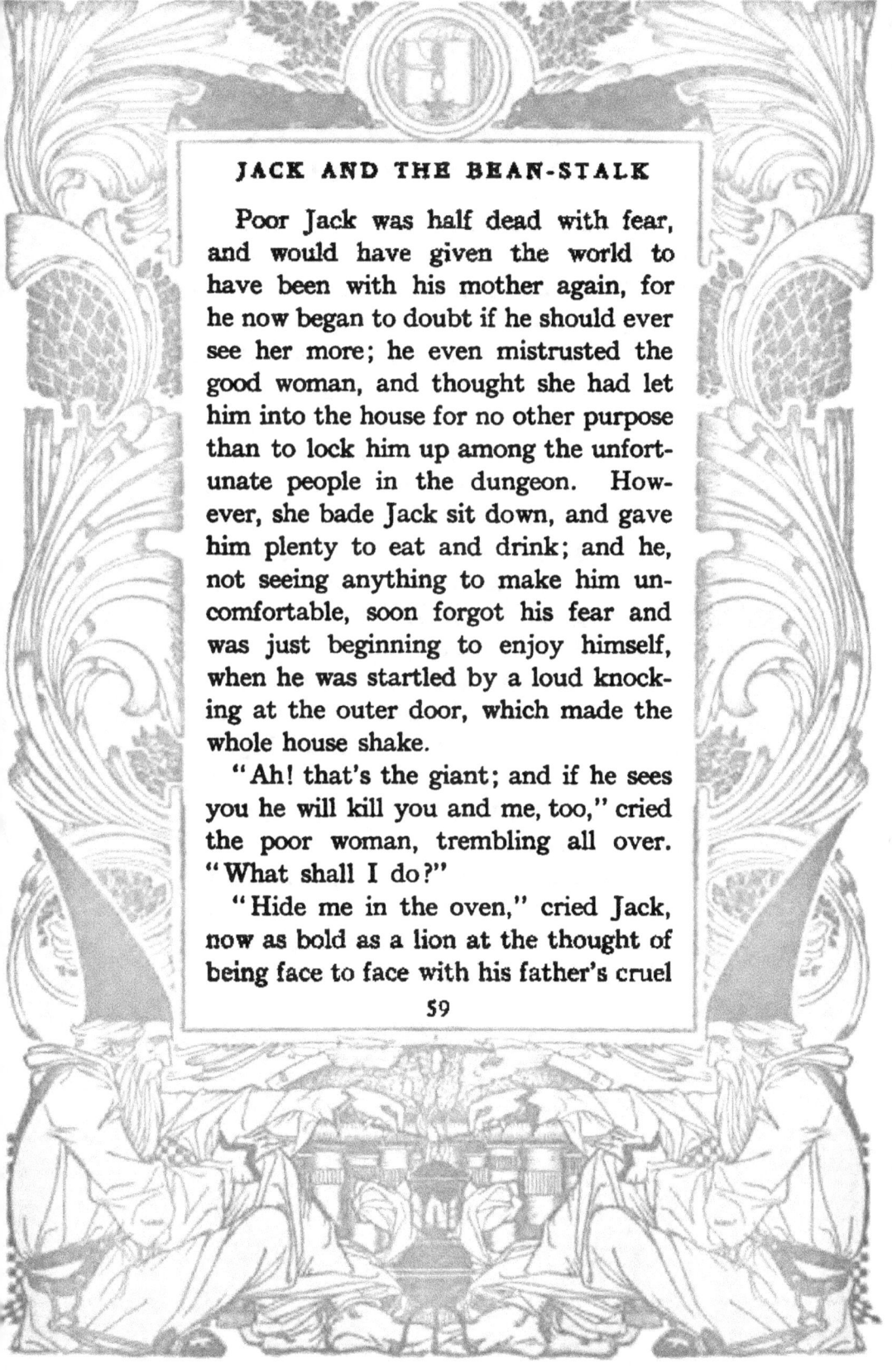

JACK AND THE BEAN-STALK

Poor Jack was half dead with fear, and would have given the world to have been with his mother again, for he now began to doubt if he should ever see her more; he even mistrusted the good woman, and thought she had let him into the house for no other purpose than to lock him up among the unfortunate people in the dungeon. However, she bade Jack sit down, and gave him plenty to eat and drink; and he, not seeing anything to make him uncomfortable, soon forgot his fear and was just beginning to enjoy himself, when he was startled by a loud knocking at the outer door, which made the whole house shake.

"Ah! that's the giant; and if he sees you he will kill you and me, too," cried the poor woman, trembling all over. "What shall I do?"

"Hide me in the oven," cried Jack, now as bold as a lion at the thought of being face to face with his father's cruel

59

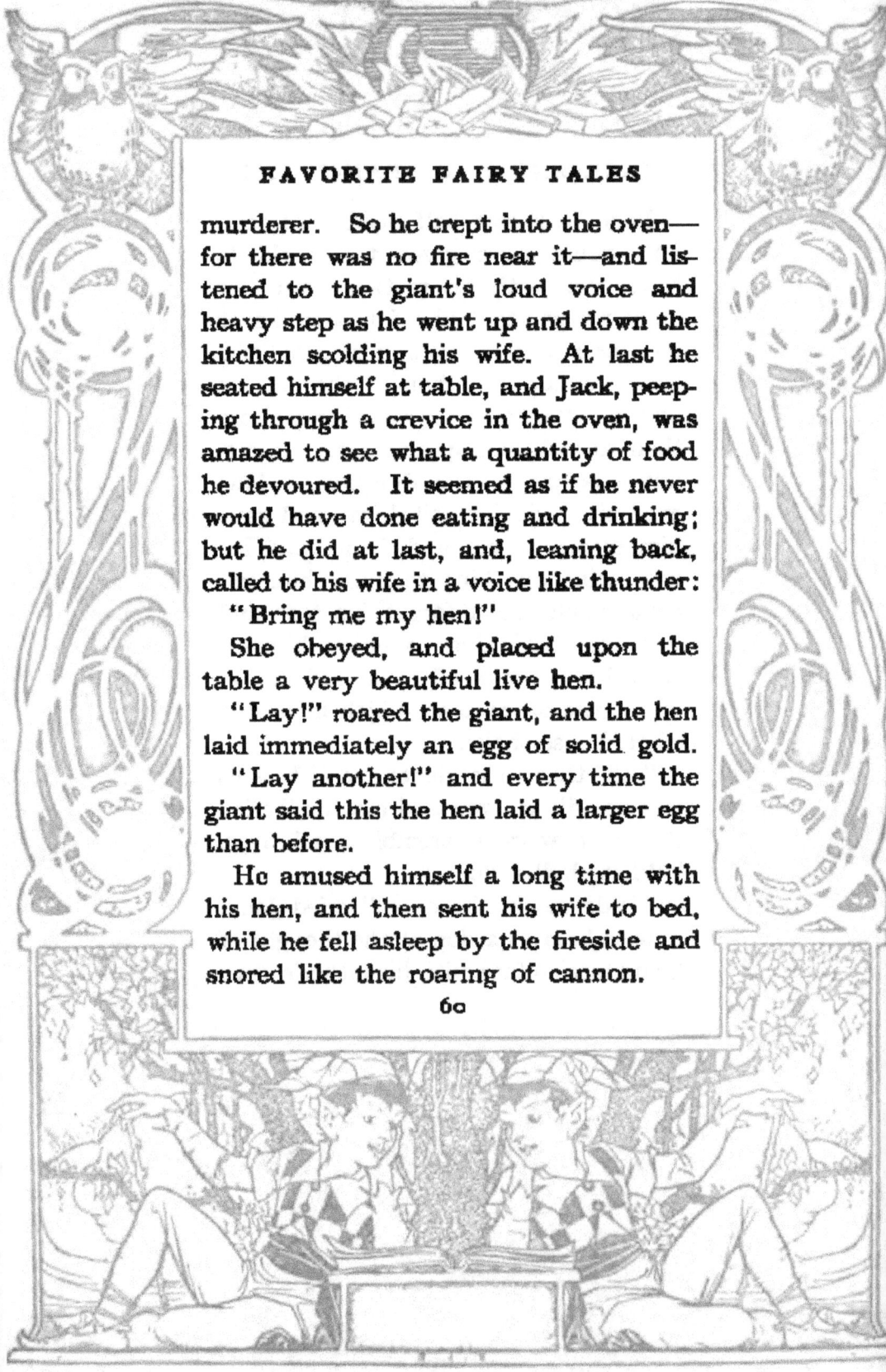

murderer. So he crept into the oven—
for there was no fire near it—and listened to the giant's loud voice and
heavy step as he went up and down the
kitchen scolding his wife. At last he
seated himself at table, and Jack, peep-
ing through a crevice in the oven, was
amazed to see what a quantity of food
he devoured. It seemed as if he never
would have done eating and drinking;
but he did at last, and, leaning back,
called to his wife in a voice like thunder:

"Bring me my hen!"

She obeyed, and placed upon the
table a very beautiful live hen.

"Lay!" roared the giant, and the hen
laid immediately an egg of solid gold.

"Lay another!" and every time the
giant said this the hen laid a larger egg
than before.

He amused himself a long time with
his hen, and then sent his wife to bed,
while he fell asleep by the fireside and
snored like the roaring of cannon.

JACK AND THE BEAN-STALK

As soon as he was asleep Jack crept out of the oven, seized the hen, and ran off with her. He got safely out of the house, and, finding his way along the road he came, reached the top of the bean - stalk, which he descended in safety.

His mother was overjoyed to see him. She thought he had come to some ill end.

"Not a bit of it, mother. Look here!" and he showed her the hen. "Now lay," and the hen obeyed him as readily as the giant, and laid as many golden eggs as he desired.

These eggs being sold, Jack and his mother got plenty of money, and for some months lived very happily together, till Jack got another great longing to climb the bean-stalk and carry away some more of the giant's riches. He had told his mother of his adventure, but had been very careful not to say a word about his father. He

61

thought of his journey again and again, but still he could not summon resolution enough to break it to his mother, being well assured that she would endeavor to prevent his going. However, one day he told her boldly that he must take another journey up the bean-stalk. She begged and prayed him not to think of it, and tried all in her power to dissuade him; she told him that the giant's wife would certainly know him again, and that the giant would desire nothing better than to get him into his power, that he might put him to a cruel death, in order to be revenged for the loss of his hen. Jack, finding that all his arguments were useless, ceased speaking, though resolved to go at all events. He had a dress prepared which would disguise him, and something to color his skin; he thought it impossible for any one to recollect him in this dress.

A few mornings after he rose very

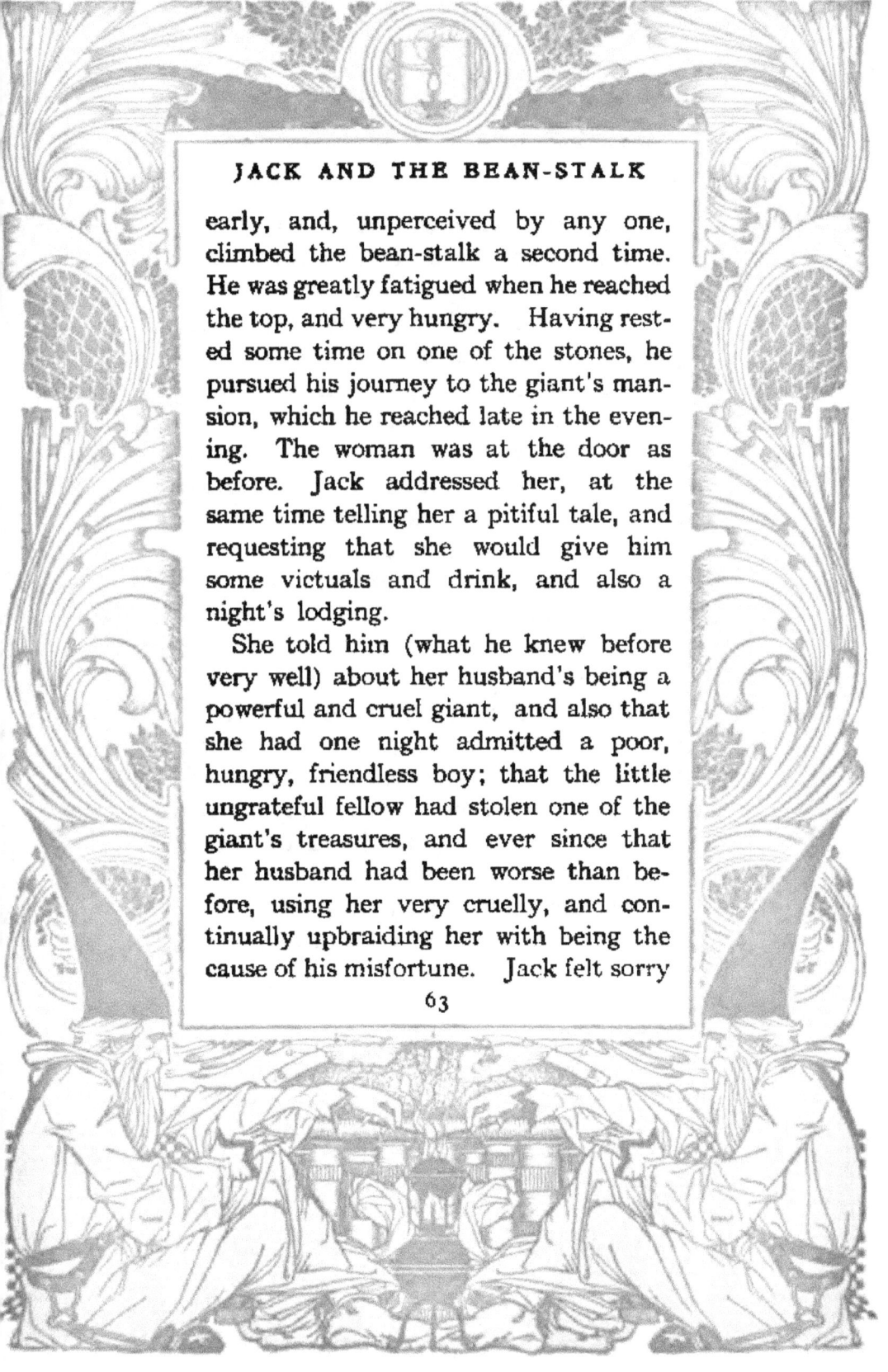

early, and, unperceived by any one, climbed the bean-stalk a second time. He was greatly fatigued when he reached the top, and very hungry. Having rested some time on one of the stones, he pursued his journey to the giant's mansion, which he reached late in the evening. The woman was at the door as before. Jack addressed her, at the same time telling her a pitiful tale, and requesting that she would give him some victuals and drink, and also a night's lodging.

She told him (what he knew before very well) about her husband's being a powerful and cruel giant, and also that she had one night admitted a poor, hungry, friendless boy; that the little ungrateful fellow had stolen one of the giant's treasures, and ever since that her husband had been worse than before, using her very cruelly, and continually upbraiding her with being the cause of his misfortune. Jack felt sorry

63

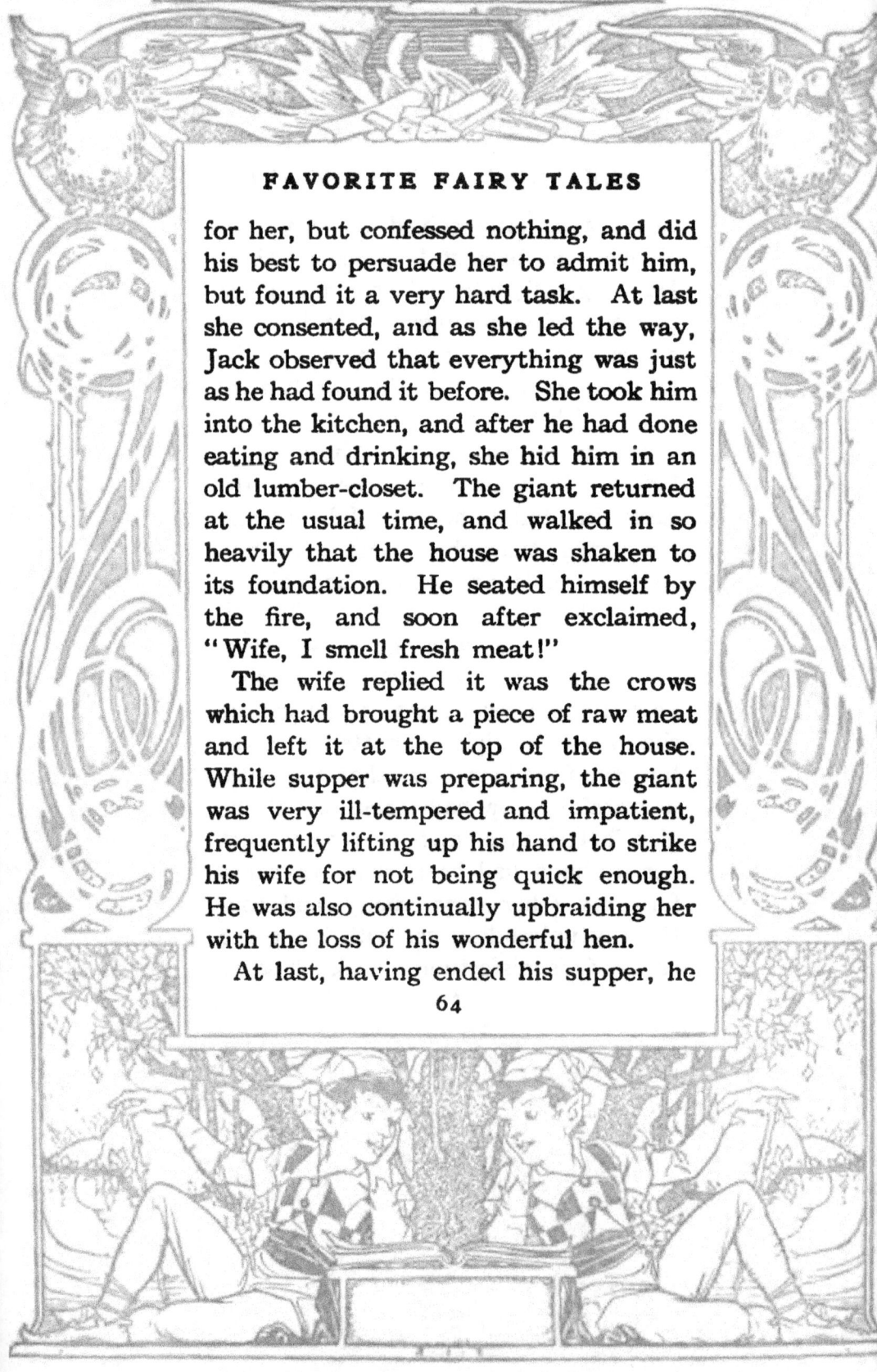

for her, but confessed nothing, and did his best to persuade her to admit him, but found it a very hard task. At last she consented, and as she led the way, Jack observed that everything was just as he had found it before. She took him into the kitchen, and after he had done eating and drinking, she hid him in an old lumber-closet. The giant returned at the usual time, and walked in so heavily that the house was shaken to its foundation. He seated himself by the fire, and soon after exclaimed, "Wife, I smell fresh meat!"

The wife replied it was the crows which had brought a piece of raw meat and left it at the top of the house. While supper was preparing, the giant was very ill-tempered and impatient, frequently lifting up his hand to strike his wife for not being quick enough. He was also continually upbraiding her with the loss of his wonderful hen.

At last, having ended his supper, he

64

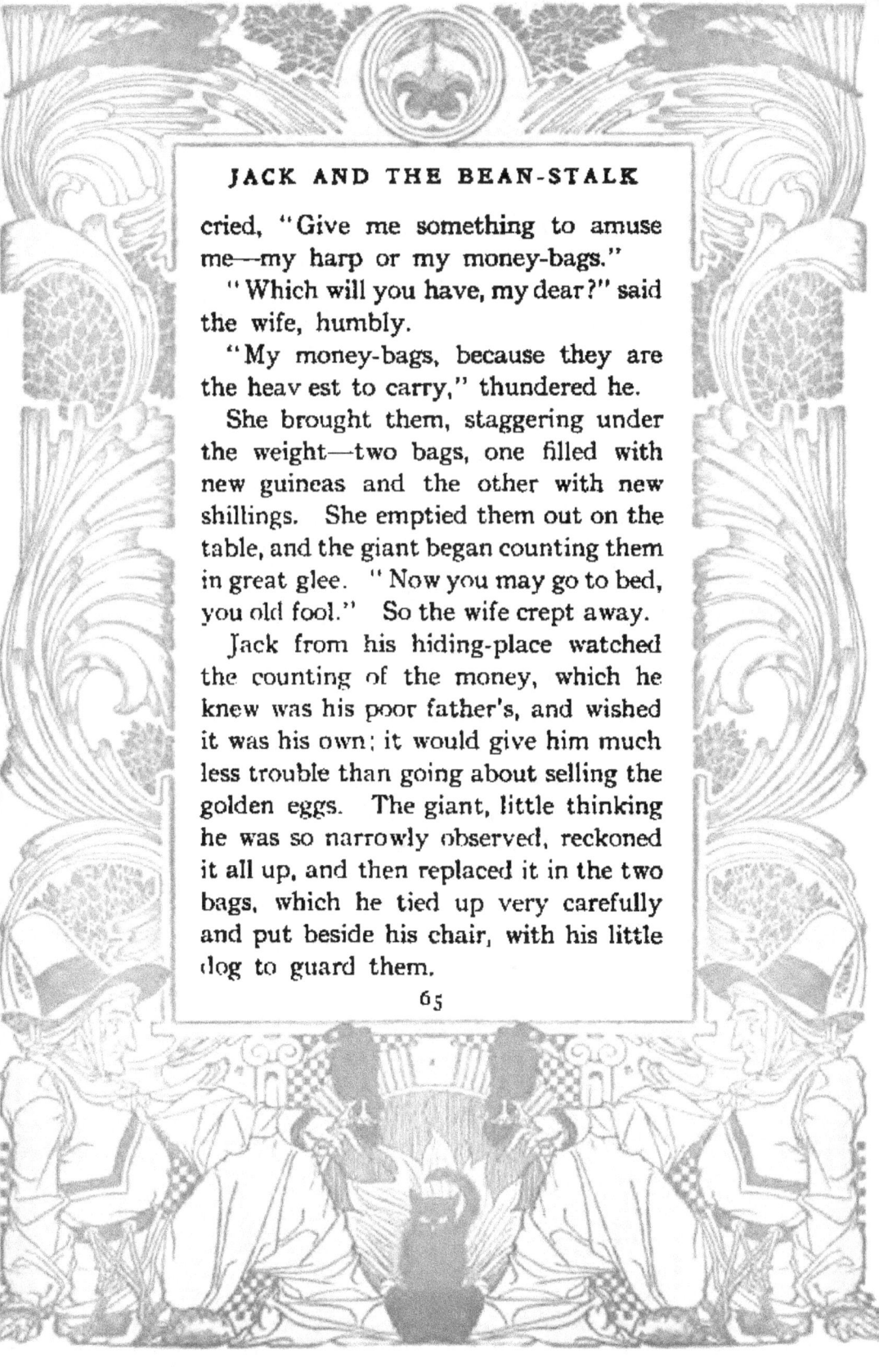

cried, "Give me something to amuse me—my harp or my money-bags."

"Which will you have, my dear?" said the wife, humbly.

"My money-bags, because they are the heav est to carry," thundered he.

She brought them, staggering under the weight—two bags, one filled with new guineas and the other with new shillings. She emptied them out on the table, and the giant began counting them in great glee. "Now you may go to bed, you old fool." So the wife crept away.

Jack from his hiding-place watched the counting of the money, which he knew was his poor father's, and wished it was his own; it would give him much less trouble than going about selling the golden eggs. The giant, little thinking he was so narrowly observed, reckoned it all up, and then replaced it in the two bags, which he tied up very carefully and put beside his chair, with his little dog to guard them.

At last he fell asleep as before, and snored so loud that Jack compared his noise to the roaring of the sea in a high wind, when the tide is coming in. At last Jack, concluding all secure, stole out, in order to carry off the two bags of money; but just as he laid his hand upon one of them, the little dog, which he had not perceived before, started from under the giant's chair and barked most furiously. Instead of endeavoring to escape, Jack stood still, though expecting his enemy to awake every instant.

Contrary, however, to his expectation, the giant continued in a sound sleep, and Jack, seeing a piece of meat, threw it to the dog, who at once ceased barking and began to devour it. So Jack carried off the bags, one on each shoulder, but they were so heavy that it took him two whole days to descend the bean-stalk and get back to his mother's door.

Just as he laid his hand upon one of them, the little dog barked
most furiously

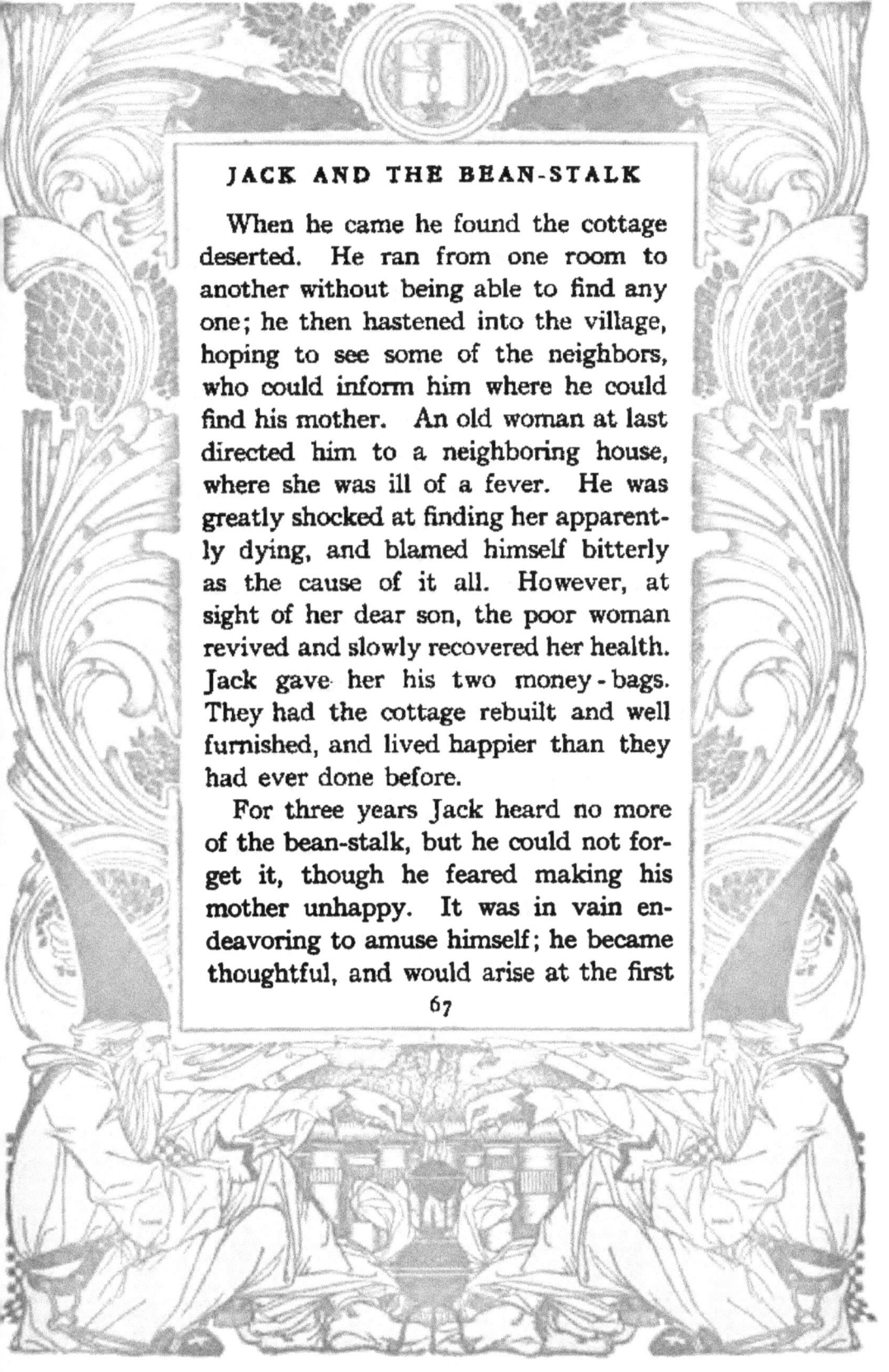

JACK AND THE BEAN-STALK

When he came he found the cottage deserted. He ran from one room to another without being able to find any one; he then hastened into the village, hoping to see some of the neighbors, who could inform him where he could find his mother. An old woman at last directed him to a neighboring house, where she was ill of a fever. He was greatly shocked at finding her apparently dying, and blamed himself bitterly as the cause of it all. However, at sight of her dear son, the poor woman revived and slowly recovered her health. Jack gave her his two money - bags. They had the cottage rebuilt and well furnished, and lived happier than they had ever done before.

For three years Jack heard no more of the bean-stalk, but he could not forget it, though he feared making his mother unhappy. It was in vain endeavoring to amuse himself; he became thoughtful, and would arise at the first

dawn of day, and sit looking at the bean-stalk for hours together. His mother saw that something preyed upon his mind, and endeavored to discover the cause; but Jack knew too well what the consequence would be should she succeed. He did his utmost, therefore, to conquer the great desire he had for another journey up the bean-stalk. Finding, however, that his inclination grew too powerful for him, he began to make secret preparations for his journey. He prepared a new disguise, better and more complete than the former, and when summer came, on the longest day he awoke as soon as it was light, and, without telling his mother, ascended the bean-stalk. He found the road, journey, etc., much as it was on the two former times. He arrived at the giant's mansion in the evening, and found the wife standing, as usual, at the door. Jack had disguised himself so completely that she did not appear to

have the least recollection of him; however, when he pleaded hunger and
poverty, in order to gain admittance,
he found it very difficult indeed to persuade her. At last he prevailed, and
was concealed in the copper. When the
giant returned he said, furiously, "I
smell fresh meat!" But Jack felt quite
composed, since the giant had said this
before and had been soon satisfied.
However, the giant started up suddenly, and, notwithstanding all his wife
could say, he searched all round the
room. While this was going forward
Jack was exceedingly terrified, wishing
himself at home a thousand times; but
when the giant approached the copper
and put his hand upon the lid, Jack
thought his death was certain.

But nothing happened; for the giant
did not take the trouble to lift up the
lid, but sat down shortly by the fireside and began to eat his enormous
supper. When he had finished he

commanded his wife to fetch down his harp. Jack peeped under the copper-lid and saw a most beautiful harp. The giant placed it on the table, said "Play!" and it played of its own accord, without anybody touching it, the most exquisite music imaginable. Jack, who was a very good musician, was delighted, and more anxious to get this than any other of his enemy's treasures. But the giant not being particularly fond of music, the harp had only the effect of lulling him to sleep earlier than usual. As for the wife, she had gone to bed as soon as ever she could.

As soon as he thought all was safe, Jack got out of the copper, and, seizing the harp, was eagerly running off with it. But the harp was enchanted by a fairy, and as soon as it found itself in strange hands it called out loudly, just as if it had been alive, "Master! Master!"

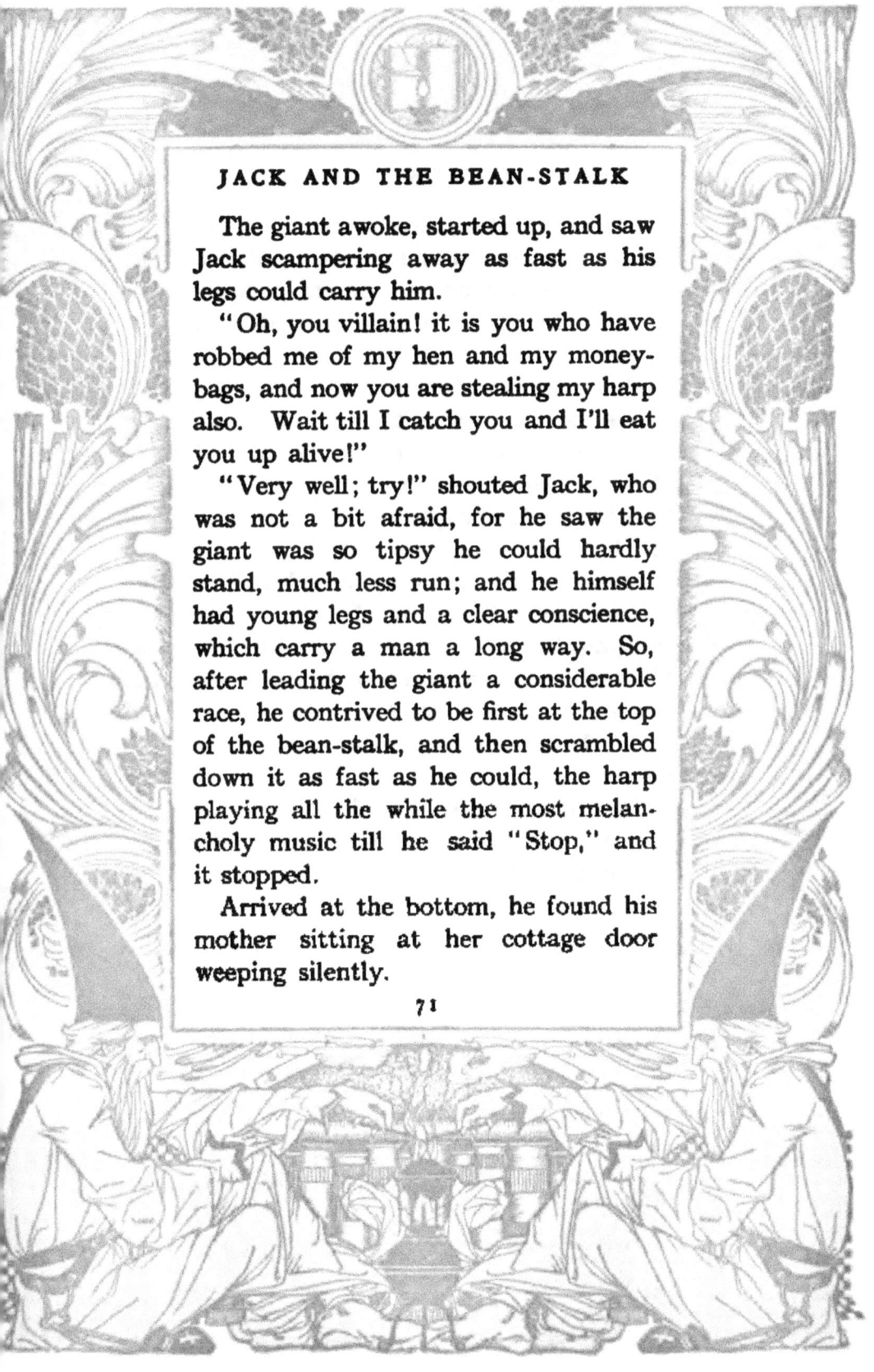

JACK AND THE BEAN-STALK

The giant awoke, started up, and saw Jack scampering away as fast as his legs could carry him.

"Oh, you villain! it is you who have robbed me of my hen and my money-bags, and now you are stealing my harp also. Wait till I catch you and I'll eat you up alive!"

"Very well; try!" shouted Jack, who was not a bit afraid, for he saw the giant was so tipsy he could hardly stand, much less run; and he himself had young legs and a clear conscience, which carry a man a long way. So, after leading the giant a considerable race, he contrived to be first at the top of the bean-stalk, and then scrambled down it as fast as he could, the harp playing all the while the most melancholy music till he said "Stop," and it stopped.

Arrived at the bottom, he found his mother sitting at her cottage door weeping silently.

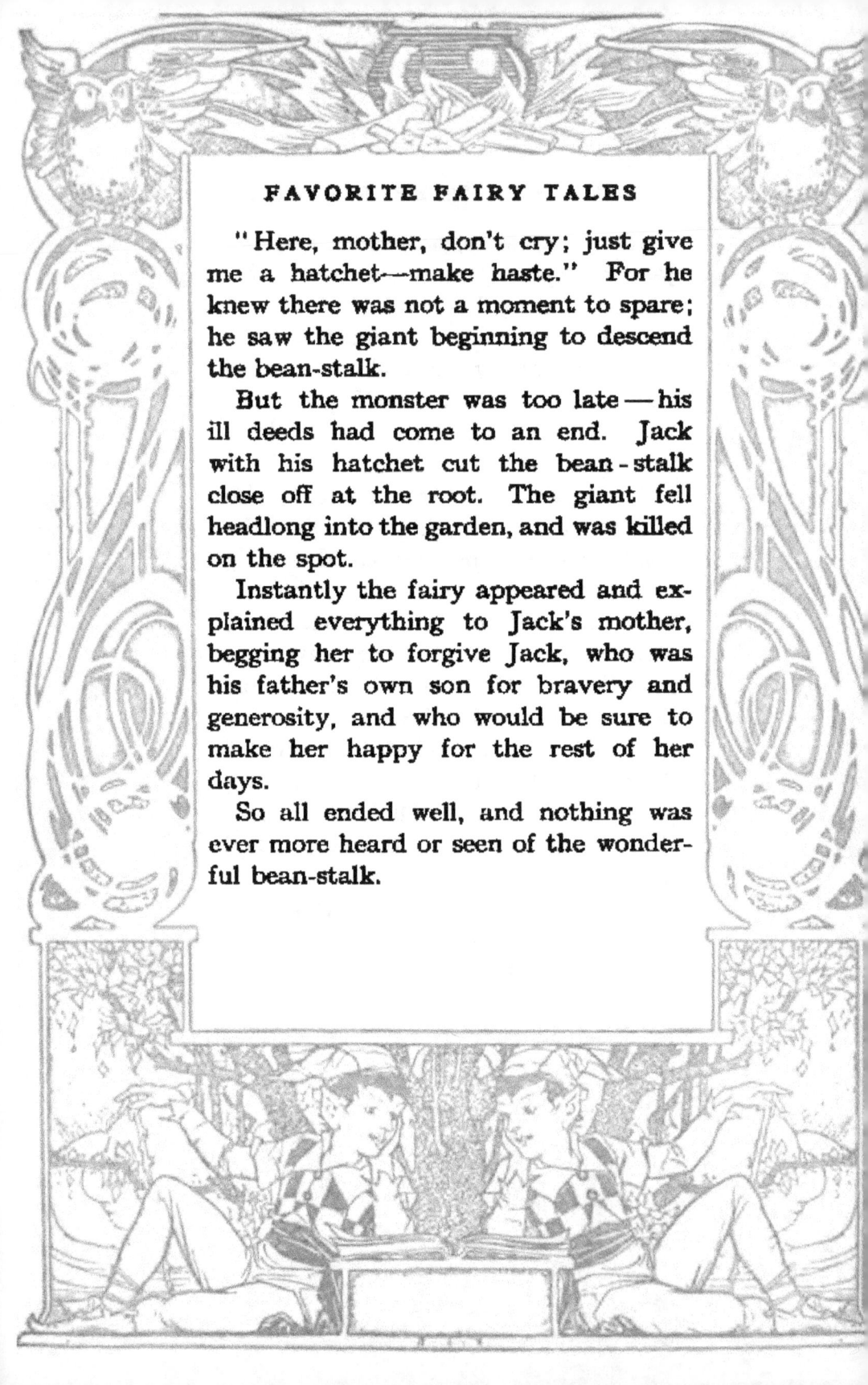

"Here, mother, don't cry; just give me a hatchet—make haste." For he knew there was not a moment to spare; he saw the giant beginning to descend the bean-stalk.

But the monster was too late—his ill deeds had come to an end. Jack with his hatchet cut the bean-stalk close off at the root. The giant fell headlong into the garden, and was killed on the spot.

Instantly the fairy appeared and explained everything to Jack's mother, begging her to forgive Jack, who was his father's own son for bravery and generosity, and who would be sure to make her happy for the rest of her days.

So all ended well, and nothing was ever more heard or seen of the wonderful bean-stalk.

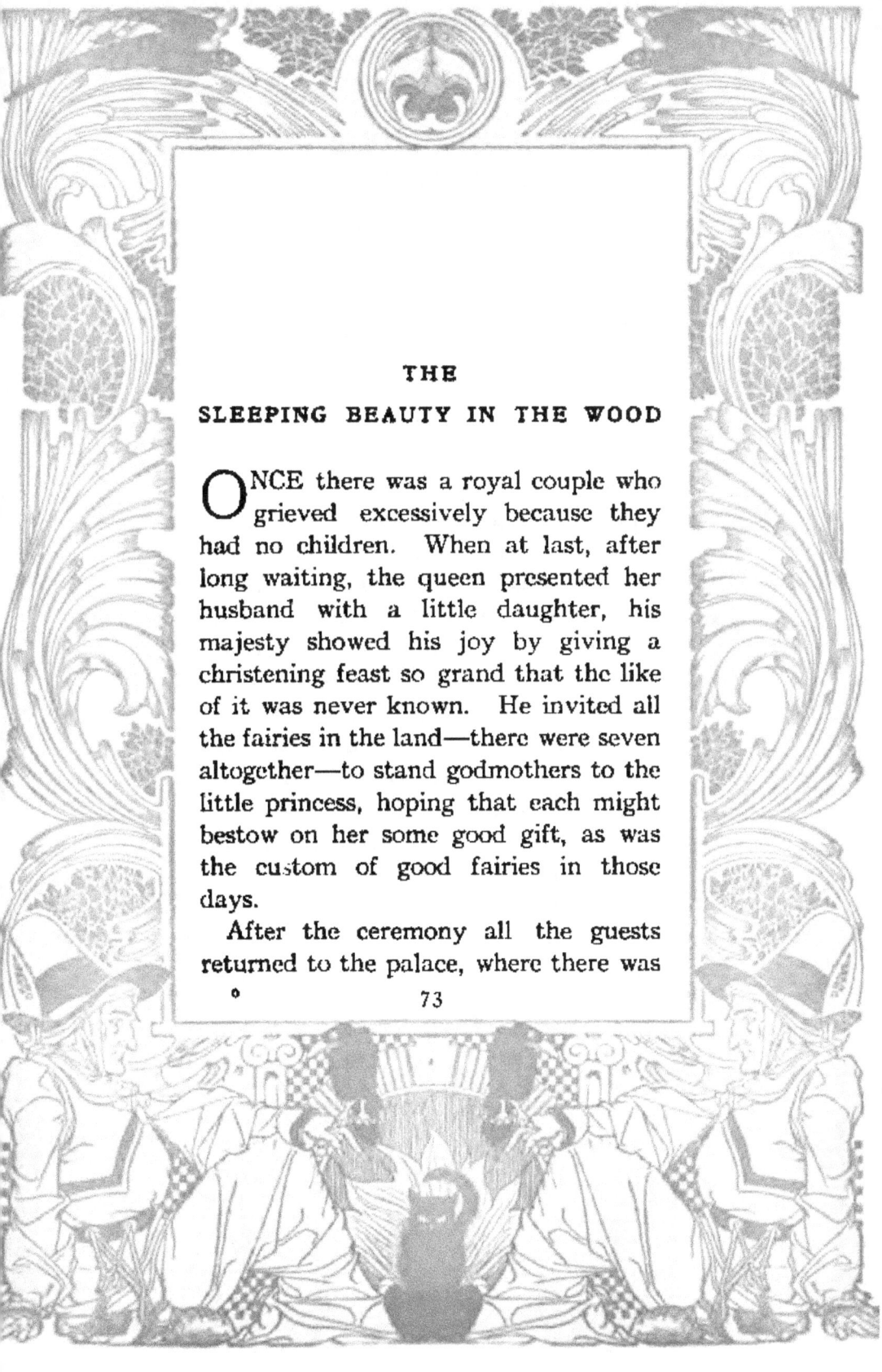

THE

SLEEPING BEAUTY IN THE WOOD

ONCE there was a royal couple who grieved excessively because they had no children. When at last, after long waiting, the queen presented her husband with a little daughter, his majesty showed his joy by giving a christening feast so grand that the like of it was never known. He invited all the fairies in the land—there were seven altogether—to stand godmothers to the little princess, hoping that each might bestow on her some good gift, as was the custom of good fairies in those days.

After the ceremony all the guests returned to the palace, where there was set before each fairy-godmother a magnificent covered dish, with an embroidered table-napkin, and a knife and fork of pure gold studded with diamonds and rubies. But alas! as they placed themselves at table there entered an old fairy who had never been invited, because more than fifty years since she had left the king's dominion on a tour of pleasure and had not been heard of until this day. His majesty, much troubled, desired a cover to be placed for her, but it was of common delf, for he had ordered from his jeweller only seven gold dishes for the seven fairies aforesaid. The elderly fairy thought herself neglected, and muttered angry menaces, which were overheard by one of the younger fairies, who chanced to sit beside her. This good godmother, afraid of harm to the pretty baby, hastened to hide herself behind the tapestry in the hall. She did this because she wished all the others to speak first—

74

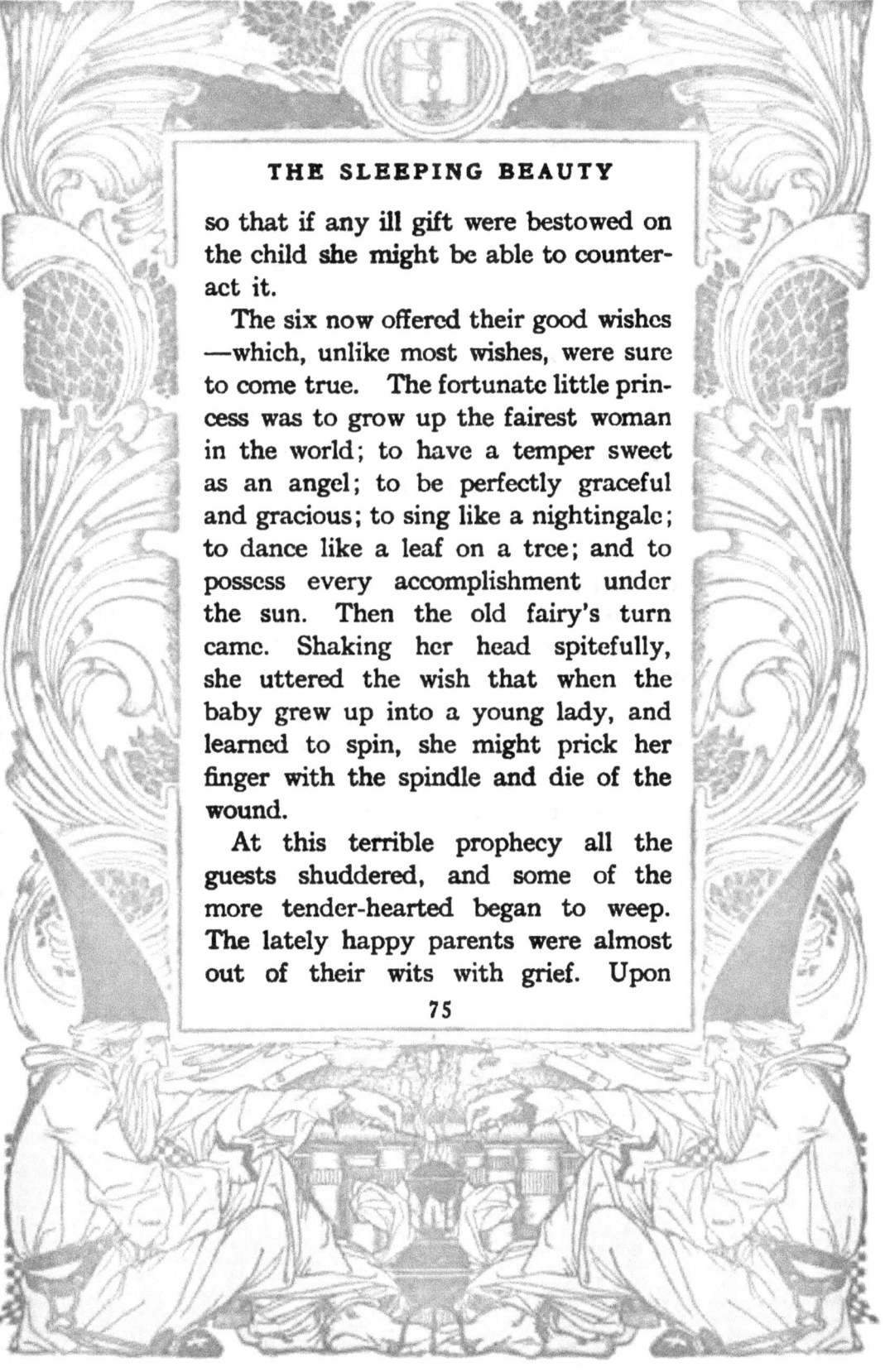

so that if any ill gift were bestowed on the child she might be able to counter-act it.

The six now offered their good wishes —which, unlike most wishes, were sure to come true. The fortunate little princess was to grow up the fairest woman in the world; to have a temper sweet as an angel; to be perfectly graceful and gracious; to sing like a nightingale; to dance like a leaf on a tree; and to possess every accomplishment under the sun. Then the old fairy's turn came. Shaking her head spitefully, she uttered the wish that when the baby grew up into a young lady, and learned to spin, she might prick her finger with the spindle and die of the wound.

At this terrible prophecy all the guests shuddered, and some of the more tender-hearted began to weep. The lately happy parents were almost out of their wits with grief. Upon

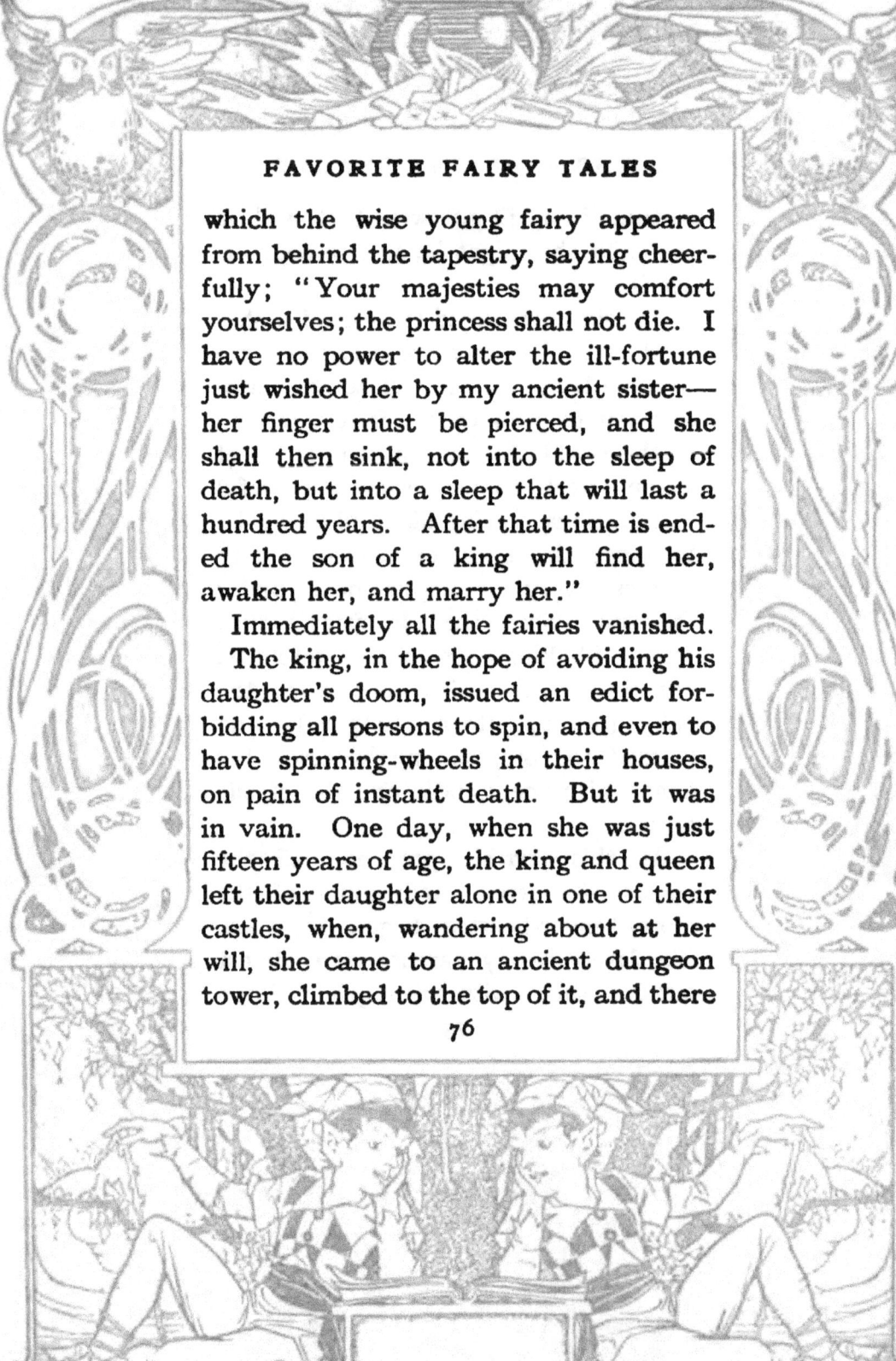

which the wise young fairy appeared from behind the tapestry, saying cheerfully; "Your majesties may comfort yourselves; the princess shall not die. I have no power to alter the ill-fortune just wished her by my ancient sister—her finger must be pierced, and she shall then sink, not into the sleep of death, but into a sleep that will last a hundred years. After that time is ended the son of a king will find her, awaken her, and marry her."

Immediately all the fairies vanished.

The king, in the hope of avoiding his daughter's doom, issued an edict forbidding all persons to spin, and even to have spinning-wheels in their houses, on pain of instant death. But it was in vain. One day, when she was just fifteen years of age, the king and queen left their daughter alone in one of their castles, when, wandering about at her will, she came to an ancient dungeon tower, climbed to the top of it, and there

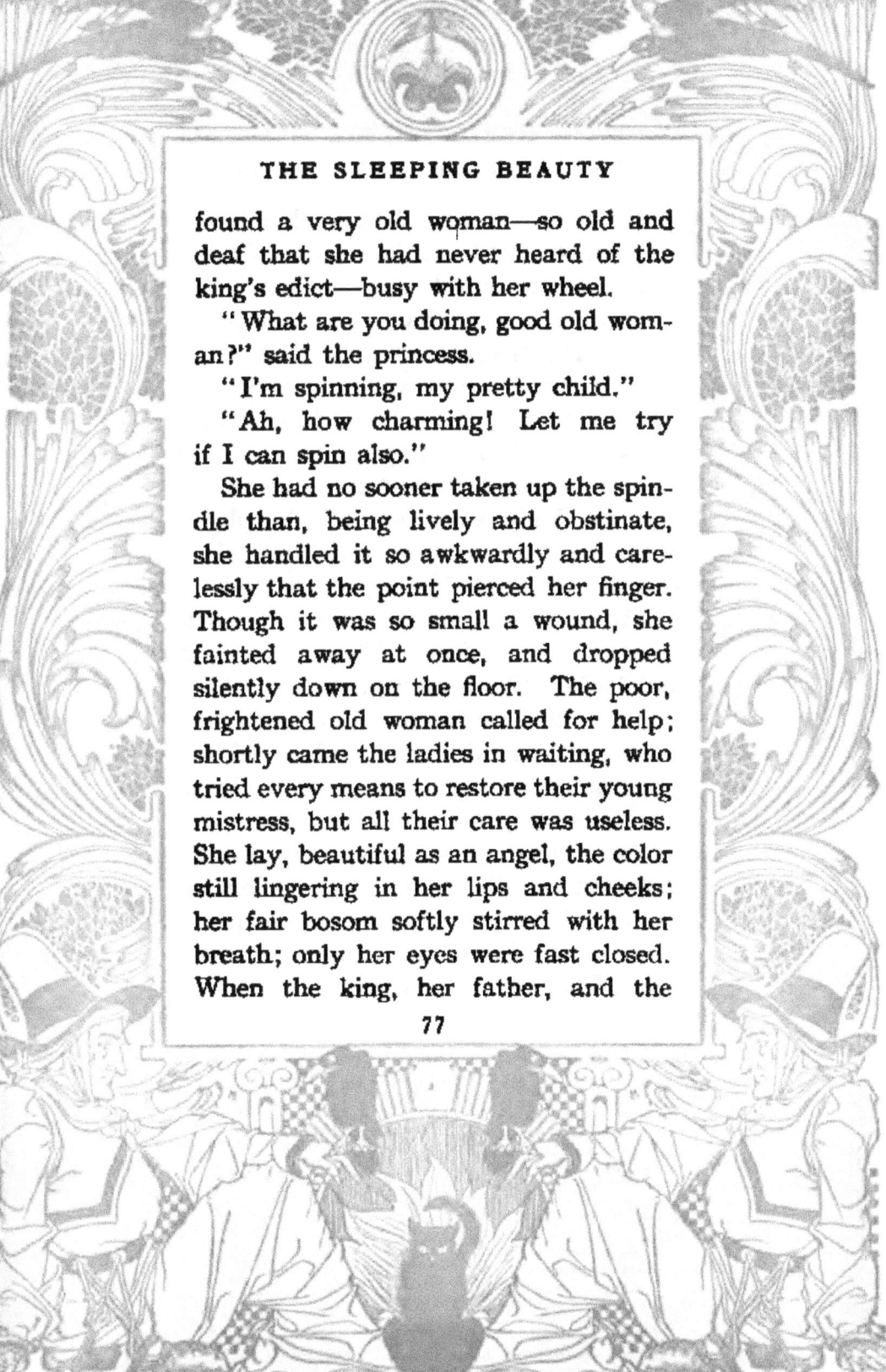

found a very old woman—so old and deaf that she had never heard of the king's edict—busy with her wheel.

"What are you doing, good old woman?" said the princess.

"I'm spinning, my pretty child."

"Ah, how charming! Let me try if I can spin also."

She had no sooner taken up the spindle than, being lively and obstinate, she handled it so awkwardly and carelessly that the point pierced her finger. Though it was so small a wound, she fainted away at once, and dropped silently down on the floor. The poor, frightened old woman called for help; shortly came the ladies in waiting, who tried every means to restore their young mistress, but all their care was useless. She lay, beautiful as an angel, the color still lingering in her lips and cheeks; her fair bosom softly stirred with her breath; only her eyes were fast closed. When the king, her father, and the queen, her mother, beheld her thus, they knew regret was idle—all had happened as the cruel fairy meant. But they also knew that their daughter would not sleep forever, though after one hundred years it was not likely they would either of them behold her awakening. Until that happy hour should arrive, they determined to leave her in repose. They sent away all the physicians and attendants, and themselves sorrowfully laid her upon a bed of embroidery, in the most elegant apartment of the palace. There she slept and looked like a sleeping angel still.

When this misfortune happened, the kindly young fairy who had saved the princess by changing her sleep of death into this sleep of a hundred years was twelve thousand leagues away in the kingdom of Mataquin. But being informed of everything, she arrived speedily in a chariot of fire drawn by dragons. The king was somewhat startled

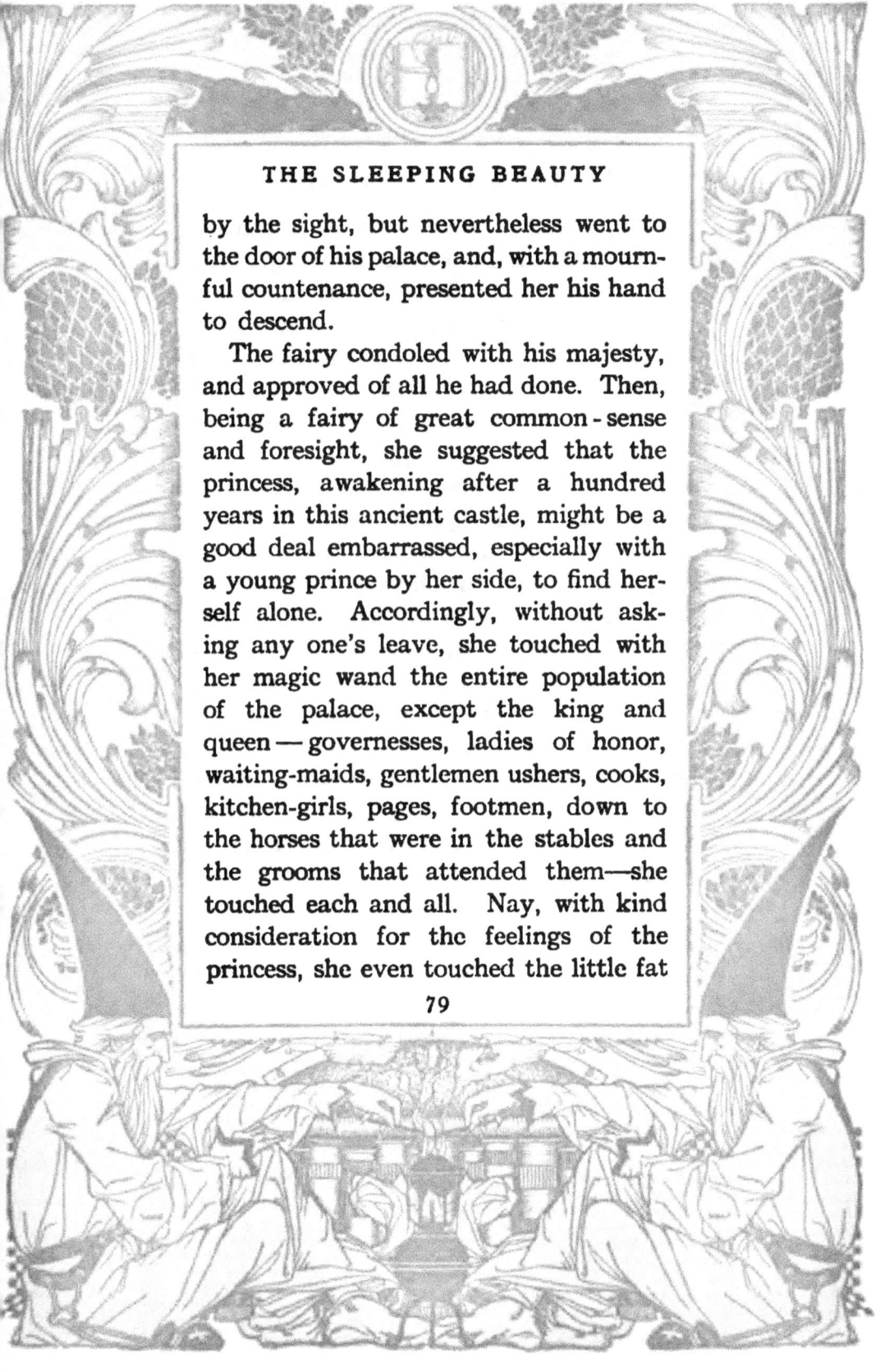

by the sight, but nevertheless went to the door of his palace, and, with a mournful countenance, presented her his hand to descend.

The fairy condoled with his majesty, and approved of all he had done. Then, being a fairy of great common-sense and foresight, she suggested that the princess, awakening after a hundred years in this ancient castle, might be a good deal embarrassed, especially with a young prince by her side, to find herself alone. Accordingly, without asking any one's leave, she touched with her magic wand the entire population of the palace, except the king and queen — governesses, ladies of honor, waiting-maids, gentlemen ushers, cooks, kitchen-girls, pages, footmen, down to the horses that were in the stables and the grooms that attended them—she touched each and all. Nay, with kind consideration for the feelings of the princess, she even touched the little fat

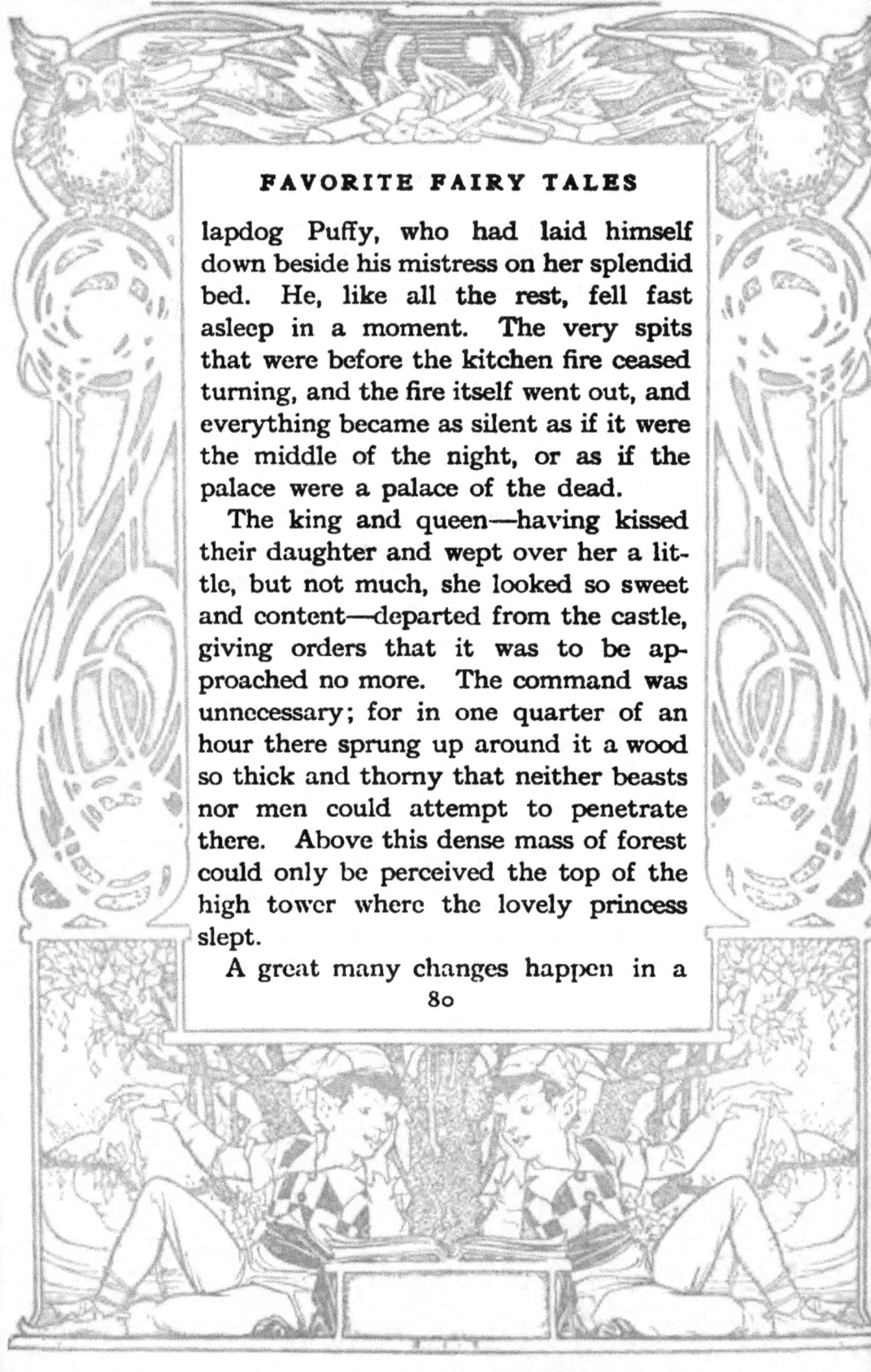

lapdog Puffy, who had laid himself down beside his mistress on her splendid bed. He, like all the rest, fell fast asleep in a moment. The very spits that were before the kitchen fire ceased turning, and the fire itself went out, and everything became as silent as if it were the middle of the night, or as if the palace were a palace of the dead.

The king and queen—having kissed their daughter and wept over her a little, but not much, she looked so sweet and content—departed from the castle, giving orders that it was to be approached no more. The command was unnecessary; for in one quarter of an hour there sprung up around it a wood so thick and thorny that neither beasts nor men could attempt to penetrate there. Above this dense mass of forest could only be perceived the top of the high tower where the lovely princess slept.

A great many changes happen in a

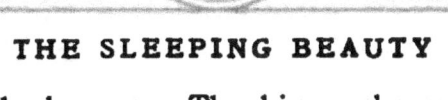

hundred years. The king, who never had a second child, died, and his throne passed into another royal family. So entirely was the story of the poor princess forgotten, that when the reigning king's son, being one day out hunting and stopped in the chase by this formidable wood, inquired what wood it was, and what were those towers which he saw appearing out of the midst of it, no one could answer him. At length an old peasant was found who remembered having heard his grandfather say to his father, that in this tower was a princess, beautiful as the day, who was doomed to sleep there for one hundred years, until awakened by a king's son, her destined bridegroom.

At this the young prince, who had the spirit of a hero, determined to find out the truth for himself. Spurred on by both generosity and curiosity, he leaped from his horse and began to force his way through the thick wood.

To his amazement the stiff branches
all gave way, and the ugly thorns
sheathed themselves of their own accord, and the brambles buried themselves in the earth to let him pass.
This done, they closed behind him,
allowing none of his suite to follow:
but, ardent and young, he went boldly
on alone. The first thing he saw was
enough to smite him with fear. Bodies
of men and horses lay extended on the
ground; but the men had faces, not
death-white, but red as peonies, and
beside them were glasses half filled with
wine, showing that they had gone to
sleep drinking. Next he entered a
large court paved with marble, where
stood rows of guards presenting arms,
but motionless as if cut out of stone;
then he passed through many chambers
where gentlemen and ladies, all in the
costume of the past century, slept at
their ease, some standing, some sitting.
The pages were lurking in corners, the

A young girl of wonderful beauty lay asleep on an embroidered bed

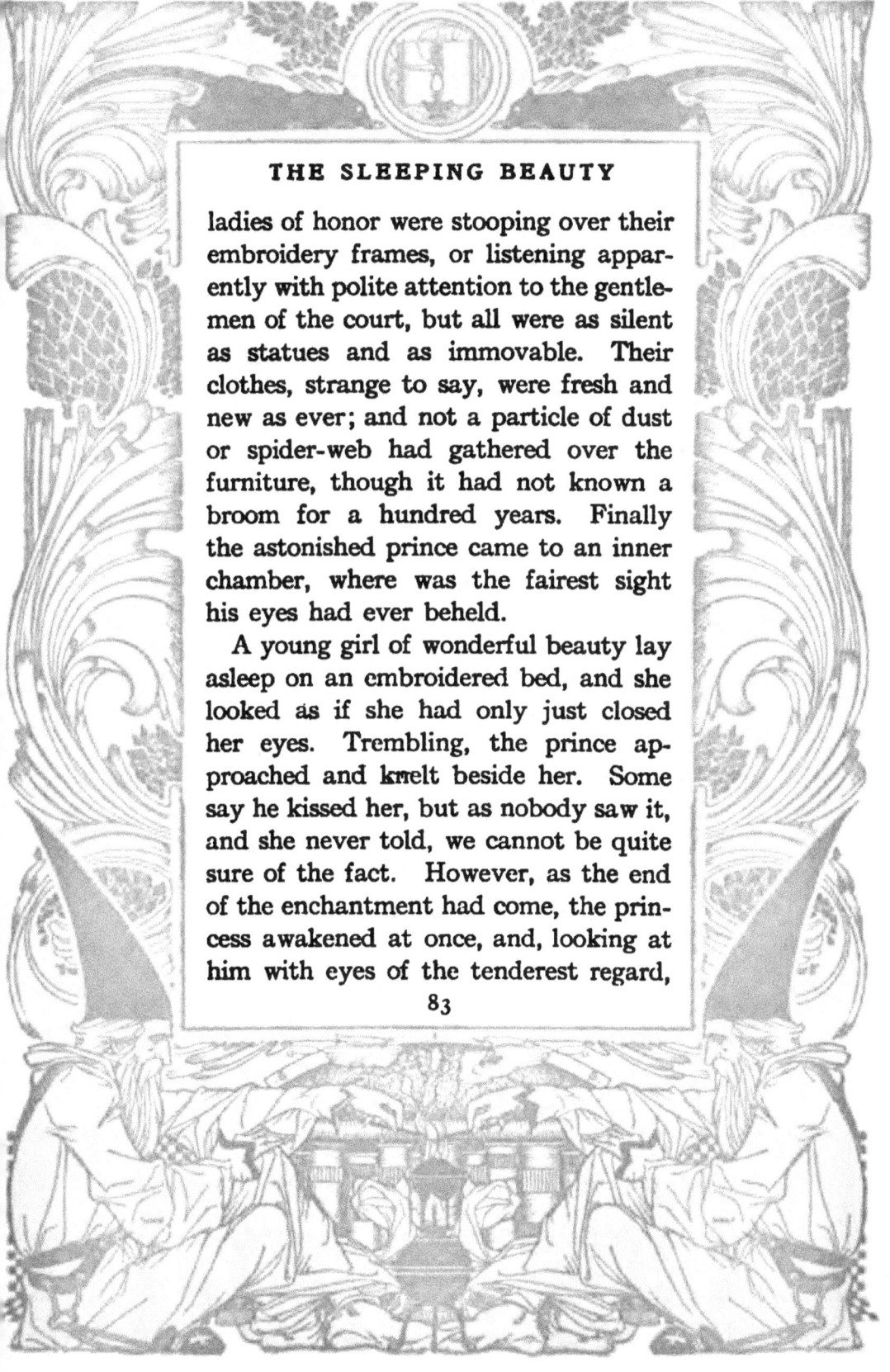

ladies of honor were stooping over their embroidery frames, or listening apparently with polite attention to the gentlemen of the court, but all were as silent as statues and as immovable. Their clothes, strange to say, were fresh and new as ever; and not a particle of dust or spider-web had gathered over the furniture, though it had not known a broom for a hundred years. Finally the astonished prince came to an inner chamber, where was the fairest sight his eyes had ever beheld.

A young girl of wonderful beauty lay asleep on an embroidered bed, and she looked as if she had only just closed her eyes. Trembling, the prince approached and knelt beside her. Some say he kissed her, but as nobody saw it, and she never told, we cannot be quite sure of the fact. However, as the end of the enchantment had come, the princess awakened at once, and, looking at him with eyes of the tenderest regard,

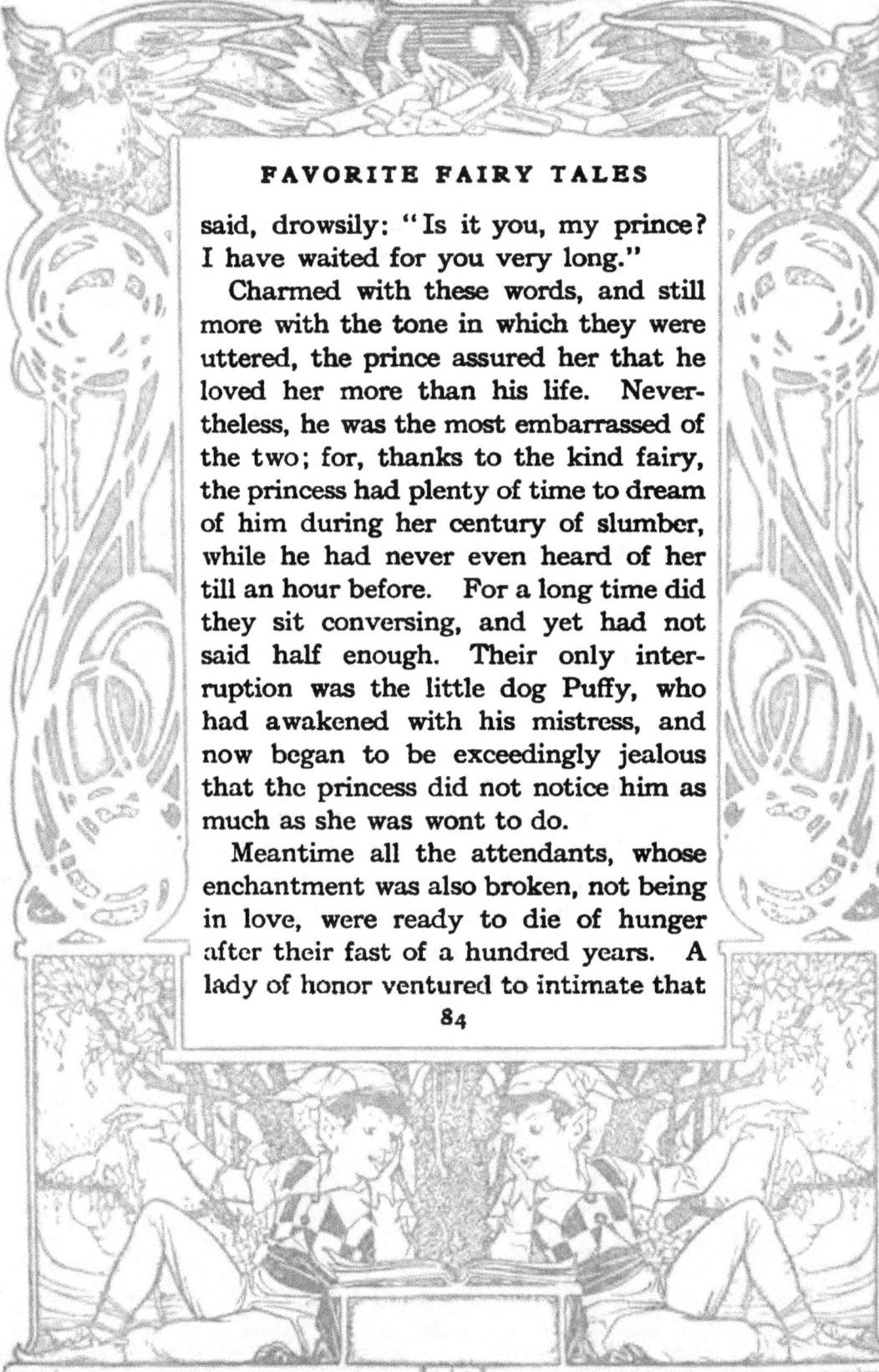

said, drowsily: "Is it you, my prince? I have waited for you very long."

Charmed with these words, and still more with the tone in which they were uttered, the prince assured her that he loved her more than his life. Nevertheless, he was the most embarrassed of the two; for, thanks to the kind fairy, the princess had plenty of time to dream of him during her century of slumber, while he had never even heard of her till an hour before. For a long time did they sit conversing, and yet had not said half enough. Their only interruption was the little dog Puffy, who had awakened with his mistress, and now began to be exceedingly jealous that the princess did not notice him as much as she was wont to do.

Meantime all the attendants, whose enchantment was also broken, not being in love, were ready to die of hunger after their fast of a hundred years. A lady of honor ventured to intimate that

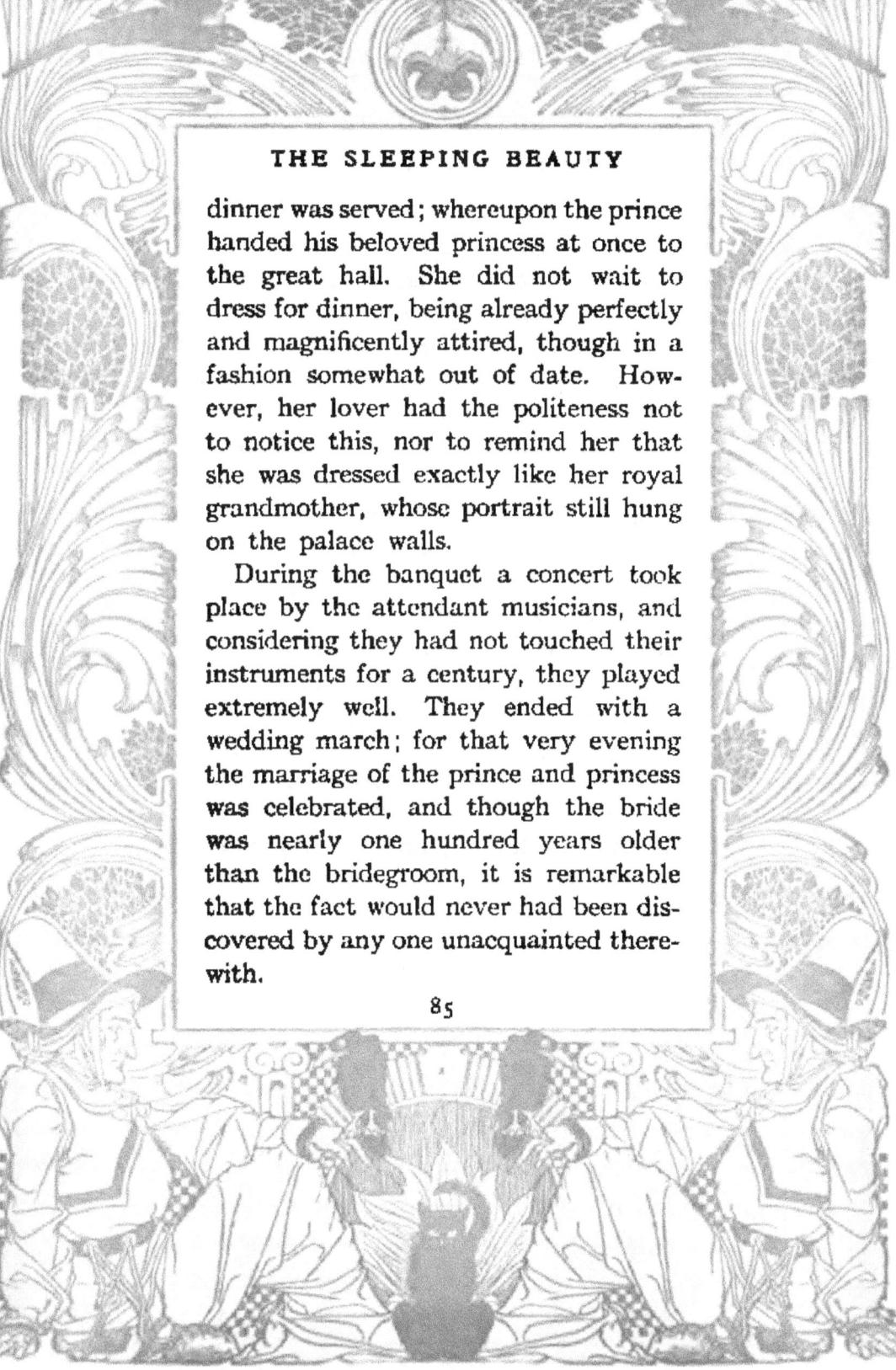

dinner was served; whereupon the prince handed his beloved princess at once to the great hall. She did not wait to dress for dinner, being already perfectly and magnificently attired, though in a fashion somewhat out of date. However, her lover had the politeness not to notice this, nor to remind her that she was dressed exactly like her royal grandmother, whose portrait still hung on the palace walls.

During the banquet a concert took place by the attendant musicians, and considering they had not touched their instruments for a century, they played extremely well. They ended with a wedding march; for that very evening the marriage of the prince and princess was celebrated, and though the bride was nearly one hundred years older than the bridegroom, it is remarkable that the fact would never had been discovered by any one unacquainted therewith.

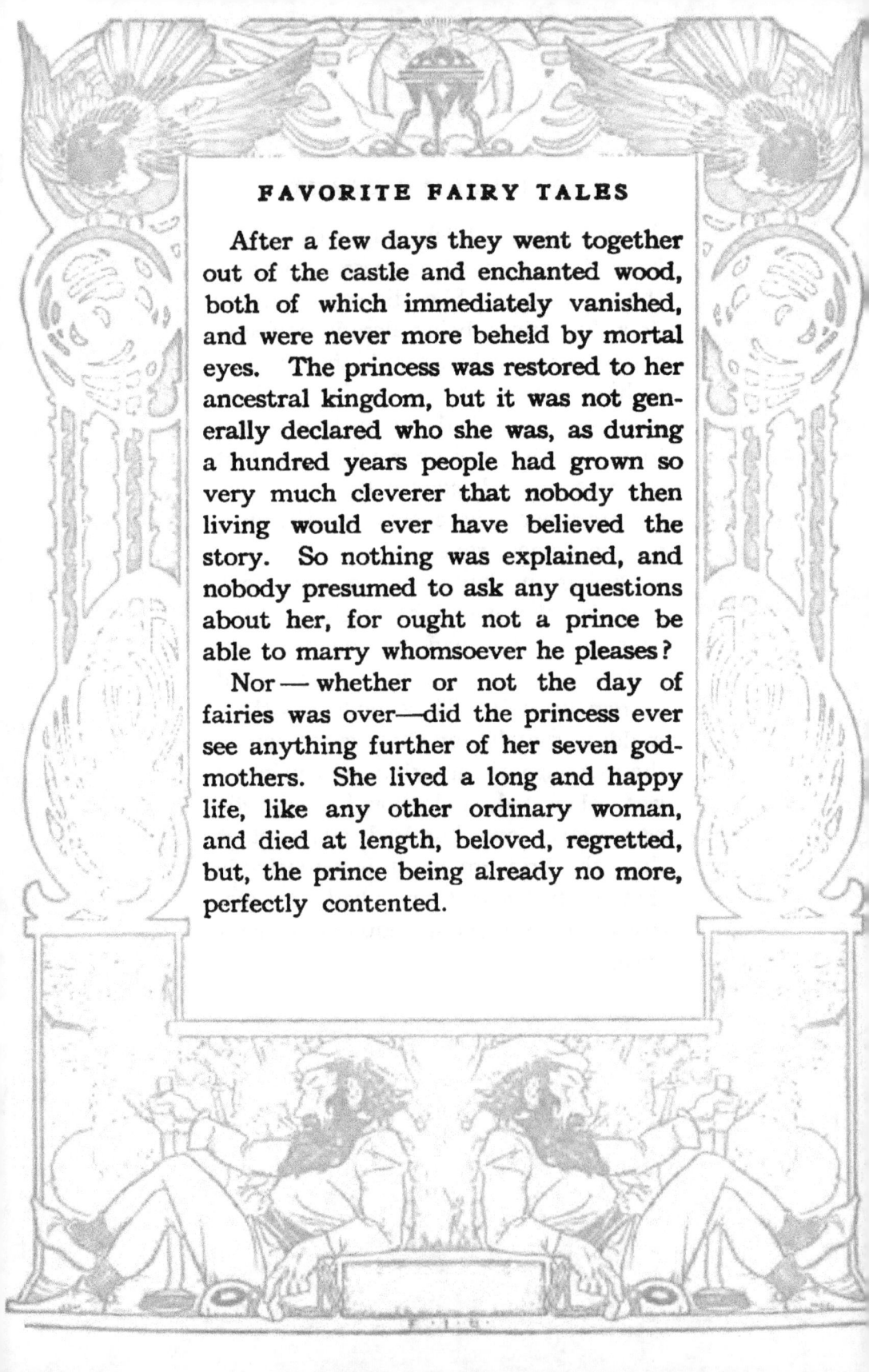

After a few days they went together out of the castle and enchanted wood, both of which immediately vanished, and were never more beheld by mortal eyes. The princess was restored to her ancestral kingdom, but it was not generally declared who she was, as during a hundred years people had grown so very much cleverer that nobody then living would ever have believed the story. So nothing was explained, and nobody presumed to ask any questions about her, for ought not a prince be able to marry whomsoever he pleases?

Nor — whether or not the day of fairies was over—did the princess ever see anything further of her seven godmothers. She lived a long and happy life, like any other ordinary woman, and died at length, beloved, regretted, but, the prince being already no more, perfectly contented.

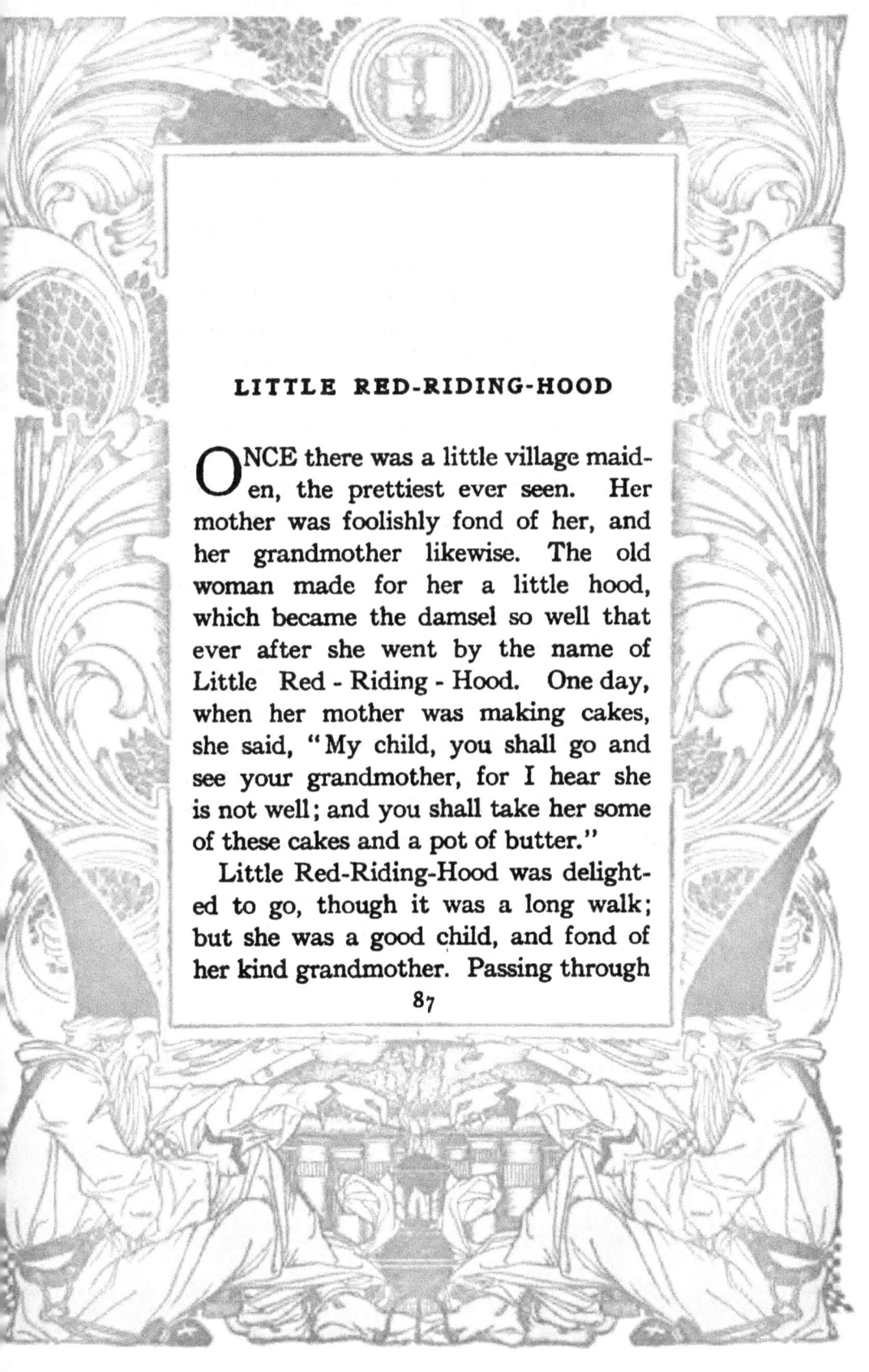

LITTLE RED-RIDING-HOOD

ONCE there was a little village maiden, the prettiest ever seen. Her mother was foolishly fond of her, and her grandmother likewise. The old woman made for her a little hood, which became the damsel so well that ever after she went by the name of Little Red - Riding - Hood. One day, when her mother was making cakes, she said, "My child, you shall go and see your grandmother, for I hear she is not well; and you shall take her some of these cakes and a pot of butter."

Little Red-Riding-Hood was delighted to go, though it was a long walk; but she was a good child, and fond of her kind grandmother. Passing through

87

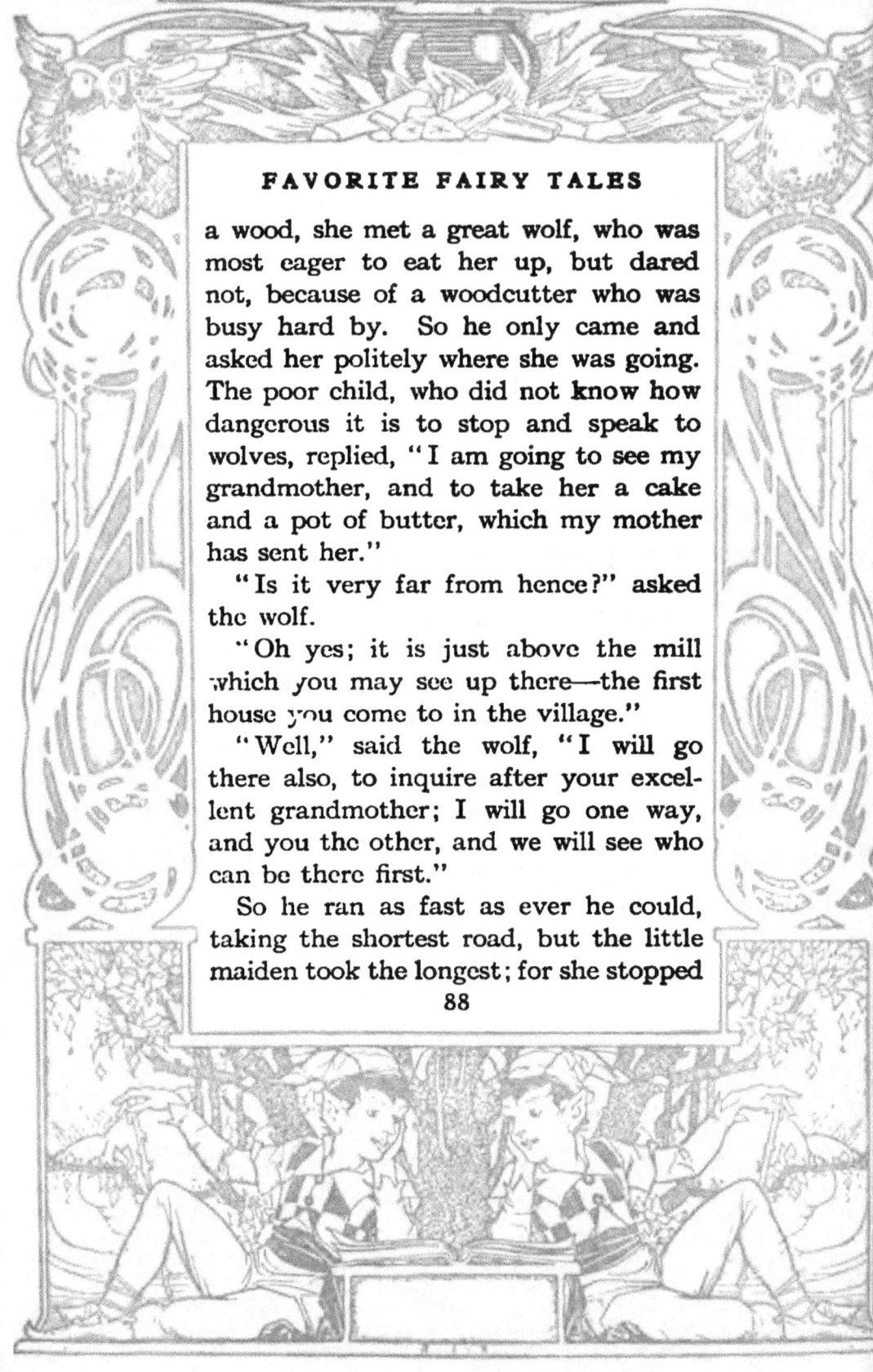

a wood, she met a great wolf, who was most eager to eat her up, but dared not, because of a woodcutter who was busy hard by. So he only came and asked her politely where she was going. The poor child, who did not know how dangerous it is to stop and speak to wolves, replied, "I am going to see my grandmother, and to take her a cake and a pot of butter, which my mother has sent her."

"Is it very far from hence?" asked the wolf.

"Oh yes; it is just above the mill which you may see up there—the first house you come to in the village."

"Well," said the wolf, "I will go there also, to inquire after your excellent grandmother; I will go one way, and you the other, and we will see who can be there first."

So he ran as fast as ever he could, taking the shortest road, but the little maiden took the longest; for she stopped

He asked her politely where she was going

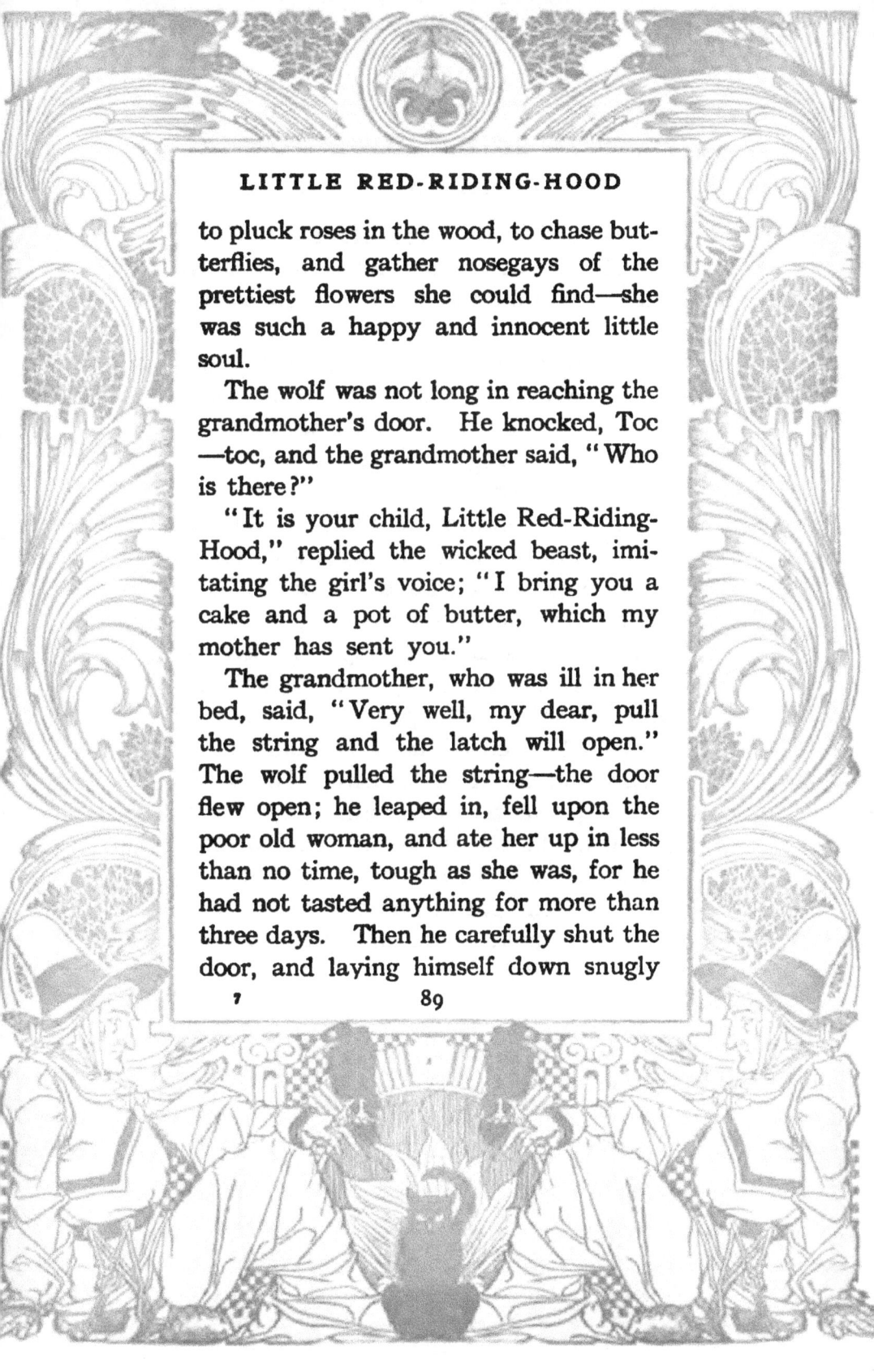

to pluck roses in the wood, to chase butterflies, and gather nosegays of the
prettiest flowers she could find—she
was such a happy and innocent little
soul.

The wolf was not long in reaching the
grandmother's door. He knocked, Toc
—toc, and the grandmother said, "Who
is there?"

"It is your child, Little Red-Riding-
Hood," replied the wicked beast, imi-
tating the girl's voice; "I bring you a
cake and a pot of butter, which my
mother has sent you."

The grandmother, who was ill in her
bed, said, "Very well, my dear, pull
the string and the latch will open."
The wolf pulled the string—the door
flew open; he leaped in, fell upon the
poor old woman, and ate her up in less
than no time, tough as she was, for he
had not tasted anything for more than
three days. Then he carefully shut the
door, and laying himself down snugly

in the bed, waited for Little Red-Rid-ing-Hood, who was not long before she came and knocked, Toc—toc, at the door.

"Who is there?" said the wolf; and the little maiden, hearing his gruff voice, felt sure that her poor grandmother must have caught a bad cold and be very ill indeed.

So she answered, cheerfully, "It is your child, Little Red-Riding-Hood, who brings you a cake and a pot of but-ter that my mother has sent you."

Then the wolf, softening his voice as much as he could, said, "Pull the string, and the latch will open."

So Little Red-Riding-Hood pulled the string and the door opened. The wolf, seeing her enter, hid himself as much as he could under the coverlid of the bed, and said in a whisper, "Put the cake and the pot of butter on the shelf, and then make haste and come to bed, for it is very late."

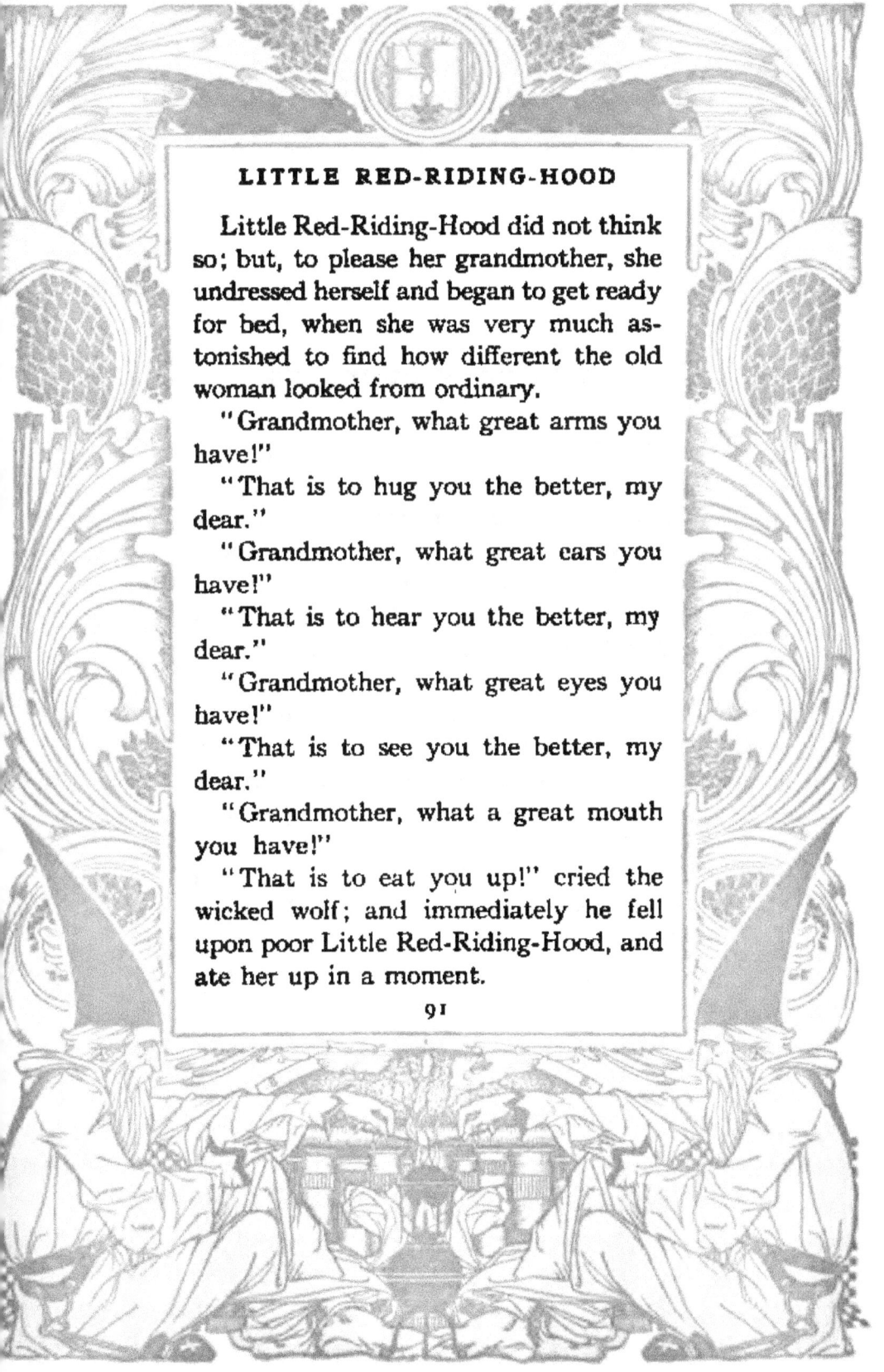

LITTLE RED-RIDING-HOOD

Little Red-Riding-Hood did not think so; but, to please her grandmother, she undressed herself and began to get ready for bed, when she was very much astonished to find how different the old woman looked from ordinary.

"Grandmother, what great arms you have!"

"That is to hug you the better, my dear."

"Grandmother, what great ears you have!"

"That is to hear you the better, my dear."

"Grandmother, what great eyes you have!"

"That is to see you the better, my dear."

"Grandmother, what a great mouth you have!"

"That is to eat you up!" cried the wicked wolf; and immediately he fell upon poor Little Red-Riding-Hood, and ate her up in a moment.

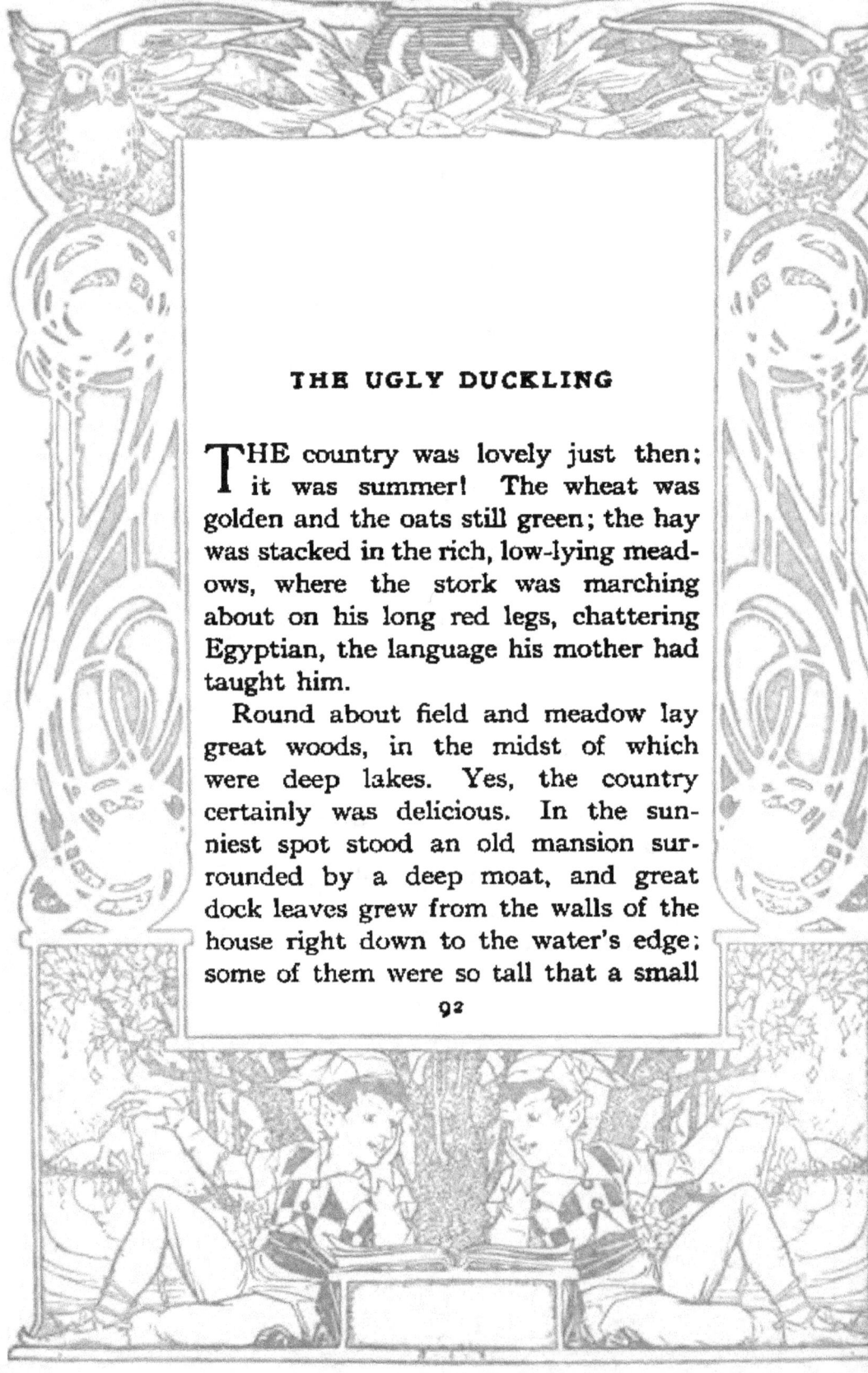

THE UGLY DUCKLING

THE country was lovely just then; it was summer! The wheat was golden and the oats still green; the hay was stacked in the rich, low-lying meadows, where the stork was marching about on his long red legs, chattering Egyptian, the language his mother had taught him.

Round about field and meadow lay great woods, in the midst of which were deep lakes. Yes, the country certainly was delicious. In the sunniest spot stood an old mansion surrounded by a deep moat, and great dock leaves grew from the walls of the house right down to the water's edge; some of them were so tall that a small

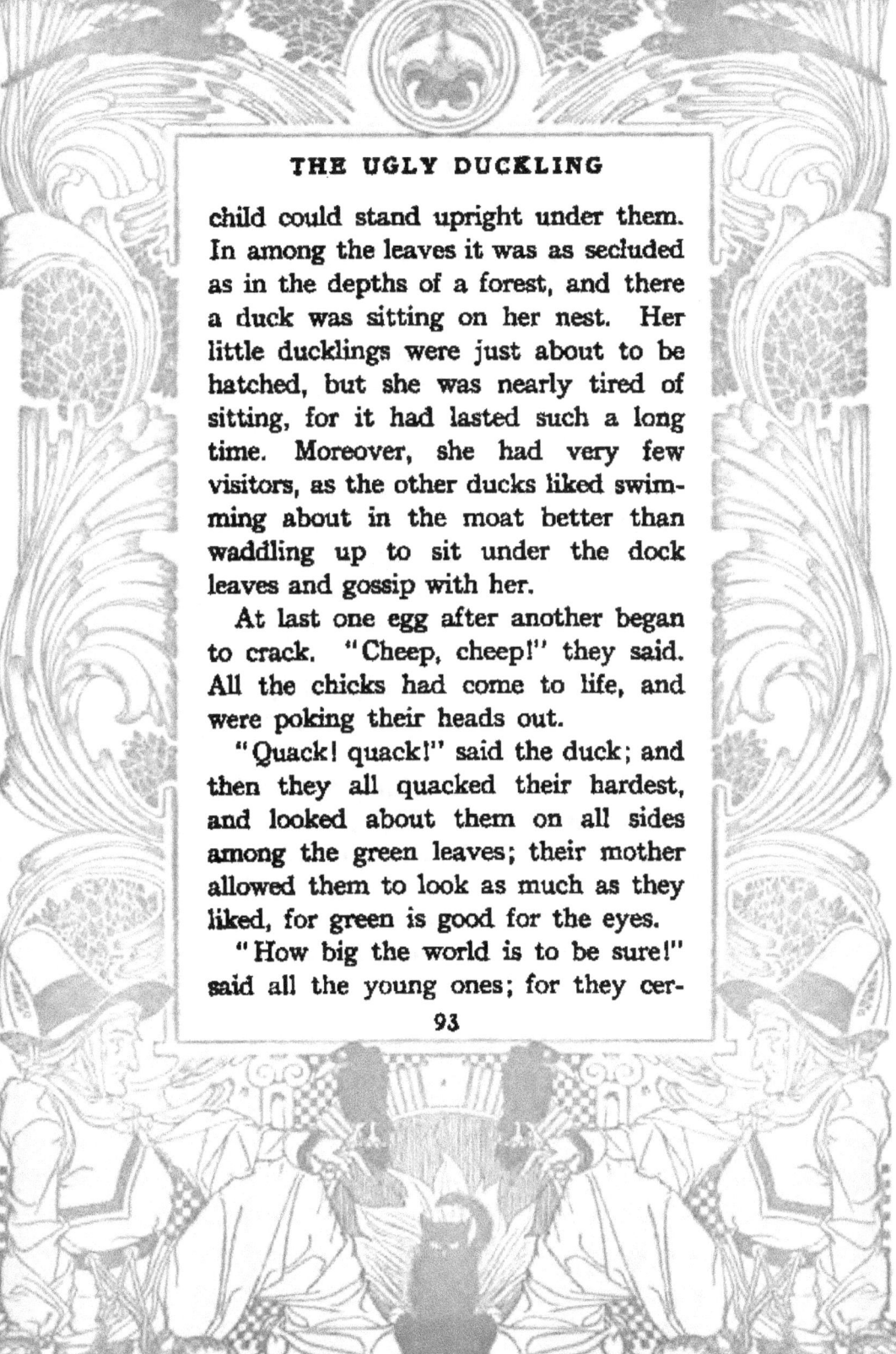

child could stand upright under them. In among the leaves it was as secluded as in the depths of a forest, and there a duck was sitting on her nest. Her little ducklings were just about to be hatched, but she was nearly tired of sitting, for it had lasted such a long time. Moreover, she had very few visitors, as the other ducks liked swimming about in the moat better than waddling up to sit under the dock leaves and gossip with her.

At last one egg after another began to crack. "Cheep, cheep!" they said. All the chicks had come to life, and were poking their heads out.

"Quack! quack!" said the duck; and then they all quacked their hardest, and looked about them on all sides among the green leaves; their mother allowed them to look as much as they liked, for green is good for the eyes.

"How big the world is to be sure!" said all the young ones; for they cer-

93

tainly had ever so much more room to move about than when they were inside the egg-shell.

"Do you imagine this is the whole world?" said the mother. "It stretches a long way on the other side of the garden, right into the parson's field; but I have never been as far as that! I suppose you are all here now?" and she got up. "No! I declare I have not got you all yet! The biggest egg is still there; how long is it going to last?" and then she settled herself on the nest again.

"Well, how are you getting on?" said an old duck who had come to pay her a visit.

"This one egg is taking such a long time," answered the sitting duck, "the shell will not crack; but now you must look at the others; they are the finest ducklings I have ever seen! they are all exactly like their father, the rascal! he never comes to see me."

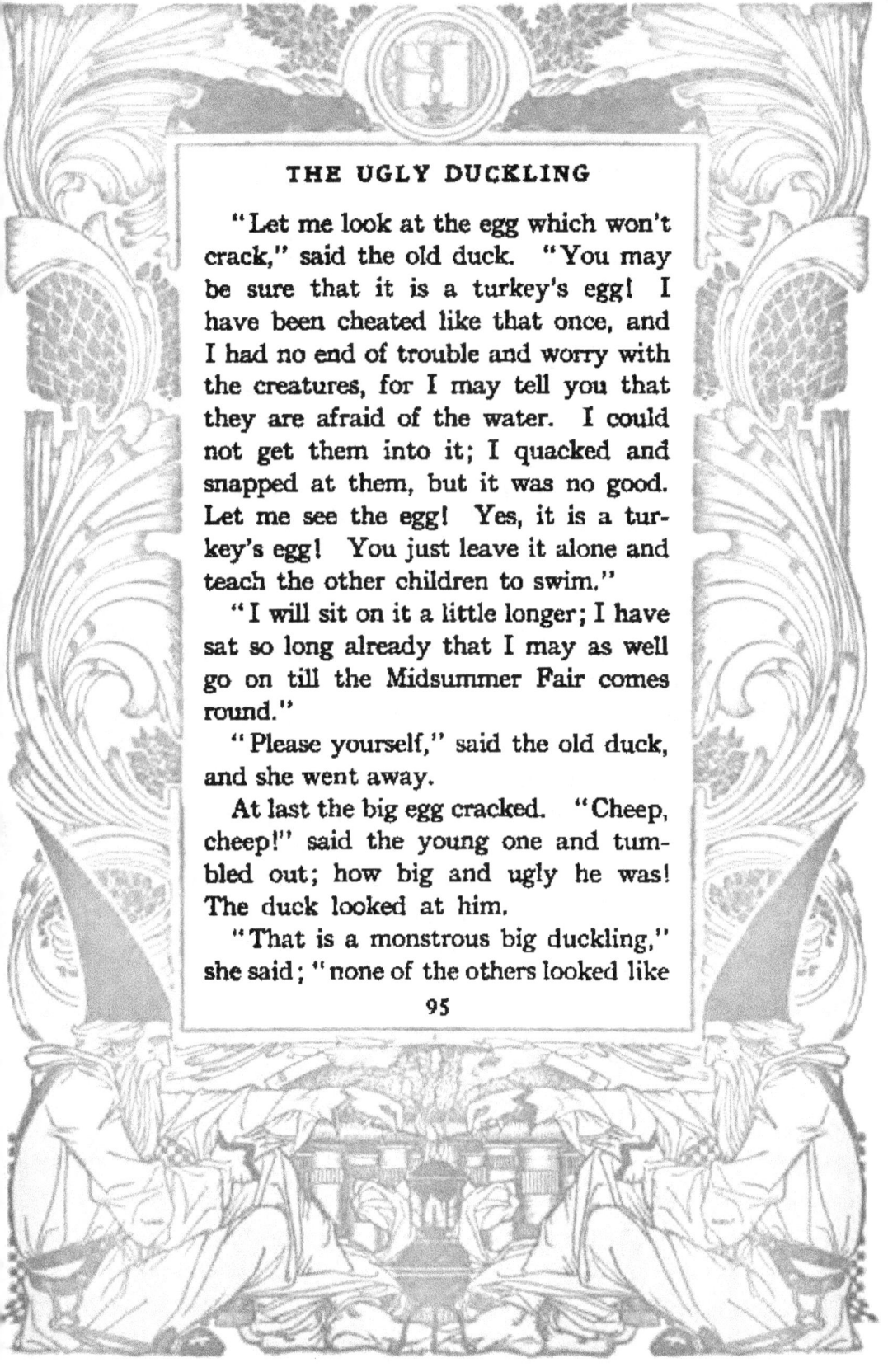

THE UGLY DUCKLING

"Let me look at the egg which won't crack," said the old duck. "You may be sure that it is a turkey's egg! I have been cheated like that once, and I had no end of trouble and worry with the creatures, for I may tell you that they are afraid of the water. I could not get them into it; I quacked and snapped at them, but it was no good. Let me see the egg! Yes, it is a turkey's egg! You just leave it alone and teach the other children to swim."

"I will sit on it a little longer; I have sat so long already that I may as well go on till the Midsummer Fair comes round."

"Please yourself," said the old duck, and she went away.

At last the big egg cracked. "Cheep, cheep!" said the young one and tumbled out; how big and ugly he was! The duck looked at him.

"That is a monstrous big duckling," she said; "none of the others looked like

95

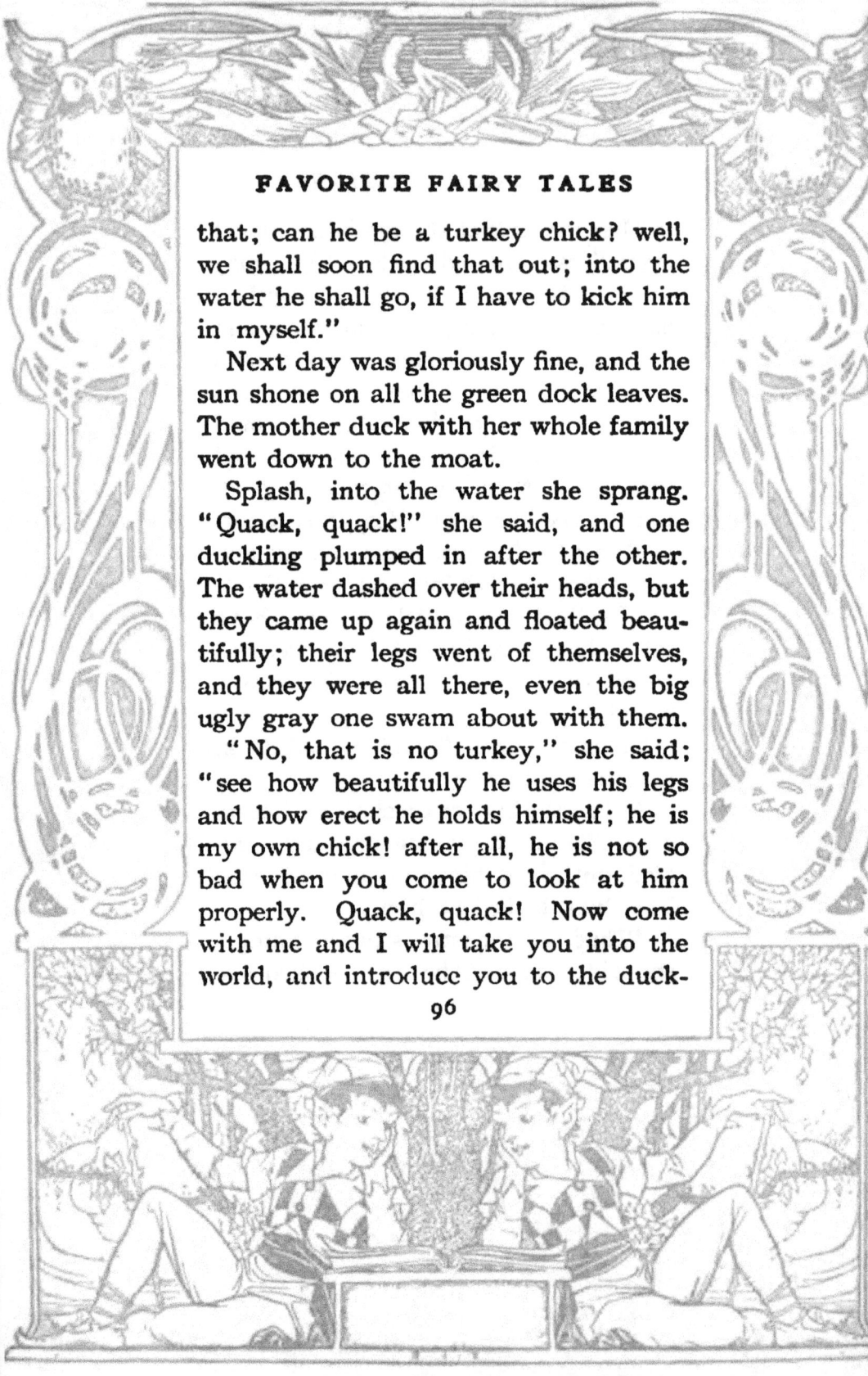

that; can he be a turkey chick? well, we shall soon find that out; into the water he shall go, if I have to kick him in myself."

Next day was gloriously fine, and the sun shone on all the green dock leaves. The mother duck with her whole family went down to the moat.

Splash, into the water she sprang. "Quack, quack!" she said, and one duckling plumped in after the other. The water dashed over their heads, but they came up again and floated beautifully; their legs went of themselves, and they were all there, even the big ugly gray one swam about with them.

"No, that is no turkey," she said; "see how beautifully he uses his legs and how erect he holds himself; he is my own chick! after all, he is not so bad when you come to look at him properly. Quack, quack! Now come with me and I will take you into the world, and introduce you to the duck-

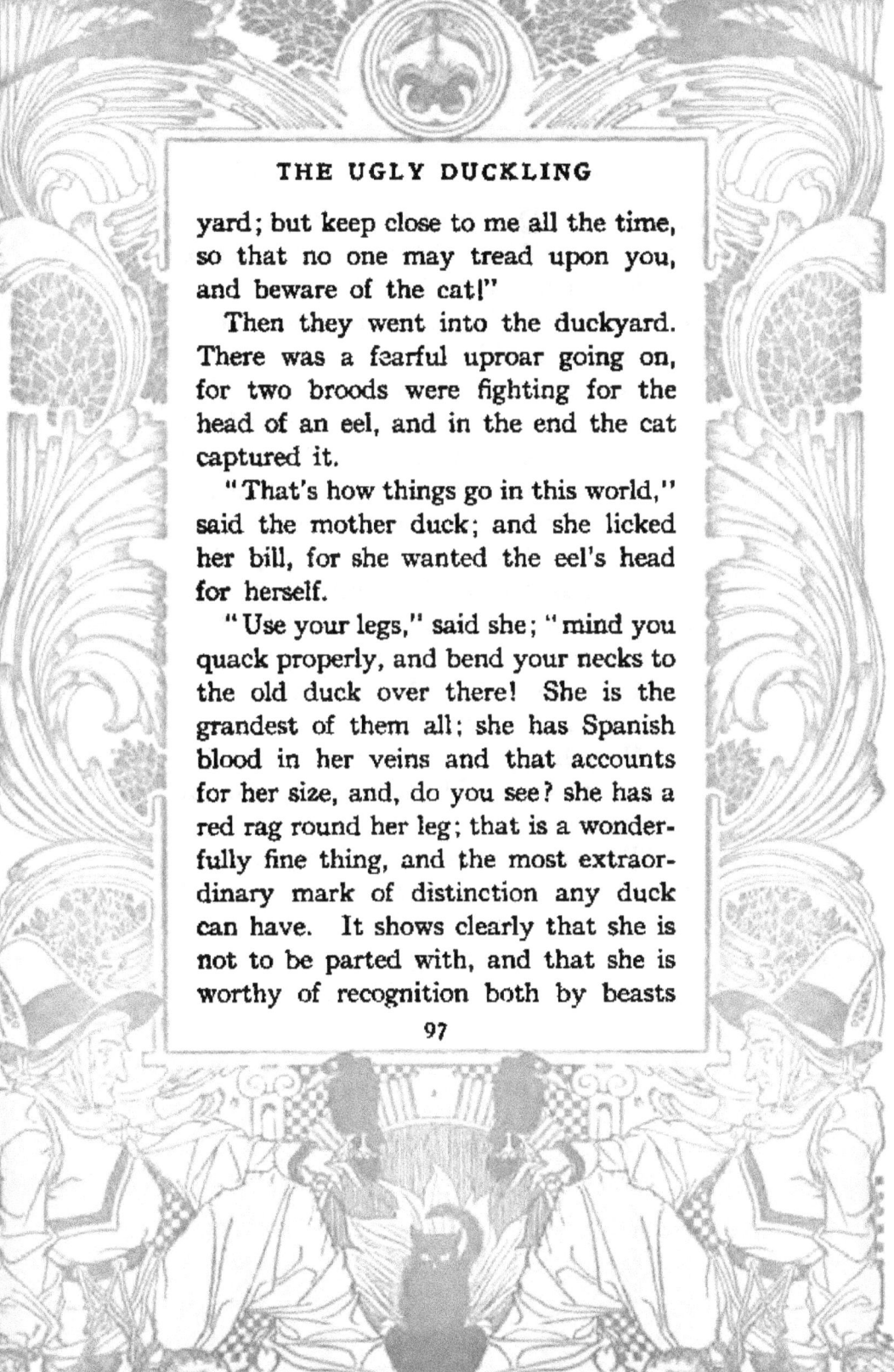

yard; but keep close to me all the time, so that no one may tread upon you, and beware of the cat!"

Then they went into the duckyard. There was a fearful uproar going on, for two broods were fighting for the head of an eel, and in the end the cat captured it.

"That's how things go in this world," said the mother duck; and she licked her bill, for she wanted the eel's head for herself.

"Use your legs," said she; "mind you quack properly, and bend your necks to the old duck over there! She is the grandest of them all; she has Spanish blood in her veins and that accounts for her size, and, do you see? she has a red rag round her leg; that is a wonderfully fine thing, and the most extraordinary mark of distinction any duck can have. It shows clearly that she is not to be parted with, and that she is worthy of recognition both by beasts

and men! Quack now! don't turn your toes in, a well brought up duckling keeps his legs wide apart just like father and mother; that's it, now bend your necks, and say quack!"

They did as they were bid, but the other ducks round about looked at them and said, quite loud: "Just look there! now we are to have that tribe! just as if there were not enough of us already, and, oh dear! how ugly that duckling is, we won't stand him!" and a duck flew at him at once and bit him in the neck.

"Let him be," said the mother; "he is doing no harm."

"Very likely not, but he is so ungainly and queer," said the biter, "he must be whacked."

"They are handsome children mother has," said the old duck with the rag round her leg; "all good looking except this one, and he is not a good specimen; it's a pity you can't make him over again."

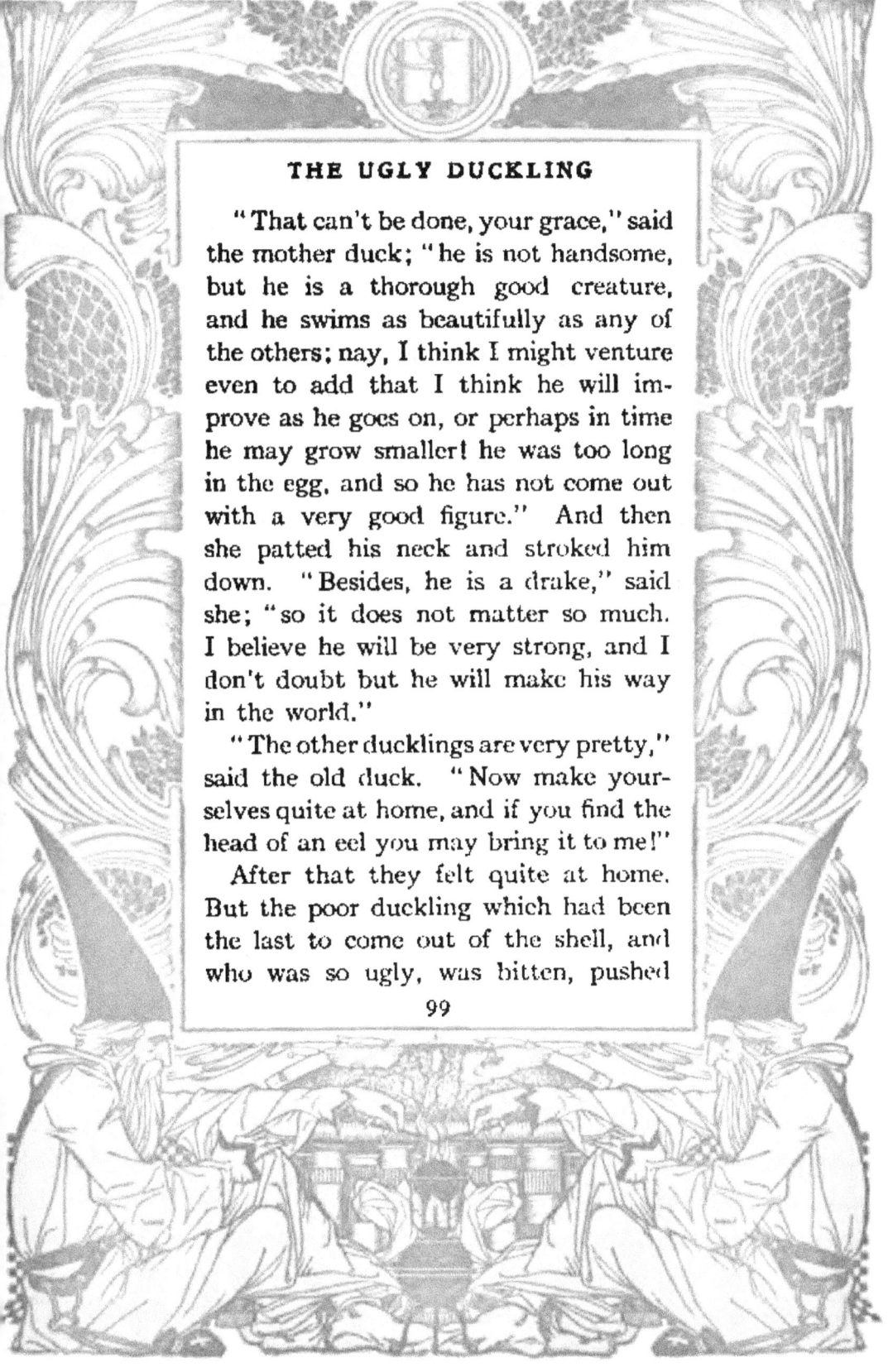

THE UGLY DUCKLING

"That can't be done, your grace," said the mother duck; "he is not handsome, but he is a thorough good creature, and he swims as beautifully as any of the others; nay, I think I might venture even to add that I think he will improve as he goes on, or perhaps in time he may grow smaller! he was too long in the egg, and so he has not come out with a very good figure." And then she patted his neck and stroked him down. "Besides, he is a drake," said she; "so it does not matter so much. I believe he will be very strong, and I don't doubt but he will make his way in the world."

"The other ducklings are very pretty," said the old duck. "Now make yourselves quite at home, and if you find the head of an eel you may bring it to me!"

After that they felt quite at home. But the poor duckling which had been the last to come out of the shell, and who was so ugly, was bitten, pushed about, and made fun of both by the ducks and the hens. "He is too big," they all said; and the turkey-cock, who was born with his spurs on, and therefore thought himself quite an emperor, puffed himself up like a vessel in full sail, made for him, and gobbled and gobbled till he became quite red in the face. The poor duckling was at his wit's end, and did not know which way to turn; he was in despair because he was so ugly and the butt of the whole duckyard.

So the first day passed, and afterwards matters grew worse and worse. The poor duckling was chased and hustled by all of them; even his brothers and sisters ill-used him, and they were always saying, "If only the cat would get hold of you, you hideous object!" Even his mother said, "I wish to goodness you were miles away." The ducks bit him, the hens pecked him, and the girl who fed them kicked him aside.

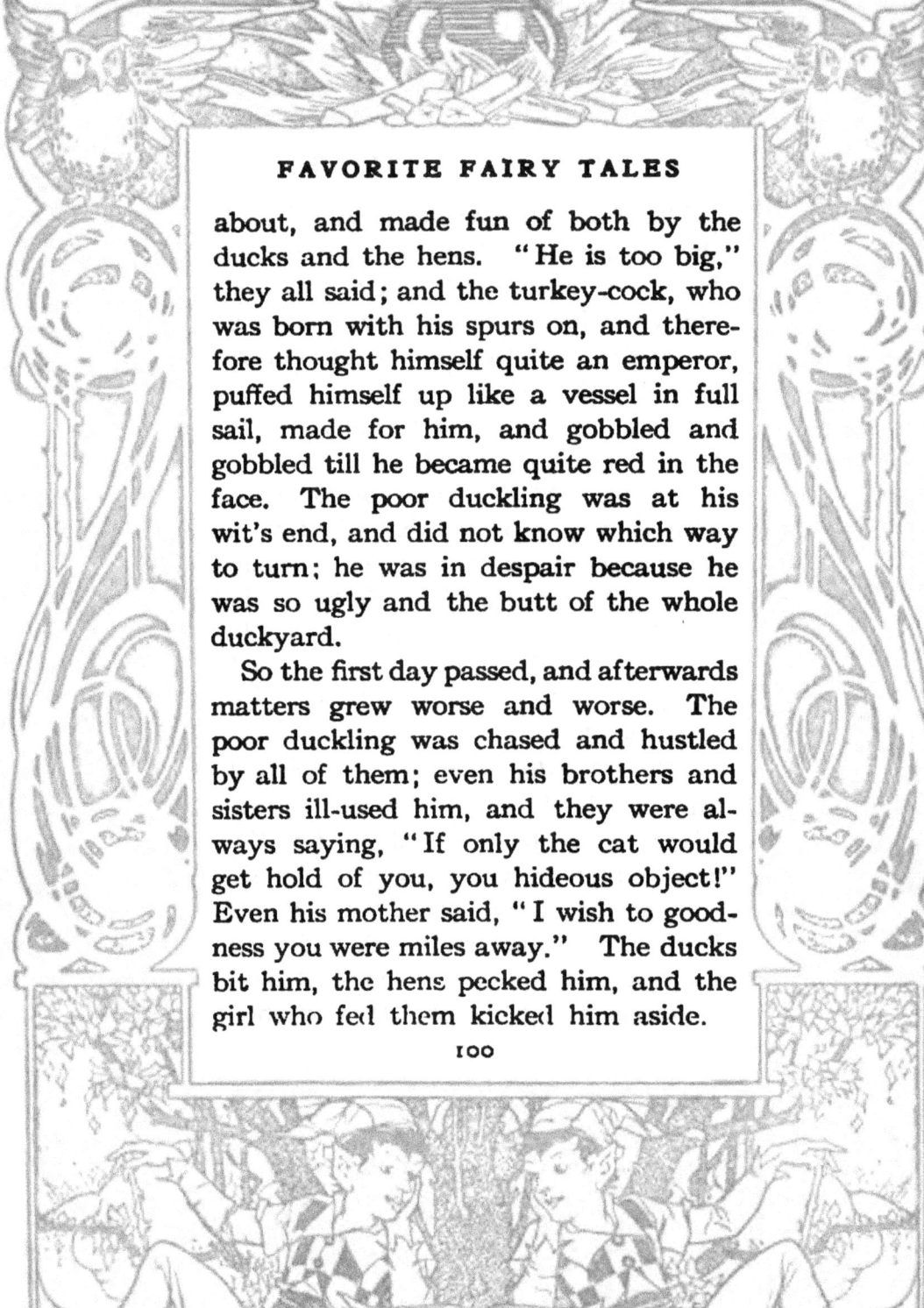

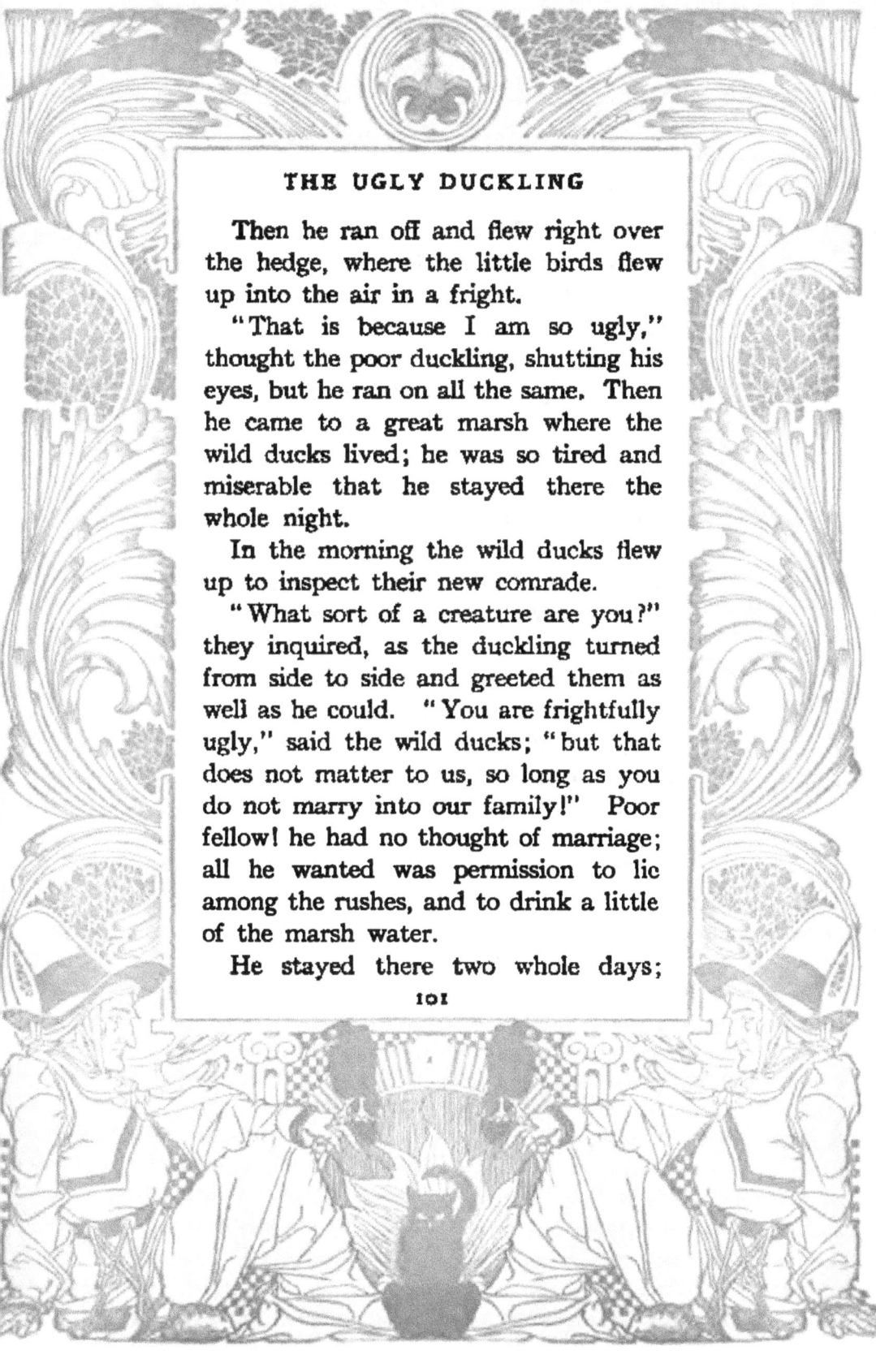

Then he ran off and flew right over the hedge, where the little birds flew up into the air in a fright.

"That is because I am so ugly," thought the poor duckling, shutting his eyes, but he ran on all the same. Then he came to a great marsh where the wild ducks lived; he was so tired and miserable that he stayed there the whole night.

In the morning the wild ducks flew up to inspect their new comrade.

"What sort of a creature are you?" they inquired, as the duckling turned from side to side and greeted them as well as he could. "You are frightfully ugly," said the wild ducks; "but that does not matter to us, so long as you do not marry into our family!" Poor fellow! he had no thought of marriage; all he wanted was permission to lie among the rushes, and to drink a little of the marsh water.

He stayed there two whole days;

then two wild geese came, or, rather, two wild ganders; they were not long out of the shell, and therefore rather pert.

"I say, comrade," they said, "you are so ugly that we have taken quite a fancy to you; will you join us and be a bird of passage? There is another marsh close by, and there are some charming wild geese there; all sweet young ladies, who can say quack! You are ugly enough to make your fortune among them." Just at that moment, bang! bang! was heard up above, and both the wild geese fell dead among the reeds, and the water turned blood red. Bang! bang! went the guns, and whole flocks of wild geese flew up from the rushes and the shot peppered among them again.

There was a grand shooting-party, and the sportsmen lay hidden round the marsh; some even sat on the branches of the trees which overhung the water;

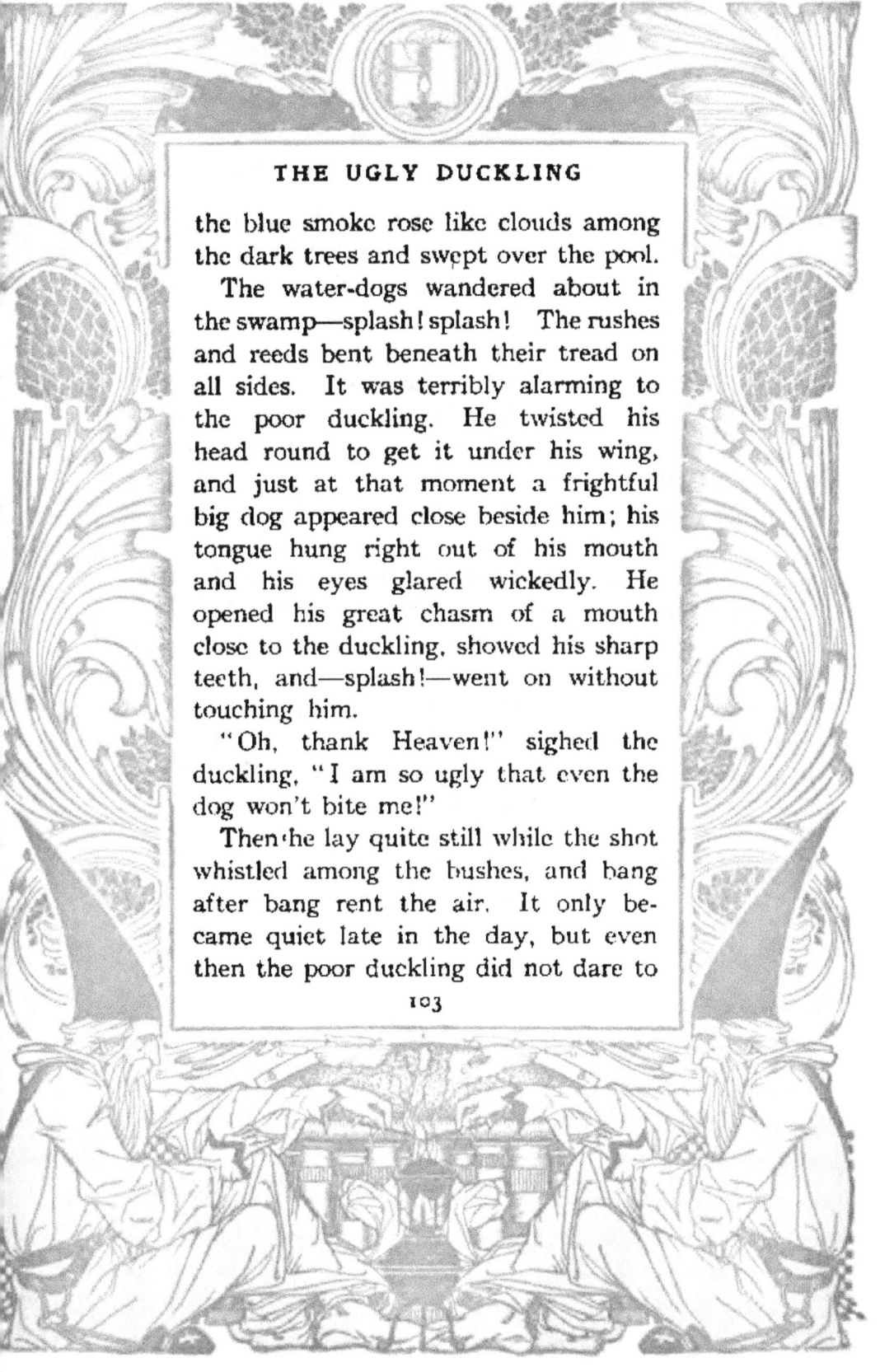

the blue smoke rose like clouds among the dark trees and swept over the pool.

The water-dogs wandered about in the swamp—splash! splash! The rushes and reeds bent beneath their tread on all sides. It was terribly alarming to the poor duckling. He twisted his head round to get it under his wing, and just at that moment a frightful big dog appeared close beside him; his tongue hung right out of his mouth and his eyes glared wickedly. He opened his great chasm of a mouth close to the duckling, showed his sharp teeth, and—splash!—went on without touching him.

"Oh, thank Heaven!" sighed the duckling, "I am so ugly that even the dog won't bite me!"

Then he lay quite still while the shot whistled among the bushes, and bang after bang rent the air. It only became quiet late in the day, but even then the poor duckling did not dare to

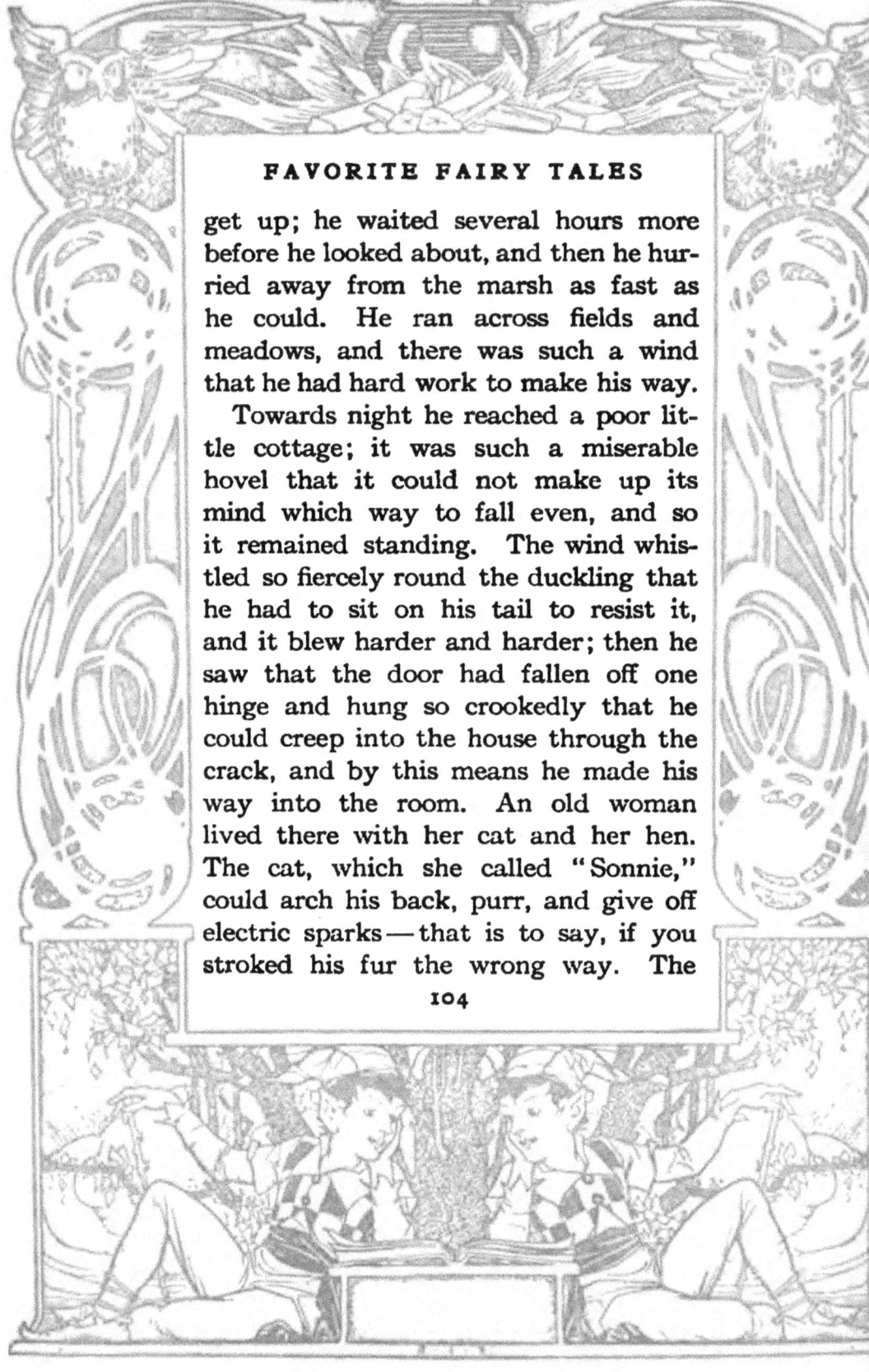

get up; he waited several hours more before he looked about, and then he hurried away from the marsh as fast as he could. He ran across fields and meadows, and there was such a wind that he had hard work to make his way.

Towards night he reached a poor little cottage; it was such a miserable hovel that it could not make up its mind which way to fall even, and so it remained standing. The wind whistled so fiercely round the duckling that he had to sit on his tail to resist it, and it blew harder and harder; then he saw that the door had fallen off one hinge and hung so crookedly that he could creep into the house through the crack, and by this means he made his way into the room. An old woman lived there with her cat and her hen. The cat, which she called "Sonnie," could arch his back, purr, and give off electric sparks—that is to say, if you stroked his fur the wrong way. The hen had quite tiny short legs, and so she was called "Chuckie-low-legs." She laid good eggs, and the old woman was as fond of her as if she had been her own child.

In the morning the strange duckling was discovered immediately, and the cat began to purr and the hen to cluck.

"What on earth is that!" said the old woman, looking round; but her sight was not good, and she thought the duckling was a fat duck which had escaped. "This is a capital find," said she; "now I shall have duck's eggs if only it is not a drake. We must find out about that!"

So she took the duckling on trial for three weeks, but no eggs made their appearance. The cat was the master of the house and the hen the mistress, and they always spoke of "we and the world," for they thought that they represented the half of the world, and that quite the better half.

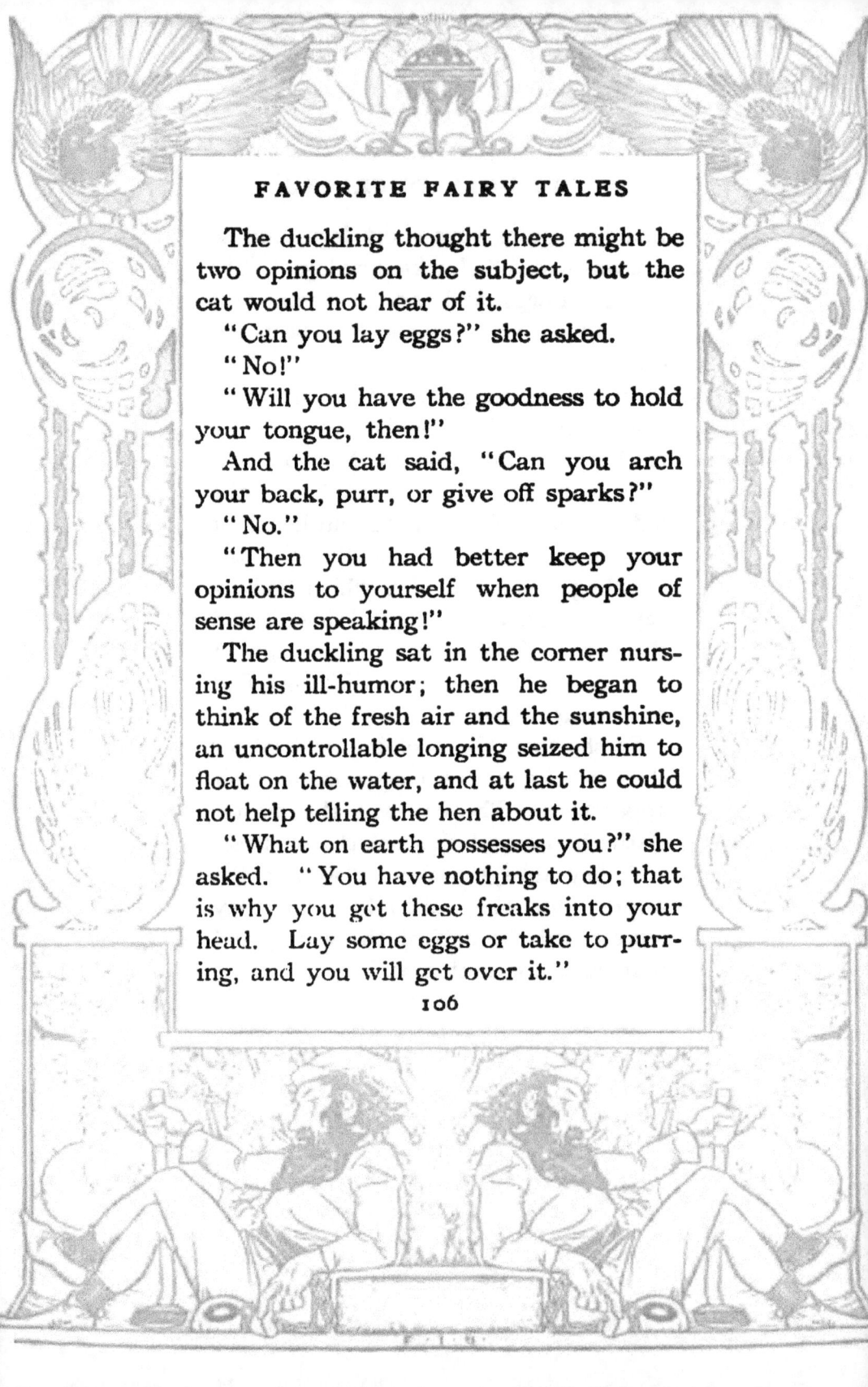

The duckling thought there might be two opinions on the subject, but the cat would not hear of it.

"Can you lay eggs?" she asked.

"No!"

"Will you have the goodness to hold your tongue, then!"

And the cat said, "Can you arch your back, purr, or give off sparks?"

"No."

"Then you had better keep your opinions to yourself when people of sense are speaking!"

The duckling sat in the corner nursing his ill-humor; then he began to think of the fresh air and the sunshine, an uncontrollable longing seized him to float on the water, and at last he could not help telling the hen about it.

"What on earth possesses you?" she asked. "You have nothing to do; that is why you get these freaks into your head. Lay some eggs or take to purring, and you will get over it."

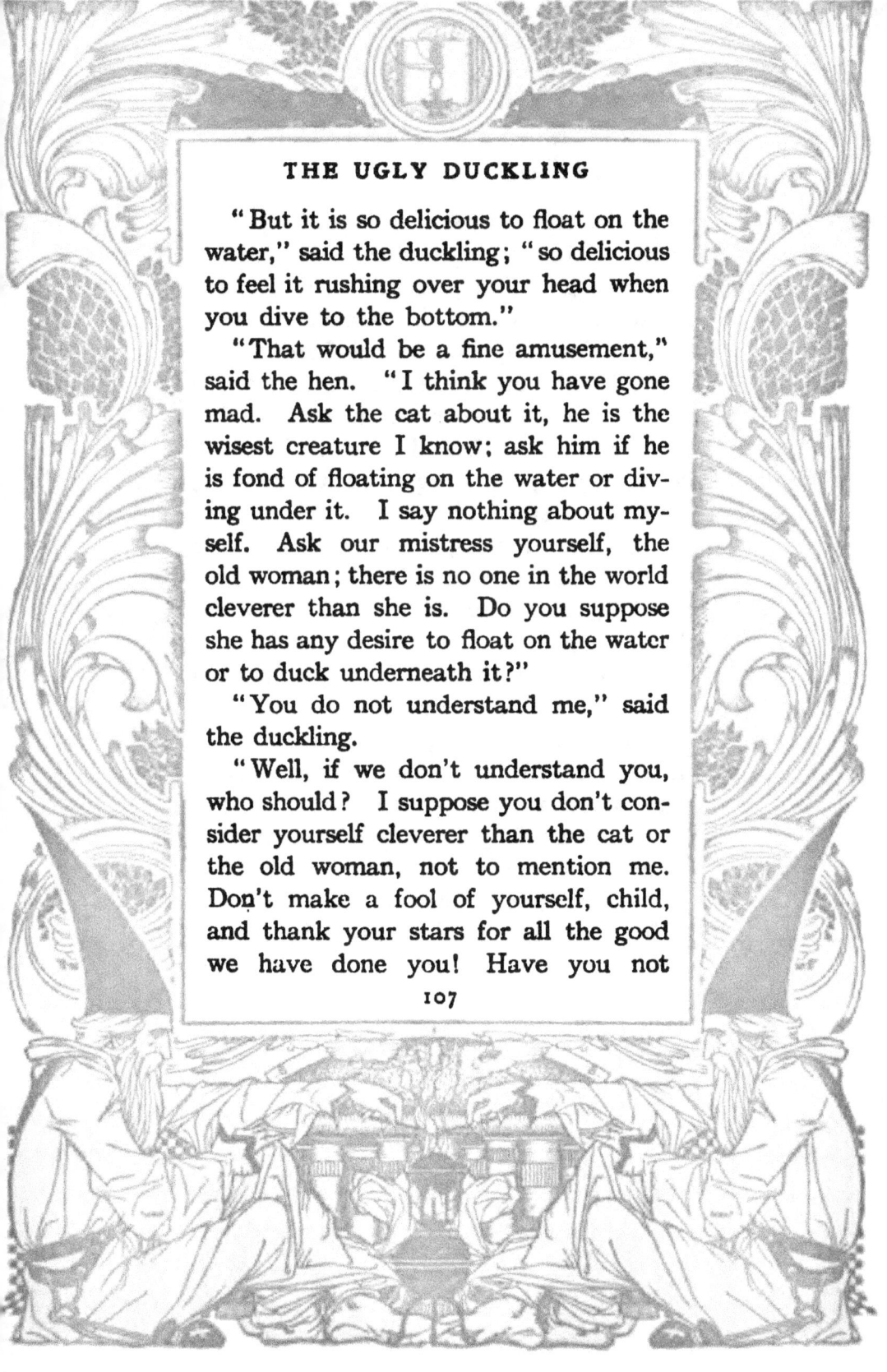

"But it is so delicious to float on the water," said the duckling; "so delicious to feel it rushing over your head when you dive to the bottom."

"That would be a fine amusement," said the hen. "I think you have gone mad. Ask the cat about it, he is the wisest creature I know; ask him if he is fond of floating on the water or diving under it. I say nothing about myself. Ask our mistress yourself, the old woman; there is no one in the world cleverer than she is. Do you suppose she has any desire to float on the water or to duck underneath it?"

"You do not understand me," said the duckling.

"Well, if we don't understand you, who should? I suppose you don't consider yourself cleverer than the cat or the old woman, not to mention me. Don't make a fool of yourself, child, and thank your stars for all the good we have done you! Have you not

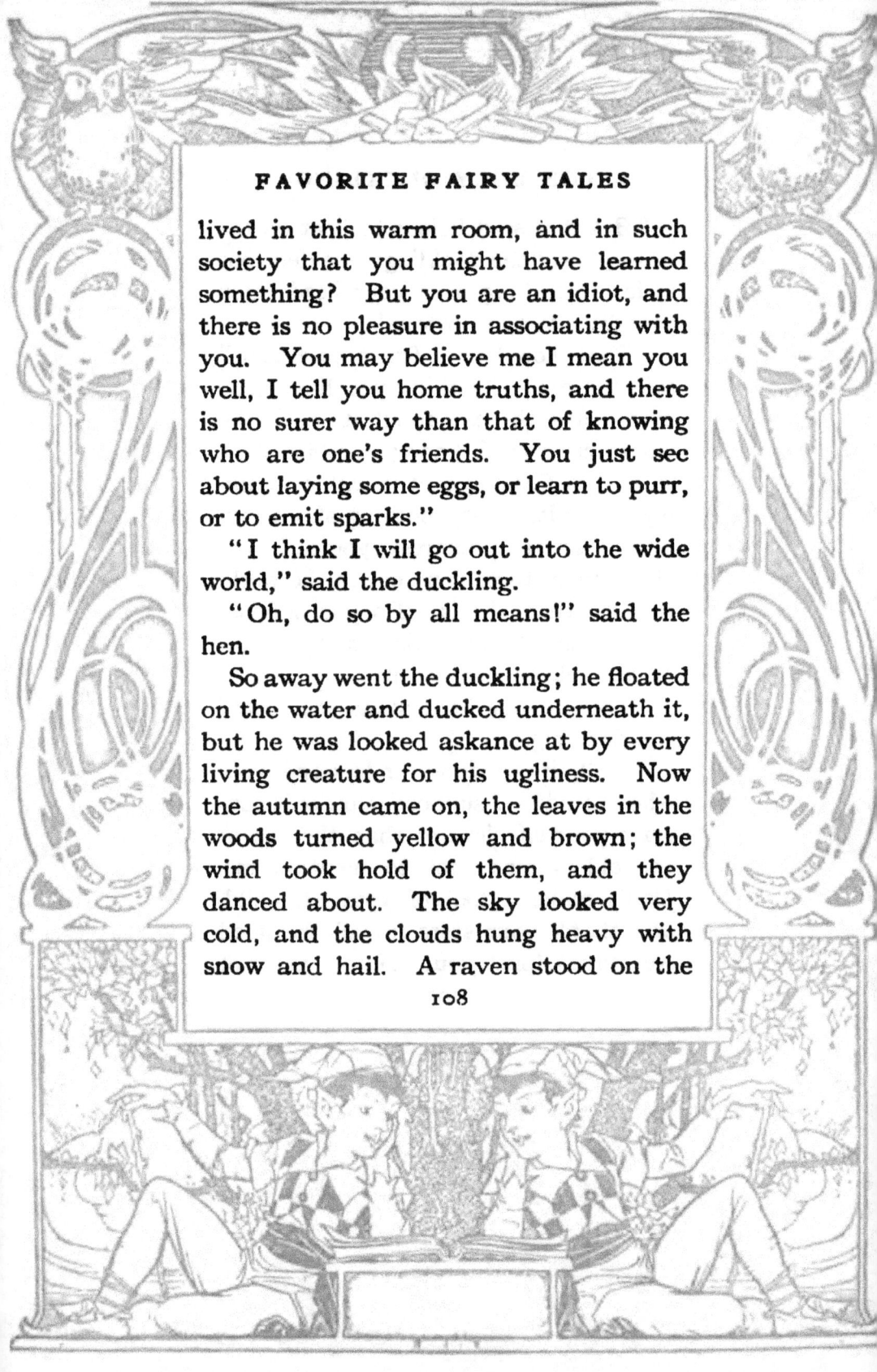

lived in this warm room, and in such society that you might have learned something? But you are an idiot, and there is no pleasure in associating with you. You may believe me I mean you well, I tell you home truths, and there is no surer way than that of knowing who are one's friends. You just see about laying some eggs, or learn to purr, or to emit sparks."

"I think I will go out into the wide world," said the duckling.

"Oh, do so by all means!" said the hen.

So away went the duckling; he floated on the water and ducked underneath it, but he was looked askance at by every living creature for his ugliness. Now the autumn came on, the leaves in the woods turned yellow and brown; the wind took hold of them, and they danced about. The sky looked very cold, and the clouds hung heavy with snow and hail. A raven stood on the

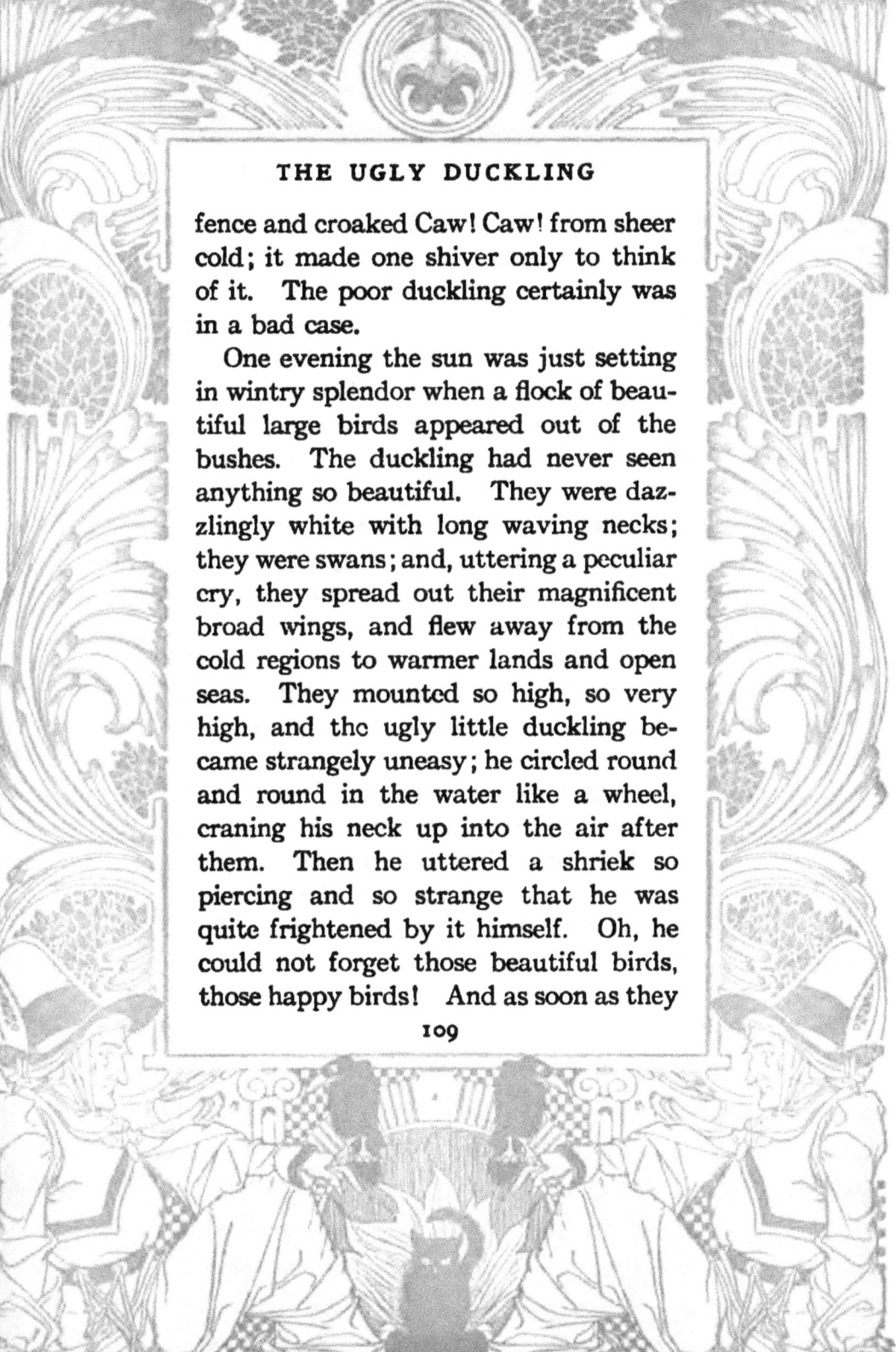

fence and croaked Caw! Caw! from sheer cold; it made one shiver only to think of it. The poor duckling certainly was in a bad case.

One evening the sun was just setting in wintry splendor when a flock of beautiful large birds appeared out of the bushes. The duckling had never seen anything so beautiful. They were dazzlingly white with long waving necks; they were swans; and, uttering a peculiar cry, they spread out their magnificent broad wings, and flew away from the cold regions to warmer lands and open seas. They mounted so high, so very high, and the ugly little duckling became strangely uneasy; he circled round and round in the water like a wheel, craning his neck up into the air after them. Then he uttered a shriek so piercing and so strange that he was quite frightened by it himself. Oh, he could not forget those beautiful birds, those happy birds! And as soon as they

were out of sight he ducked right down to the bottom, and when he came up again he was quite beside himself. He did not know what the birds were or whither they flew, but all the same he was more drawn towards them than he had ever been by any creatures before. He did not even envy them in the least. How could it occur to him even to wish to be such a marvel of beauty; he would have been thankful if only the ducks would have tolerated him among them —the poor ugly creature!

The winter was so bitterly cold that the duckling was obliged to swim about in the water to keep it from freezing, but every night the hole in which he swam got smaller and smaller. Then it froze so hard that the surface ice cracked, and the duckling had to use his legs all the time, so that the ice should not close in round him; at last he was so weary that he could move no more, and he was frozen fast into the ice.

THE UGLY DUCKLING

Early in the morning a peasant came along and saw him; he went out onto the ice and hammered a hole in it with his heavy wooden shoe, and carried the duckling home to his wife. There it soon revived. The children wanted to play with it, but the duckling thought they were going to ill-use him, and rushed in his fright into the milk pan, and the milk spurted out all over the room. The woman shrieked and threw up her hands; then it flew into the butter cask, and down into the meal tub and out again. Just imagine what it looked like by this time! The woman screamed and tried to hit it with the tongs, and the children tumbled over one another in trying to catch it, and they screamed with laughter. By good luck the door stood open, and the duckling flew out among the bushes and the new fallen snow, and it lay there thoroughly exhausted.

But it would be too sad to mention

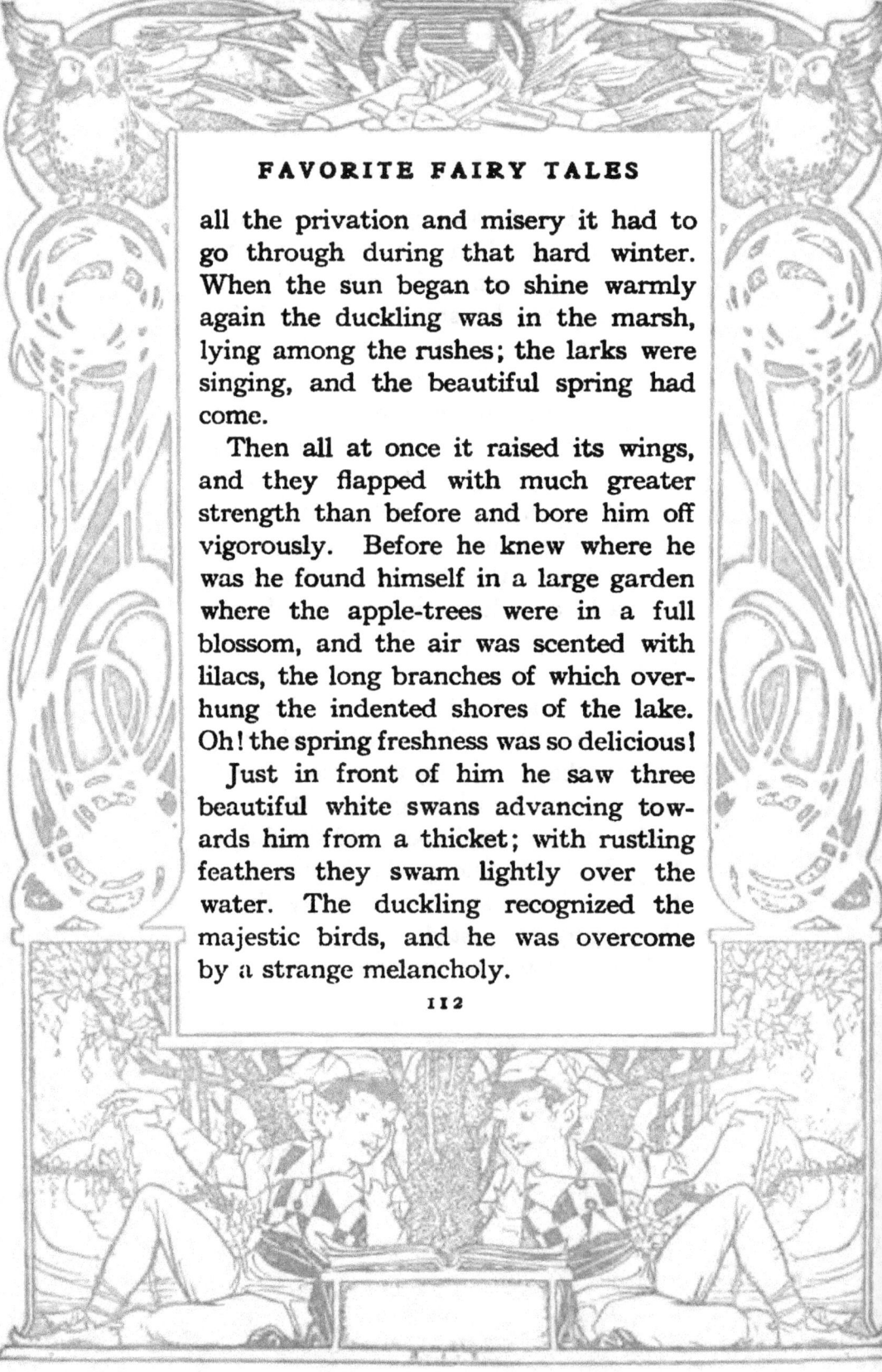

all the privation and misery it had to go through during that hard winter. When the sun began to shine warmly again the duckling was in the marsh, lying among the rushes; the larks were singing, and the beautiful spring had come.

Then all at once it raised its wings, and they flapped with much greater strength than before and bore him off vigorously. Before he knew where he was he found himself in a large garden where the apple-trees were in a full blossom, and the air was scented with lilacs, the long branches of which overhung the indented shores of the lake. Oh! the spring freshness was so delicious!

Just in front of him he saw three beautiful white swans advancing towards him from a thicket; with rustling feathers they swam lightly over the water. The duckling recognized the majestic birds, and he was overcome by a strange melancholy.

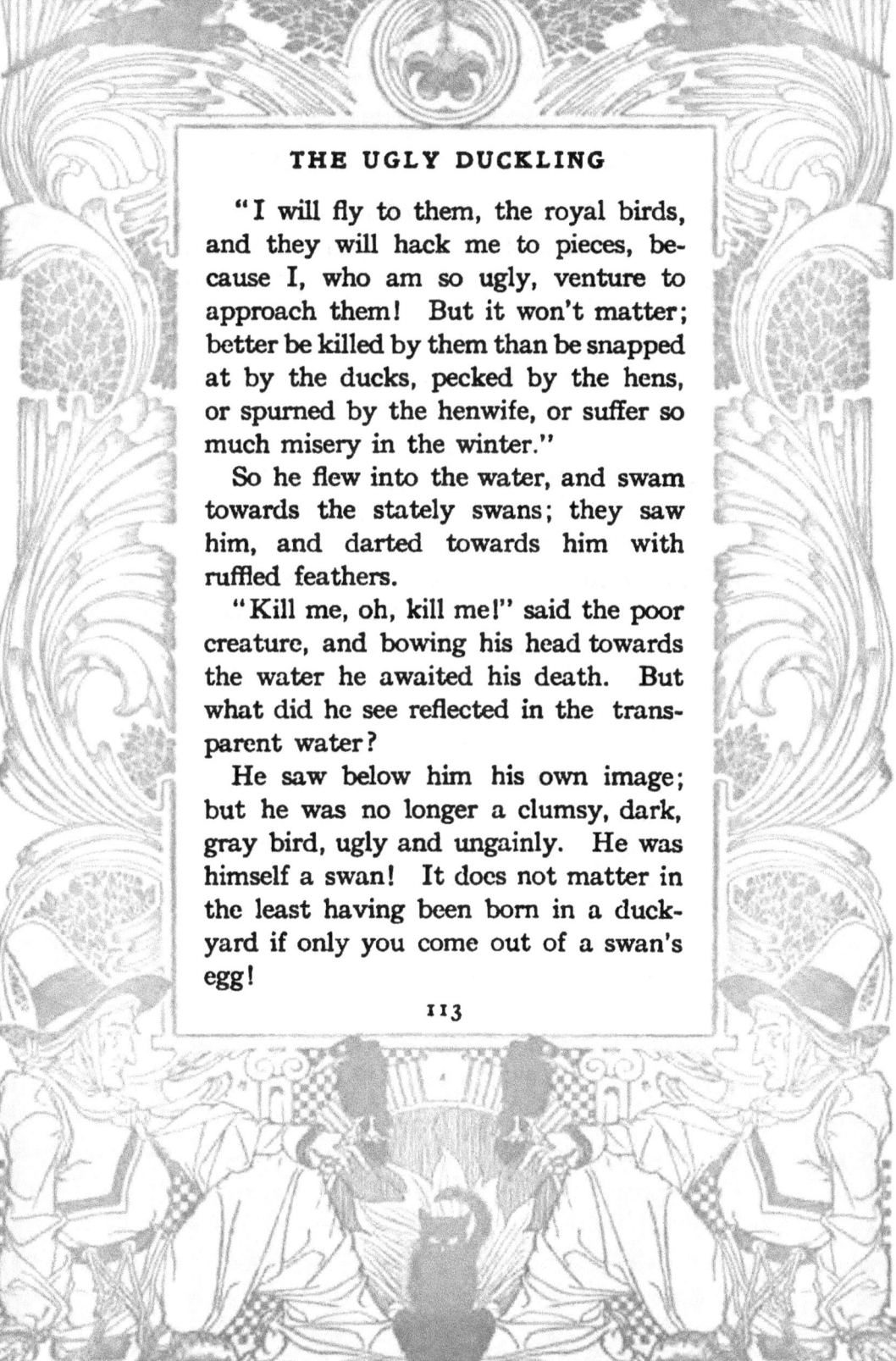

THE UGLY DUCKLING

"I will fly to them, the royal birds, and they will hack me to pieces, because I, who am so ugly, venture to approach them! But it won't matter; better be killed by them than be snapped at by the ducks, pecked by the hens, or spurned by the henwife, or suffer so much misery in the winter."

So he flew into the water, and swam towards the stately swans; they saw him, and darted towards him with ruffled feathers.

"Kill me, oh, kill me!" said the poor creature, and bowing his head towards the water he awaited his death. But what did he see reflected in the transparent water?

He saw below him his own image; but he was no longer a clumsy, dark, gray bird, ugly and ungainly. He was himself a swan! It does not matter in the least having been born in a duck-yard if only you come out of a swan's egg!

He felt quite glad of all the misery and tribulation he had gone through; he was the better able to appreciate his good-fortune now, and all the beauty which greeted him. The big swans swam round and round him, and stroked him with their bills.

Some little children came into the garden with corn and pieces of bread, which they threw into the water; and the smallest one cried out: "There is a new one!" The other children shouted with joy: "Yes, a new one has come!" And they clapped their hands and danced about, running after their father and mother. They threw the bread into the water, and one and all said that "the new one was the prettiest; he was so young and handsome." And the old swans bent their heads and did homage before him.

He felt quite shy, and hid his head under his wing; he did not know what to think; he was so very happy, but

Some little children threw pieces of bread into the water

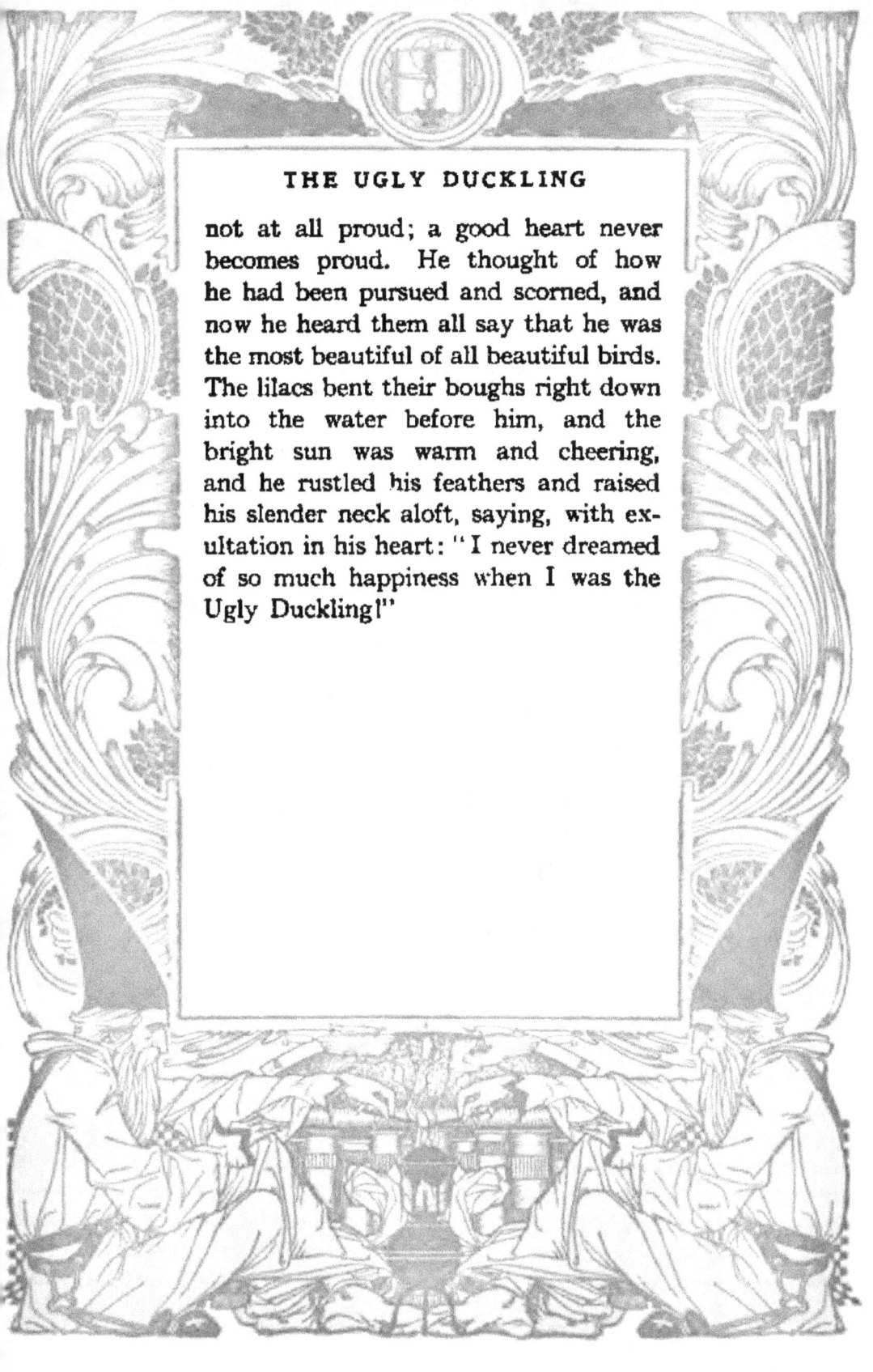

not at all proud; a good heart never becomes proud. He thought of how he had been pursued and scorned, and now he heard them all say that he was the most beautiful of all beautiful birds. The lilacs bent their boughs right down into the water before him, and the bright sun was warm and cheering, and he rustled his feathers and raised his slender neck aloft, saying, with exultation in his heart: "I never dreamed of so much happiness when I was the Ugly Duckling!"

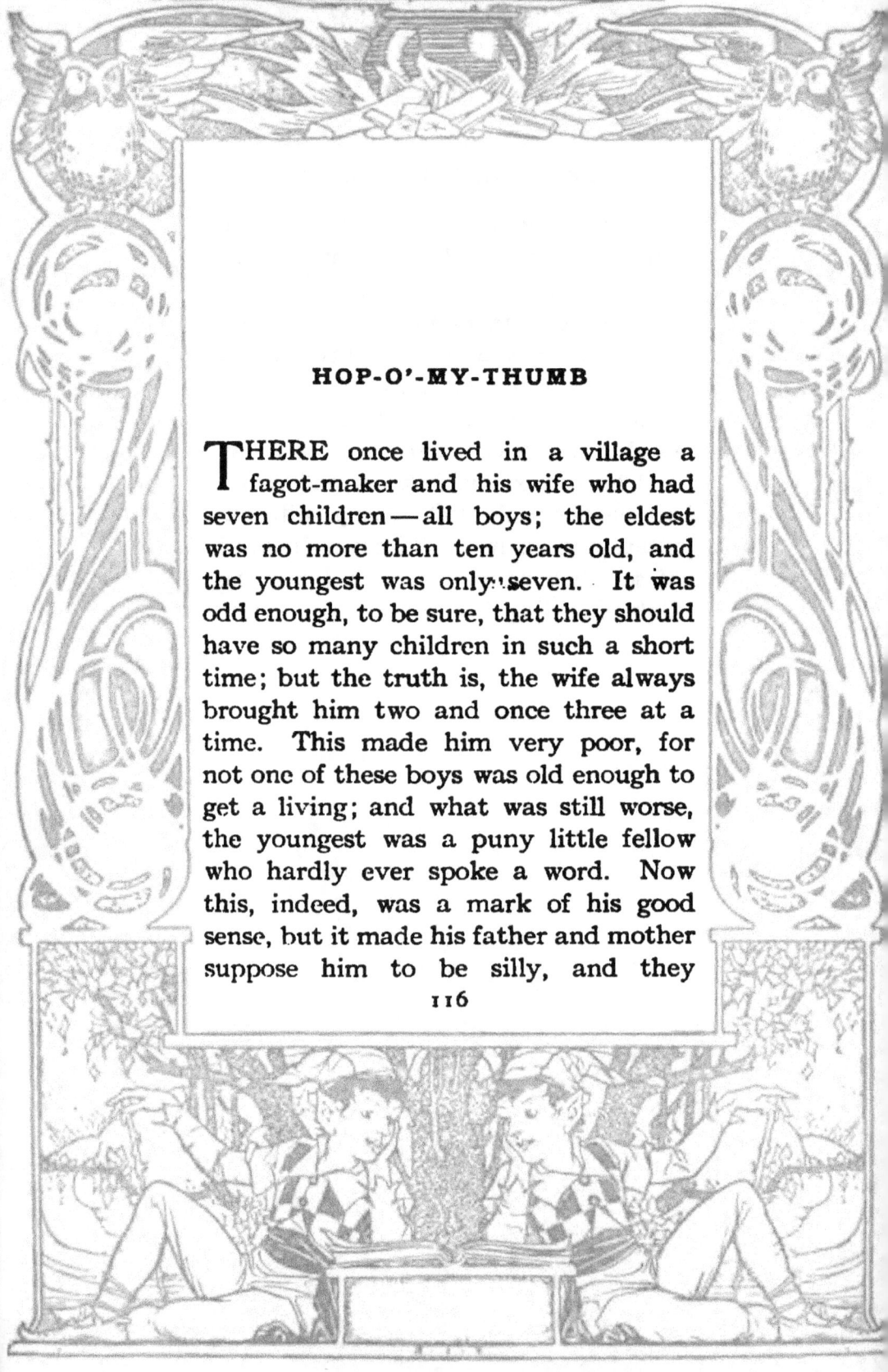

HOP-O'-MY-THUMB

THERE once lived in a village a
fagot-maker and his wife who had
seven children — all boys; the eldest
was no more than ten years old, and
the youngest was only seven. It was
odd enough, to be sure, that they should
have so many children in such a short
time; but the truth is, the wife always
brought him two and once three at a
time. This made him very poor, for
not one of these boys was old enough to
get a living; and what was still worse,
the youngest was a puny little fellow
who hardly ever spoke a word. Now
this, indeed, was a mark of his good
sense, but it made his father and mother
suppose him to be silly, and they

116

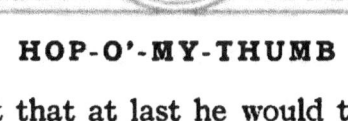

thought that at last he would turn out
quite a fool. This boy was the least
size ever seen; for when he was born
he was no bigger than a man's thumb,
which made him be christened by the
name of Hop-o'-my-Thumb. The poor
child was the drudge of the whole house,
and always bore the blame of everything that was done wrong. For all
this, Hop-o'-my-Thumb was far more
clever than any of his brothers; and
though he spoke but little he heard
and knew more than people thought.
It happened just at this time that for
want of rain the fields had grown but
half as much corn and potatoes as they
used to grow; so that the fagot-maker
and his wife could not give the boys
the food they had before, which was
always either bread or potatoes.

After the father and mother had
grieved some time, they thought that
as they could contrive no other way to
live they must somehow get rid of their

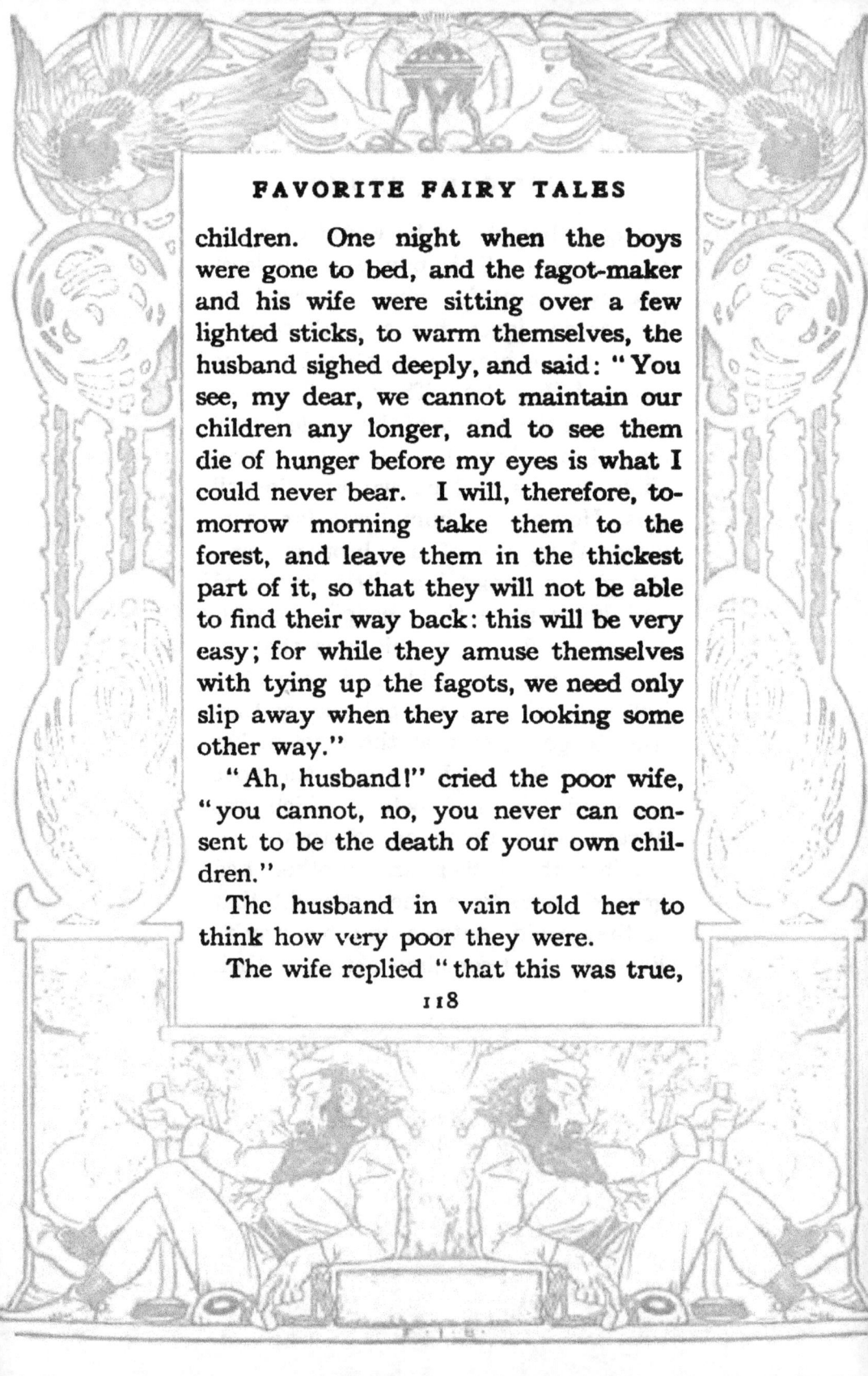

children. One night when the boys
were gone to bed, and the fagot-maker
and his wife were sitting over a few
lighted sticks, to warm themselves, the
husband sighed deeply, and said: "You
see, my dear, we cannot maintain our
children any longer, and to see them
die of hunger before my eyes is what I
could never bear. I will, therefore, to-
morrow morning take them to the
forest, and leave them in the thickest
part of it, so that they will not be able
to find their way back: this will be very
easy; for while they amuse themselves
with tying up the fagots, we need only
slip away when they are looking some
other way."

"Ah, husband!" cried the poor wife,
"you cannot, no, you never can consent to be the death of your own children."

The husband in vain told her to
think how very poor they were.

The wife replied "that this was true,

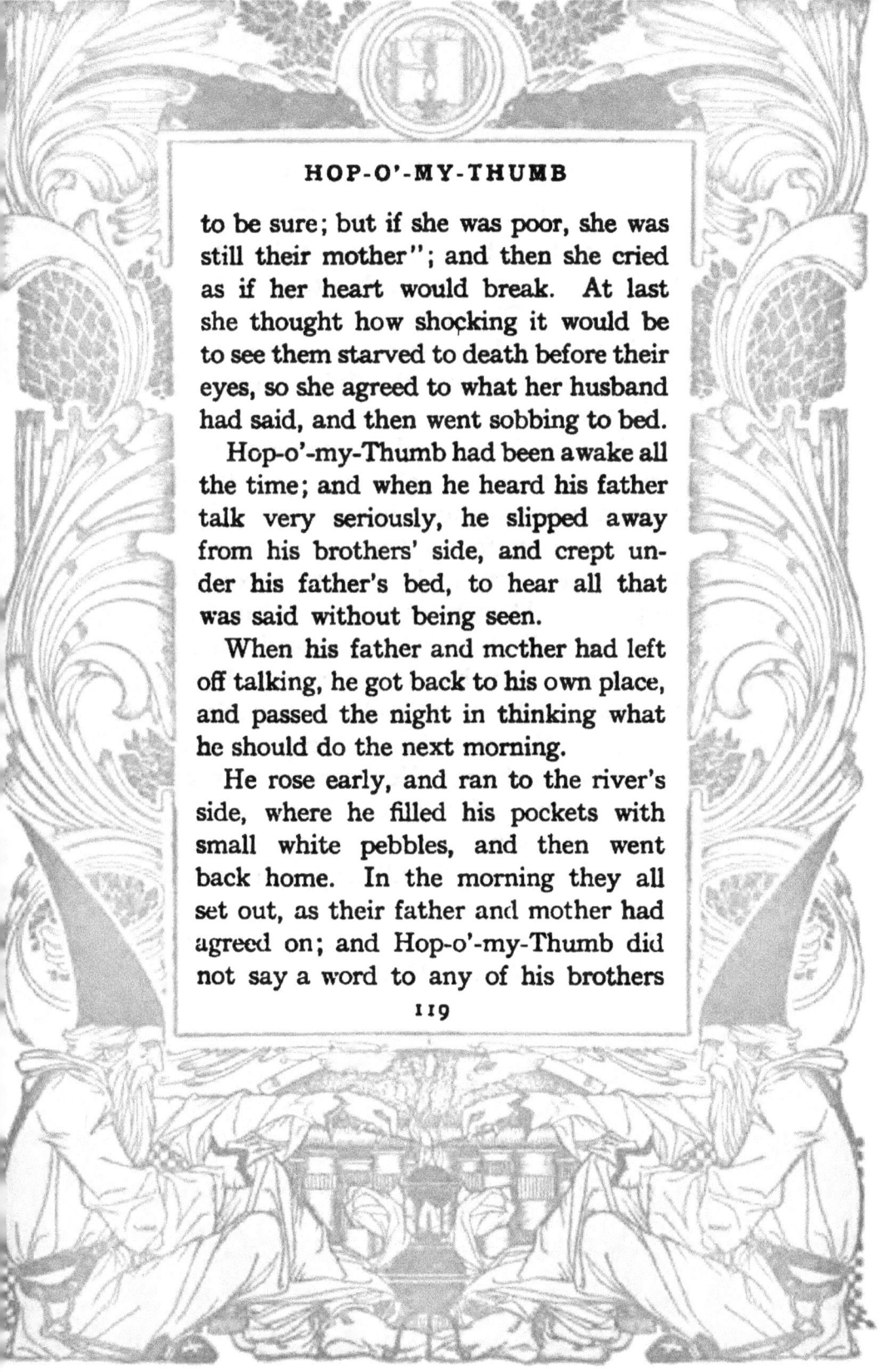

to be sure; but if she was poor, she was
still their mother"; and then she cried
as if her heart would break. At last
she thought how shocking it would be
to see them starved to death before their
eyes, so she agreed to what her husband
had said, and then went sobbing to bed.

Hop-o'-my-Thumb had been awake all
the time; and when he heard his father
talk very seriously, he slipped away
from his brothers' side, and crept under his father's bed, to hear all that
was said without being seen.

When his father and mother had left
off talking, he got back to his own place,
and passed the night in thinking what
he should do the next morning.

He rose early, and ran to the river's
side, where he filled his pockets with
small white pebbles, and then went
back home. In the morning they all
set out, as their father and mother had
agreed on; and Hop-o'-my-Thumb did
not say a word to any of his brothers

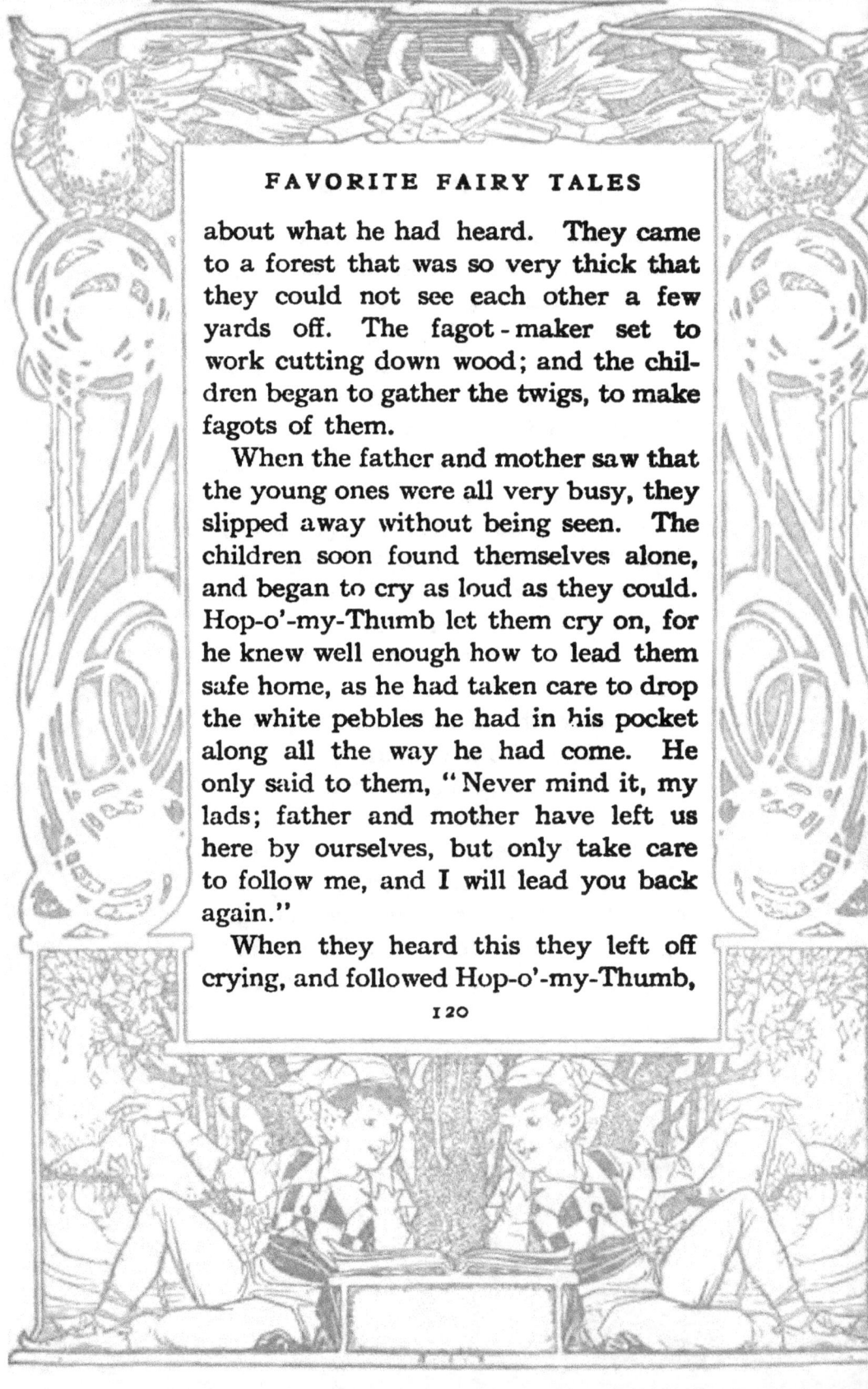

about what he had heard. They came
to a forest that was so very thick that
they could not see each other a few
yards off. The fagot-maker set to
work cutting down wood; and the children began to gather the twigs, to make
fagots of them.

When the father and mother saw that
the young ones were all very busy, they
slipped away without being seen. The
children soon found themselves alone,
and began to cry as loud as they could.
Hop-o'-my-Thumb let them cry on, for
he knew well enough how to lead them
safe home, as he had taken care to drop
the white pebbles he had in his pocket
along all the way he had come. He
only said to them, "Never mind it, my
lads; father and mother have left us
here by ourselves, but only take care
to follow me, and I will lead you back
again."

When they heard this they left off
crying, and followed Hop-o'-my-Thumb,

The children began to cry as loud as they could

who soon brought them to their father's house by the very same path which they had come along. At first they had not the courage to go in, but stood at the door to hear what their parents were talking about. Just as the fagot-maker and his wife had come home without their children a great gentleman of the village sent to pay them two guineas for work they had done for him, which he had owed them so long that they never thought of getting a farthing of it. This money made them quite happy; for the poor creatures were very hungry, and had no other way of getting anything to eat.

The fagot-maker sent his wife out immediately to buy some meat; and as it was a long time since she had made a hearty meal, she bought as much meat as would have been enough for six or eight persons. The truth was, when she was thinking what would be enough for dinner, she forgot that her

children were not at home; but as soon as she and her husband had done eating, she cried out: "Alas! where are our poor children? How they would feast on what we have left! It was all your fault, husband! I told you we should repent leaving them to starve in the forest! Oh, mercy! perhaps they have already been eaten by the hungry wolves!" The poor woman shed plenty of tears. "Alas! alas!" said she, over and over again, "what is become of my dear children?"

The children, who were all at the door, cried out together, "Here we are, mother, here we are!"

She flew like lightning to let them in, and kissed every one of them.

The fagot-maker and his wife were charmed at having their children once more with them, and their joy for this lasted till their money was all spent; but then they found themselves quite as ill off as before. So by degrees they again thought of leaving them in the forest: and that the young ones might not come back a second time, they said they would take them a great deal farther than they did at first. They could not talk about this matter so sly-ly but that Hop-o'-my-Thumb found means to hear all that passed between them; but he cared very little about it, for he thought it would be easy for him to do just the same as he had done be-fore. But although he got up very early the next morning to go to the river's side to get the pebbles, a thing which he had not thought of hindered him; for he found that the house door was double locked. Hop-o'-my-Thumb was now quite at a loss what to do; but soon after this his mother gave each of the children a piece of bread for breakfast and then it came into his head that he could make his share do as well as the pebbles by dropping crumbs of it all the way as he went.

123

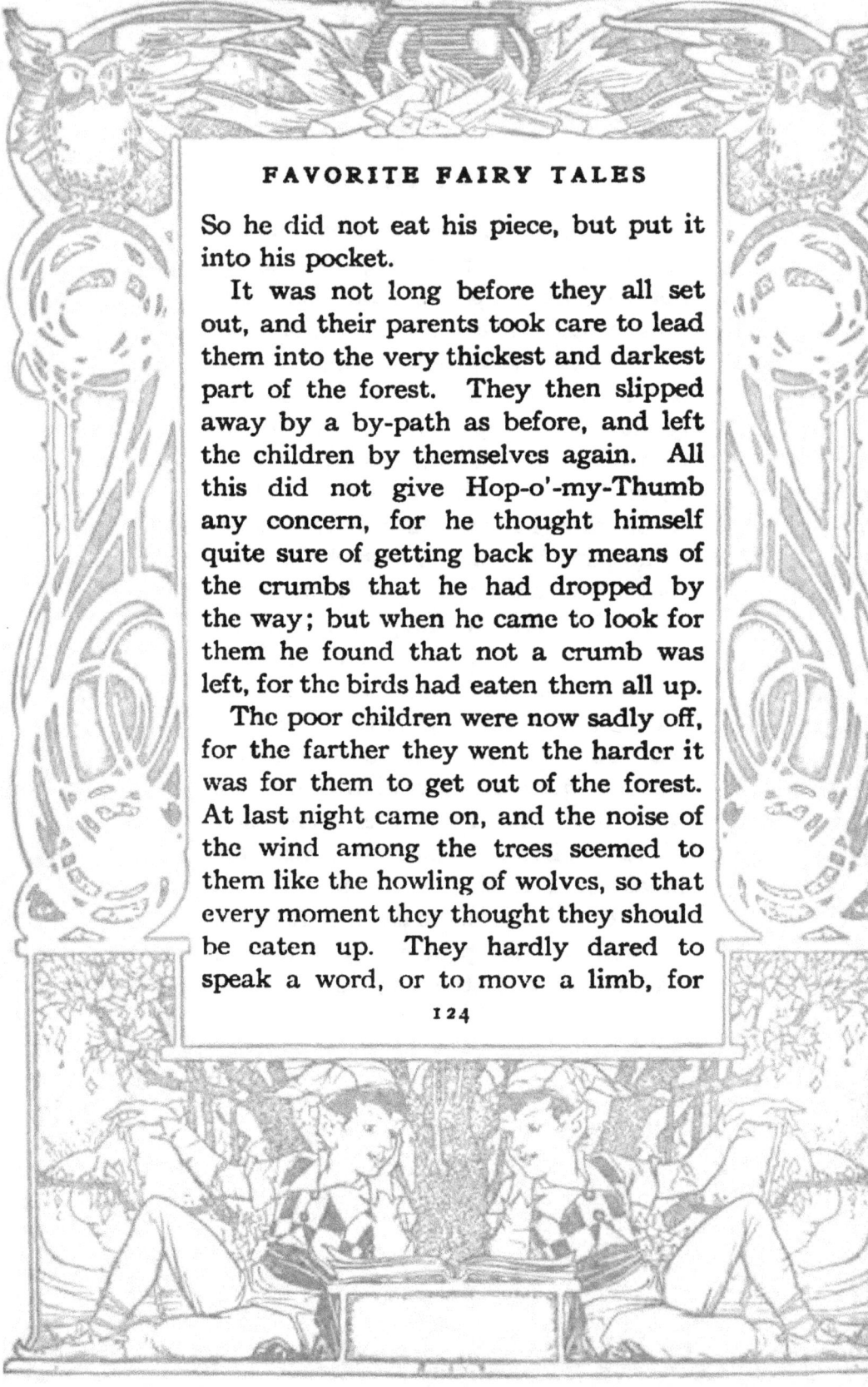

So he did not eat his piece, but put it into his pocket.

It was not long before they all set out, and their parents took care to lead them into the very thickest and darkest part of the forest. They then slipped away by a by-path as before, and left the children by themselves again. All this did not give Hop-o'-my-Thumb any concern, for he thought himself quite sure of getting back by means of the crumbs that he had dropped by the way; but when he came to look for them he found that not a crumb was left, for the birds had eaten them all up.

The poor children were now sadly off, for the farther they went the harder it was for them to get out of the forest. At last night came on, and the noise of the wind among the trees seemed to them like the howling of wolves, so that every moment they thought they should be eaten up. They hardly dared to speak a word, or to move a limb, for

124

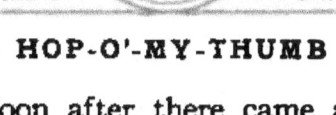

fear. Soon after there came a heavy
rain which wetted them to the very
skin, and made the ground so slippery
that they fell down at almost every
step and got dirty all over.

Before it was quite dark Hop-o'-
my-Thumb climbed up to the top of a
tree, and looked round on all sides to
see if he could find any way of getting
help. He saw a small light, like that
of a candle, but it was a very great
way off, and beyond the forest. He
then came down from the tree, to try
to find the way to it; but he could not
see it when he was on the ground, and
he was in the utmost trouble what to
do next. They walked on towards the
place where he had seen the light, and
at last reached the end of the forest,
and got sight of it again. They now
walked faster; and after being much
tired and vexed (for every time they
got into lower ground they lost sight
of the light), came to the house it was

125

in. They knocked at the door, which was opened by a very poor-natured-looking lady, who asked what brought them there. Hop-o'-my-Thumb told her that they were poor children who had lost their way in the forest, and begged that she would give them a bed till morning. When the lady saw that they had such pretty faces she began to shed tears, and said: "Ah, my poor children, you do not know what place you are come to. This is the house of an Ogre, who eats up little boys and girls."

"Alas! madam," replied Hop-o'-my-Thumb, who trembled from head to foot, "what shall we do? If we go back to the forest we are sure of being torn to pieces by the wolves; we would rather, therefore, be eaten by the gentleman. Besides, when he sees us, perhaps he may take pity on us and spare our lives."

The Ogre's wife thought she could

contrive to hide them from her husband till morning; so she let them go in and warm themselves by a good fire, before which there was a whole sheep roasting for the Ogre's supper. When they had stood a short time by the fire there came a loud knocking at the door: this was the Ogre come home. His wife hurried the children under the bed and told them to lie still, and she then let her husband in.

The Ogre asked if supper were ready, and if the wine were fetched from the cellar; and then he sat down at the table. The sheep was not quite done, but he liked it much better half raw. In a minute or two the Ogre began to snuff to his right and left, and said he smelt child's flesh.

"It must be this calf, which has just been killed," said his wife.

"I smell child's flesh, I tell thee once more!" cried the Ogre, looking all about the room—"I smell child's flesh; there

127

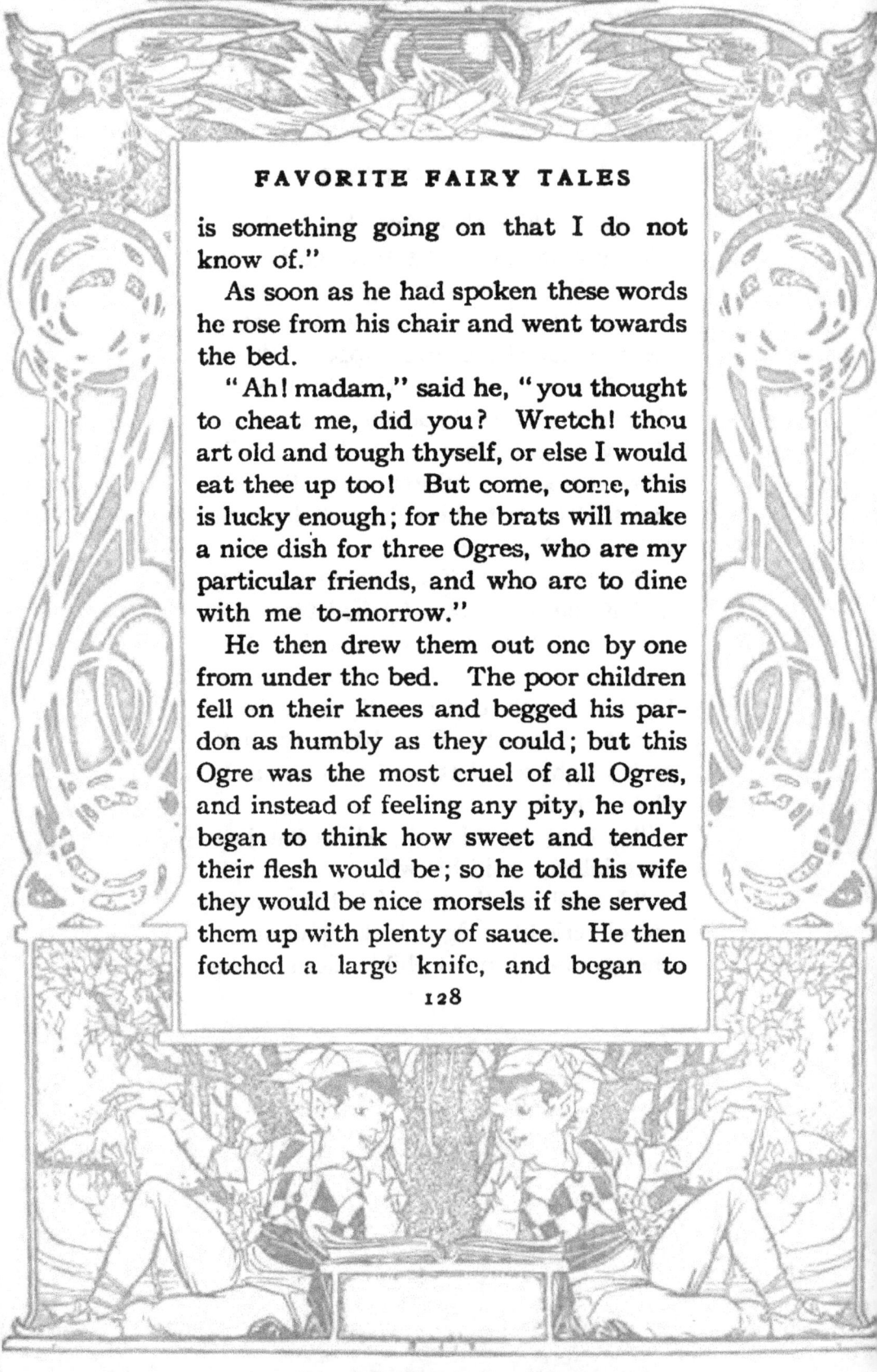

is something going on that I do not know of."

As soon as he had spoken these words he rose from his chair and went towards the bed.

"Ah! madam," said he, "you thought to cheat me, did you? Wretch! thou art old and tough thyself, or else I would eat thee up too! But come, come, this is lucky enough; for the brats will make a nice dish for three Ogres, who are my particular friends, and who are to dine with me to-morrow."

He then drew them out one by one from under the bed. The poor children fell on their knees and begged his pardon as humbly as they could; but this Ogre was the most cruel of all Ogres, and instead of feeling any pity, he only began to think how sweet and tender their flesh would be; so he told his wife they would be nice morsels if she served them up with plenty of sauce. He then fetched a large knife, and began to

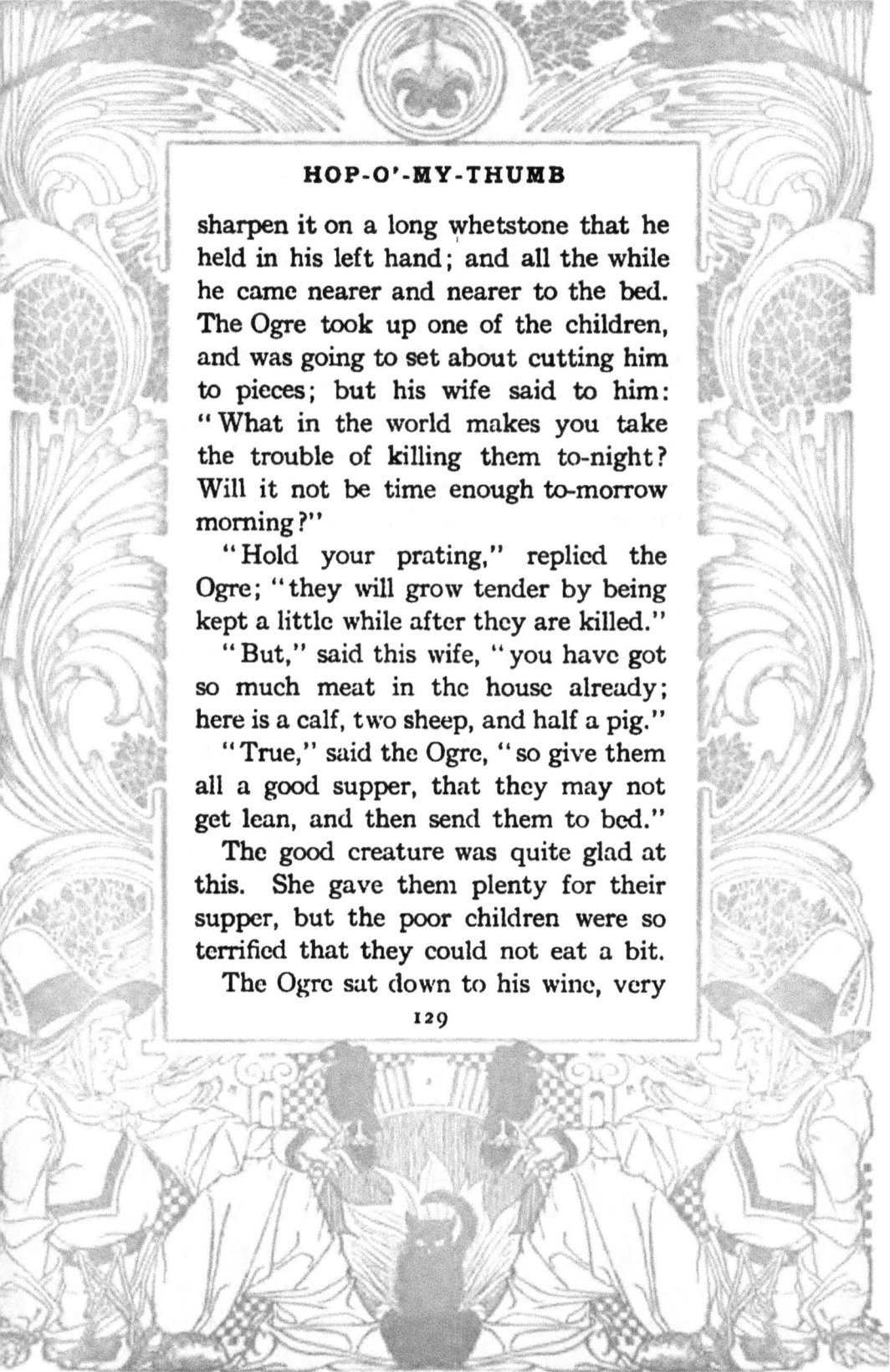

sharpen it on a long whetstone that he
held in his left hand; and all the while
he came nearer and nearer to the bed.
The Ogre took up one of the children,
and was going to set about cutting him
to pieces; but his wife said to him:
"What in the world makes you take
the trouble of killing them to-night?
Will it not be time enough to-morrow
morning?"

"Hold your prating," replied the
Ogre; "they will grow tender by being
kept a little while after they are killed."

"But," said this wife, "you have got
so much meat in the house already;
here is a calf, two sheep, and half a pig."

"True," said the Ogre, "so give them
all a good supper, that they may not
get lean, and then send them to bed."

The good creature was quite glad at
this. She gave them plenty for their
supper, but the poor children were so
terrified that they could not eat a bit.

The Ogre sat down to his wine, very

much pleased with the thought of giving his friends such a dainty dish: this made him drink rather more than common, and he was soon obliged to go to bed himself. Now the Ogre had seven daughters, who were all very young like Hop-o'-my-Thumb and his brothers. These young Ogresses had fair skins, because they fed on raw meat like their father; but they had small gray eyes, quite round, and sunk in their heads, hooked noses, wide mouths, and very long, sharp teeth, standing a great way off each other. They were too young as yet to do much mischief; but they showed that if they lived to be as old as their father they would grow quite as cruel as he was, for they took pleasure already in biting young children and sucking their blood. The Ogresses had been put to bed very early that night; they were all in one bed, which was very large, and every one of them had a crown of gold on her head. There

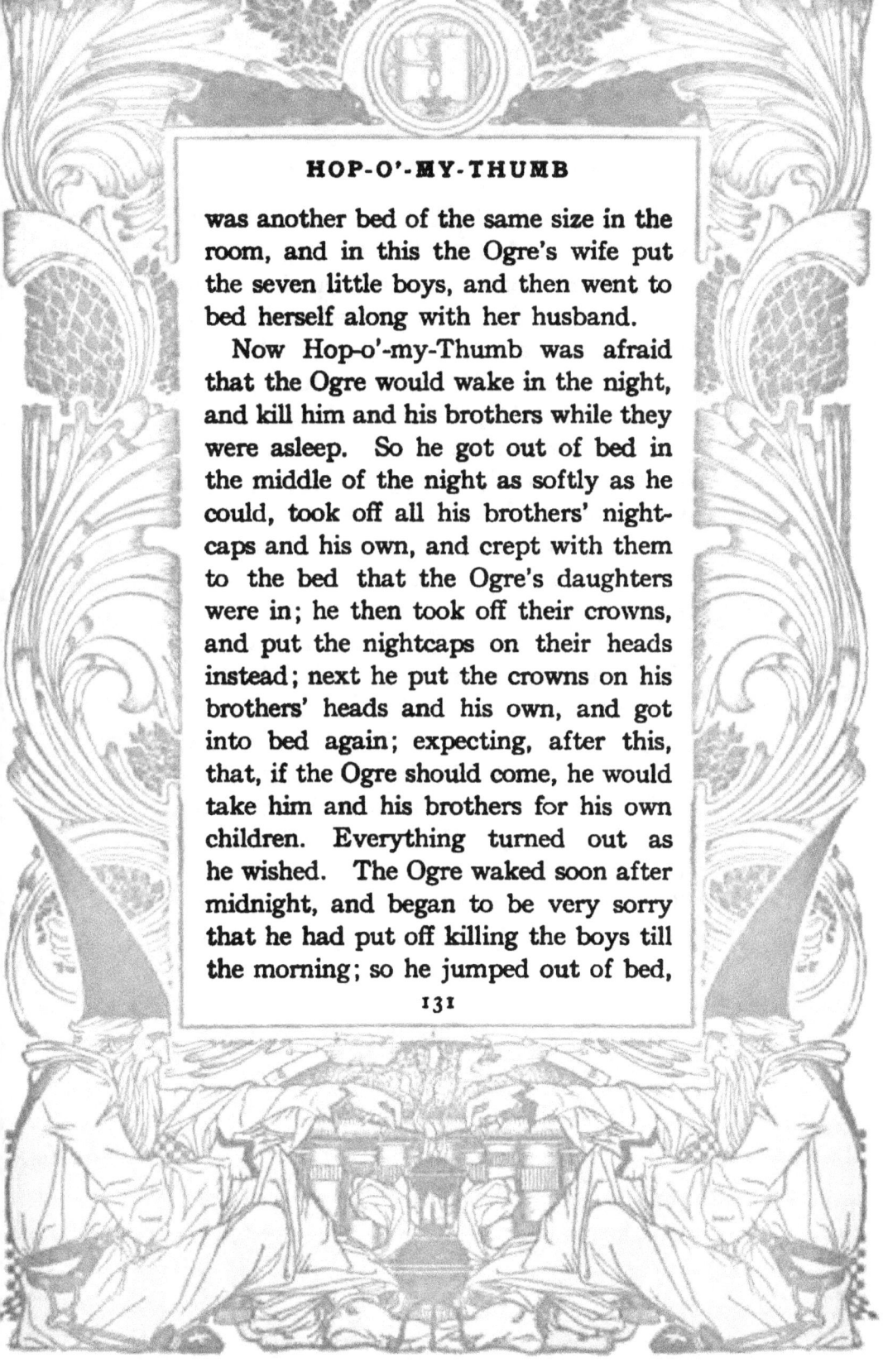

was another bed of the same size in the room, and in this the Ogre's wife put the seven little boys, and then went to bed herself along with her husband.

Now Hop-o'-my-Thumb was afraid that the Ogre would wake in the night, and kill him and his brothers while they were asleep. So he got out of bed in the middle of the night as softly as he could, took off all his brothers' night-caps and his own, and crept with them to the bed that the Ogre's daughters were in; he then took off their crowns, and put the nightcaps on their heads instead; next he put the crowns on his brothers' heads and his own, and got into bed again; expecting, after this, that, if the Ogre should come, he would take him and his brothers for his own children. Everything turned out as he wished. The Ogre waked soon after midnight, and began to be very sorry that he had put off killing the boys till the morning; so he jumped out of bed,

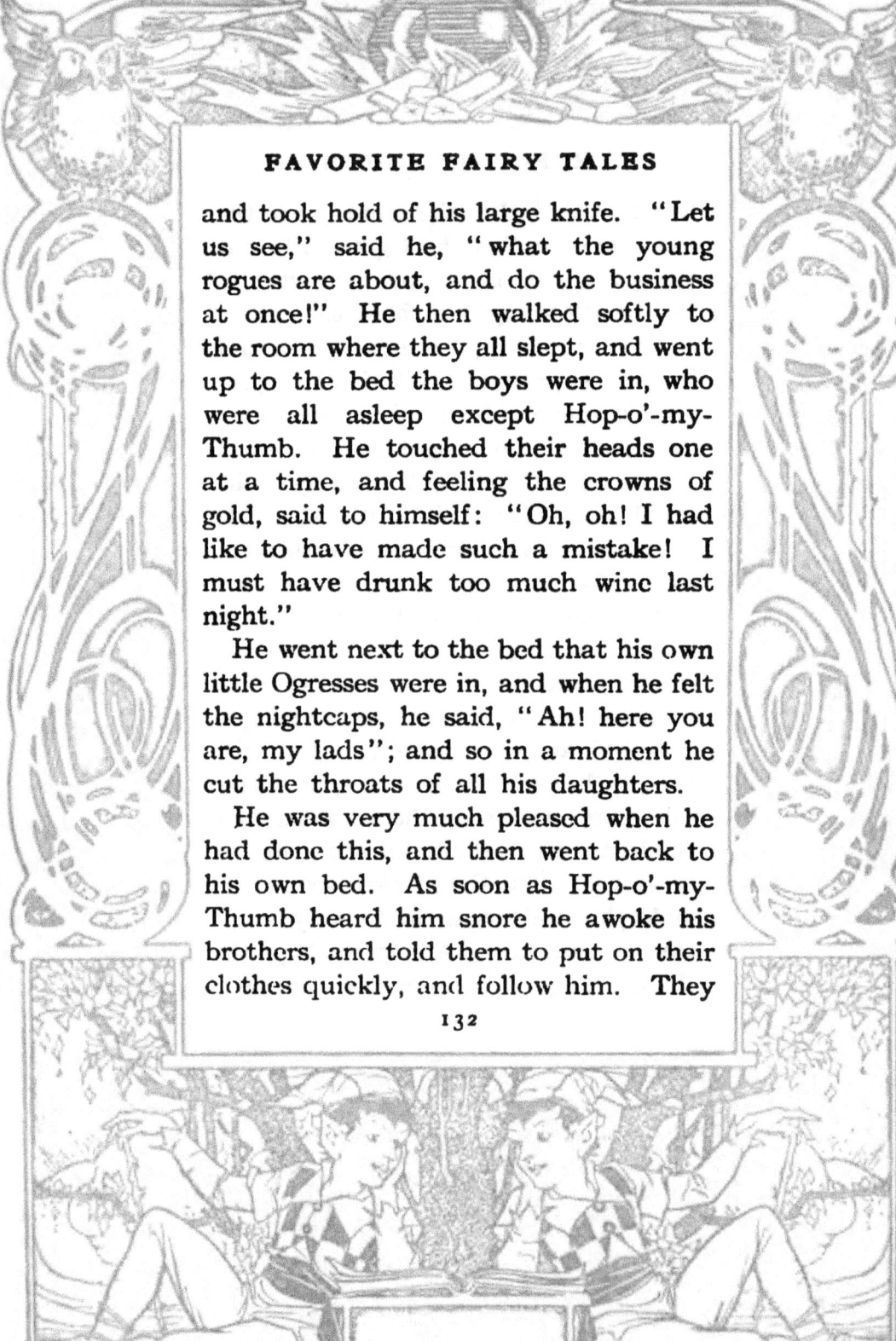

and took hold of his large knife. "Let us see," said he, "what the young rogues are about, and do the business at once!" He then walked softly to the room where they all slept, and went up to the bed the boys were in, who were all asleep except Hop-o'-my-Thumb. He touched their heads one at a time, and feeling the crowns of gold, said to himself: "Oh, oh! I had like to have made such a mistake! I must have drunk too much wine last night."

He went next to the bed that his own little Ogresses were in, and when he felt the nightcaps, he said, "Ah! here you are, my lads"; and so in a moment he cut the throats of all his daughters.

He was very much pleased when he had done this, and then went back to his own bed. As soon as Hop-o'-my-Thumb heard him snore he awoke his brothers, and told them to put on their clothes quickly, and follow him. They

stole down softly into the garden, and then jumped from the wall into the road; they ran as fast as their legs could carry them, but were so much afraid all the while that they hardly knew which way to take. When the Ogre waked in the morning he said to his wife, grinning: "My dear, go and dress the young rogues I saw last night."

The wife was quite surprised at hearing her husband speak so kindly, and did not dream of the real meaning of his words. She supposed he wanted her to help them to put on their clothes; so she went up-stairs, and the first thing she saw was her seven daughters with their throats cut and all over blood. This threw her into a fainting fit. The Ogre was afraid his wife might be too long in doing what he had set her about, so he went himself to help her; but he was as much shocked as she had been at the dreadful sight of his bleeding children. "Ah! what have I done?"

he cried. "But the little rascals shall pay for it, I warrant them."

He first threw some water on his wife's face; and, as soon as she came to herself, he said to her: "Bring me quickly my seven-league boots, that I may go and catch the little vipers."

The Ogre then put on these boots, and set out with all speed. He strided over many parts of the country, and at last turned into the very road in which the poor children were. For they had set off towards the fagot-maker's cottage, which they had almost reached. They watched the Ogre stepping from mountain to mountain at one step, and crossing rivers as if they had been tiny brooks. At this Hop-o'-my-Thumb thought a little what was to be done; and spying a hollow place under a large rock, he made his brothers get into it. He then crept in himself, but kept his eye fixed on the Ogre, to see what he would do next.

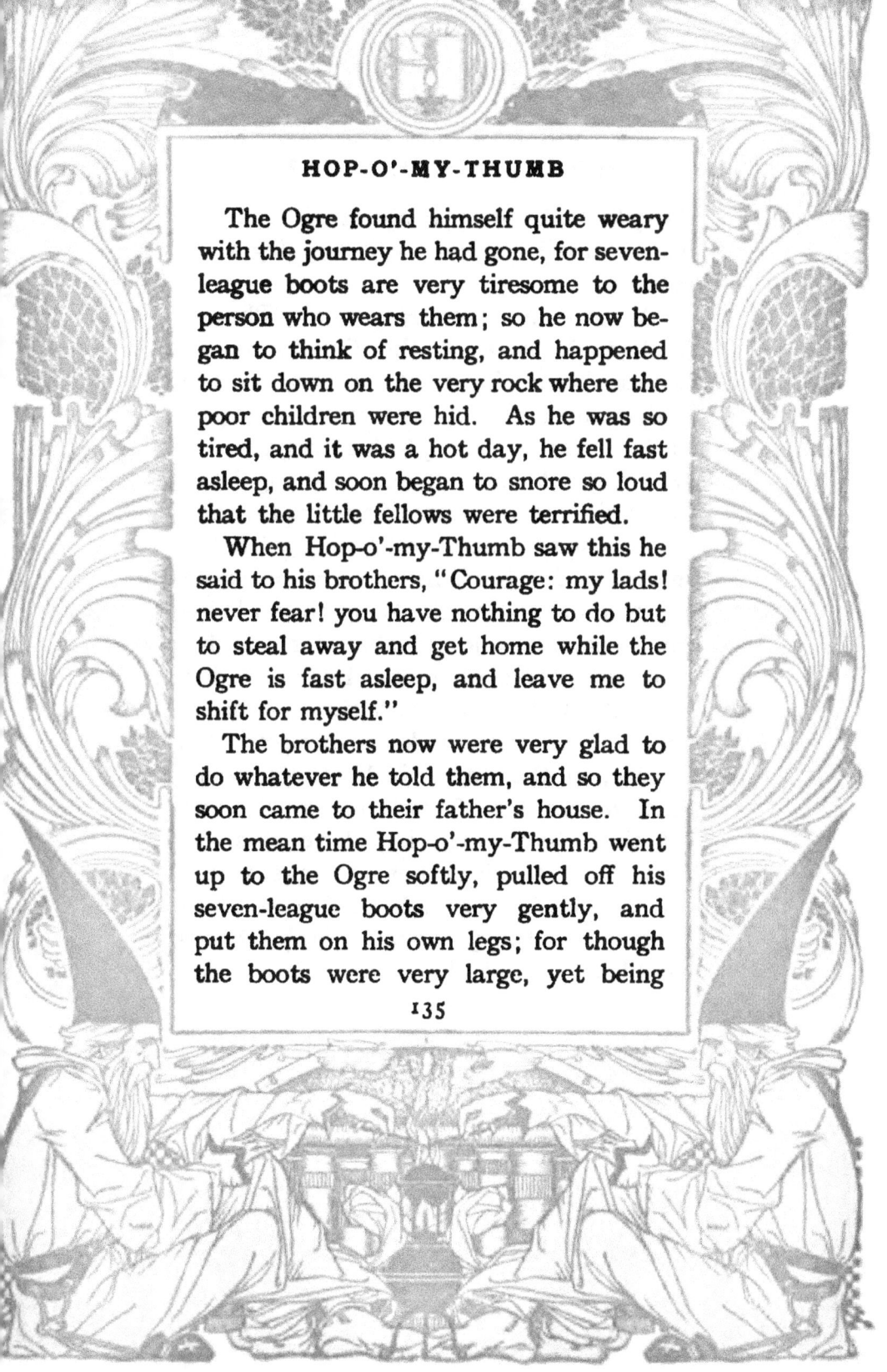

HOP-O'-MY-THUMB

The Ogre found himself quite weary with the journey he had gone, for seven-league boots are very tiresome to the person who wears them; so he now began to think of resting, and happened to sit down on the very rock where the poor children were hid. As he was so tired, and it was a hot day, he fell fast asleep, and soon began to snore so loud that the little fellows were terrified.

When Hop-o'-my-Thumb saw this he said to his brothers, "Courage: my lads! never fear! you have nothing to do but to steal away and get home while the Ogre is fast asleep, and leave me to shift for myself."

The brothers now were very glad to do whatever he told them, and so they soon came to their father's house. In the mean time Hop-o'-my-Thumb went up to the Ogre softly, pulled off his seven-league boots very gently, and put them on his own legs; for though the boots were very large, yet being

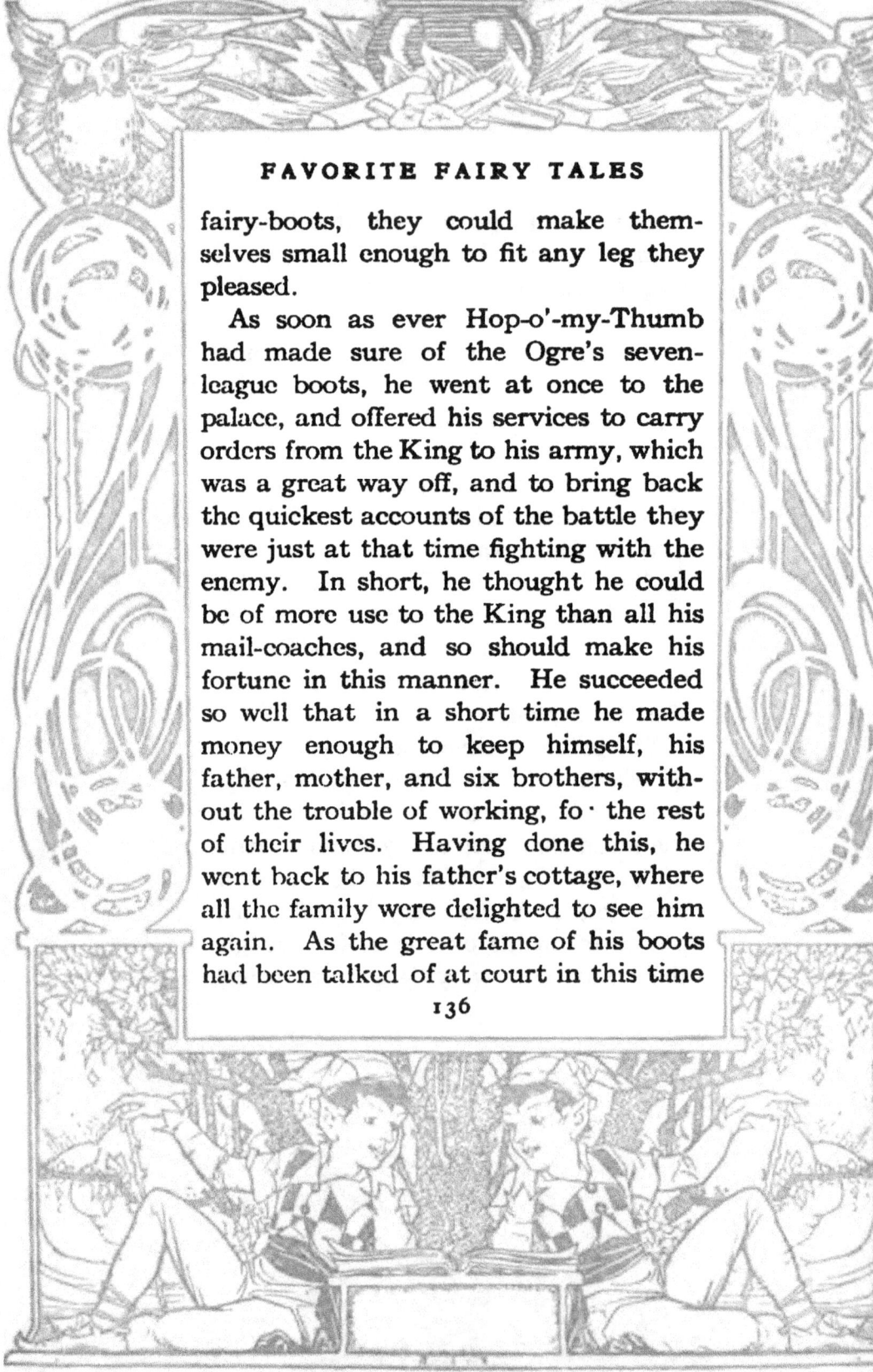

fairy-boots, they could make themselves small enough to fit any leg they
pleased.

As soon as ever Hop-o'-my-Thumb
had made sure of the Ogre's seven-
league boots, he went at once to the
palace, and offered his services to carry
orders from the King to his army, which
was a great way off, and to bring back
the quickest accounts of the battle they
were just at that time fighting with the
enemy. In short, he thought he could
be of more use to the King than all his
mail-coaches, and so should make his
fortune in this manner. He succeeded
so well that in a short time he made
money enough to keep himself, his
father, mother, and six brothers, without the trouble of working, fo· the rest
of their lives. Having done this, he
went back to his father's cottage, where
all the family were delighted to see him
again. As the great fame of his boots
had been talked of at court in this time

the King sent for him, and indeed employed him very often in the greatest affairs of the state, so that he became one of the richest men in the kingdom.

And now let us see what became of the wicked Ogre. He slept so soundly that he never discovered the loss of his boots; but having an evil conscience and bad dreams, he fell in his sleep from the corner of the rock where Hop-o'-my-Thumb and his brothers had left him, and bruised himself so much from head to foot that he could not stir; so he was forced to stretch himself out at full length, and wait for some one to come and help him.

Now a good many fagot-makers passed near the place where the Ogre lay, and when they heard him groan they went up to ask him what was the matter. But the Ogre had eaten such a great number of children in his lifetime that he had grown so very big and fat that these men could not even have carried one of his legs, so they were forced to leave him there. At last night came on, and then a large serpent came out of a wood just by and stung him, so that he died in great pain.

By and by, Hop-o'-my-Thumb, who had become the King's first favorite, heard of the Ogre's death; and the first thing he did was to tell his Majesty all that the good-natured Ogress had done to save the lives of himself and brothers. The King was so much pleased at what he heard that he asked Hop-o'-my-Thumb if there was any favor he could bestow upon her. Hop-o'-my-Thumb thanked the King, and desired that the Ogress might have the noble title of Duchess of Draggletail given to her, which was no sooner asked than granted. The Ogress then came to court, and lived very happily for many years, enjoying the vast fortune she had found in the Ogre's chests. As for Hop-o'-

138

HOP-O'-MY-THUMB

my-Thumb, he every day grew more witty and brave; till at last the King made him the greatest lord in the kingdom, and set him over all his affairs.

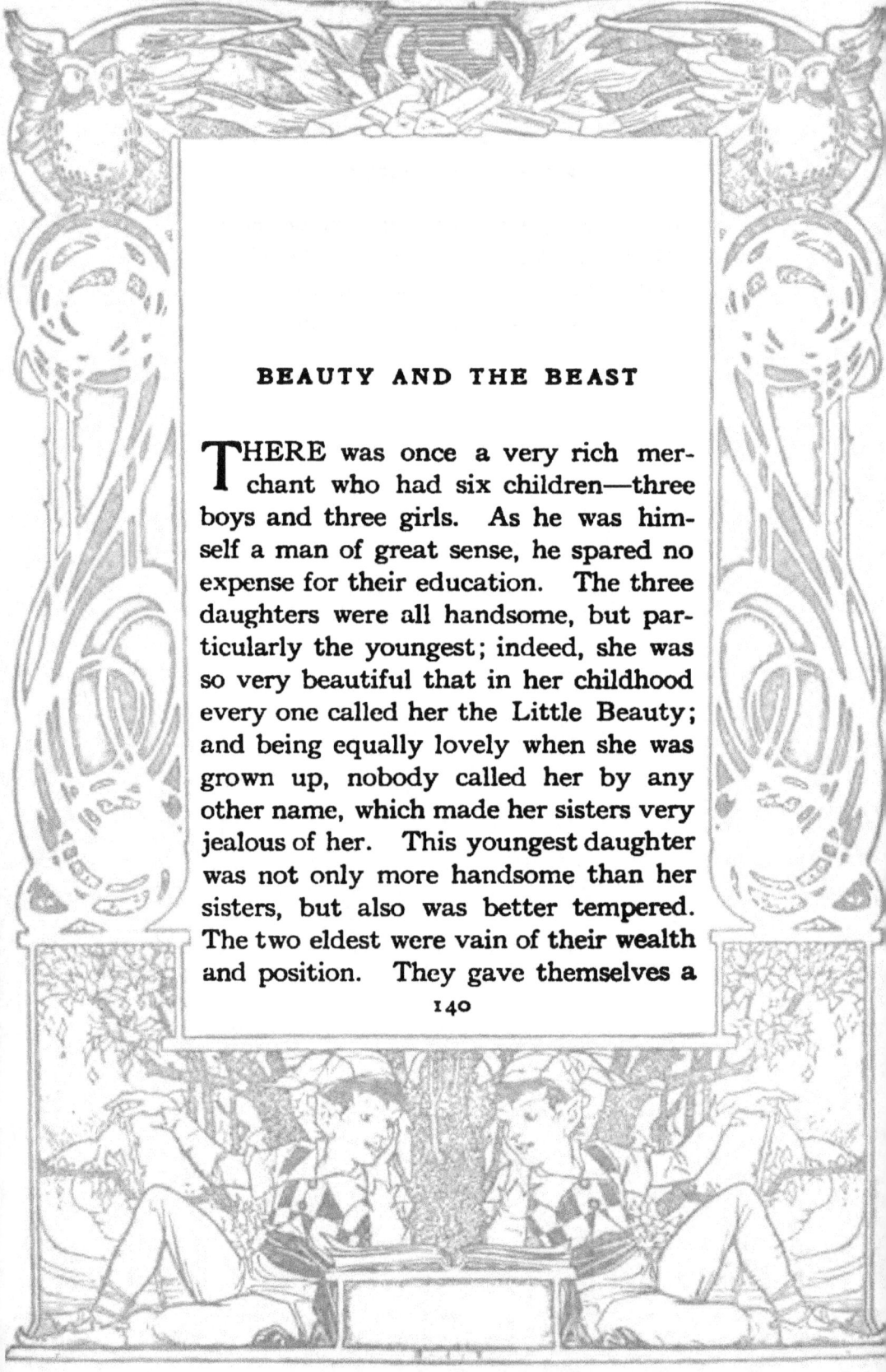

BEAUTY AND THE BEAST

THERE was once a very rich merchant who had six children—three
boys and three girls. As he was himself a man of great sense, he spared no
expense for their education. The three
daughters were all handsome, but particularly the youngest; indeed, she was
so very beautiful that in her childhood
every one called her the Little Beauty;
and being equally lovely when she was
grown up, nobody called her by any
other name, which made her sisters very
jealous of her. This youngest daughter
was not only more handsome than her
sisters, but also was better tempered.
The two eldest were vain of their wealth
and position. They gave themselves a

140

thousand airs, and refused to visit other merchants' daughters; nor would they condescend to be seen except with persons of quality. They went every day to balls, plays, and public walks, and always made game of their youngest sister for spending her time in reading or other useful employments. As it was well known that these young ladies would have large fortunes, many great merchants wished to get them for wives: but the two eldest always answered that, for their parts, they had no thoughts of marrying any one below a duke or an earl at least. Beauty had quite as many offers as her sisters, but she always answered, with the greatest civility, that though she was much obliged to her lovers, she would rather live some years longer with her father, as she thought herself too young to marry.

It happened that, by some unlucky accident, the merchant suddenly lost all his fortune, and had nothing left but a small cottage in the country. Upon this he said to his daughters, while the tears ran down his cheeks, "My children, we must now go and dwell in the cottage, and try to get a living by labor, for we have no other means of support." The two eldest replied that they did not know how to work, and would not leave town; for they had lovers enough who would be glad to marry them, though they had no longer any fortune. But in this they were mistaken; for when the lovers heard what had happened, they said, "The girls were so proud and ill-tempered that all we wanted was their fortune; we are not sorry at all to see their pride brought down; let them show off their airs to their cows and sheep." But everybody pitied poor Beauty, because she was so sweet-tempered and kind to all, and several gentlemen offered to marry her, though she had not a penny; but Beauty

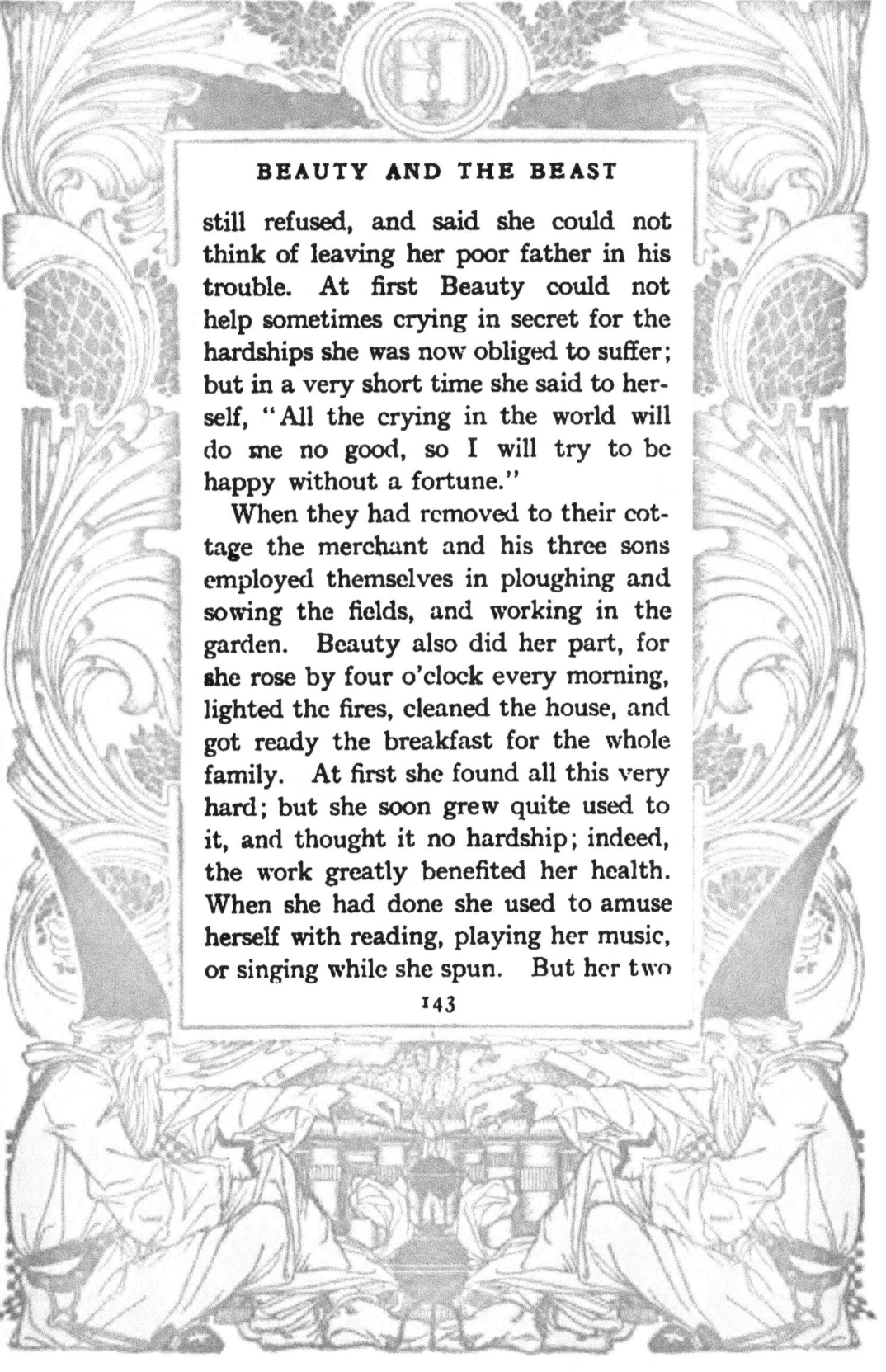

still refused, and said she could not think of leaving her poor father in his trouble. At first Beauty could not help sometimes crying in secret for the hardships she was now obliged to suffer; but in a very short time she said to herself, "All the crying in the world will do me no good, so I will try to be happy without a fortune."

When they had removed to their cottage the merchant and his three sons employed themselves in ploughing and sowing the fields, and working in the garden. Beauty also did her part, for she rose by four o'clock every morning, lighted the fires, cleaned the house, and got ready the breakfast for the whole family. At first she found all this very hard; but she soon grew quite used to it, and thought it no hardship; indeed, the work greatly benefited her health. When she had done she used to amuse herself with reading, playing her music, or singing while she spun. But her two

sisters were at a loss what to do to pass the time away: they had their breakfast in bed, and did not rise till ten o'clock. Then they commonly walked out, but always found themselves very soon tired, when they would often sit down under a shady tree, and grieve for the loss of their carriage and fine clothes, and say to each other, "What a mean-spirited, poor, stupid creature our young sister is, to be so content with this low way of life!" But their father thought differently, and loved and admired his youngest child more than ever.

After they had lived in this manner about a year the merchant received a letter, which informed him that one of his richest ships, which he thought was lost, had just come into port. This news made the two eldest sisters almost mad with joy, for they thought they should now leave the cottage, and have all their finery again. When they found that their father must take a

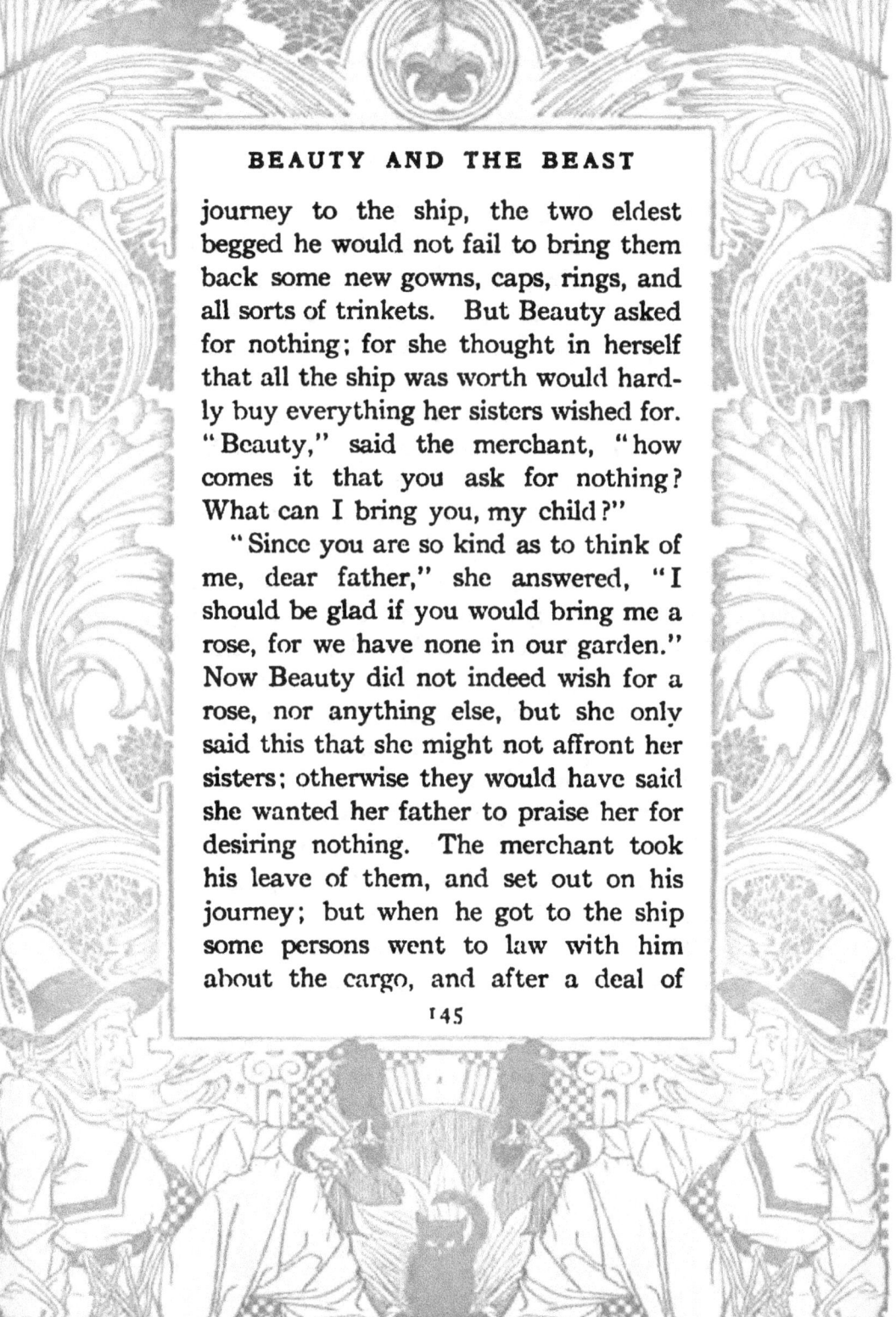

journey to the ship, the two eldest
begged he would not fail to bring them
back some new gowns, caps, rings, and
all sorts of trinkets. But Beauty asked
for nothing; for she thought in herself
that all the ship was worth would hardly buy everything her sisters wished for.
"Beauty," said the merchant, "how
comes it that you ask for nothing?
What can I bring you, my child?"

"Since you are so kind as to think of
me, dear father," she answered, "I
should be glad if you would bring me a
rose, for we have none in our garden."
Now Beauty did not indeed wish for a
rose, nor anything else, but she only
said this that she might not affront her
sisters; otherwise they would have said
she wanted her father to praise her for
desiring nothing. The merchant took
his leave of them, and set out on his
journey; but when he got to the ship
some persons went to law with him
about the cargo, and after a deal of

trouble he came back to his cottage as poor as he had left it. When he was within thirty miles of his home, and thinking of the joy of again meeting his children, he lost his way in the midst of a dense forest. It rained and snowed very hard, and, besides, the wind was so high as to throw him twice from his horse. Night came on, and he feared he should die of cold and hunger, or be torn to pieces by the wolves that he heard howling round him. All at once he cast his eyes towards a long avenue, and saw at the end a light, but it seemed a great way off. He made the best of his way towards it, and found that it came from a splendid palace, the windows of which were all blazing with light. It had great bronze gates, standing wide open, and fine court-yards, through which the merchant passed; but not a living soul was to be seen. There were stables too, which his poor, starved horse, less scrupulous than him-

146

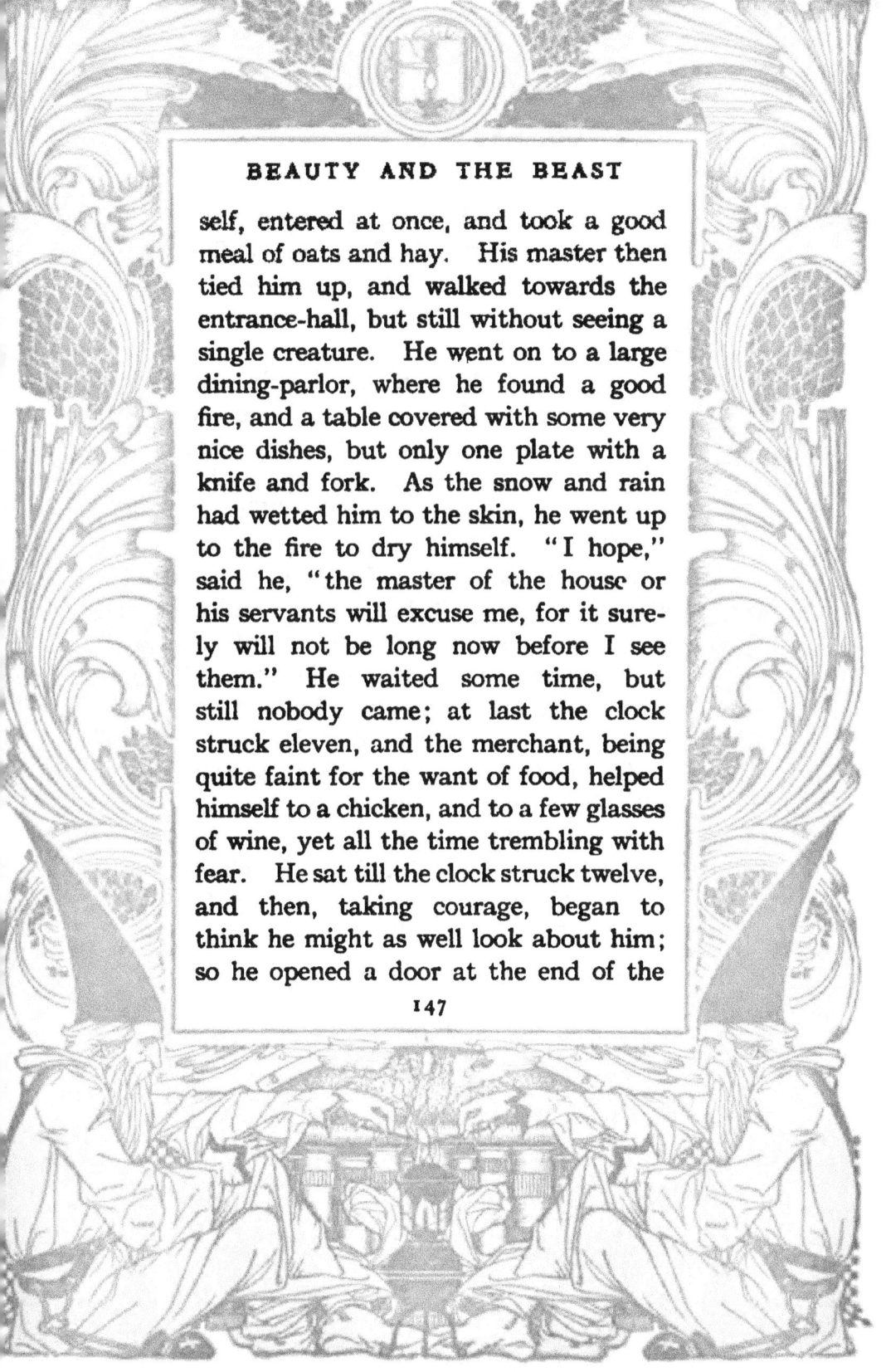

self, entered at once, and took a good meal of oats and hay. His master then tied him up, and walked towards the entrance-hall, but still without seeing a single creature. He went on to a large dining-parlor, where he found a good fire, and a table covered with some very nice dishes, but only one plate with a knife and fork. As the snow and rain had wetted him to the skin, he went up to the fire to dry himself. "I hope," said he, "the master of the house or his servants will excuse me, for it surely will not be long now before I see them." He waited some time, but still nobody came; at last the clock struck eleven, and the merchant, being quite faint for the want of food, helped himself to a chicken, and to a few glasses of wine, yet all the time trembling with fear. He sat till the clock struck twelve, and then, taking courage, began to think he might as well look about him; so he opened a door at the end of the

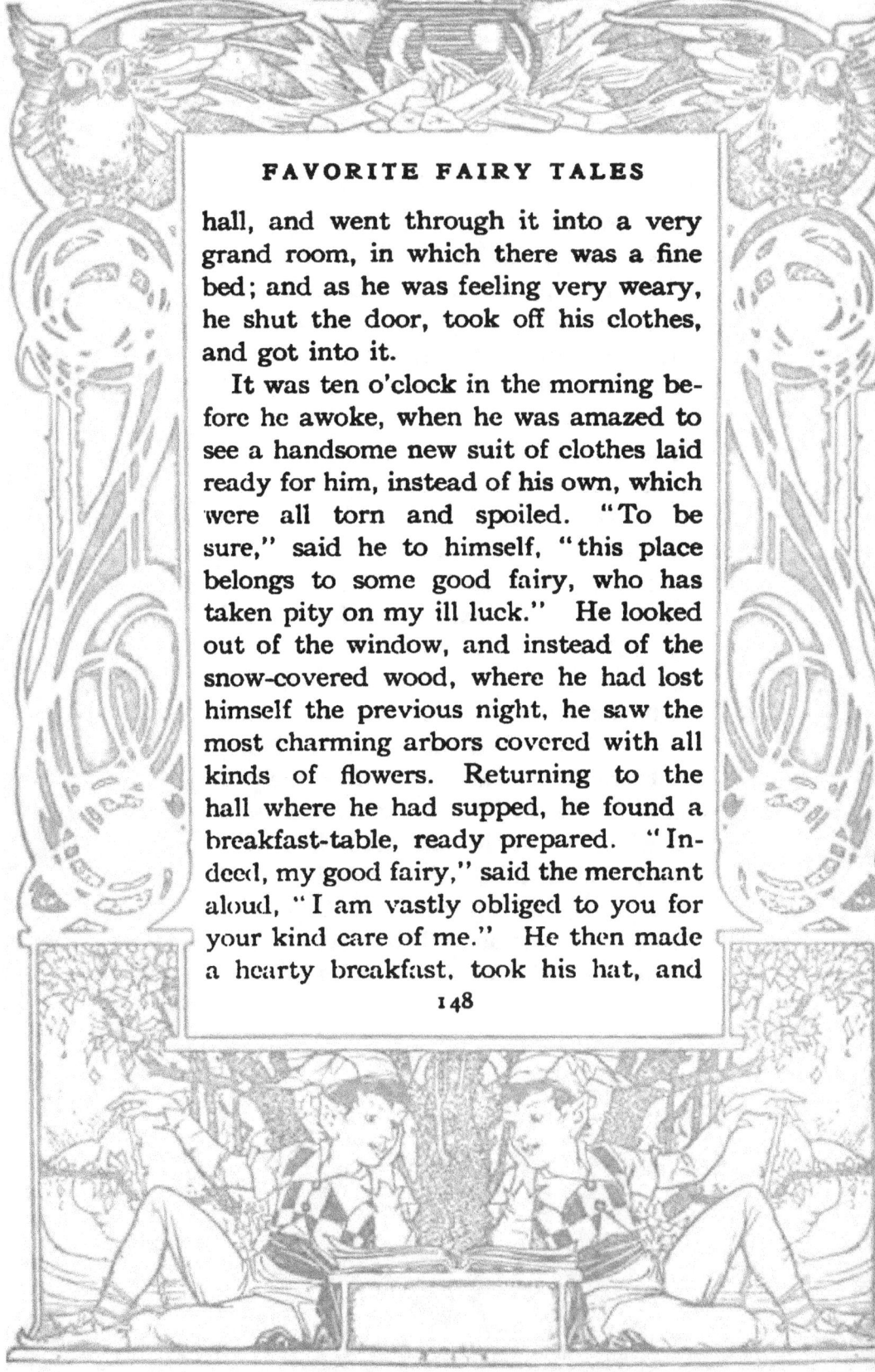

hall, and went through it into a very grand room, in which there was a fine bed; and as he was feeling very weary, he shut the door, took off his clothes, and got into it.

It was ten o'clock in the morning before he awoke, when he was amazed to see a handsome new suit of clothes laid ready for him, instead of his own, which were all torn and spoiled. "To be sure," said he to himself, "this place belongs to some good fairy, who has taken pity on my ill luck." He looked out of the window, and instead of the snow-covered wood, where he had lost himself the previous night, he saw the most charming arbors covered with all kinds of flowers. Returning to the hall where he had supped, he found a breakfast-table, ready prepared. "Indeed, my good fairy," said the merchant aloud, "I am vastly obliged to you for your kind care of me." He then made a hearty breakfast, took his hat, and

148

was going to the stable to pay his horse a visit; but as he passed under one of the arbors, which was loaded with roses, he thought of what Beauty had asked him to bring back to her, and so he took a bunch of roses to carry home. At the same moment he heard a loud noise, and saw coming towards him a beast, so frightful to look at that he was ready to faint with fear. "Ungrateful man!" said the beast, in a terrible voice, "I have saved your life by admitting you into my palace, and in return you steal my roses, which I value more than anything I possess. But you shall atone for your fault: you shall die in a quarter of an hour."

The merchant fell on his knees, and, clasping his hands, said, "Sir, I humbly beg your pardon. I did not think it would offend you to gather a rose for one of my daughters, who had entreated me to bring her one home. Do not kill me, my lord!"

"I am not a lord, but a beast," replied the monster; "I hate false compliments, so do not fancy that you can coax me by any such ways. You tell me that you have daughters; now I will suffer you to escape if one of them will come and die in your stead. If not, promise that you will yourself return in three months, to be dealt with as I may choose."

The tender-hearted merchant had no thoughts of letting any one of his daughters die for his sake; but he knew that if he seemed to accept the beast's terms, he should at least have the pleasure of seeing them once again. So he gave his promise, and was told he might set off as soon as he liked. "But," said the beast, "I do not wish you to go back empty-handed. Go to the room you slept in, and you will find a chest there; fill it with whatsoever you like best, and I will have it taken to your own house for you."

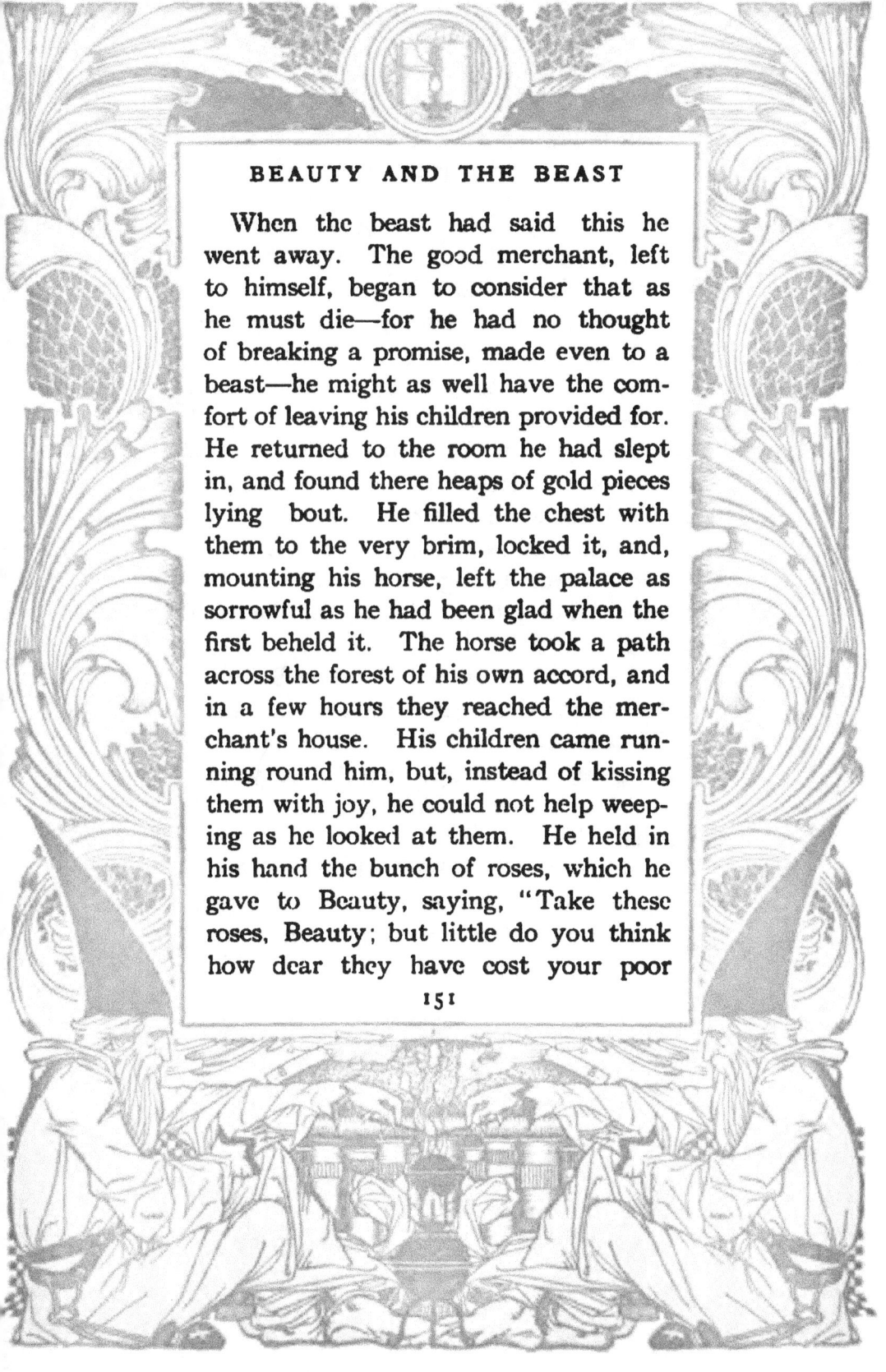

BEAUTY AND THE BEAST

When the beast had said this he
went away. The good merchant, left
to himself, began to consider that as
he must die—for he had no thought
of breaking a promise, made even to a
beast—he might as well have the comfort of leaving his children provided for.
He returned to the room he had slept
in, and found there heaps of gold pieces
lying bout. He filled the chest with
them to the very brim, locked it, and,
mounting his horse, left the palace as
sorrowful as he had been glad when the
first beheld it. The horse took a path
across the forest of his own accord, and
in a few hours they reached the merchant's house. His children came running round him, but, instead of kissing
them with joy, he could not help weeping as he looked at them. He held in
his hand the bunch of roses, which he
gave to Beauty, saying, "Take these
roses, Beauty; but little do you think
how dear they have cost your poor

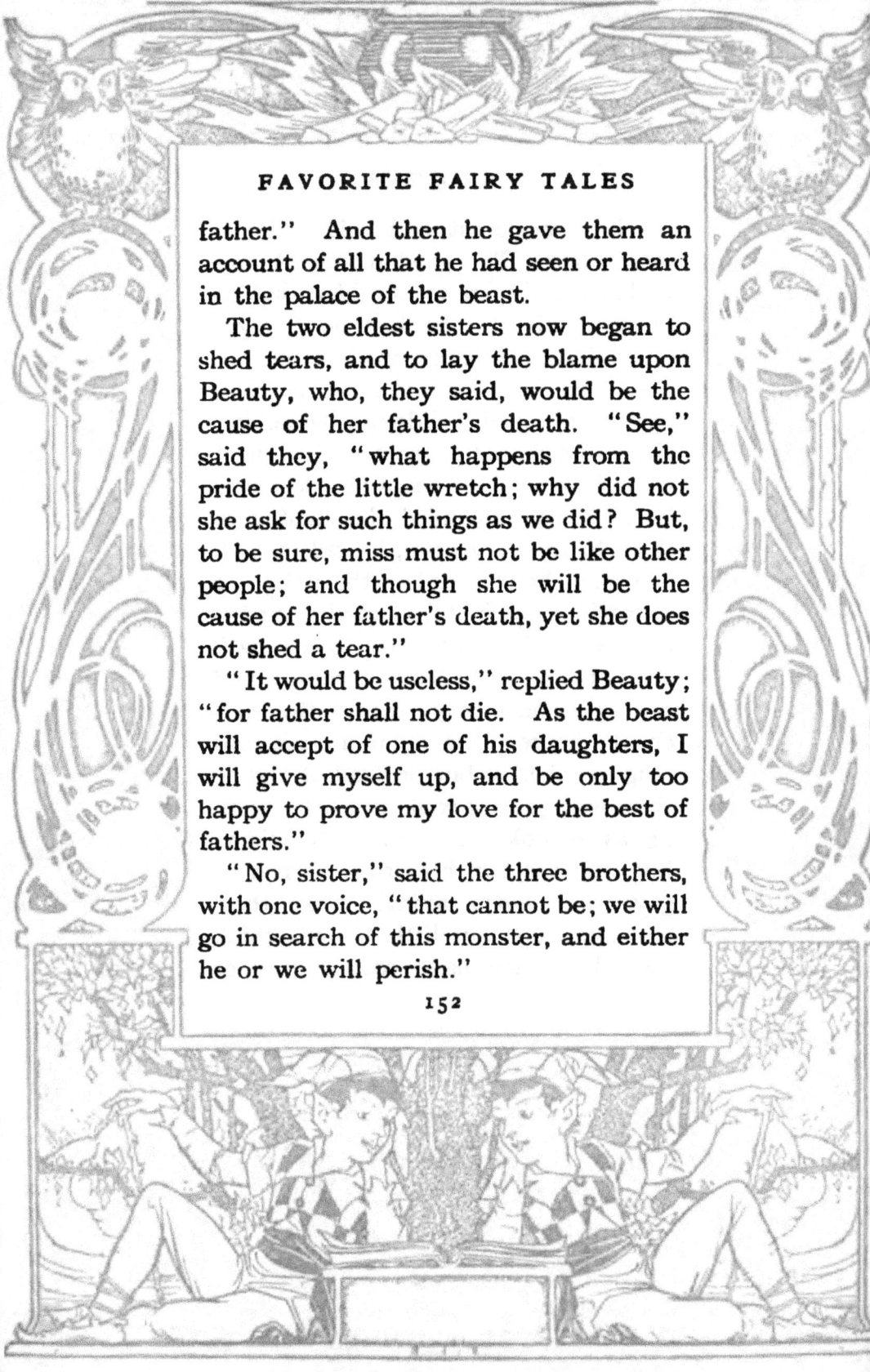

father." And then he gave them an account of all that he had seen or heard in the palace of the beast.

The two eldest sisters now began to shed tears, and to lay the blame upon Beauty, who, they said, would be the cause of her father's death. "See," said they, "what happens from the pride of the little wretch; why did not she ask for such things as we did? But, to be sure, miss must not be like other people; and though she will be the cause of her father's death, yet she does not shed a tear."

"It would be useless," replied Beauty; "for father shall not die. As the beast will accept of one of his daughters, I will give myself up, and be only too happy to prove my love for the best of fathers."

"No, sister," said the three brothers, with one voice, "that cannot be; we will go in search of this monster, and either he or we will perish."

"Do not hope to kill him," said the merchant; "his power is far too great. But Beauty's young life shall not be sacrificed; I am old, and cannot expect to live much longer; so I shall but give up a few years of my life, and shall only grieve for the sake of my children."

"Never, father!" cried Beauty; "if you go back to the palace, you cannot hinder my going after you; though young, I am not over-fond of life; and I would much rather be eaten up by the monster than die of grief for your loss."

The merchant in vain tried to reason with Beauty, who still obstinately kept to her purpose; which, in truth, made her two sisters glad, for they were jealous of her, because everybody loved her.

The merchant was so grieved at the thoughts of losing his child that he never once thought of the chest filled with gold, but at night, to his great surprise, he found it standing by his bedside. He said nothing about his riches to his eldest daughters, for he knew very well it would at once make them want to return to town; but he told Beauty his secret, and she then said that while he was away two gentlemen had been on a visit at their cottage who had fallen in love with her two sisters. She entreated her father to marry them without delay, for she was so sweet-natured she only wished them to be happy.

Three months went by only too fast, and then the merchant and Beauty got ready to set out for the palace of the beast. Upon this the two sisters rubbed their eyes with an onion to make believe they were crying; both the merchant and his sons cried in earnest. Only Beauty shed no tears. They reached the palace in a very few hours, and the horse, without bidding, went into the same stable as before. The merchant and Beauty walked towards the large hall, where they found a table

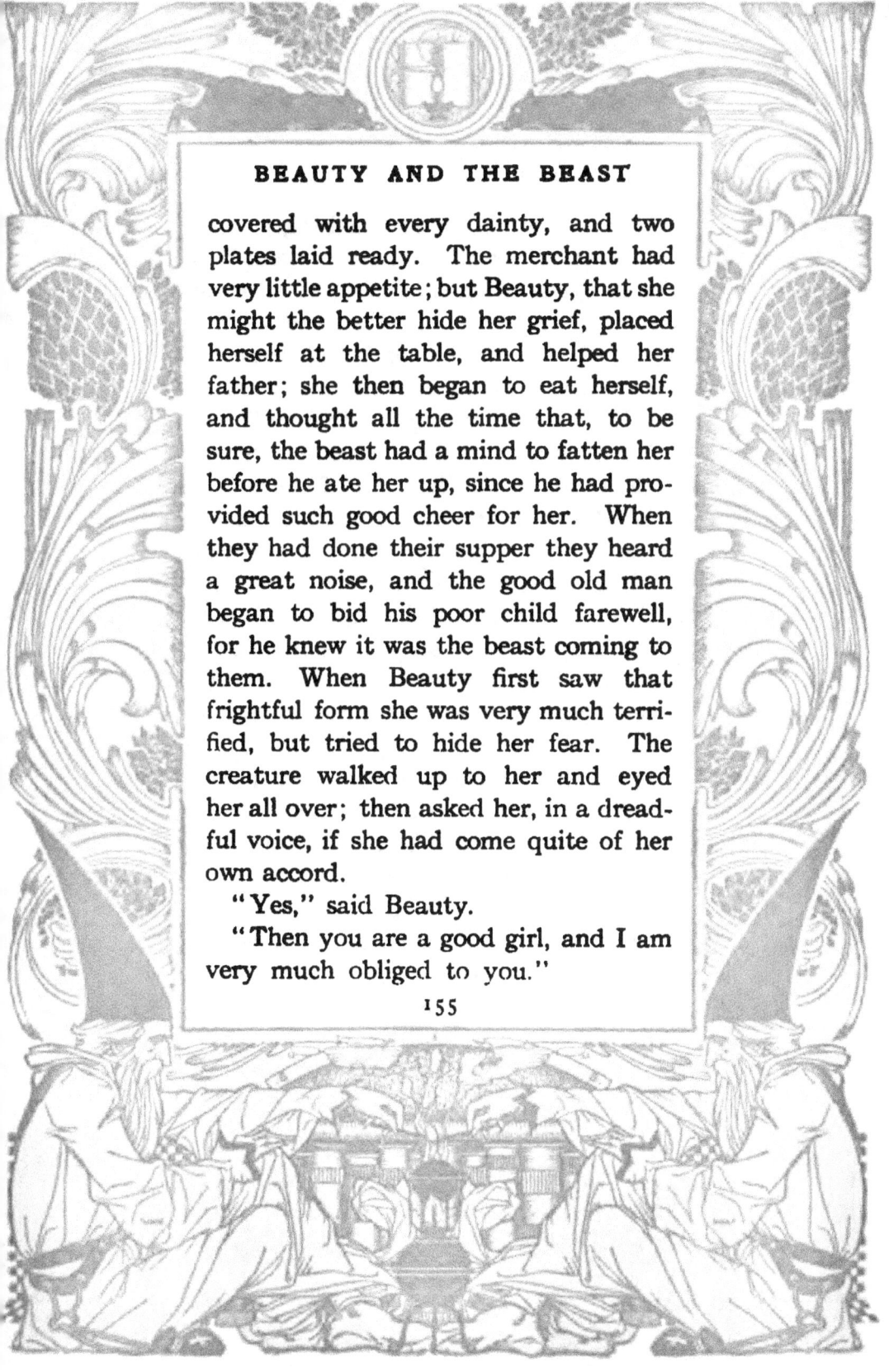

covered with every dainty, and two plates laid ready. The merchant had very little appetite; but Beauty, that she might the better hide her grief, placed herself at the table, and helped her father; she then began to eat herself, and thought all the time that, to be sure, the beast had a mind to fatten her before he ate her up, since he had provided such good cheer for her. When they had done their supper they heard a great noise, and the good old man began to bid his poor child farewell, for he knew it was the beast coming to them. When Beauty first saw that frightful form she was very much terrified, but tried to hide her fear. The creature walked up to her and eyed her all over; then asked her, in a dreadful voice, if she had come quite of her own accord.

"Yes," said Beauty.

"Then you are a good girl, and I am very much obliged to you."

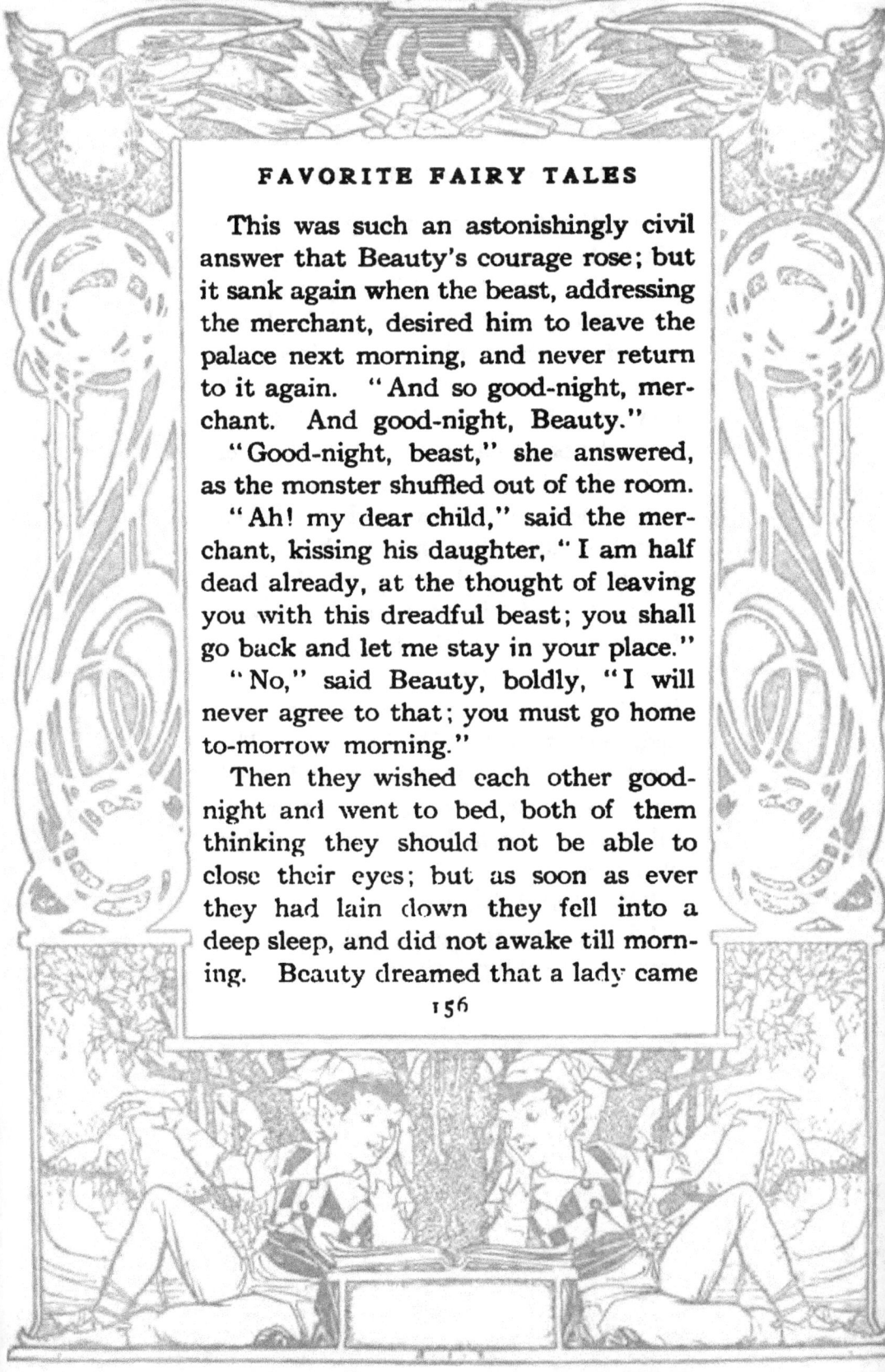

This was such an astonishingly civil answer that Beauty's courage rose; but it sank again when the beast, addressing the merchant, desired him to leave the palace next morning, and never return to it again. "And so good-night, merchant. And good-night, Beauty."

"Good-night, beast," she answered, as the monster shuffled out of the room.

"Ah! my dear child," said the merchant, kissing his daughter, "I am half dead already, at the thought of leaving you with this dreadful beast; you shall go back and let me stay in your place."

"No," said Beauty, boldly, "I will never agree to that; you must go home to-morrow morning."

Then they wished each other good-night and went to bed, both of them thinking they should not be able to close their eyes; but as soon as ever they had lain down they fell into a deep sleep, and did not awake till morning. Beauty dreamed that a lady came

156

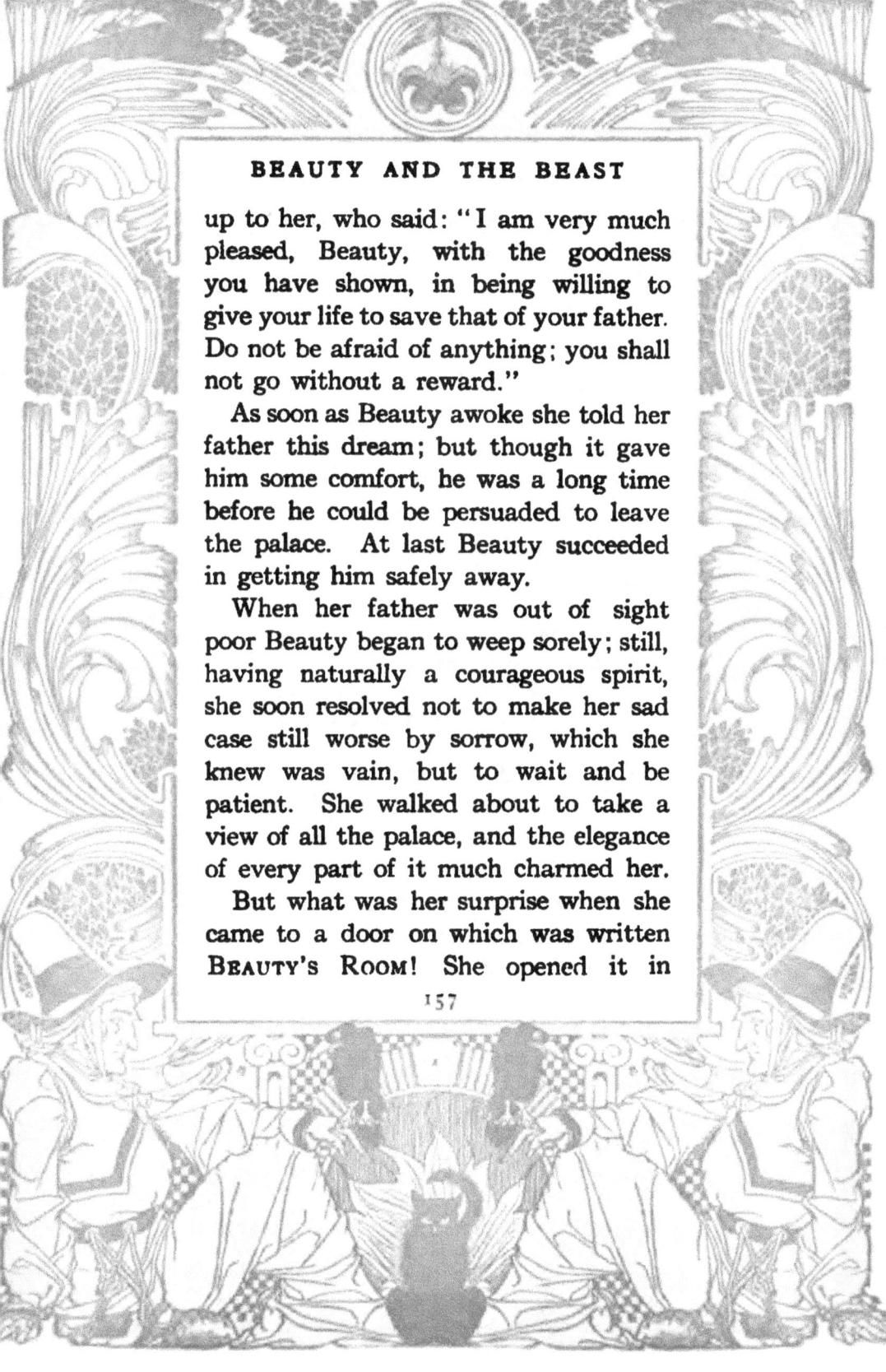

up to her, who said: "I am very much pleased, Beauty, with the goodness you have shown, in being willing to give your life to save that of your father. Do not be afraid of anything; you shall not go without a reward."

As soon as Beauty awoke she told her father this dream; but though it gave him some comfort, he was a long time before he could be persuaded to leave the palace. At last Beauty succeeded in getting him safely away.

When her father was out of sight poor Beauty began to weep sorely; still, having naturally a courageous spirit, she soon resolved not to make her sad case still worse by sorrow, which she knew was vain, but to wait and be patient. She walked about to take a view of all the palace, and the elegance of every part of it much charmed her.

But what was her surprise when she came to a door on which was written BEAUTY'S ROOM! She opened it in

haste, and her eyes were dazzled by the splendor and taste of the apartment. What made her wonder more than all the rest was a large library filled with books, a harpsichord, and many pieces of music. "The beast surely does not mean to eat me up immediately," said she, "since he takes care I shall not be at a loss how to amuse myself." She opened the library, and saw these verses written in letters of gold on the back of one of the books:

" Beauteous lady, dry your tears,
    Here's no cause for sighs or fears.
    Command as freely as you may,
    For you command and I obey."

"Alas!" said she, sighing, "I wish I could only command a sight of my poor father, and to know what he is doing at this moment." Just then, by chance, she cast her eyes on a looking-glass that stood near her, and in it she saw a picture of her old home, and her

158

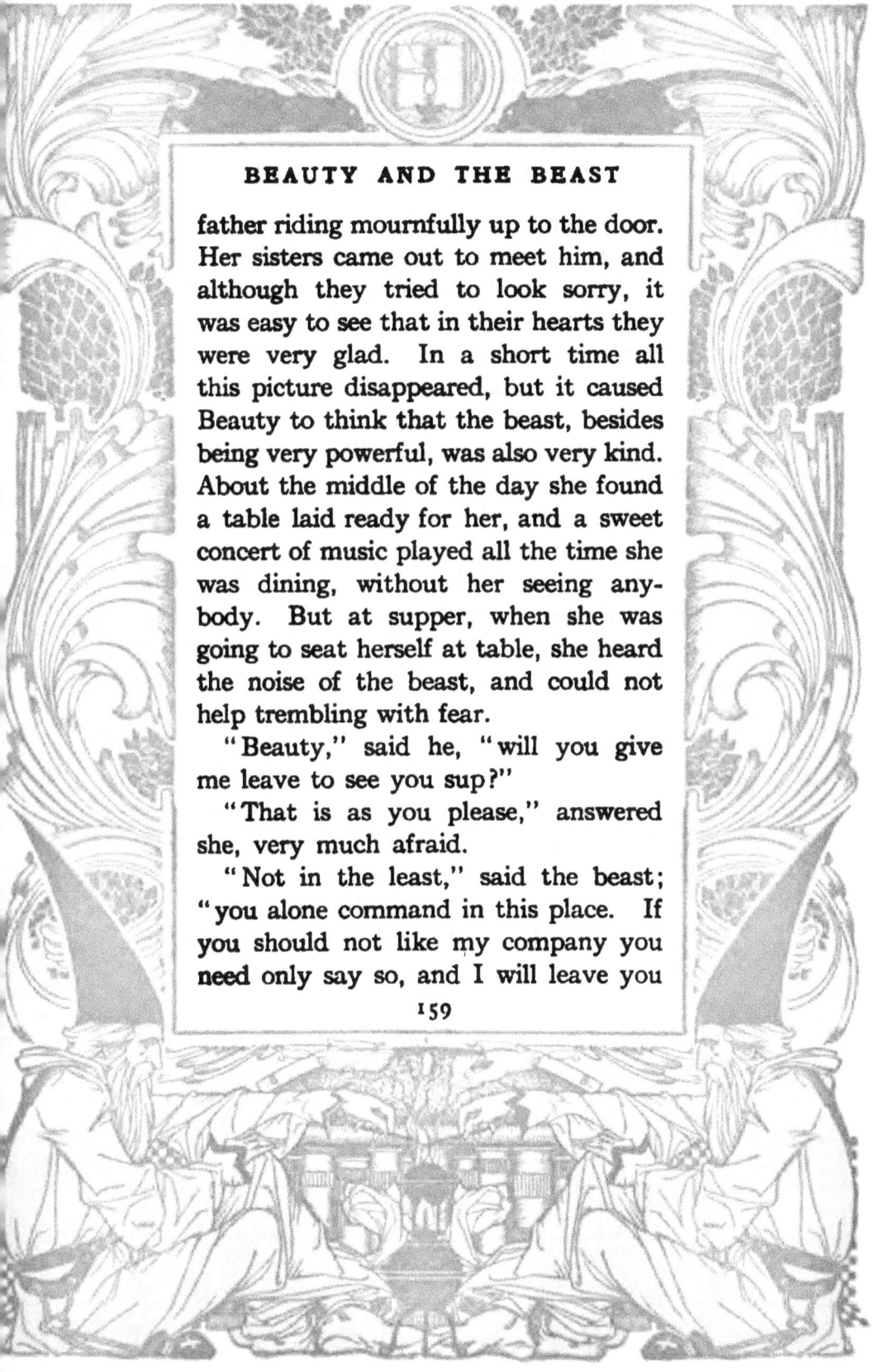

father riding mournfully up to the door.
Her sisters came out to meet him, and
although they tried to look sorry, it
was easy to see that in their hearts they
were very glad. In a short time all
this picture disappeared, but it caused
Beauty to think that the beast, besides
being very powerful, was also very kind.
About the middle of the day she found
a table laid ready for her, and a sweet
concert of music played all the time she
was dining, without her seeing anybody. But at supper, when she was
going to seat herself at table, she heard
the noise of the beast, and could not
help trembling with fear.

"Beauty," said he, "will you give
me leave to see you sup?"

"That is as you please," answered
she, very much afraid.

"Not in the least," said the beast;
"you alone command in this place. If
you should not like my company you
need only say so, and I will leave you

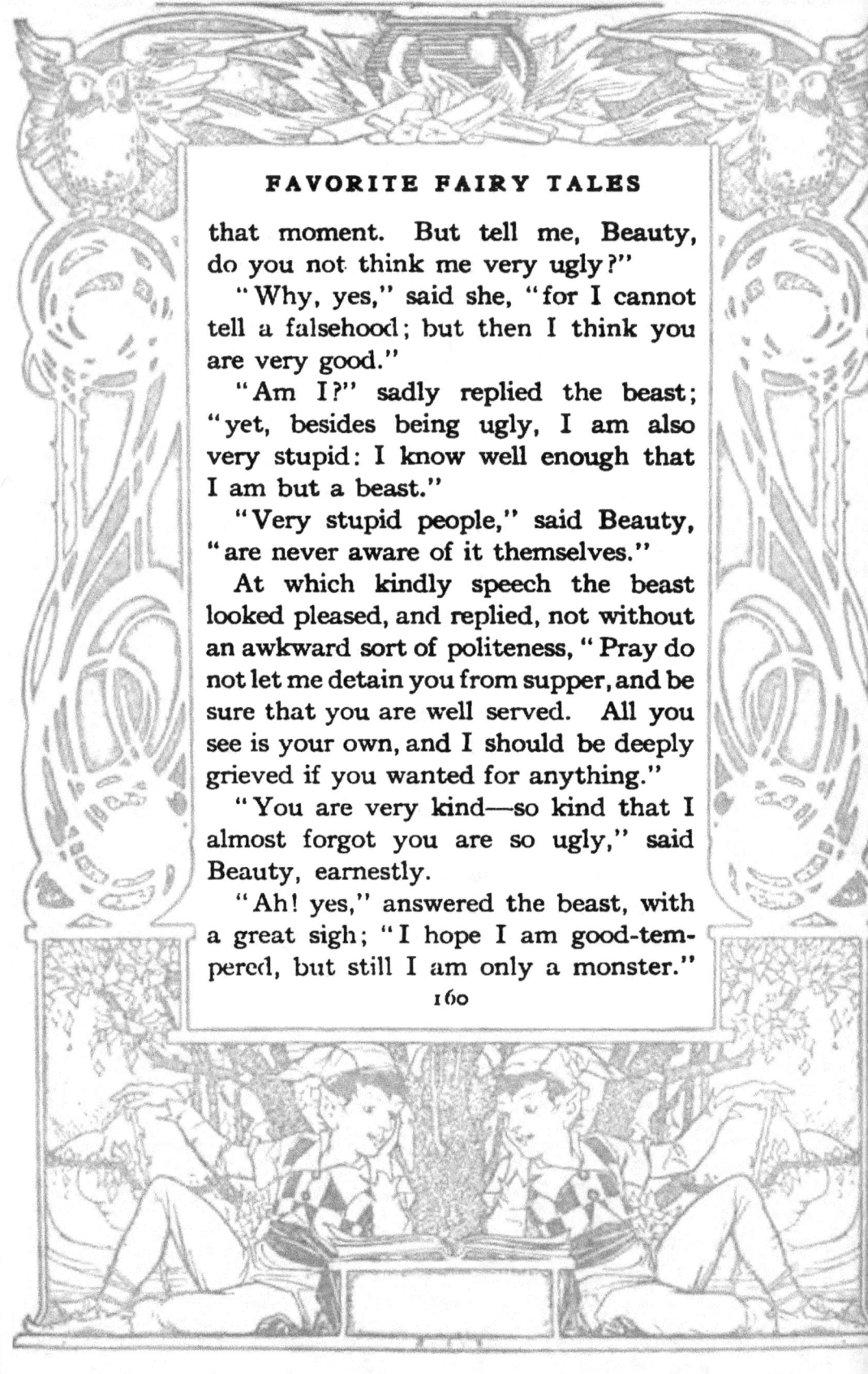

that moment. But tell me, Beauty, do you not think me very ugly?"

"Why, yes," said she, "for I cannot tell a falsehood; but then I think you are very good."

"Am I?" sadly replied the beast; "yet, besides being ugly, I am also very stupid: I know well enough that I am but a beast."

"Very stupid people," said Beauty, "are never aware of it themselves."

At which kindly speech the beast looked pleased, and replied, not without an awkward sort of politeness, "Pray do not let me detain you from supper, and be sure that you are well served. All you see is your own, and I should be deeply grieved if you wanted for anything."

"You are very kind—so kind that I almost forgot you are so ugly," said Beauty, earnestly.

"Ah! yes," answered the beast, with a great sigh; "I hope I am good-tempered, but still I am only a monster."

160

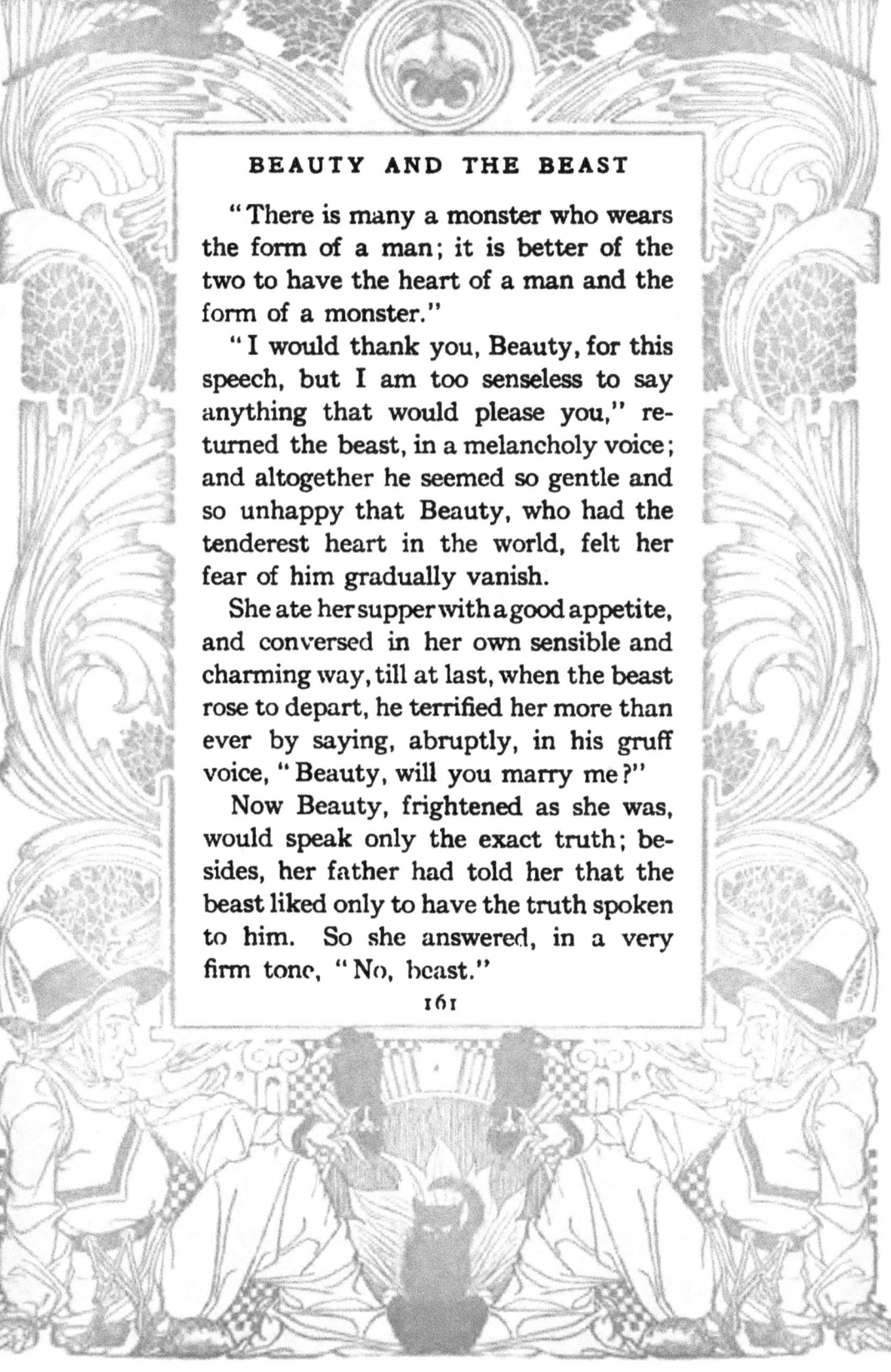

BEAUTY AND THE BEAST

"There is many a monster who wears the form of a man; it is better of the two to have the heart of a man and the form of a monster."

"I would thank you, Beauty, for this speech, but I am too senseless to say anything that would please you," returned the beast, in a melancholy voice; and altogether he seemed so gentle and so unhappy that Beauty, who had the tenderest heart in the world, felt her fear of him gradually vanish.

She ate her supper with a good appetite, and conversed in her own sensible and charming way, till at last, when the beast rose to depart, he terrified her more than ever by saying, abruptly, in his gruff voice, "Beauty, will you marry me?"

Now Beauty, frightened as she was, would speak only the exact truth; besides, her father had told her that the beast liked only to have the truth spoken to him. So she answered, in a very firm tone, "No, beast."

He did not go into a passion, or do anything but sigh deeply, and depart.

When Beauty found herself alone she began to feel pity for the poor beast. "Oh!" said she, "what a sad thing it is that he should be so very frightful, since he is so good-tempered!"

Beauty lived three months in this palace very well pleased. The beast came to see her every night, and talked with her while she supped; and though what he said was not very clever, yet, as she saw in him every day some new goodness, instead of dreading the time of his coming, she soon began continually looking at her watch, to see if it were nine o'clock; for that was the hour when he never failed to visit her. One thing only vexed her, which was that every night before he went away he always made it a rule to ask her if she would be his wife, and seemed very much grieved at her steadfastly replying "No." At last, one night, she said

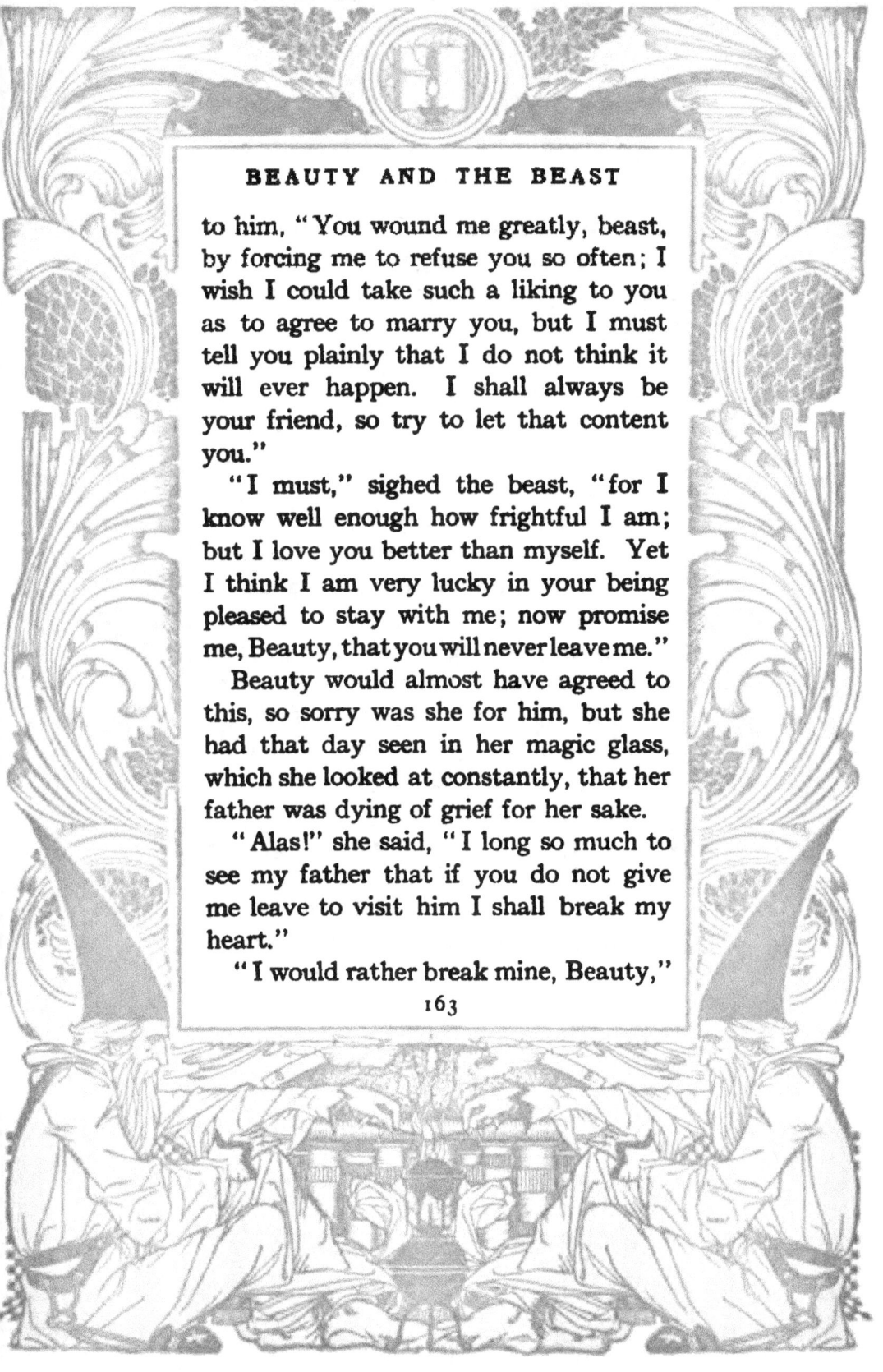

to him, "You wound me greatly, beast, by forcing me to refuse you so often; I wish I could take such a liking to you as to agree to marry you, but I must tell you plainly that I do not think it will ever happen. I shall always be your friend, so try to let that content you."

"I must," sighed the beast, "for I know well enough how frightful I am; but I love you better than myself. Yet I think I am very lucky in your being pleased to stay with me; now promise me, Beauty, that you will never leave me."

Beauty would almost have agreed to this, so sorry was she for him, but she had that day seen in her magic glass, which she looked at constantly, that her father was dying of grief for her sake.

"Alas!" she said, "I long so much to see my father that if you do not give me leave to visit him I shall break my heart."

"I would rather break mine, Beauty,"

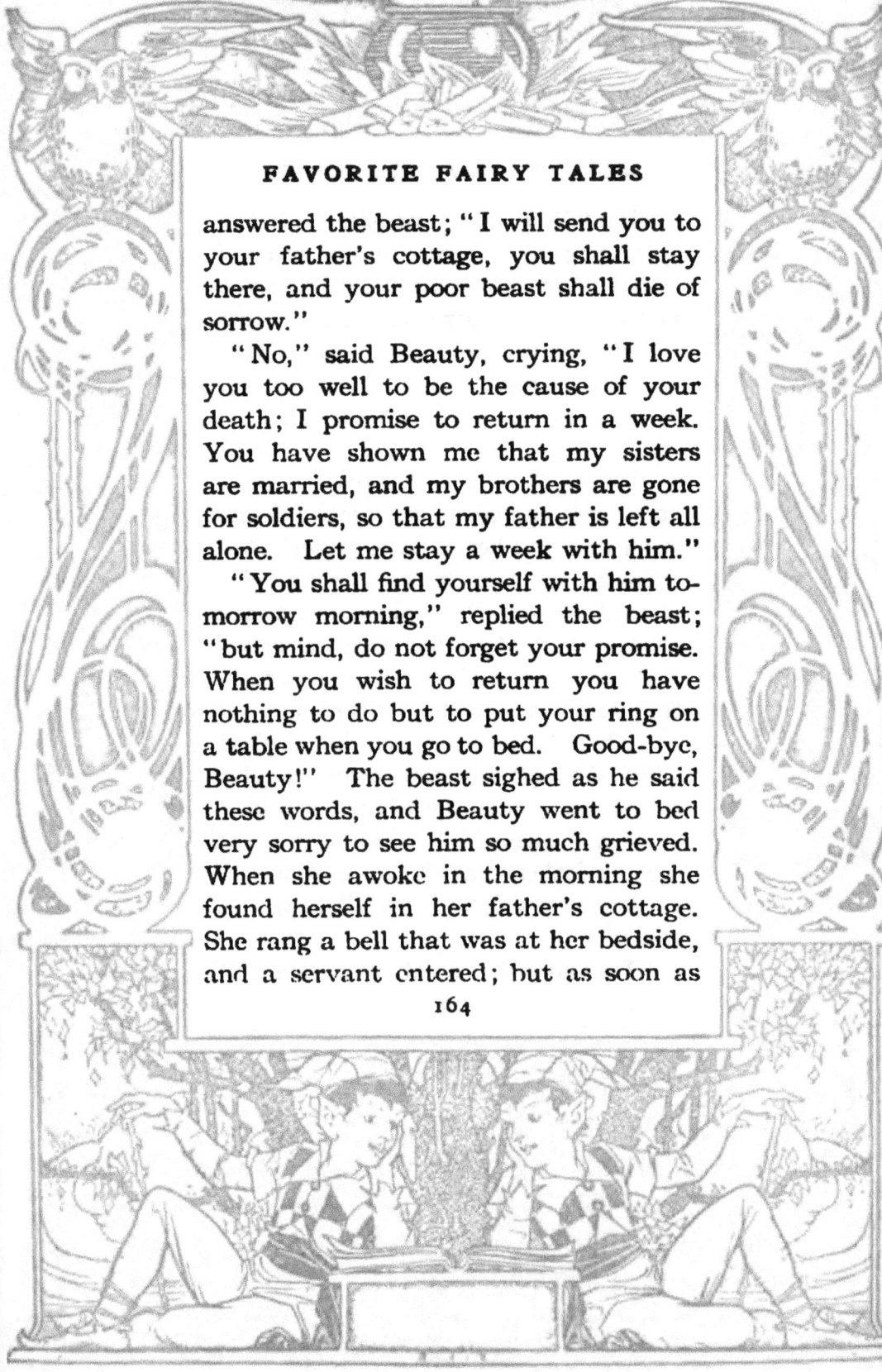

answered the beast; "I will send you to your father's cottage, you shall stay there, and your poor beast shall die of sorrow."

"No," said Beauty, crying, "I love you too well to be the cause of your death; I promise to return in a week. You have shown me that my sisters are married, and my brothers are gone for soldiers, so that my father is left all alone. Let me stay a week with him."

"You shall find yourself with him to-morrow morning," replied the beast; "but mind, do not forget your promise. When you wish to return you have nothing to do but to put your ring on a table when you go to bed. Good-bye, Beauty!" The beast sighed as he said these words, and Beauty went to bed very sorry to see him so much grieved. When she awoke in the morning she found herself in her father's cottage. She rang a bell that was at her bedside, and a servant entered; but as soon as

she saw Beauty the woman gave a loud
shriek; upon which the merchant ran
up-stairs, and when he beheld his daughter he ran to her and kissed her a hundred times. At last Beauty began to
remember that she had brought no
clothes with her to put on; but the servant told her she had just found in the
next room a large chest full of dresses,
trimmed all over with gold, and adorned
with pearls and diamonds.

Beauty, in her own mind, thanked
the beast for his kindness, and put on
the plainest gown she could find among
them all. She then desired the servant
to lay the rest aside, for she intended to
give them to her sisters; but, as soon
as she had spoken these words, the chest
was gone out of sight in a moment. Her
father then suggested perhaps the beast
chose for her to keep them all for herself; and as soon as he had said this,
they saw the chest standing again in
the same place. While Beauty was

dressing herself a servant brought word
to her that her sisters were come with
their husbands to pay her a visit. They
both lived unhappily with the gentlemen they had married. The husband
of the eldest was very handsome, but
was so proud of this that he thought of
nothing else from morning till night,
and did not care a pin for the beauty of
his wife. The second had married a
man of great learning; but he made no
use of it, except to torment and affront
all his friends, and his wife more than
any of them. The two sisters were
ready to burst with spite when they saw
Beauty dressed like a princess, and looking so very charming. All the kindness
that she showed them was of no use;
for they were vexed more than ever
when she told them how happy she
lived at the palace of the beast. The
spiteful creatures went by themselves
into the garden, where they cried to
think of her good-fortune.

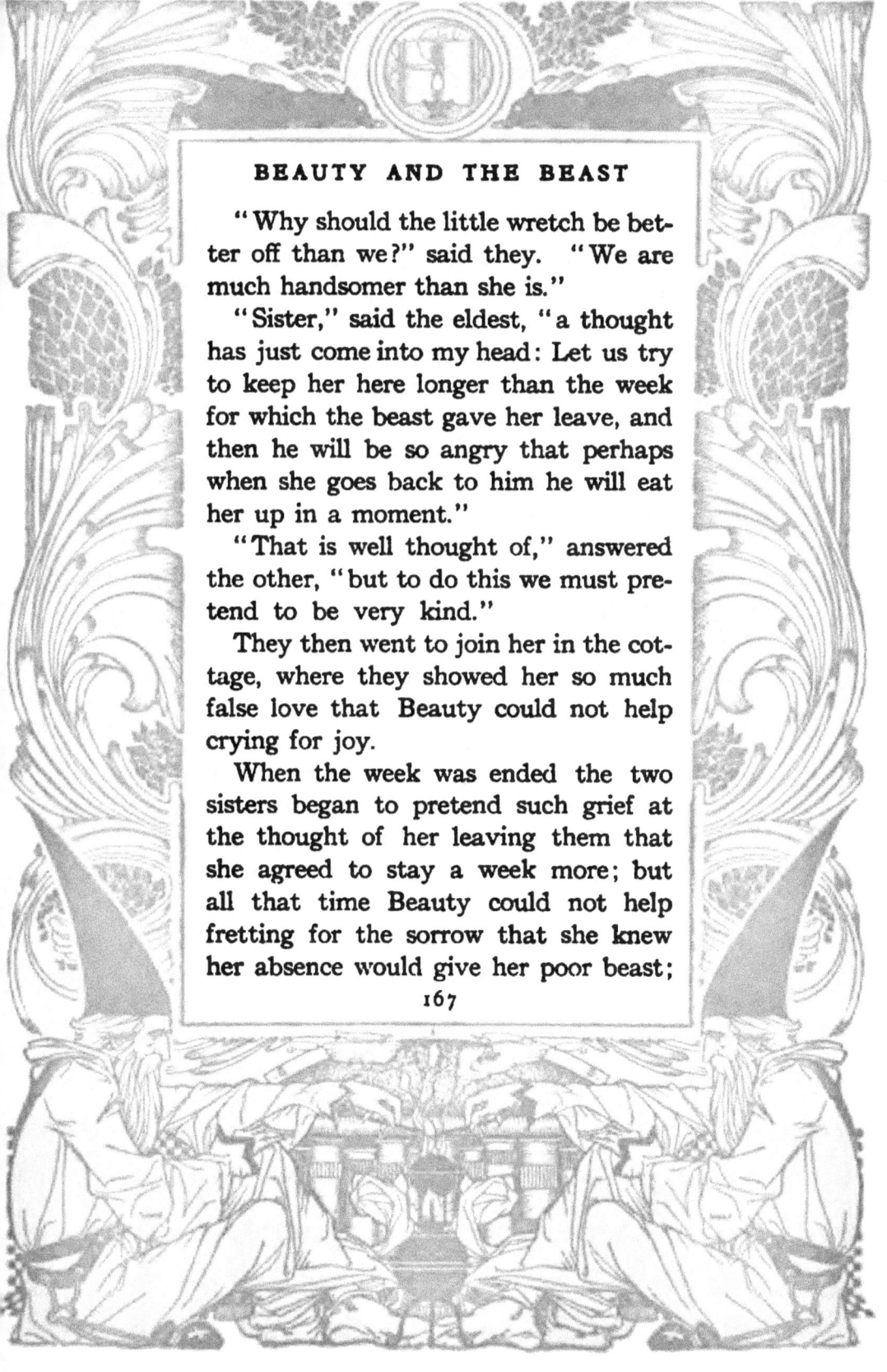

BEAUTY AND THE BEAST

"Why should the little wretch be better off than we?" said they. "We are much handsomer than she is."

"Sister," said the eldest, "a thought has just come into my head: Let us try to keep her here longer than the week for which the beast gave her leave, and then he will be so angry that perhaps when she goes back to him he will eat her up in a moment."

"That is well thought of," answered the other, "but to do this we must pretend to be very kind."

They then went to join her in the cottage, where they showed her so much false love that Beauty could not help crying for joy.

When the week was ended the two sisters began to pretend such grief at the thought of her leaving them that she agreed to stay a week more; but all that time Beauty could not help fretting for the sorrow that she knew her absence would give her poor beast;

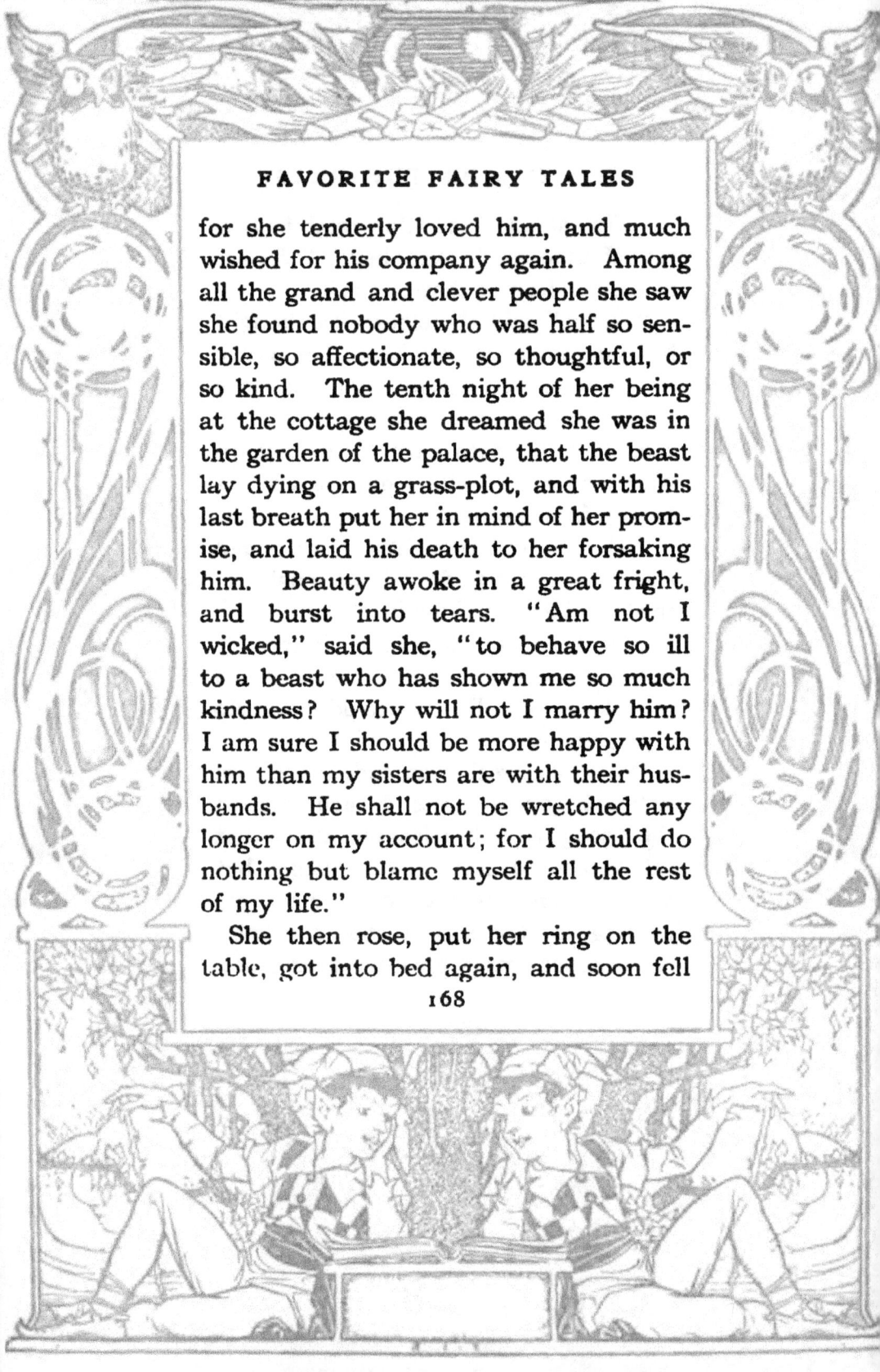

for she tenderly loved him, and much wished for his company again. Among all the grand and clever people she saw she found nobody who was half so sensible, so affectionate, so thoughtful, or so kind. The tenth night of her being at the cottage she dreamed she was in the garden of the palace, that the beast lay dying on a grass-plot, and with his last breath put her in mind of her promise, and laid his death to her forsaking him. Beauty awoke in a great fright, and burst into tears. "Am not I wicked," said she, "to behave so ill to a beast who has shown me so much kindness? Why will not I marry him? I am sure I should be more happy with him than my sisters are with their husbands. He shall not be wretched any longer on my account; for I should do nothing but blame myself all the rest of my life."

She then rose, put her ring on the table, got into bed again, and soon fell

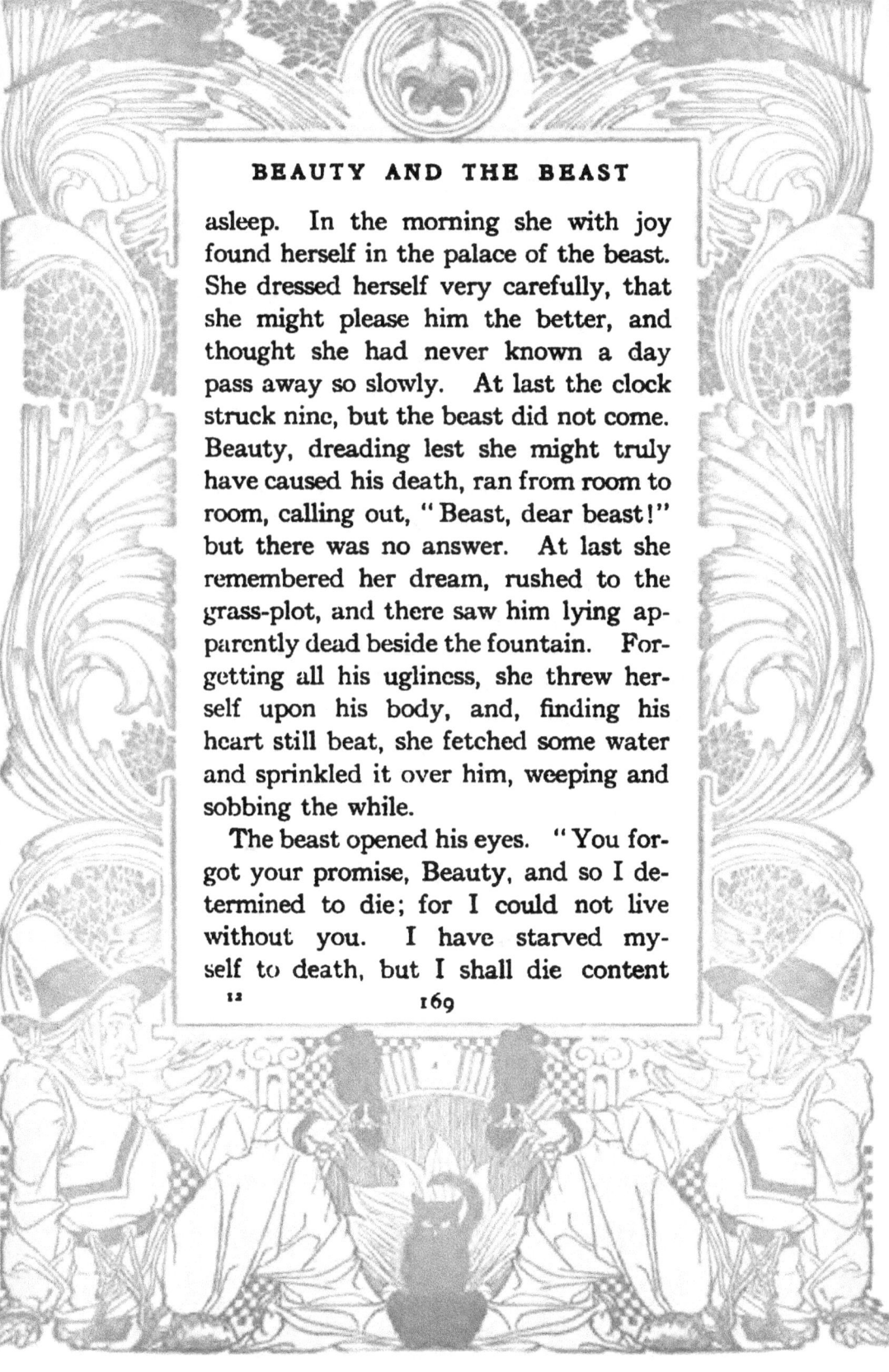

asleep. In the morning she with joy
found herself in the palace of the beast.
She dressed herself very carefully, that
she might please him the better, and
thought she had never known a day
pass away so slowly. At last the clock
struck nine, but the beast did not come.
Beauty, dreading lest she might truly
have caused his death, ran from room to
room, calling out, "Beast, dear beast!"
but there was no answer. At last she
remembered her dream, rushed to the
grass-plot, and there saw him lying apparently dead beside the fountain. For-
getting all his ugliness, she threw herself upon his body, and, finding his
heart still beat, she fetched some water
and sprinkled it over him, weeping and
sobbing the while.

The beast opened his eyes. "You forgot your promise, Beauty, and so I determined to die; for I could not live
without you. I have starved myself to death, but I shall die content

since I have seen your face once
more."

"No, dear beast," cried Beauty, pas-
sionately, "you shall not die; you shall
live to be my husband! I thought it
was only friendship I felt for you, but
now I know it was love."

The moment Beauty had spoken these
words the palace was suddenly lighted
up, and all kinds of rejoicings were heard
around them, none of which she noticed,
but hung over her dear beast with the
utmost tenderness. At last, unable to
restrain herself, she dropped her head
over her hands, covered her eyes, and
cried for joy; and, when she looked up
again, the beast was gone. In his stead
she saw at her feet a handsome, graceful young prince, who thanked her with
the tenderest expressions for having
freed him from enchantment.

"But where is my poor beast? I
only want him and nobody else," sobbed Beauty.

She saw at her feet a handsome, graceful young prince

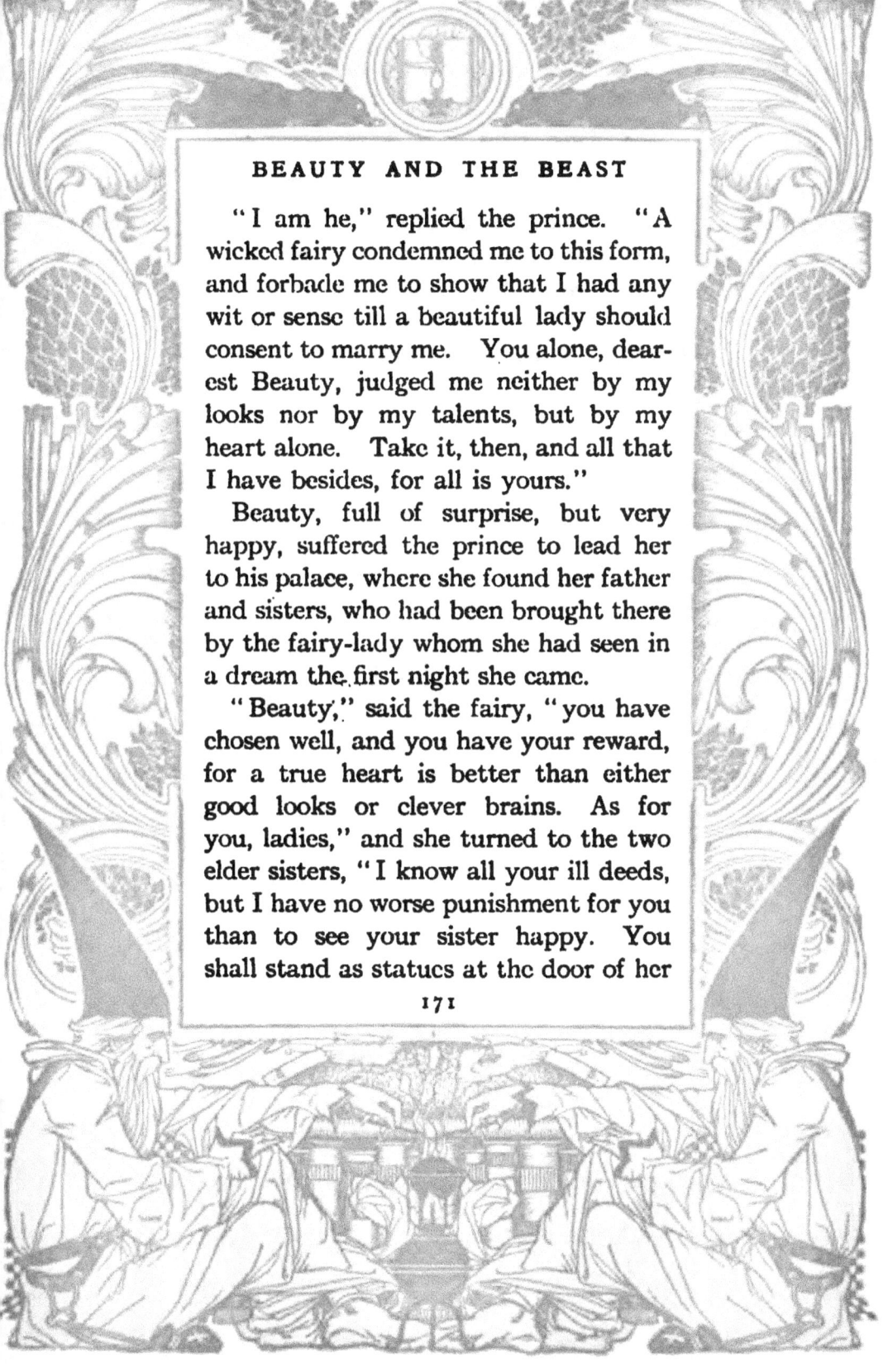

BEAUTY AND THE BEAST

"I am he," replied the prince. "A wicked fairy condemned me to this form, and forbade me to show that I had any wit or sense till a beautiful lady should consent to marry me. You alone, dearest Beauty, judged me neither by my looks nor by my talents, but by my heart alone. Take it, then, and all that I have besides, for all is yours."

Beauty, full of surprise, but very happy, suffered the prince to lead her to his palace, where she found her father and sisters, who had been brought there by the fairy-lady whom she had seen in a dream the first night she came.

"Beauty," said the fairy, "you have chosen well, and you have your reward, for a true heart is better than either good looks or clever brains. As for you, ladies," and she turned to the two elder sisters, "I know all your ill deeds, but I have no worse punishment for you than to see your sister happy. You shall stand as statues at the door of her

171

palace, and when you repent of and have amended your faults, you shall become women again. But, to tell you the truth, I very much fear you will remain statues forever."

LITTLE SNOWDROP

ONCE upon a time, in the middle of winter, when the flakes of snow fell like feathers from the sky, a queen sat at a window set in an ebony frame, and sewed. While she was sewing and watching the snow fall, she pricked her finger with her needle, and three drops of blood dropped on the snow. And because the crimson looked so beautiful on the white snow, she thought: "Oh that I had a child as white as snow, as red as blood, and as black as the wood of this ebony frame!"

Soon afterwards she had a little daughter, who was as white as snow, as red as blood, and had hair as black

173

as ebony. And when the child was born the queen died.

After a year had gone by the king took another wife. She was a handsome lady, but proud and haughty, and could not endure that any one should surpass her in beauty. She had a wonderful mirror, and whenever she walked up to it, and looked at herself in it, she said:

> "Little glass upon the wall,
> Who is fairest among us all?"

Then the mirror replied:

> "Lady queen, so grand and tall,
> Thou art the fairest of them all."

And she was satisfied, for she knew the mirror always told the truth. But Snowdrop grew ever taller and fairer, and at seven years old was beautiful as the day, and more beautiful than the queen herself. So once, when the queen asked of her mirror:

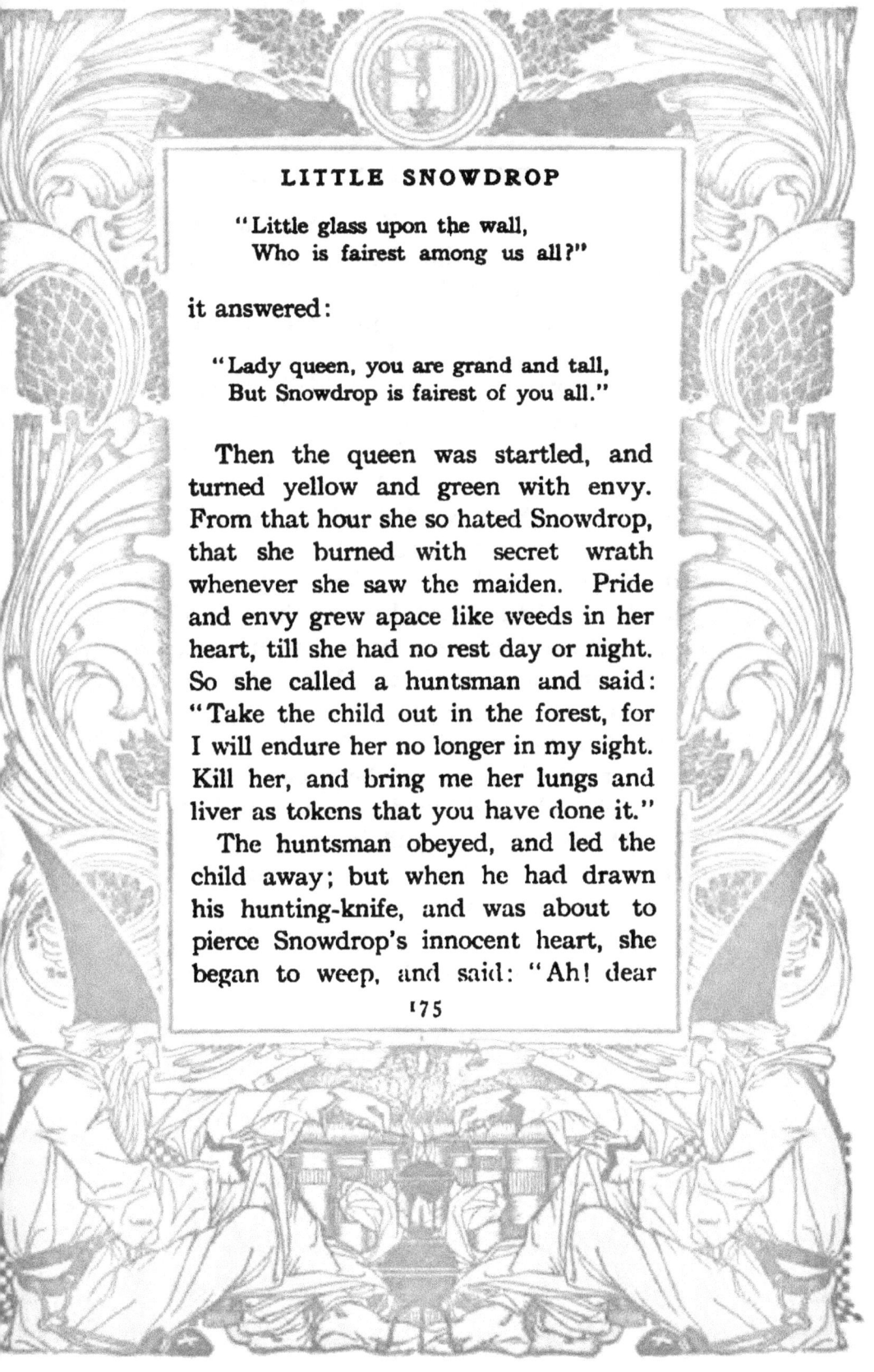

LITTLE SNOWDROP

"Little glass upon the wall,
  Who is fairest among us all?"

it answered:

"Lady queen, you are grand and tall,
  But Snowdrop is fairest of you all."

Then the queen was startled, and turned yellow and green with envy. From that hour she so hated Snowdrop, that she burned with secret wrath whenever she saw the maiden. Pride and envy grew apace like weeds in her heart, till she had no rest day or night. So she called a huntsman and said: "Take the child out in the forest, for I will endure her no longer in my sight. Kill her, and bring me her lungs and liver as tokens that you have done it."

The huntsman obeyed, and led the child away; but when he had drawn his hunting-knife, and was about to pierce Snowdrop's innocent heart, she began to weep, and said: "Ah! dear

175

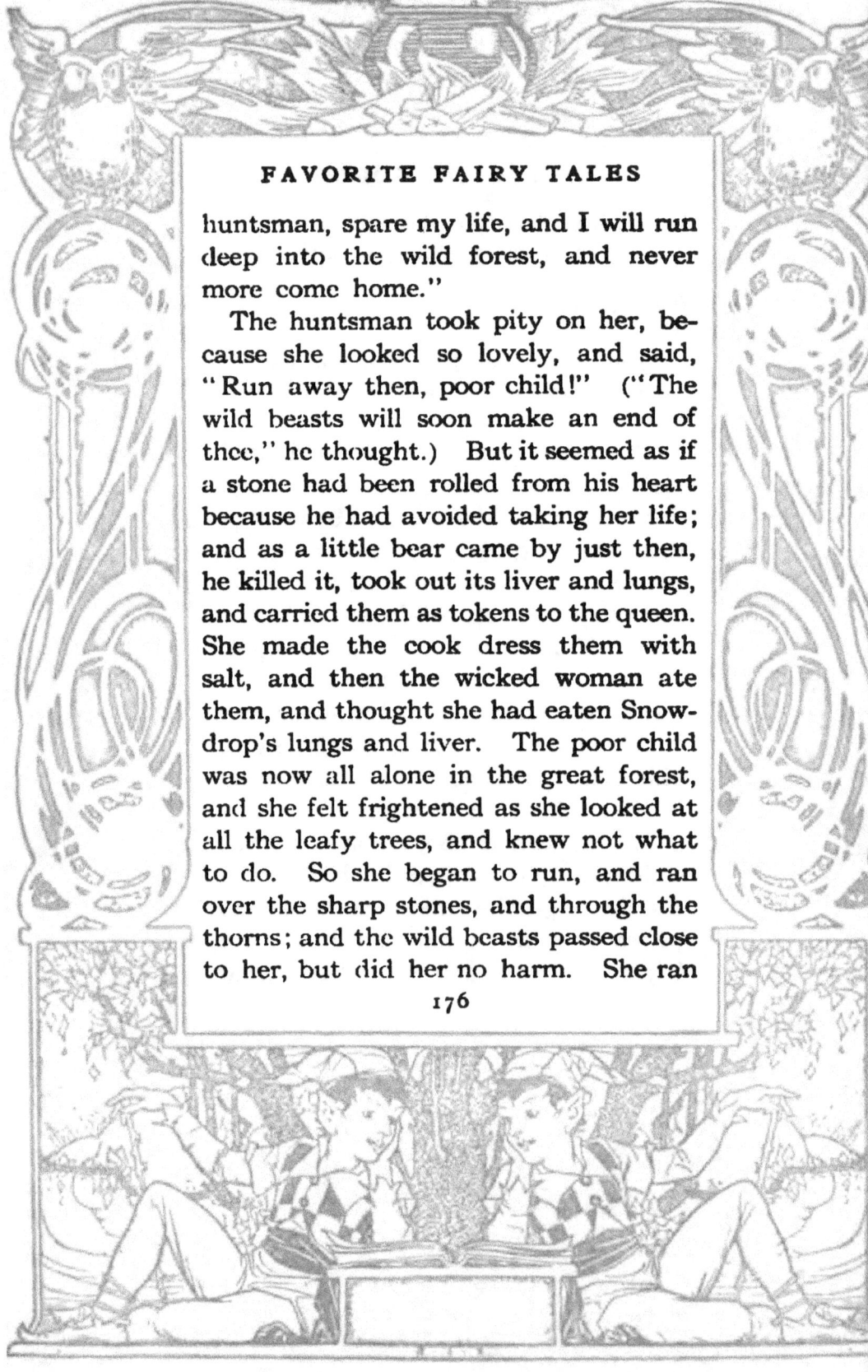

huntsman, spare my life, and I will run deep into the wild forest, and never more come home."

The huntsman took pity on her, because she looked so lovely, and said, "Run away then, poor child!" ("The wild beasts will soon make an end of thee," he thought.) But it seemed as if a stone had been rolled from his heart because he had avoided taking her life; and as a little bear came by just then, he killed it, took out its liver and lungs, and carried them as tokens to the queen. She made the cook dress them with salt, and then the wicked woman ate them, and thought she had eaten Snow-drop's lungs and liver. The poor child was now all alone in the great forest, and she felt frightened as she looked at all the leafy trees, and knew not what to do. So she began to run, and ran over the sharp stones, and through the thorns; and the wild beasts passed close to her, but did her no harm. She ran

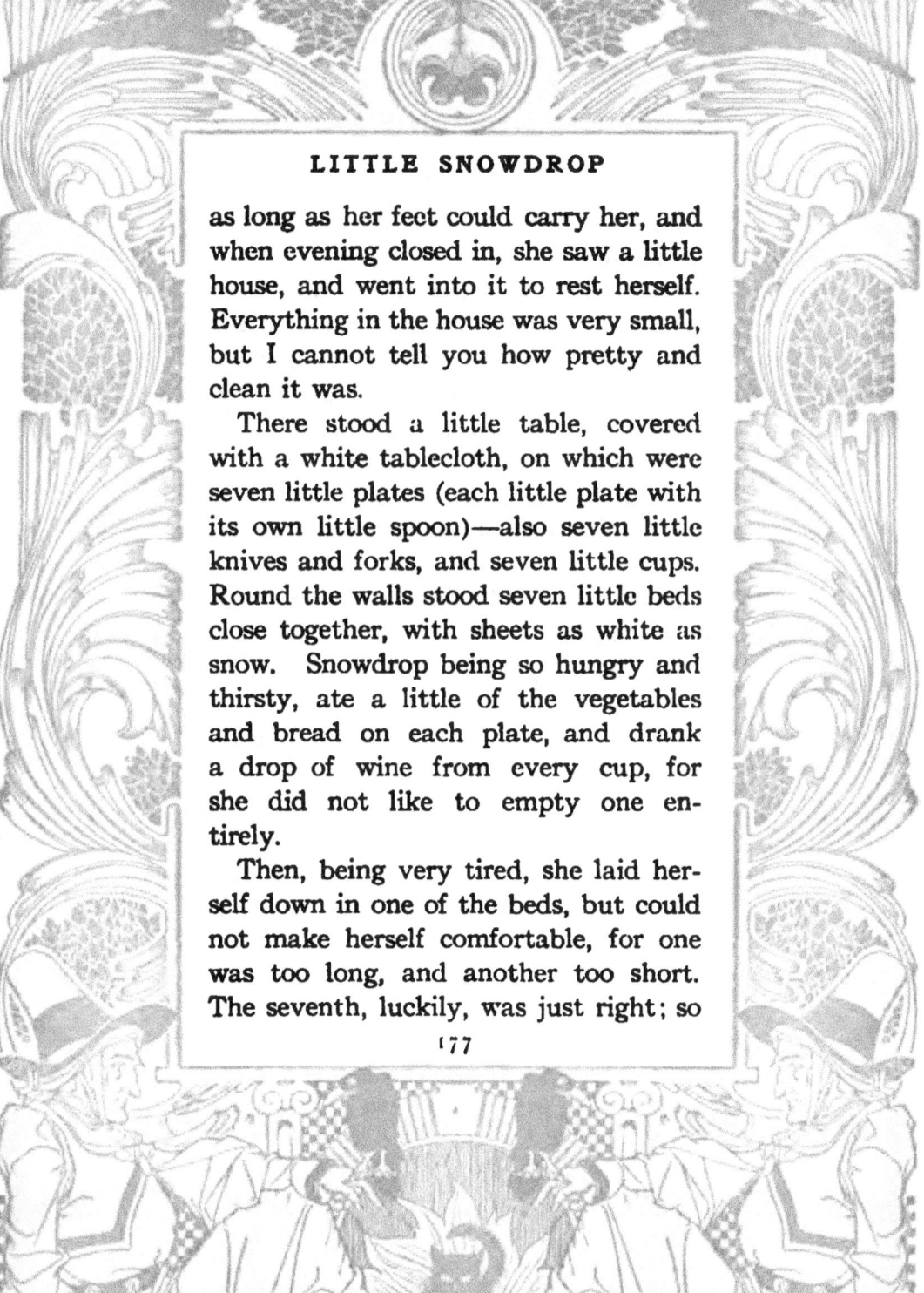

as long as her feet could carry her, and when evening closed in, she saw a little house, and went into it to rest herself. Everything in the house was very small, but I cannot tell you how pretty and clean it was.

There stood a little table, covered with a white tablecloth, on which were seven little plates (each little plate with its own little spoon)—also seven little knives and forks, and seven little cups. Round the walls stood seven little beds close together, with sheets as white as snow. Snowdrop being so hungry and thirsty, ate a little of the vegetables and bread on each plate, and drank a drop of wine from every cup, for she did not like to empty one entirely.

Then, being very tired, she laid herself down in one of the beds, but could not make herself comfortable, for one was too long, and another too short. The seventh, luckily, was just right; so

177

there she stayed, said her prayers, and fell asleep.

When it was grown quite dark, home came the masters of the house, seven dwarfs, who delved and mined for iron among the mountains. They lighted their seven candles, and as soon as there was a light in the kitchen, they saw that some one had been there, for it was not quite so orderly as they had left it.

The first said, "Who has been sitting on my stool?"

The second, "Who has eaten off my plate?"

The third, "Who has taken part of my loaf?"

The fourth, "Who has touched my vegetables?"

The fifth, "Who has used my fork?"

The sixth, "Who has cut with my knife?"

The seventh, "Who has drunk out of my little cup?"

178

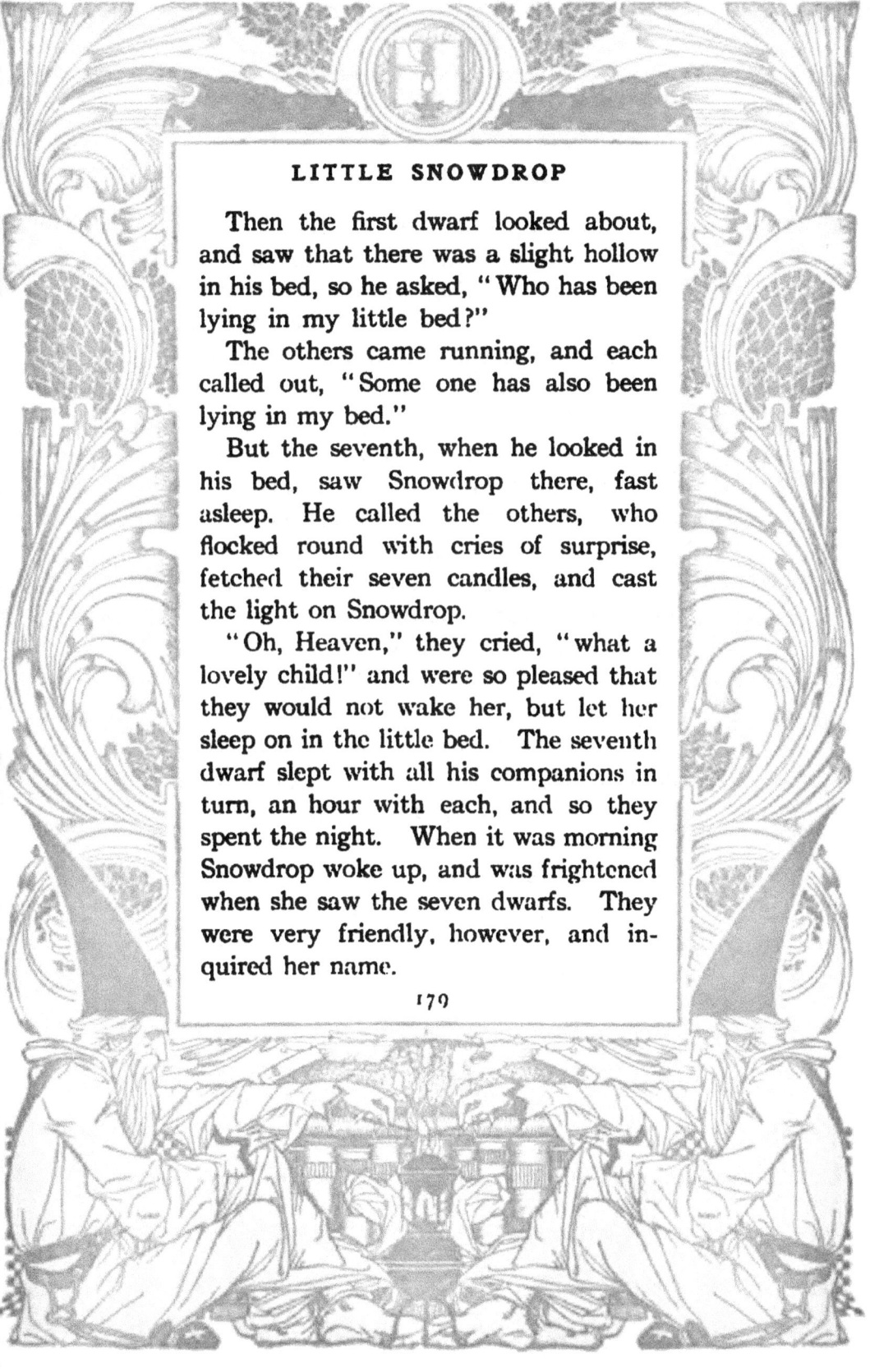

LITTLE SNOWDROP

Then the first dwarf looked about, and saw that there was a slight hollow in his bed, so he asked, "Who has been lying in my little bed?"

The others came running, and each called out, "Some one has also been lying in my bed."

But the seventh, when he looked in his bed, saw Snowdrop there, fast asleep. He called the others, who flocked round with cries of surprise, fetched their seven candles, and cast the light on Snowdrop.

"Oh, Heaven," they cried, "what a lovely child!" and were so pleased that they would not wake her, but let her sleep on in the little bed. The seventh dwarf slept with all his companions in turn, an hour with each, and so they spent the night. When it was morning Snowdrop woke up, and was frightened when she saw the seven dwarfs. They were very friendly, however, and inquired her name.

179

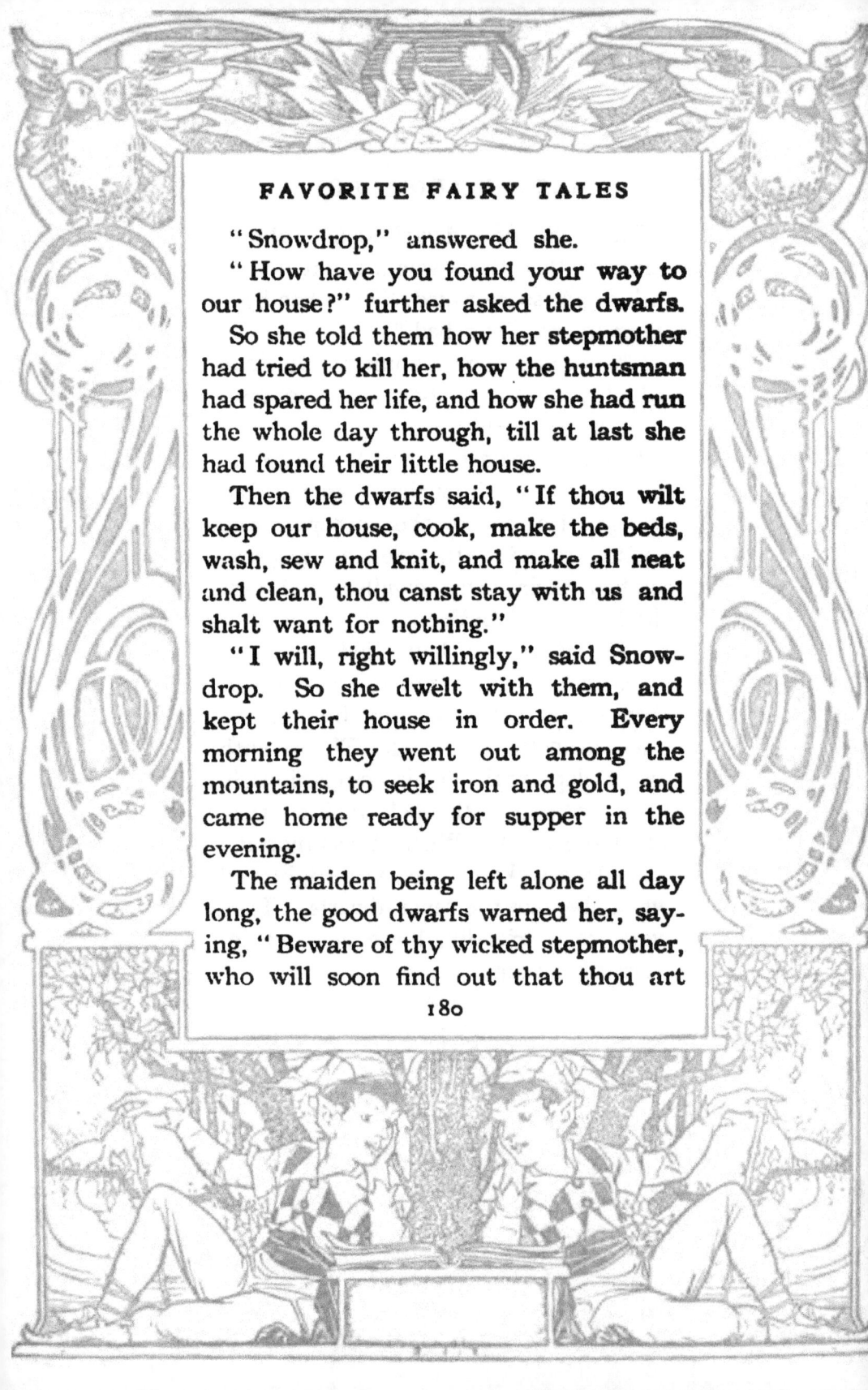

"Snowdrop," answered she.

"How have you found your way to our house?" further asked the dwarfs.

So she told them how her stepmother had tried to kill her, how the huntsman had spared her life, and how she had run the whole day through, till at last she had found their little house.

Then the dwarfs said, "If thou wilt keep our house, cook, make the beds, wash, sew and knit, and make all neat and clean, thou canst stay with us and shalt want for nothing."

"I will, right willingly," said Snowdrop. So she dwelt with them, and kept their house in order. Every morning they went out among the mountains, to seek iron and gold, and came home ready for supper in the evening.

The maiden being left alone all day long, the good dwarfs warned her, saying, "Beware of thy wicked stepmother, who will soon find out that thou art

"Oh, Heaven," they cried, "what a lovely child!"

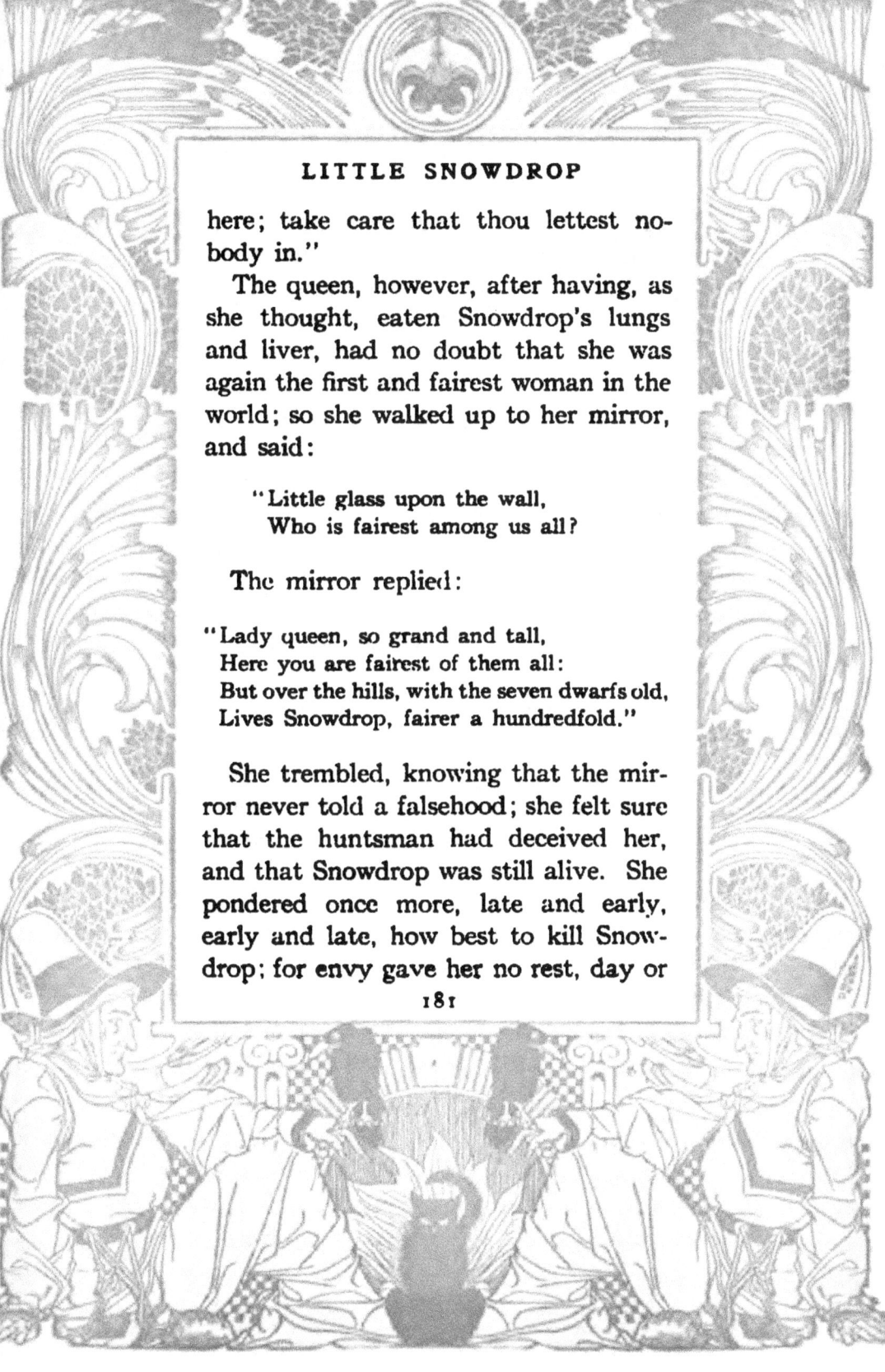

here; take care that thou lettest no-body in."

The queen, however, after having, as she thought, eaten Snowdrop's lungs and liver, had no doubt that she was again the first and fairest woman in the world; so she walked up to her mirror, and said:

> "Little glass upon the wall,
> Who is fairest among us all?

The mirror replied:

> "Lady queen, so grand and tall,
> Here you are fairest of them all:
> But over the hills, with the seven dwarfs old,
> Lives Snowdrop, fairer a hundredfold."

She trembled, knowing that the mirror never told a falsehood; she felt sure that the huntsman had deceived her, and that Snowdrop was still alive. She pondered once more, late and early, early and late, how best to kill Snow-drop; for envy gave her no rest, day or

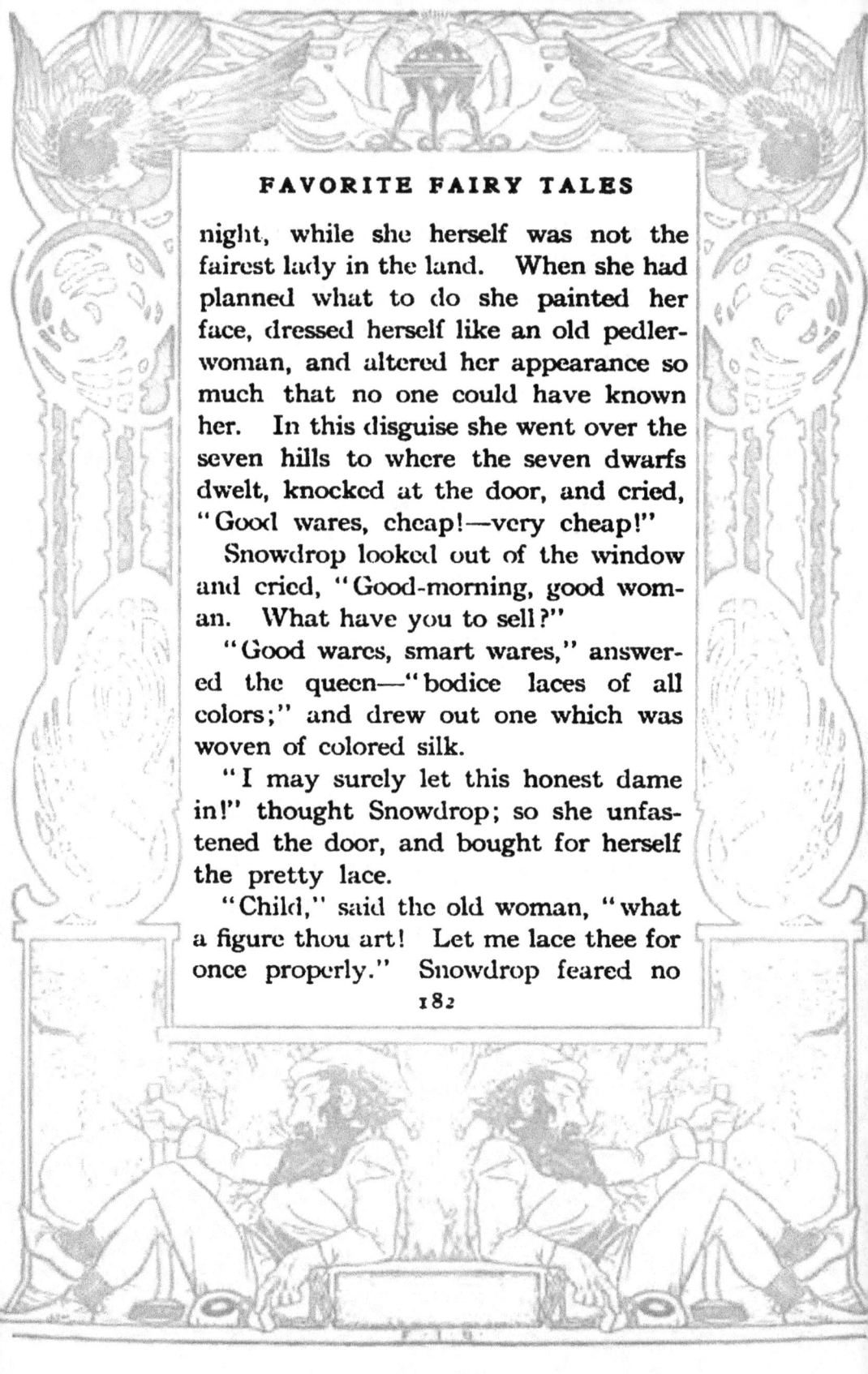

night, while she herself was not the fairest lady in the land. When she had planned what to do she painted her face, dressed herself like an old pedler-woman, and altered her appearance so much that no one could have known her. In this disguise she went over the seven hills to where the seven dwarfs dwelt, knocked at the door, and cried, "Good wares, cheap!—very cheap!"

Snowdrop looked out of the window and cried, "Good-morning, good woman. What have you to sell?"

"Good wares, smart wares," answered the queen—"bodice laces of all colors;" and drew out one which was woven of colored silk.

"I may surely let this honest dame in!" thought Snowdrop; so she unfastened the door, and bought for herself the pretty lace.

"Child," said the old woman, "what a figure thou art! Let me lace thee for once properly." Snowdrop feared no

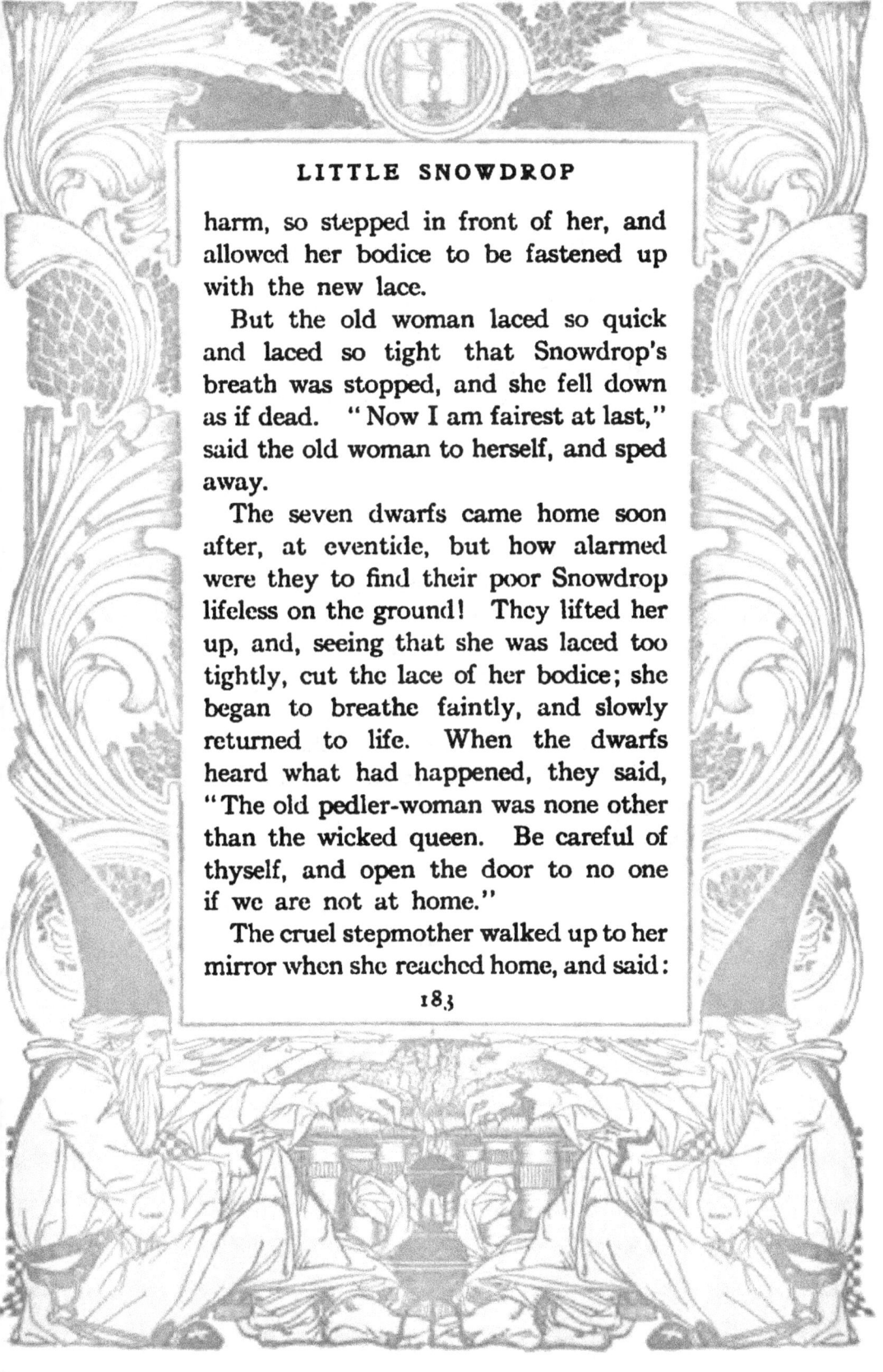

harm, so stepped in front of her, and allowed her bodice to be fastened up with the new lace.

But the old woman laced so quick and laced so tight that Snowdrop's breath was stopped, and she fell down as if dead. "Now I am fairest at last," said the old woman to herself, and sped away.

The seven dwarfs came home soon after, at eventide, but how alarmed were they to find their poor Snowdrop lifeless on the ground! They lifted her up, and, seeing that she was laced too tightly, cut the lace of her bodice; she began to breathe faintly, and slowly returned to life. When the dwarfs heard what had happened, they said, "The old pedler-woman was none other than the wicked queen. Be careful of thyself, and open the door to no one if we are not at home."

The cruel stepmother walked up to her mirror when she reached home, and said:

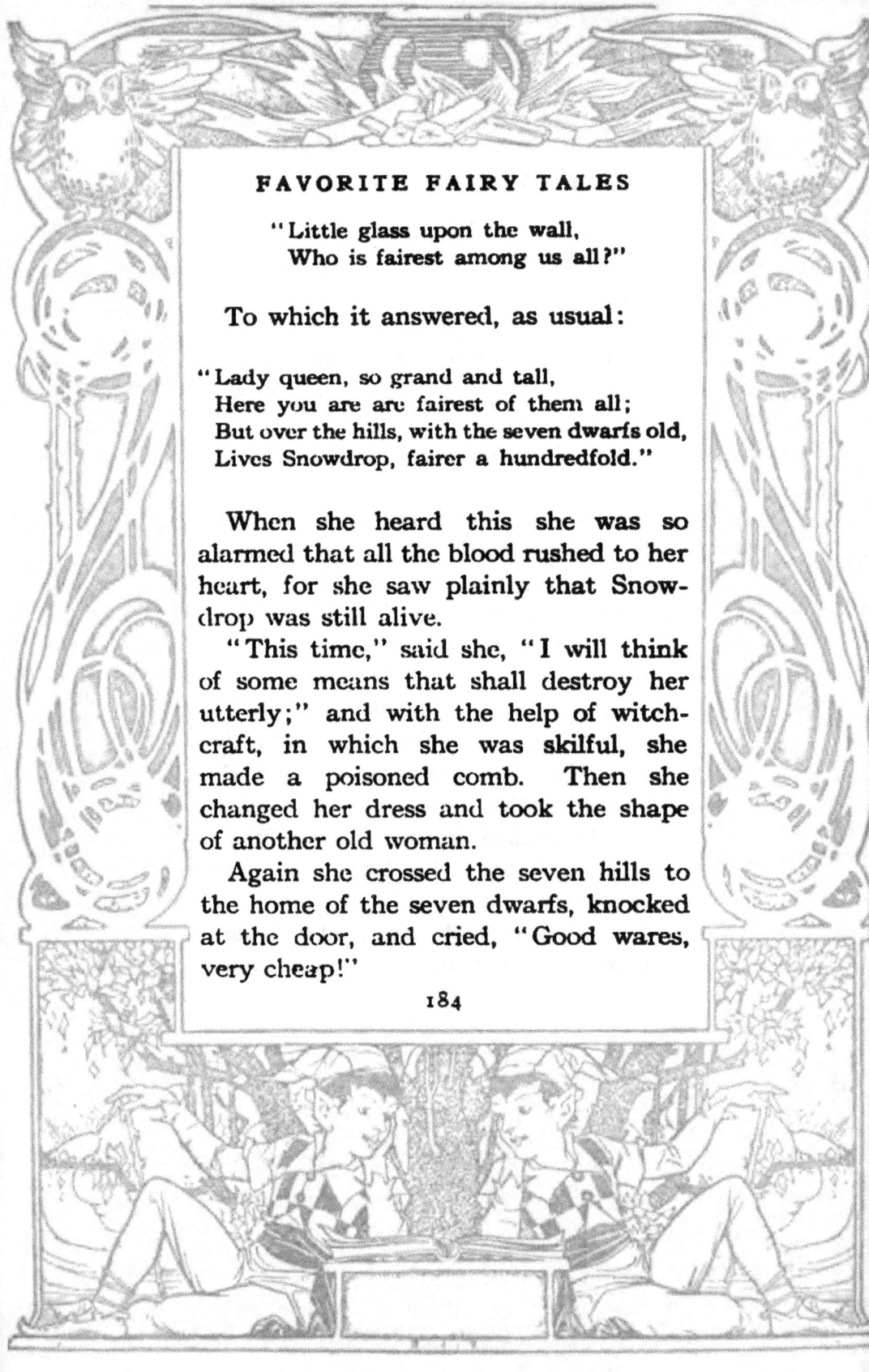

FAVORITE FAIRY TALES

"Little glass upon the wall,
  Who is fairest among us all?"

To which it answered, as usual:

"Lady queen, so grand and tall,
  Here you are are fairest of them all;
  But over the hills, with the seven dwarfs old,
  Lives Snowdrop, fairer a hundredfold."

When she heard this she was so alarmed that all the blood rushed to her heart, for she saw plainly that Snowdrop was still alive.

"This time," said she, "I will think of some means that shall destroy her utterly;" and with the help of witchcraft, in which she was skilful, she made a poisoned comb. Then she changed her dress and took the shape of another old woman.

Again she crossed the seven hills to the home of the seven dwarfs, knocked at the door, and cried, "Good wares, very cheap!"

184

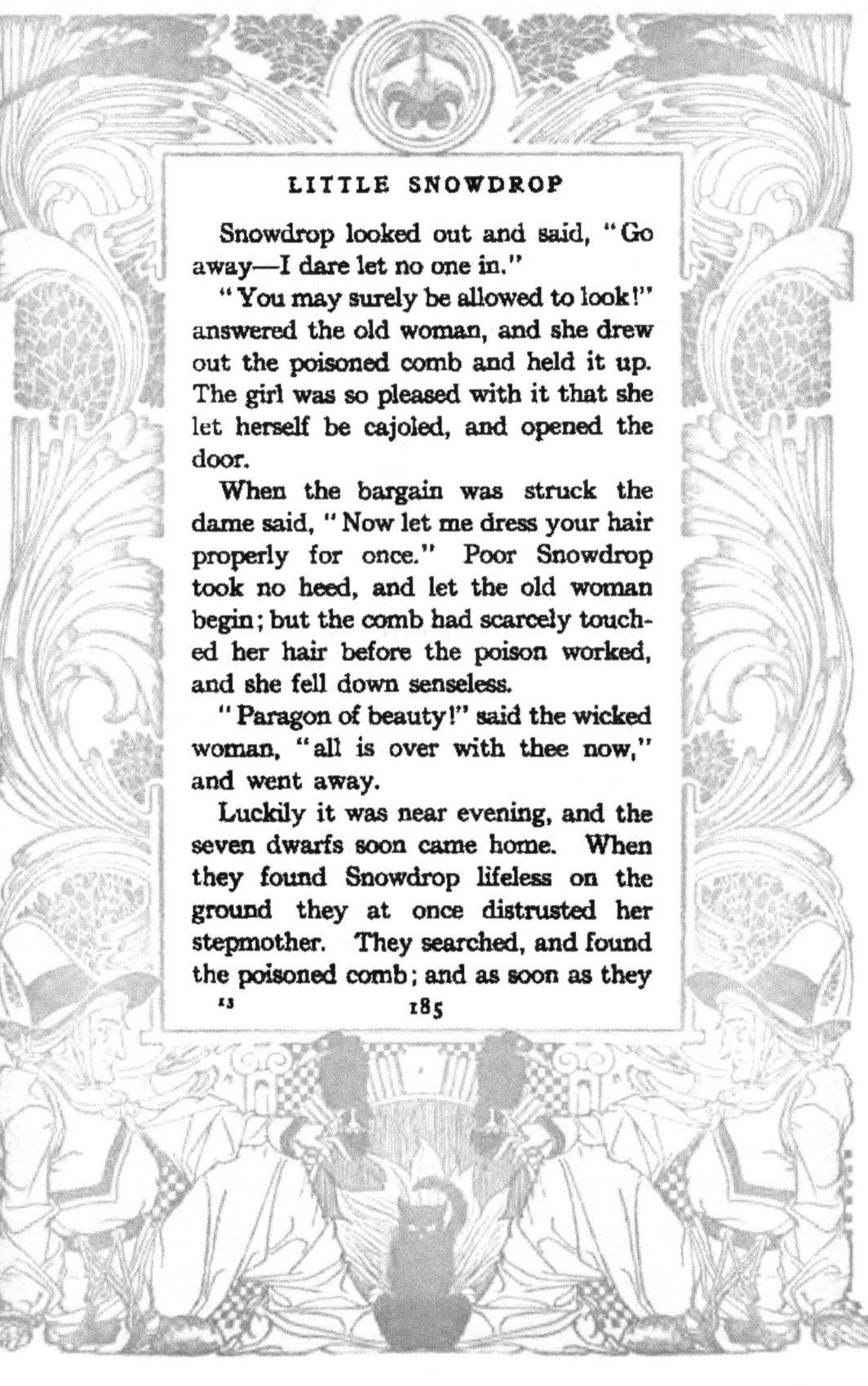

Snowdrop looked out and said, "Go away—I dare let no one in."

"You may surely be allowed to look!" answered the old woman, and she drew out the poisoned comb and held it up. The girl was so pleased with it that she let herself be cajoled, and opened the door.

When the bargain was struck the dame said, "Now let me dress your hair properly for once." Poor Snowdrop took no heed, and let the old woman begin; but the comb had scarcely touched her hair before the poison worked, and she fell down senseless.

"Paragon of beauty!" said the wicked woman, "all is over with thee now," and went away.

Luckily it was near evening, and the seven dwarfs soon came home. When they found Snowdrop lifeless on the ground they at once distrusted her stepmother. They searched, and found the poisoned comb; and as soon as they

had drawn it out, Snowdrop came to herself, and told them what had happened. Again they warned her to be careful, and open the door to no one.

The queen placed herself before the mirror at home and said:

> "Little glass upon the wall,
>   Who is fairest among us all?"

But it again answered:

> "Lady queen, so grand and tall,
>   Here, you are fairest of them all?"
> But over the hills, with the seven dwarfs old,
>   Lives Snowdrop, fairer a thousandfold."

When she heard the mirror speak thus she quivered with rage. "Snowdrop shall die," she cried, "if it costs my own life!"

Then she went to a secret and lonely chamber, where no one ever disturbed her, and compounded an apple of deadly poison. Ripe and rosy cheeked, it was so beautiful to look upon that all who saw

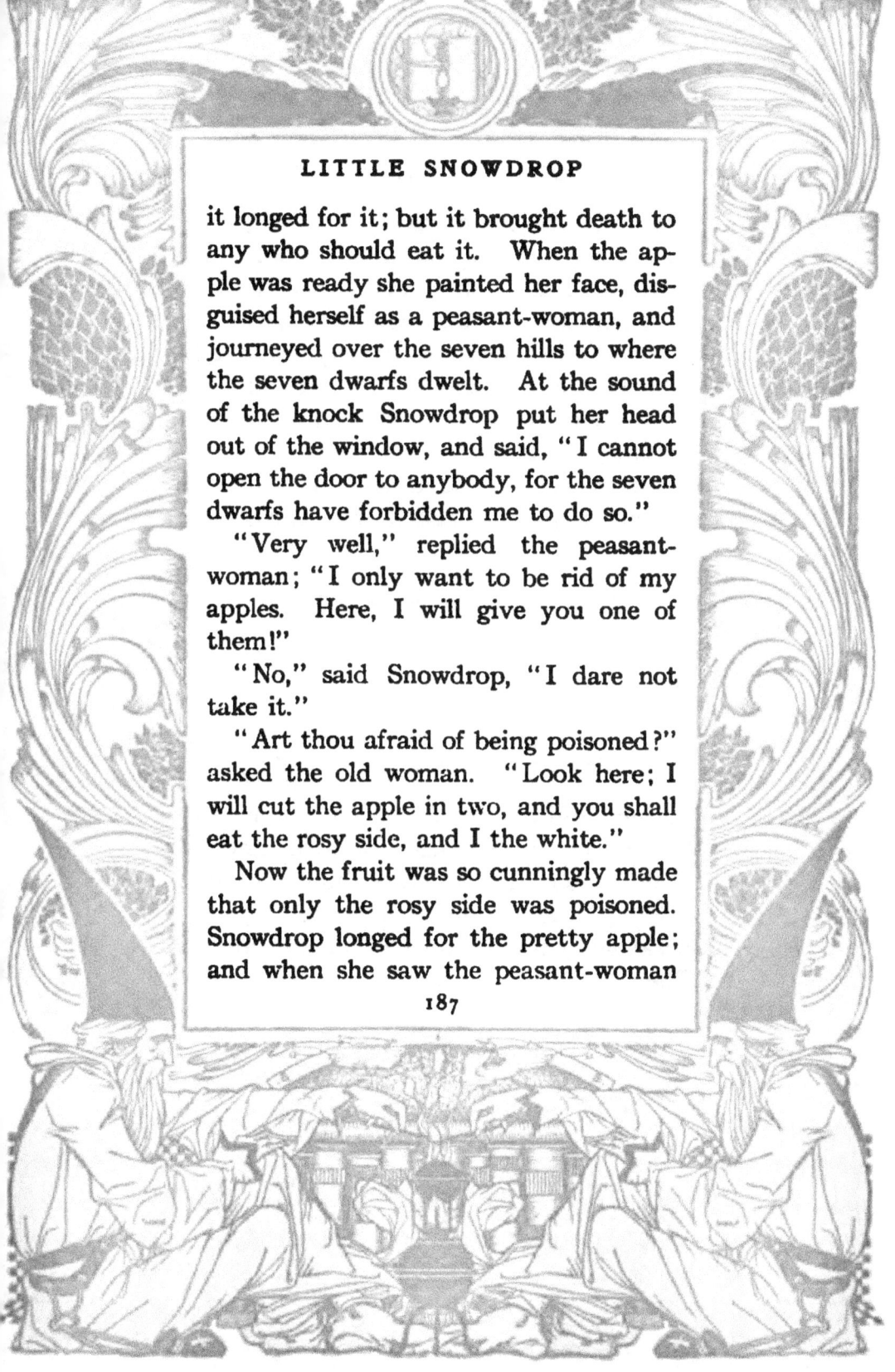

it longed for it; but it brought death to any who should eat it. When the apple was ready she painted her face, disguised herself as a peasant-woman, and journeyed over the seven hills to where the seven dwarfs dwelt. At the sound of the knock Snowdrop put her head out of the window, and said, "I cannot open the door to anybody, for the seven dwarfs have forbidden me to do so."

"Very well," replied the peasant-woman; "I only want to be rid of my apples. Here, I will give you one of them!"

"No," said Snowdrop, "I dare not take it."

"Art thou afraid of being poisoned?" asked the old woman. "Look here; I will cut the apple in two, and you shall eat the rosy side, and I the white."

Now the fruit was so cunningly made that only the rosy side was poisoned. Snowdrop longed for the pretty apple; and when she saw the peasant-woman

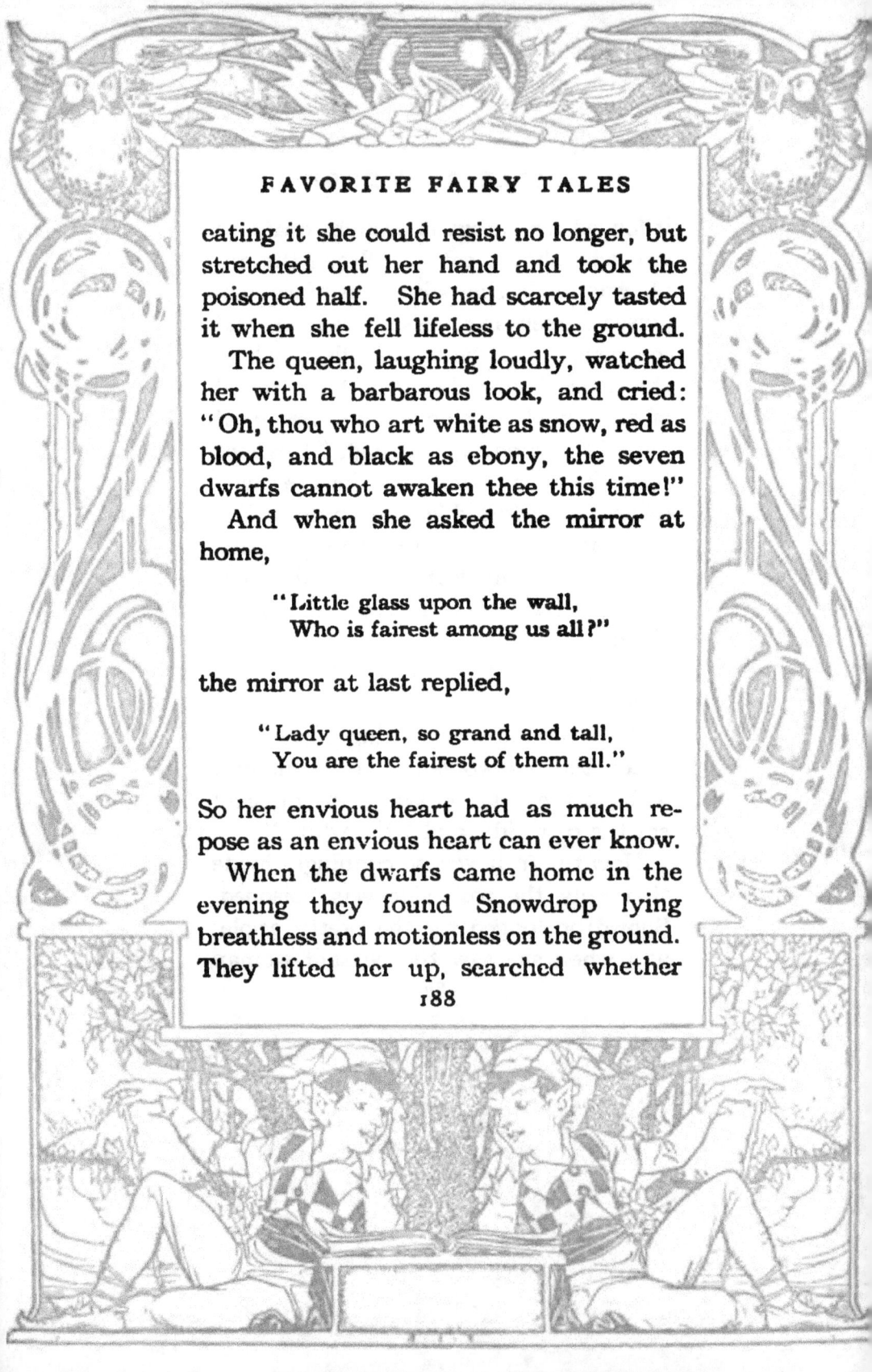

eating it she could resist no longer, but stretched out her hand and took the poisoned half. She had scarcely tasted it when she fell lifeless to the ground.

The queen, laughing loudly, watched her with a barbarous look, and cried: "Oh, thou who art white as snow, red as blood, and black as ebony, the seven dwarfs cannot awaken thee this time!"

And when she asked the mirror at home,

"Little glass upon the wall,
Who is fairest among us all?"

the mirror at last replied,

"Lady queen, so grand and tall,
You are the fairest of them all."

So her envious heart had as much repose as an envious heart can ever know.

When the dwarfs came home in the evening they found Snowdrop lying breathless and motionless on the ground. They lifted her up, searched whether

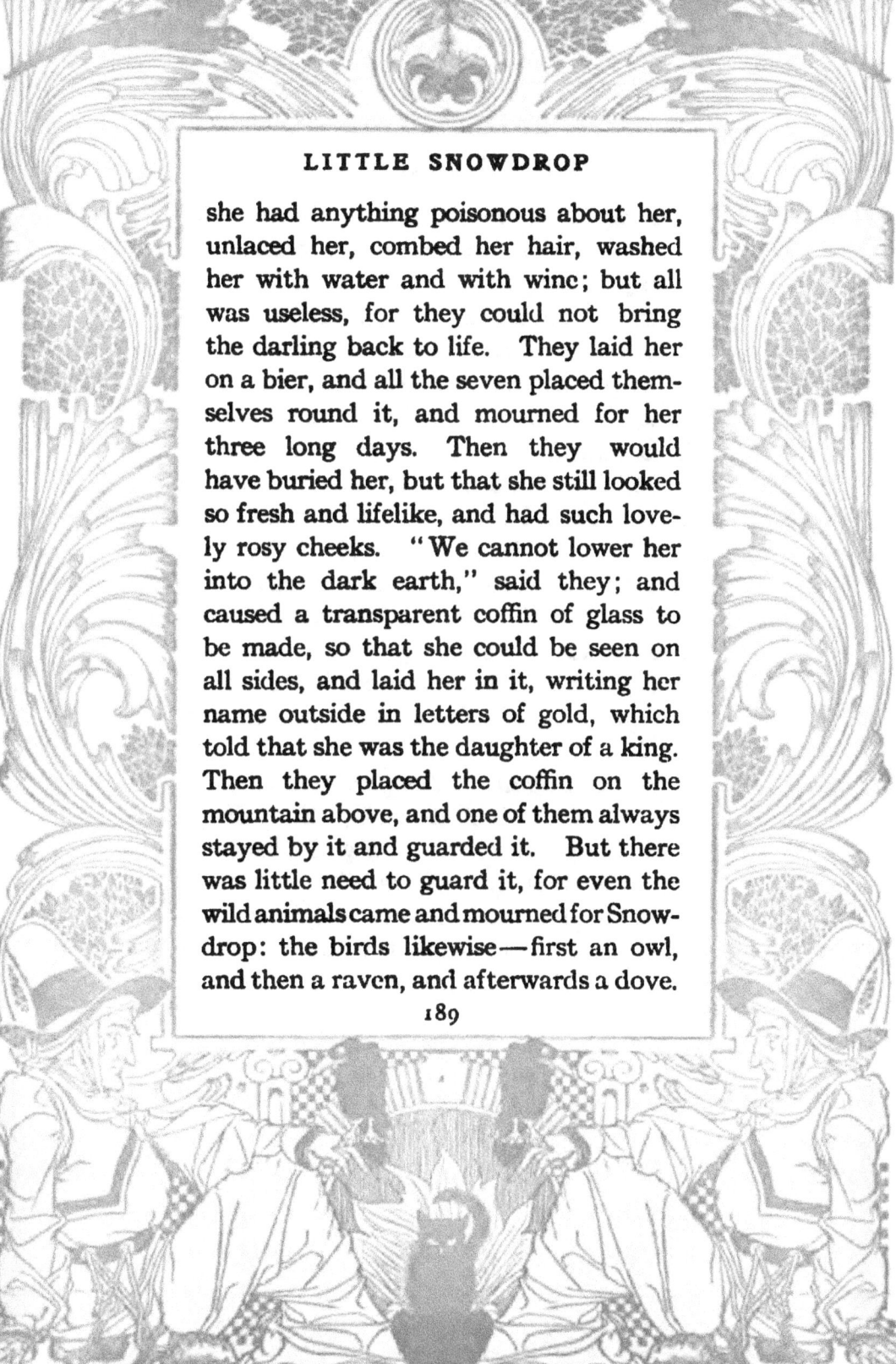

she had anything poisonous about her, unlaced her, combed her hair, washed her with water and with wine; but all was useless, for they could not bring the darling back to life. They laid her on a bier, and all the seven placed themselves round it, and mourned for her three long days. Then they would have buried her, but that she still looked so fresh and lifelike, and had such lovely rosy cheeks. "We cannot lower her into the dark earth," said they; and caused a transparent coffin of glass to be made, so that she could be seen on all sides, and laid her in it, writing her name outside in letters of gold, which told that she was the daughter of a king. Then they placed the coffin on the mountain above, and one of them always stayed by it and guarded it. But there was little need to guard it, for even the wild animals came and mourned for Snowdrop: the birds likewise—first an owl, and then a raven, and afterwards a dove.

189

Long, long years did Snowdrop lie in her coffin unchanged, looking as though asleep, for she was still white as snow, red as blood, and her hair was as black as ebony. At last the son of a king chanced to wander into the forest, and came to the dwarf's house for a night's shelter. He saw the coffin on the mountain with the beautiful Snowdrop in it, and read what was written there in letters of gold. Then he said to the dwarfs, "Let me have the coffin! I will give you whatever you like to ask for it."

But the dwarfs answered, "We would not part with it for all the gold in the world."

He said again, "Yet give it me; for I cannot live without seeing Snowdrop, and though she is dead, I will prize and honor her as my beloved."

Then the good dwarfs took pity on him, and gave him the coffin. The prince had it borne away by his ser-

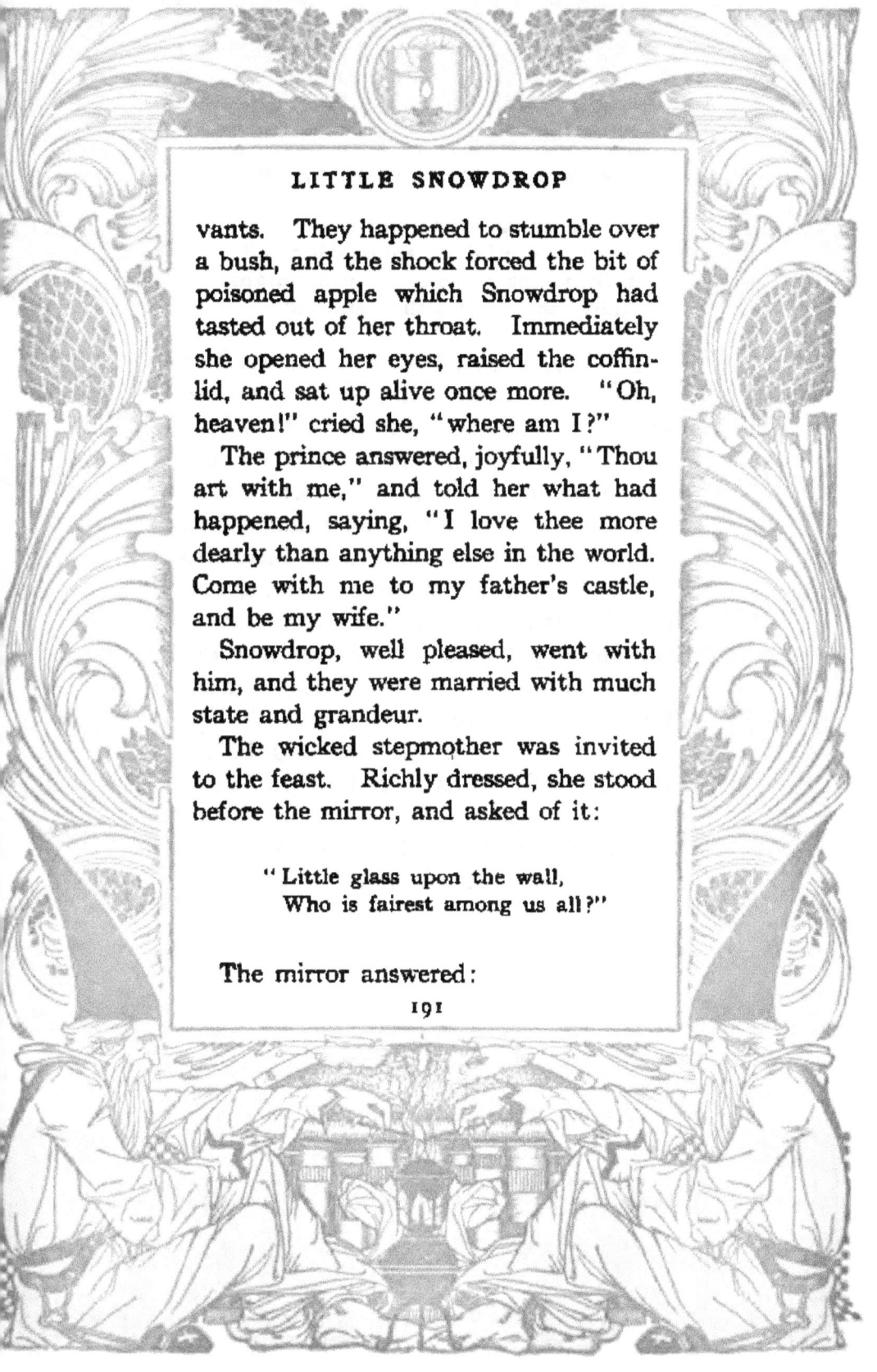

vants. They happened to stumble over a bush, and the shock forced the bit of poisoned apple which Snowdrop had tasted out of her throat. Immediately she opened her eyes, raised the coffin-lid, and sat up alive once more. "Oh, heaven!" cried she, "where am I?"

The prince answered, joyfully, "Thou art with me," and told her what had happened, saying, "I love thee more dearly than anything else in the world. Come with me to my father's castle, and be my wife."

Snowdrop, well pleased, went with him, and they were married with much state and grandeur.

The wicked stepmother was invited to the feast. Richly dressed, she stood before the mirror, and asked of it:

> "Little glass upon the wall,
> Who is fairest among us all?"

The mirror answered:

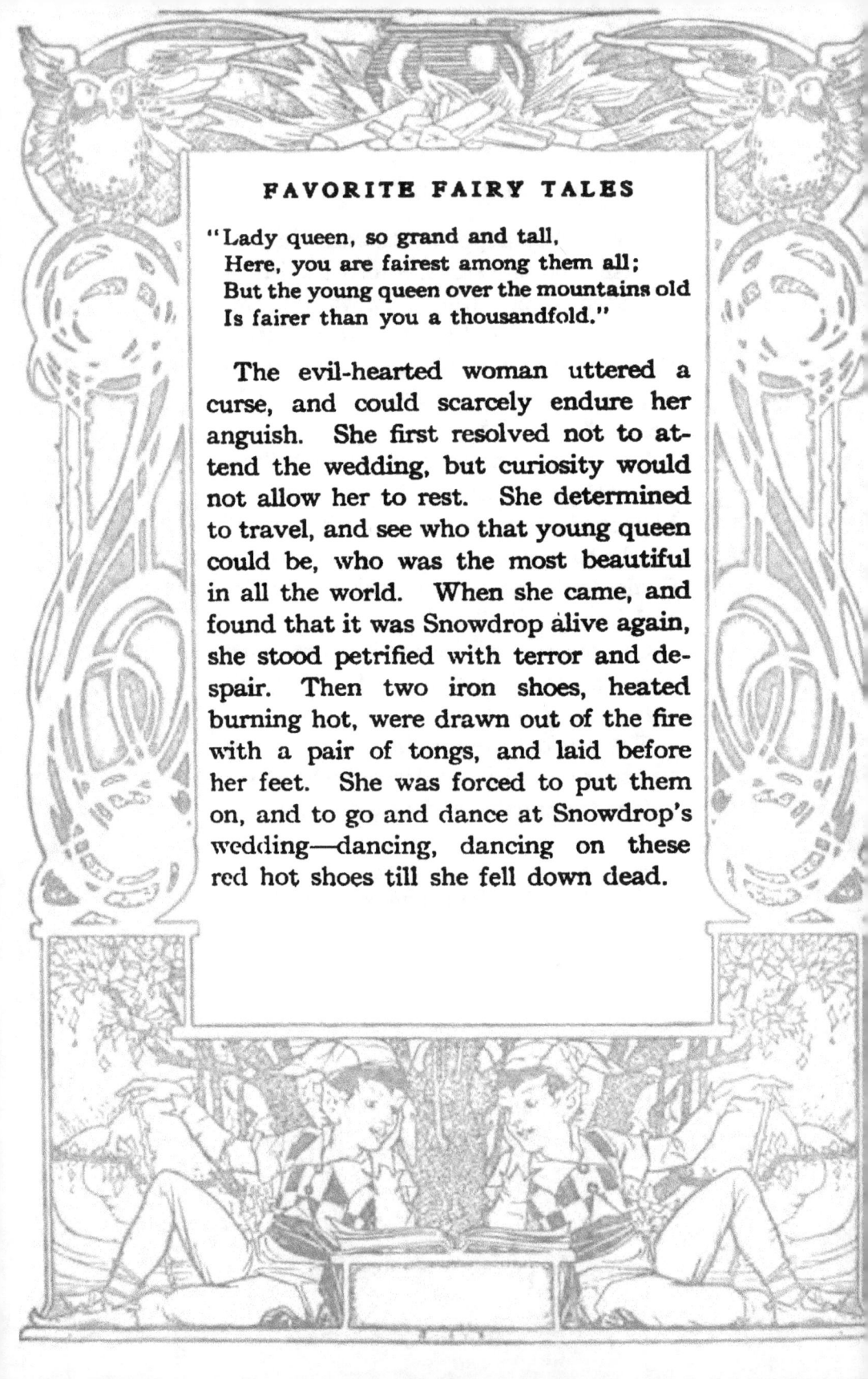

"Lady queen, so grand and tall,
  Here, you are fairest among them all;
  But the young queen over the mountains old
  Is fairer than you a thousandfold."

The evil-hearted woman uttered a curse, and could scarcely endure her anguish. She first resolved not to attend the wedding, but curiosity would not allow her to rest. She determined to travel, and see who that young queen could be, who was the most beautiful in all the world. When she came, and found that it was Snowdrop alive again, she stood petrified with terror and despair. Then two iron shoes, heated burning hot, were drawn out of the fire with a pair of tongs, and laid before her feet. She was forced to put them on, and to go and dance at Snowdrop's wedding—dancing, dancing on these red hot shoes till she fell down dead.

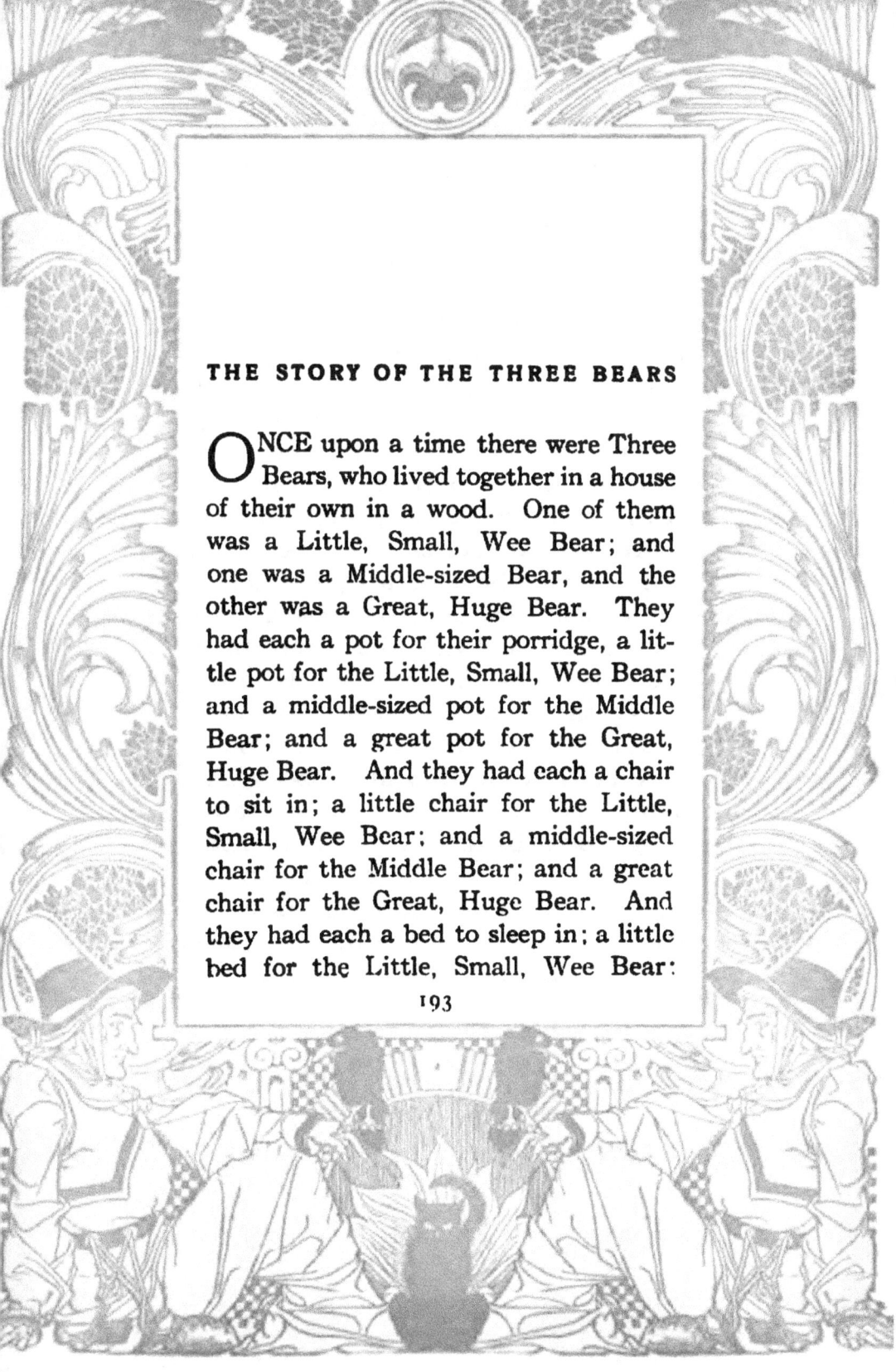

THE STORY OF THE THREE BEARS

ONCE upon a time there were Three Bears, who lived together in a house of their own in a wood. One of them was a Little, Small, Wee Bear; and one was a Middle-sized Bear, and the other was a Great, Huge Bear. They had each a pot for their porridge, a little pot for the Little, Small, Wee Bear; and a middle-sized pot for the Middle Bear; and a great pot for the Great, Huge Bear. And they had each a chair to sit in; a little chair for the Little, Small, Wee Bear; and a middle-sized chair for the Middle Bear; and a great chair for the Great, Huge Bear. And they had each a bed to sleep in; a little bed for the Little, Small, Wee Bear:

and a middle-sized bed for the Middle Bear; and a great bed for the Great, Huge Bear.

One day, after they had made the porridge for their breakfast, and poured it into their porridge-pots, they walked out into the wood while the porridge was cooling, that they might not burn their mouths by beginning too soon to eat it. And while they were walking a little old woman came to the house. She could not have been a good, honest old woman; for, first, she looked in at the window, and then she peeped in at the key-hole; and, seeing nobody in the house, she lifted the latch. The door was not fastened, because the bears were good bears, who did nobody any harm, and never suspected that anybody would harm them. So the little old woman opened the door and went in, and well pleased she was when she saw the porridge on the table. If she had been a good little old woman she

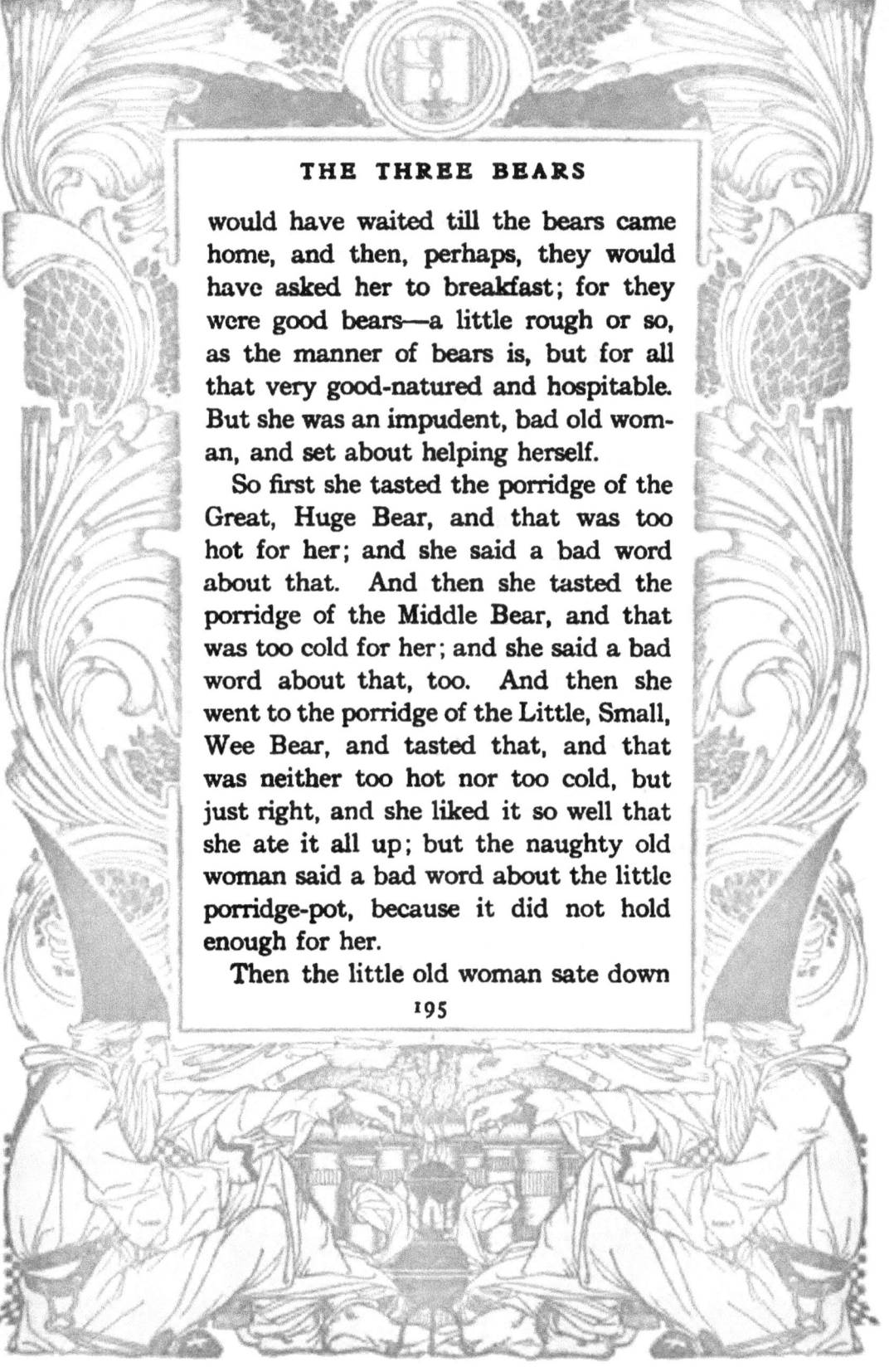

would have waited till the bears came
home, and then, perhaps, they would
have asked her to breakfast; for they
were good bears—a little rough or so,
as the manner of bears is, but for all
that very good-natured and hospitable.
But she was an impudent, bad old woman, and set about helping herself.

So first she tasted the porridge of the
Great, Huge Bear, and that was too
hot for her; and she said a bad word
about that. And then she tasted the
porridge of the Middle Bear, and that
was too cold for her; and she said a bad
word about that, too. And then she
went to the porridge of the Little, Small,
Wee Bear, and tasted that, and that
was neither too hot nor too cold, but
just right, and she liked it so well that
she ate it all up; but the naughty old
woman said a bad word about the little
porridge-pot, because it did not hold
enough for her.

Then the little old woman sate down

in the chair of the Great, Huge Bear,
and that was too hard for her. And
then she sate down in the chair of the
Middle Bear, and that was too soft for
her. And then she sate down in the
chair of the Little, Small, Wee Bear, and
that was neither too hard nor too soft,
but just right. So she seated herself
in it, and there she sate till the bottom
of the chair came out, and down came
she, plump upon the ground. And the
naughty old woman said a wicked word
about that, too.

Then the little old woman went up-
stairs into the bedchamber in which
the three bears slept. And first she
lay down upon the bed of the Great,
Huge Bear; but that was too high at
the head for her. And next she lay
down upon the bed of the Middle Bear;
and that was too high at the foot for
her. And then she lay down upon the
bed of the Little, Small, Wee Bear; and
that was neither too high at the head

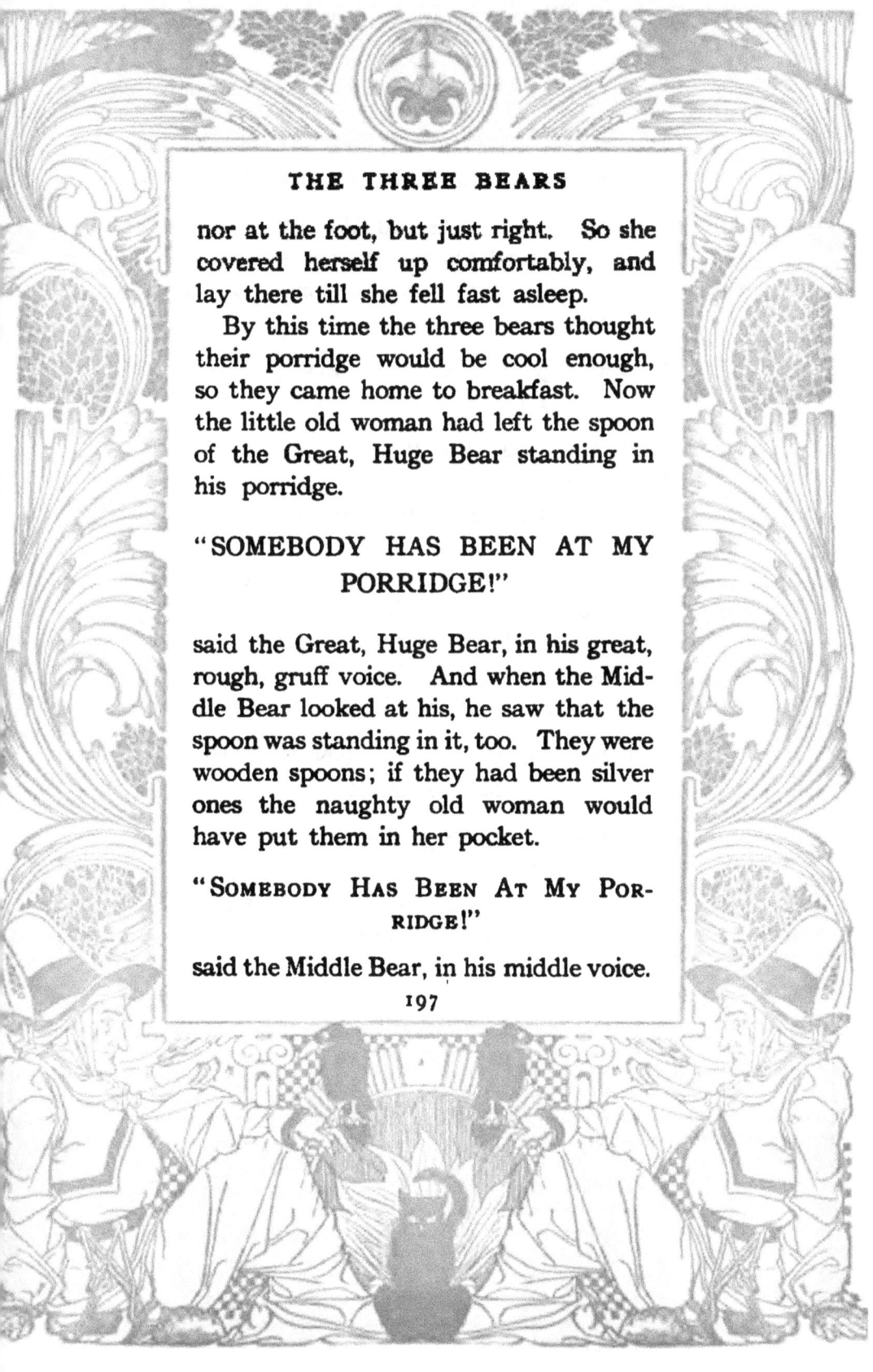

nor at the foot, but just right. So she covered herself up comfortably, and lay there till she fell fast asleep.

By this time the three bears thought their porridge would be cool enough, so they came home to breakfast. Now the little old woman had left the spoon of the Great, Huge Bear standing in his porridge.

"SOMEBODY HAS BEEN AT MY PORRIDGE!"

said the Great, Huge Bear, in his great, rough, gruff voice. And when the Middle Bear looked at his, he saw that the spoon was standing in it, too. They were wooden spoons; if they had been silver ones the naughty old woman would have put them in her pocket.

"SOMEBODY HAS BEEN AT MY PORRIDGE!"

said the Middle Bear, in his middle voice.

197

Then the Little, Small, Wee Bear looked at his, and there was the spoon in the porridge-pot, but the porridge was all gone.

"Somebody has been at my porridge, and has eaten it all up!"

said the Little, Small, Wee Bear, in his little, small, wee voice.

Upon this the three bears, seeing that some one had entered their house, and eaten up the Little, Small, Wee Bear's breakfast, began to look about them. Now the little old woman had not put the hard cushion straight when she rose from the chair of the Great, Huge Bear.

"SOMEBODY HAS BEEN SITTING IN MY CHAIR!"

said the Great, Huge Bear, in his great, rough, gruff voice.

And the little old woman had squatted down the soft cushion of the Middle Bear.

THE THREE BEARS

"SOMEBODY HAS BEEN SITTING IN MY CHAIR!"

said the Middle Bear, in his middle voice.

And you know what the little old woman had done to the third chair.

"Somebody has been sitting in my chair, and has sate the bottom of it out!"

said the Little, Small, Wee Bear, in his little, small, wee voice.

Then the three bears thought it necessary that they should make further search, so they went up-stairs into their bedchamber. Now the little old woman had pulled the pillow of the Great, Huge Bear out of its place.

"SOMEBODY HAS BEEN LYING IN MY BED!"

said the Great, Huge Bear, in his great, rough, gruff voice.

And the little old woman had pulled

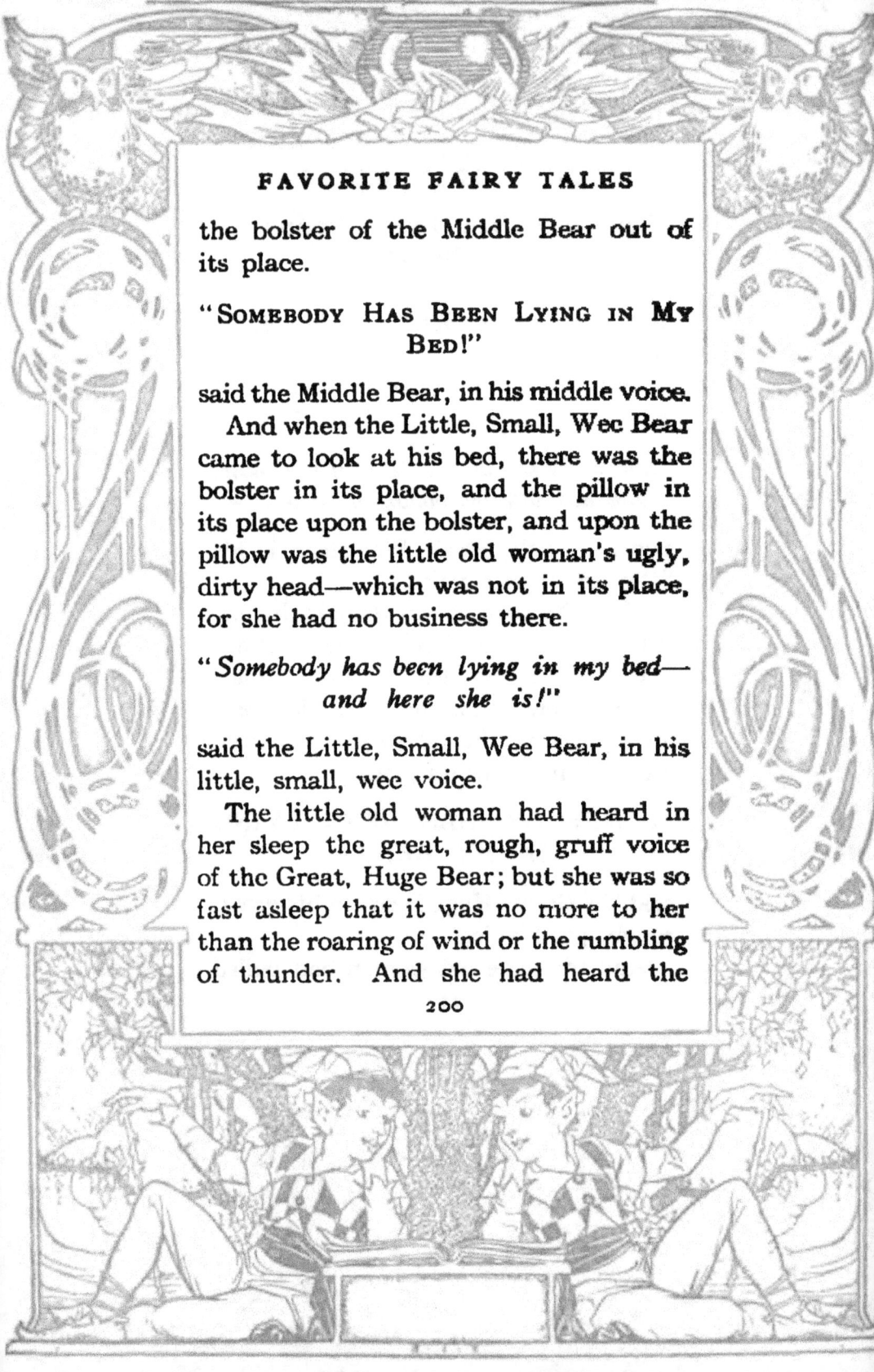

the bolster of the Middle Bear out of
its place.

"SOMEBODY HAS BEEN LYING IN MY
BED!"

said the Middle Bear, in his middle voice.

And when the Little, Small, Wee Bear
came to look at his bed, there was the
bolster in its place, and the pillow in
its place upon the bolster, and upon the
pillow was the little old woman's ugly,
dirty head—which was not in its place,
for she had no business there.

*"Somebody has been lying in my bed—
and here she is!"*

said the Little, Small, Wee Bear, in his
little, small, wee voice.

The little old woman had heard in
her sleep the great, rough, gruff voice
of the Great, Huge Bear; but she was so
fast asleep that it was no more to her
than the roaring of wind or the rumbling
of thunder. And she had heard the

The voice of the little, small, wee bear awakened her at once

middle voice of the Middle Bear, but it was only as if she had heard some one speaking in a dream. But when she heard the little, small, wee voice of the Little, Small, Wee Bear, it was so sharp and so shrill that it awakened her at once. Up she started; and when she saw the Three Bears on one side of the bed she tumbled herself out at the other and ran to the window. Now the window was open, because the bears, like good, tidy bears as they were, always opened their bedchamber window when they got up in the morning. Out the little old woman jumped; and whether she broke her neck in the fall, or ran into the wood and was lost there, or found her way out of the wood and was taken up by the constable and sent to the House of Correction for a vagrant as she was, I cannot tell. But the Three Bears never saw anything more of her.

From " The Green Fairy Book," edited by Andrew Lang, by the courtesy of Longmans, Green & Co.

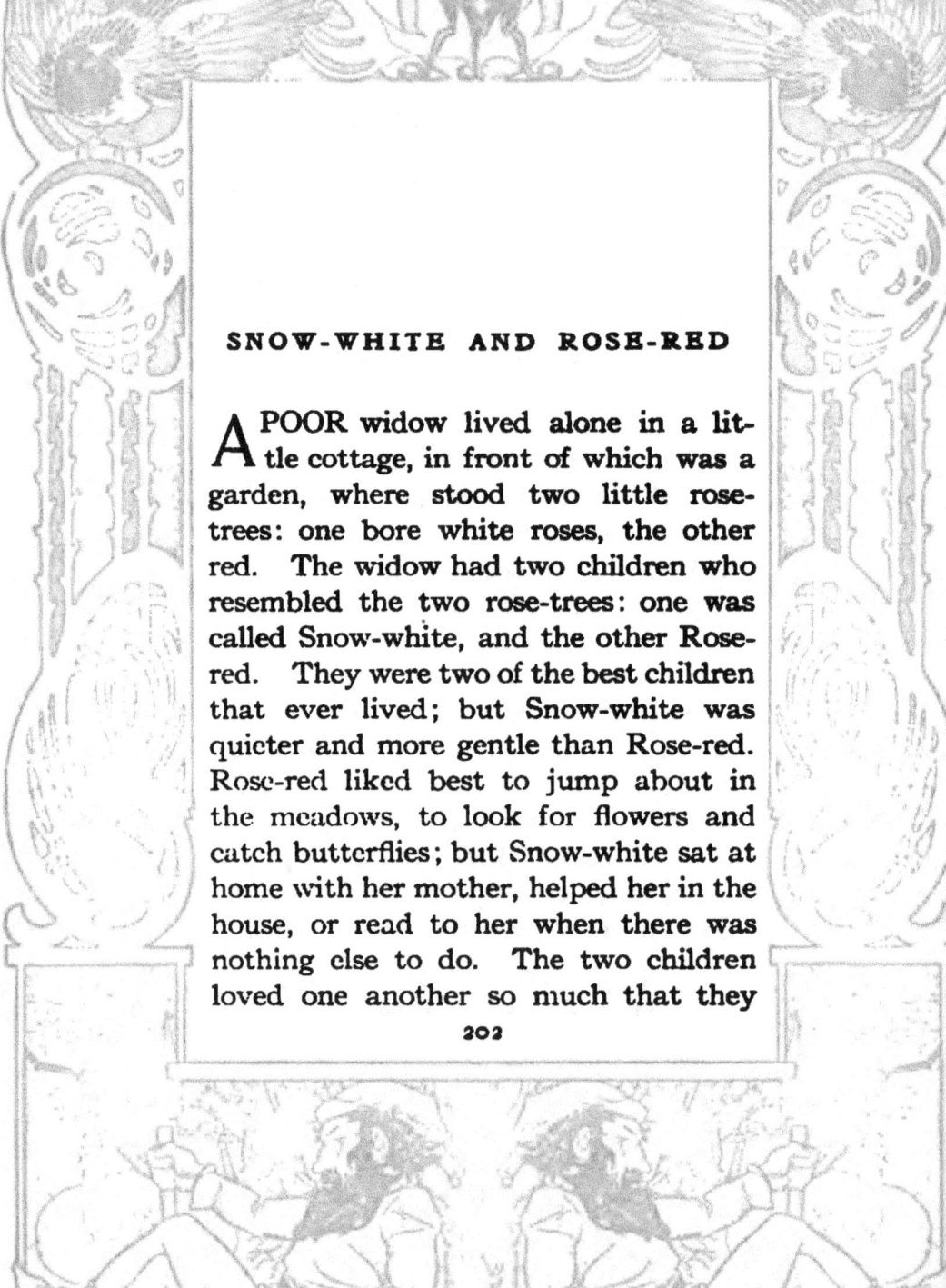

SNOW-WHITE AND ROSE-RED

A POOR widow lived alone in a little cottage, in front of which was a garden, where stood two little rose-trees: one bore white roses, the other red. The widow had two children who resembled the two rose-trees: one was called Snow-white, and the other Rose-red. They were two of the best children that ever lived; but Snow-white was quieter and more gentle than Rose-red. Rose-red liked best to jump about in the meadows, to look for flowers and catch butterflies; but Snow-white sat at home with her mother, helped her in the house, or read to her when there was nothing else to do. The two children loved one another so much that they

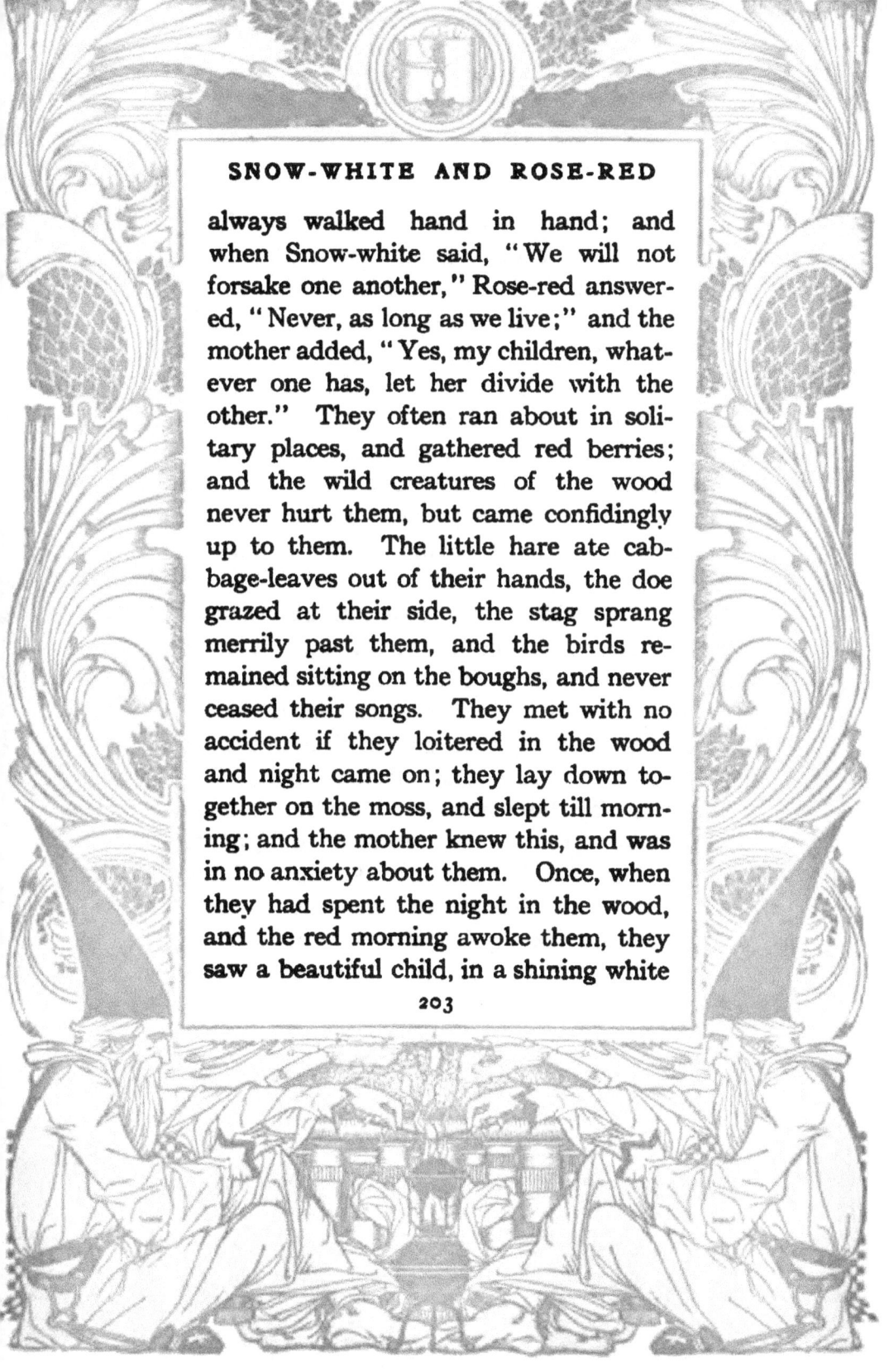

always walked hand in hand; and
when Snow-white said, "We will not
forsake one another," Rose-red answered, "Never, as long as we live;" and the
mother added, "Yes, my children, whatever one has, let her divide with the
other." They often ran about in solitary places, and gathered red berries;
and the wild creatures of the wood
never hurt them, but came confidingly
up to them. The little hare ate cab-
bage-leaves out of their hands, the doe
grazed at their side, the stag sprang
merrily past them, and the birds remained sitting on the boughs, and never
ceased their songs. They met with no
accident if they loitered in the wood
and night came on; they lay down together on the moss, and slept till morning; and the mother knew this, and was
in no anxiety about them. Once, when
they had spent the night in the wood,
and the red morning awoke them, they
saw a beautiful child, in a shining white

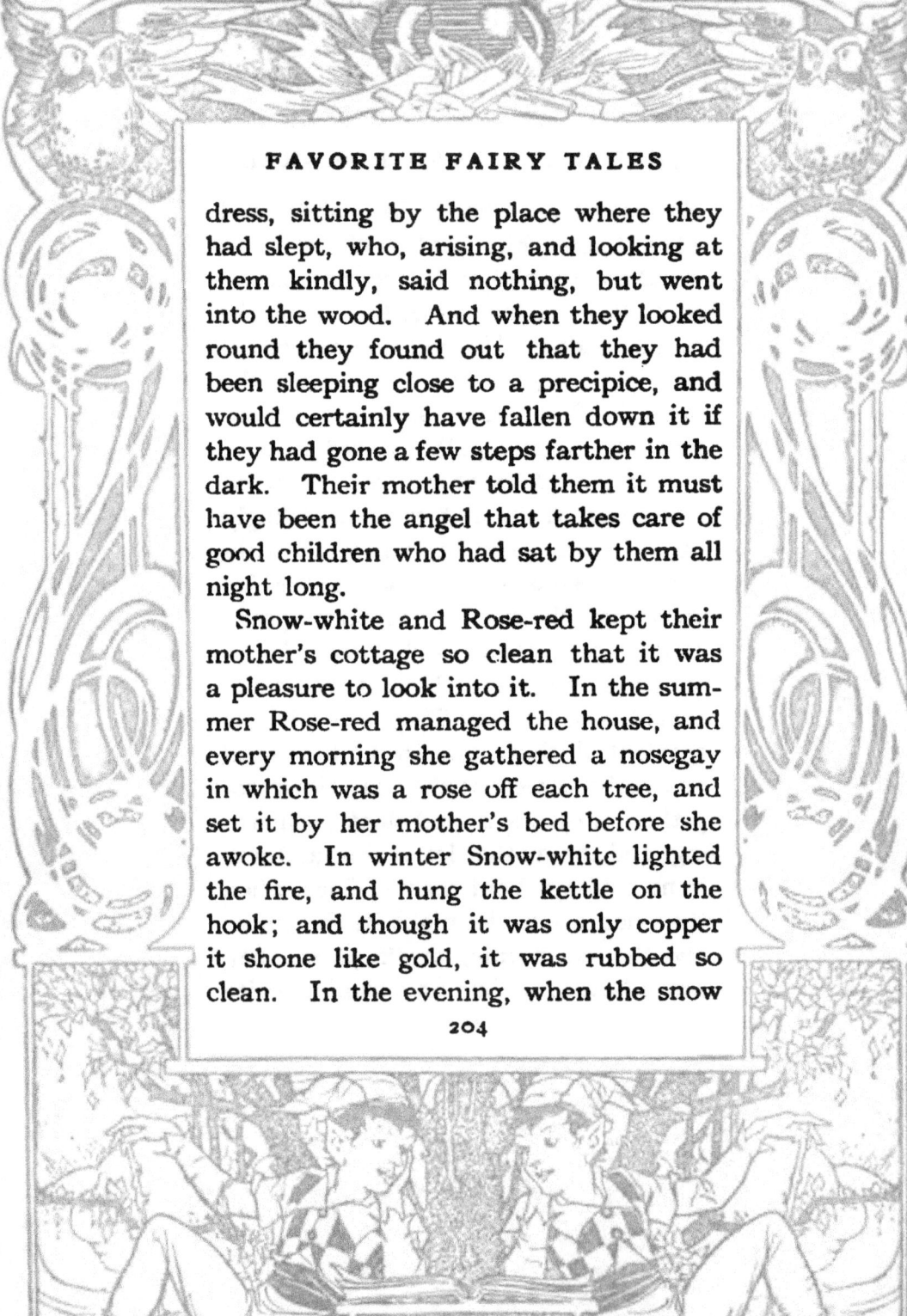

dress, sitting by the place where they had slept, who, arising, and looking at them kindly, said nothing, but went into the wood. And when they looked round they found out that they had been sleeping close to a precipice, and would certainly have fallen down it if they had gone a few steps farther in the dark. Their mother told them it must have been the angel that takes care of good children who had sat by them all night long.

Snow-white and Rose-red kept their mother's cottage so clean that it was a pleasure to look into it. In the summer Rose-red managed the house, and every morning she gathered a nosegay in which was a rose off each tree, and set it by her mother's bed before she awoke. In winter Snow-white lighted the fire, and hung the kettle on the hook; and though it was only copper it shone like gold, it was rubbed so clean. In the evening, when the snow

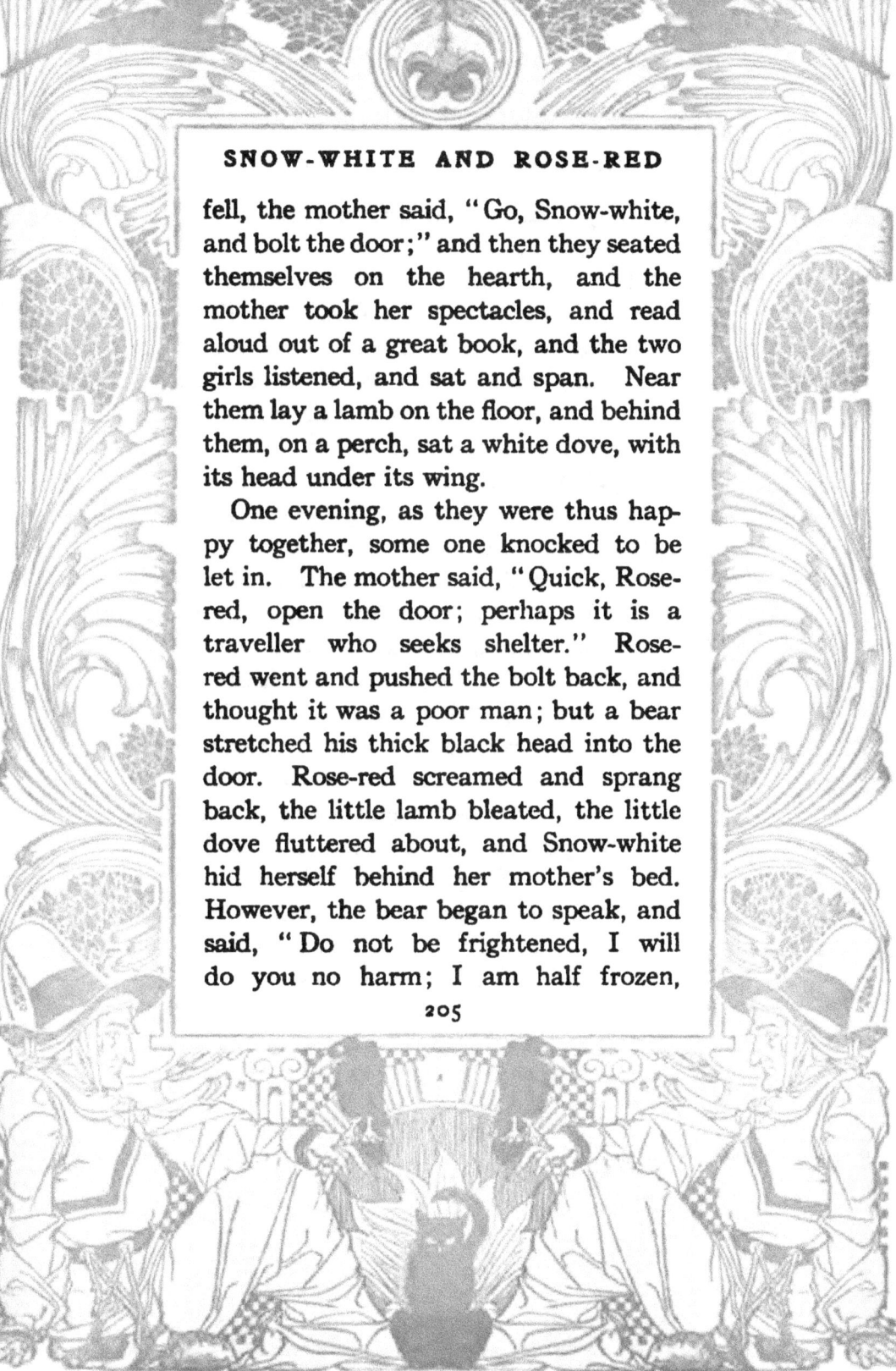

fell, the mother said, "Go, Snow-white,
and bolt the door;" and then they seated
themselves on the hearth, and the
mother took her spectacles, and read
aloud out of a great book, and the two
girls listened, and sat and span. Near
them lay a lamb on the floor, and behind
them, on a perch, sat a white dove, with
its head under its wing.

One evening, as they were thus happy together, some one knocked to be
let in. The mother said, "Quick, Rose-
red, open the door; perhaps it is a
traveller who seeks shelter." Rose-
red went and pushed the bolt back, and
thought it was a poor man; but a bear
stretched his thick black head into the
door. Rose-red screamed and sprang
back, the little lamb bleated, the little
dove fluttered about, and Snow-white
hid herself behind her mother's bed.
However, the bear began to speak, and
said, "Do not be frightened, I will
do you no harm; I am half frozen,

205

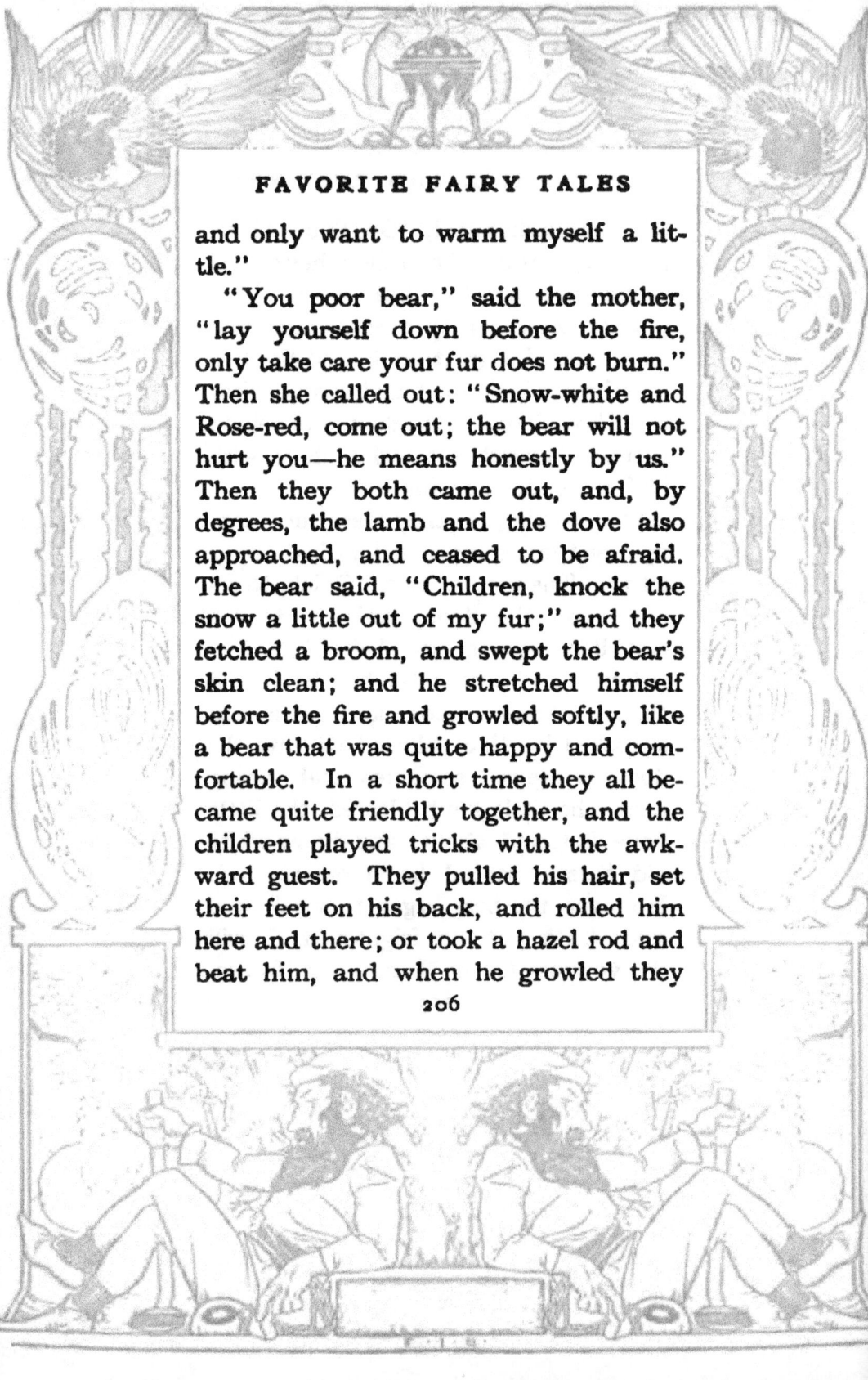

and only want to warm myself a little."

"You poor bear," said the mother, "lay yourself down before the fire, only take care your fur does not burn." Then she called out: "Snow-white and Rose-red, come out; the bear will not hurt you—he means honestly by us." Then they both came out, and, by degrees, the lamb and the dove also approached, and ceased to be afraid. The bear said, "Children, knock the snow a little out of my fur;" and they fetched a broom, and swept the bear's skin clean; and he stretched himself before the fire and growled softly, like a bear that was quite happy and comfortable. In a short time they all became quite friendly together, and the children played tricks with the awkward guest. They pulled his hair, set their feet on his back, and rolled him here and there; or took a hazel rod and beat him, and when he growled they

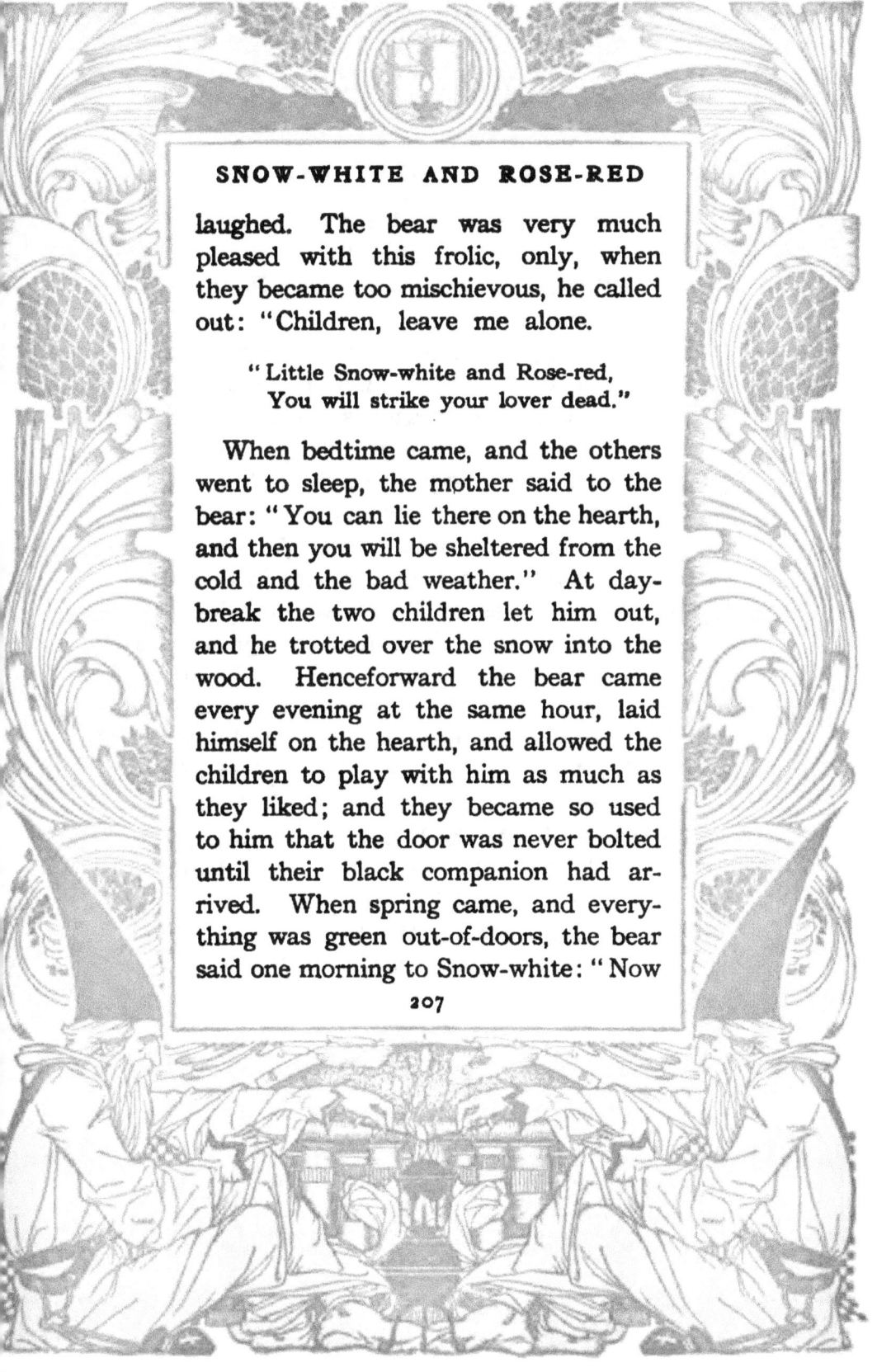

laughed. The bear was very much pleased with this frolic, only, when they became too mischievous, he called out: "Children, leave me alone.

"Little Snow-white and Rose-red,
  You will strike your lover dead."

When bedtime came, and the others went to sleep, the mother said to the bear: "You can lie there on the hearth, and then you will be sheltered from the cold and the bad weather." At daybreak the two children let him out, and he trotted over the snow into the wood. Henceforward the bear came every evening at the same hour, laid himself on the hearth, and allowed the children to play with him as much as they liked; and they became so used to him that the door was never bolted until their black companion had arrived. When spring came, and everything was green out-of-doors, the bear said one morning to Snow-white: " Now

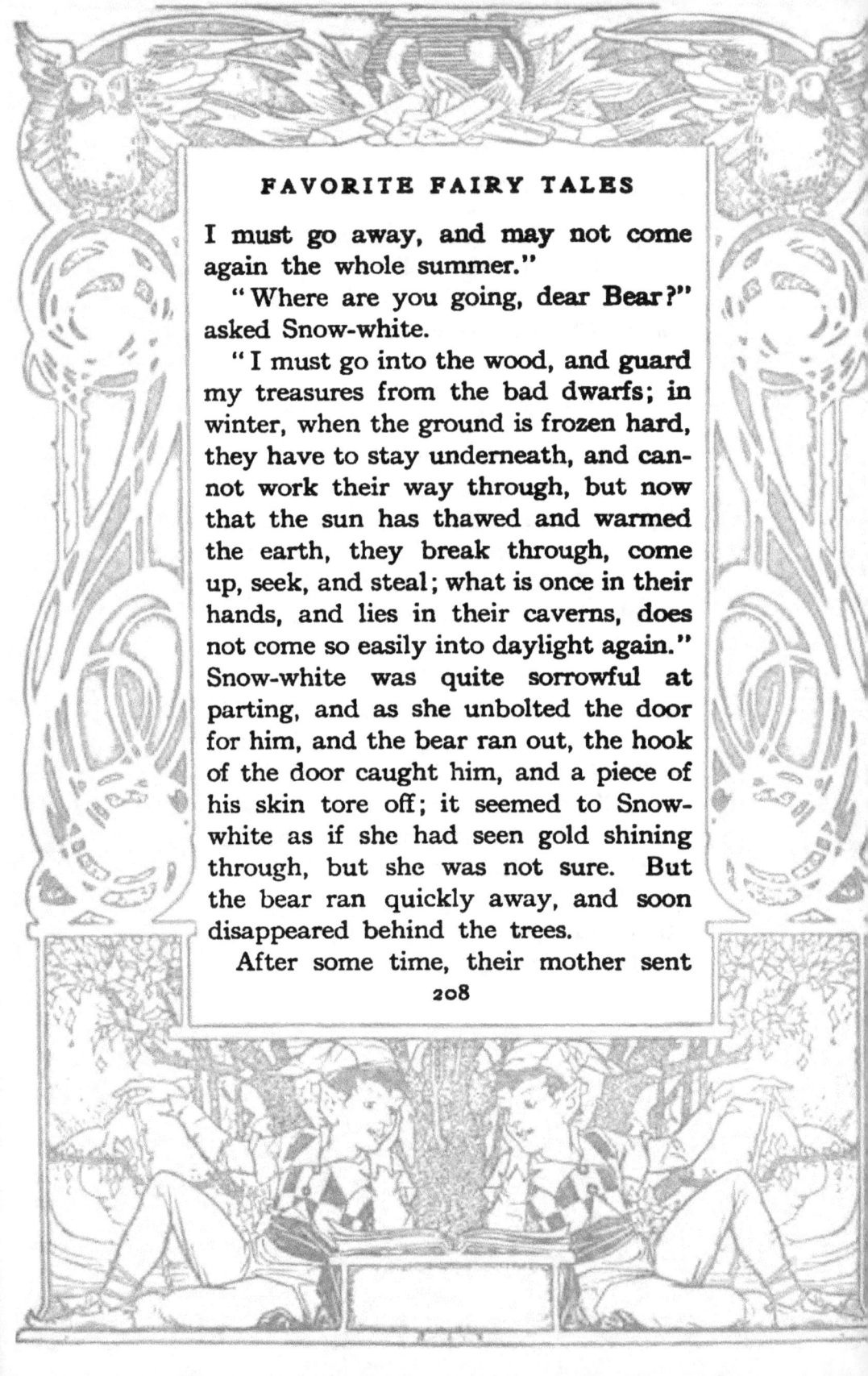

I must go away, and may not come again the whole summer."

"Where are you going, dear Bear?" asked Snow-white.

"I must go into the wood, and guard my treasures from the bad dwarfs; in winter, when the ground is frozen hard, they have to stay underneath, and cannot work their way through, but now that the sun has thawed and warmed the earth, they break through, come up, seek, and steal; what is once in their hands, and lies in their caverns, does not come so easily into daylight again." Snow-white was quite sorrowful at parting, and as she unbolted the door for him, and the bear ran out, the hook of the door caught him, and a piece of his skin tore off; it seemed to Snow-white as if she had seen gold shining through, but she was not sure. But the bear ran quickly away, and soon disappeared behind the trees.

After some time, their mother sent

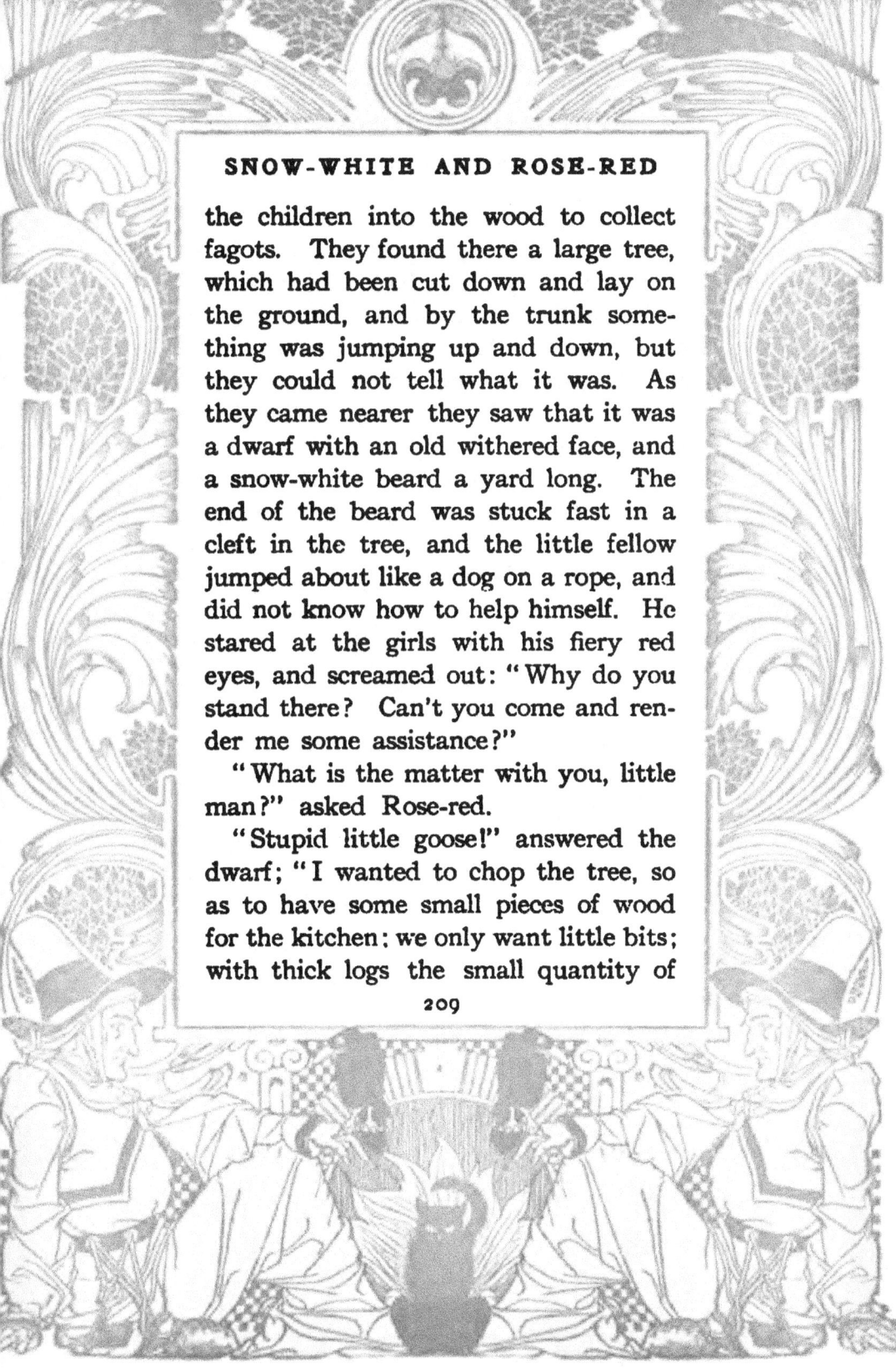

the children into the wood to collect fagots. They found there a large tree, which had been cut down and lay on the ground, and by the trunk something was jumping up and down, but they could not tell what it was. As they came nearer they saw that it was a dwarf with an old withered face, and a snow-white beard a yard long. The end of the beard was stuck fast in a cleft in the tree, and the little fellow jumped about like a dog on a rope, and did not know how to help himself. He stared at the girls with his fiery red eyes, and screamed out: "Why do you stand there? Can't you come and render me some assistance?"

"What is the matter with you, little man?" asked Rose-red.

"Stupid little goose!" answered the dwarf; "I wanted to chop the tree, so as to have some small pieces of wood for the kitchen: we only want little bits; with thick logs the small quantity of

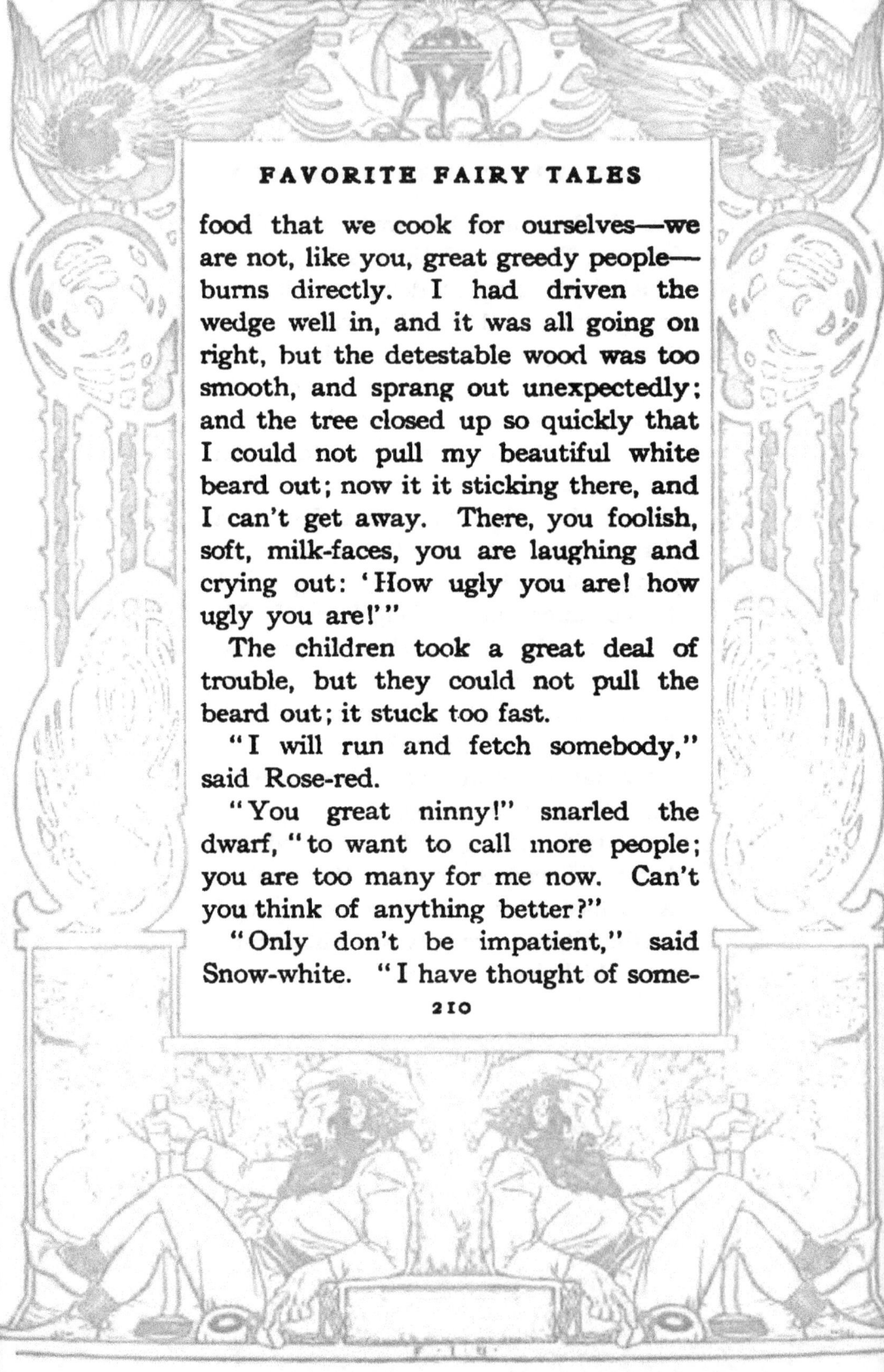

food that we cook for ourselves—we are not, like you, great greedy people— burns directly. I had driven the wedge well in, and it was all going on right, but the detestable wood was too smooth, and sprang out unexpectedly; and the tree closed up so quickly that I could not pull my beautiful white beard out; now it it sticking there, and I can't get away. There, you foolish, soft, milk-faces, you are laughing and crying out: 'How ugly you are! how ugly you are!'"

The children took a great deal of trouble, but they could not pull the beard out; it stuck too fast.

"I will run and fetch somebody," said Rose-red.

"You great ninny!" snarled the dwarf, "to want to call more people; you are too many for me now. Can't you think of anything better?"

"Only don't be impatient," said Snow-white. "I have thought of some-

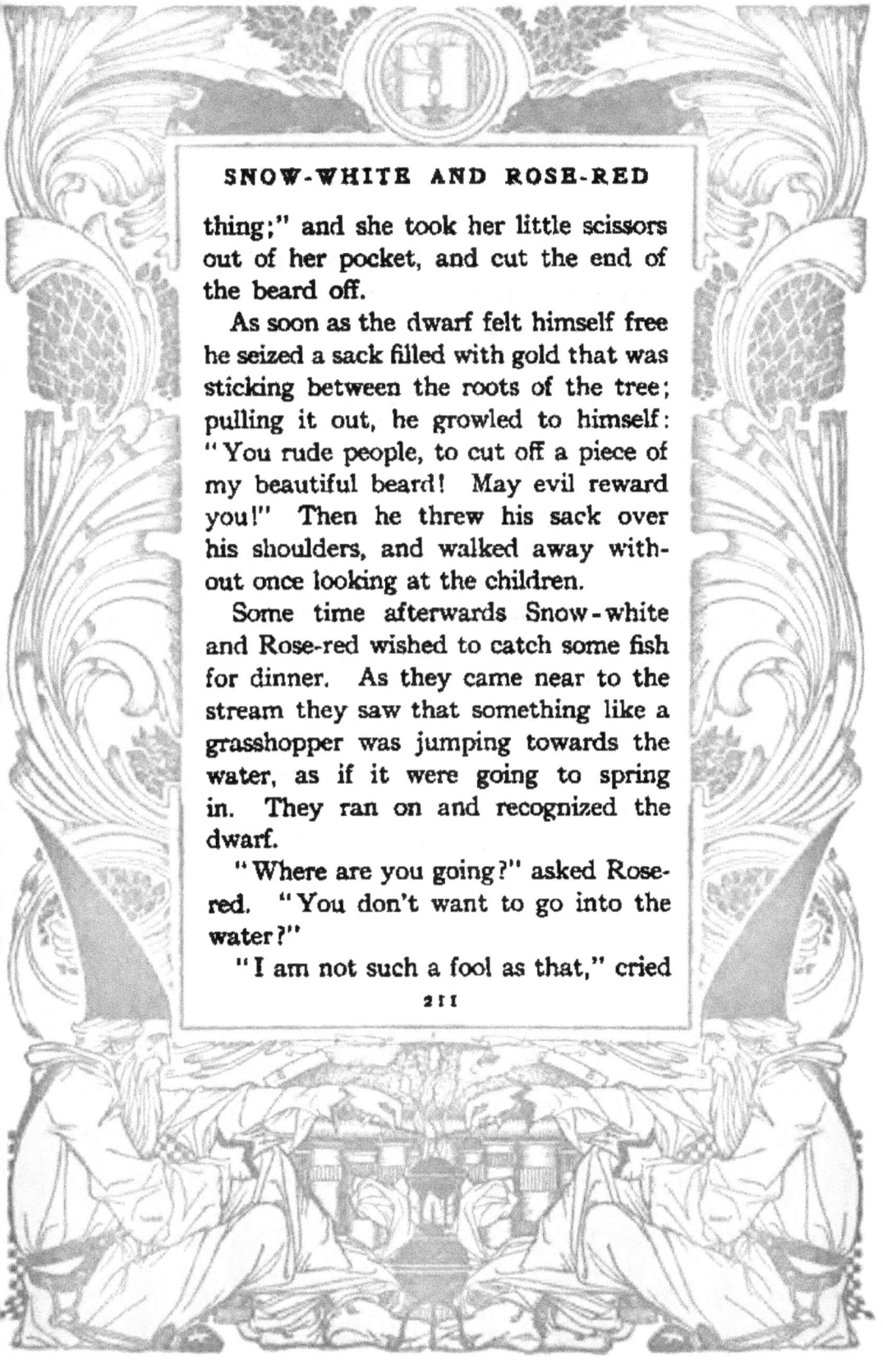

thing;" and she took her little scissors out of her pocket, and cut the end of the beard off.

As soon as the dwarf felt himself free he seized a sack filled with gold that was sticking between the roots of the tree; pulling it out, he growled to himself: "You rude people, to cut off a piece of my beautiful beard! May evil reward you!" Then he threw his sack over his shoulders, and walked away without once looking at the children.

Some time afterwards Snow-white and Rose-red wished to catch some fish for dinner. As they came near to the stream they saw that something like a grasshopper was jumping towards the water, as if it were going to spring in. They ran on and recognized the dwarf.

"Where are you going?" asked Rose-red. "You don't want to go into the water?"

"I am not such a fool as that," cried

211

the dwarf. "Don't you see the detestable fish wants to pull me in?"

The little fellow had been sitting there fishing, and, unluckily, the wind had entangled his beard with the line. When directly afterwards a great fish bit at his hook the weak creature could not pull him out, so the fish was pulling the dwarf into the water. It is true he caught hold of all the reeds and rushes, but that did not help him much; he had to follow all the movements of the fish, and was in imminent danger of being drowned. The girls, coming at the right time, held him fast and tried to get the beard loose from the line, but in vain—beard and line were entangled fast together. There was nothing to do but to pull out the scissors and to cut off the beard, in doing which a little piece of it was lost. When the dwarf saw that, he cried out: "Is that manners, you goose! to disfigure one's face so? Is it not enough that you once

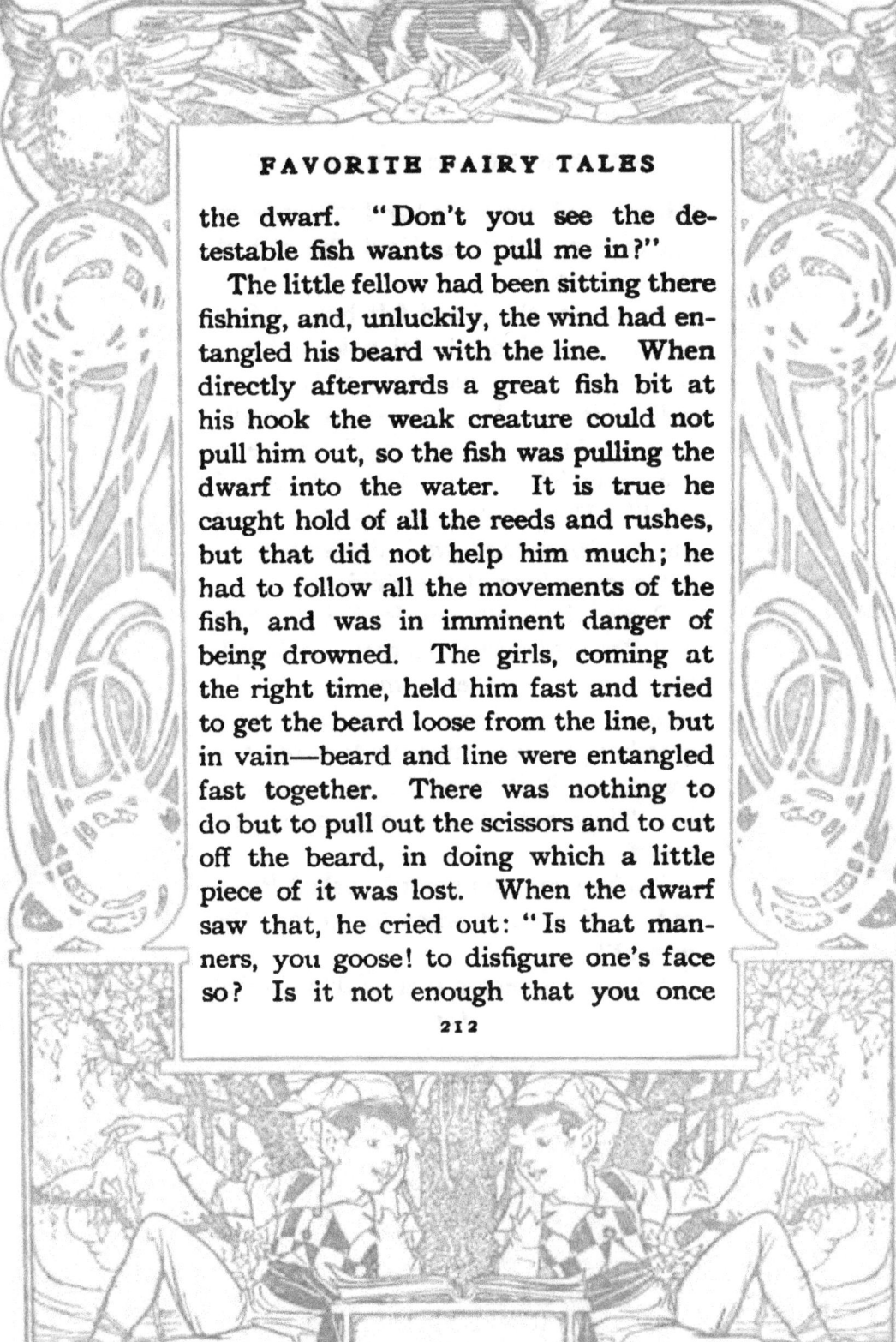

cut my beard shorter? But now you have cut the best part of it off, I dare not be seen by my people. I wish you had had to run, and had lost the soles of your shoes!" Then he fetched a sack of pearls that lay among the rushes, and, without saying a word more, he dragged it away and disappeared behind a stone.

Soon after the mother sent the two girls to the town to buy cotton, needles, cord, and tape. The road led them by a heath, scattered over which lay great masses of rock. There they saw a large bird hovering in the air; it flew round and round just above them, always sinking lower and lower, and at last it settled down by a rock not far distant. Directly after they heard a piercing, wailing cry. They ran up, and saw with horror that the eagle had seized their old acquaintance, the dwarf, and was going to carry him off. The compassionate children instantly seized hold of the little man, held him fast, and struggled so long that the eagle let his prey go.

When the dwarf had recovered from his first fright, he called out, in his shrill voice: "Could not you deal rather more gently with me? You have torn my thin coat all in tatters, awkward, clumsy creatures that you are!" Then he took a sack of precious stones, and slipped behind the rock again into his den. The girls, who were used to his ingratitude, went on their way, and completed their business in the town. As they were coming home again over the heath they surprised the dwarf, who had emptied his sack of precious stones on a little clean place, and had not thought that any one would come by there so late. The evening sun shone on the glittering stones, which looked so beautiful in all their colors that the children could not help standing still to gaze.

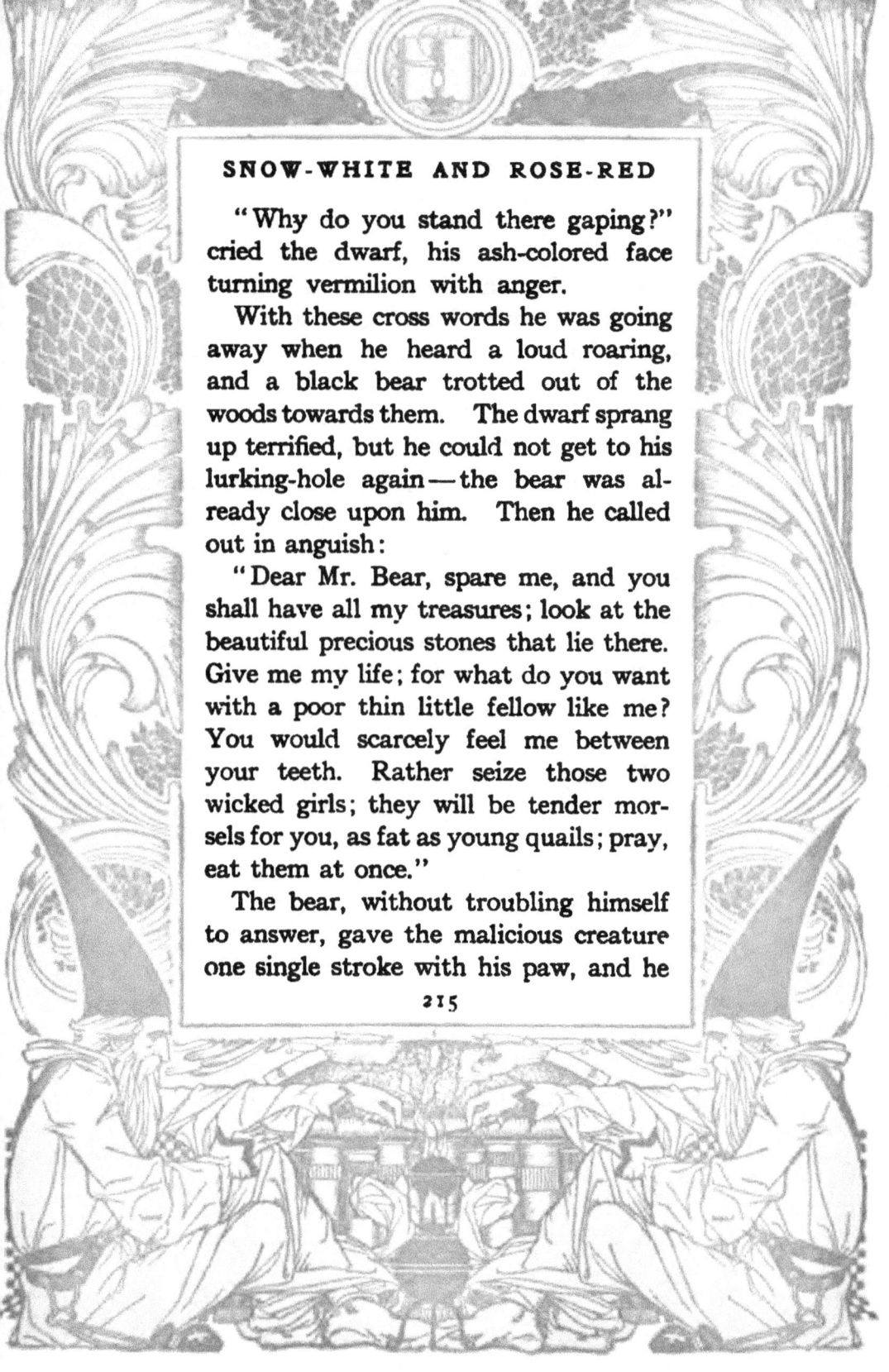

"Why do you stand there gaping?" cried the dwarf, his ash-colored face turning vermilion with anger.

With these cross words he was going away when he heard a loud roaring, and a black bear trotted out of the woods towards them. The dwarf sprang up terrified, but he could not get to his lurking-hole again — the bear was already close upon him. Then he called out in anguish:

"Dear Mr. Bear, spare me, and you shall have all my treasures; look at the beautiful precious stones that lie there. Give me my life; for what do you want with a poor thin little fellow like me? You would scarcely feel me between your teeth. Rather seize those two wicked girls; they will be tender morsels for you, as fat as young quails; pray, eat them at once."

The bear, without troubling himself to answer, gave the malicious creature one single stroke with his paw, and he

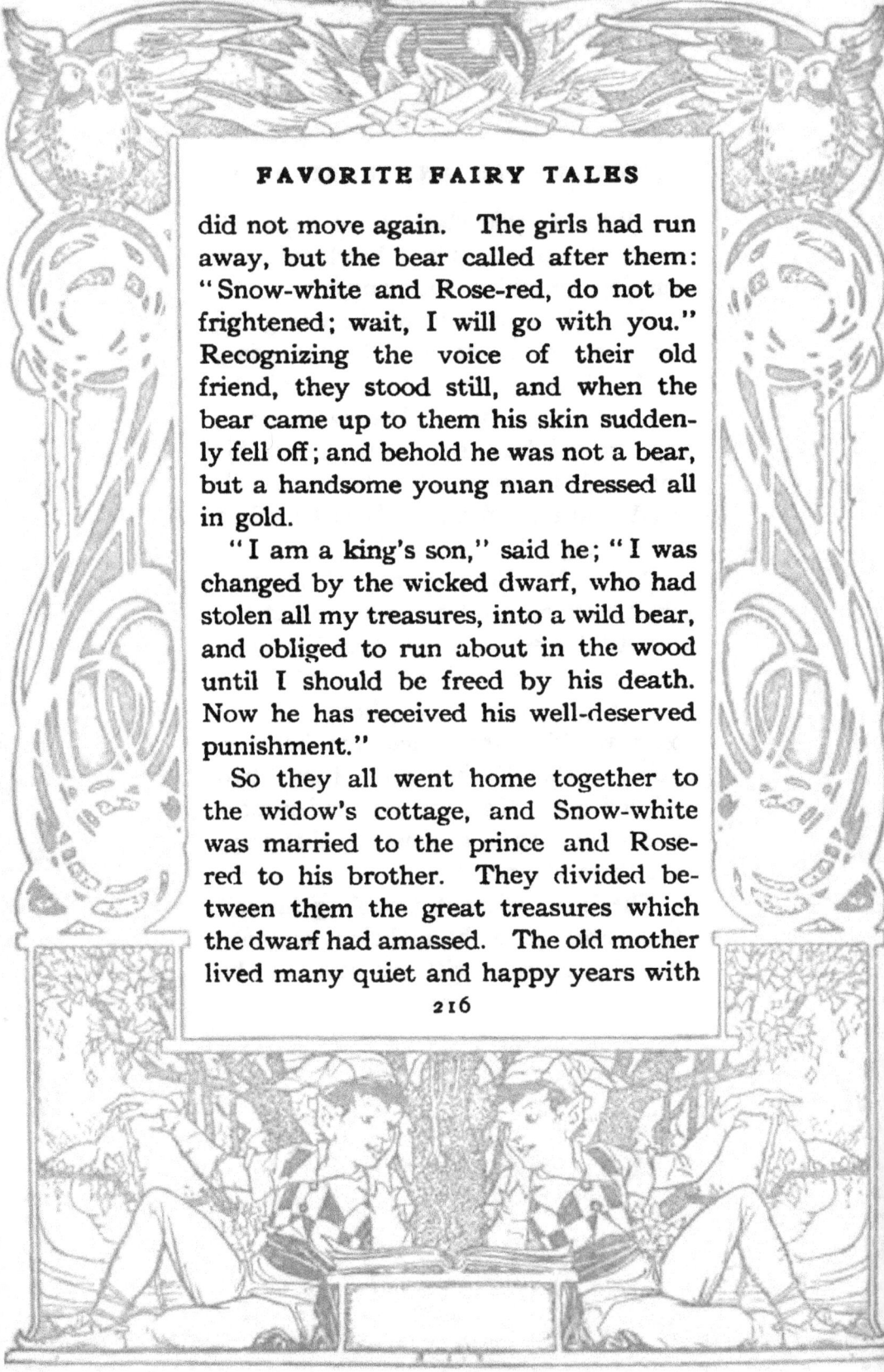

did not move again. The girls had run away, but the bear called after them: "Snow-white and Rose-red, do not be frightened; wait, I will go with you." Recognizing the voice of their old friend, they stood still, and when the bear came up to them his skin suddenly fell off; and behold he was not a bear, but a handsome young man dressed all in gold.

"I am a king's son," said he; "I was changed by the wicked dwarf, who had stolen all my treasures, into a wild bear, and obliged to run about in the wood until I should be freed by his death. Now he has received his well-deserved punishment."

So they all went home together to the widow's cottage, and Snow-white was married to the prince and Rose-red to his brother. They divided between them the great treasures which the dwarf had amassed. The old mother lived many quiet and happy years with

her children; but when she left her cottage for the palace she took the two rose-trees with her, and they stood before her window and bore every year the most beautiful roses—one white and the other red.

15

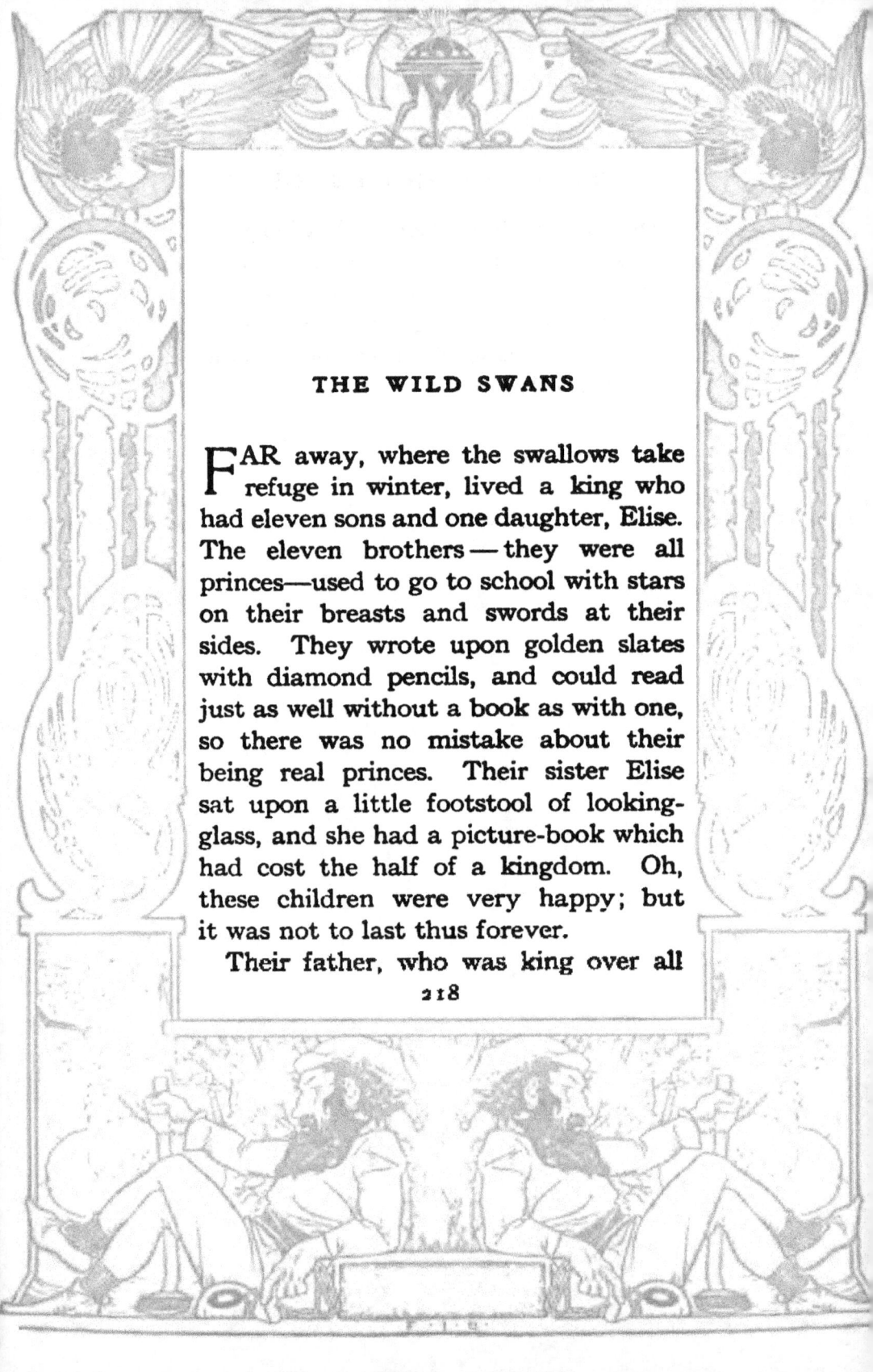

THE WILD SWANS

FAR away, where the swallows take refuge in winter, lived a king who had eleven sons and one daughter, Elise. The eleven brothers — they were all princes—used to go to school with stars on their breasts and swords at their sides. They wrote upon golden slates with diamond pencils, and could read just as well without a book as with one, so there was no mistake about their being real princes. Their sister Elise sat upon a little footstool of looking-glass, and she had a picture-book which had cost the half of a kingdom. Oh, these children were very happy; but it was not to last thus forever.

Their father, who was king over all

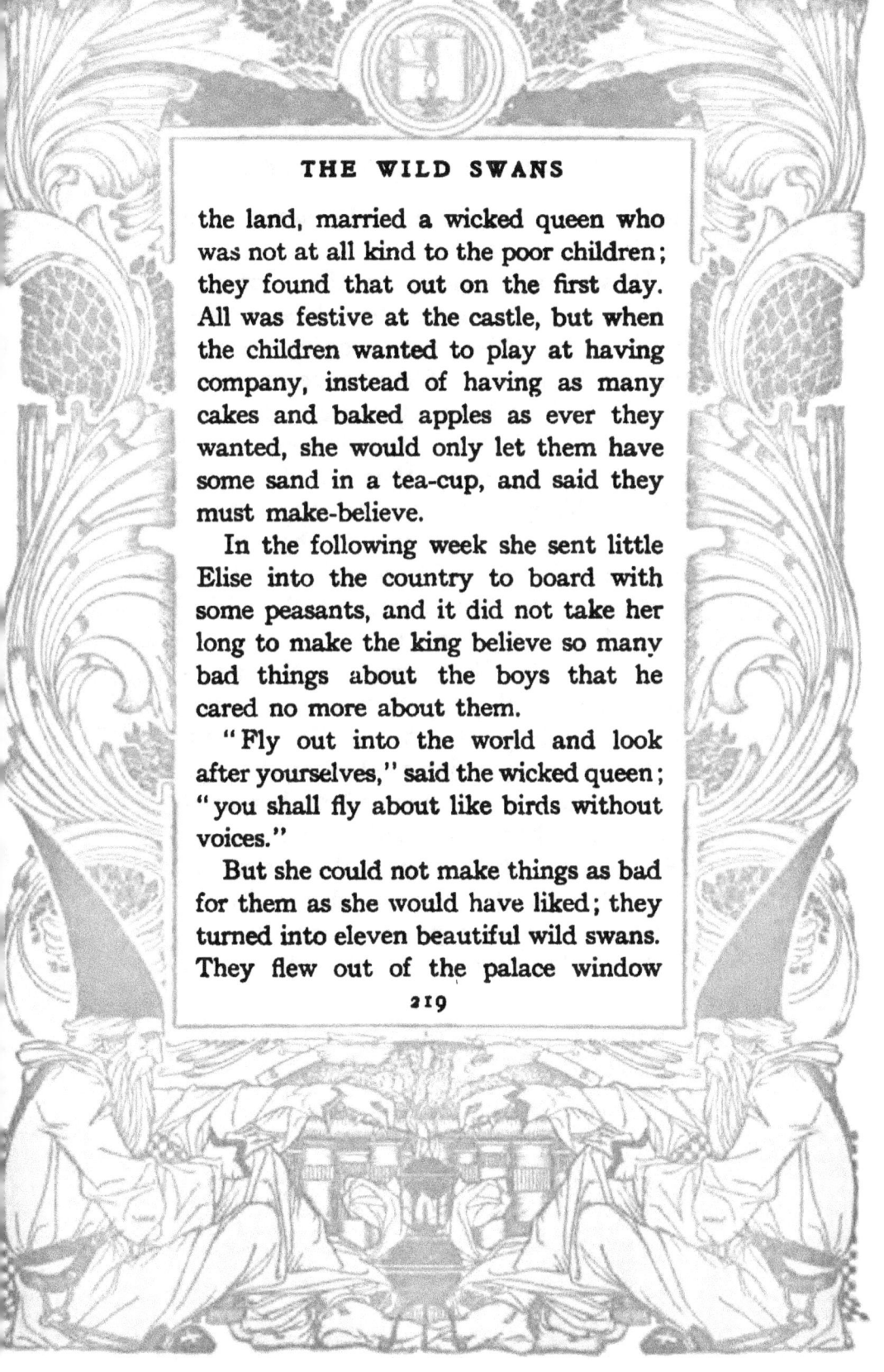

the land, married a wicked queen who was not at all kind to the poor children; they found that out on the first day. All was festive at the castle, but when the children wanted to play at having company, instead of having as many cakes and baked apples as ever they wanted, she would only let them have some sand in a tea-cup, and said they must make-believe.

In the following week she sent little Elise into the country to board with some peasants, and it did not take her long to make the king believe so many bad things about the boys that he cared no more about them.

"Fly out into the world and look after yourselves," said the wicked queen; "you shall fly about like birds without voices."

But she could not make things as bad for them as she would have liked; they turned into eleven beautiful wild swans. They flew out of the palace window

219

with a weird scream, right across the park and the woods.

It was very early in the morning when they came to the place where their sister Elise was sleeping in the peasant's house. They hovered over the roof of the house, turning and twisting their long necks, and flapping their wings; but no one either heard or saw them. They had to fly away again, and they soared up towards the clouds, far out into the wide world, and they settled in a big, dark wood, which stretched right down to the shore.

Poor little Elise stood in the peasant's room, playing with a green leaf, for she had no other toys. She made a little hole in it, which she looked through at the sun, and it seemed to her as if she saw her brothers' bright eyes. Every time the warm sunbeams shone upon her cheek it reminded her of their kisses. One day passed just like another. When the wind whistled through the rose-hedges outside the house, it whispered to the roses: "Who can be prettier than you are?" But the roses shook their heads and answered: "Elise!" And when the old woman sat in the doorway reading her Psalms the wind turned over the leaves and said to the book: "Who can be more pious than you?" "Elise!" answered the book. Both the roses and the book of Psalms only spoke the truth.

She was to go home when she was fifteen, but when the queen saw how pretty she was she got very angry, and her heart was filled with hatred. She would willingly have turned her into a wild swan too, like her brothers, but she did not dare to do it at once, for the king wanted to see his daughter. The queen always went to the bath in the early morning. It was built of marble, and adorned with soft cushions and beautiful carpets.

She took three toads, kissed them,

and said to the first: "Sit upon Elise's head when she comes to the bath, so that she may become sluggish like yourself." "Sit upon her forehead," she said to the second, "that she may become ugly like you, and then her father won't know her! Rest upon her heart," she whispered to the third. "Let an evil spirit come over her, which may be a burden to her." Then she put the toads into the clean water, and a green tinge immediately came over it. She called Elise, undressed her, and made her go into the bath; when she ducked under the water, one of the toads got among her hair, the other got onto her forehead, and the third onto her bosom. But when she stood up three scarlet poppies floated on the water; had not the creatures been poisonous, and kissed by the sorceress, they would have been changed into crimson roses, but yet they became flowers from merely having rested a

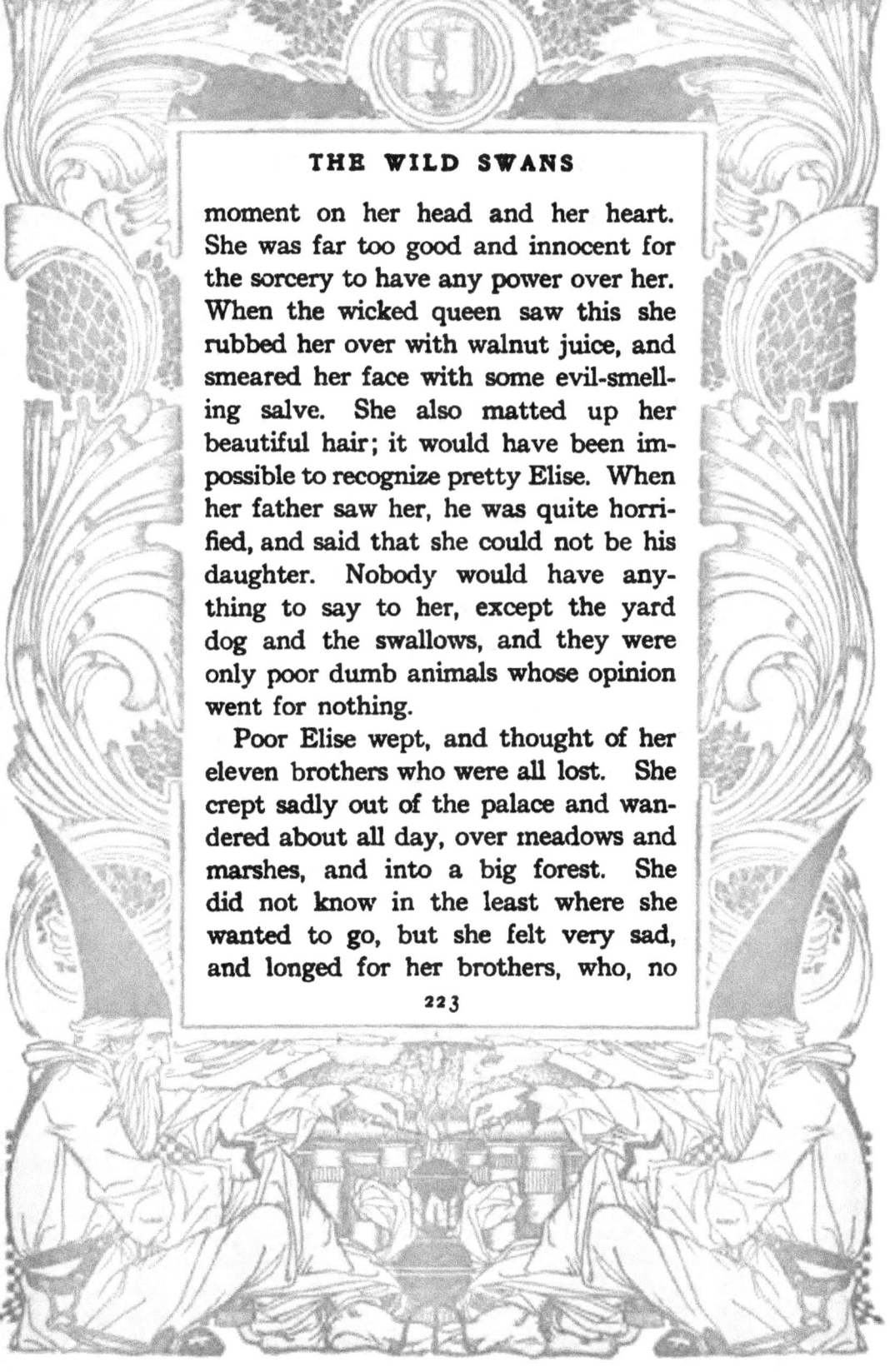

moment on her head and her heart. She was far too good and innocent for the sorcery to have any power over her. When the wicked queen saw this she rubbed her over with walnut juice, and smeared her face with some evil-smelling salve. She also matted up her beautiful hair; it would have been impossible to recognize pretty Elise. When her father saw her, he was quite horrified, and said that she could not be his daughter. Nobody would have anything to say to her, except the yard dog and the swallows, and they were only poor dumb animals whose opinion went for nothing.

Poor Elise wept, and thought of her eleven brothers who were all lost. She crept sadly out of the palace and wandered about all day, over meadows and marshes, and into a big forest. She did not know in the least where she wanted to go, but she felt very sad, and longed for her brothers, who, no

223

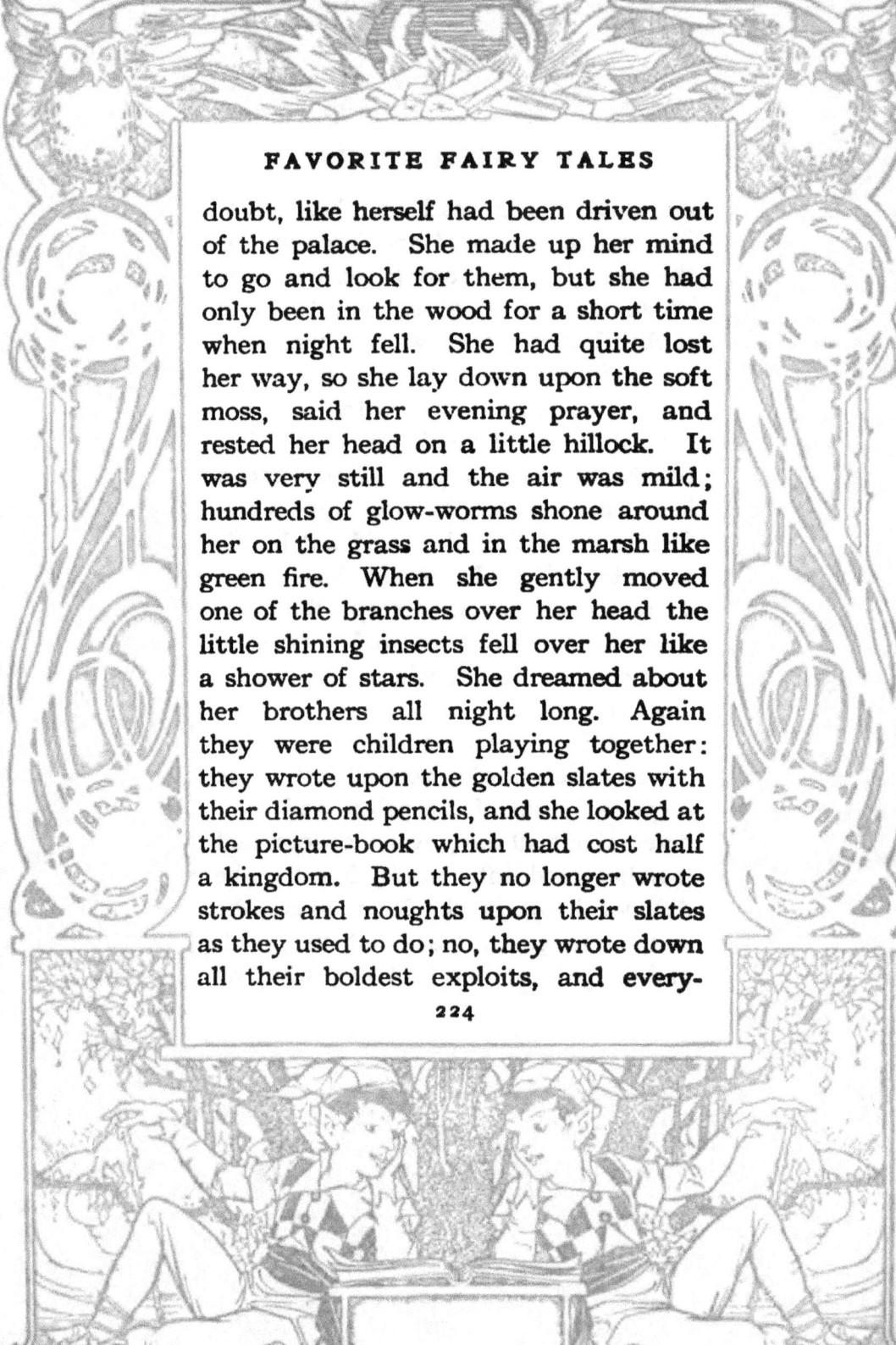

doubt, like herself had been driven out of the palace. She made up her mind to go and look for them, but she had only been in the wood for a short time when night fell. She had quite lost her way, so she lay down upon the soft moss, said her evening prayer, and rested her head on a little hillock. It was very still and the air was mild; hundreds of glow-worms shone around her on the grass and in the marsh like green fire. When she gently moved one of the branches over her head the little shining insects fell over her like a shower of stars. She dreamed about her brothers all night long. Again they were children playing together: they wrote upon the golden slates with their diamond pencils, and she looked at the picture-book which had cost half a kingdom. But they no longer wrote strokes and noughts upon their slates as they used to do; no, they wrote down all their boldest exploits, and every-

thing that they had seen and experienced. Everything in the picture-book was alive, the birds sang, and the people walked out of the book, and spoke to Elise and her brothers. When she turned over a page they skipped back into their places again, so that there should be no confusion among the pictures.

When she woke the sun was already high; it is true she could not see it very well through the thick branches of the lofty forest trees, but the sunbeams cast a golden shimmer around beyond the forest. There was a fresh, delicious scent of grass and herbs in the air, and the birds were almost ready to perch upon her shoulders. She could hear the splashing of water, for there were many springs around, which all flowed into a pond with a lovely sandy bottom. It was surrounded with thick bushes, but there was one place which the stags had trampled down, and Elise passed through the opening to the

water side. It was so transparent that had not the branches been moved by the breeze she must have thought that they were painted on the bottom, so plainly was every leaf reflected, both those on which the sun played, and those which were in shade.

When she saw her own face she was quite frightened, it was so brown and ugly; but when she wet her little hand and rubbed her eyes and forehead her white skin shone through again. Then she took off all her clothes and went into the fresh water. A more beautiful royal child than she could not be found in all the world.

When she had put on her clothes again and plaited her long hair she went to a sparkling spring, and drank some of the water out of the hollow of her hand. Then she wandered farther into the wood, though where she was going she had not the least idea. She thought of her brothers, and she thought

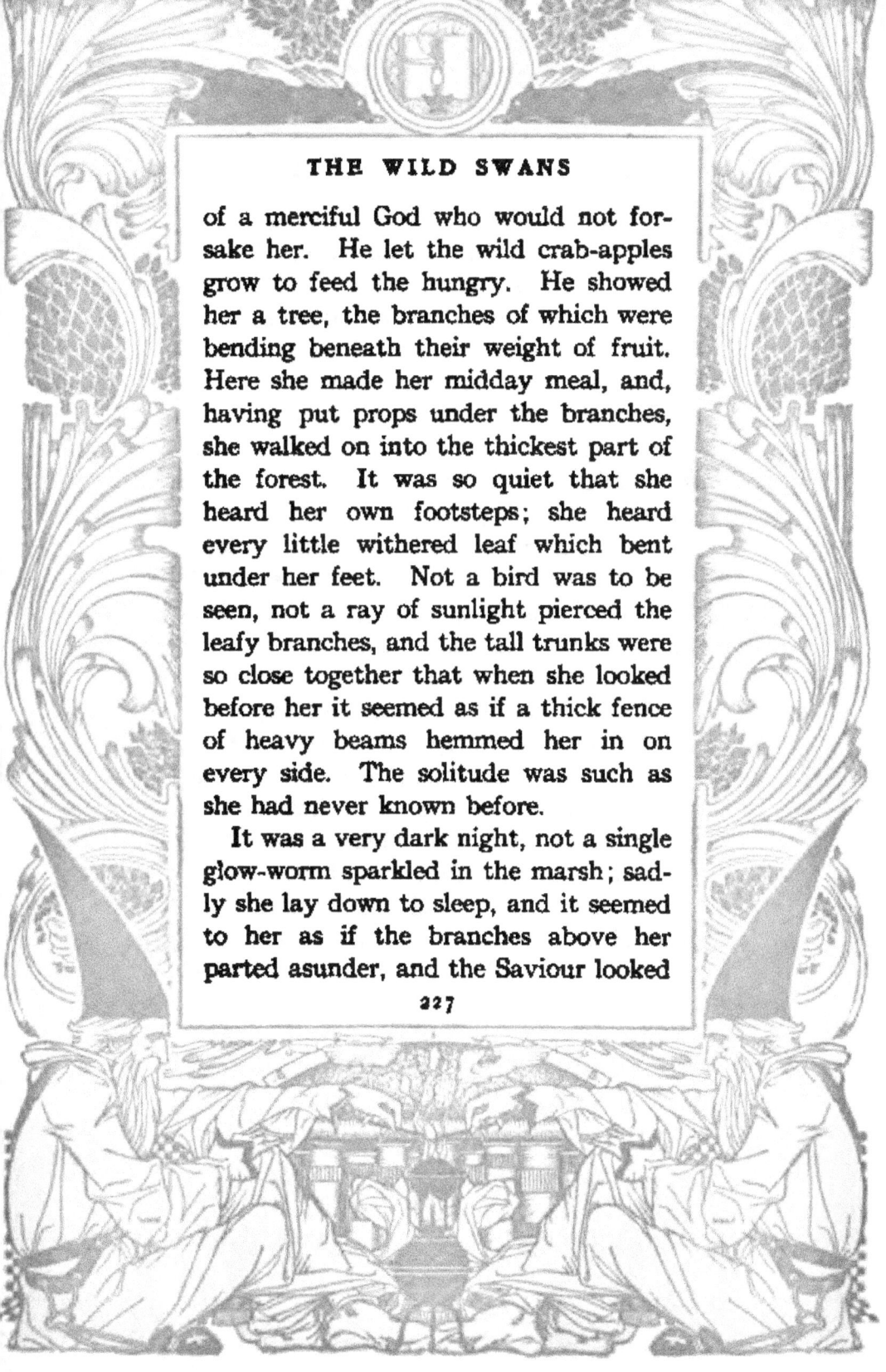

of a merciful God who would not forsake her. He let the wild crab-apples
grow to feed the hungry. He showed
her a tree, the branches of which were
bending beneath their weight of fruit.
Here she made her midday meal, and,
having put props under the branches,
she walked on into the thickest part of
the forest. It was so quiet that she
heard her own footsteps; she heard
every little withered leaf which bent
under her feet. Not a bird was to be
seen, not a ray of sunlight pierced the
leafy branches, and the tall trunks were
so close together that when she looked
before her it seemed as if a thick fence
of heavy beams hemmed her in on
every side. The solitude was such as
she had never known before.

It was a very dark night, not a single
glow-worm sparkled in the marsh; sadly she lay down to sleep, and it seemed
to her as if the branches above her
parted asunder, and the Saviour looked

down upon her with His loving eyes, and little angels' heads peeped out above His head and under His arms.

When she woke in the morning she was not sure if she had dreamed this, or whether it was really true.

She walked a little farther, when she met an old woman with a basket full of berries, of which she gave her some. Elise asked if she had seen eleven princes ride through the wood. "No," said the old woman, "but yesterday I saw eleven swans, with golden crowns upon their heads, swimming in the stream close by here."

She led Elise a little farther to a slope, at the foot of which the stream meandered. The trees on either bank stretched out their rich, leafy branches towards each other, and where, from their natural growth, they could not reach each other, they had torn their roots out of the ground, and leaned over the water so as to interlace their branches.

228

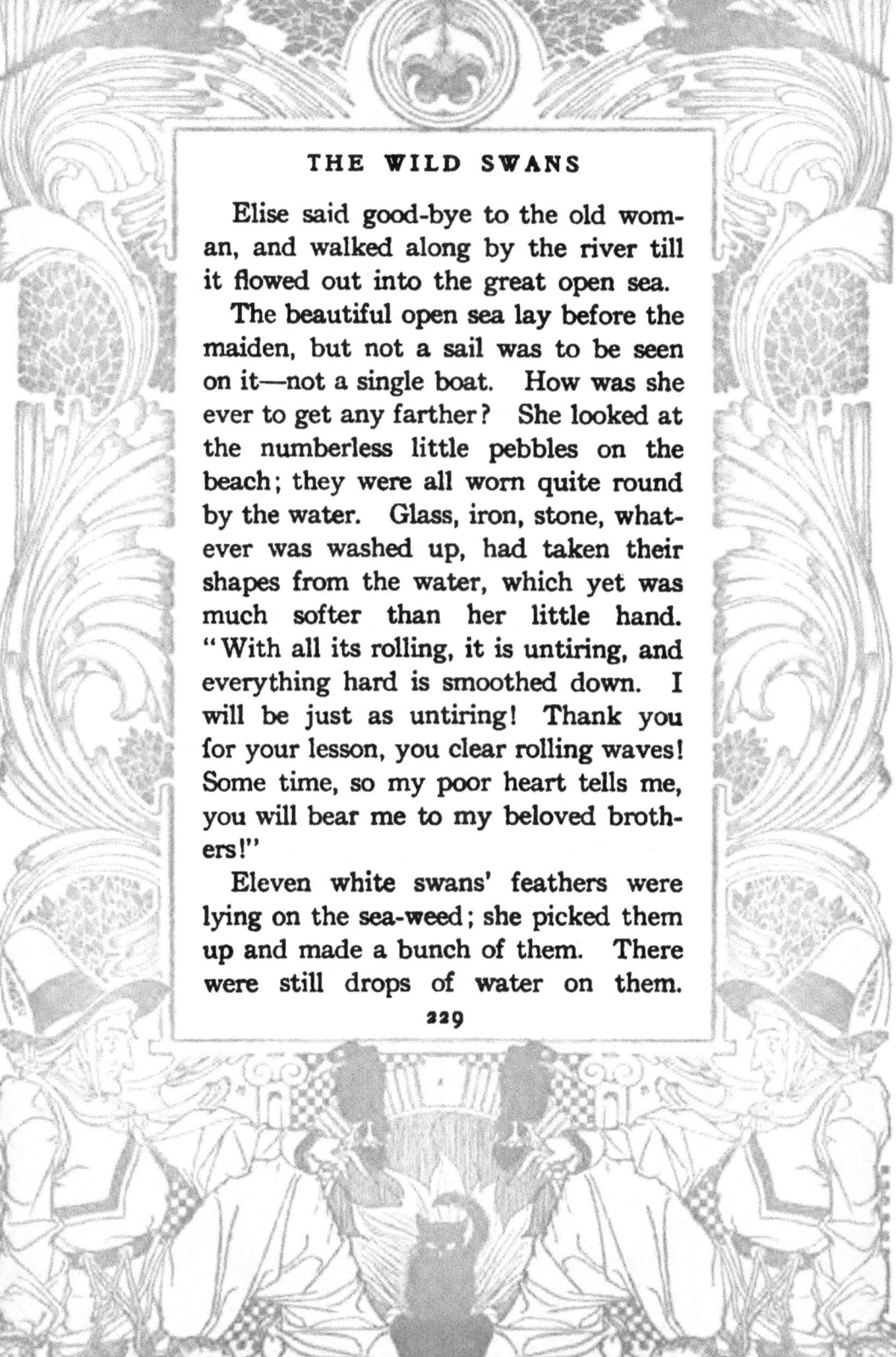

THE WILD SWANS

Elise said good-bye to the old woman, and walked along by the river till it flowed out into the great open sea.

The beautiful open sea lay before the maiden, but not a sail was to be seen on it—not a single boat. How was she ever to get any farther? She looked at the numberless little pebbles on the beach; they were all worn quite round by the water. Glass, iron, stone, whatever was washed up, had taken their shapes from the water, which yet was much softer than her little hand. "With all its rolling, it is untiring, and everything hard is smoothed down. I will be just as untiring! Thank you for your lesson, you clear rolling waves! Some time, so my poor heart tells me, you will bear me to my beloved brothers!"

Eleven white swans' feathers were lying on the sea-weed; she picked them up and made a bunch of them. There were still drops of water on them.

Whether these were dew or tears no one could tell. It was very lonely there by the shore, but she did not feel it, for the sea was ever changing. There were more changes on it in the course of a few hours than could be seen on an inland fresh-water lake in a year. If a big black cloud arose it was just as if the sea wanted to say, "I can look black too," and then the wind blew up and the waves showed their white crests. But if the clouds were red and the wind dropped, the sea looked like a rose-leaf, now white, now green. But, however still it was, there was always a little gentle motion just by the shore; the water rose and fell softly, like the bosom of a sleeping child.

When the sun was just about to go down, Elise saw eleven wild swans with golden crowns upon their heads flying towards the shore. They flew in a swaying line, one behind the other, like a white ribbon streamer. Elise climb-

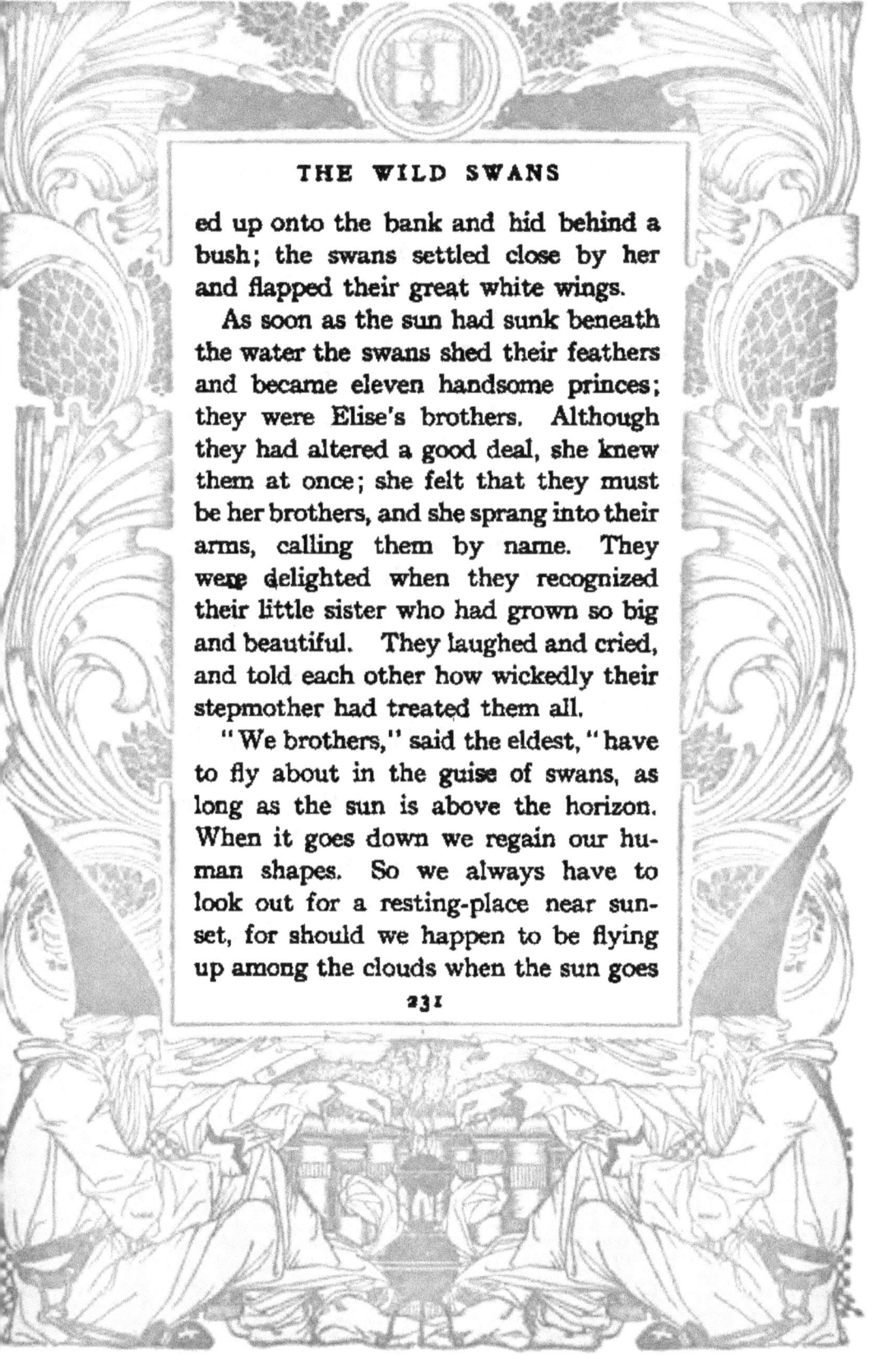

ed up onto the bank and hid behind a bush; the swans settled close by her and flapped their great white wings.

As soon as the sun had sunk beneath the water the swans shed their feathers and became eleven handsome princes; they were Elise's brothers. Although they had altered a good deal, she knew them at once; she felt that they must be her brothers, and she sprang into their arms, calling them by name. They were delighted when they recognized their little sister who had grown so big and beautiful. They laughed and cried, and told each other how wickedly their stepmother had treated them all.

"We brothers," said the eldest, "have to fly about in the guise of swans, as long as the sun is above the horizon. When it goes down we regain our human shapes. So we always have to look out for a resting-place near sunset, for should we happen to be flying up among the clouds when the sun goes down we should be hurled to the depths below. We do not live here; there is another land, just as beautiful as this, beyond the sea; but the way to it is very long, and we have to cross the mighty ocean to get to it. There is not a single island on the way where we can spend the night; only one solitary little rock juts up above the water midway. It is only just big enough for us to stand upon close together, and if there is a heavy sea the water splashes over us, yet we thank our God for it. We stay there over night in our human forms, and without it we could never revisit our beloved Fatherland, for our flight takes two of the longest days in the year. We are only permitted to visit the home of our fathers once a year, and we dare only stay for eleven days. We hover over this big forest from whence we catch a glimpse of the palace where we were born, and where our father lives; beyond it we can see

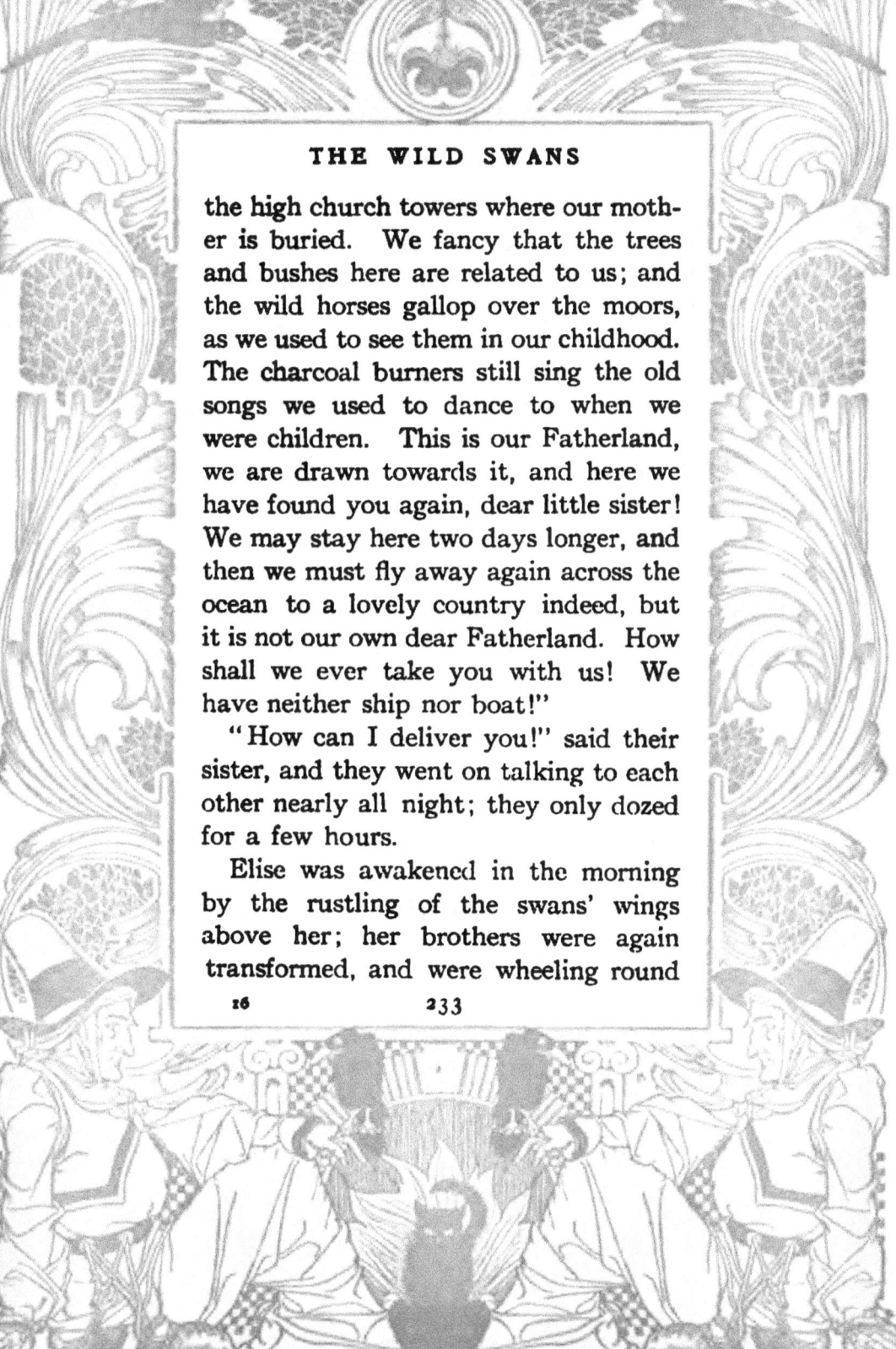

the high church towers where our mother is buried. We fancy that the trees and bushes here are related to us; and the wild horses gallop over the moors, as we used to see them in our childhood. The charcoal burners still sing the old songs we used to dance to when we were children. This is our Fatherland, we are drawn towards it, and here we have found you again, dear little sister! We may stay here two days longer, and then we must fly away again across the ocean to a lovely country indeed, but it is not our own dear Fatherland. How shall we ever take you with us! We have neither ship nor boat!"

"How can I deliver you!" said their sister, and they went on talking to each other nearly all night; they only dozed for a few hours.

Elise was awakened in the morning by the rustling of the swans' wings above her; her brothers were again transformed, and were wheeling round

in great circles till she lost sight of them in the distance. One of them, the youngest, stayed behind. He laid his head against her bosom, and she caressed it with her fingers. They remained together all day. Towards evening the others came back, and as soon as the sun went down they took their natural forms.

"To-morrow we must fly away, and we dare not come back for a whole year, but we can't leave you like this! Have you courage to go with us? My arm is strong enough to carry you over the forest, so surely our united strength ought to be sufficient to bear you across the ocean."

"Oh yes; take me with you," said Elise.

They spent the whole night in weaving a kind of net of the elastic bark of the willow bound together with tough rushes; they made it both large and strong. Elise lay down upon it, and

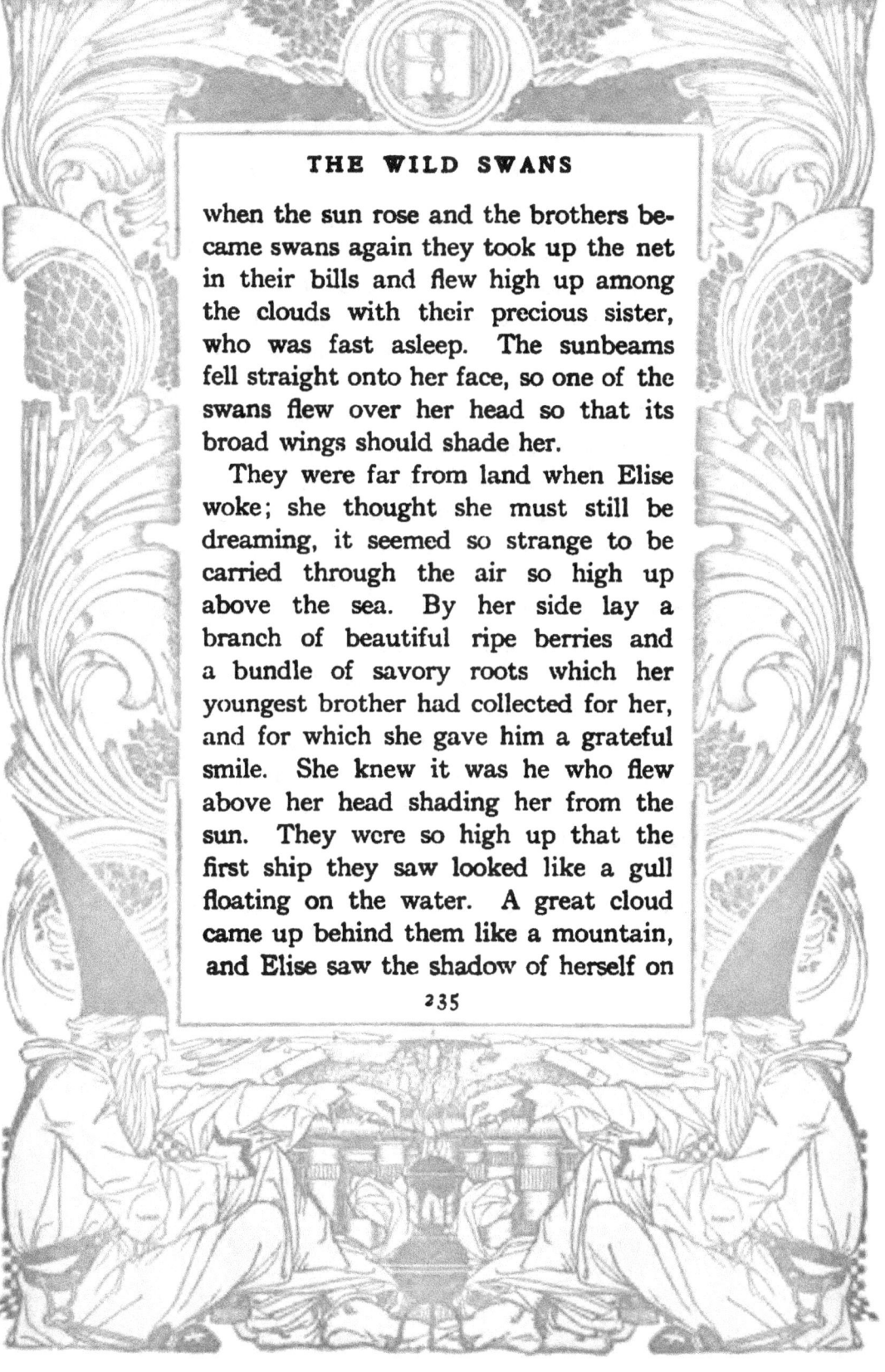

when the sun rose and the brothers became swans again they took up the net in their bills and flew high up among the clouds with their precious sister, who was fast asleep. The sunbeams fell straight onto her face, so one of the swans flew over her head so that its broad wings should shade her.

They were far from land when Elise woke; she thought she must still be dreaming, it seemed so strange to be carried through the air so high up above the sea. By her side lay a branch of beautiful ripe berries and a bundle of savory roots which her youngest brother had collected for her, and for which she gave him a grateful smile. She knew it was he who flew above her head shading her from the sun. They were so high up that the first ship they saw looked like a gull floating on the water. A great cloud came up behind them like a mountain, and Elise saw the shadow of herself on it, and those of the eleven swans looking like giants. It was a more beautiful picture than any she had ever seen before, but as the sun rose higher, the cloud fell behind, and the shadow picture disappeared.

They flew on and on all day like an arrow whizzing through the air, but they went slower than usual, for now they had their sister to carry. A storm came up, and night was drawing on; Elise saw the sun sinking with terror in her heart, for the solitary rock was nowhere to be seen. The swans seemed to be taking stronger strokes than ever; alas! she was the cause of their not being able to get on faster; as soon as the sun went down they would become men, and they would all be hurled into the sea and drowned. She prayed to God from the bottom of her heart, but still no rock was to be seen! Black clouds gathered, and strong gusts of wind announced a storm; the clouds looked like

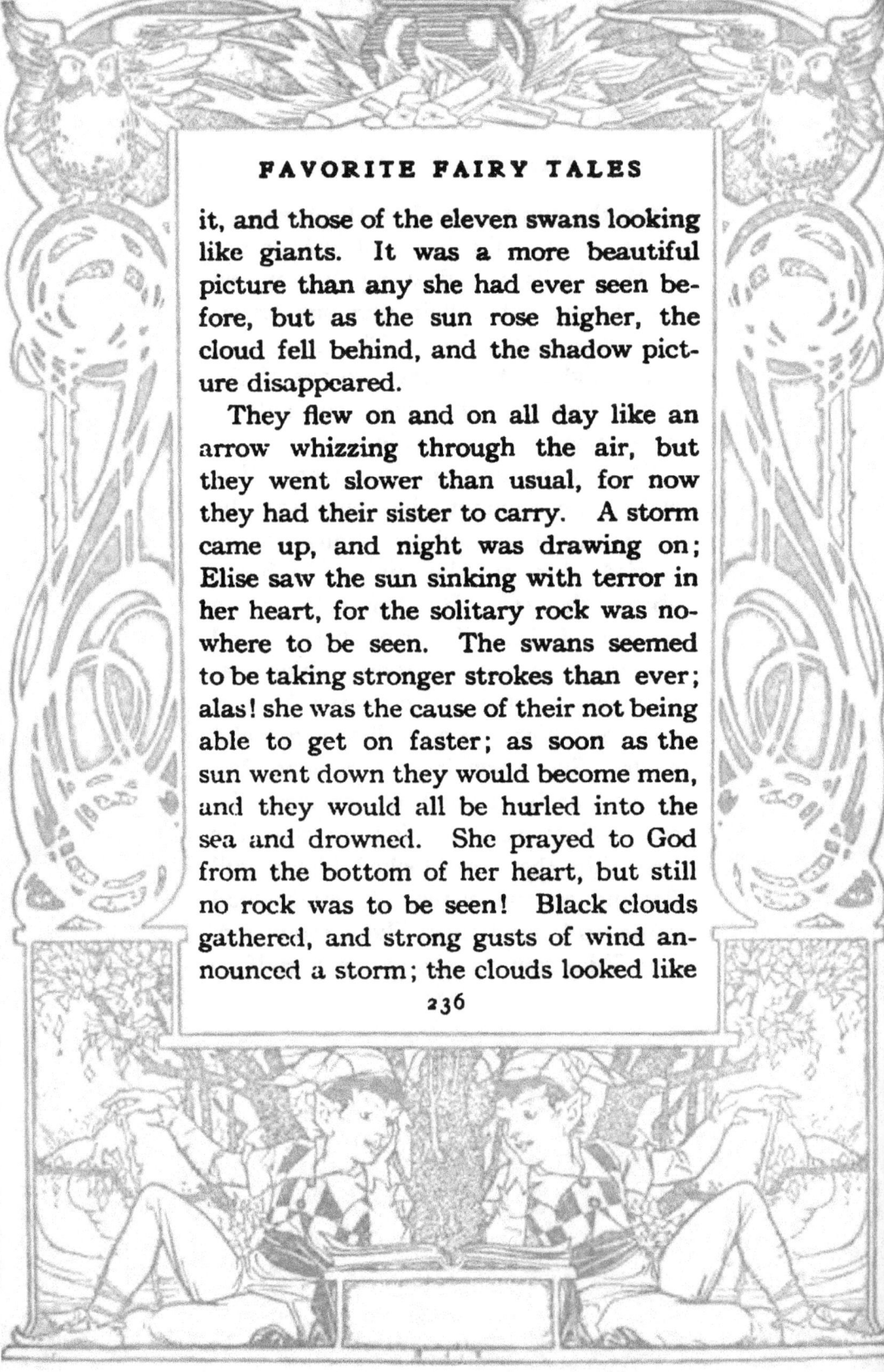

a great threatening leaden wave, and the flashes of lightning followed each other rapidly.

The sun was now at the edge of the sea. Elise's heart quaked, when suddenly the swans shot downward so suddenly that she thought they were falling then they hovered again. Half of the sun was below the horizon, and there for the first time she saw the little rock below, which did not look bigger than the head of a seal above the water. The sun sank very quickly, it was no bigger than a star, but her foot touched solid earth. The sun went out like the last sparks of a bit of burning paper; she saw her brothers stand arm in arm around her, but there was only just room enough for them. The waves beat upon the rock and washed over them like drenching rain. The heavens shone with continuous fire, and the thunder rolled, peal upon peal. But the sister and brothers held one another's

237

hands and sang a psalm which gave them comfort and courage.

The air was pure and still at dawn. As soon as the sun rose the swans flew off with Elise, away from the islet. The sea still ran high; it looked from where they were as if the white foam on the dark green water were millions of swans floating on the waves.

When the sun rose higher Elise saw before her, half floating in the air, great masses of ice, with shining glaciers on the heights. A palace was perched midway a mile in length, with one bold colonnade built above another. Beneath them swayed palm-trees and gorgeous blossoms as big as mill wheels. She asked if this was the land to which she was going, but the swans shook their heads, because what she saw was a mirage—the beautiful and ever-changing palace of Fata Morgana. No mortal dared enter it. Elise gazed at it; but as she gazed the palace, gardens,

Elsie saw an ice palace, with one bold colonnade built above another

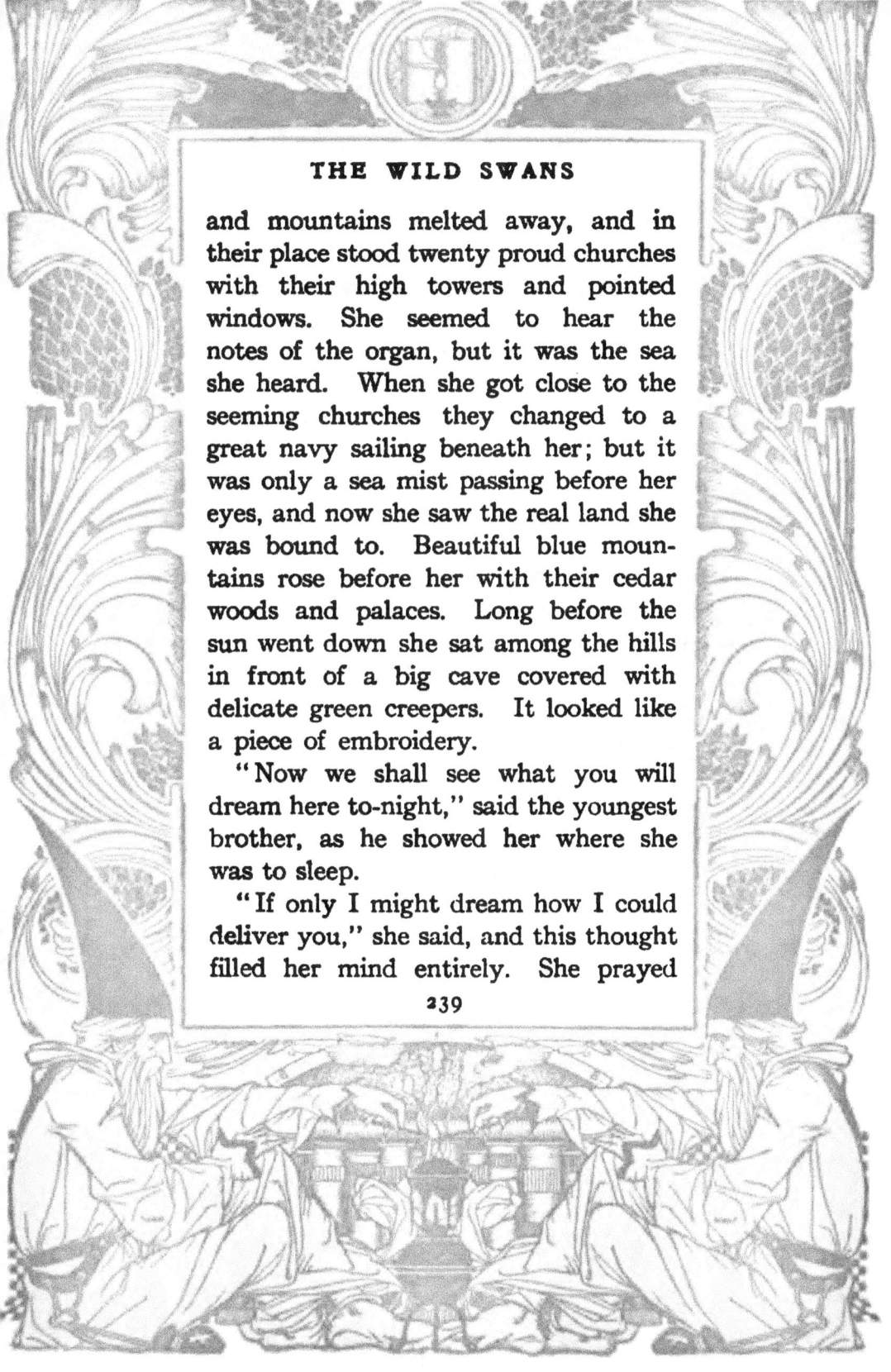

and mountains melted away, and in their place stood twenty proud churches with their high towers and pointed windows. She seemed to hear the notes of the organ, but it was the sea she heard. When she got close to the seeming churches they changed to a great navy sailing beneath her; but it was only a sea mist passing before her eyes, and now she saw the real land she was bound to. Beautiful blue mountains rose before her with their cedar woods and palaces. Long before the sun went down she sat among the hills in front of a big cave covered with delicate green creepers. It looked like a piece of embroidery.

"Now we shall see what you will dream here to-night," said the youngest brother, as he showed her where she was to sleep.

"If only I might dream how I could deliver you," she said, and this thought filled her mind entirely. She prayed

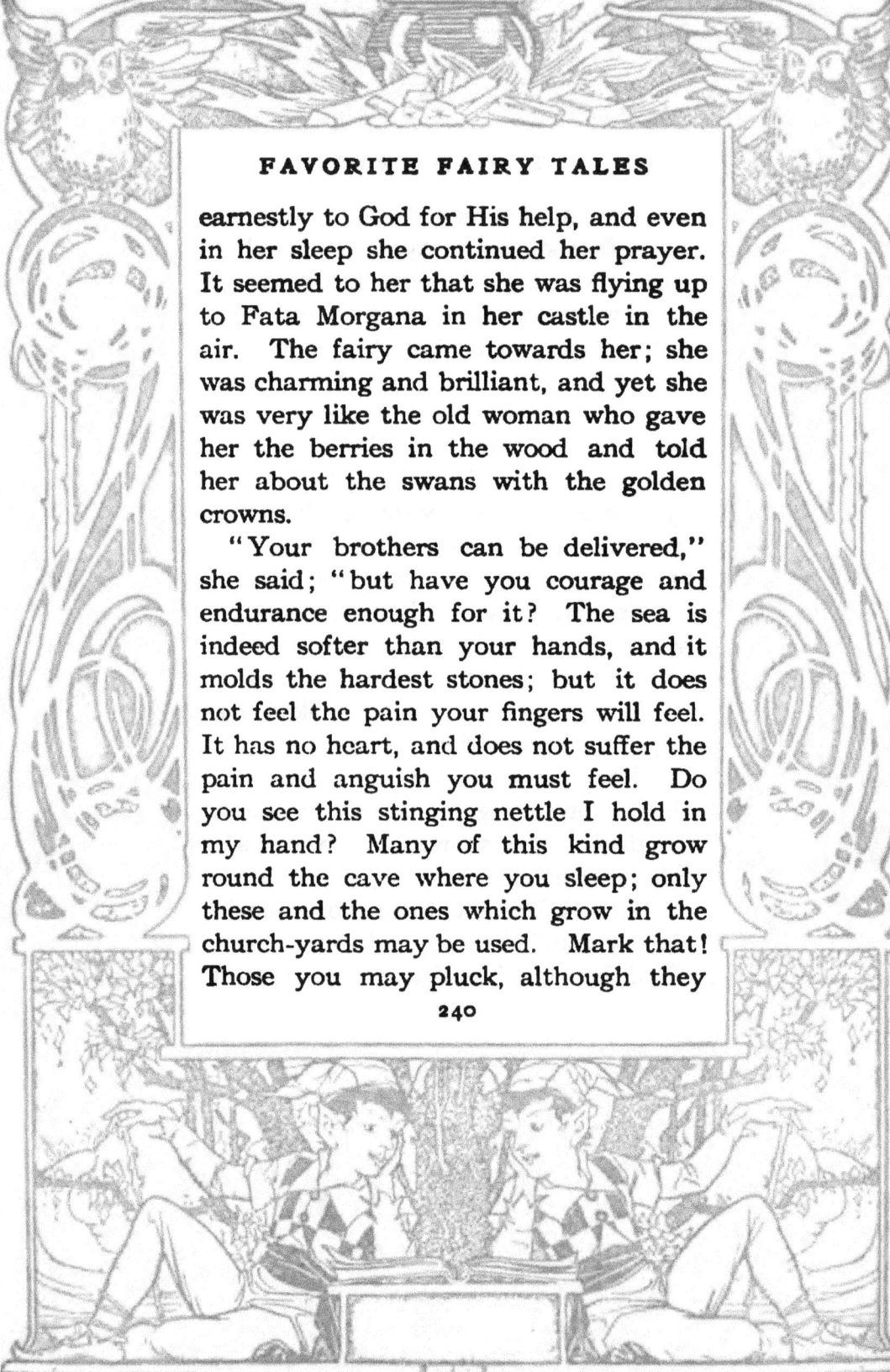

earnestly to God for His help, and even in her sleep she continued her prayer. It seemed to her that she was flying up to Fata Morgana in her castle in the air. The fairy came towards her; she was charming and brilliant, and yet she was very like the old woman who gave her the berries in the wood and told her about the swans with the golden crowns.

"Your brothers can be delivered," she said; "but have you courage and endurance enough for it? The sea is indeed softer than your hands, and it molds the hardest stones; but it does not feel the pain your fingers will feel. It has no heart, and does not suffer the pain and anguish you must feel. Do you see this stinging nettle I hold in my hand? Many of this kind grow round the cave where you sleep; only these and the ones which grow in the church-yards may be used. Mark that! Those you may pluck, although they

will burn and blister your hands. Crush the nettles with your feet and you will have flax, and of this you must weave eleven coats of mail with long sleeves. Throw these over the eleven wild swans and the charm is broken! But remember that from the moment you begin this work till it is finished, even if it takes years, you must not utter a word! The first word you say will fall like a murderer's dagger into the hearts of your brothers. Their lives hang on your tongue. Mark this well!"

She touched her hand at the same moment—it was like burning fire—and woke Elise. It was bright daylight, and close to where she slept lay a nettle like those in her dream. She fell upon her knees with thanks to God, and left the cave to begin her work.

She seized the horrid nettles with her delicate hands, and they burnt like fire; great blisters rose on her hands

and arms, but she suffered it willingly if only it would deliver her beloved brothers. She crushed every nettle with her ba c feet, and twisted it into green flax.

When the sun went down and the brothers came back they were alarmed at finding her mute; they thought it was some new witchcraft exercised by their wicked stepmother. But when they saw her hands they understood that it was for their sakes; the youngest brother wept, and wherever his tears fell she felt no more pain and the blisters disappeared.

She spent the whole night at her work, for she could not rest till she had delivered her dear brothers. All the following day while her brothers were away she sat solitary, but never had the time flown so fast. One coat of mail was finished, and she began the next. Then a hunting-horn sounded among the mountains; she was much

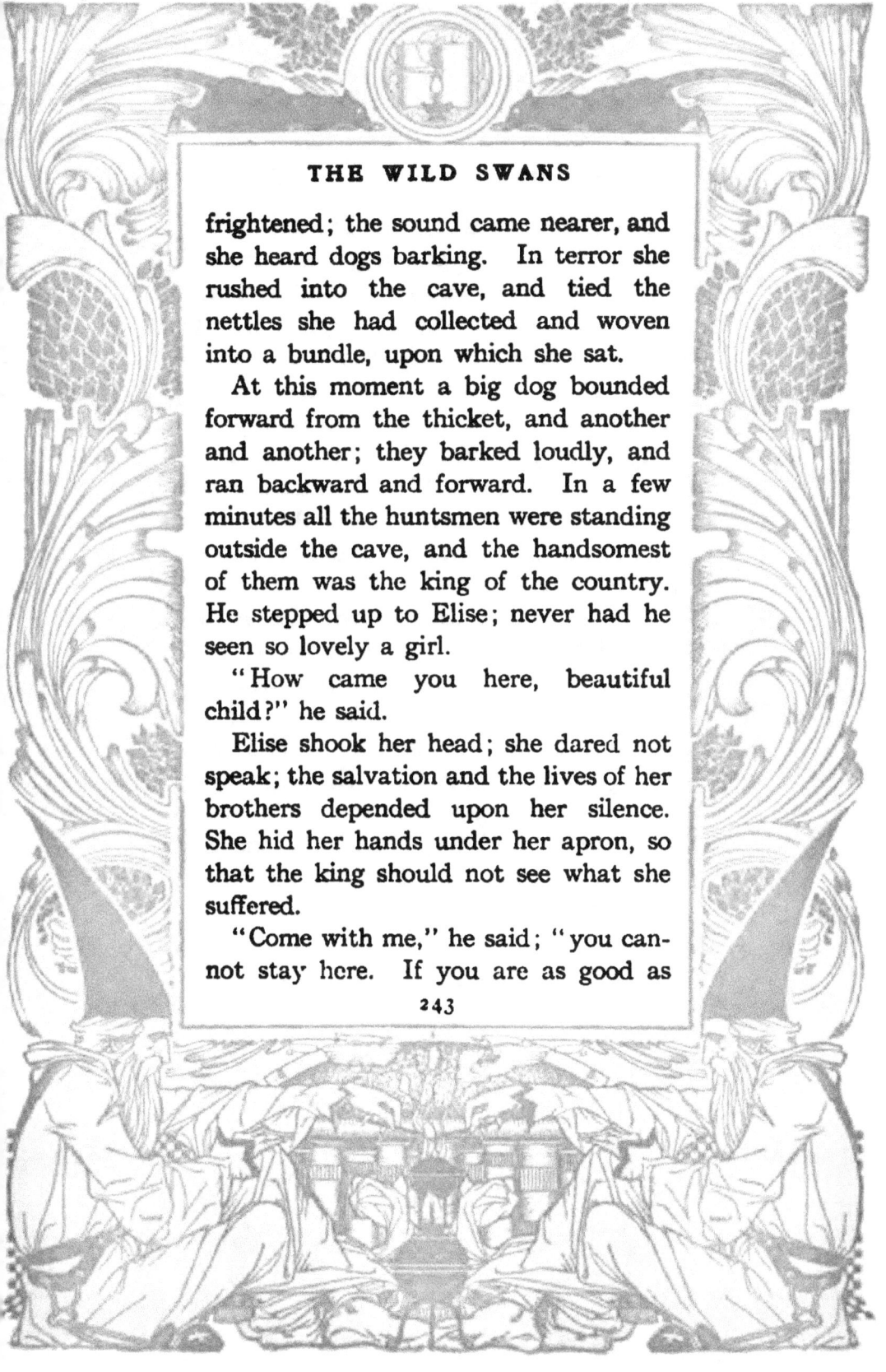

frightened; the sound came nearer, and she heard dogs barking. In terror she rushed into the cave, and tied the nettles she had collected and woven into a bundle, upon which she sat.

At this moment a big dog bounded forward from the thicket, and another and another; they barked loudly, and ran backward and forward. In a few minutes all the huntsmen were standing outside the cave, and the handsomest of them was the king of the country. He stepped up to Elise; never had he seen so lovely a girl.

"How came you here, beautiful child?" he said.

Elise shook her head; she dared not speak; the salvation and the lives of her brothers depended upon her silence. She hid her hands under her apron, so that the king should not see what she suffered.

"Come with me," he said; "you cannot stay here. If you are as good as

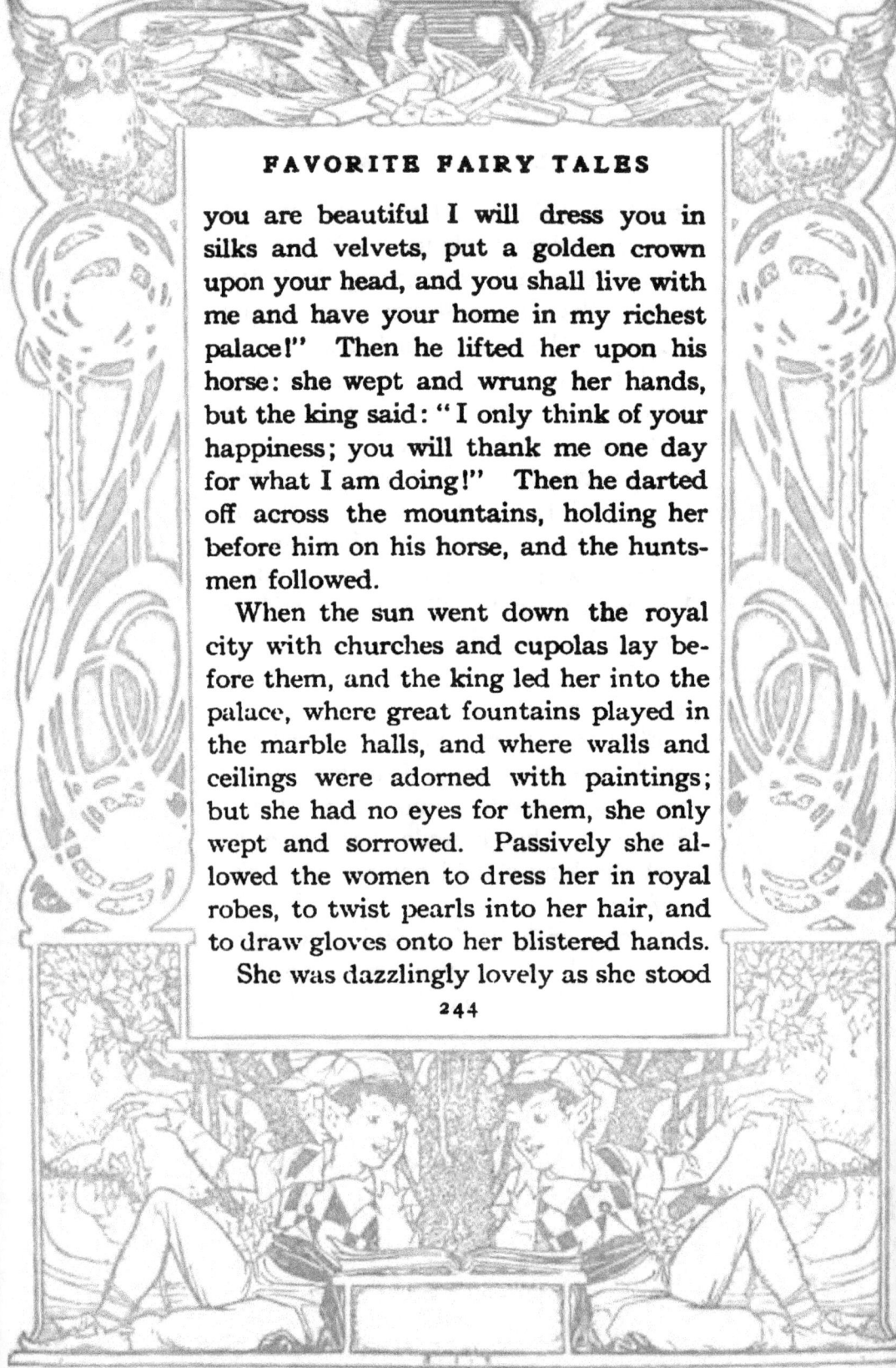

you are beautiful I will dress you in
silks and velvets, put a golden crown
upon your head, and you shall live with
me and have your home in my richest
palace!" Then he lifted her upon his
horse: she wept and wrung her hands,
but the king said: "I only think of your
happiness; you will thank me one day
for what I am doing!" Then he darted
off across the mountains, holding her
before him on his horse, and the huntsmen followed.

When the sun went down the royal
city with churches and cupolas lay before them, and the king led her into the
palace, where great fountains played in
the marble halls, and where walls and
ceilings were adorned with paintings;
but she had no eyes for them, she only
wept and sorrowed. Passively she allowed the women to dress her in royal
robes, to twist pearls into her hair, and
to draw gloves onto her blistered hands.

She was dazzlingly lovely as she stood

there in all her magnificence; the court-
iers bent low before her, and the king
wooed her as his bride, although the
archbishop shook his head, and whispered that he feared the beautiful wood
maiden was a witch who had dazzled
their eyes and infatuated the king.

The king refused to listen to him; he
ordered the music to play, the richest
food to be brought, and the loveliest
girls to dance before her. She was led
through scented gardens into gorgeous
apartments, but nothing brought a
smile to her lips or into her eyes; sorrow
sat there like a heritage and a possession
for all time. Last of all, the king
opened the door of a little chamber
close by the room where she was to
sleep. It was adorned with costly
green carpets, and made to exactly re-
semble the cave where he found her.
On the floor lay the bundle of flax she
had spun from the nettles, and from
the ceiling hung the shirt of mail which

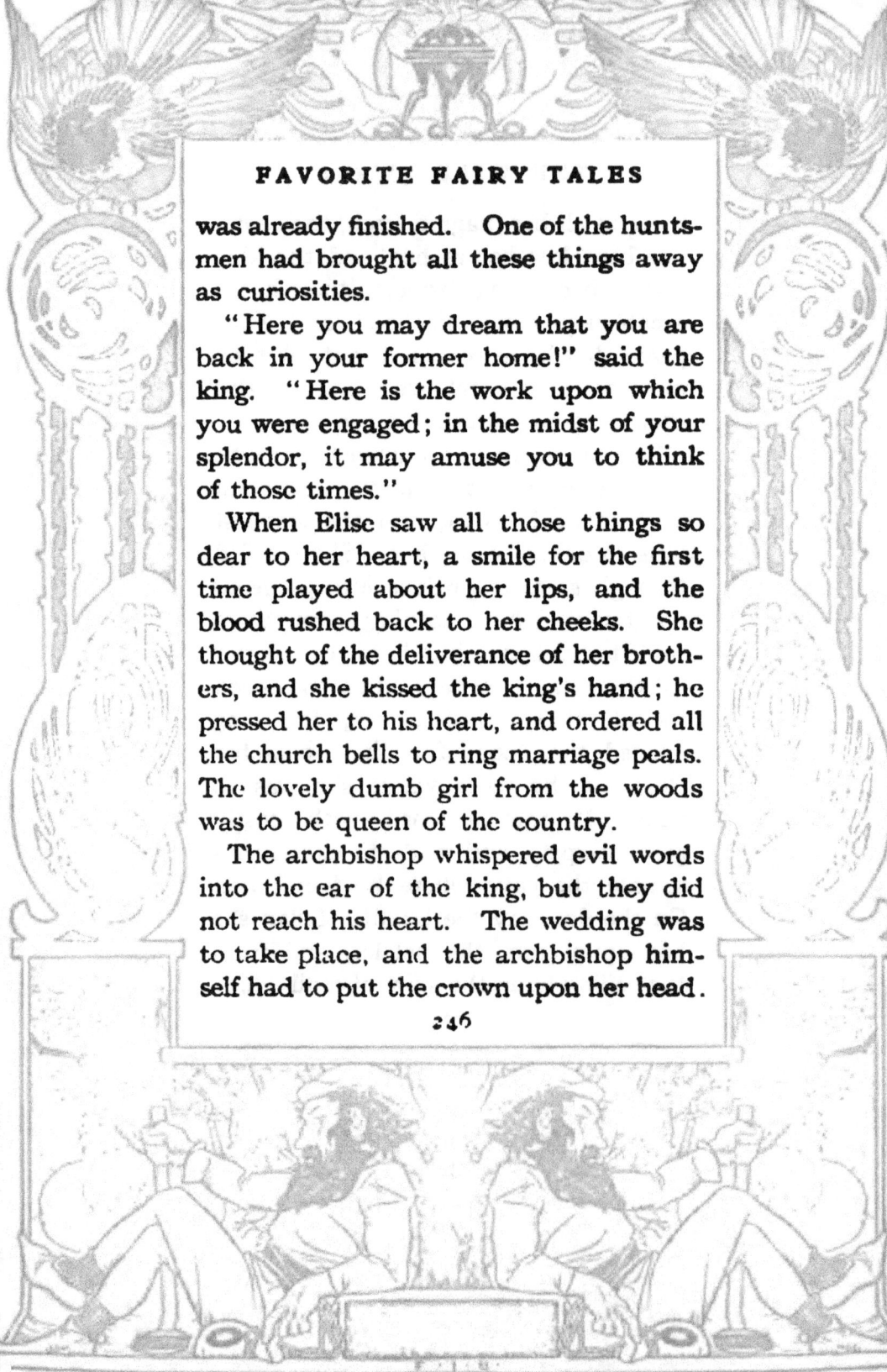

was already finished. One of the huntsmen had brought all these things away as curiosities.

"Here you may dream that you are back in your former home!" said the king. "Here is the work upon which you were engaged; in the midst of your splendor, it may amuse you to think of those times."

When Elise saw all those things so dear to her heart, a smile for the first time played about her lips, and the blood rushed back to her cheeks. She thought of the deliverance of her brothers, and she kissed the king's hand; he pressed her to his heart, and ordered all the church bells to ring marriage peals. The lovely dumb girl from the woods was to be queen of the country.

The archbishop whispered evil words into the ear of the king, but they did not reach his heart. The wedding was to take place, and the archbishop himself had to put the crown upon her head.

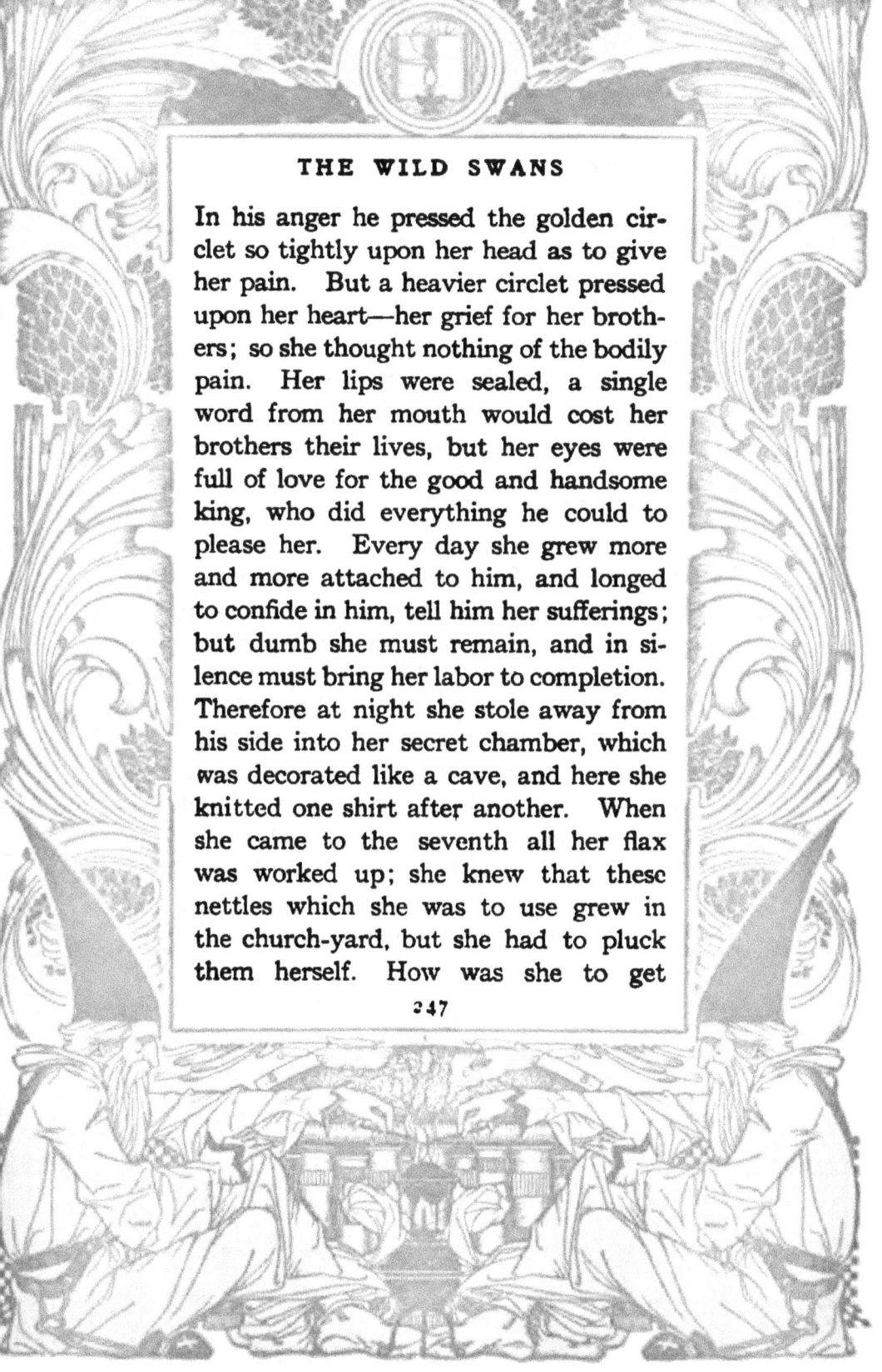

THE WILD SWANS

In his anger he pressed the golden circlet so tightly upon her head as to give her pain. But a heavier circlet pressed upon her heart—her grief for her brothers; so she thought nothing of the bodily pain. Her lips were sealed, a single word from her mouth would cost her brothers their lives, but her eyes were full of love for the good and handsome king, who did everything he could to please her. Every day she grew more and more attached to him, and longed to confide in him, tell him her sufferings; but dumb she must remain, and in silence must bring her labor to completion. Therefore at night she stole away from his side into her secret chamber, which was decorated like a cave, and here she knitted one shirt after another. When she came to the seventh all her flax was worked up; she knew that these nettles which she was to use grew in the church-yard, but she had to pluck them herself. How was she to get

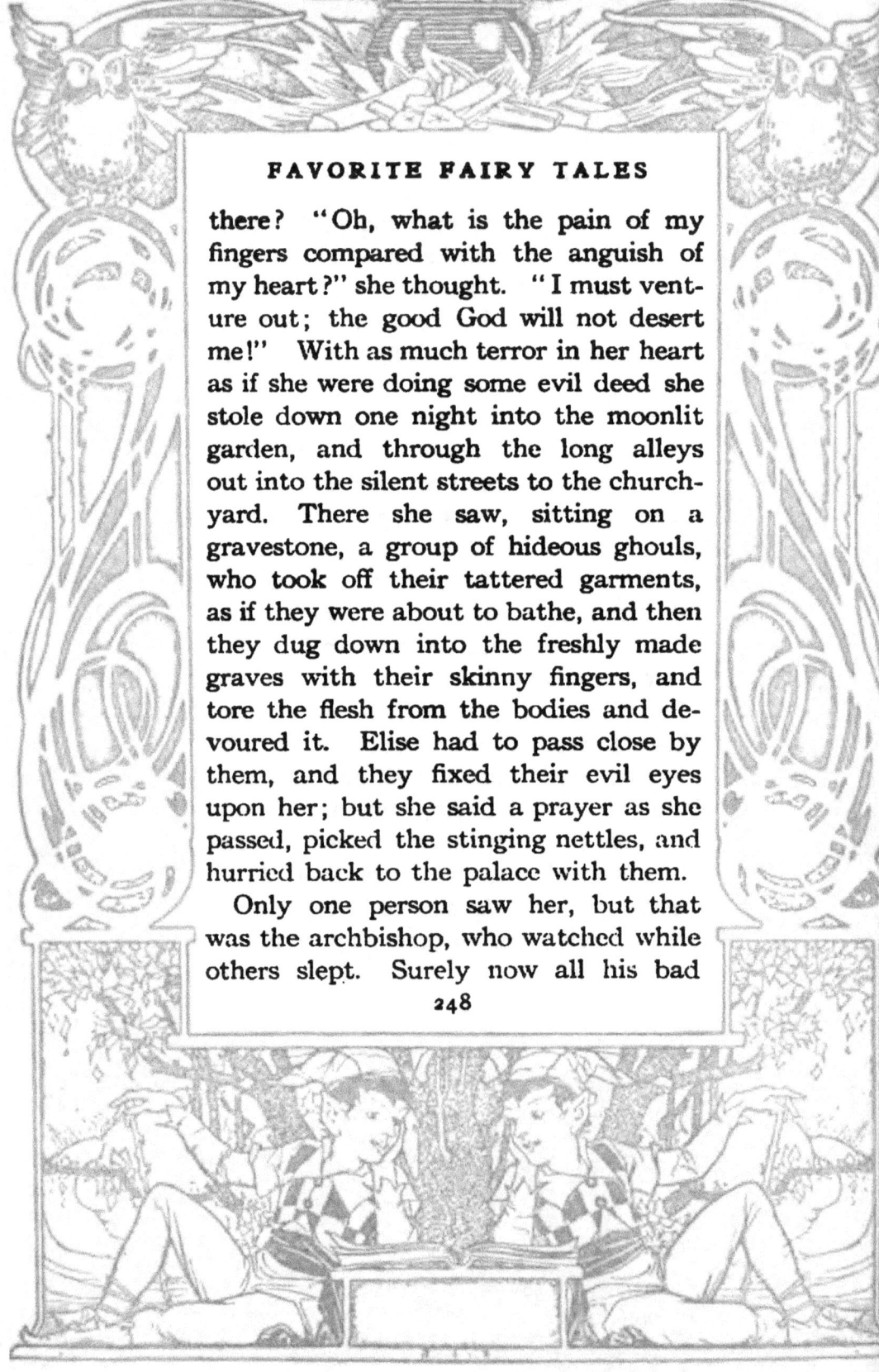

there? "Oh, what is the pain of my fingers compared with the anguish of my heart?" she thought. "I must venture out; the good God will not desert me!" With as much terror in her heart as if she were doing some evil deed she stole down one night into the moonlit garden, and through the long alleys out into the silent streets to the churchyard. There she saw, sitting on a gravestone, a group of hideous ghouls, who took off their tattered garments, as if they were about to bathe, and then they dug down into the freshly made graves with their skinny fingers, and tore the flesh from the bodies and devoured it. Elise had to pass close by them, and they fixed their evil eyes upon her; but she said a prayer as she passed, picked the stinging nettles, and hurried back to the palace with them.

Only one person saw her, but that was the archbishop, who watched while others slept. Surely now all his bad

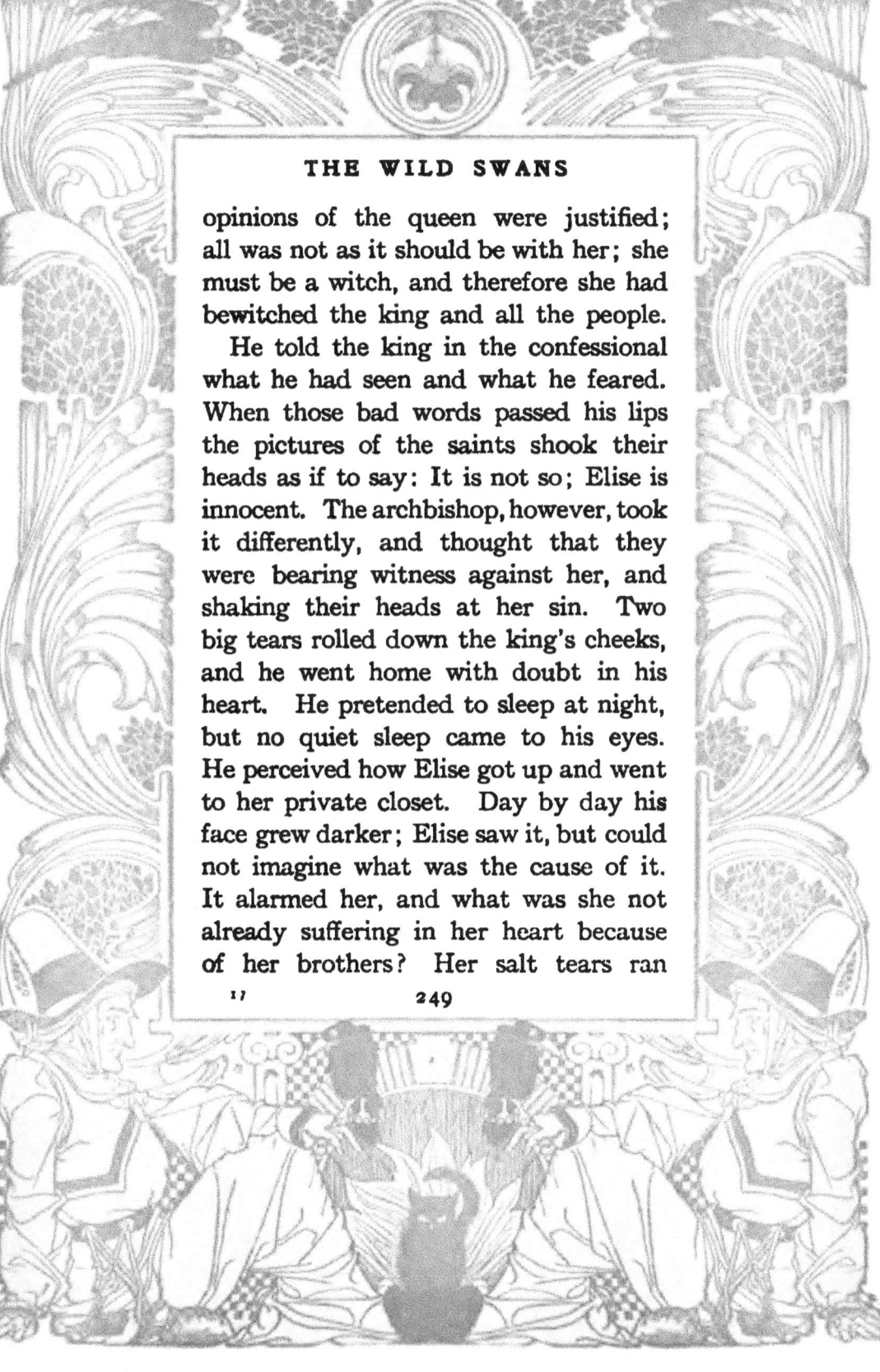

opinions of the queen were justified; all was not as it should be with her; she must be a witch, and therefore she had bewitched the king and all the people.

He told the king in the confessional what he had seen and what he feared. When those bad words passed his lips the pictures of the saints shook their heads as if to say: It is not so; Elise is innocent. The archbishop, however, took it differently, and thought that they were bearing witness against her, and shaking their heads at her sin. Two big tears rolled down the king's cheeks, and he went home with doubt in his heart. He pretended to sleep at night, but no quiet sleep came to his eyes. He perceived how Elise got up and went to her private closet. Day by day his face grew darker; Elise saw it, but could not imagine what was the cause of it. It alarmed her, and what was she not already suffering in her heart because of her brothers? Her salt tears ran down upon the royal purple velvet, they lay upon it like sparkling diamonds, and all who saw their splendor wished to be queen.

She had, however, almost reached the end of her labors, only one shirt of mail was wanting; but again she had no more flax, and not a single nettle was left. Once more, for the last time, she must go to the church-yard to pluck a few handfuls. She thought with dread of the solitary walk and the horrible ghouls, but her will was as strong as her trust in God.

Elise went, but the king and the archbishop followed her; they saw her disappear within the grated gateway of the church-yard. When they followed they saw the ghouls sitting on the grave-stone as Elise had see them before; and the king turned away his head because he thought she was among them—she, whose head this very evening had rested on his breast.

250

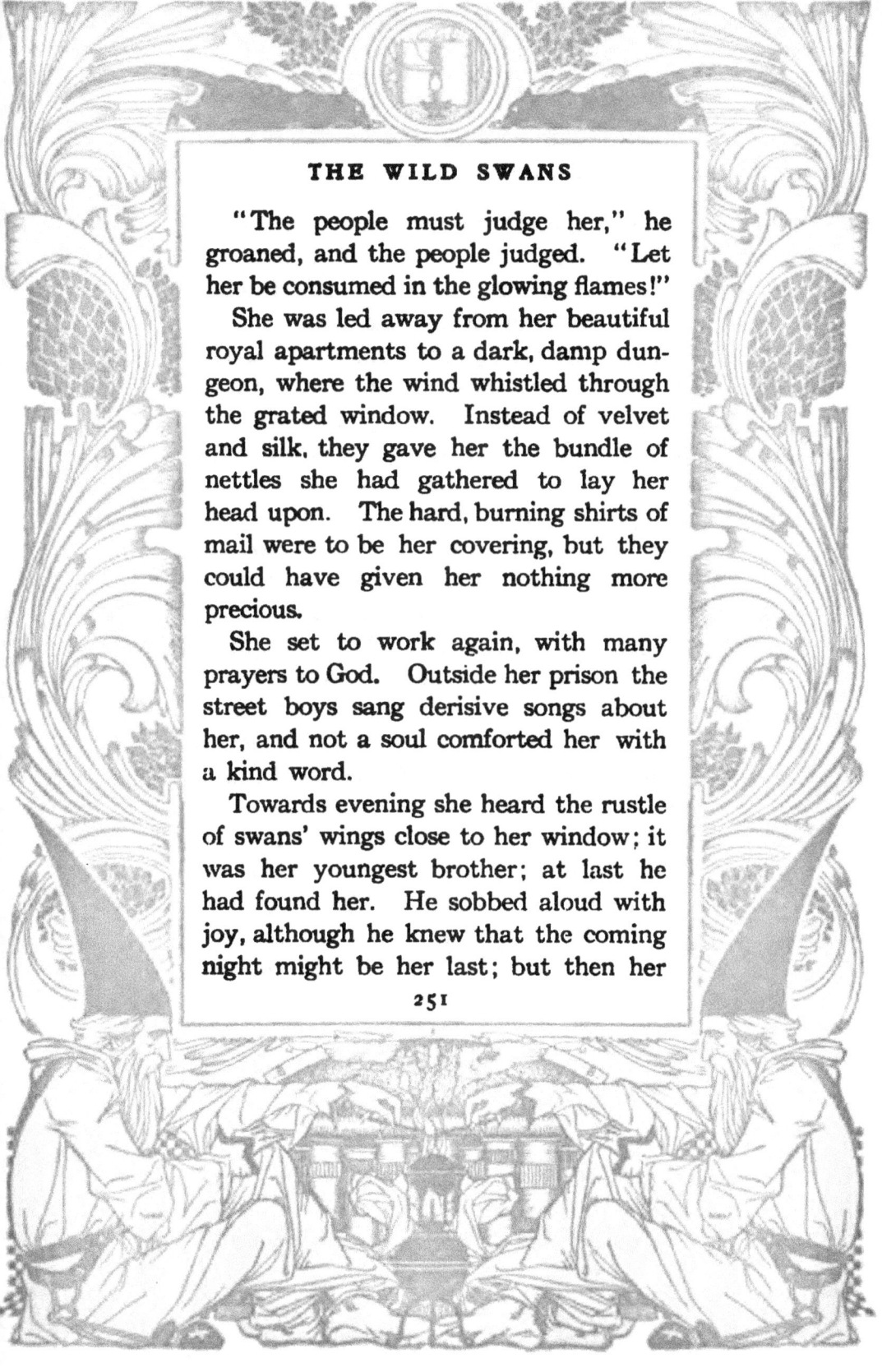

THE WILD SWANS

"The people must judge her," he groaned, and the people judged. "Let her be consumed in the glowing flames!"

She was led away from her beautiful royal apartments to a dark, damp dungeon, where the wind whistled through the grated window. Instead of velvet and silk, they gave her the bundle of nettles she had gathered to lay her head upon. The hard, burning shirts of mail were to be her covering, but they could have given her nothing more precious.

She set to work again, with many prayers to God. Outside her prison the street boys sang derisive songs about her, and not a soul comforted her with a kind word.

Towards evening she heard the rustle of swans' wings close to her window; it was her youngest brother; at last he had found her. He sobbed aloud with joy, although he knew that the coming night might be her last; but then her

work was almost done, and her brothers were there.

The archbishop came to spend his last hours with her, as he had promised the king. She shook her head at him, and by looks and gestures begged him to leave her. She had only this night in which to finish her work, or else all would be wasted, all — her pain, tears, and sleepless nights. The archbishop went away with bitter words against her, but poor Elise knew that she was innocent, and she went on with her work.

The little mice ran about the floor bringing nettles to her feet, so as to give what help they could, and a thrush sat on the grating of the window where he sang all night as merrily as he could to keep up her courage.

It was still only dawn and the sun would not rise for an hour when the eleven brothers stood at the gate of the palace, begging to be taken to the king. This could not be done was the answer, for it was still night; the king was asleep, and no one dared wake him. All their entreaties and threats were useless; the watch turned out, and even the king himself came to see what was the matter; but just then the sun rose, and no more brothers were to be seen—only eleven wild swans hovering over the palace.

The whole populace streamed out of the town gates; they were all anxious to see the witch burned. A miserable horse drew the cart in which Elise was seated. They had put upon her a smock of green sacking, and all her beautiful long hair hung loose from the lovely head. Her cheeks were deathly pale, and her lips moved softly, while her fingers unceasingly twisted the green yarn. Even on the way to her death she could not abandon her unfinished work. Ten shirts lay completed at her feet; she labored away at the eleventh amid the scoffing insults of the populace.

"Look at the witch; how she mutters! She has never a book of psalms in her hands; no, there she sits with her loathsome sorcery. Tear it away from her into a thousand bits!"

The crowd pressed around her to destroy her work, but just then eleven white swans flew down and perched upon the cart flapping their wings. The crowd gave way before them in terror.

"It is a sign from Heaven! She is innocent!" they whispered, but they dared not say it aloud.

The executioner seized her by the hand. But she hastily threw the eleven shirts over the swans, who were immediately transformed to eleven handsome princes; but the youngest had a swan's wing in place of an arm, for one sleeve was wanting to his shirt of mail; she had not been able to finish it.

"Now I may speak! I am innocent." The populace who saw what had hap-

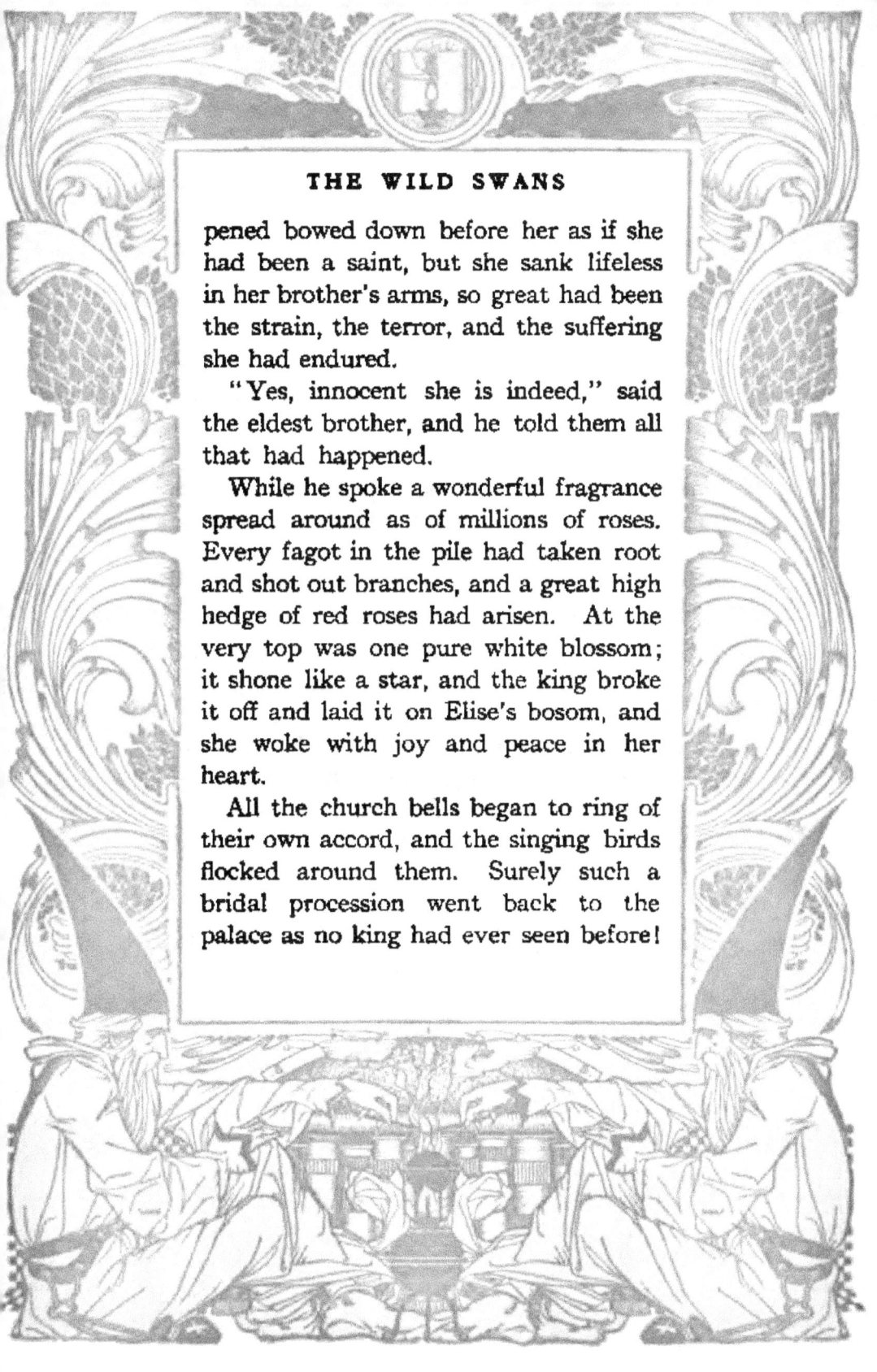

pened bowed down before her as if she had been a saint, but she sank lifeless in her brother's arms, so great had been the strain, the terror, and the suffering she had endured.

"Yes, innocent she is indeed," said the eldest brother, and he told them all that had happened.

While he spoke a wonderful fragrance spread around as of millions of roses. Every fagot in the pile had taken root and shot out branches, and a great high hedge of red roses had arisen. At the very top was one pure white blossom; it shone like a star, and the king broke it off and laid it on Elise's bosom, and she woke with joy and peace in her heart.

All the church bells began to ring of their own accord, and the singing birds flocked around them. Surely such a bridal procession went back to the palace as no king had ever seen before!

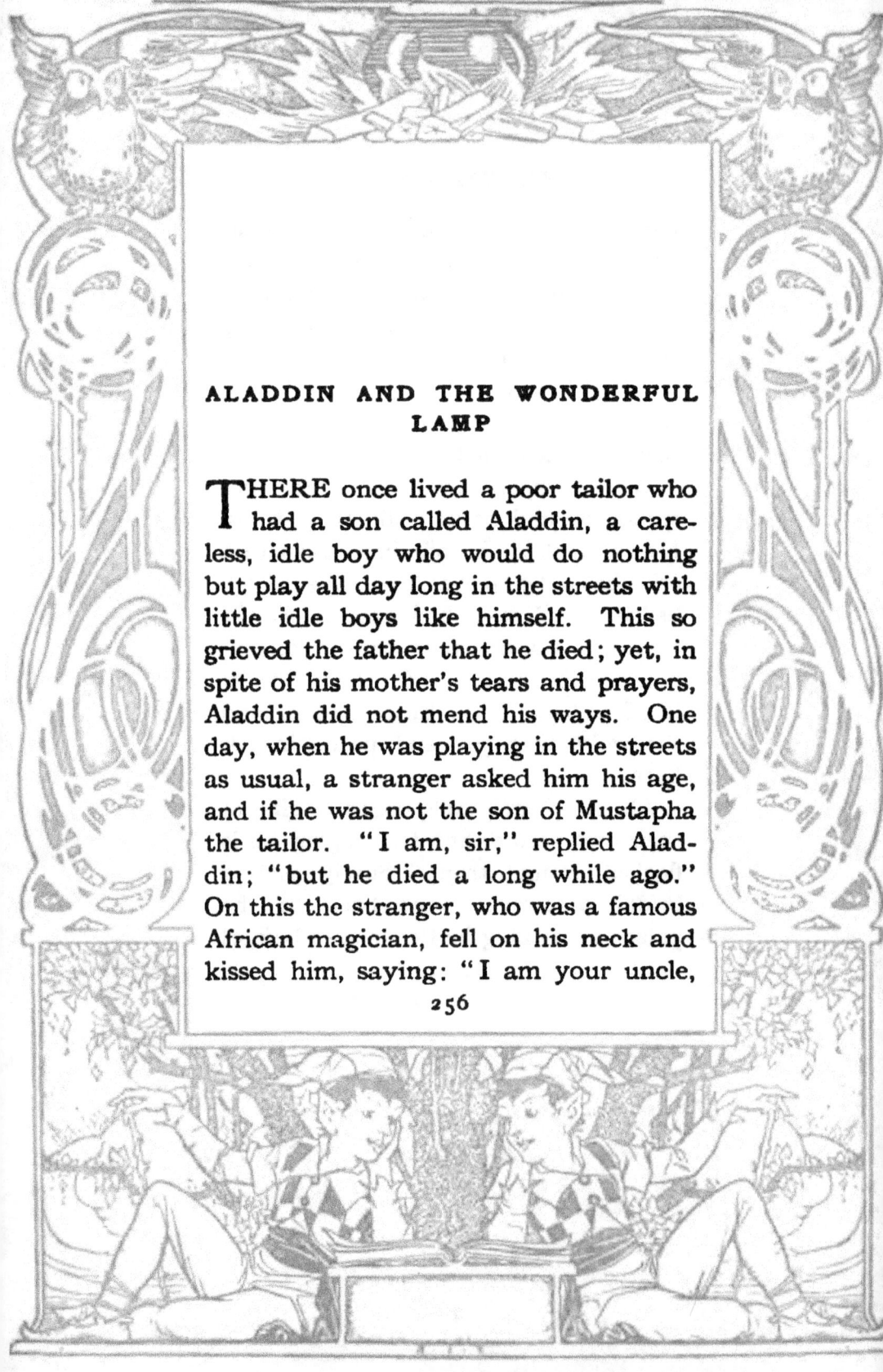

ALADDIN AND THE WONDERFUL LAMP

THERE once lived a poor tailor who had a son called Aladdin, a careless, idle boy who would do nothing but play all day long in the streets with little idle boys like himself. This so grieved the father that he died; yet, in spite of his mother's tears and prayers, Aladdin did not mend his ways. One day, when he was playing in the streets as usual, a stranger asked him his age, and if he was not the son of Mustapha the tailor. "I am, sir," replied Aladdin; "but he died a long while ago." On this the stranger, who was a famous African magician, fell on his neck and kissed him, saying: "I am your uncle,

256

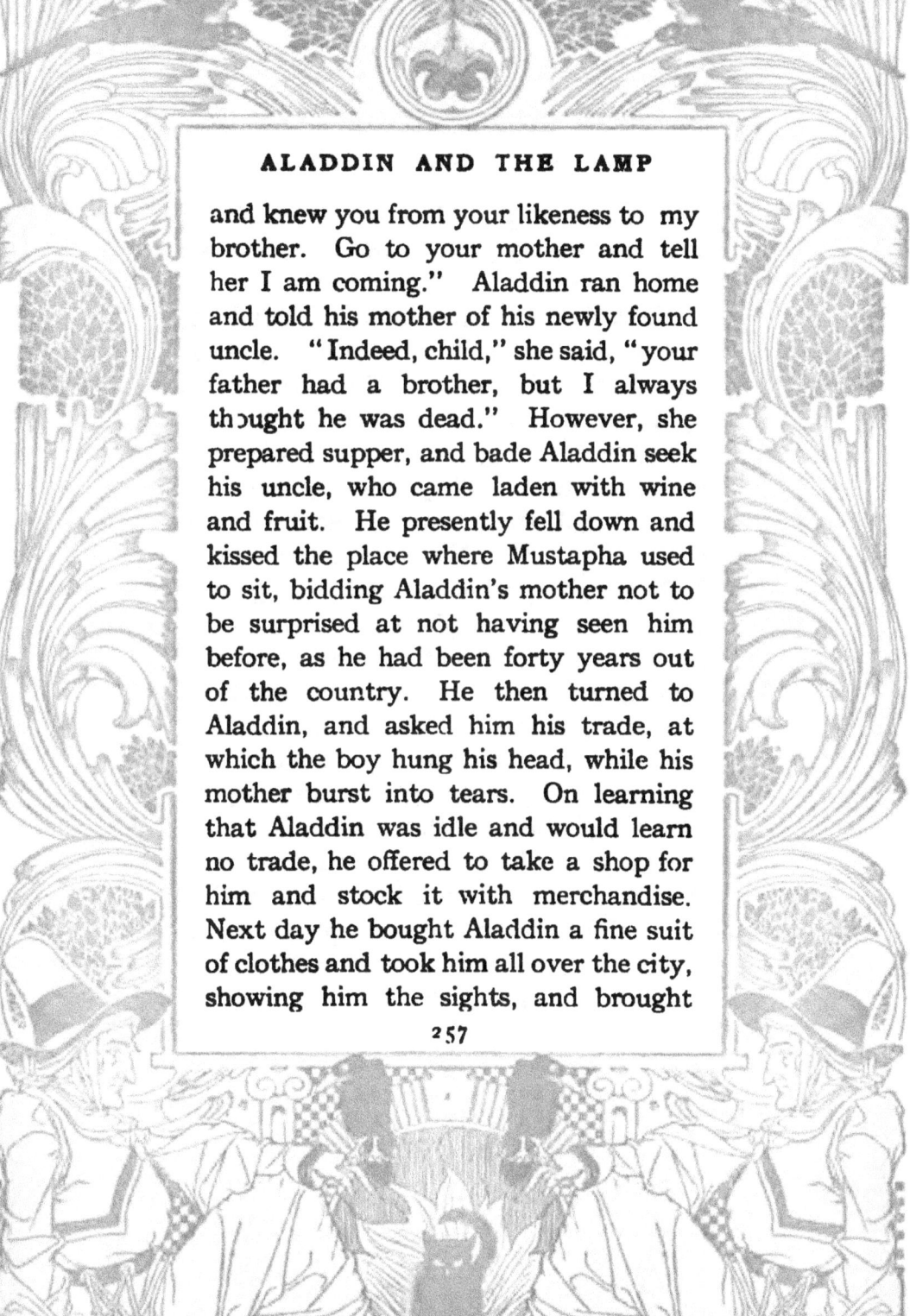

and knew you from your likeness to my
brother. Go to your mother and tell
her I am coming." Aladdin ran home
and told his mother of his newly found
uncle. "Indeed, child," she said, "your
father had a brother, but I always
thought he was dead." However, she
prepared supper, and bade Aladdin seek
his uncle, who came laden with wine
and fruit. He presently fell down and
kissed the place where Mustapha used
to sit, bidding Aladdin's mother not to
be surprised at not having seen him
before, as he had been forty years out
of the country. He then turned to
Aladdin, and asked him his trade, at
which the boy hung his head, while his
mother burst into tears. On learning
that Aladdin was idle and would learn
no trade, he offered to take a shop for
him and stock it with merchandise.
Next day he bought Aladdin a fine suit
of clothes and took him all over the city,
showing him the sights, and brought

257

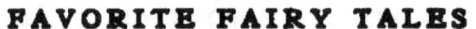

him home at nightfall to his mother,
who was overjoyed to see her son so
fine.

Next day the magician led Aladdin
into some beautiful gardens a long way
outside the city gates. They sat down
by a fountain, and the magician pulled
a cake from his girdle which he divided
between them. They then journeyed
onward till they almost reached the
mountains. Aladdin was so tired that
he begged to go back, but the magician
beguiled him with pleasant stories, and
led him on in spite of himself. At last
they came to two mountains divided by
a narrow valley. "We will go no farther," said the false uncle. "I will show
you something wonderful; only do you
gather up sticks while I kindle a fire."
When it was lit the magician threw on
it a powder he had about him, at the
same time saying some magical words.
The earth trembled a little and opened
in front of them, disclosing a square

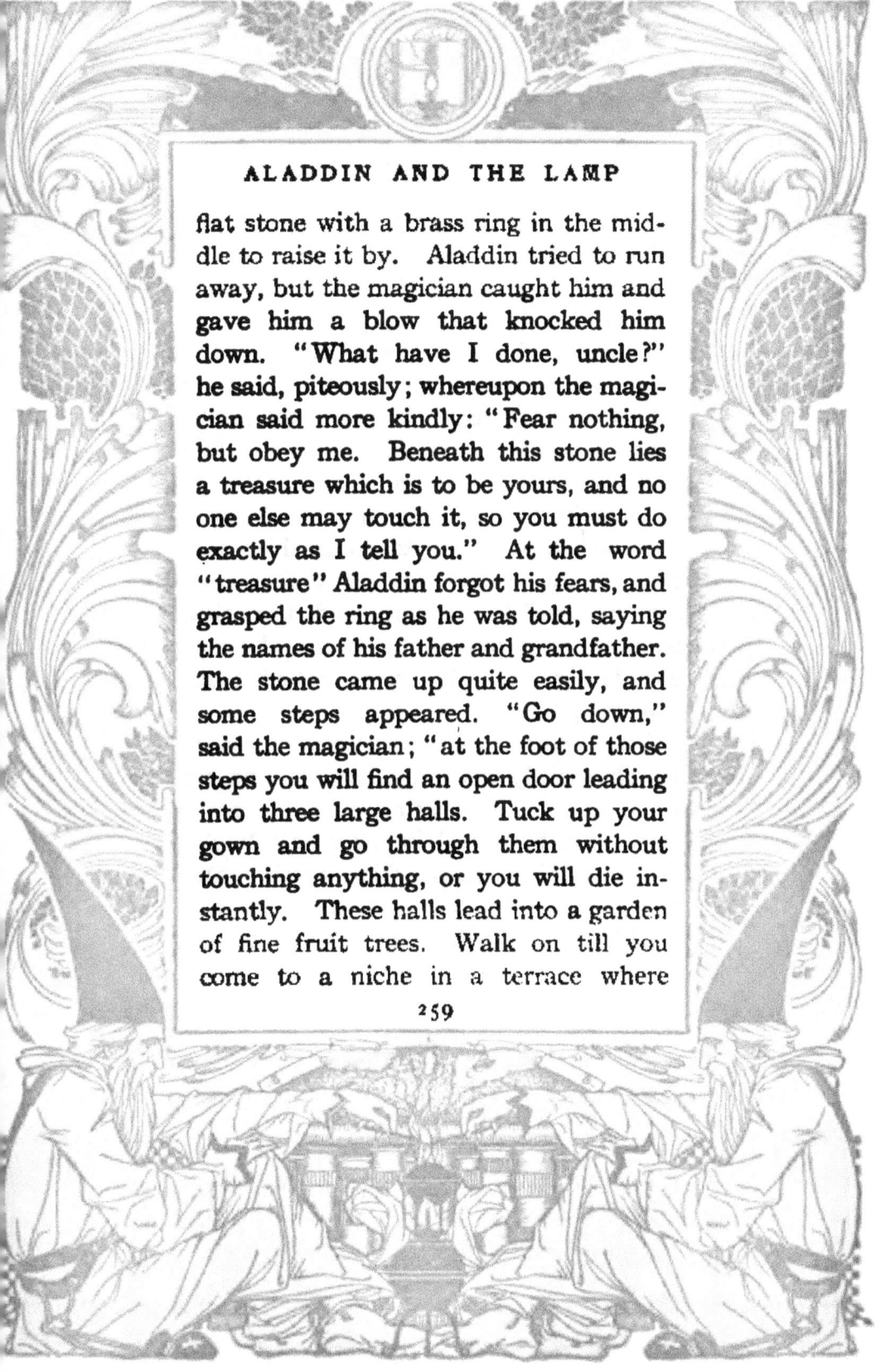

flat stone with a brass ring in the middle to raise it by. Aladdin tried to run away, but the magician caught him and gave him a blow that knocked him down. "What have I done, uncle?" he said, piteously; whereupon the magician said more kindly: "Fear nothing, but obey me. Beneath this stone lies a treasure which is to be yours, and no one else may touch it, so you must do exactly as I tell you." At the word "treasure" Aladdin forgot his fears, and grasped the ring as he was told, saying the names of his father and grandfather. The stone came up quite easily, and some steps appeared. "Go down," said the magician; "at the foot of those steps you will find an open door leading into three large halls. Tuck up your gown and go through them without touching anything, or you will die instantly. These halls lead into a garden of fine fruit trees. Walk on till you come to a niche in a terrace where

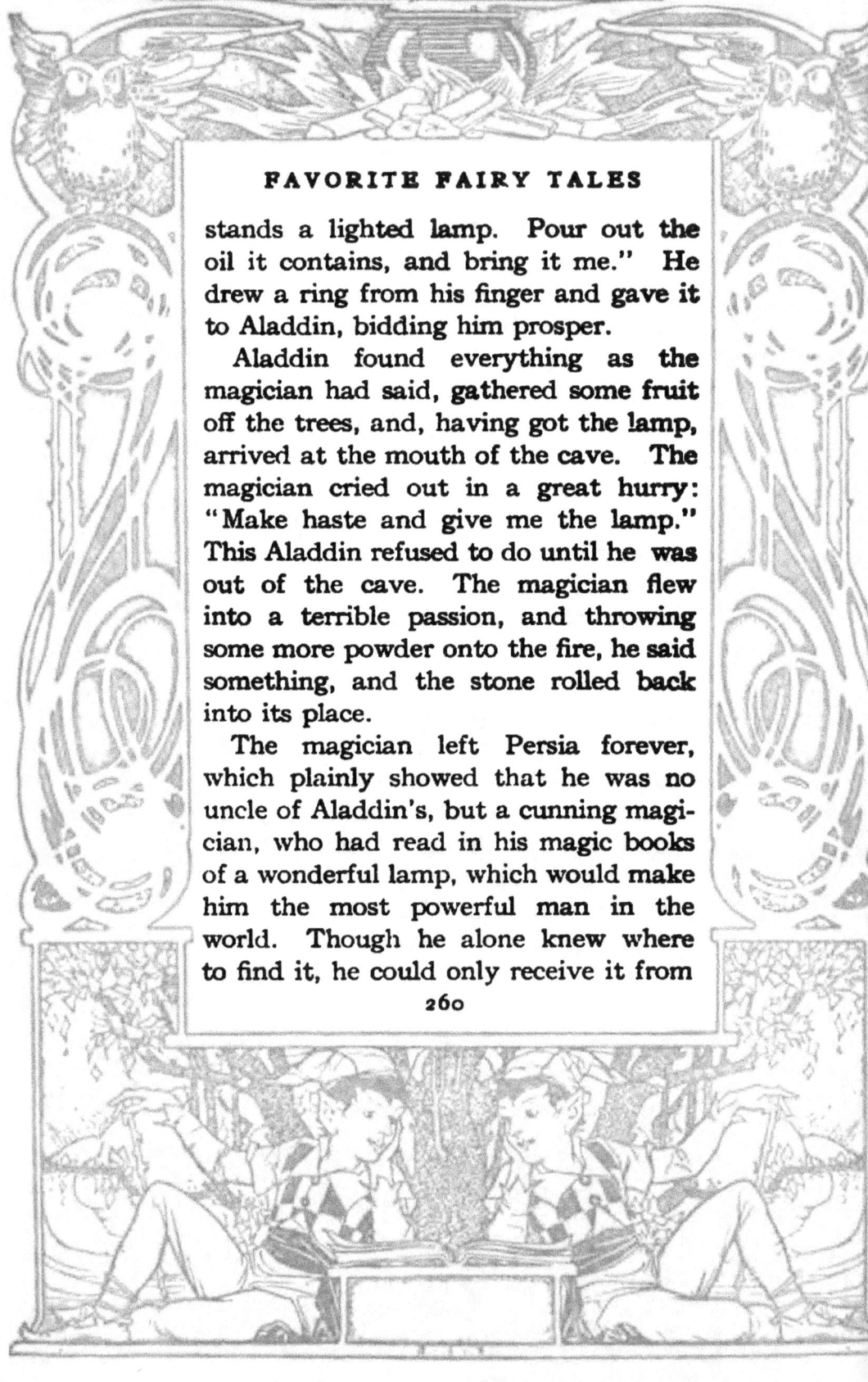

stands a lighted lamp. Pour out the
oil it contains, and bring it me." He
drew a ring from his finger and gave it
to Aladdin, bidding him prosper.

Aladdin found everything as the
magician had said, gathered some fruit
off the trees, and, having got the lamp,
arrived at the mouth of the cave. The
magician cried out in a great hurry:
"Make haste and give me the lamp."
This Aladdin refused to do until he was
out of the cave. The magician flew
into a terrible passion, and throwing
some more powder onto the fire, he said
something, and the stone rolled back
into its place.

The magician left Persia forever,
which plainly showed that he was no
uncle of Aladdin's, but a cunning magician, who had read in his magic books
of a wonderful lamp, which would make
him the most powerful man in the
world. Though he alone knew where
to find it, he could only receive it from

"I am the Slave of the Ring, and will obey thee in all things"

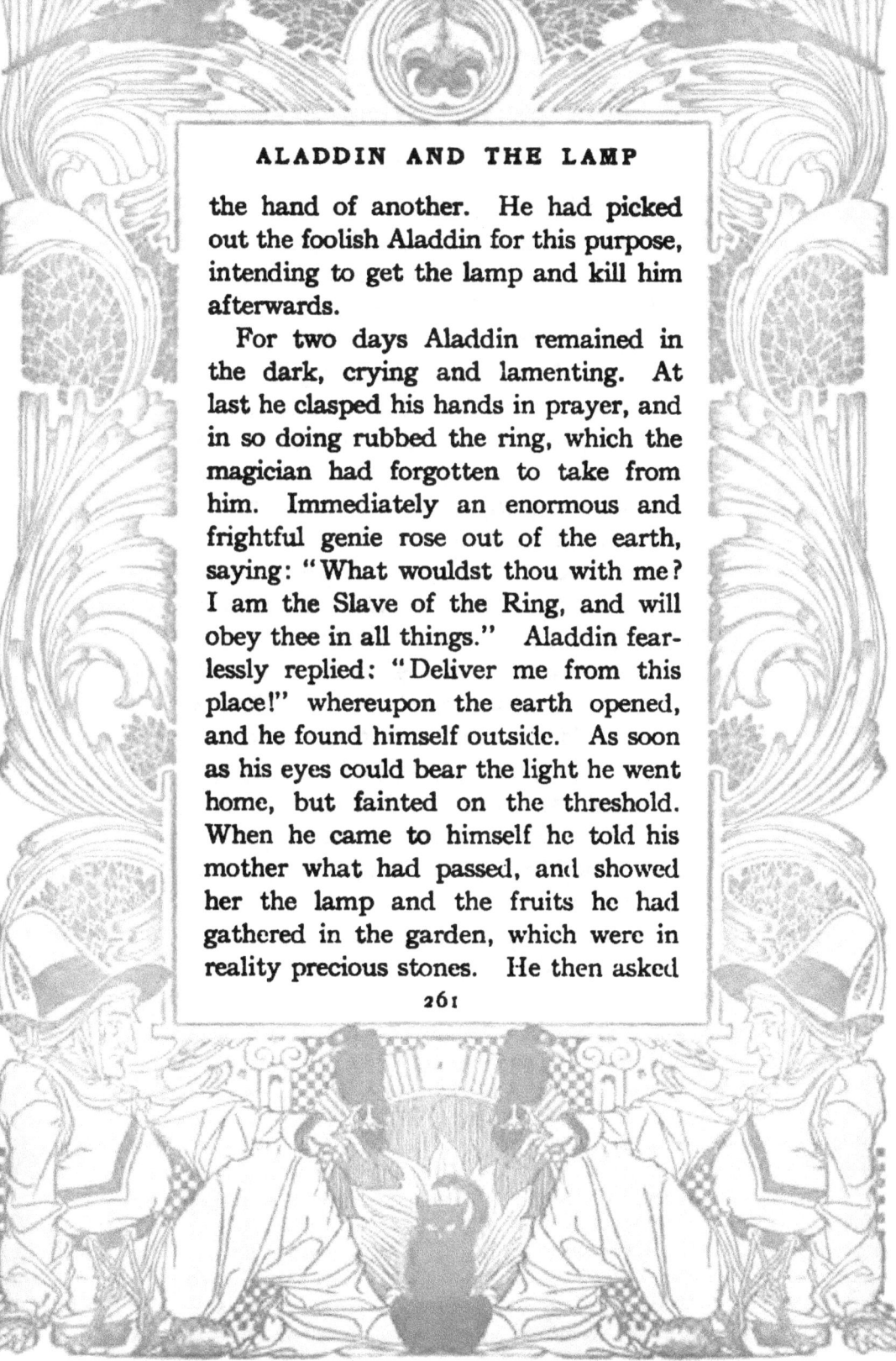

the hand of another. He had picked out the foolish Aladdin for this purpose, intending to get the lamp and kill him afterwards.

For two days Aladdin remained in the dark, crying and lamenting. At last he clasped his hands in prayer, and in so doing rubbed the ring, which the magician had forgotten to take from him. Immediately an enormous and frightful genie rose out of the earth, saying: "What wouldst thou with me? I am the Slave of the Ring, and will obey thee in all things." Aladdin fearlessly replied: "Deliver me from this place!" whereupon the earth opened, and he found himself outside. As soon as his eyes could bear the light he went home, but fainted on the threshold. When he came to himself he told his mother what had passed, and showed her the lamp and the fruits he had gathered in the garden, which were in reality precious stones. He then asked for some food. "Alas! child," she said, "I have nothing in the house, but I have spun a little cotton and will go and sell it." Aladdin bade her keep her cotton, for he would sell the lamp instead. As it was very dirty she began to rub it, that it might fetch a higher price. Instantly a hideous genie appeared, and asked what she would have. She fainted away, but Aladdin, snatchthe lamp, said boldly: "Fetch me something to eat!" The genie returned with a silver bowl, twelve silver plates containing rich meats, two silver cups, and two bottles of wine. Aladdin's mother, when she came to herself, said: "Whence comes this splendid feast?" "Ask not, but eat," replied Aladdin. So they sat at breakfast till it was dinner-time, and Aladdin told his mother about the lamp. She begged him to sell it, and have nothing to do with devils. "No," said Aladdin, "since chance hath made us aware of its virtues, we will use it, and

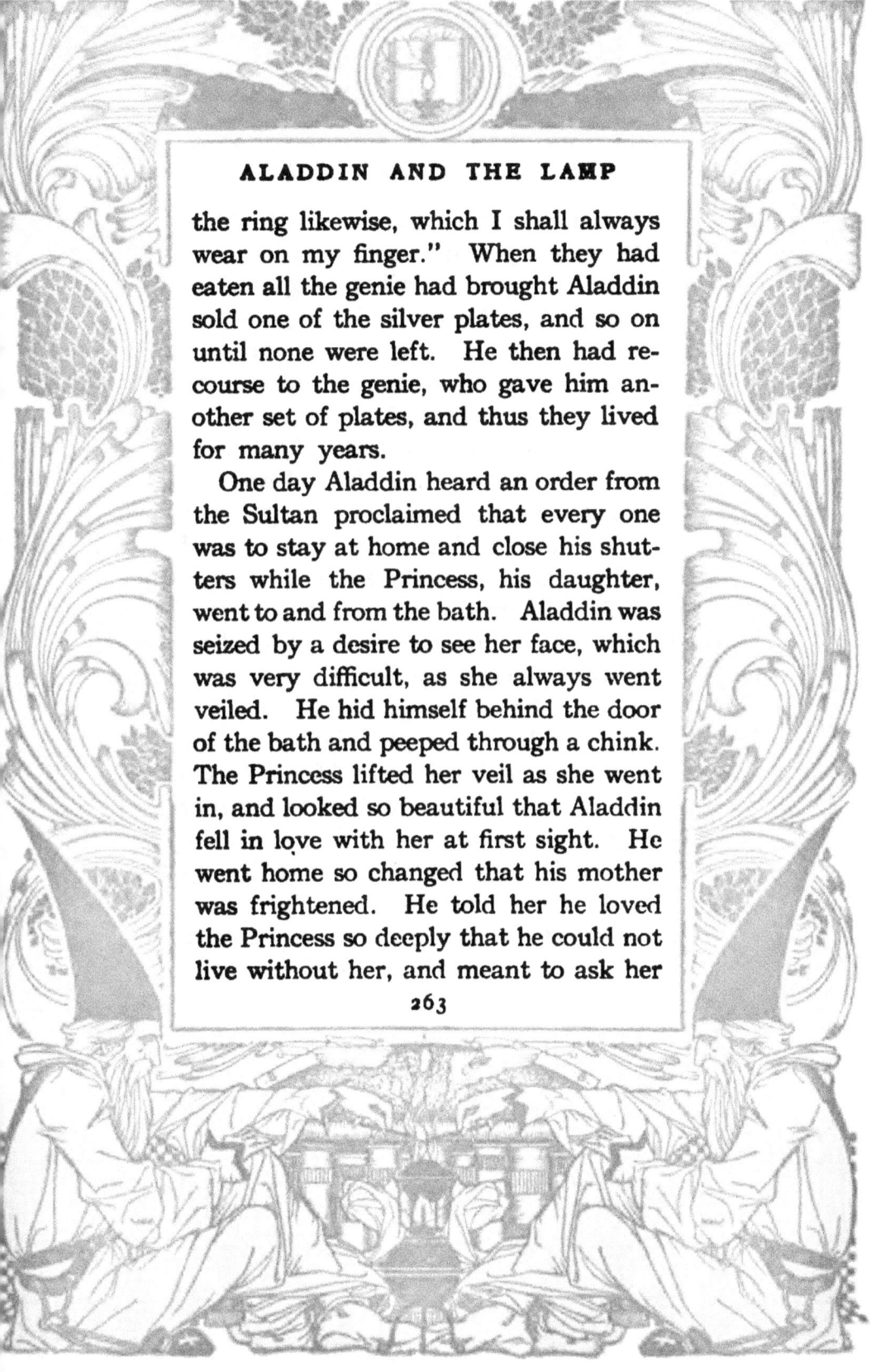

the ring likewise, which I shall always
wear on my finger." When they had
eaten all the genie had brought Aladdin
sold one of the silver plates, and so on
until none were left. He then had recourse to the genie, who gave him another set of plates, and thus they lived
for many years.

One day Aladdin heard an order from
the Sultan proclaimed that every one
was to stay at home and close his shut-
ters while the Princess, his daughter,
went to and from the bath. Aladdin was
seized by a desire to see her face, which
was very difficult, as she always went
veiled. He hid himself behind the door
of the bath and peeped through a chink.
The Princess lifted her veil as she went
in, and looked so beautiful that Aladdin
fell in love with her at first sight. He
went home so changed that his mother
was frightened. He told her he loved
the Princess so deeply that he could not
live without her, and meant to ask her

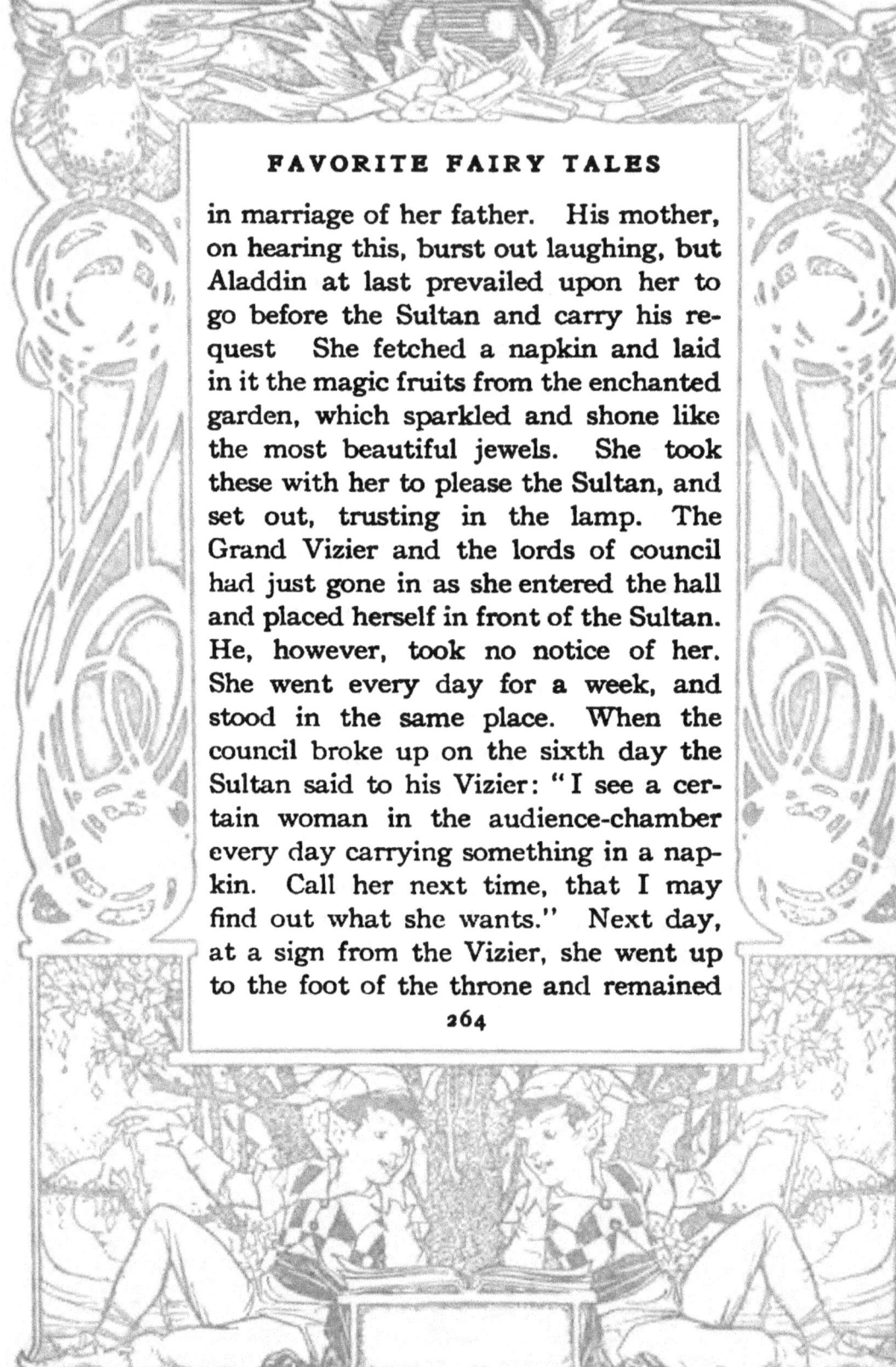

in marriage of her father. His mother, on hearing this, burst out laughing, but Aladdin at last prevailed upon her to go before the Sultan and carry his request She fetched a napkin and laid in it the magic fruits from the enchanted garden, which sparkled and shone like the most beautiful jewels. She took these with her to please the Sultan, and set out, trusting in the lamp. The Grand Vizier and the lords of council had just gone in as she entered the hall and placed herself in front of the Sultan. He, however, took no notice of her. She went every day for a week, and stood in the same place. When the council broke up on the sixth day the Sultan said to his Vizier: "I see a certain woman in the audience-chamber every day carrying something in a napkin. Call her next time, that I may find out what she wants." Next day, at a sign from the Vizier, she went up to the foot of the throne and remained

kneeling till the Sultan said to her:
"Rise, good woman, and tell me what
you want." She hesitated, so the Sultan sent away all but the Vizier, and
bade her speak freely, promising to forgive her beforehand for anything she
might say. She then told him of her
son's violent love for the Princess. "I
prayed him to forget her," she said,
"but in vain; he threatened to do some
desperate deed if I refused to go and
ask your Majesty for the hand of the
Princess. Now I pray you to forgive
not me alone, but my son Aladdin."
The Sultan asked her kindly what she
had in the napkin, whereupon she un-
folded the jewels and presented them.
He was thunderstruck, and turning to
the Vizier said: "What sayest thou?
Ought I not to bestow the Princess on
one who values her at such a price?"
The Vizier, who wanted her for his own
son, begged the Sultan to withhold her
for three months, in the course of which

he hoped his son would contrive to make him a richer present. The Sultan granted this, and told Aladdin's mother that, though he consented to the marriage, she must not appear before him again for three months.

Aladdin waited patiently for nearly three months, but after two had elapsed his mother, going into the city to buy oil, found every one rejoicing, and asked what was going on. "Do you not know," was the answer, "that the son of the Grand Vizier is to marry the Sultan's daughter to-night?" Breathless, she ran and told Aladdin, who was overwhelmed at first, but presently bethought him of the lamp. He rubbed it, and the genie appeared, saying: "What is thy will?" Aladdin replied: "The Sultan, as thou knowest, has broken his promise to me, and the Vizier's son is to have the Princess. My command is that to-night you bring hither the bride and bridegroom." "Master,

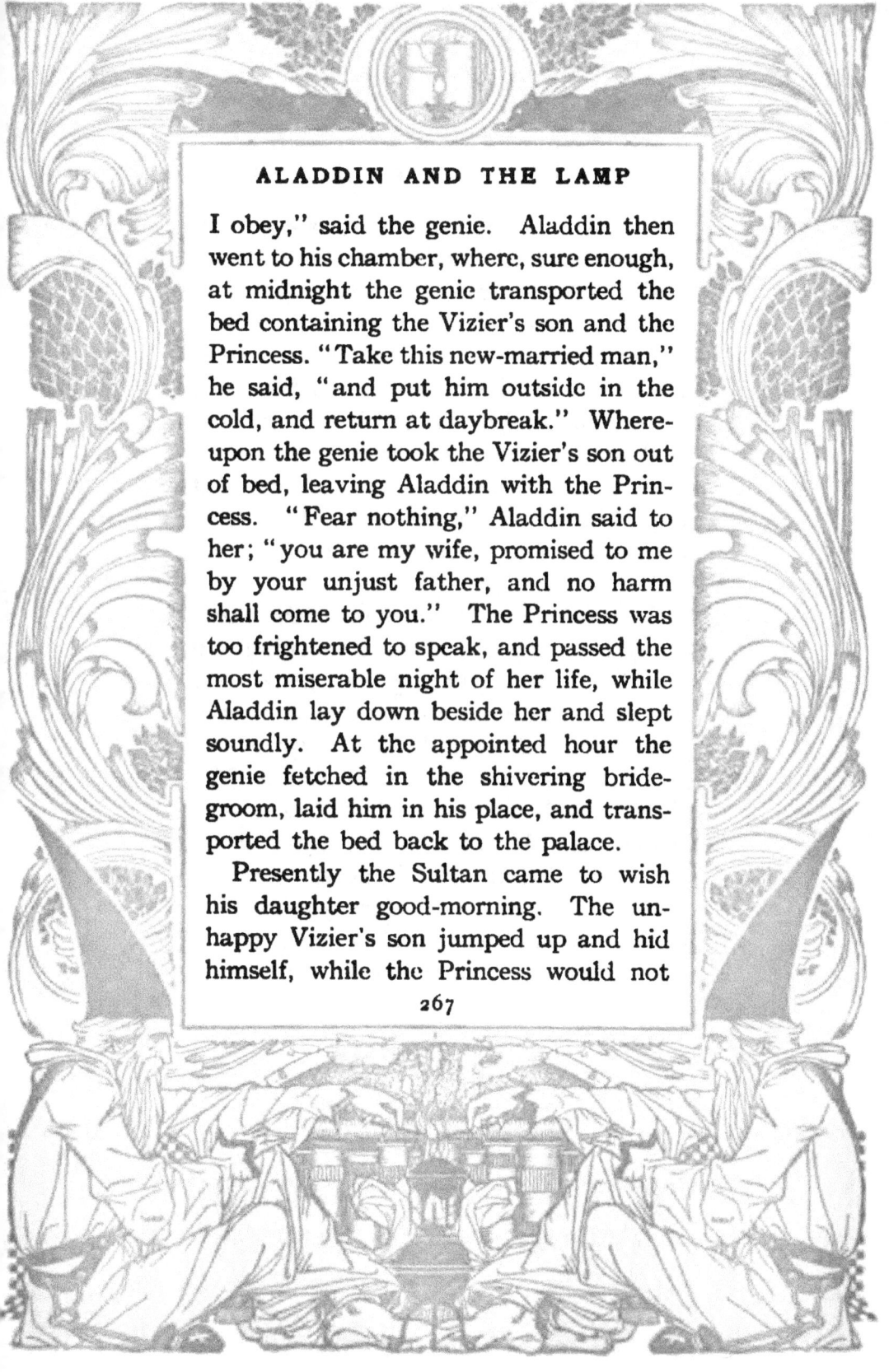

ALADDIN AND THE LAMP

I obey," said the genie. Aladdin then
went to his chamber, where, sure enough,
at midnight the genie transported the
bed containing the Vizier's son and the
Princess. "Take this new-married man,"
he said, "and put him outside in the
cold, and return at daybreak." Whereupon the genie took the Vizier's son out
of bed, leaving Aladdin with the Princess. "Fear nothing," Aladdin said to
her; "you are my wife, promised to me
by your unjust father, and no harm
shall come to you." The Princess was
too frightened to speak, and passed the
most miserable night of her life, while
Aladdin lay down beside her and slept
soundly. At the appointed hour the
genie fetched in the shivering bridegroom, laid him in his place, and transported the bed back to the palace.

Presently the Sultan came to wish
his daughter good-morning. The unhappy Vizier's son jumped up and hid
himself, while the Princess would not

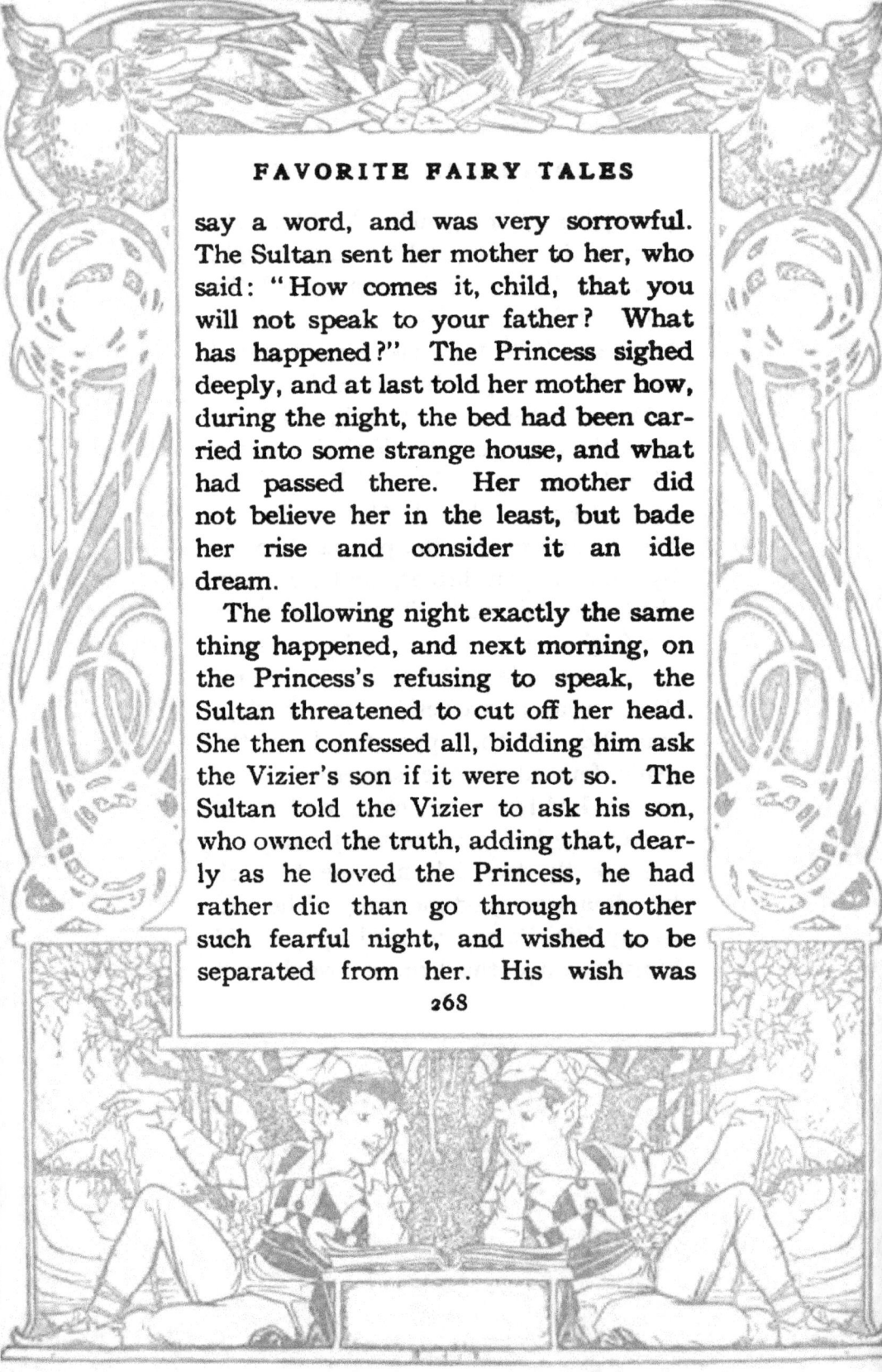

say a word, and was very sorrowful. The Sultan sent her mother to her, who said: "How comes it, child, that you will not speak to your father? What has happened?" The Princess sighed deeply, and at last told her mother how, during the night, the bed had been carried into some strange house, and what had passed there. Her mother did not believe her in the least, but bade her rise and consider it an idle dream.

The following night exactly the same thing happened, and next morning, on the Princess's refusing to speak, the Sultan threatened to cut off her head. She then confessed all, bidding him ask the Vizier's son if it were not so. The Sultan told the Vizier to ask his son, who owned the truth, adding that, dearly as he loved the Princess, he had rather die than go through another such fearful night, and wished to be separated from her. His wish was

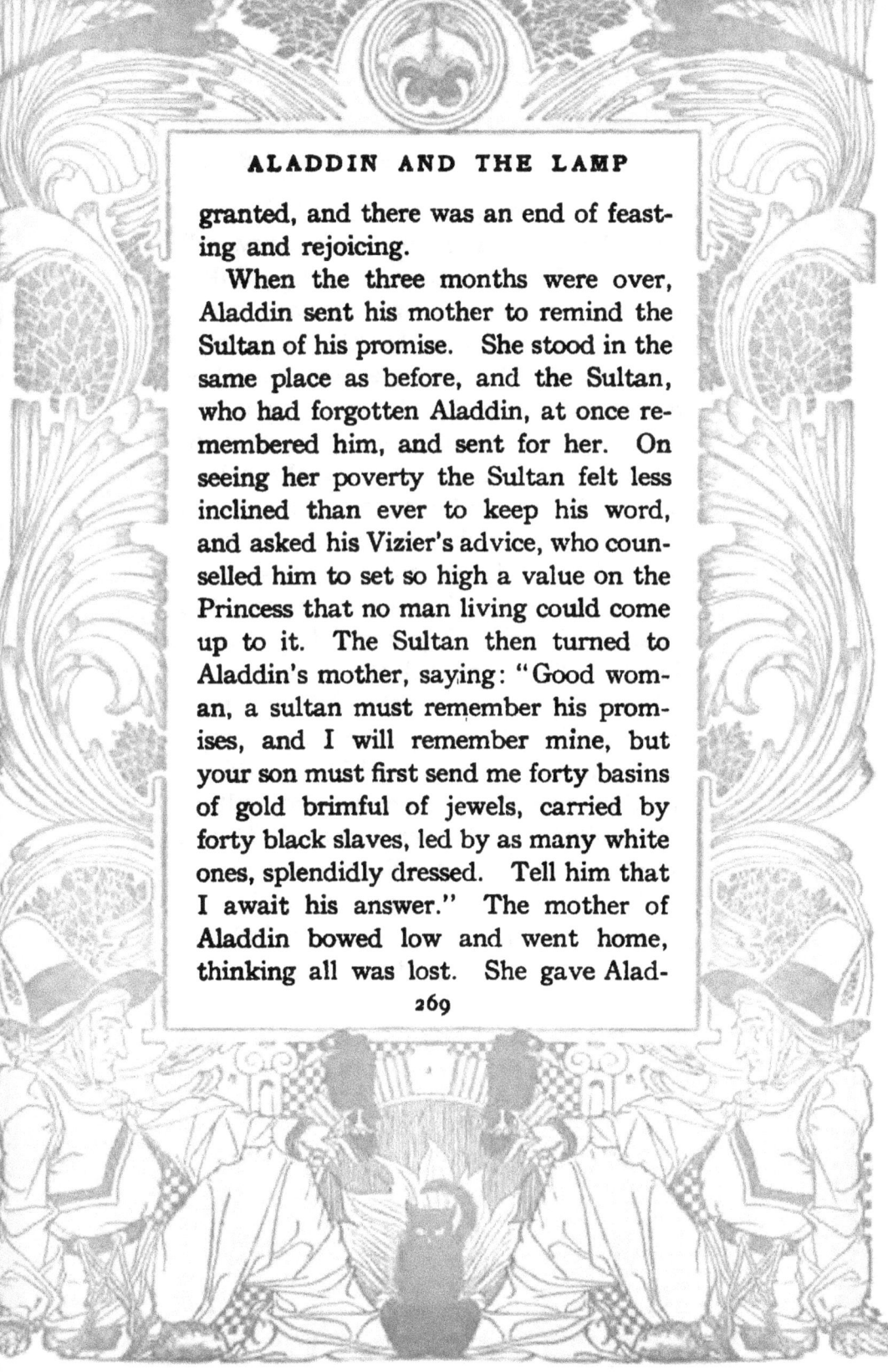

granted, and there was an end of feasting and rejoicing.

When the three months were over, Aladdin sent his mother to remind the Sultan of his promise. She stood in the same place as before, and the Sultan, who had forgotten Aladdin, at once remembered him, and sent for her. On seeing her poverty the Sultan felt less inclined than ever to keep his word, and asked his Vizier's advice, who counselled him to set so high a value on the Princess that no man living could come up to it. The Sultan then turned to Aladdin's mother, saying: "Good woman, a sultan must remember his promises, and I will remember mine, but your son must first send me forty basins of gold brimful of jewels, carried by forty black slaves, led by as many white ones, splendidly dressed. Tell him that I await his answer." The mother of Aladdin bowed low and went home, thinking all was lost. She gave Aladdin the message, adding: "He may wait long enough for your answer!" "Not so long, mother, as you think," her son replied. "I would do a great deal more than that for the Princess." He summoned the genie, and in a few moments the eighty slaves arrived, and filled up the small house and garden. Aladdin made them set out to the palace two and two, followed by his mother. They were so richly dressed, with such splendid jewels in their girdles, that every one crowded to see them and the basins of gold they carried on their heads. They entered the palace, and, after kneeling before the Sultan, stood in a half-circle round the throne with their arms crossed, while Aladdin's mother presented them to the Sultan. He hesitated no longer, but said: "Good woman, return and tell your son that I wait for him with open arms." She lost no time in telling Aladdin, bidding him make haste. But Aladdin first

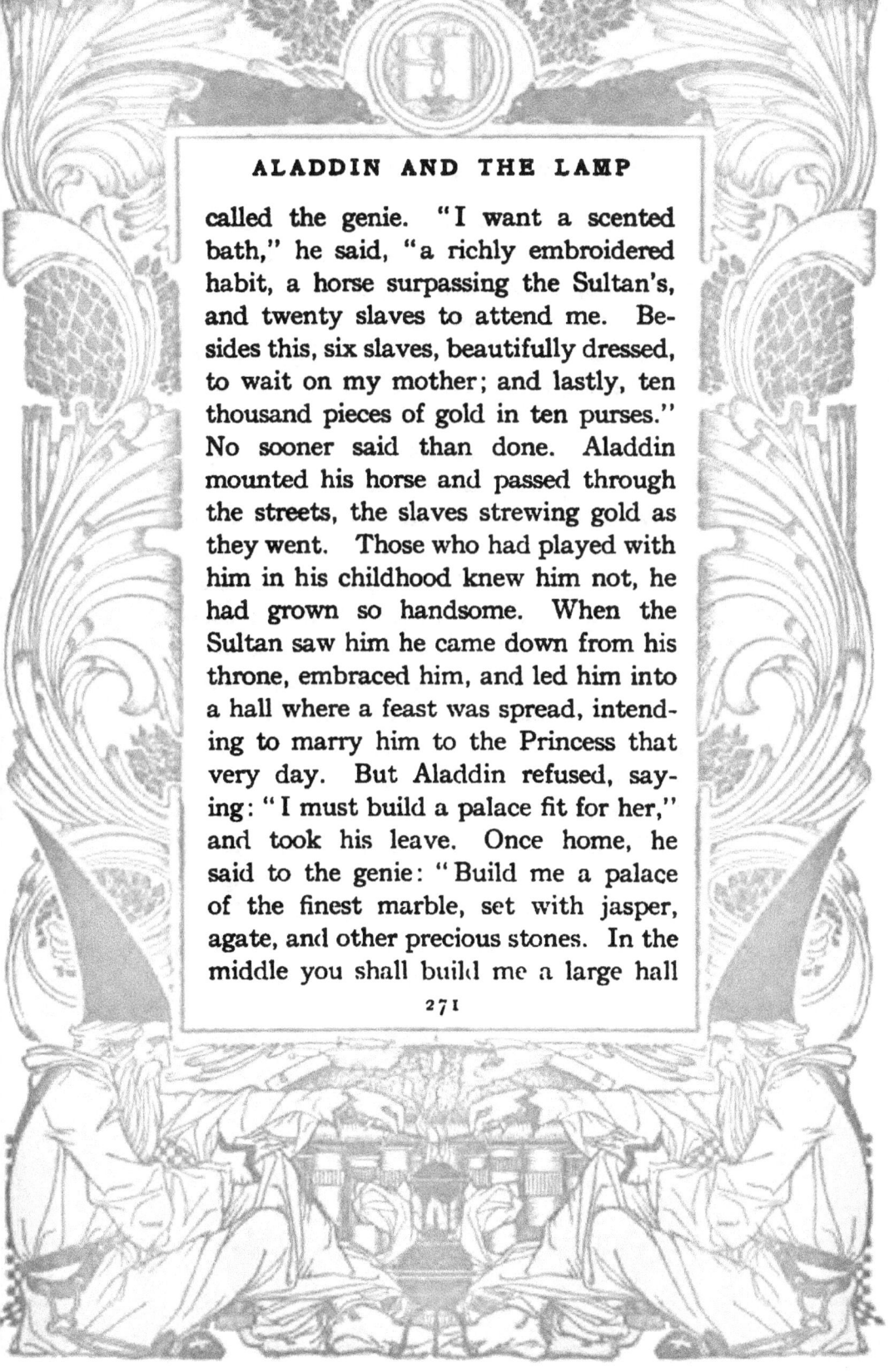

called the genie. "I want a scented
bath," he said, "a richly embroidered
habit, a horse surpassing the Sultan's,
and twenty slaves to attend me. Besides this, six slaves, beautifully dressed,
to wait on my mother; and lastly, ten
thousand pieces of gold in ten purses."
No sooner said than done. Aladdin
mounted his horse and passed through
the streets, the slaves strewing gold as
they went. Those who had played with
him in his childhood knew him not, he
had grown so handsome. When the
Sultan saw him he came down from his
throne, embraced him, and led him into
a hall where a feast was spread, intending to marry him to the Princess that
very day. But Aladdin refused, saying: "I must build a palace fit for her,"
and took his leave. Once home, he
said to the genie: "Build me a palace
of the finest marble, set with jasper,
agate, and other precious stones. In the
middle you shall build me a large hall

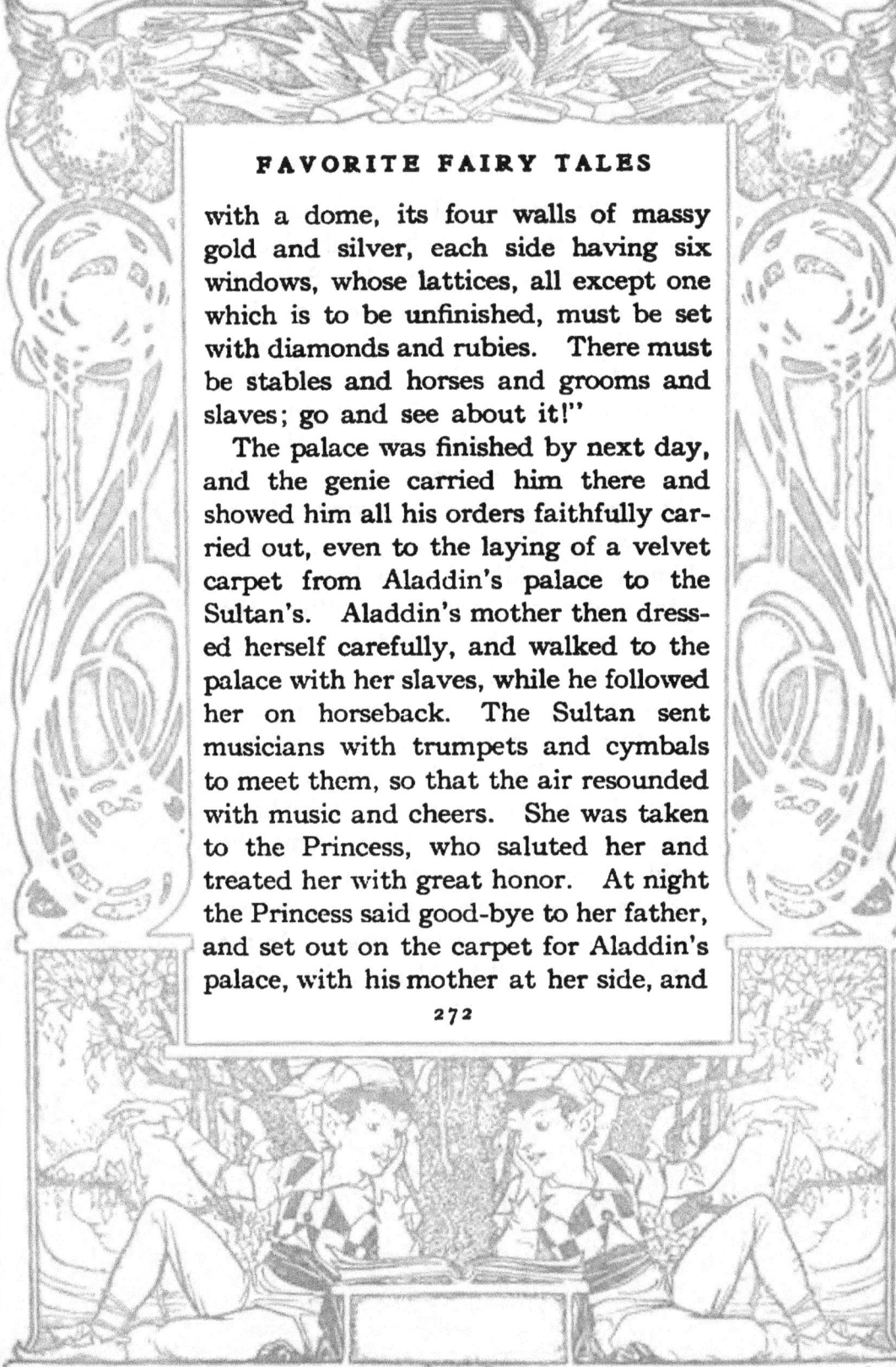

with a dome, its four walls of massy gold and silver, each side having six windows, whose lattices, all except one which is to be unfinished, must be set with diamonds and rubies. There must be stables and horses and grooms and slaves; go and see about it!"

The palace was finished by next day, and the genie carried him there and showed him all his orders faithfully carried out, even to the laying of a velvet carpet from Aladdin's palace to the Sultan's. Aladdin's mother then dressed herself carefully, and walked to the palace with her slaves, while he followed her on horseback. The Sultan sent musicians with trumpets and cymbals to meet them, so that the air resounded with music and cheers. She was taken to the Princess, who saluted her and treated her with great honor. At night the Princess said good-bye to her father, and set out on the carpet for Aladdin's palace, with his mother at her side, and

272

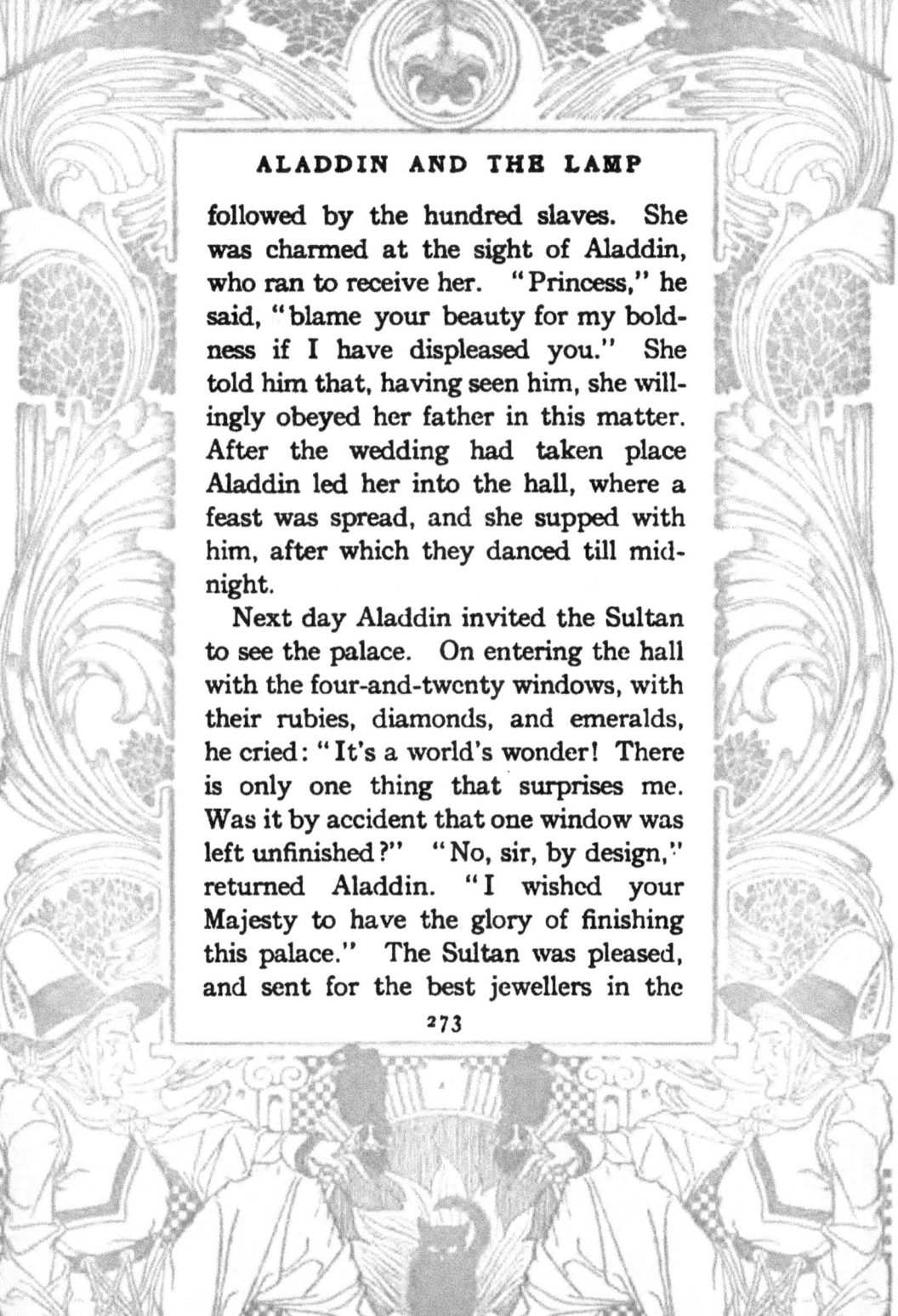

followed by the hundred slaves. She was charmed at the sight of Aladdin, who ran to receive her. "Princess," he said, "blame your beauty for my boldness if I have displeased you." She told him that, having seen him, she willingly obeyed her father in this matter. After the wedding had taken place Aladdin led her into the hall, where a feast was spread, and she supped with him, after which they danced till midnight.

Next day Aladdin invited the Sultan to see the palace. On entering the hall with the four-and-twenty windows, with their rubies, diamonds, and emeralds, he cried: "It's a world's wonder! There is only one thing that surprises me. Was it by accident that one window was left unfinished?" "No, sir, by design," returned Aladdin. "I wished your Majesty to have the glory of finishing this palace." The Sultan was pleased, and sent for the best jewellers in the

273

city. He showed them the unfinished window, and bade them fit it up like the others. "Sir," replied their spokesman, "we cannot find jewels enough." The Sultan had his own fetched, which they soon used, but to no purpose, for in a month's time the work was not half done. Aladdin, knowing that their task was vain, bade them undo their work and carry the jewels back, and the genie finished the window at his command. The Sultan was surprised to receive his jewels again, and visited Aladdin, who showed him the window finished. The Sultan embraced him, the envious Vizier meanwhile hinting that it was the work of enchantment.

Aladdin had won the hearts of the people by his gentle bearing. He was made captain of the Sultan's armies, and won several battles for him, but remained modest and courteous as before, and lived thus in peace and content for several years.

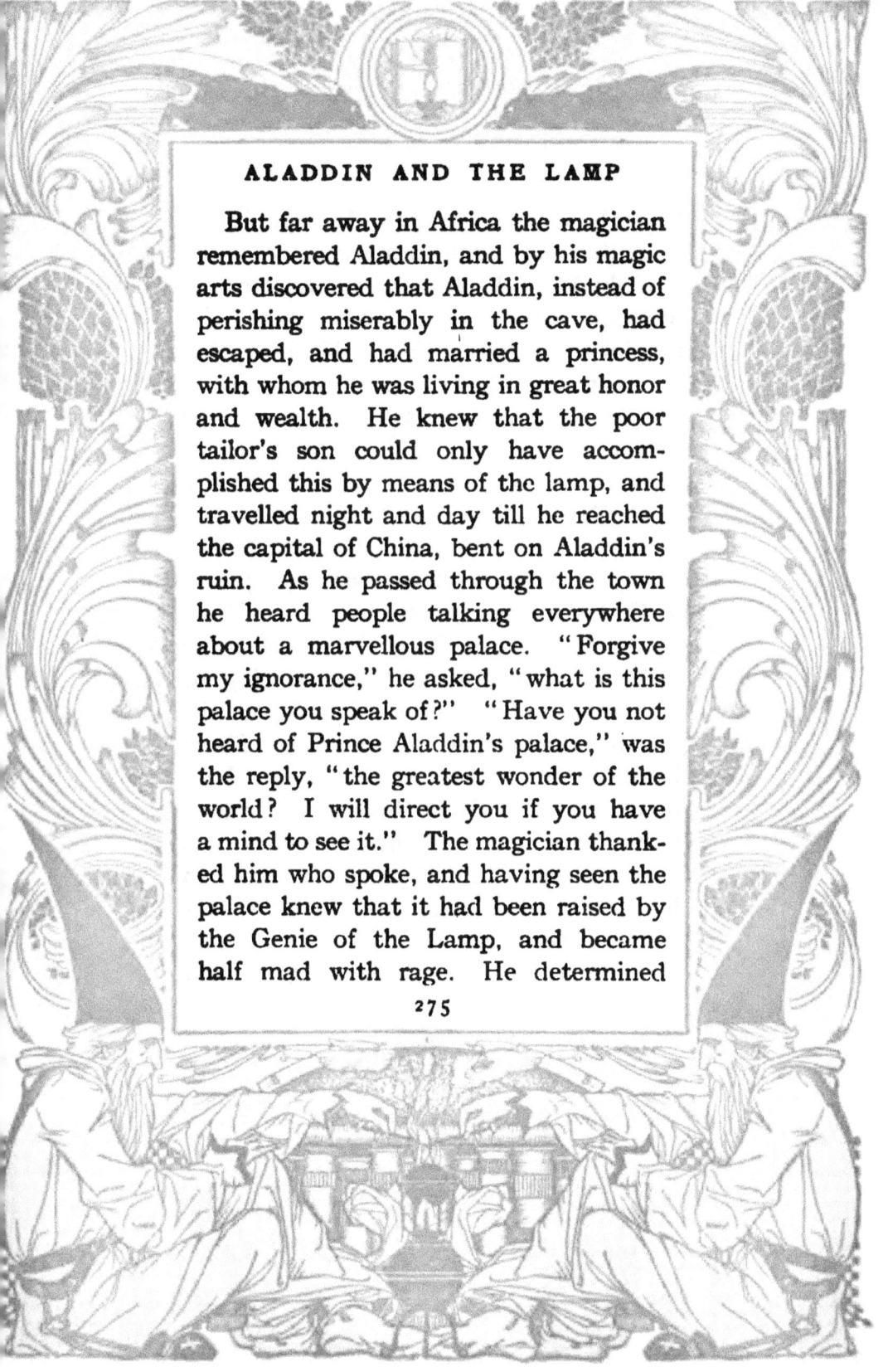

ALADDIN AND THE LAMP

But far away in Africa the magician remembered Aladdin, and by his magic arts discovered that Aladdin, instead of perishing miserably in the cave, had escaped, and had married a princess, with whom he was living in great honor and wealth. He knew that the poor tailor's son could only have accomplished this by means of the lamp, and travelled night and day till he reached the capital of China, bent on Aladdin's ruin. As he passed through the town he heard people talking everywhere about a marvellous palace. "Forgive my ignorance," he asked, "what is this palace you speak of?" "Have you not heard of Prince Aladdin's palace," was the reply, "the greatest wonder of the world? I will direct you if you have a mind to see it." The magician thanked him who spoke, and having seen the palace knew that it had been raised by the Genie of the Lamp, and became half mad with rage. He determined

275

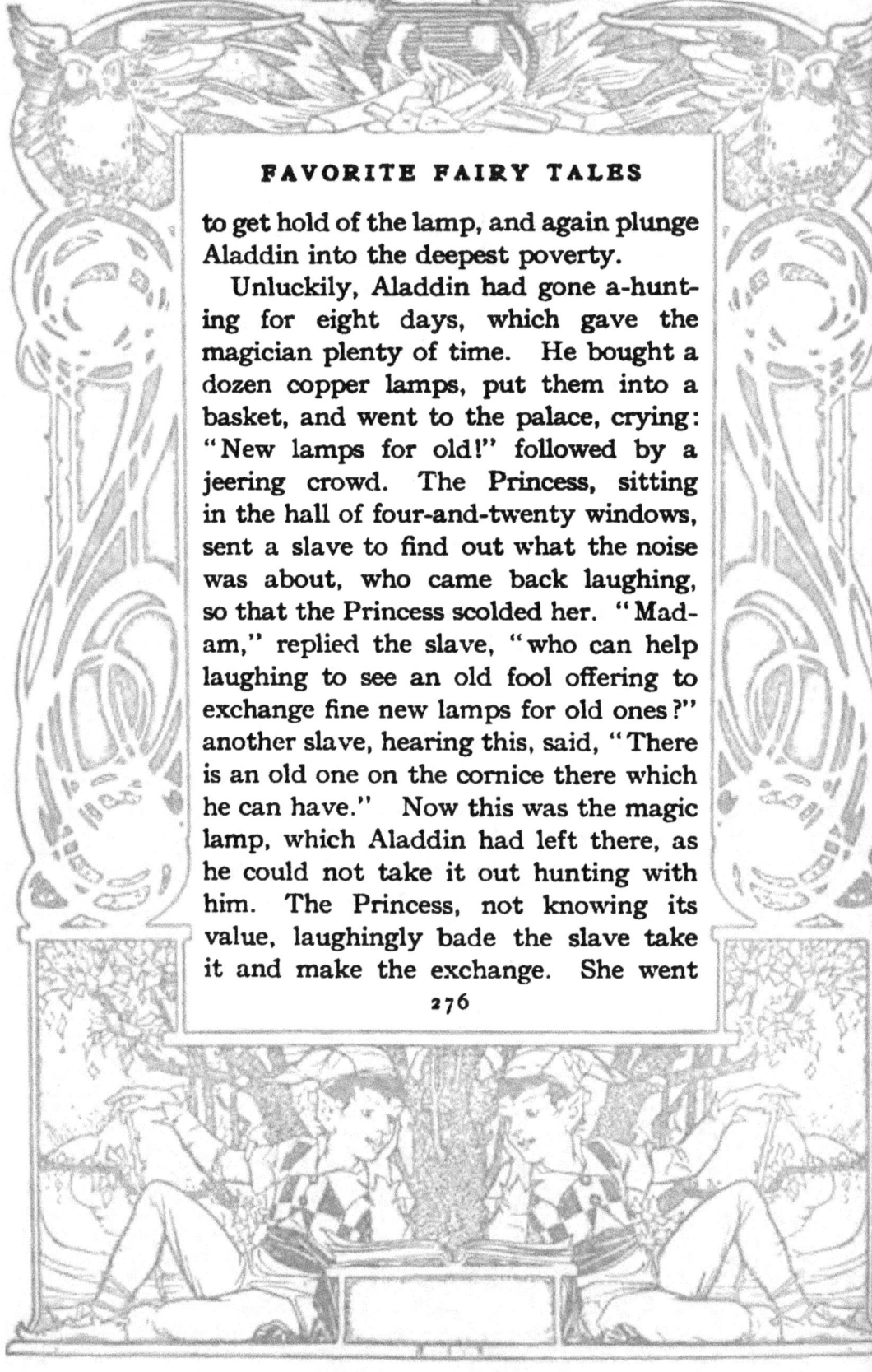

to get hold of the lamp, and again plunge Aladdin into the deepest poverty.

Unluckily, Aladdin had gone a-hunting for eight days, which gave the magician plenty of time. He bought a dozen copper lamps, put them into a basket, and went to the palace, crying: "New lamps for old!" followed by a jeering crowd. The Princess, sitting in the hall of four-and-twenty windows, sent a slave to find out what the noise was about, who came back laughing, so that the Princess scolded her. "Madam," replied the slave, "who can help laughing to see an old fool offering to exchange fine new lamps for old ones?" another slave, hearing this, said, "There is an old one on the cornice there which he can have." Now this was the magic lamp, which Aladdin had left there, as he could not take it out hunting with him. The Princess, not knowing its value, laughingly bade the slave take it and make the exchange. She went

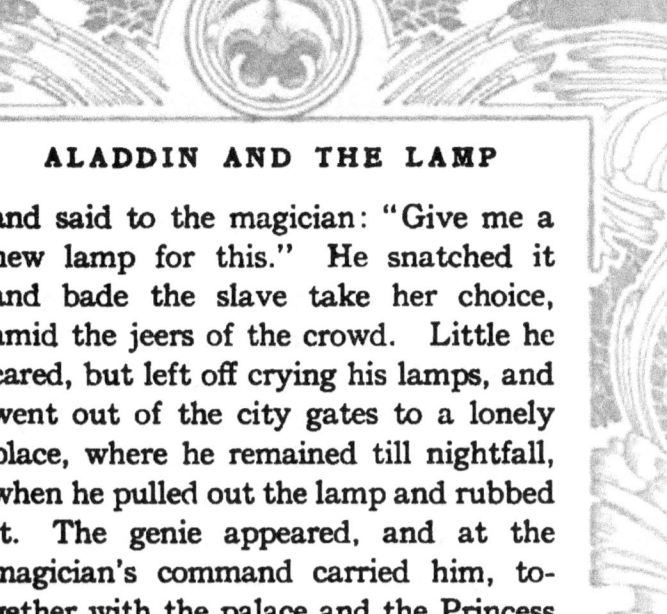

and said to the magician: "Give me a new lamp for this." He snatched it and bade the slave take her choice, amid the jeers of the crowd. Little he cared, but left off crying his lamps, and went out of the city gates to a lonely place, where he remained till nightfall, when he pulled out the lamp and rubbed it. The genie appeared, and at the magician's command carried him, together with the palace and the Princess in it, to a lonely place in Africa.

Next morning the Sultan looked out of the window towards Aladdin's palace and rubbed his eyes, for it was gone. He sent for the Vizier and asked what had become of the palace. The Vizier looked out, too, and was lost in astonishment. He again put it down to enchantment, and this time the Sultan believed him, and sent thirty men on horseback to fetch Aladdin in chains. They met him riding home, bound him, and forced him to go with them on foot.

The people, however, who loved him, followed, armed, to see that he came to no harm. He was carried before the Sultan, who ordered the executioner to cut off his head. The executioner made Aladdin kneel down, bandaged his eyes, and raised his scimitar to strike. At that instant the Vizier, who saw that the crowd had forced their way into the court-yard and were scaling the walls to rescue Aladdin, called to the executioner to stay his hand. The people, indeed, looked so threatening that the Sultan gave way and ordered Aladdin to be unbound, and pardoned him in the sight of the crowd. Aladdin now begged to know what he had done. "False wretch!" said the Sultan, "come hither," and showed him from the window the place where his palace had stood. Aladdin was so amazed that he could not say a word. "Where is my palace and my daughter?" demanded the Sultan. "For the first I am not so

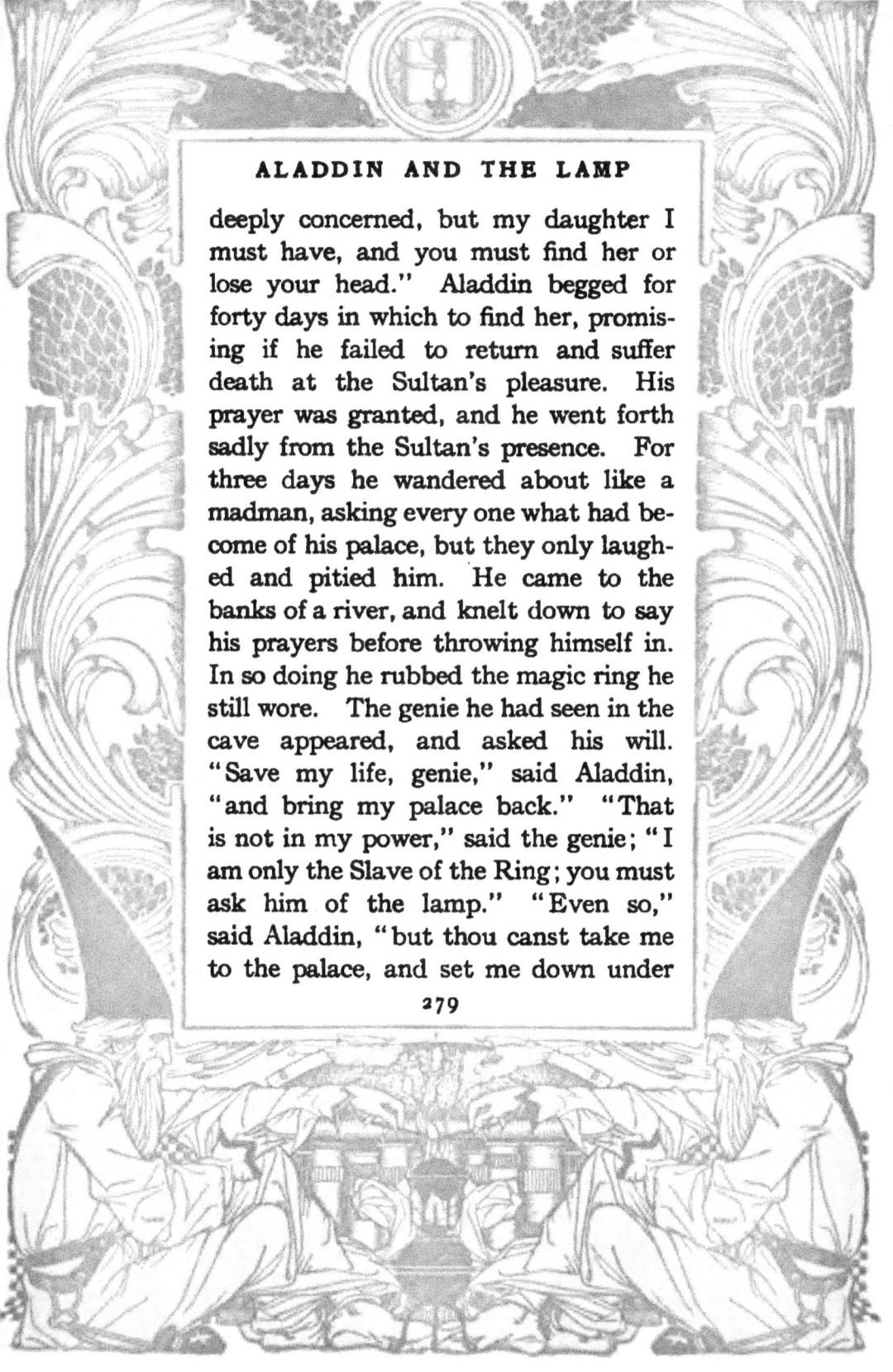

deeply concerned, but my daughter I must have, and you must find her or lose your head." Aladdin begged for forty days in which to find her, promising if he failed to return and suffer death at the Sultan's pleasure. His prayer was granted, and he went forth sadly from the Sultan's presence. For three days he wandered about like a madman, asking every one what had become of his palace, but they only laughed and pitied him. He came to the banks of a river, and knelt down to say his prayers before throwing himself in. In so doing he rubbed the magic ring he still wore. The genie he had seen in the cave appeared, and asked his will. "Save my life, genie," said Aladdin, "and bring my palace back." "That is not in my power," said the genie; "I am only the Slave of the Ring; you must ask him of the lamp." "Even so," said Aladdin, "but thou canst take me to the palace, and set me down under

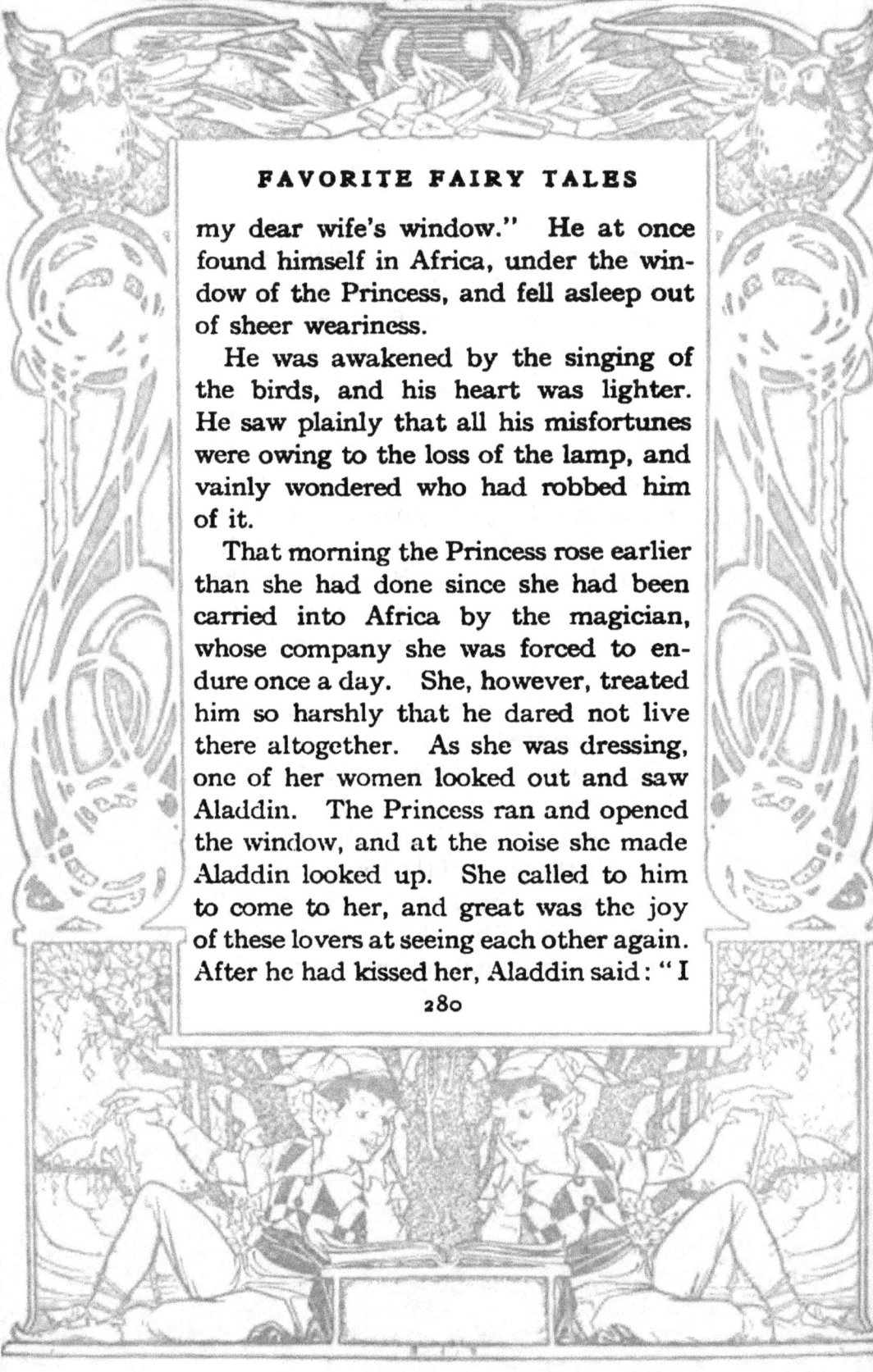

my dear wife's window." He at once
found himself in Africa, under the window of the Princess, and fell asleep out
of sheer weariness.

He was awakened by the singing of
the birds, and his heart was lighter.
He saw plainly that all his misfortunes
were owing to the loss of the lamp, and
vainly wondered who had robbed him
of it.

That morning the Princess rose earlier
than she had done since she had been
carried into Africa by the magician,
whose company she was forced to endure once a day. She, however, treated
him so harshly that he dared not live
there altogether. As she was dressing,
one of her women looked out and saw
Aladdin. The Princess ran and opened
the window, and at the noise she made
Aladdin looked up. She called to him
to come to her, and great was the joy
of these lovers at seeing each other again.
After he had kissed her, Aladdin said: "I

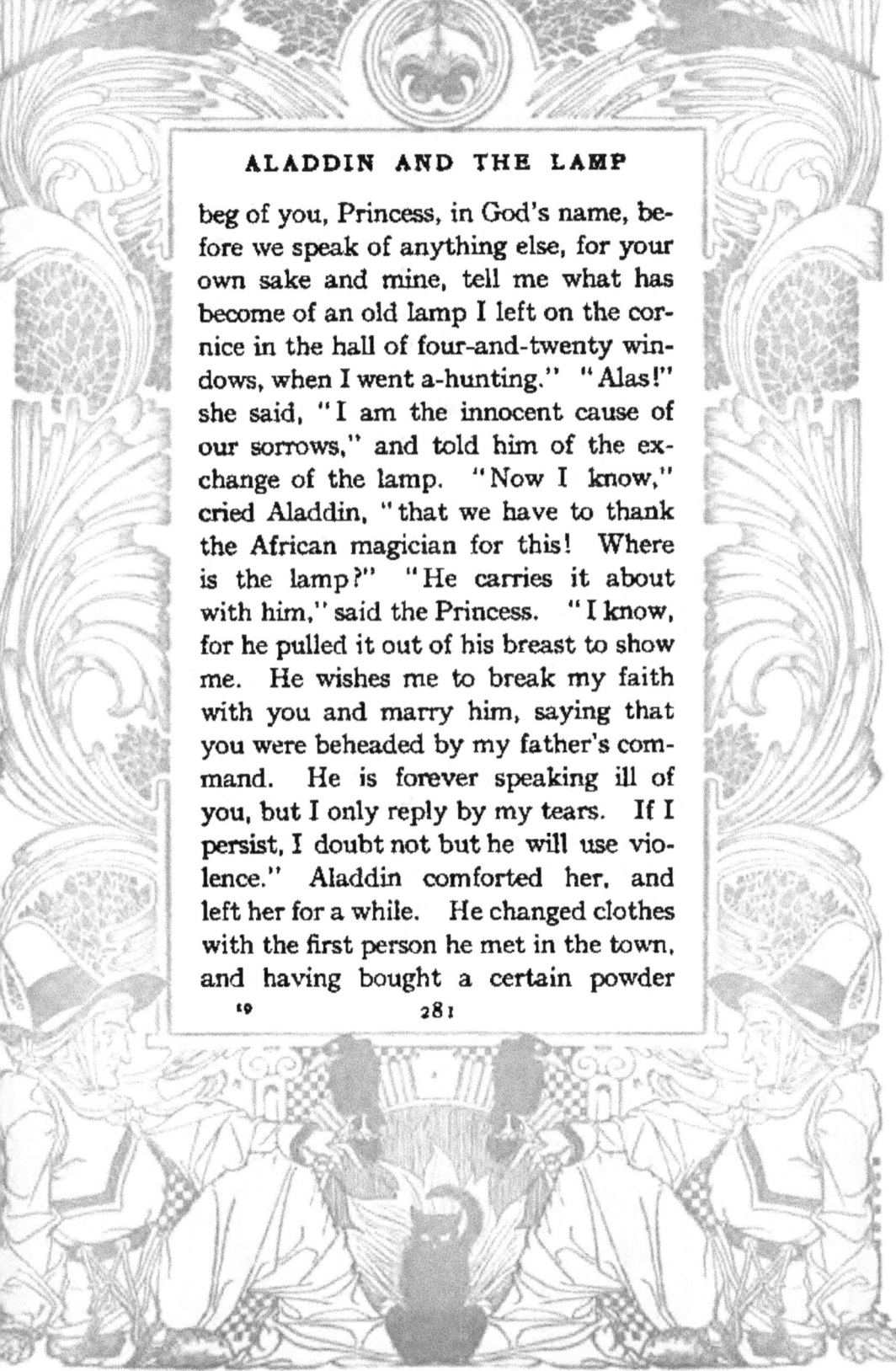

beg of you, Princess, in God's name, before we speak of anything else, for your own sake and mine, tell me what has become of an old lamp I left on the cornice in the hall of four-and-twenty windows, when I went a-hunting." "Alas!" she said, "I am the innocent cause of our sorrows," and told him of the exchange of the lamp. "Now I know," cried Aladdin, "that we have to thank the African magician for this! Where is the lamp?" "He carries it about with him," said the Princess. "I know, for he pulled it out of his breast to show me. He wishes me to break my faith with you and marry him, saying that you were beheaded by my father's command. He is forever speaking ill of you, but I only reply by my tears. If I persist, I doubt not but he will use violence." Aladdin comforted her, and left her for a while. He changed clothes with the first person he met in the town, and having bought a certain powder returned to the Princess, who let him in by a little side door. "Put on your most beautiful dress," he said to her, "and receive the magician with smiles, leading him to believe that you have forgotten me. Invite him to sup with you, and say you wish to taste the wine of his country. He will go for some and while he is gone I will tell you what to do." She listened carefully to Aladdin, and when he left her arrayed herself gayly for the first time since she left China. She put on a girdle and head-dress of diamonds, and seeing in a glass that she was more beautiful than ever, received the magician, saying, to his great amazement: "I have made up my mind that Aladdin is dead, and that all my tears will not bring him back to me, so I am resolved to mourn no more, and have therefore invited you to sup with me; but I am tired of the wines of China, and would fain taste those of Africa." The magician flew to his cel-

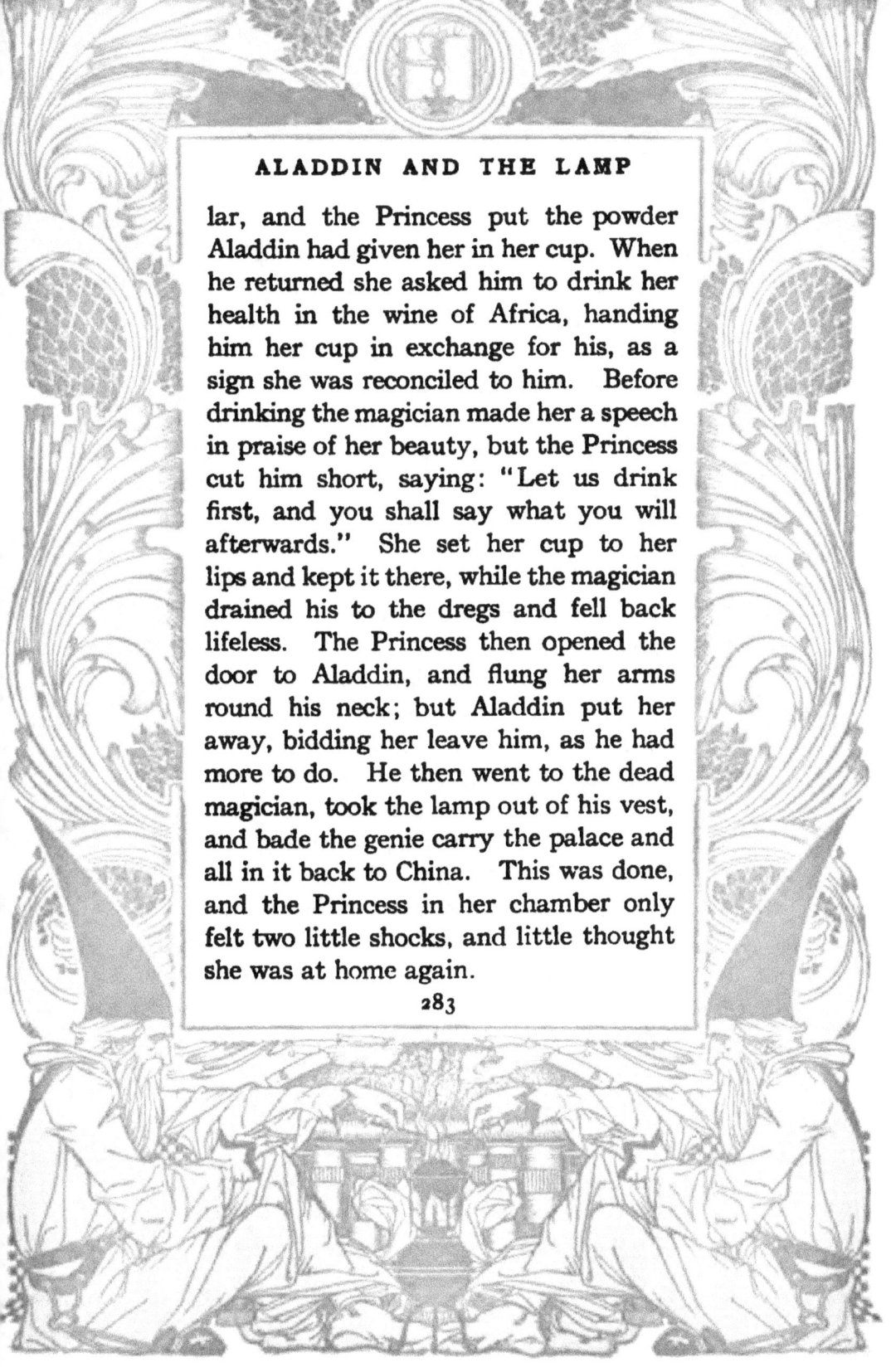

lar, and the Princess put the powder Aladdin had given her in her cup. When he returned she asked him to drink her health in the wine of Africa, handing him her cup in exchange for his, as a sign she was reconciled to him. Before drinking the magician made her a speech in praise of her beauty, but the Princess cut him short, saying: "Let us drink first, and you shall say what you will afterwards." She set her cup to her lips and kept it there, while the magician drained his to the dregs and fell back lifeless. The Princess then opened the door to Aladdin, and flung her arms round his neck; but Aladdin put her away, bidding her leave him, as he had more to do. He then went to the dead magician, took the lamp out of his vest, and bade the genie carry the palace and all in it back to China. This was done, and the Princess in her chamber only felt two little shocks, and little thought she was at home again.

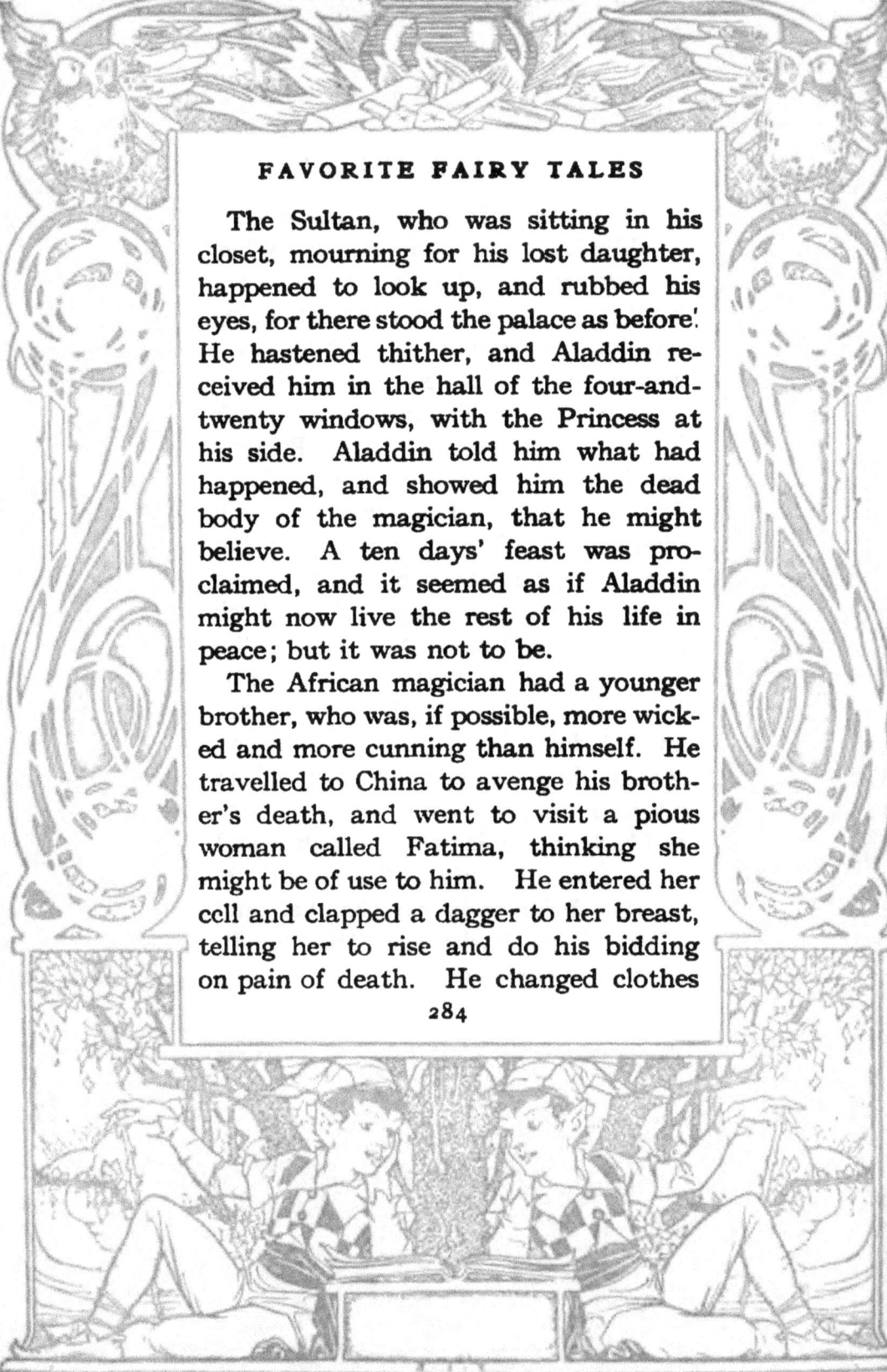

The Sultan, who was sitting in his closet, mourning for his lost daughter, happened to look up, and rubbed his eyes, for there stood the palace as before! He hastened thither, and Aladdin received him in the hall of the four-and-twenty windows, with the Princess at his side. Aladdin told him what had happened, and showed him the dead body of the magician, that he might believe. A ten days' feast was proclaimed, and it seemed as if Aladdin might now live the rest of his life in peace; but it was not to be.

The African magician had a younger brother, who was, if possible, more wicked and more cunning than himself. He travelled to China to avenge his brother's death, and went to visit a pious woman called Fatima, thinking she might be of use to him. He entered her cell and clapped a dagger to her breast, telling her to rise and do his bidding on pain of death. He changed clothes

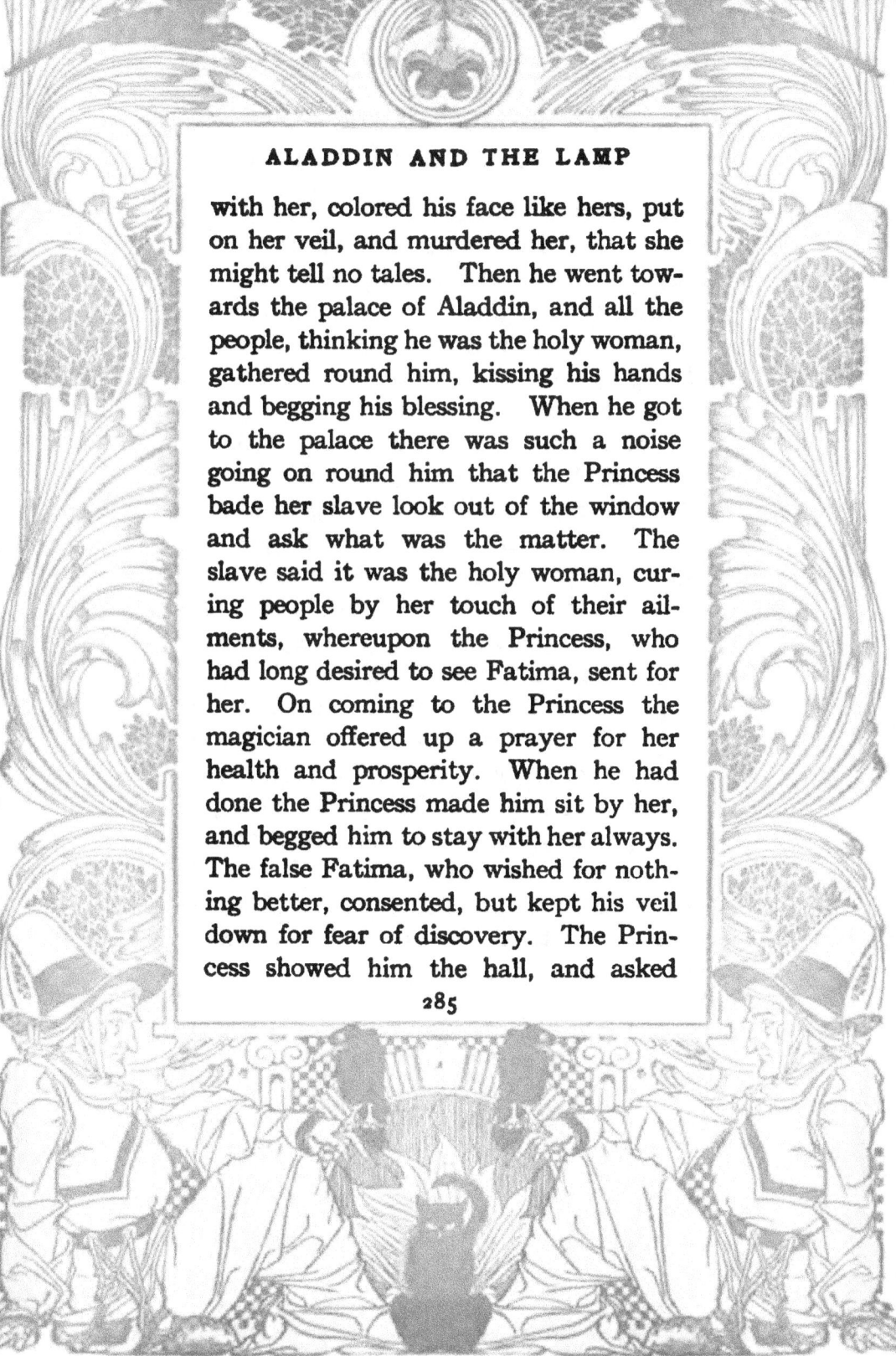

with her, colored his face like hers, put on her veil, and murdered her, that she might tell no tales. Then he went towards the palace of Aladdin, and all the people, thinking he was the holy woman, gathered round him, kissing his hands and begging his blessing. When he got to the palace there was such a noise going on round him that the Princess bade her slave look out of the window and ask what was the matter. The slave said it was the holy woman, curing people by her touch of their ailments, whereupon the Princess, who had long desired to see Fatima, sent for her. On coming to the Princess the magician offered up a prayer for her health and prosperity. When he had done the Princess made him sit by her, and begged him to stay with her always. The false Fatima, who wished for nothing better, consented, but kept his veil down for fear of discovery. The Princess showed him the hall, and asked

him what he thought of it. "It is truly beautiful," said the false Fatima. "In my mind it wants but one thing." "And what is that?" said the Princess. "If only a roc's egg," replied he, "were hung up from the middle of this dome, it would be the wonder of the world."

After this the Princess could think of nothing but the roc's egg, and when Aladdin returned from hunting he found her in a very ill humor. He begged to know what was amiss, and she told him that all her pleasure in the hall was spoiled for the want of a roc's egg hanging from the dome. "If that is all," replied Aladdin, "you shall soon be happy." He left her and rubbed the lamp, and when the genie appeared commanded him to bring a roc's egg. The genie gave such a loud and terrible shriek that the hall shook. "Wretch!" he cried, "is it not enough that I have done everything for you but you must command me to bring my master and

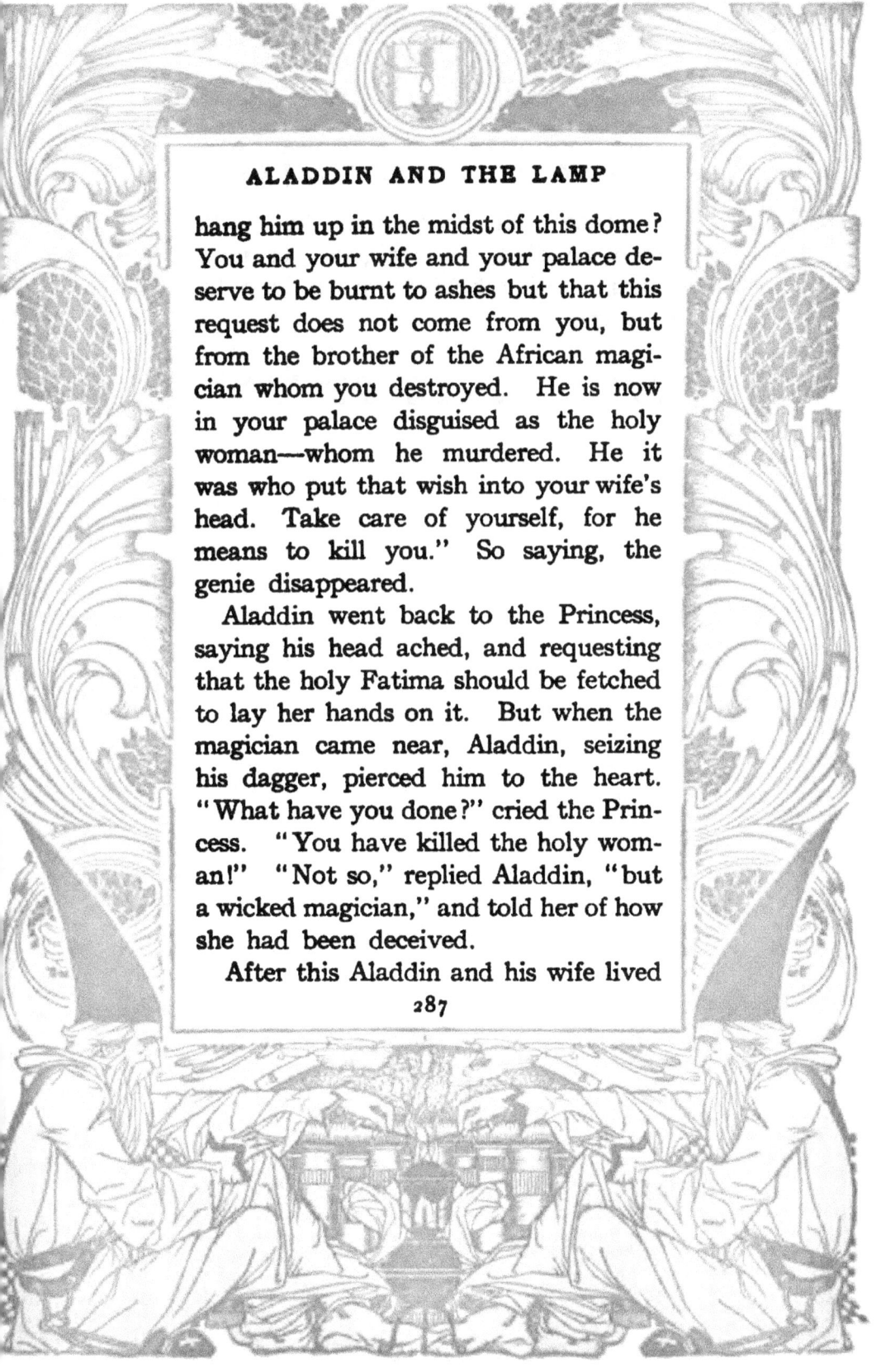

hang him up in the midst of this dome?
You and your wife and your palace deserve to be burnt to ashes but that this
request does not come from you, but
from the brother of the African magician whom you destroyed. He is now
in your palace disguised as the holy
woman—whom he murdered. He it
was who put that wish into your wife's
head. Take care of yourself, for he
means to kill you." So saying, the
genie disappeared.

Aladdin went back to the Princess,
saying his head ached, and requesting
that the holy Fatima should be fetched
to lay her hands on it. But when the
magician came near, Aladdin, seizing
his dagger, pierced him to the heart.
"What have you done?" cried the Princess. "You have killed the holy woman!" "Not so," replied Aladdin, "but
a wicked magician," and told her of how
she had been deceived.

After this Aladdin and his wife lived

FAVORITE FAIRY TALES

in peace. He succeeded the Sultan when he died, and reigned for many years, leaving behind him a long line of kings.

From " The Blue Fairy Book," edited by Andrew Lang, by permission of Messrs. Longmans, Green & Co.

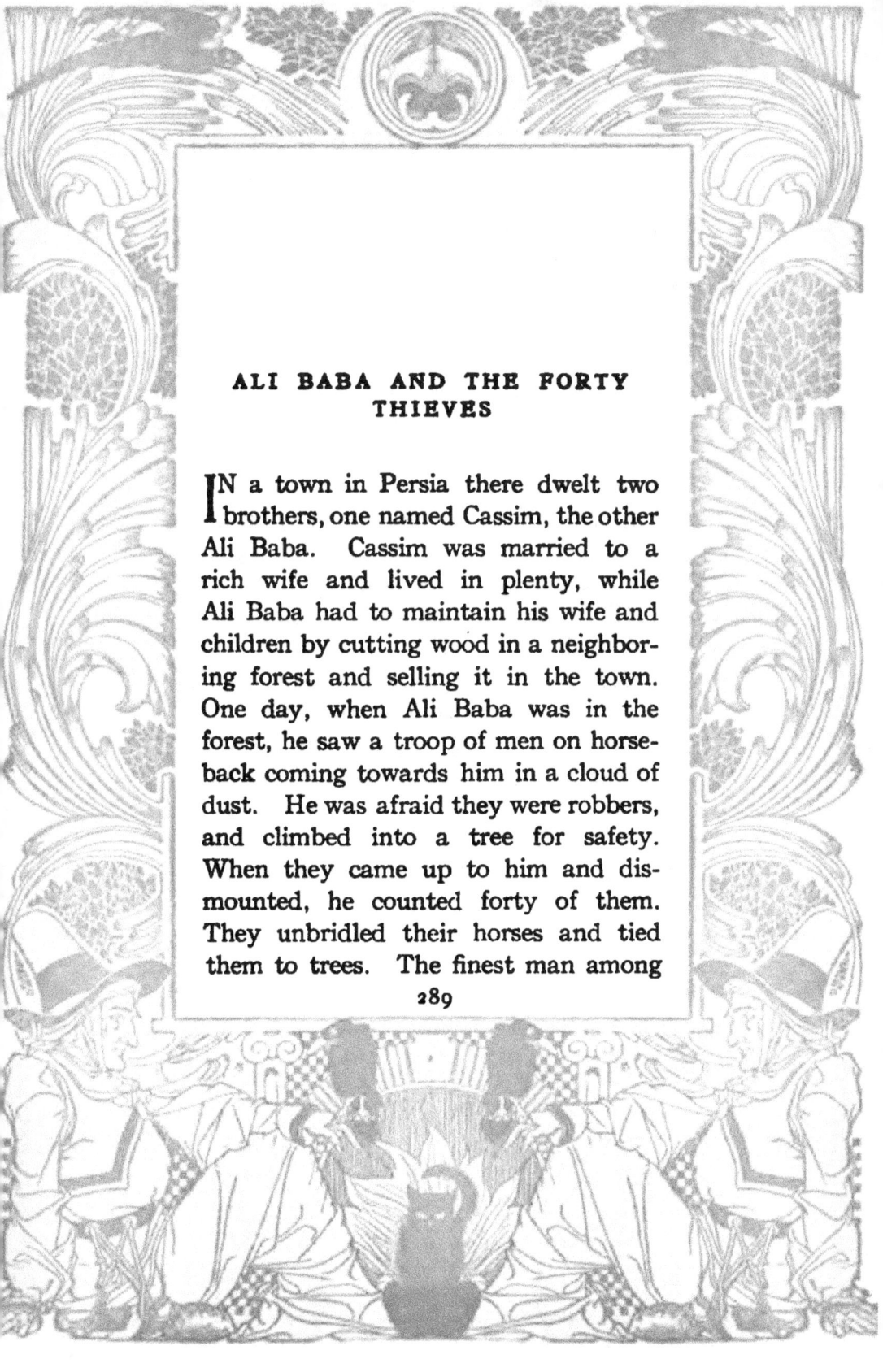

ALI BABA AND THE FORTY THIEVES

IN a town in Persia there dwelt two brothers, one named Cassim, the other Ali Baba. Cassim was married to a rich wife and lived in plenty, while Ali Baba had to maintain his wife and children by cutting wood in a neighboring forest and selling it in the town. One day, when Ali Baba was in the forest, he saw a troop of men on horseback coming towards him in a cloud of dust. He was afraid they were robbers, and climbed into a tree for safety. When they came up to him and dismounted, he counted forty of them. They unbridled their horses and tied them to trees. The finest man among

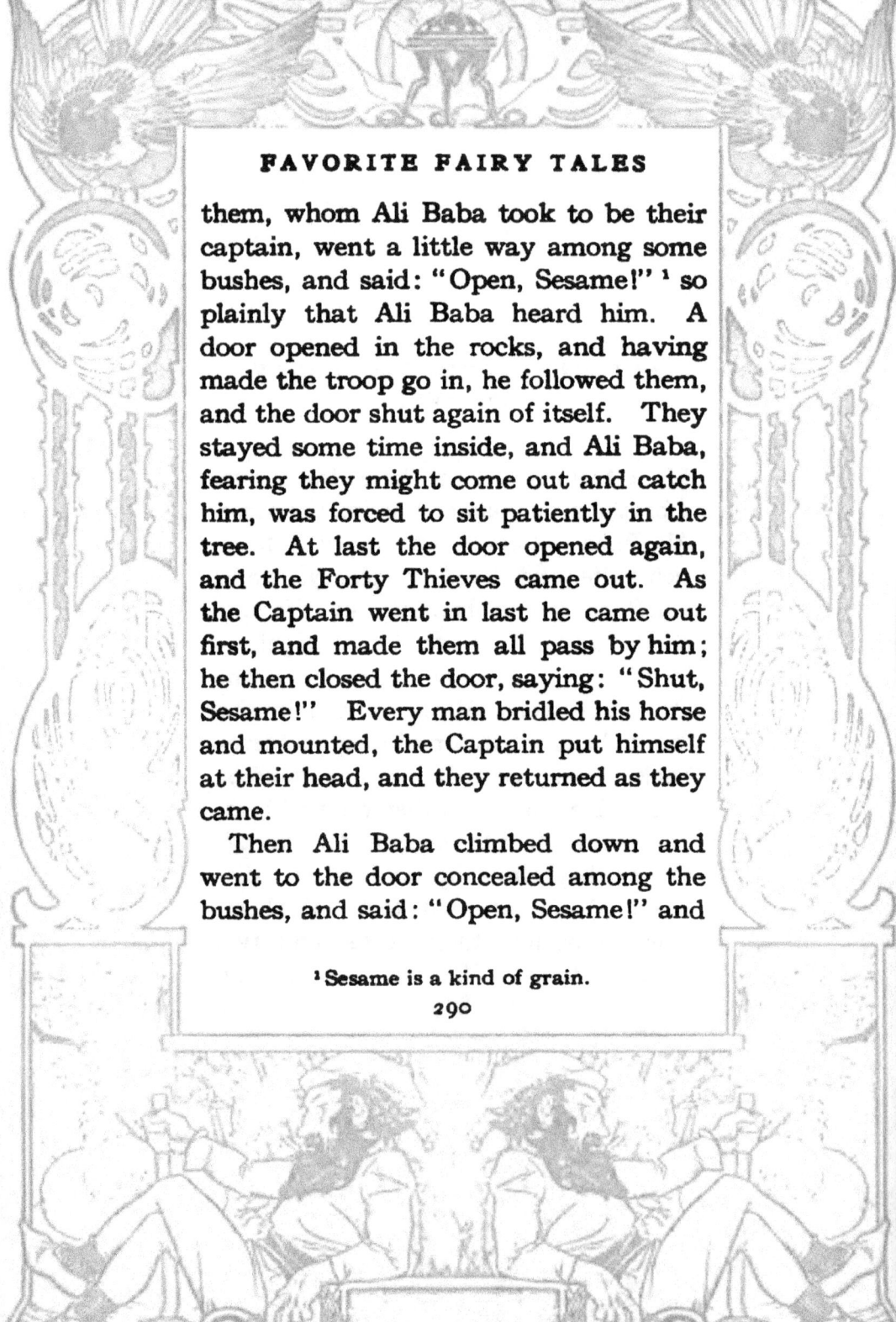

them, whom Ali Baba took to be their captain, went a little way among some bushes, and said: "Open, Sesame!" [1] so plainly that Ali Baba heard him. A door opened in the rocks, and having made the troop go in, he followed them, and the door shut again of itself. They stayed some time inside, and Ali Baba, fearing they might come out and catch him, was forced to sit patiently in the tree. At last the door opened again, and the Forty Thieves came out. As the Captain went in last he came out first, and made them all pass by him; he then closed the door, saying: "Shut, Sesame!" Every man bridled his horse and mounted, the Captain put himself at their head, and they returned as they came.

Then Ali Baba climbed down and went to the door concealed among the bushes, and said: "Open, Sesame!" and

[1] Sesame is a kind of grain.

it flew open. Ali Baba, who expected a dull, dismal place, was greatly surprised to find it large and well lighted, and hollowed by the hand of man in the form of a vault, which received the light from an opening in the ceiling. He saw rich bales of merchandise—silk, stuff-brocades, all piled together, and gold and silver in heaps, and money in leather purses. He went in and the door shut behind him. He did not look at the silver, but brought out as many bags of gold as he thought his asses, which were browsing outside, could carry, loaded them with the bags, and hid it all with fagots. Using the words: "Shut, Sesame!" he closed the door and went home.

Then he drove his asses into the yard, shut the gates, carried the money-bags to his wife, and emptied them out before her. He bade her keep the secret, and he would go and bury the gold. "Let me first measure it," said his wife.

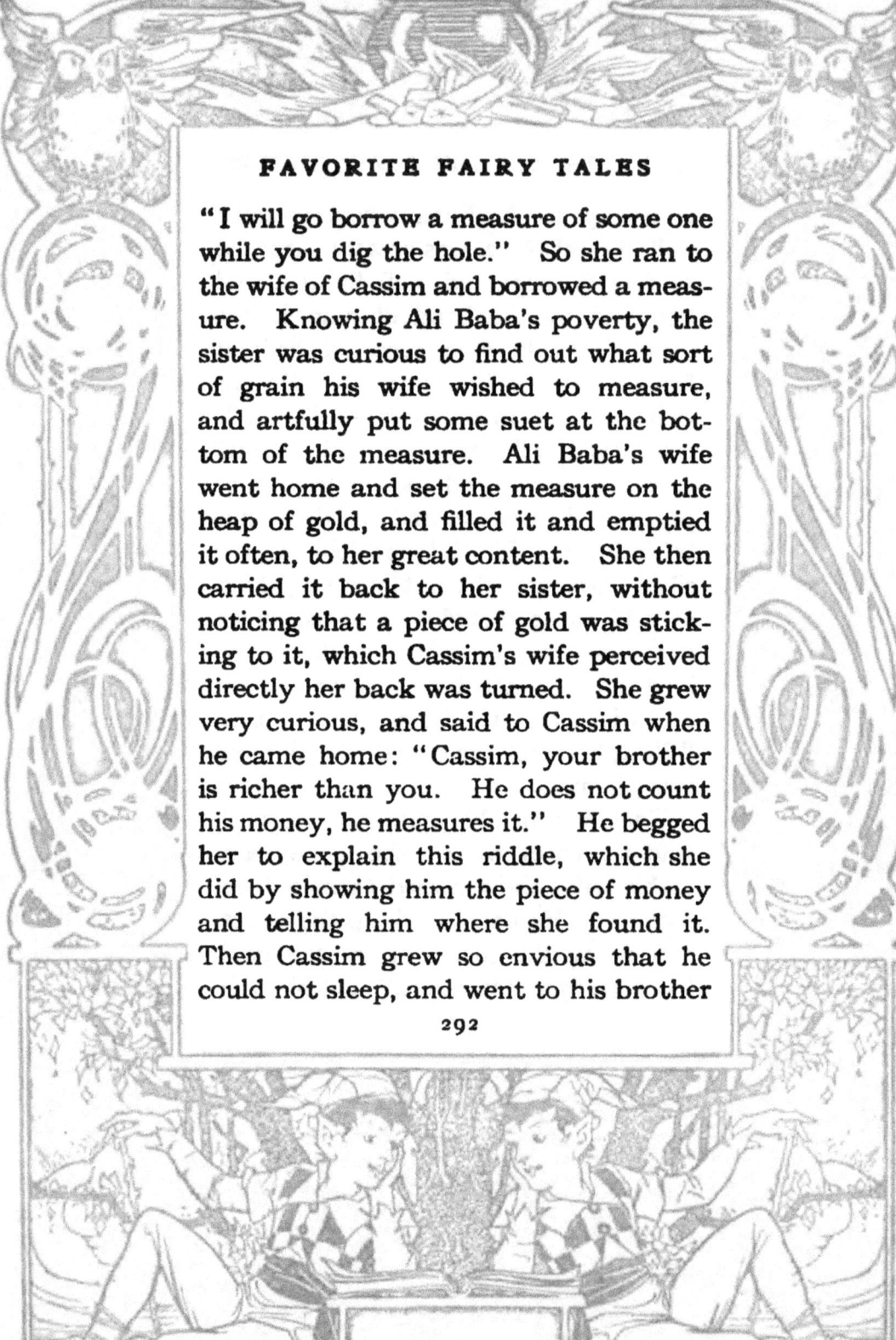

"I will go borrow a measure of some one while you dig the hole." So she ran to the wife of Cassim and borrowed a measure. Knowing Ali Baba's poverty, the sister was curious to find out what sort of grain his wife wished to measure, and artfully put some suet at the bottom of the measure. Ali Baba's wife went home and set the measure on the heap of gold, and filled it and emptied it often, to her great content. She then carried it back to her sister, without noticing that a piece of gold was sticking to it, which Cassim's wife perceived directly her back was turned. She grew very curious, and said to Cassim when he came home: "Cassim, your brother is richer than you. He does not count his money, he measures it." He begged her to explain this riddle, which she did by showing him the piece of money and telling him where she found it. Then Cassim grew so envious that he could not sleep, and went to his brother in the morning before sunrise. "Ali Baba," he said, showing him the gold piece, "you pretend to be poor and yet you measure gold." By this Ali Baba perceived that through his wife's folly Cassim and his wife knew their secret, so he confessed all and offered Cassim a share. "That I expect," said Cassim; "but I must know where to find the treasure, otherwise I will discover all, and you will lose all." Ali Baba, more out of kindness than fear, told him of the cave, and the very words to use. Cassim left Ali Baba, meaning to be beforehand with him and get the treasure himself. He rose early next morning, and set out with ten mules loaded with great chests. He soon found the place, and the door in the rock. He said: "Open, Sesame!" and the door opened and shut behind him. He could have feasted his eyes all day on the treasures, but he now hastened to gather together as much of it as possible; but when he

293

was ready to go he could not remember what to say for thinking of his great riches. Instead of "Sesame," he said: "Open, Barley!" and the door remained fast. He named several different sorts of grain, all but the right one, and the door still stuck fast. He was so frightened at the danger he was in that he had as much forgotten the word as if he had never heard it.

About noon the robbers returned to their cave, and saw Cassim's mules roving about with great chests on their backs. This gave them the alarm; they drew their sabres, and went to the door, which opened on their Captain's saying: "Open, Sesame!" Cassim, who had heard the trampling of their horses' feet, resolved to sell his life dearly, so when the door opened he leaped out and threw the Captain down. In vain, however, for the robbers with their sabres soon killed him. On entering the cave they saw all the bags laid ready,

Cassim forgets the magic word

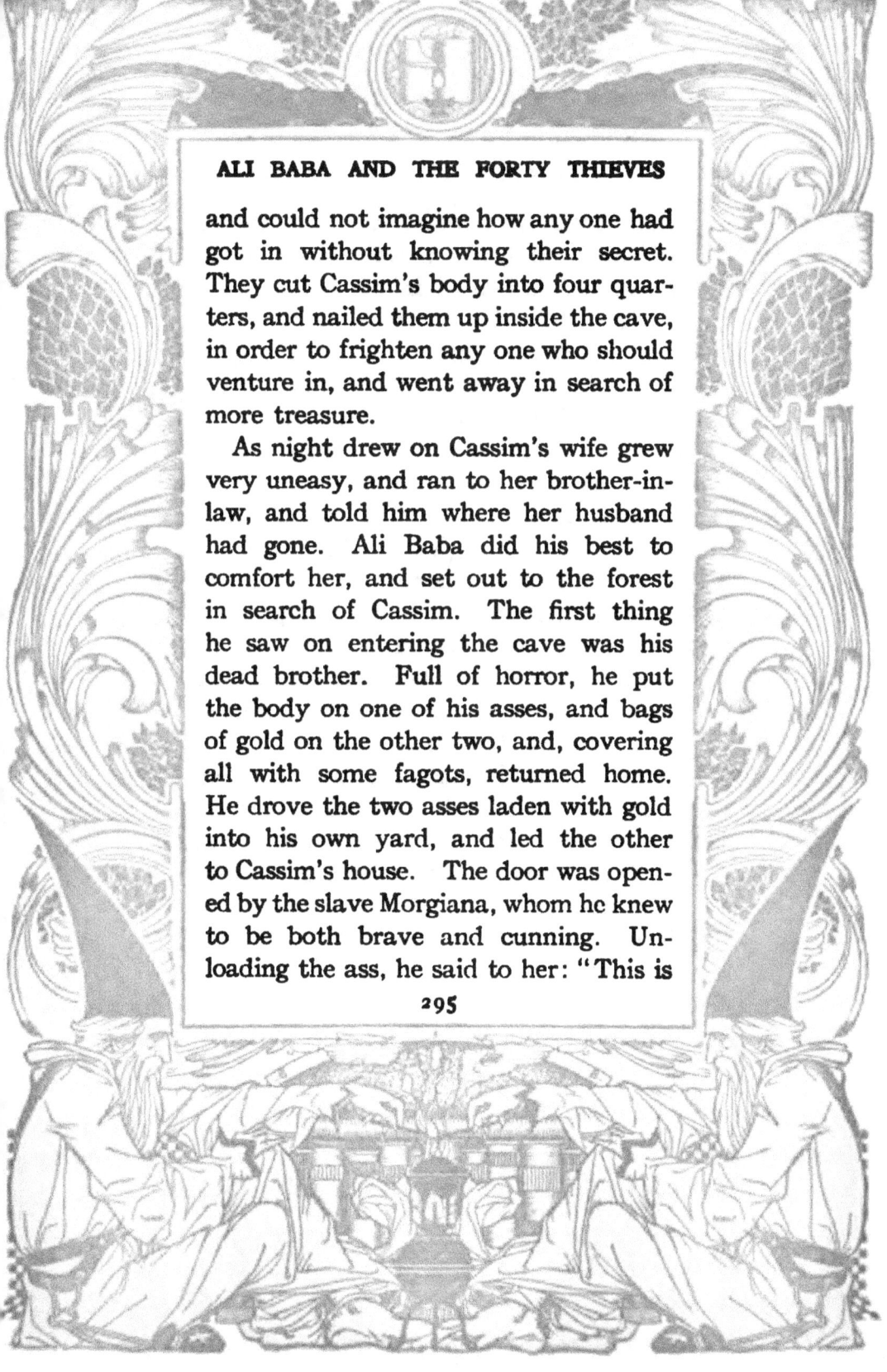

and could not imagine how any one had got in without knowing their secret. They cut Cassim's body into four quarters, and nailed them up inside the cave, in order to frighten any one who should venture in, and went away in search of more treasure.

As night drew on Cassim's wife grew very uneasy, and ran to her brother-in-law, and told him where her husband had gone. Ali Baba did his best to comfort her, and set out to the forest in search of Cassim. The first thing he saw on entering the cave was his dead brother. Full of horror, he put the body on one of his asses, and bags of gold on the other two, and, covering all with some fagots, returned home. He drove the two asses laden with gold into his own yard, and led the other to Cassim's house. The door was opened by the slave Morgiana, whom he knew to be both brave and cunning. Unloading the ass, he said to her: "This is

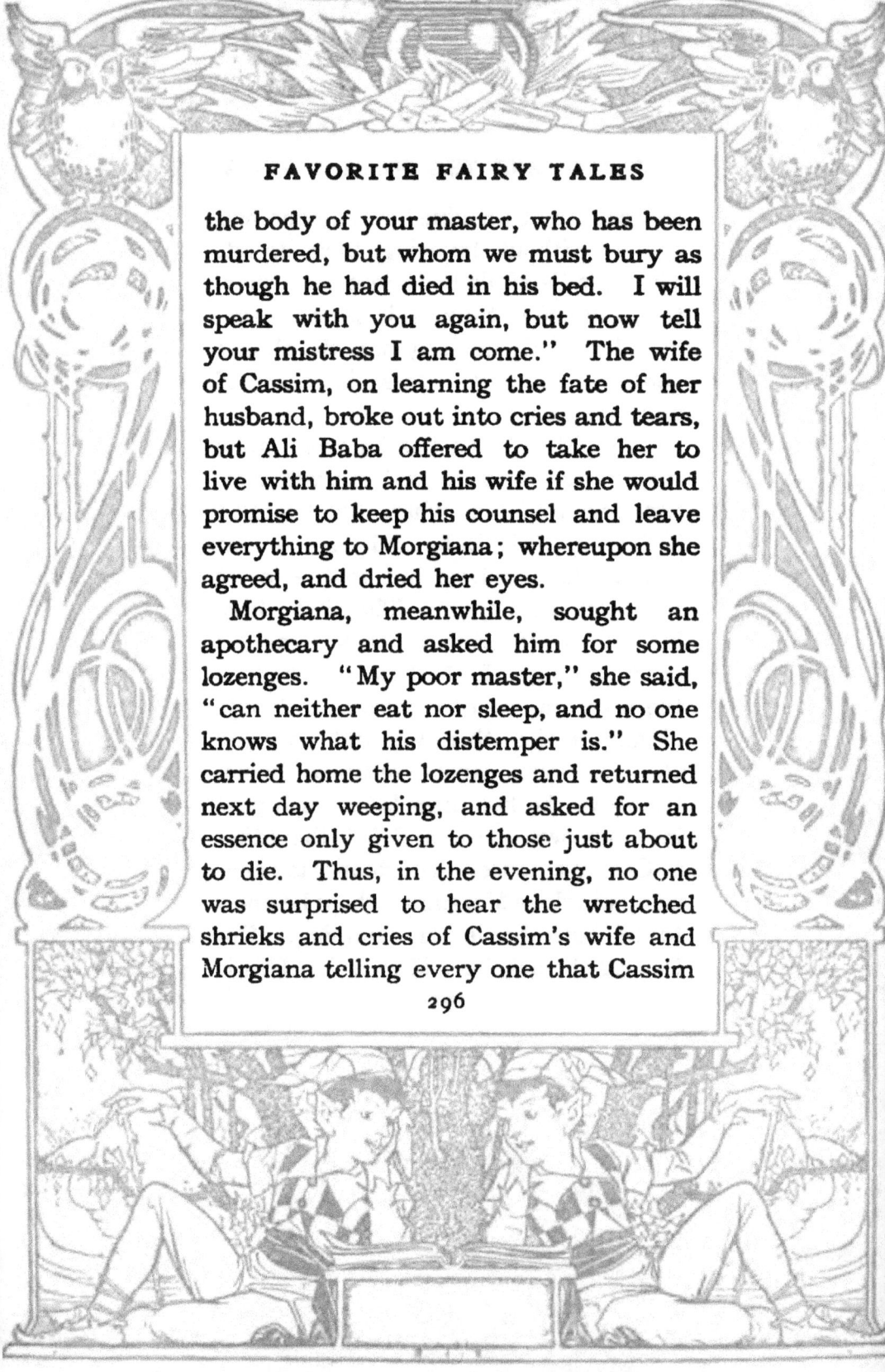

the body of your master, who has been murdered, but whom we must bury as though he had died in his bed. I will speak with you again, but now tell your mistress I am come." The wife of Cassim, on learning the fate of her husband, broke out into cries and tears, but Ali Baba offered to take her to live with him and his wife if she would promise to keep his counsel and leave everything to Morgiana; whereupon she agreed, and dried her eyes.

Morgiana, meanwhile, sought an apothecary and asked him for some lozenges. "My poor master," she said, "can neither eat nor sleep, and no one knows what his distemper is." She carried home the lozenges and returned next day weeping, and asked for an essence only given to those just about to die. Thus, in the evening, no one was surprised to hear the wretched shrieks and cries of Cassim's wife and Morgiana telling every one that Cassim

was dead. The day after, Morgiana went to an old cobbler near the gates of the town who opened his stall early, put a piece of gold in his hand, and bade him follow with his needle and thread. Having bound his eyes with a handkerchief, she took him to the room where the body lay, pulled off the bandage, and bade him sew the quarters together, after which she covered his eyes again and led him home. Then they buried Cassim, and Morgiana his slave followed him to the grave, weeping and tearing her hair, while Cassim's wife stayed at home uttering lamentable cries. Next day she went to live with Ali Baba, who gave Cassim's shop to his eldest son.

The Forty Thieves, on their return to the cave, were much astonished to find Cassim's body gone and some of their money-bags. "We are certainly discovered," said the Captain, "and shall be undone if we cannot find out who it is that knows our secret. Two

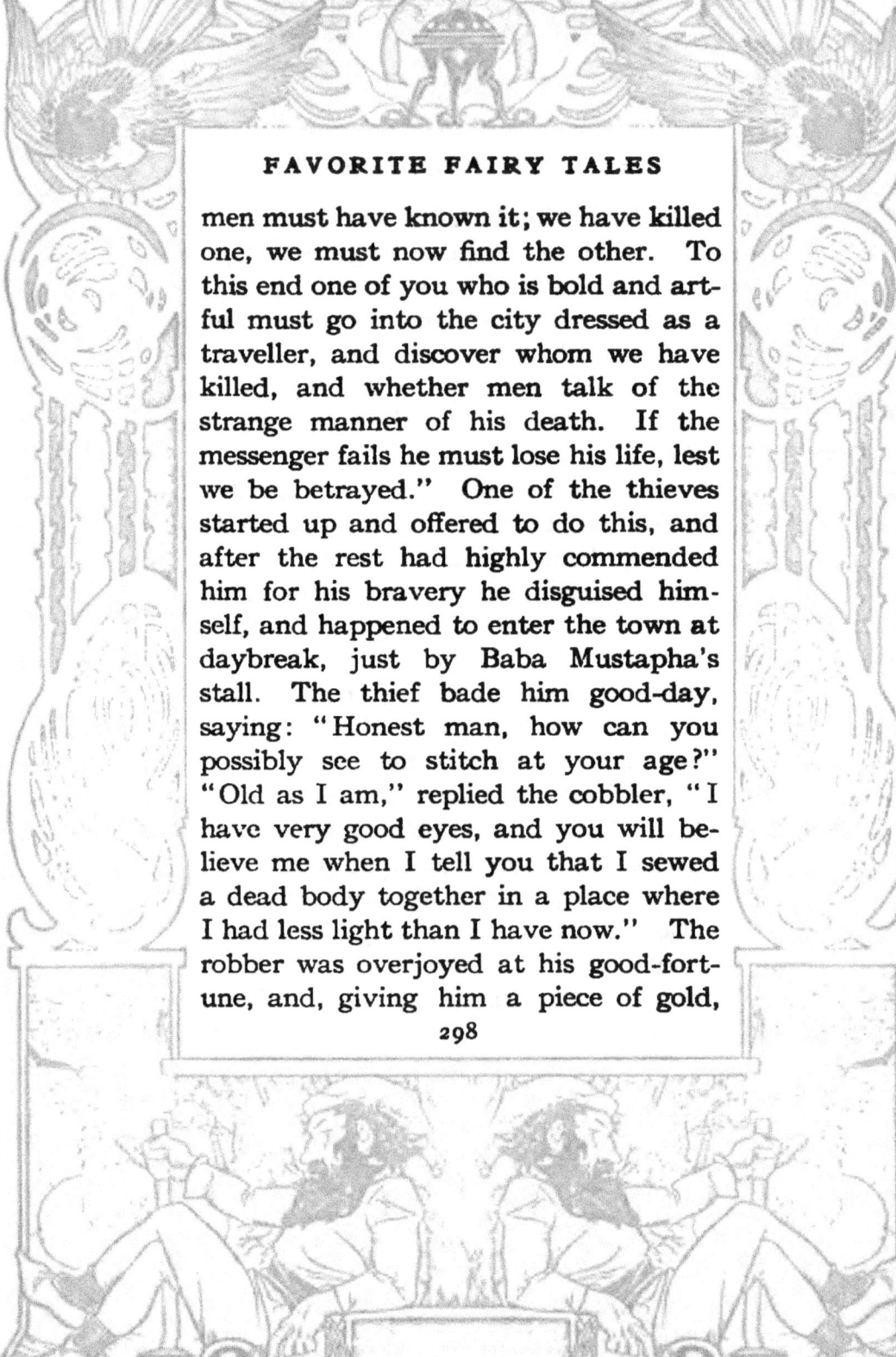

men must have known it; we have killed one, we must now find the other. To this end one of you who is bold and artful must go into the city dressed as a traveller, and discover whom we have killed, and whether men talk of the strange manner of his death. If the messenger fails he must lose his life, lest we be betrayed." One of the thieves started up and offered to do this, and after the rest had highly commended him for his bravery he disguised himself, and happened to enter the town at daybreak, just by Baba Mustapha's stall. The thief bade him good-day, saying: "Honest man, how can you possibly see to stitch at your age?" "Old as I am," replied the cobbler, "I have very good eyes, and you will believe me when I tell you that I sewed a dead body together in a place where I had less light than I have now." The robber was overjoyed at his good-fortune, and, giving him a piece of gold,

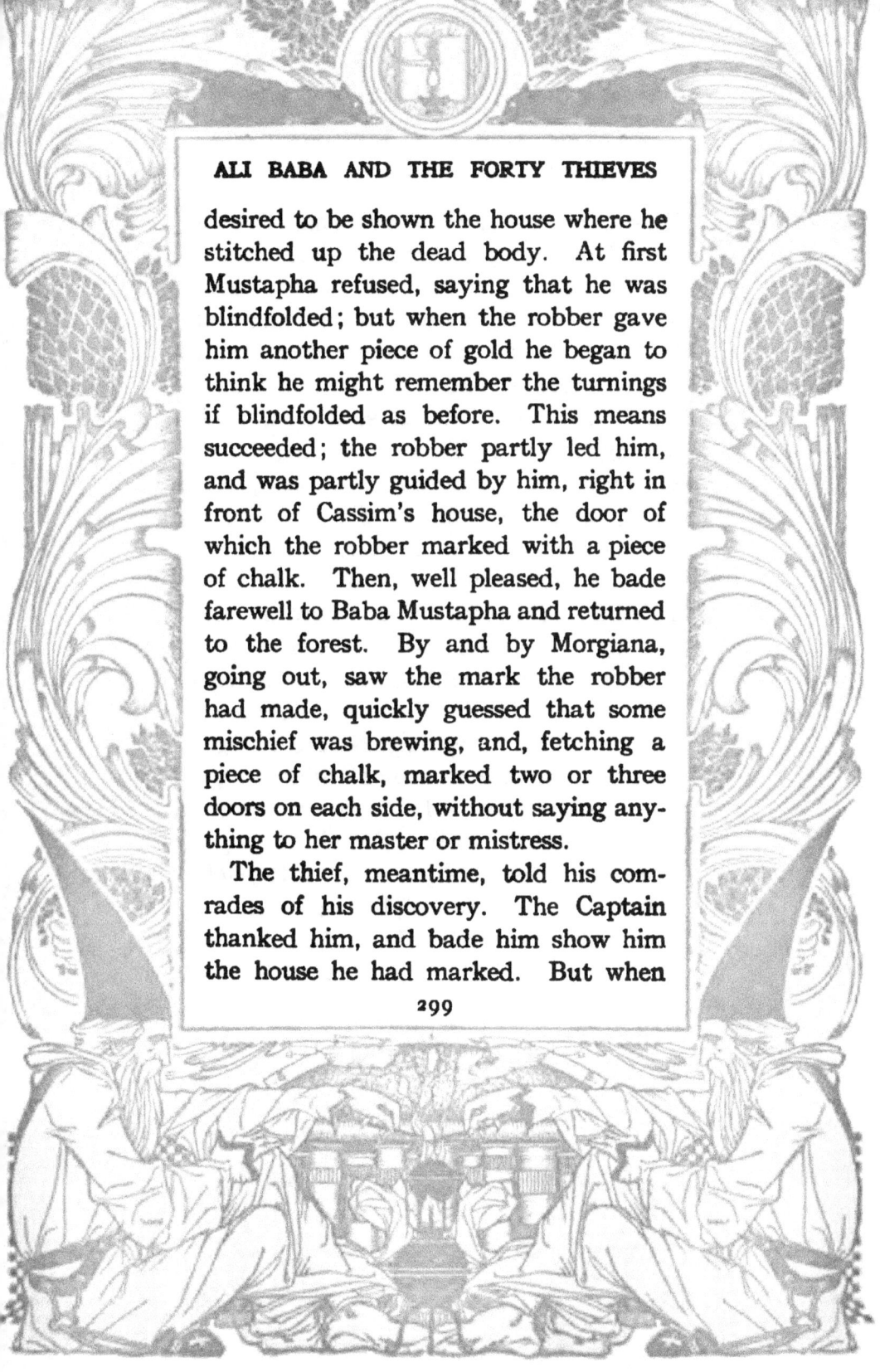

desired to be shown the house where he stitched up the dead body. At first Mustapha refused, saying that he was blindfolded; but when the robber gave him another piece of gold he began to think he might remember the turnings if blindfolded as before. This means succeeded; the robber partly led him, and was partly guided by him, right in front of Cassim's house, the door of which the robber marked with a piece of chalk. Then, well pleased, he bade farewell to Baba Mustapha and returned to the forest. By and by Morgiana, going out, saw the mark the robber had made, quickly guessed that some mischief was brewing, and, fetching a piece of chalk, marked two or three doors on each side, without saying anything to her master or mistress.

The thief, meantime, told his comrades of his discovery. The Captain thanked him, and bade him show him the house he had marked. But when they came to it they saw that five or six of the houses were chalked in the same manner. The guide was so confounded that he knew not what answer to make, and when they returned he was at once beheaded for having failed. Another robber was despatched, and, having won over Baba Mustapha, marked the house in red chalk; but Morgiana being again too clever for them, the second messenger was put to death also. The Captain now resolved to go himself, but, wiser than the others, he did not mark the house, but looked at it so closely that he could not fail to remember it. He returned, and ordered his men to go into the neighboring villages and buy nineteen mules, and thirty-eight leather jars, all empty, except one which was full of oil. The Captain put one of his men, fully armed, into each, rubbing the outside of the jars with oil from the full vessel. Then the nineteen mules were loaded with thirty-seven

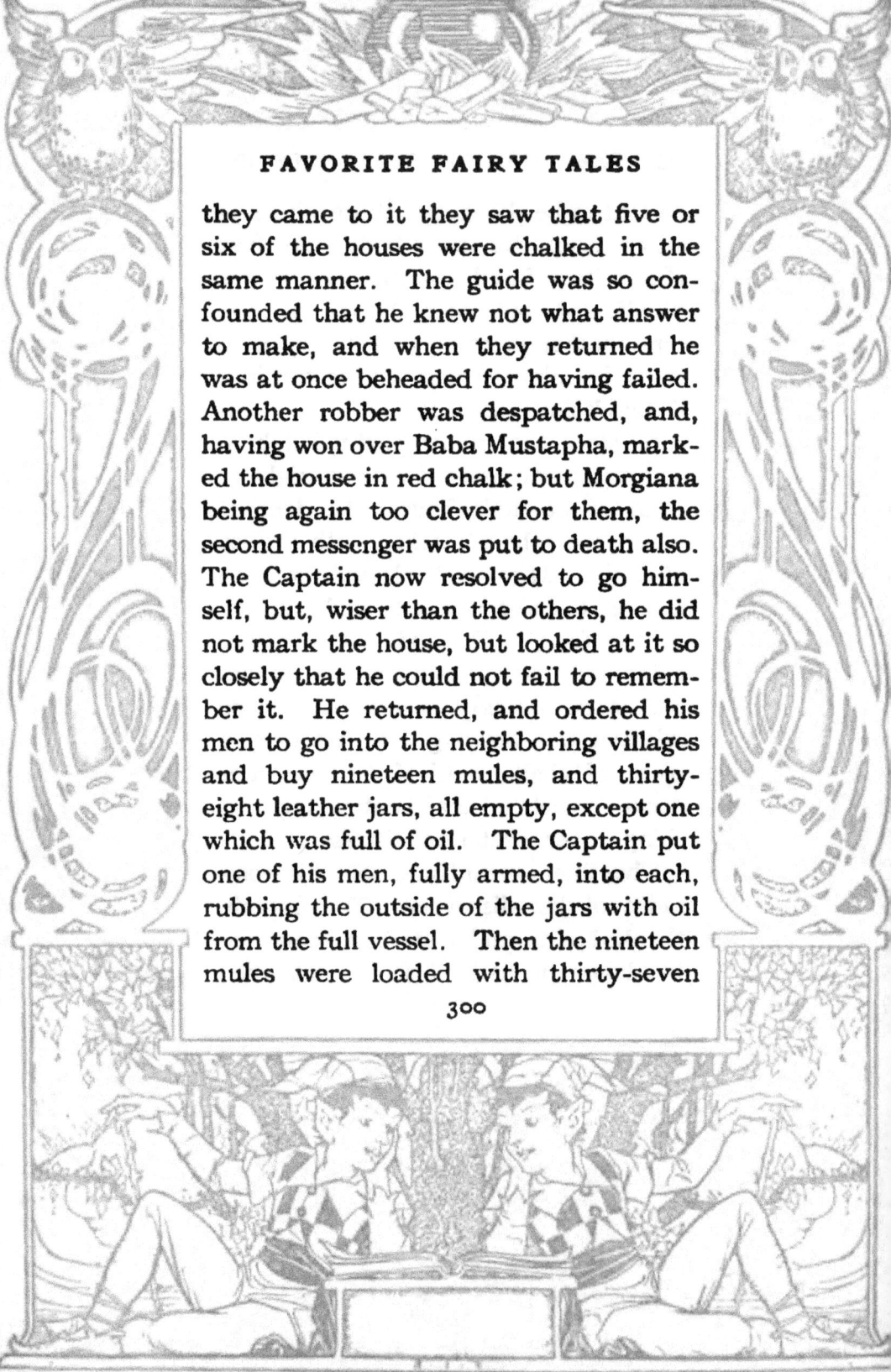

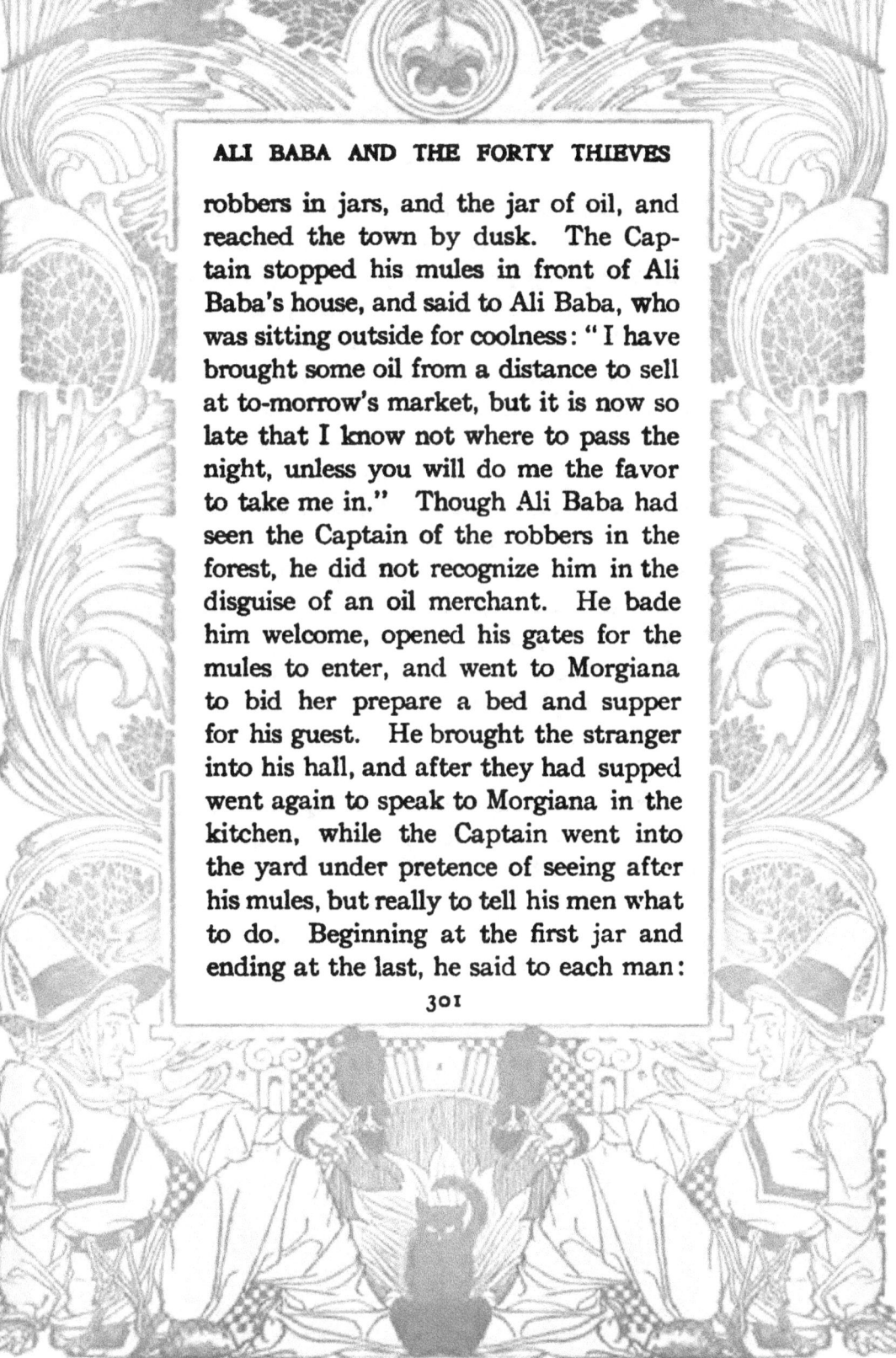

robbers in jars, and the jar of oil, and reached the town by dusk. The Captain stopped his mules in front of Ali Baba's house, and said to Ali Baba, who was sitting outside for coolness: " I have brought some oil from a distance to sell at to-morrow's market, but it is now so late that I know not where to pass the night, unless you will do me the favor to take me in." Though Ali Baba had seen the Captain of the robbers in the forest, he did not recognize him in the disguise of an oil merchant. He bade him welcome, opened his gates for the mules to enter, and went to Morgiana to bid her prepare a bed and supper for his guest. He brought the stranger into his hall, and after they had supped went again to speak to Morgiana in the kitchen, while the Captain went into the yard under pretence of seeing after his mules, but really to tell his men what to do. Beginning at the first jar and ending at the last, he said to each man:

"As soon as I throw some stones from the window of the chamber where I lie, cut the jars open with your knives and come out, and I will be with you in a trice." He returned to the house, and Morgiana led him to his chamber. She then told Abdallah, her fellow-slave, to set on the pot to make some broth for her master, who had gone to bed. Meanwhile her lamp went out, and she had no more oil in the house. "Do not be uneasy," said Abdallah; "go into the yard and take some out of one of those jars." Morgiana thanked him for his advice, took the oil-pot, and went into the yard. When she came to the first jar the robber inside said softly: "Is it time?"

Any other slave but Morgiana, on finding a man in the jar instead of the oil she wanted, would have screamed, and made a noise; but she, knowing the danger her master was in, bethought herself of a plan, and answered quietly:

302

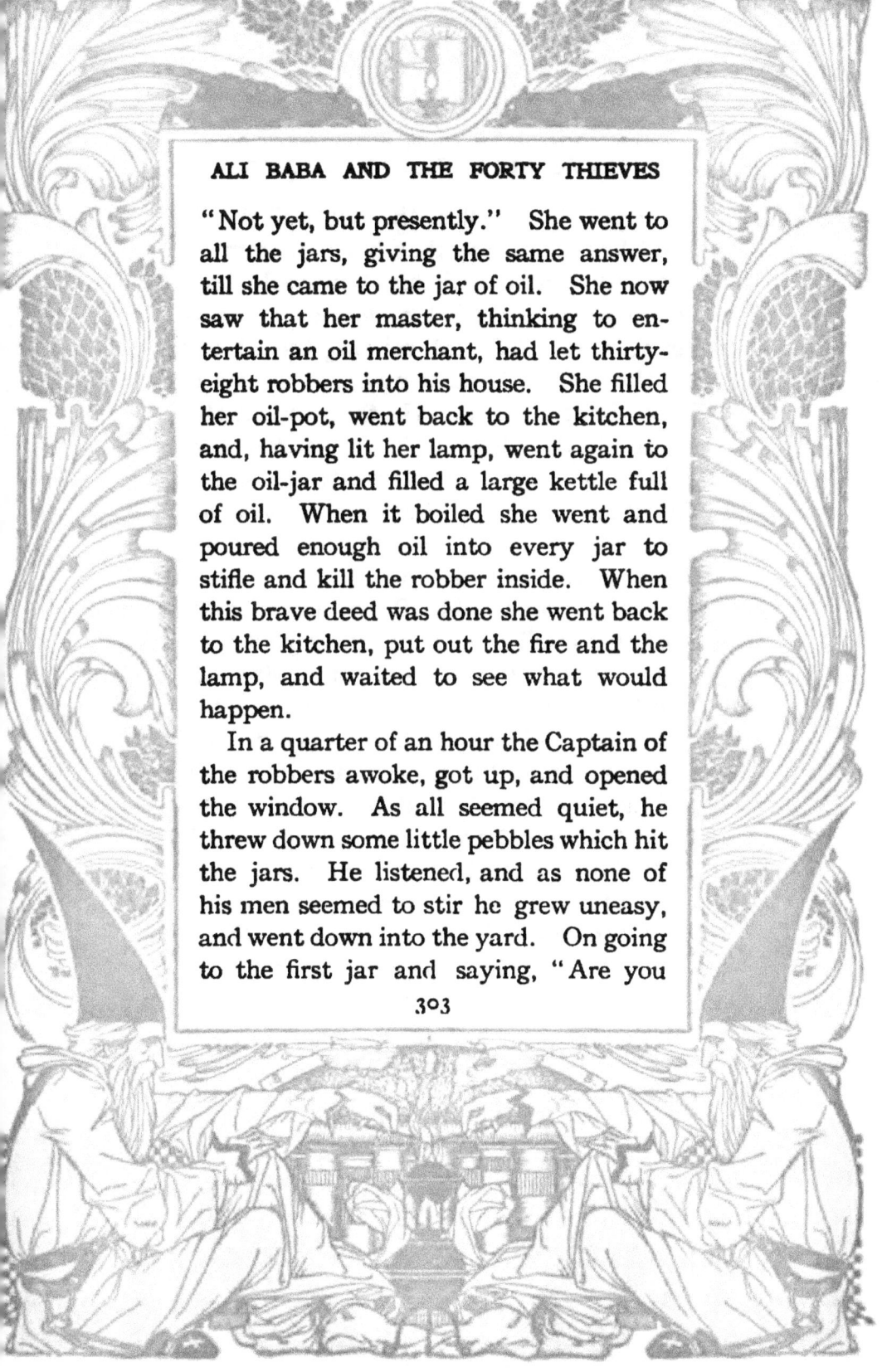

"Not yet, but presently." She went to
all the jars, giving the same answer,
till she came to the jar of oil. She now
saw that her master, thinking to en-
tertain an oil merchant, had let thirty-
eight robbers into his house. She filled
her oil-pot, went back to the kitchen,
and, having lit her lamp, went again to
the oil-jar and filled a large kettle full
of oil. When it boiled she went and
poured enough oil into every jar to
stifle and kill the robber inside. When
this brave deed was done she went back
to the kitchen, put out the fire and the
lamp, and waited to see what would
happen.

In a quarter of an hour the Captain of
the robbers awoke, got up, and opened
the window. As all seemed quiet, he
threw down some little pebbles which hit
the jars. He listened, and as none of
his men seemed to stir he grew uneasy,
and went down into the yard. On going
to the first jar and saying, "Are you

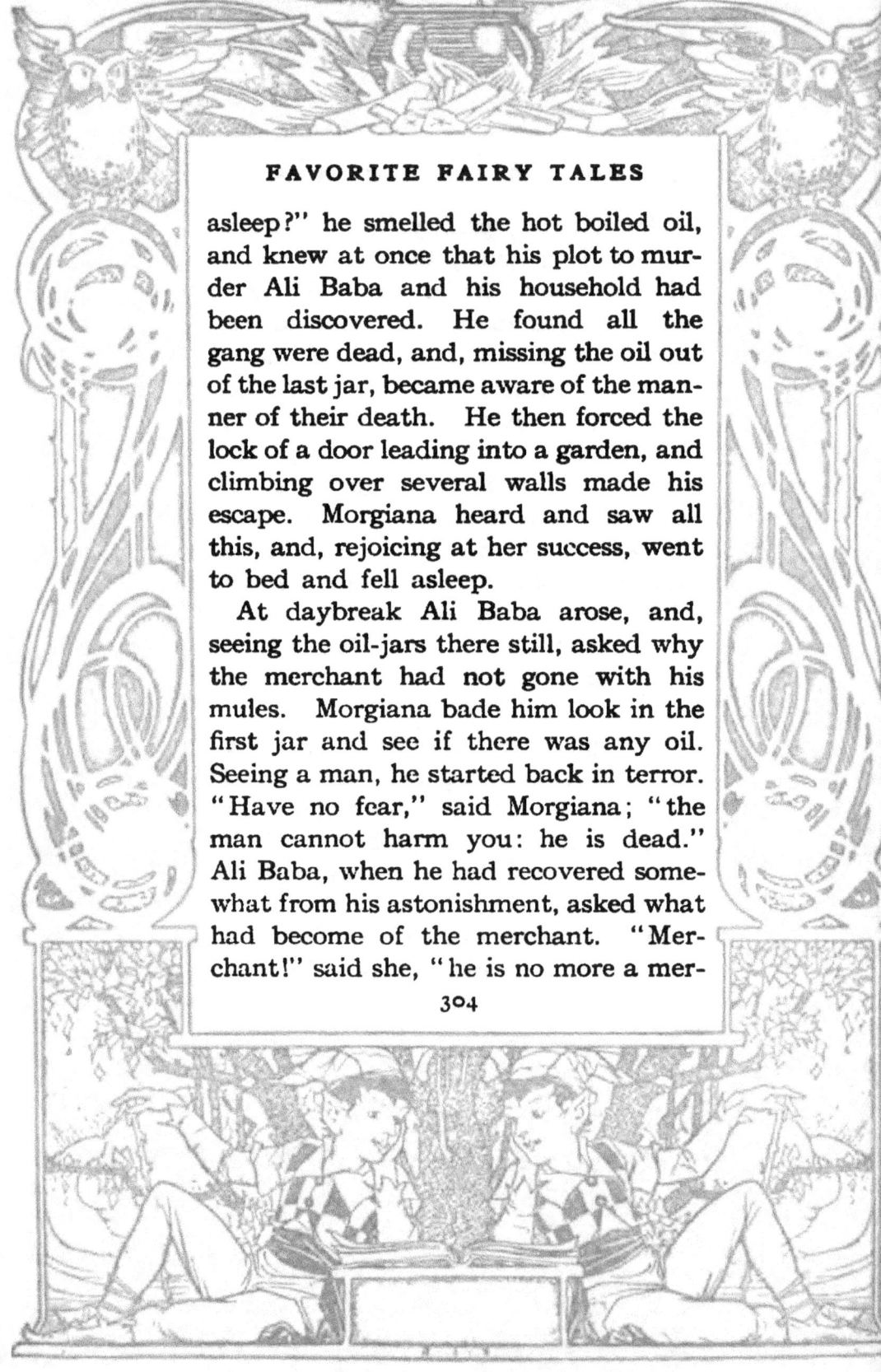

asleep?" he smelled the hot boiled oil,
and knew at once that his plot to murder Ali Baba and his household had
been discovered. He found all the
gang were dead, and, missing the oil out
of the last jar, became aware of the manner of their death. He then forced the
lock of a door leading into a garden, and
climbing over several walls made his
escape. Morgiana heard and saw all
this, and, rejoicing at her success, went
to bed and fell asleep.

At daybreak Ali Baba arose, and,
seeing the oil-jars there still, asked why
the merchant had not gone with his
mules. Morgiana bade him look in the
first jar and see if there was any oil.
Seeing a man, he started back in terror.
"Have no fear," said Morgiana; "the
man cannot harm you: he is dead."
Ali Baba, when he had recovered somewhat from his astonishment, asked what
had become of the merchant. "Merchant!" said she, "he is no more a mer-

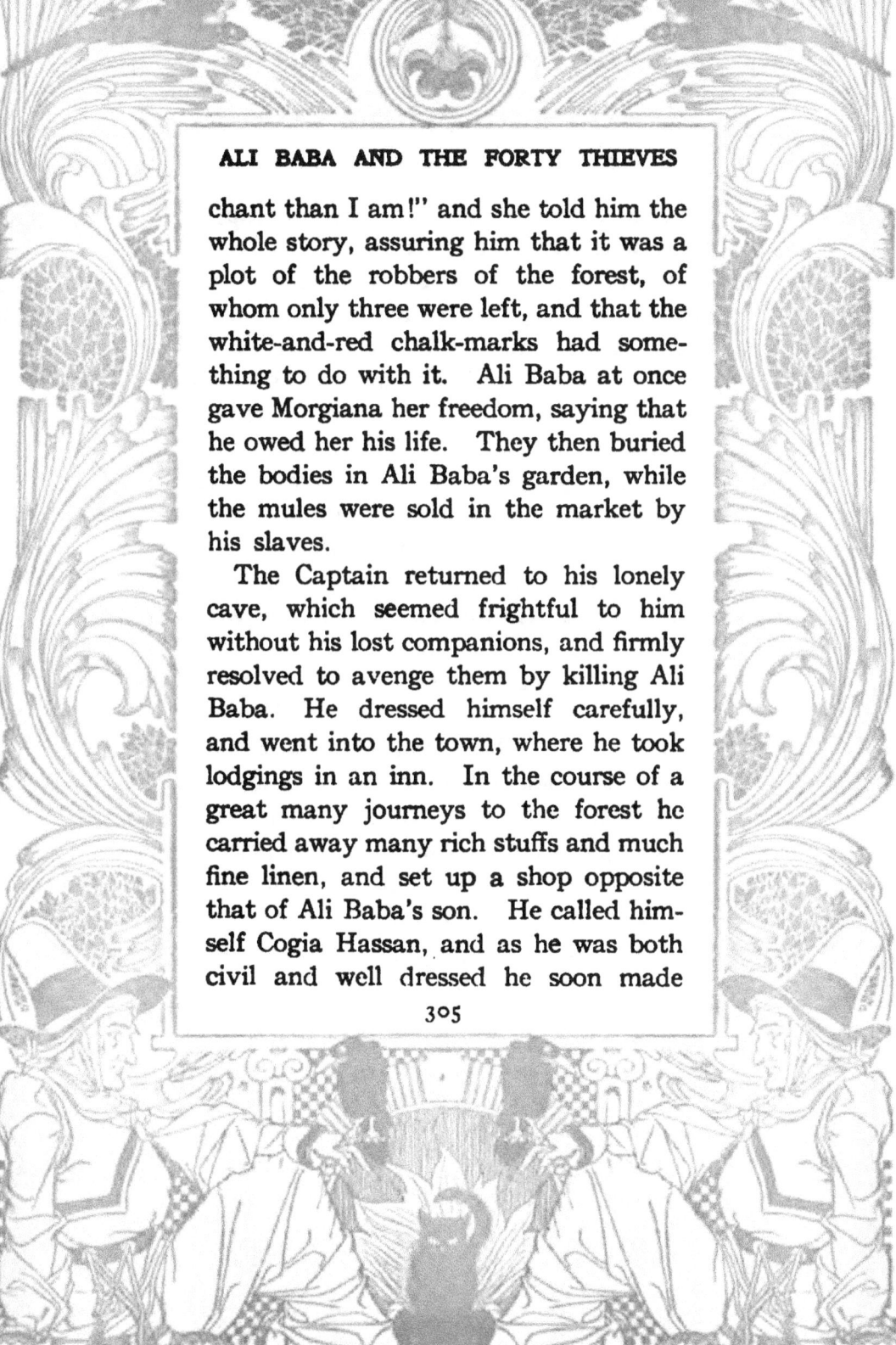

chant than I am!" and she told him the whole story, assuring him that it was a plot of the robbers of the forest, of whom only three were left, and that the white-and-red chalk-marks had something to do with it. Ali Baba at once gave Morgiana her freedom, saying that he owed her his life. They then buried the bodies in Ali Baba's garden, while the mules were sold in the market by his slaves.

The Captain returned to his lonely cave, which seemed frightful to him without his lost companions, and firmly resolved to avenge them by killing Ali Baba. He dressed himself carefully, and went into the town, where he took lodgings in an inn. In the course of a great many journeys to the forest he carried away many rich stuffs and much fine linen, and set up a shop opposite that of Ali Baba's son. He called himself Cogia Hassan, and as he was both civil and well dressed he soon made

305

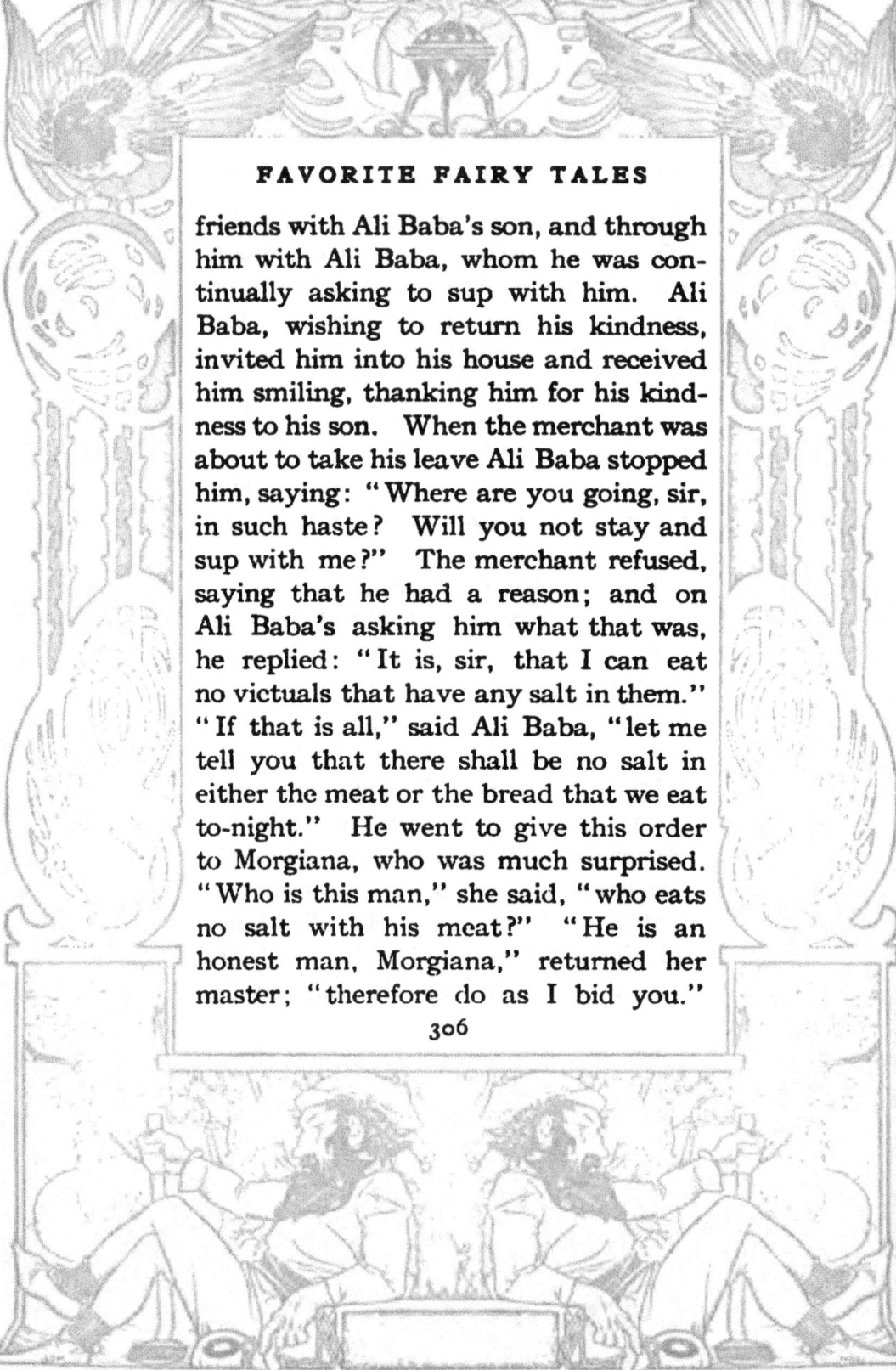

friends with Ali Baba's son, and through
him with Ali Baba, whom he was continually asking to sup with him. Ali
Baba, wishing to return his kindness,
invited him into his house and received
him smiling, thanking him for his kindness to his son. When the merchant was
about to take his leave Ali Baba stopped
him, saying: "Where are you going, sir,
in such haste? Will you not stay and
sup with me?" The merchant refused,
saying that he had a reason; and on
Ali Baba's asking him what that was,
he replied: "It is, sir, that I can eat
no victuals that have any salt in them."
"If that is all," said Ali Baba, "let me
tell you that there shall be no salt in
either the meat or the bread that we eat
to-night." He went to give this order
to Morgiana, who was much surprised.
"Who is this man," she said, "who eats
no salt with his meat?" "He is an
honest man, Morgiana," returned her
master; "therefore do as I bid you."

306

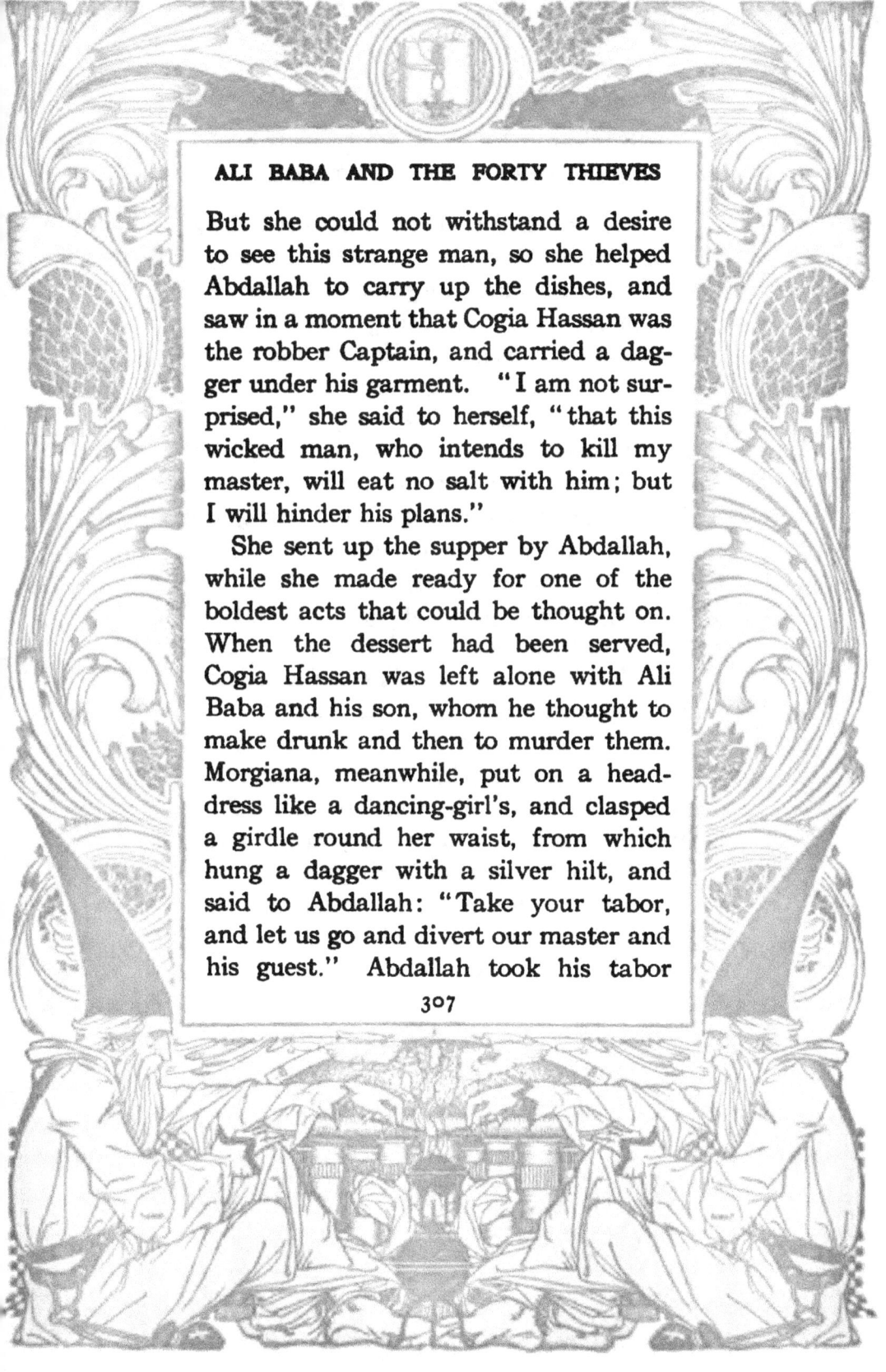

ALI BABA AND THE FORTY THIEVES

But she could not withstand a desire to see this strange man, so she helped Abdallah to carry up the dishes, and saw in a moment that Cogia Hassan was the robber Captain, and carried a dagger under his garment. "I am not surprised," she said to herself, "that this wicked man, who intends to kill my master, will eat no salt with him; but I will hinder his plans."

She sent up the supper by Abdallah, while she made ready for one of the boldest acts that could be thought on. When the dessert had been served, Cogia Hassan was left alone with Ali Baba and his son, whom he thought to make drunk and then to murder them. Morgiana, meanwhile, put on a headdress like a dancing-girl's, and clasped a girdle round her waist, from which hung a dagger with a silver hilt, and said to Abdallah: "Take your tabor, and let us go and divert our master and his guest." Abdallah took his tabor

307

and played before Morgiana until they came to the door, where Abdallah stopped playing and Morgiana made a low courtesy. "Come in, Morgiana," said Ali Baba, "and let Cogia Hassan see what you can do." And, turning to Cogia Hassan, he said: "She's my slave and my housekeeper." Cogia Hassan was by no means pleased, for he feared that his chance of killing Ali Baba was gone for the present; but he pretended great eagerness to see Morgiana, and Abdallah began to play and Morgiana to dance. After she had performed several dances, she drew her dagger and made passes with it, sometimes pointing it at her own breast, sometimes at her master's, as if it were part of the dance. Suddenly, out of breath, she snatched the tabor from Abdallah with her left hand, and, holding the dagger in her right, held out the tabor to her master. Ali Baba and his son put a piece of gold into it, and Cogia Hassan, seeing that she was coming to him, pulled out his purse to make her a present; but while he was putting his hand into it, Morgiana plunged the dagger into his heart.

"Unhappy girl!" cried Ali Baba and his son, "what have you done to ruin us?" "It was to preserve you, master, not to ruin you," answered Morgiana. "See here," opening the false merchant's garment and showing the dagger; "see what an enemy you have entertained! Remember, he would eat no salt with you, and what more would you have? Look at him! he is both the false oil merchant and the Captain of the Forty Thieves."

Ali Baba was so grateful to Morgiana for thus saving his life that he offered her to his son in marriage, who readily consented, and a few days after the wedding was celebrated with great splendor. At the end of a year Ali Baba, hearing nothing of the two remaining robbers, judged they were dead,

309

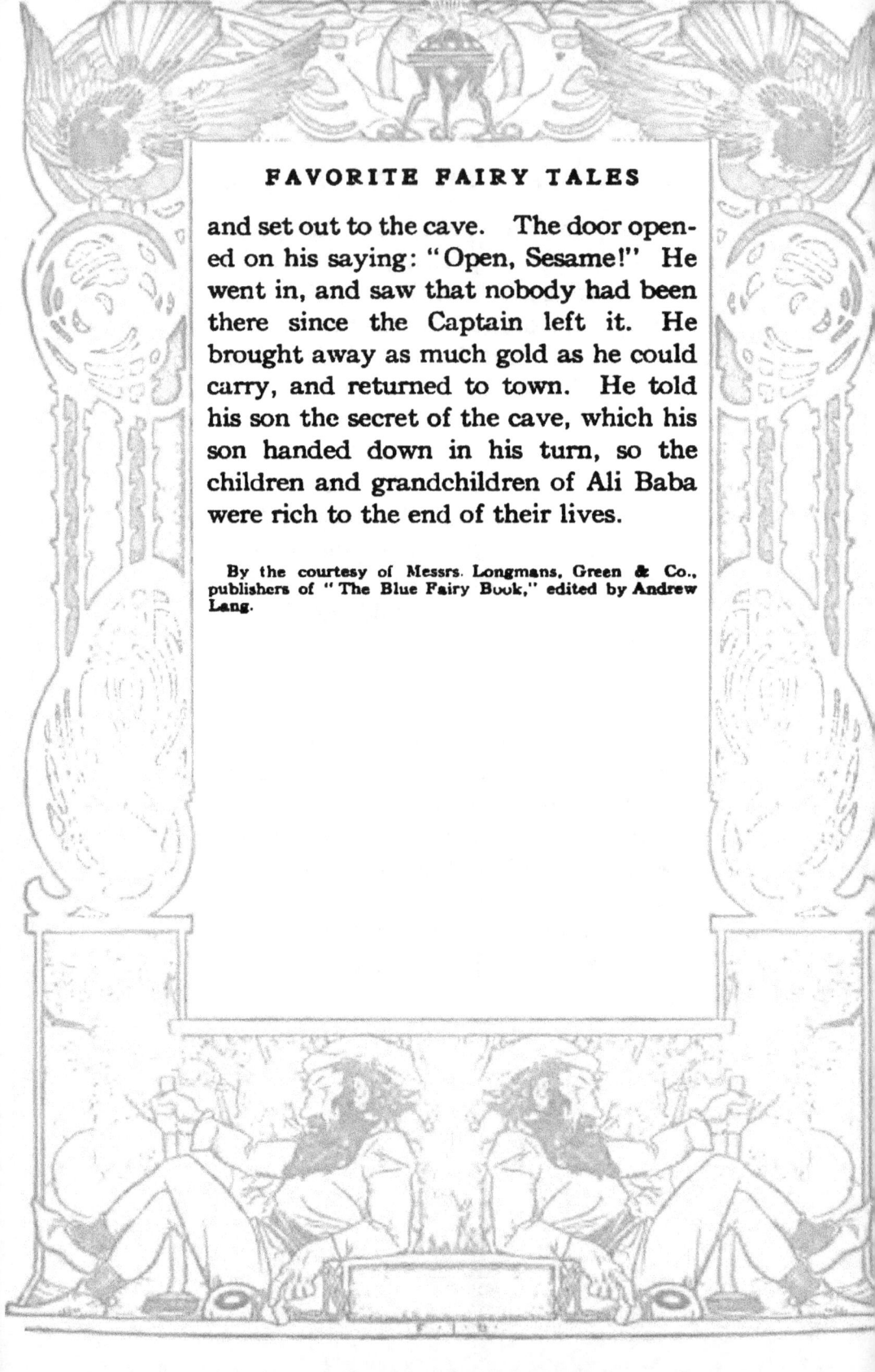

FAVORITE FAIRY TALES

and set out to the cave. The door opened on his saying: "Open, Sesame!" He went in, and saw that nobody had been there since the Captain left it. He brought away as much gold as he could carry, and returned to town. He told his son the secret of the cave, which his son handed down in his turn, so the children and grandchildren of Ali Baba were rich to the end of their lives.

By the courtesy of Messrs. Longmans, Green & Co., publishers of "The Blue Fairy Book," edited by Andrew Lang.

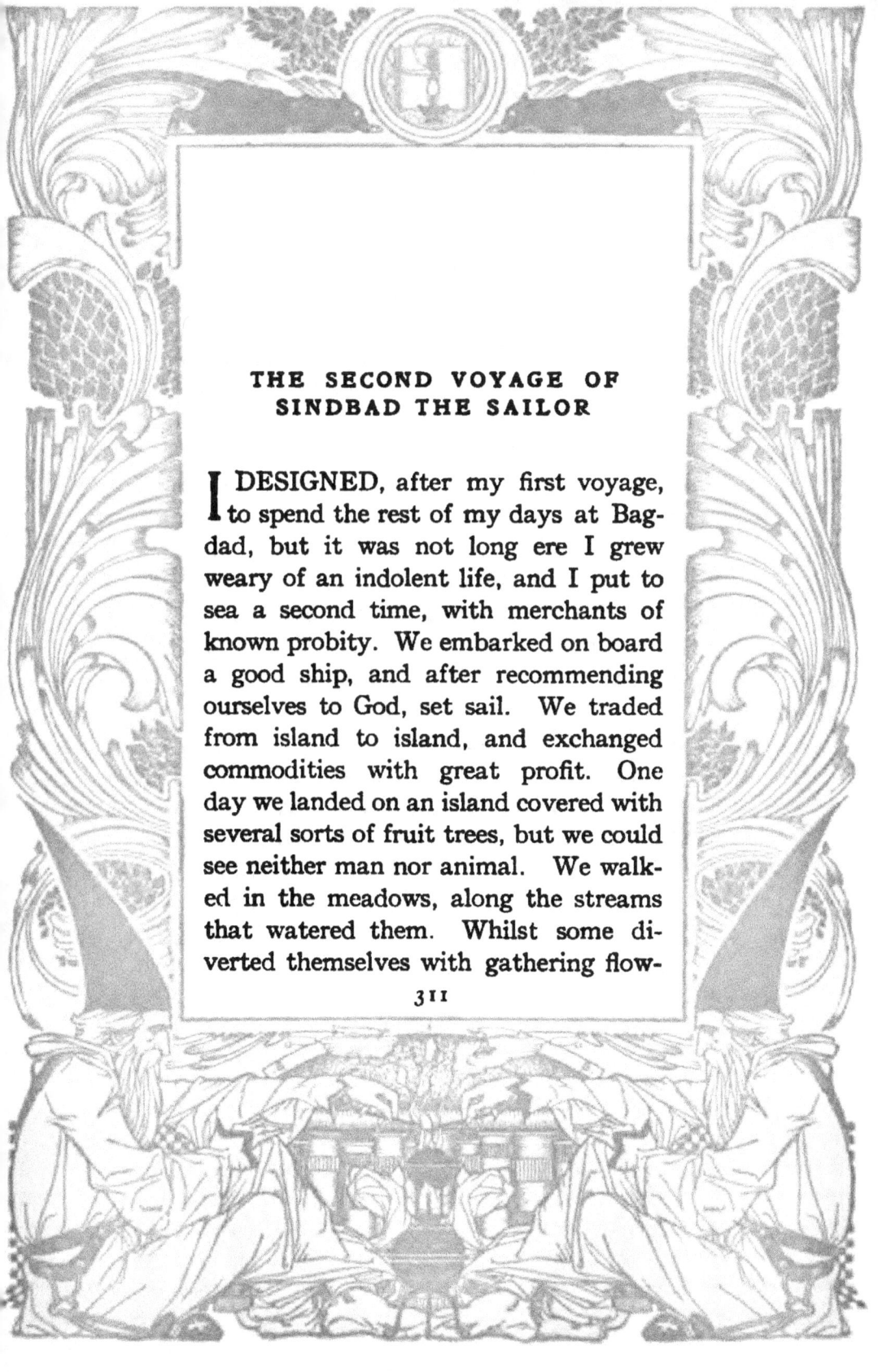

THE SECOND VOYAGE OF
SINDBAD THE SAILOR

I DESIGNED, after my first voyage, to spend the rest of my days at Bagdad, but it was not long ere I grew weary of an indolent life, and I put to sea a second time, with merchants of known probity. We embarked on board a good ship, and after recommending ourselves to God, set sail. We traded from island to island, and exchanged commodities with great profit. One day we landed on an island covered with several sorts of fruit trees, but we could see neither man nor animal. We walked in the meadows, along the streams that watered them. Whilst some diverted themselves with gathering flow-

311

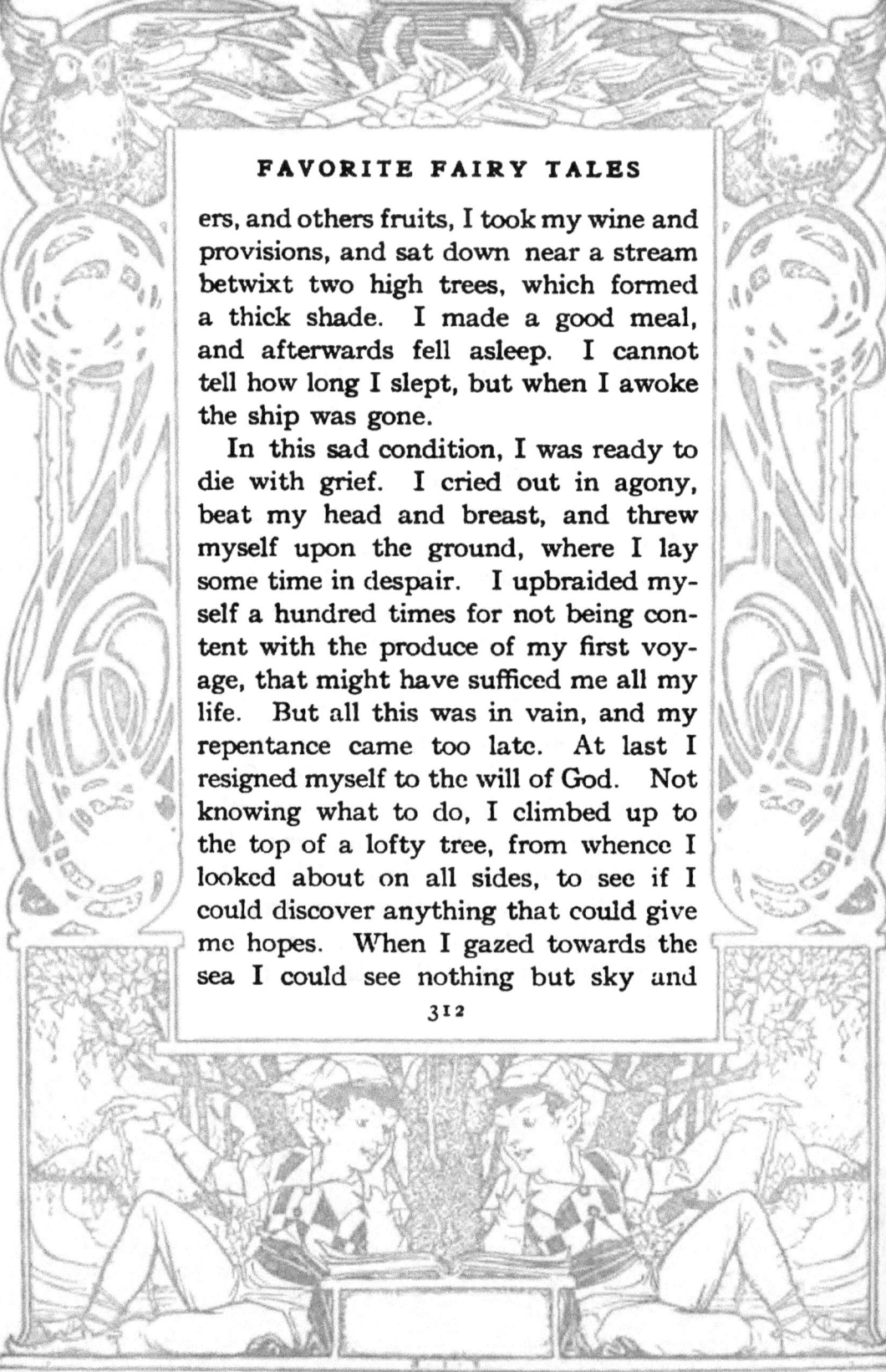

ers, and others fruits, I took my wine and provisions, and sat down near a stream betwixt two high trees, which formed a thick shade. I made a good meal, and afterwards fell asleep. I cannot tell how long I slept, but when I awoke the ship was gone.

In this sad condition, I was ready to die with grief. I cried out in agony, beat my head and breast, and threw myself upon the ground, where I lay some time in despair. I upbraided myself a hundred times for not being content with the produce of my first voyage, that might have sufficed me all my life. But all this was in vain, and my repentance came too late. At last I resigned myself to the will of God. Not knowing what to do, I climbed up to the top of a lofty tree, from whence I looked about on all sides, to see if I could discover anything that could give me hopes. When I gazed towards the sea I could see nothing but sky and

water; but looking over the land I beheld something white; and coming down, I took what provision I had left, and went towards it, the distance being so great that I could not distinguish what it was.

As I approached, I thought it to be a white dome, of a prodigious height and extent; and when I came up to it, I touched it, and found it to be very smooth. I went round to see if it was open on any side, but saw it was not, and that there was no climbing up to the top, as it was so smooth. It was at least fifty paces round.

By this time the sun was about to set, and all of a sudden the sky became as dark as if it had been covered with a thick cloud. I was much astonished at this sudden darkness, but much more when I found it occasioned by a bird of a monstrous size, that came flying towards me. I remembered that I had often heard mariners speak of a miracu-

lous bird called the roc, and conceived that the great dome which I so much admired must be its egg. In short, the bird alighted, and sat over the egg. As I perceived her coming I crept close to the egg, so that I had before me one of the legs of the bird, which was as big as the trunk of a tree. I tied myself strongly to it with my turban, in hopes that the roc next morning would carry me with her out of this desert island. After having passed the night in this condition, the bird flew away as soon as it was daylight, and carried me so high that I could not discern the earth; she afterwards descended with so much rapidity that I lost my senses. But when I found myself on the ground I speedily untied the knot, and had scarcely done so when the roc, having taken up a serpent of a monstrous length in her bill, flew away.

The spot where it left me was encompassed on all sides by mountains that

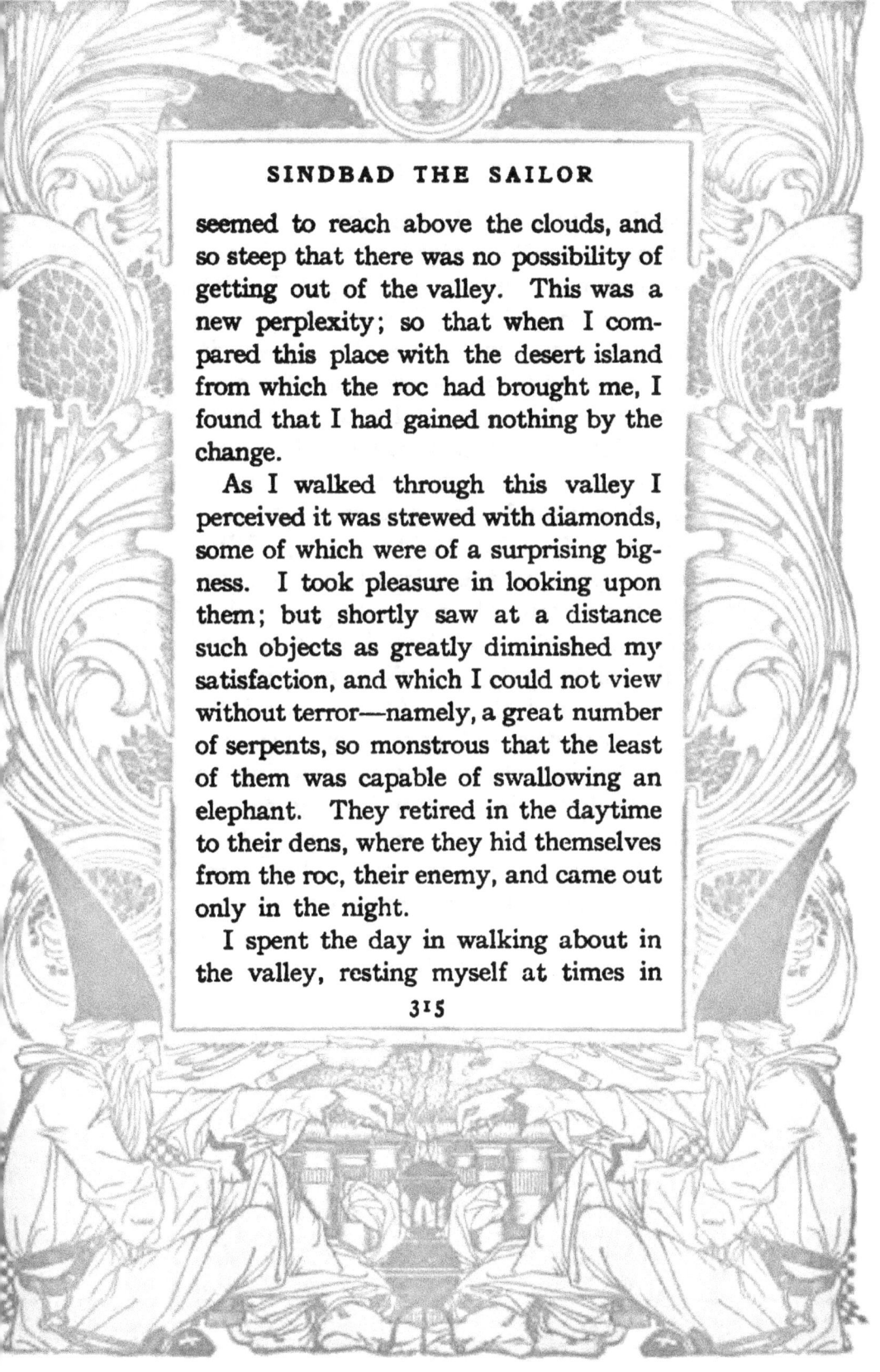

seemed to reach above the clouds, and so steep that there was no possibility of getting out of the valley. This was a new perplexity; so that when I compared this place with the desert island from which the roc had brought me, I found that I had gained nothing by the change.

As I walked through this valley I perceived it was strewed with diamonds, some of which were of a surprising bigness. I took pleasure in looking upon them; but shortly saw at a distance such objects as greatly diminished my satisfaction, and which I could not view without terror—namely, a great number of serpents, so monstrous that the least of them was capable of swallowing an elephant. They retired in the daytime to their dens, where they hid themselves from the roc, their enemy, and came out only in the night.

I spent the day in walking about in the valley, resting myself at times in

315

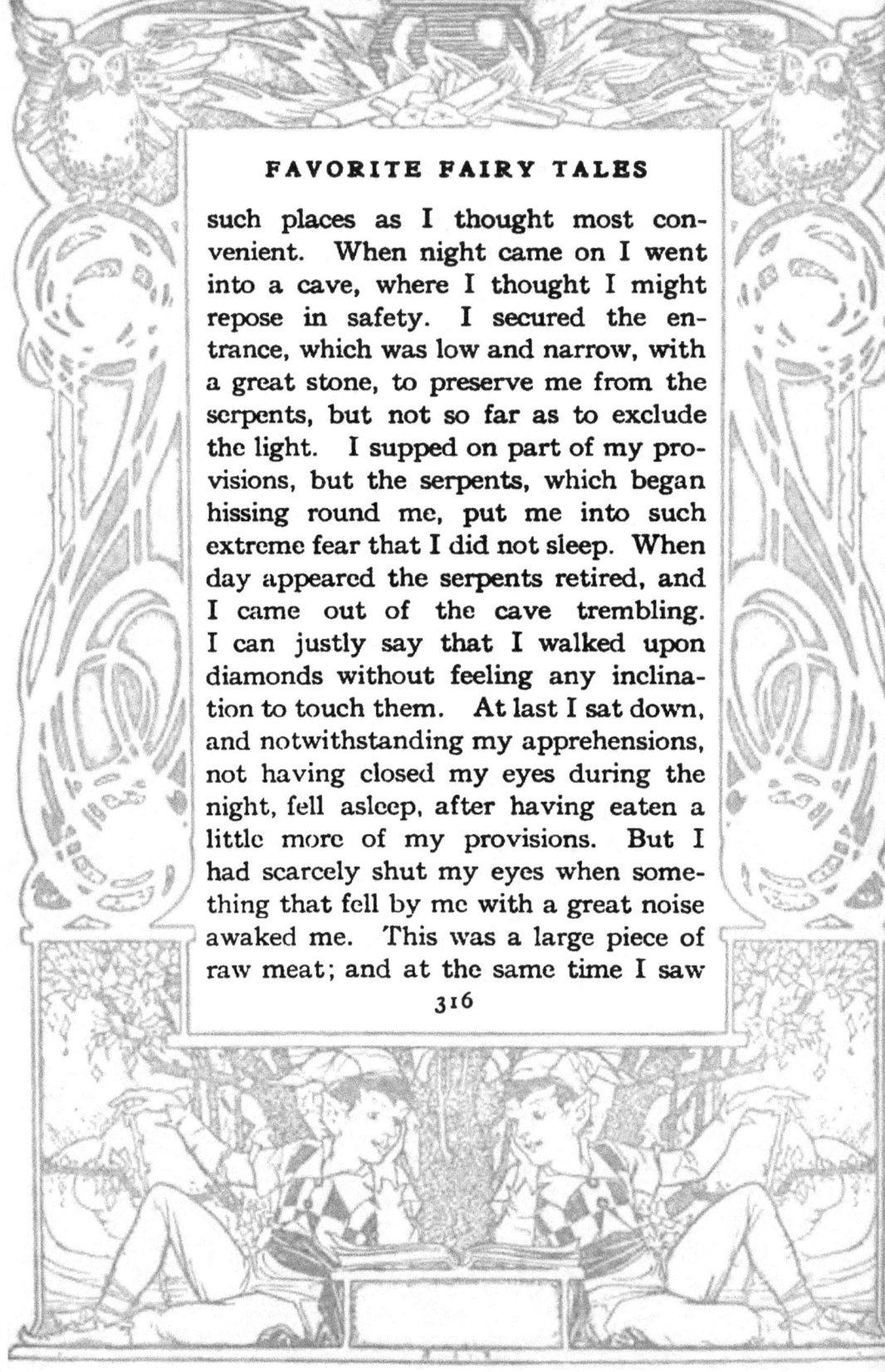

such places as I thought most convenient. When night came on I went into a cave, where I thought I might repose in safety. I secured the entrance, which was low and narrow, with a great stone, to preserve me from the serpents, but not so far as to exclude the light. I supped on part of my provisions, but the serpents, which began hissing round me, put me into such extreme fear that I did not sleep. When day appeared the serpents retired, and I came out of the cave trembling. I can justly say that I walked upon diamonds without feeling any inclination to touch them. At last I sat down, and notwithstanding my apprehensions, not having closed my eyes during the night, fell asleep, after having eaten a little more of my provisions. But I had scarcely shut my eyes when something that fell by me with a great noise awaked me. This was a large piece of raw meat; and at the same time I saw

several others fall down from the rocks in different places.

I had always regarded as fabulous what I had heard sailors and others relate of the valley of diamonds, and of the stratagems employed by merchants to obtain jewels from thence; but now I found that they had stated nothing but the truth. For the fact is that the merchants come to the neighborhood of this valley, when the eagles have young ones, and throwing great joints of meat into the valley, the diamonds, upon whose points they fall, stick to them; the eagles, which are stronger in this country than anywhere else, pounce with great force upon those pieces of meat, and carry them to their nests on the precipices of the rocks to feed their young; the merchants at this time run to their nests, disturb and drive off the eagles by their shouts, and take away the diamonds that stick to the meat.

I perceived in this device the means of my deliverance.

Having collected together the largest diamonds I could find, and put them into the leather bag in which I used to carry my provisions, I took the largest of the pieces of meat, tied it close round me with the cloth of my turban, and then laid myself upon the ground with my face downward, the bag of diamonds being made fast to my girdle.

I had scarcely placed myself in this posture when one of the eagles, having taken me up with the piece of meat to which I was fastened, carried me to his nest on the top of the mountain. The merchants immediately began their shouting to frighten the eagles; and when they had obliged them to quit their prey, one of them came to the nest where I was. He was much alarmed when he saw me; but, recovering himself, instead of inquiring how I came thither, began to quarrel with me, and

318

The merchants began their shouting to frighten the eagles

The mountains began their shooting as before. ...

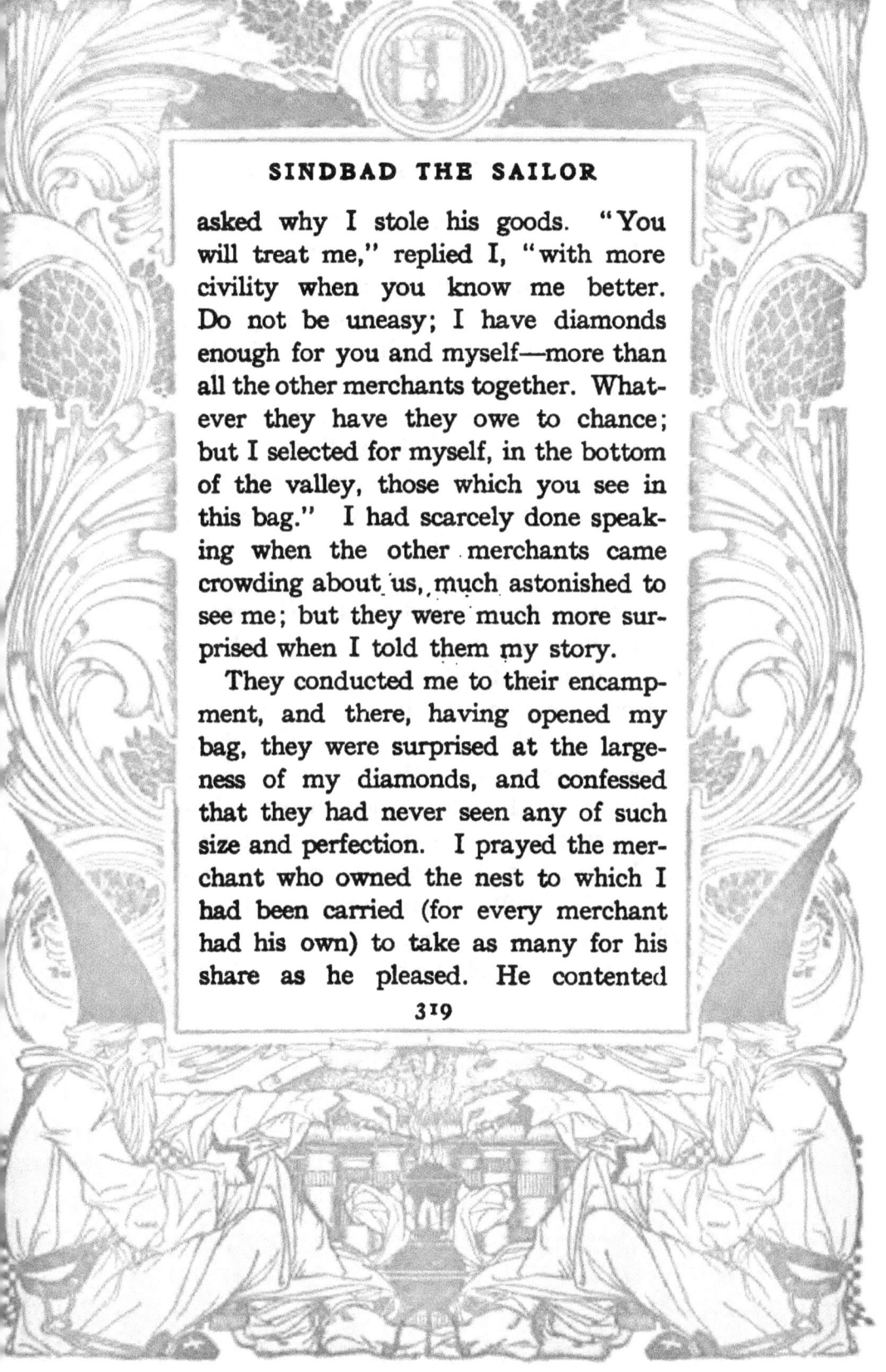

asked why I stole his goods. "You will treat me," replied I, "with more civility when you know me better. Do not be uneasy; I have diamonds enough for you and myself—more than all the other merchants together. Whatever they have they owe to chance; but I selected for myself, in the bottom of the valley, those which you see in this bag." I had scarcely done speaking when the other merchants came crowding about us, much astonished to see me; but they were much more surprised when I told them my story.

They conducted me to their encampment, and there, having opened my bag, they were surprised at the largeness of my diamonds, and confessed that they had never seen any of such size and perfection. I prayed the merchant who owned the nest to which I had been carried (for every merchant had his own) to take as many for his share as he pleased. He contented

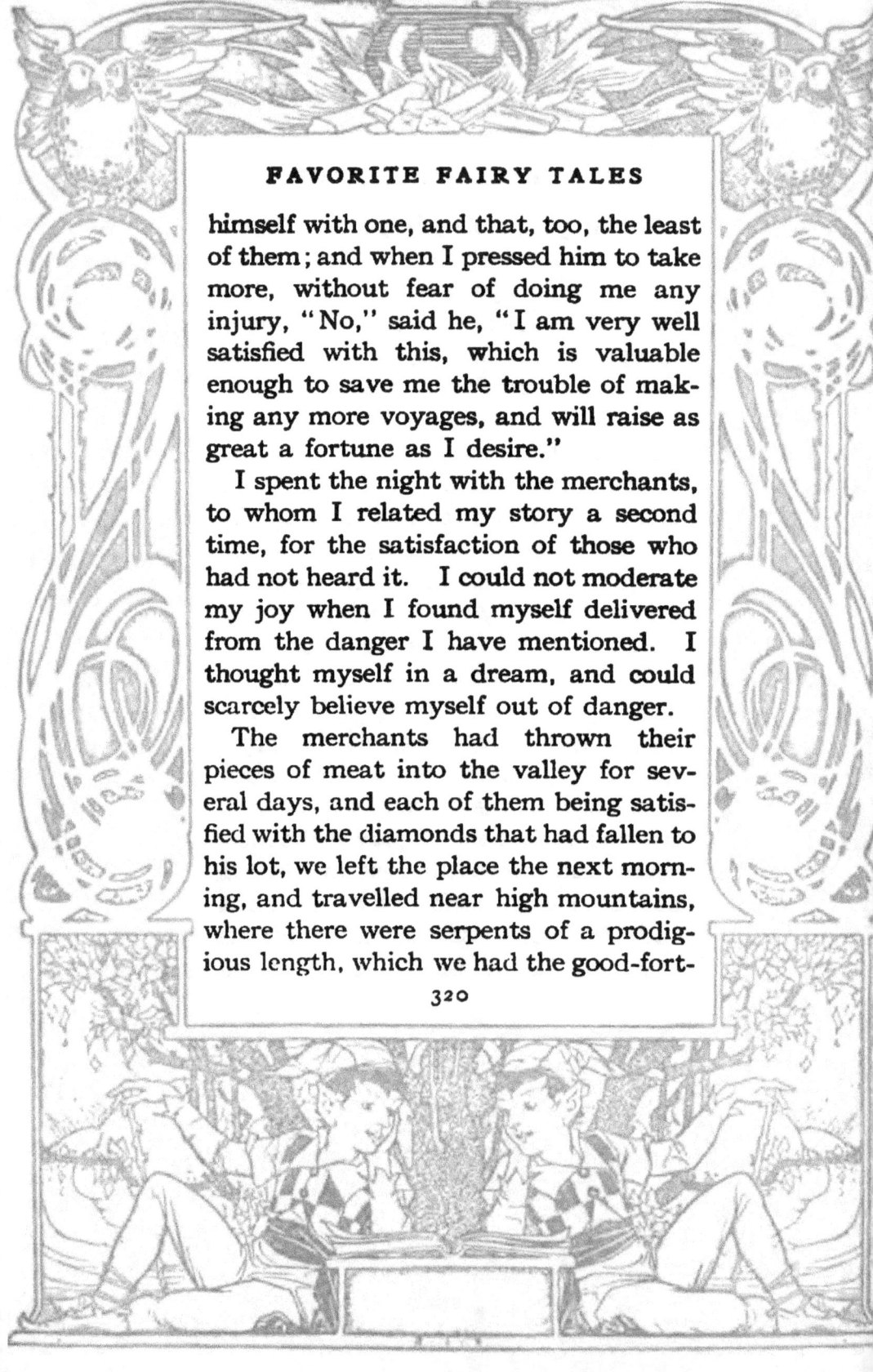

himself with one, and that, too, the least of them; and when I pressed him to take more, without fear of doing me any injury, "No," said he, "I am very well satisfied with this, which is valuable enough to save me the trouble of making any more voyages, and will raise as great a fortune as I desire."

I spent the night with the merchants, to whom I related my story a second time, for the satisfaction of those who had not heard it. I could not moderate my joy when I found myself delivered from the danger I have mentioned. I thought myself in a dream, and could scarcely believe myself out of danger.

The merchants had thrown their pieces of meat into the valley for several days, and each of them being satisfied with the diamonds that had fallen to his lot, we left the place the next morning, and travelled near high mountains, where there were serpents of a prodigious length, which we had the good-fort-

une to escape. We took shipping at the first port we reached, and touched at the isle of Roha, where the trees grow that yield camphor. The tree it so large, and its branches so thick, that one hundred men may easily sit under its shade. The juice, of which the camphor is made, exudes from a hole bored in the upper part of the tree, is received in a vessel, where it thickens to a consistency, and becomes what we call camphor. After the juice is thus drawn out, the tree withers and dies.

In this island is also found the rhinoceros, an animal less than the elephant, but larger than the buffalo. It has a horn upon its nose, which is solid, and cleft through the middle. The rhinoceros fights with the elephant, runs his horn into his belly, and carries him off upon his head; but the blood and the fat of the elephant running into his eyes and making him blind, he falls to the ground, and then, strange to relate,

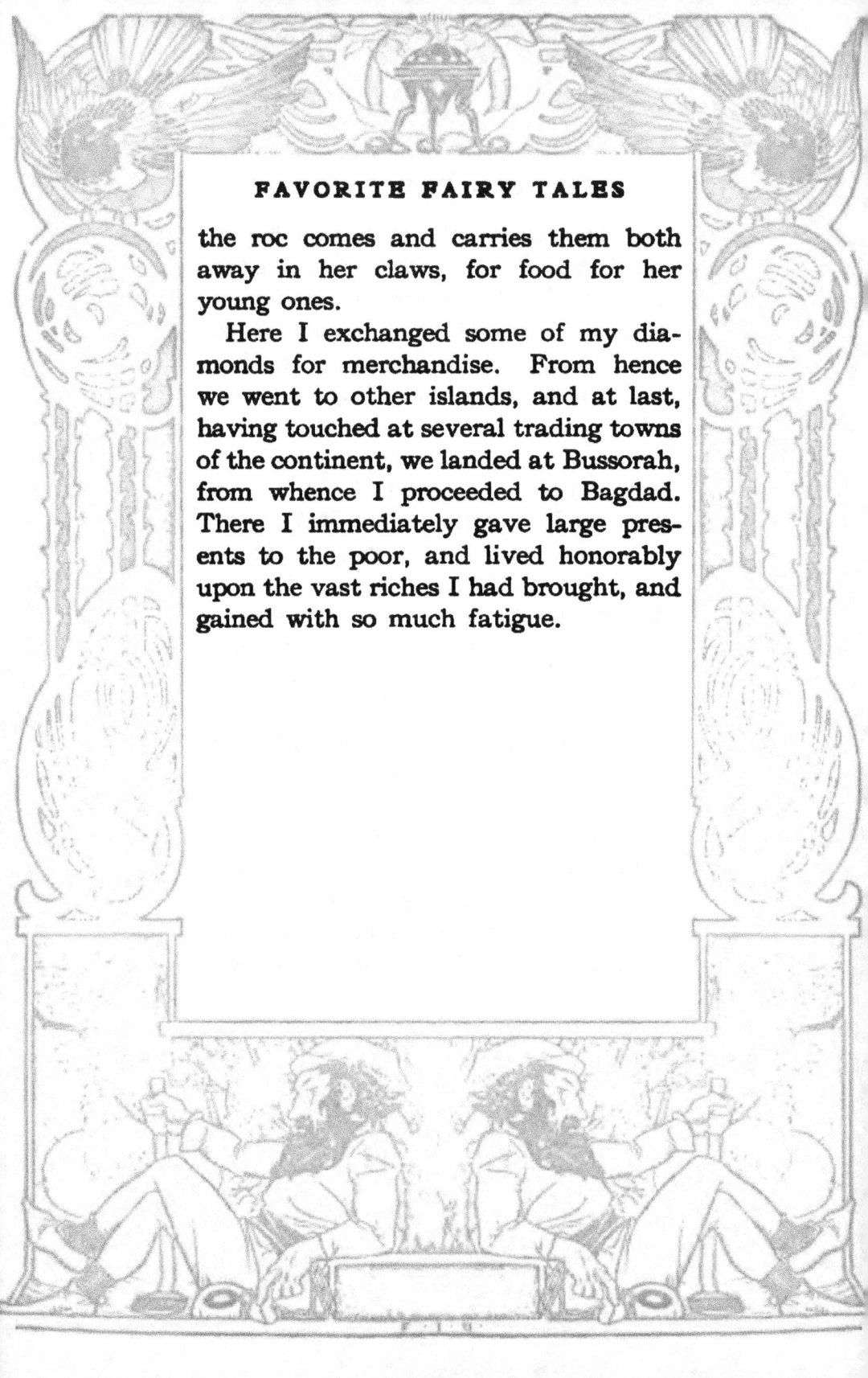

the roc comes and carries them both away in her claws, for food for her young ones.

Here I exchanged some of my diamonds for merchandise. From hence we went to other islands, and at last, having touched at several trading towns of the continent, we landed at Bussorah, from whence I proceeded to Bagdad. There I immediately gave large presents to the poor, and lived honorably upon the vast riches I had brought, and gained with so much fatigue.

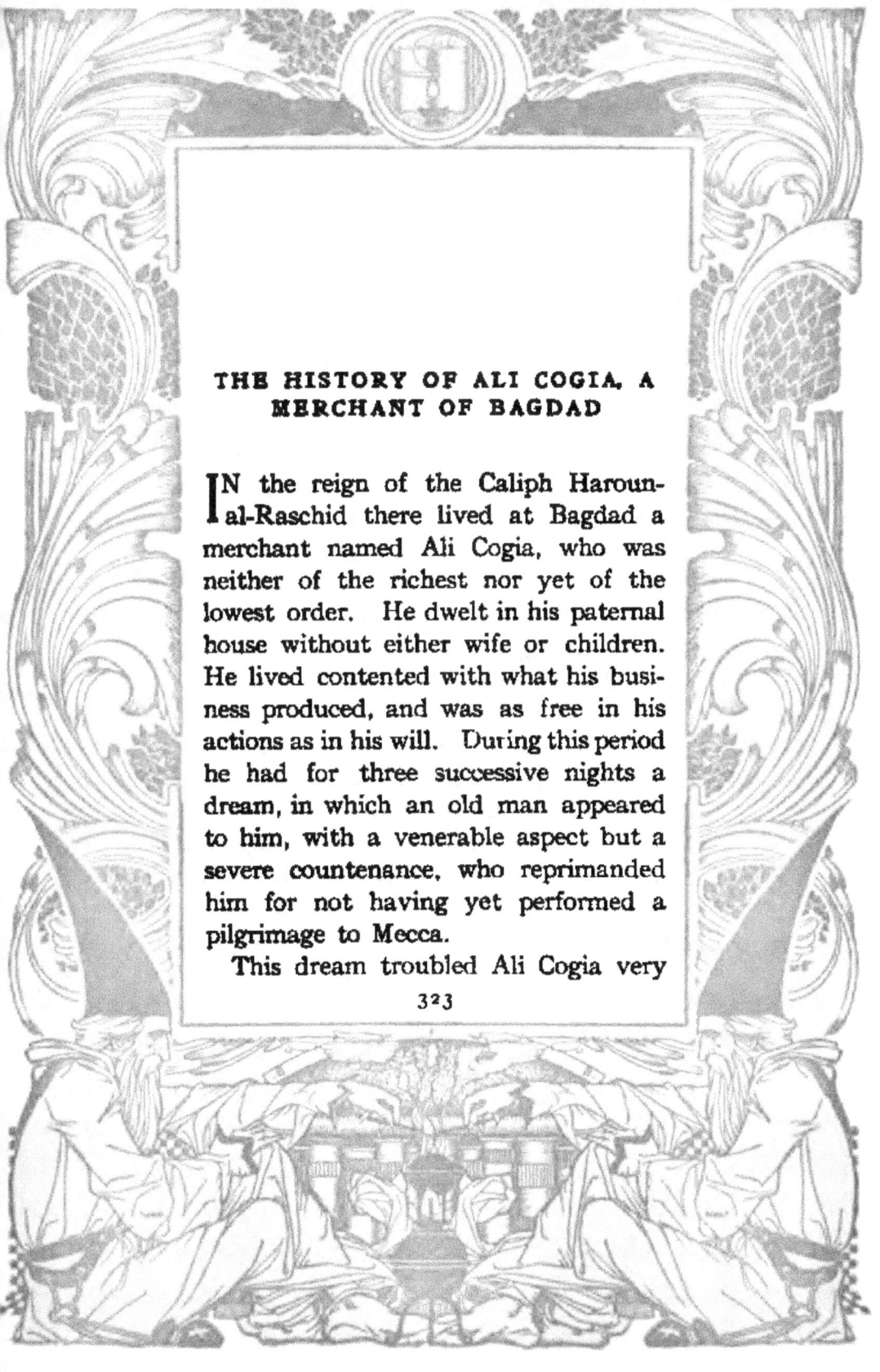

THE HISTORY OF ALI COGIA, A MERCHANT OF BAGDAD

IN the reign of the Caliph Haroun-al-Raschid there lived at Bagdad a merchant named Ali Cogia, who was neither of the richest nor yet of the lowest order. He dwelt in his paternal house without either wife or children. He lived contented with what his business produced, and was as free in his actions as in his will. During this period he had for three successive nights a dream, in which an old man appeared to him, with a venerable aspect but a severe countenance, who reprimanded him for not having yet performed a pilgrimage to Mecca.

This dream troubled Ali Cogia very

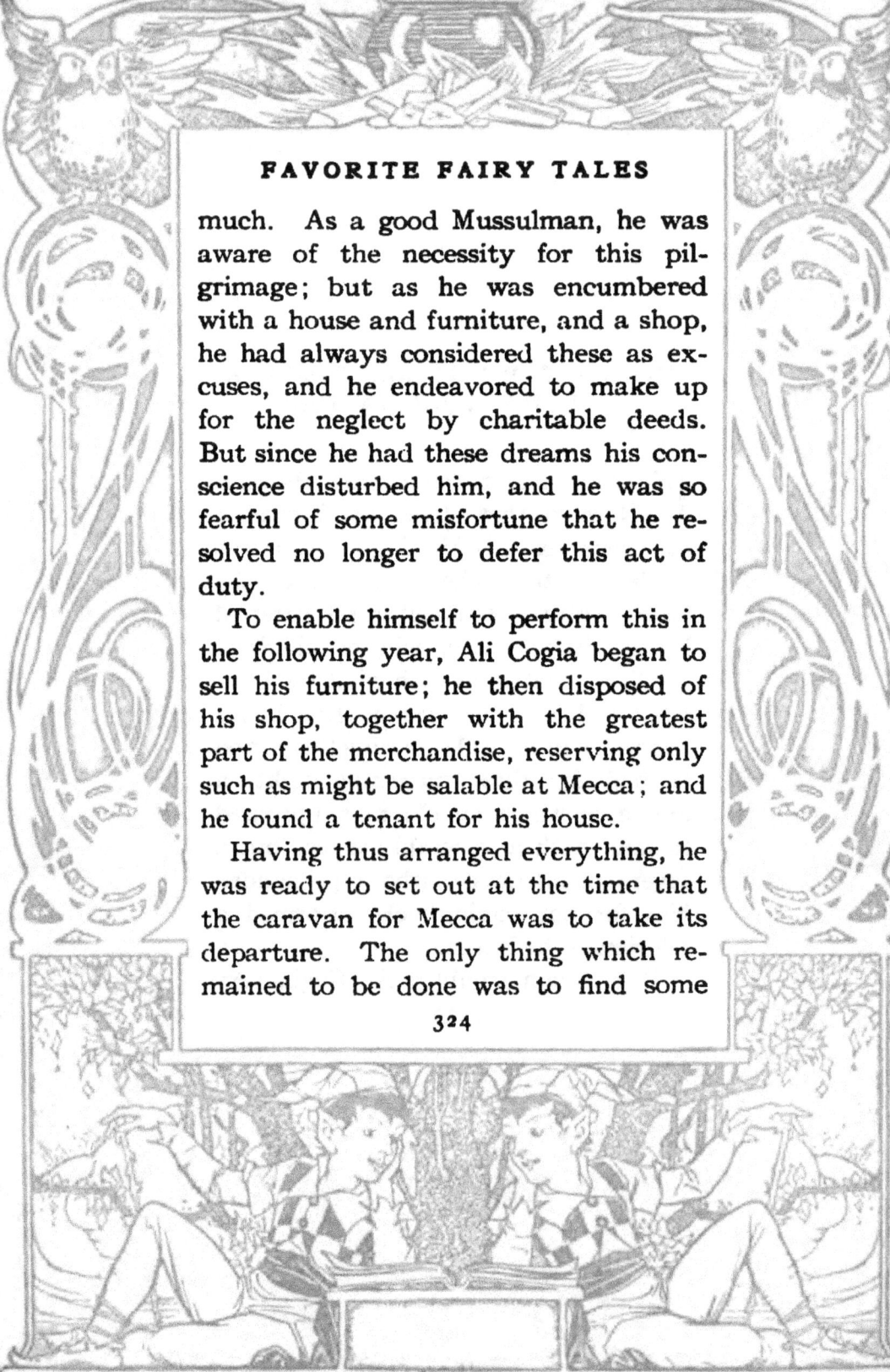

much. As a good Mussulman, he was aware of the necessity for this pilgrimage; but as he was encumbered with a house and furniture, and a shop, he had always considered these as excuses, and he endeavored to make up for the neglect by charitable deeds. But since he had these dreams his conscience disturbed him, and he was so fearful of some misfortune that he resolved no longer to defer this act of duty.

To enable himself to perform this in the following year, Ali Cogia began to sell his furniture; he then disposed of his shop, together with the greatest part of the merchandise, reserving only such as might be salable at Mecca; and he found a tenant for his house.

Having thus arranged everything, he was ready to set out at the time that the caravan for Mecca was to take its departure. The only thing which remained to be done was to find some

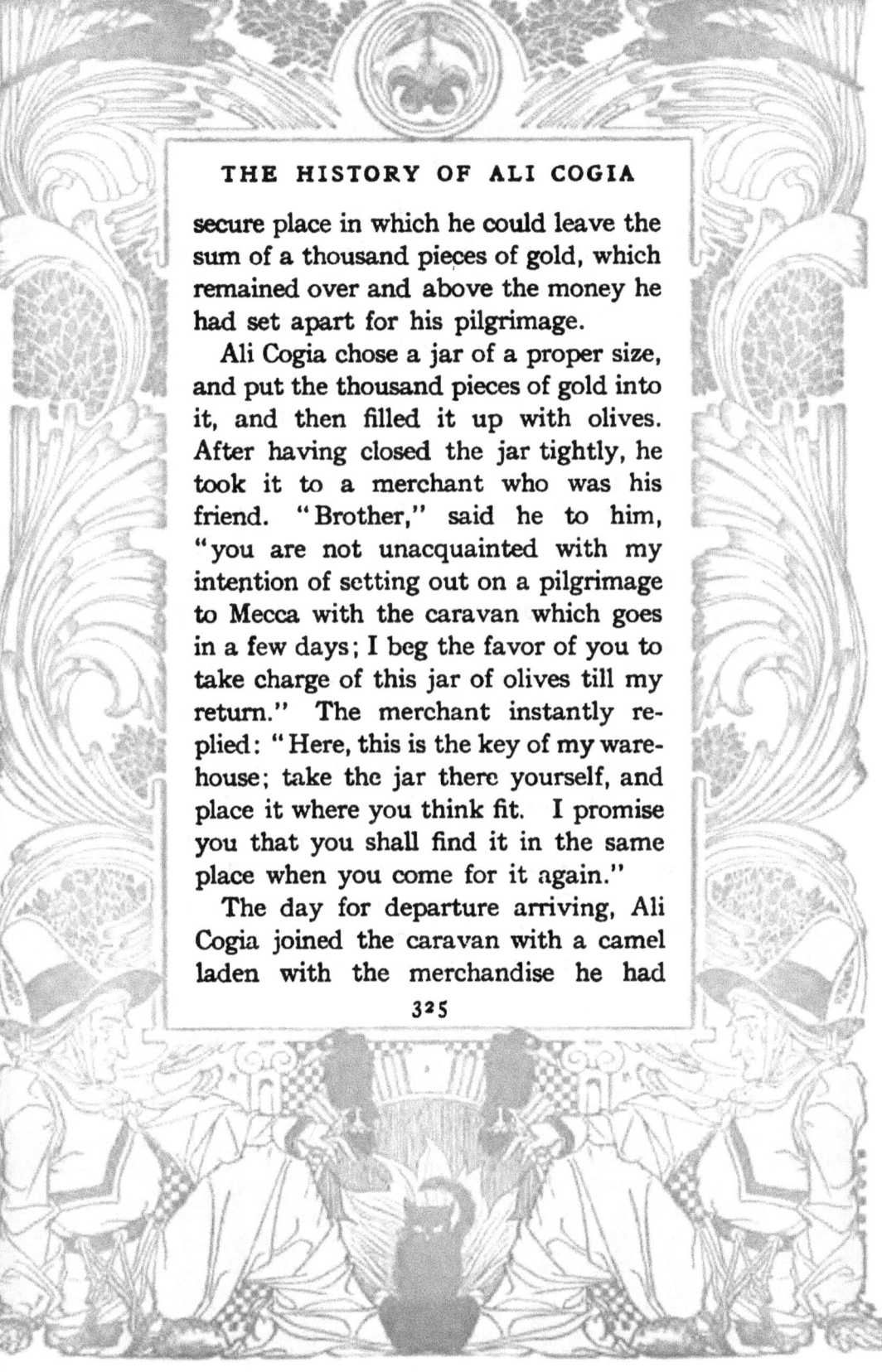

secure place in which he could leave the sum of a thousand pieces of gold, which remained over and above the money he had set apart for his pilgrimage.

Ali Cogia chose a jar of a proper size, and put the thousand pieces of gold into it, and then filled it up with olives. After having closed the jar tightly, he took it to a merchant who was his friend. "Brother," said he to him, "you are not unacquainted with my intention of setting out on a pilgrimage to Mecca with the caravan which goes in a few days; I beg the favor of you to take charge of this jar of olives till my return." The merchant instantly replied: "Here, this is the key of my warehouse; take the jar there yourself, and place it where you think fit. I promise you that you shall find it in the same place when you come for it again."

The day for departure arriving, Ali Cogia joined the caravan with a camel laden with the merchandise he had

made choice of, which also served him as a sort of saddle to ride on, and he arrived in perfect safety at Mecca. He, together with the other pilgrims, visited the temple—that edifice, so celebrated and so frequented every year by all the Mussulman nations, who repair thither from all parts of the globe, to observe the religious ceremonies which are required of them. When he had acquitted himself of the duties of his pilgrimage, he exposed the merchandise he had brought with him for sale.

Two merchants, who were passing that way, and saw the goods of Ali Cogia, found them so beautiful that they stopped to look at them, although they did not want to purchase them. When they had satisfied their curiosity, one said to the other as he was walking away: "If this merchant knew the profit he could make of his goods at Cairo, he would take them there in preference to

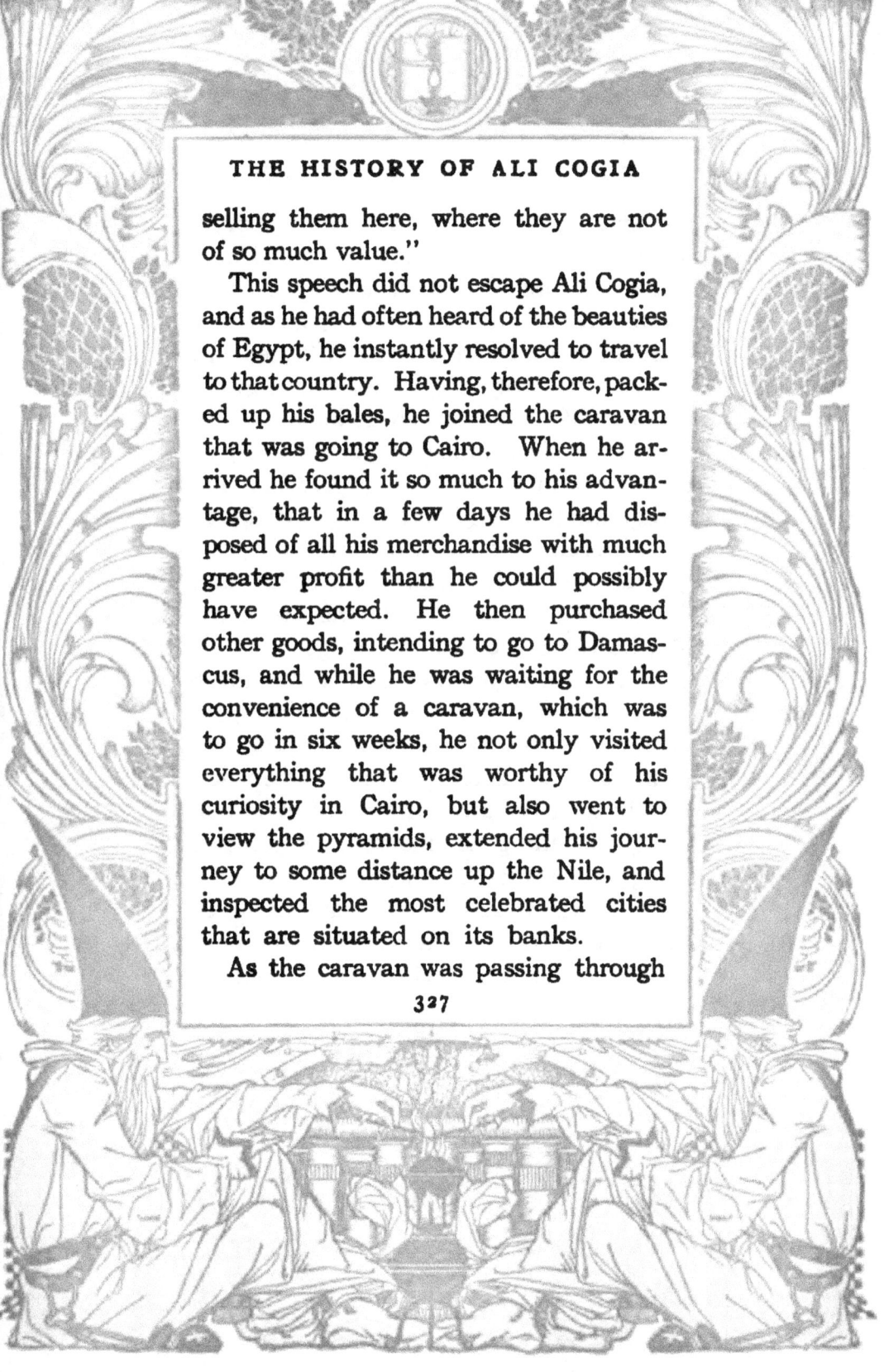

selling them here, where they are not of so much value."

This speech did not escape Ali Cogia, and as he had often heard of the beauties of Egypt, he instantly resolved to travel to that country. Having, therefore, packed up his bales, he joined the caravan that was going to Cairo. When he arrived he found it so much to his advantage, that in a few days he had disposed of all his merchandise with much greater profit than he could possibly have expected. He then purchased other goods, intending to go to Damascus, and while he was waiting for the convenience of a caravan, which was to go in six weeks, he not only visited everything that was worthy of his curiosity in Cairo, but also went to view the pyramids, extended his journey to some distance up the Nile, and inspected the most celebrated cities that are situated on its banks.

As the caravan was passing through

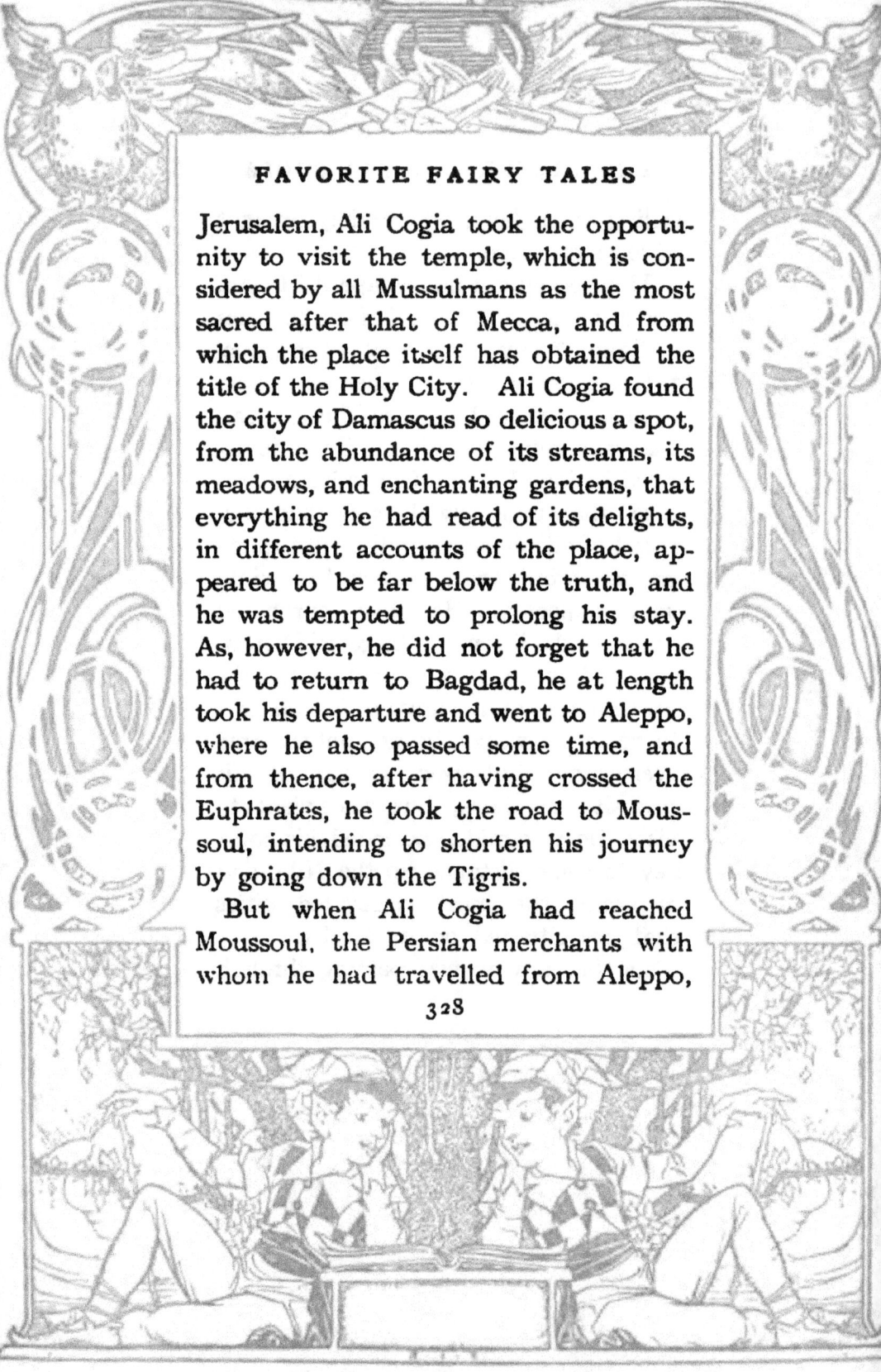

Jerusalem, Ali Cogia took the opportunity to visit the temple, which is considered by all Mussulmans as the most sacred after that of Mecca, and from which the place itself has obtained the title of the Holy City. Ali Cogia found the city of Damascus so delicious a spot, from the abundance of its streams, its meadows, and enchanting gardens, that everything he had read of its delights, in different accounts of the place, appeared to be far below the truth, and he was tempted to prolong his stay. As, however, he did not forget that he had to return to Bagdad, he at length took his departure and went to Aleppo, where he also passed some time, and from thence, after having crossed the Euphrates, he took the road to Moussoul, intending to shorten his journey by going down the Tigris.

But when Ali Cogia had reached Moussoul, the Persian merchants with whom he had travelled from Aleppo, and had formed an intimacy, gained so great an ascendancy over his mind by their obliging manners and agreeable conversation, that they had no difficulty in persuading him to accompany them to Shiraz, from whence it would be easy for him to return to Bagdad, and with considerable profit. They took him through the cities of Sultania, Reï, Coam, Kaschan, Ispahan, and then to Shiraz, where he was induced to go with them to India, and then return again to Shiraz.

In this way, reckoning also the time Ali Cogia resided in each city, it was now nearly seven years since he had quitted Bagdad, and he determined to return. Till this period the friend to whom he had intrusted the jar of olives before he left that city had never thought more of him or his jar. At the very time that Ali Cogia was on his return with a caravan from Shiraz, one evening as his friend the merchant was at supper with

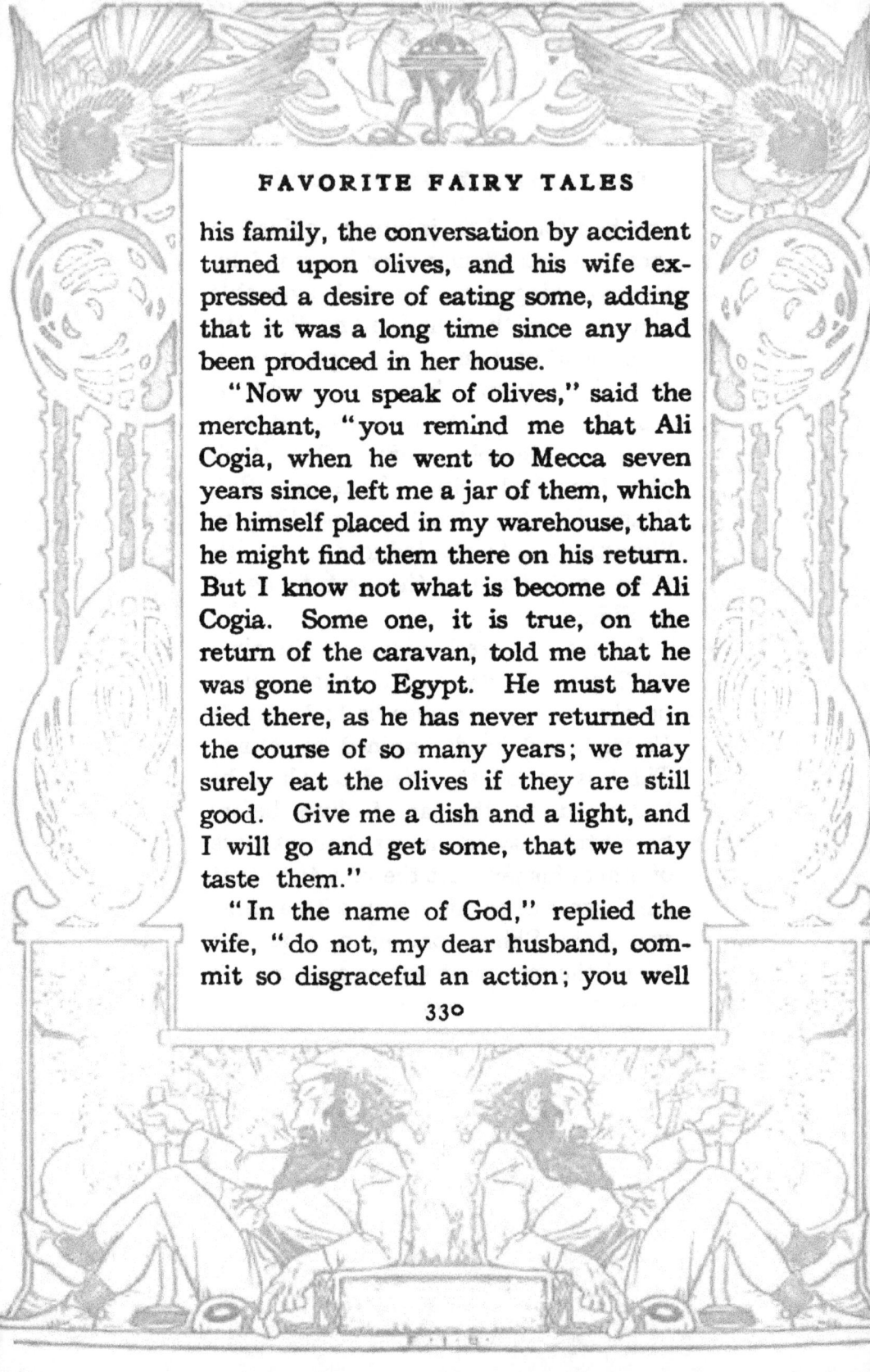

his family, the conversation by accident turned upon olives, and his wife expressed a desire of eating some, adding that it was a long time since any had been produced in her house.

"Now you speak of olives," said the merchant, "you remind me that Ali Cogia, when he went to Mecca seven years since, left me a jar of them, which he himself placed in my warehouse, that he might find them there on his return. But I know not what is become of Ali Cogia. Some one, it is true, on the return of the caravan, told me that he was gone into Egypt. He must have died there, as he has never returned in the course of so many years; we may surely eat the olives if they are still good. Give me a dish and a light, and I will go and get some, that we may taste them."

"In the name of God," replied the wife, "do not, my dear husband, commit so disgraceful an action; you well

330

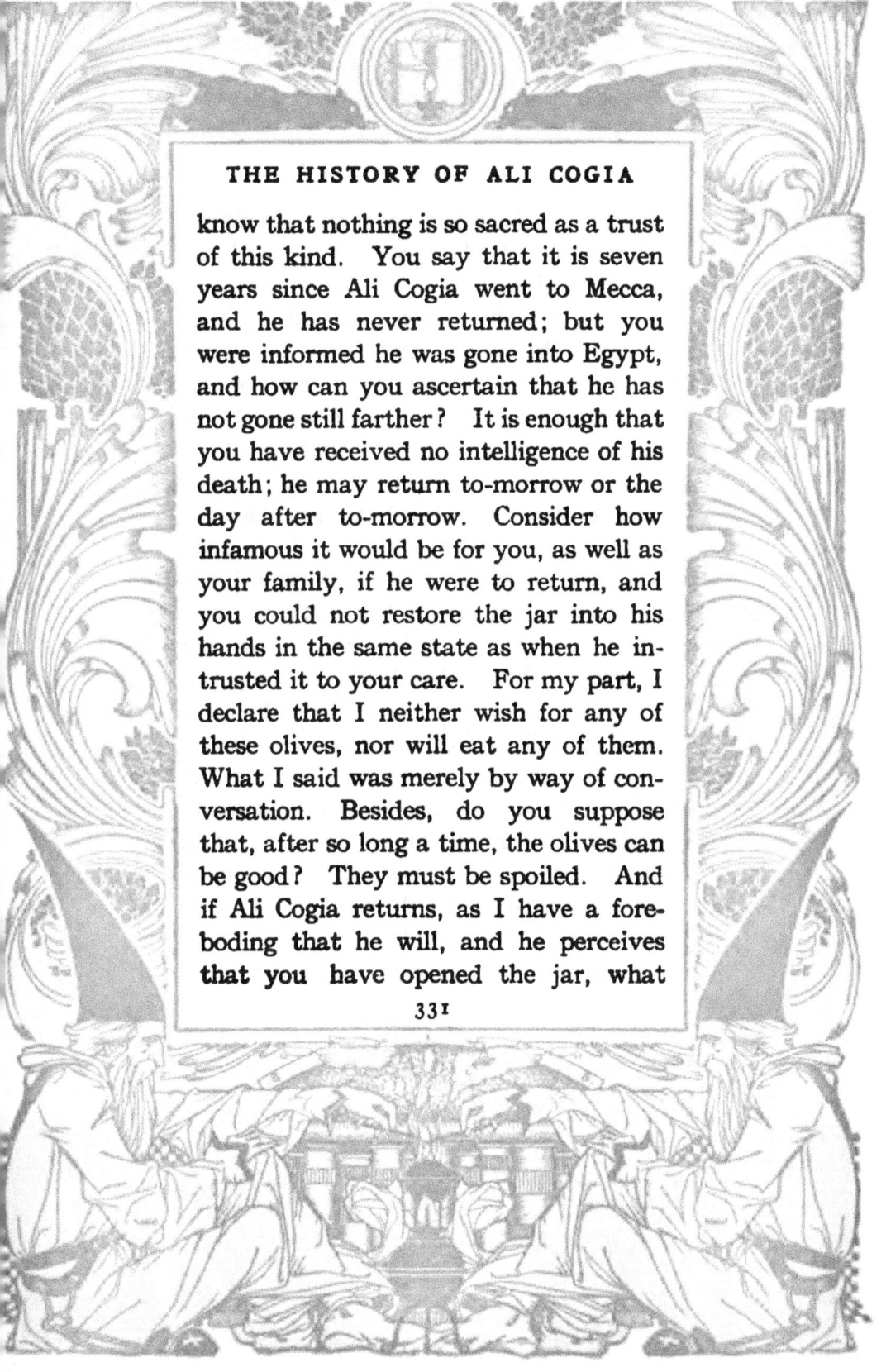

know that nothing is so sacred as a trust of this kind. You say that it is seven years since Ali Cogia went to Mecca, and he has never returned; but you were informed he was gone into Egypt, and how can you ascertain that he has not gone still farther? It is enough that you have received no intelligence of his death; he may return to-morrow or the day after to-morrow. Consider how infamous it would be for you, as well as your family, if he were to return, and you could not restore the jar into his hands in the same state as when he intrusted it to your care. For my part, I declare that I neither wish for any of these olives, nor will eat any of them. What I said was merely by way of conversation. Besides, do you suppose that, after so long a time, the olives can be good? They must be spoiled. And if Ali Cogia returns, as I have a foreboding that he will, and he perceives that you have opened the jar, what

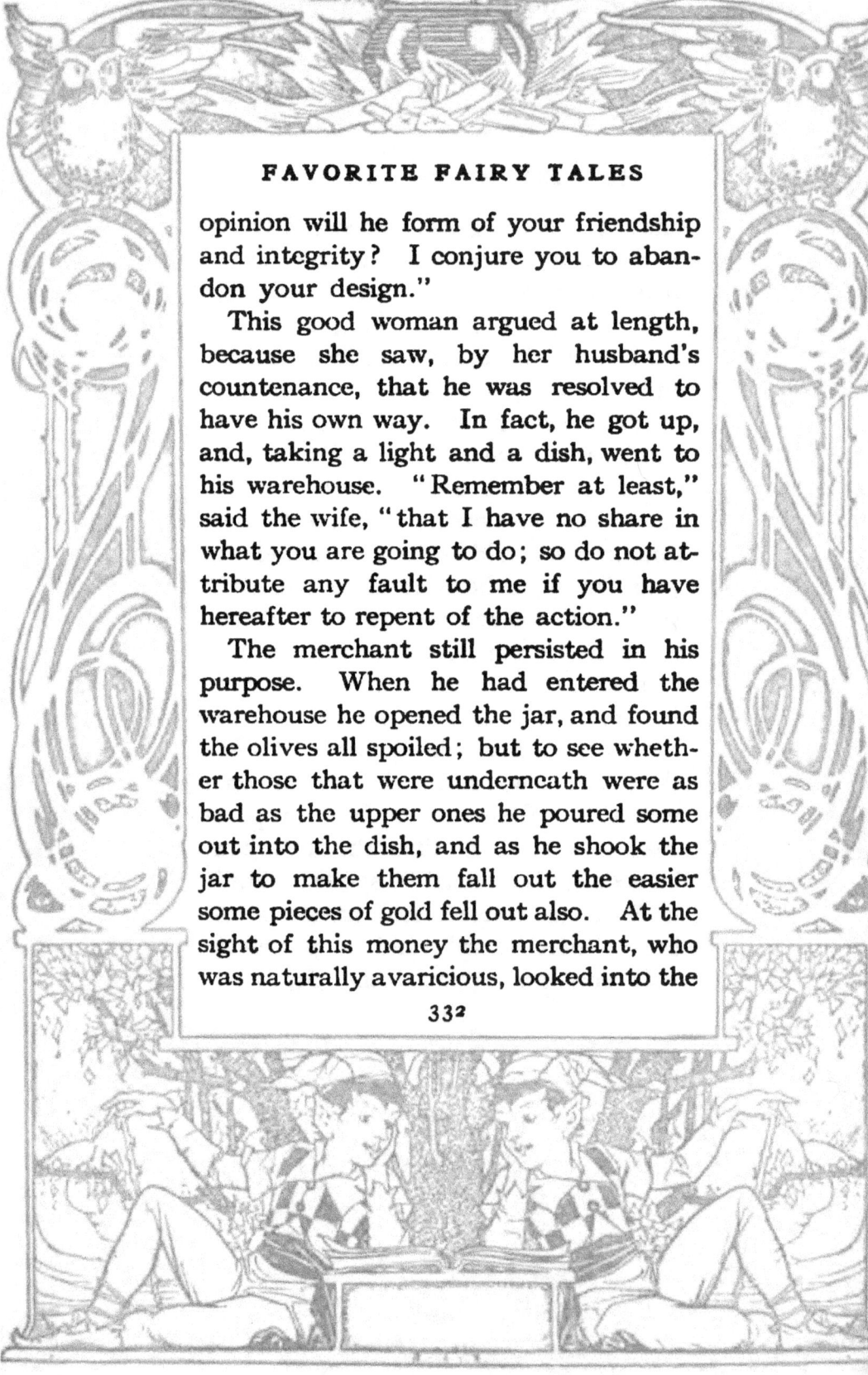

opinion will he form of your friendship
and integrity? I conjure you to abandon your design."

This good woman argued at length,
because she saw, by her husband's
countenance, that he was resolved to
have his own way. In fact, he got up,
and, taking a light and a dish, went to
his warehouse. "Remember at least,"
said the wife, "that I have no share in
what you are going to do; so do not at-
tribute any fault to me if you have
hereafter to repent of the action."

The merchant still persisted in his
purpose. When he had entered the
warehouse he opened the jar, and found
the olives all spoiled; but to see whether those that were underneath were as
bad as the upper ones he poured some
out into the dish, and as he shook the
jar to make them fall out the easier
some pieces of gold fell out also. At the
sight of this money the merchant, who
was naturally avaricious, looked into the

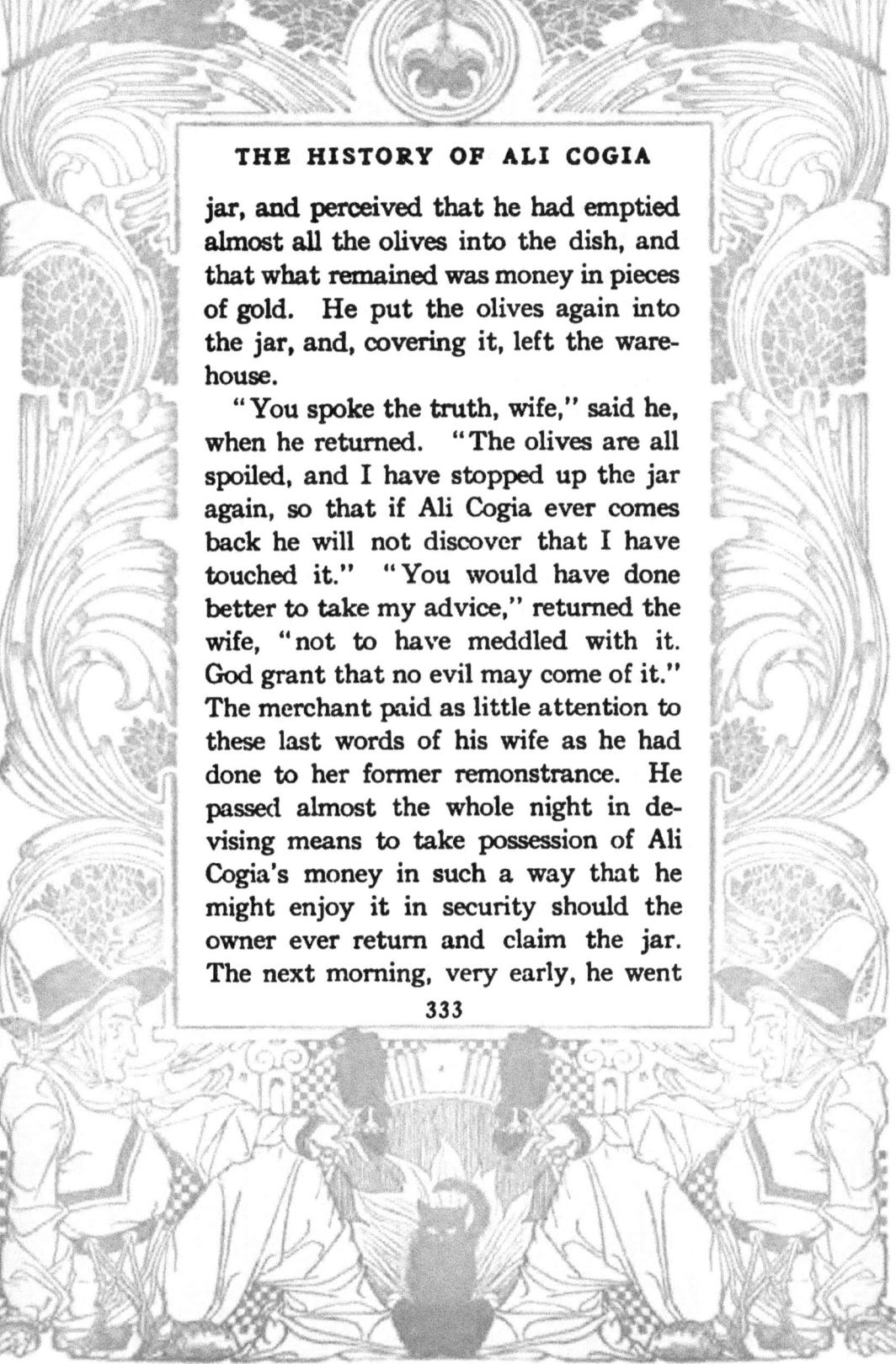

jar, and perceived that he had emptied almost all the olives into the dish, and that what remained was money in pieces of gold. He put the olives again into the jar, and, covering it, left the warehouse.

"You spoke the truth, wife," said he, when he returned. "The olives are all spoiled, and I have stopped up the jar again, so that if Ali Cogia ever comes back he will not discover that I have touched it." "You would have done better to take my advice," returned the wife, "not to have meddled with it. God grant that no evil may come of it." The merchant paid as little attention to these last words of his wife as he had done to her former remonstrance. He passed almost the whole night in devising means to take possession of Ali Cogia's money in such a way that he might enjoy it in security should the owner ever return and claim the jar. The next morning, very early, he went

out to buy some olives of that year's growth. He threw away those which had been in Ali Cogia's jar, and, taking out the gold, he put it in a place of safety; then filling the jar with the fresh olives he had just bought he put on the same cover, and placed it in the same spot where Ali Cogia had left it.

About a month after the merchant had committed this treacherous act Ali Cogia arrived at Bagdad, after his long absence from that city. As he had leased his house before his departure he alighted at a khan, where he took a lodging until he had informed his tenant of his return, that the latter might procure himself another residence.

The next day Ali Cogia went to see his friend the merchant, who received him with open arms, testifying the utmost joy at seeing him again, after an absence of so many years, which he said almost made him despair of ever beholding him any more.

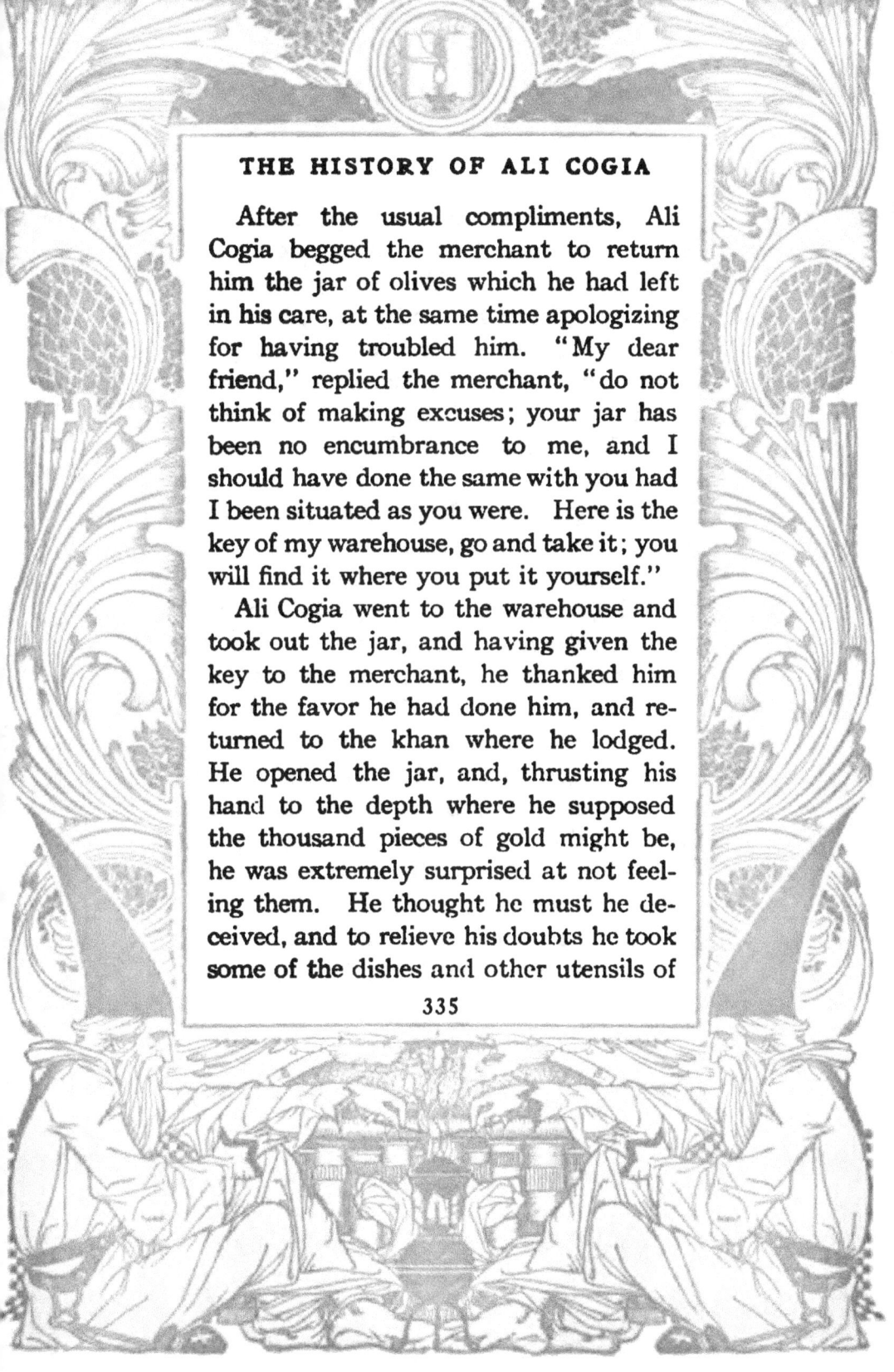

THE HISTORY OF ALI COGIA

After the usual compliments, Ali Cogia begged the merchant to return him the jar of olives which he had left in his care, at the same time apologizing for having troubled him. "My dear friend," replied the merchant, "do not think of making excuses; your jar has been no encumbrance to me, and I should have done the same with you had I been situated as you were. Here is the key of my warehouse, go and take it; you will find it where you put it yourself."

Ali Cogia went to the warehouse and took out the jar, and having given the key to the merchant, he thanked him for the favor he had done him, and returned to the khan where he lodged. He opened the jar, and, thrusting his hand to the depth where he supposed the thousand pieces of gold might be, he was extremely surprised at not feeling them. He thought he must he deceived, and to relieve his doubts he took some of the dishes and other utensils of

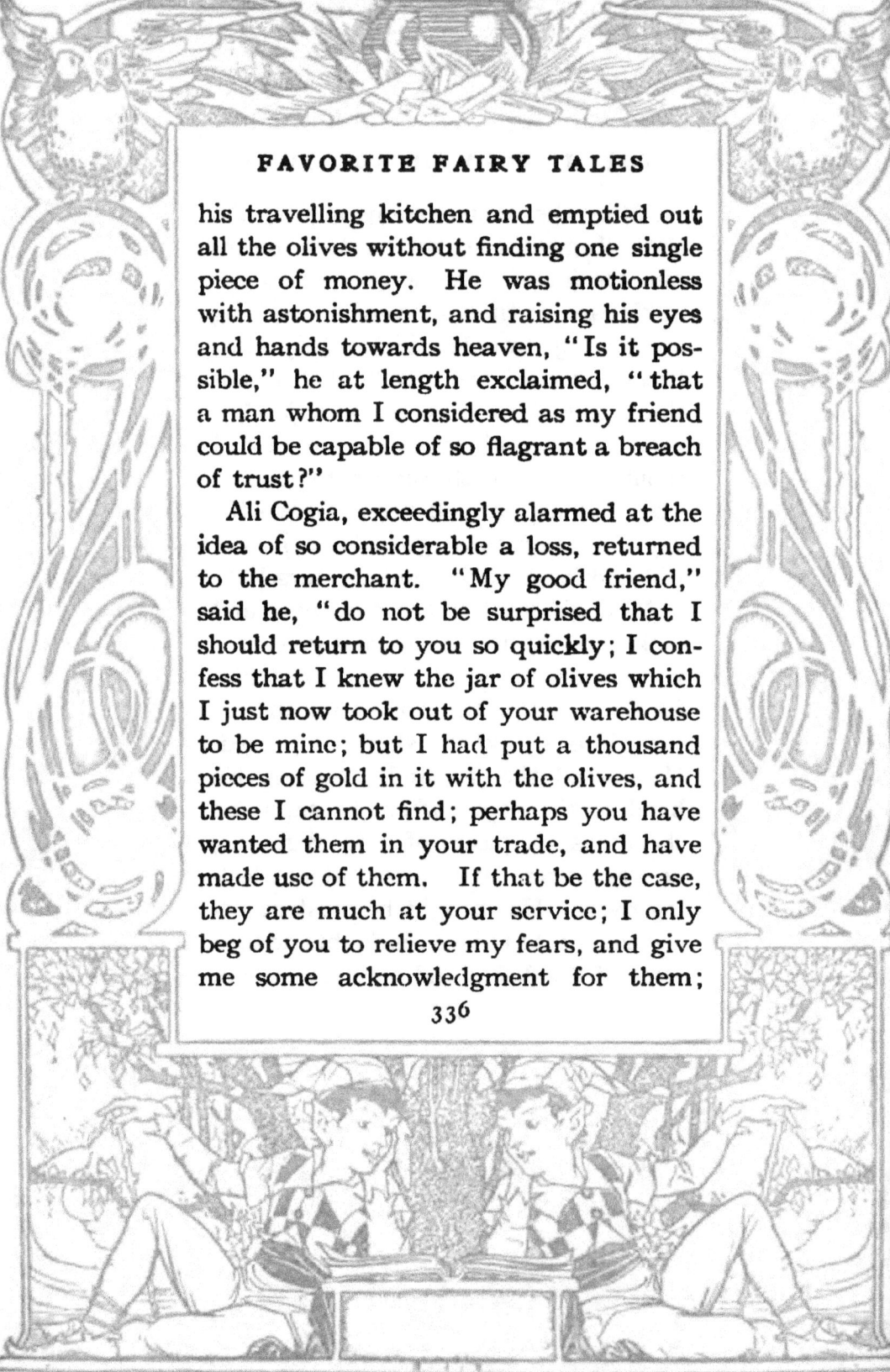

his travelling kitchen and emptied out all the olives without finding one single piece of money. He was motionless with astonishment, and raising his eyes and hands towards heaven, "Is it possible," he at length exclaimed, "that a man whom I considered as my friend could be capable of so flagrant a breach of trust?"

Ali Cogia, exceedingly alarmed at the idea of so considerable a loss, returned to the merchant. "My good friend," said he, "do not be surprised that I should return to you so quickly; I confess that I knew the jar of olives which I just now took out of your warehouse to be mine; but I had put a thousand pieces of gold in it with the olives, and these I cannot find; perhaps you have wanted them in your trade, and have made use of them. If that be the case, they are much at your service; I only beg of you to relieve my fears, and give me some acknowledgment for them;

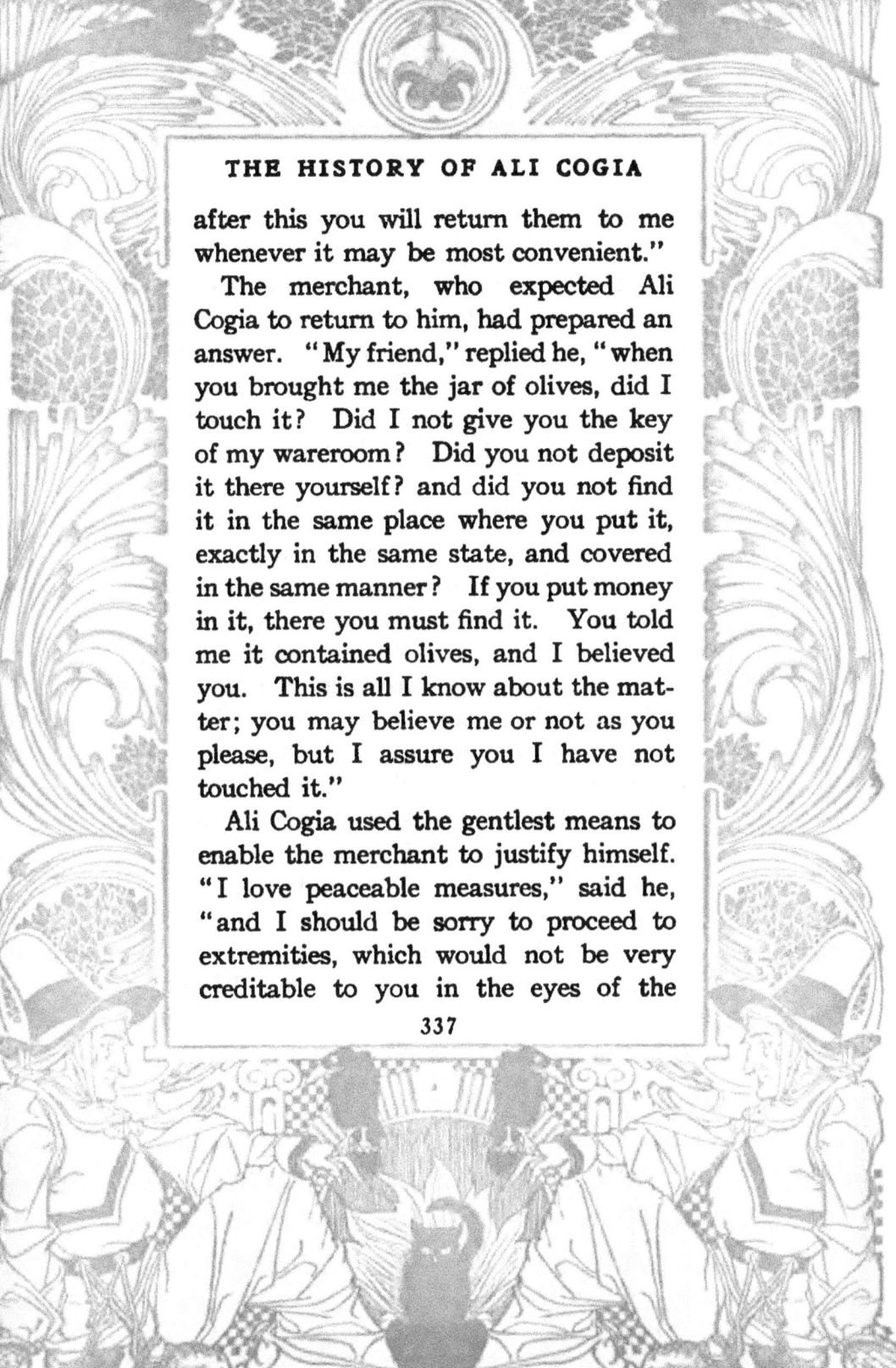

after this you will return them to me whenever it may be most convenient."

The merchant, who expected Ali Cogia to return to him, had prepared an answer. "My friend," replied he, "when you brought me the jar of olives, did I touch it? Did I not give you the key of my wareroom? Did you not deposit it there yourself? and did you not find it in the same place where you put it, exactly in the same state, and covered in the same manner? If you put money in it, there you must find it. You told me it contained olives, and I believed you. This is all I know about the matter; you may believe me or not as you please, but I assure you I have not touched it."

Ali Cogia used the gentlest means to enable the merchant to justify himself. "I love peaceable measures," said he, "and I should be sorry to proceed to extremities, which would not be very creditable to you in the eyes of the

337

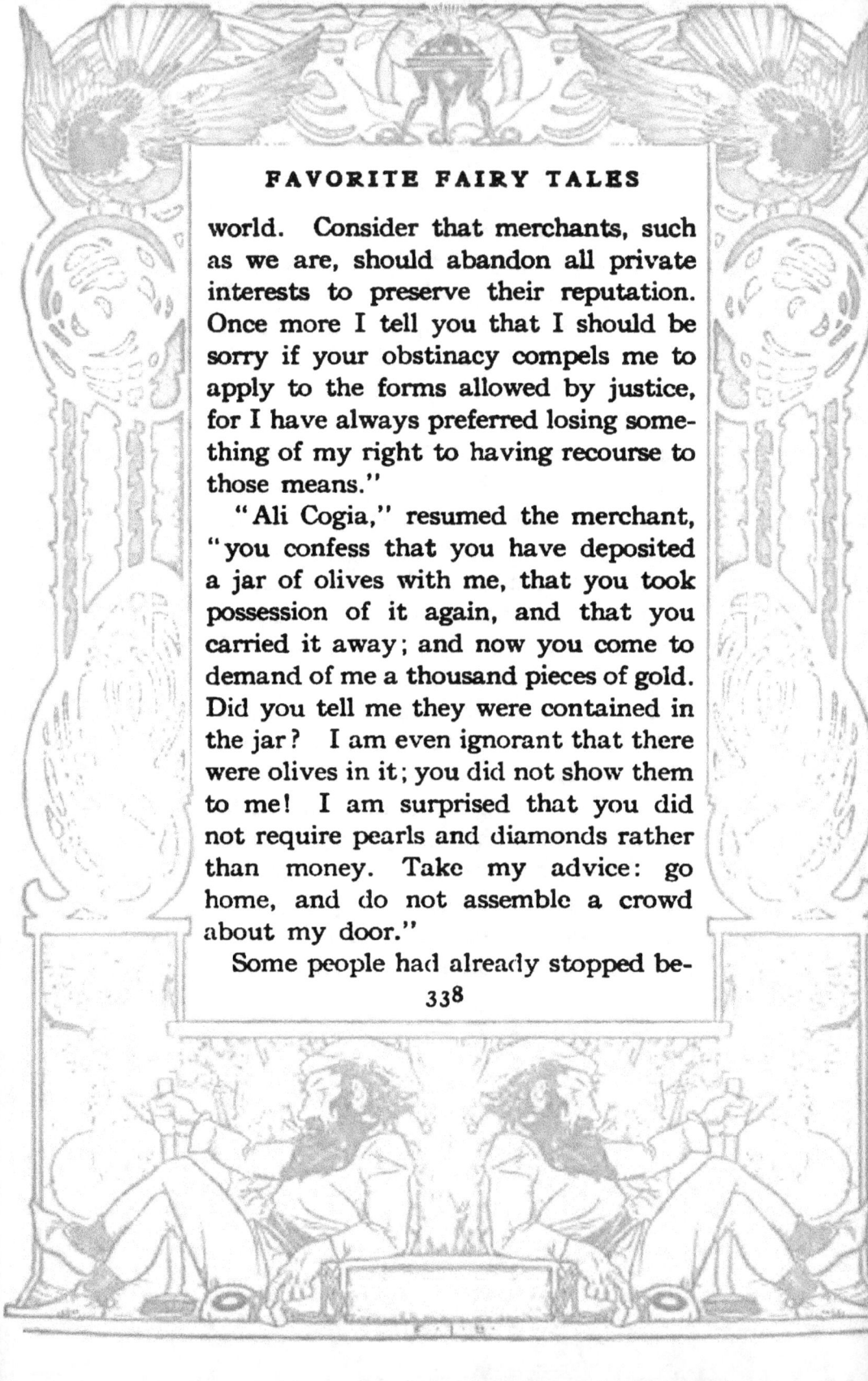

world. Consider that merchants, such as we are, should abandon all private interests to preserve their reputation. Once more I tell you that I should be sorry if your obstinacy compels me to apply to the forms allowed by justice, for I have always preferred losing something of my right to having recourse to those means."

"Ali Cogia," resumed the merchant, "you confess that you have deposited a jar of olives with me, that you took possession of it again, and that you carried it away; and now you come to demand of me a thousand pieces of gold. Did you tell me they were contained in the jar? I am even ignorant that there were olives in it; you did not show them to me! I am surprised that you did not require pearls and diamonds rather than money. Take my advice: go home, and do not assemble a crowd about my door."

Some people had already stopped be-

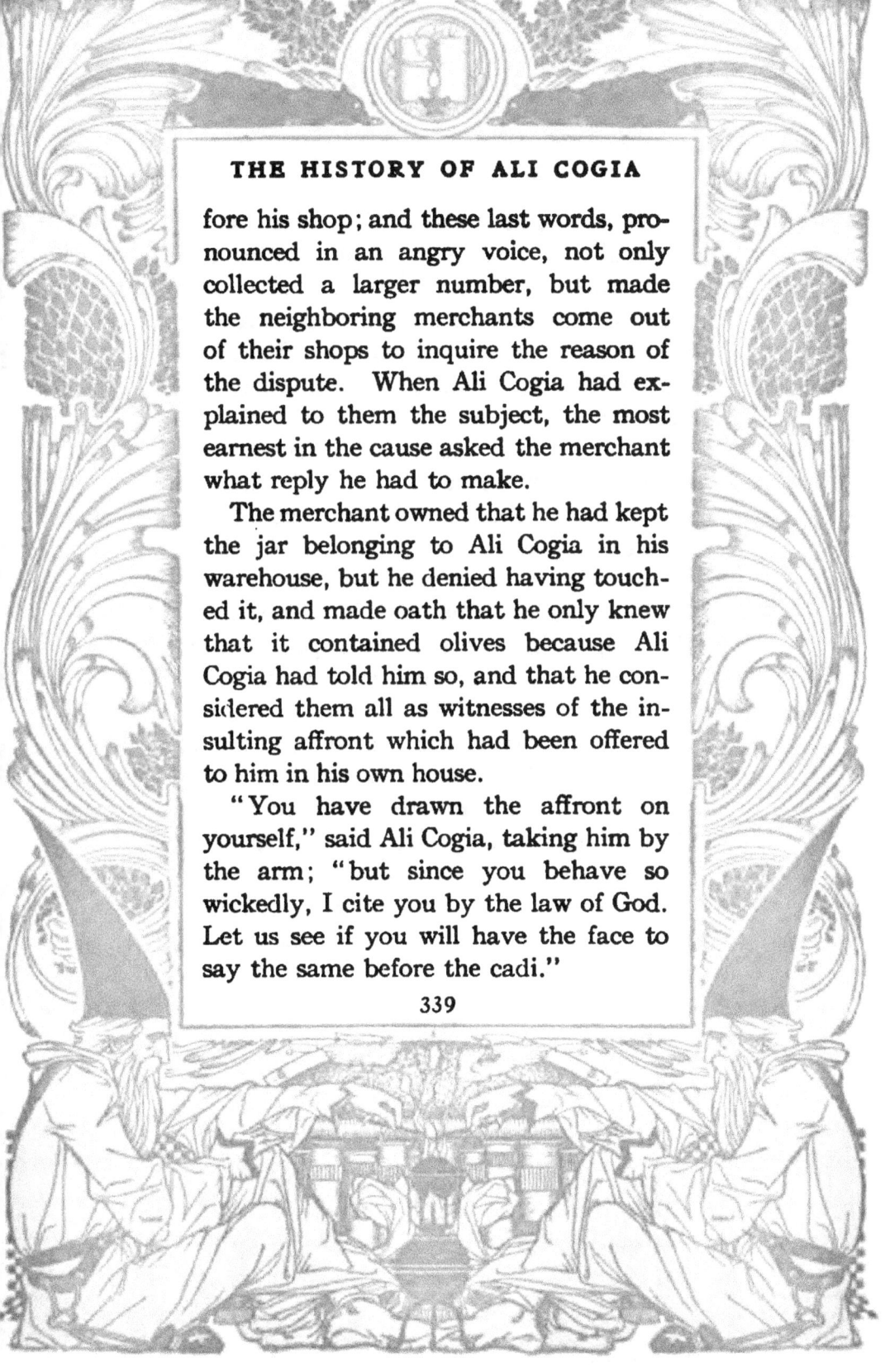

fore his shop; and these last words, pronounced in an angry voice, not only collected a larger number, but made the neighboring merchants come out of their shops to inquire the reason of the dispute. When Ali Cogia had explained to them the subject, the most earnest in the cause asked the merchant what reply he had to make.

The merchant owned that he had kept the jar belonging to Ali Cogia in his warehouse, but he denied having touched it, and made oath that he only knew that it contained olives because Ali Cogia had told him so, and that he considered them all as witnesses of the insulting affront which had been offered to him in his own house.

"You have drawn the affront on yourself," said Ali Cogia, taking him by the arm; "but since you behave so wickedly, I cite you by the law of God. Let us see if you will have the face to say the same before the cadi."

339

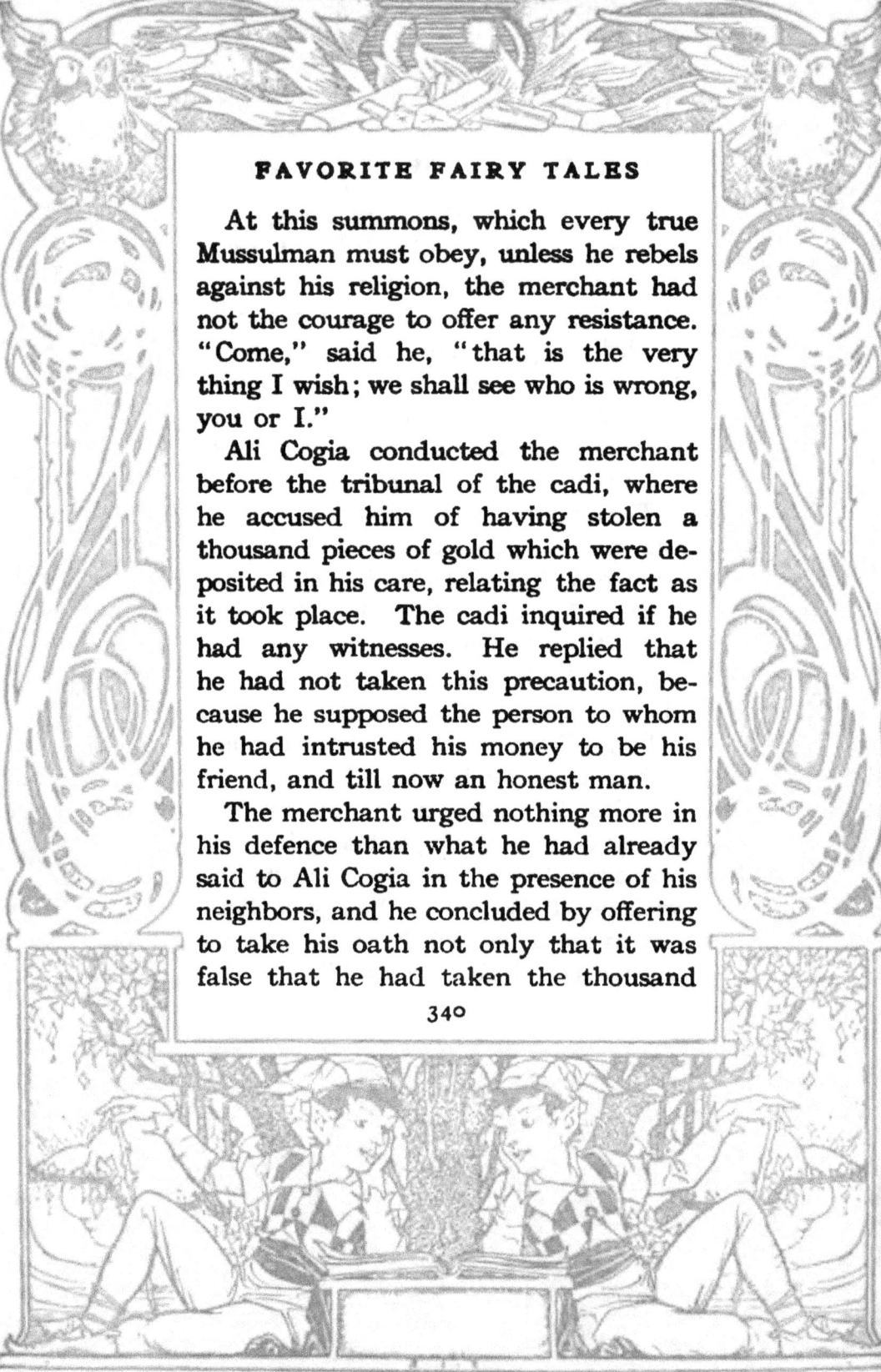

At this summons, which every true Mussulman must obey, unless he rebels against his religion, the merchant had not the courage to offer any resistance. "Come," said he, "that is the very thing I wish; we shall see who is wrong, you or I."

Ali Cogia conducted the merchant before the tribunal of the cadi, where he accused him of having stolen a thousand pieces of gold which were deposited in his care, relating the fact as it took place. The cadi inquired if he had any witnesses. He replied that he had not taken this precaution, because he supposed the person to whom he had intrusted his money to be his friend, and till now an honest man.

The merchant urged nothing more in his defence than what he had already said to Ali Cogia in the presence of his neighbors, and he concluded by offering to take his oath not only that it was false that he had taken the thousand

340

pieces of gold, but even that he had any knowledge of their being in his possession. The cadi accepted the oath, after which he was dismissed as innocent.

Ali Cogia, extremely mortified to find himself condemned to suffer so considerable a loss, protested against the sentence, and declared to the cadi that he would lay his complaint before the Caliph Haroun-al-Raschid, who would do him justice; but the cadi did not regard this threat, and he considered it merely as the effect of the resentment natural to all who lose their cause, and he thought he had performed his duty by acquitting one who was accused without any witnesses to prove the fact.

While the merchant was triumphing in his success over Ali Cogia, and indulging his joy at having made so good a bargain of the thousand pieces of gold, Ali Cogia went to draw up a petition. And the next day, having chosen

341

the time when the caliph should return from midday prayers, he placed himself in a street which led to the mosque, and when he passed, held out his hand with the petition. An officer to whom this function belongs, who was walking before the caliph, instantly left his place and came to take it, that he might present it to his master.

As Ali Cogia knew that it was the usual custom of the Caliph Haroun-al-Raschid, when he returned to his palace, to examine with his own eyes all the petitions that were presented to him in this way, he therefore followed the procession, went into the palace, and waited till the officer who had taken the petition should come out of the apartment of the caliph. When he made his appearance he told Ali Cogia that the caliph had read his petition, and appointed the following day to give him an audience; and having inquired of him where the merchant

The caliph listening to the children's court

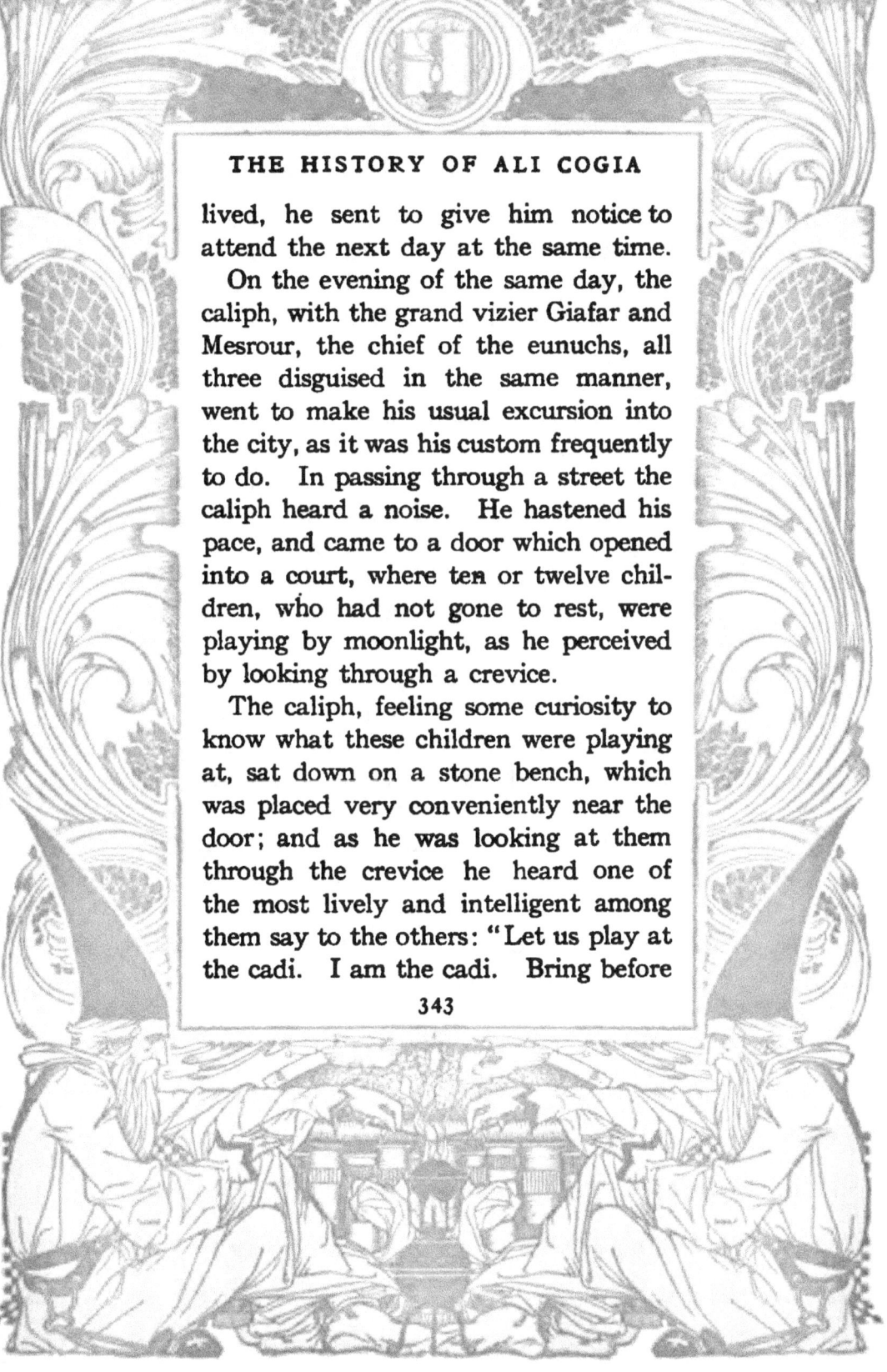

lived, he sent to give him notice to attend the next day at the same time.

On the evening of the same day, the caliph, with the grand vizier Giafar and Mesrour, the chief of the eunuchs, all three disguised in the same manner, went to make his usual excursion into the city, as it was his custom frequently to do. In passing through a street the caliph heard a noise. He hastened his pace, and came to a door which opened into a court, where ten or twelve children, who had not gone to rest, were playing by moonlight, as he perceived by looking through a crevice.

The caliph, feeling some curiosity to know what these children were playing at, sat down on a stone bench, which was placed very conveniently near the door; and as he was looking at them through the crevice he heard one of the most lively and intelligent among them say to the others: "Let us play at the cadi. I am the cadi. Bring before

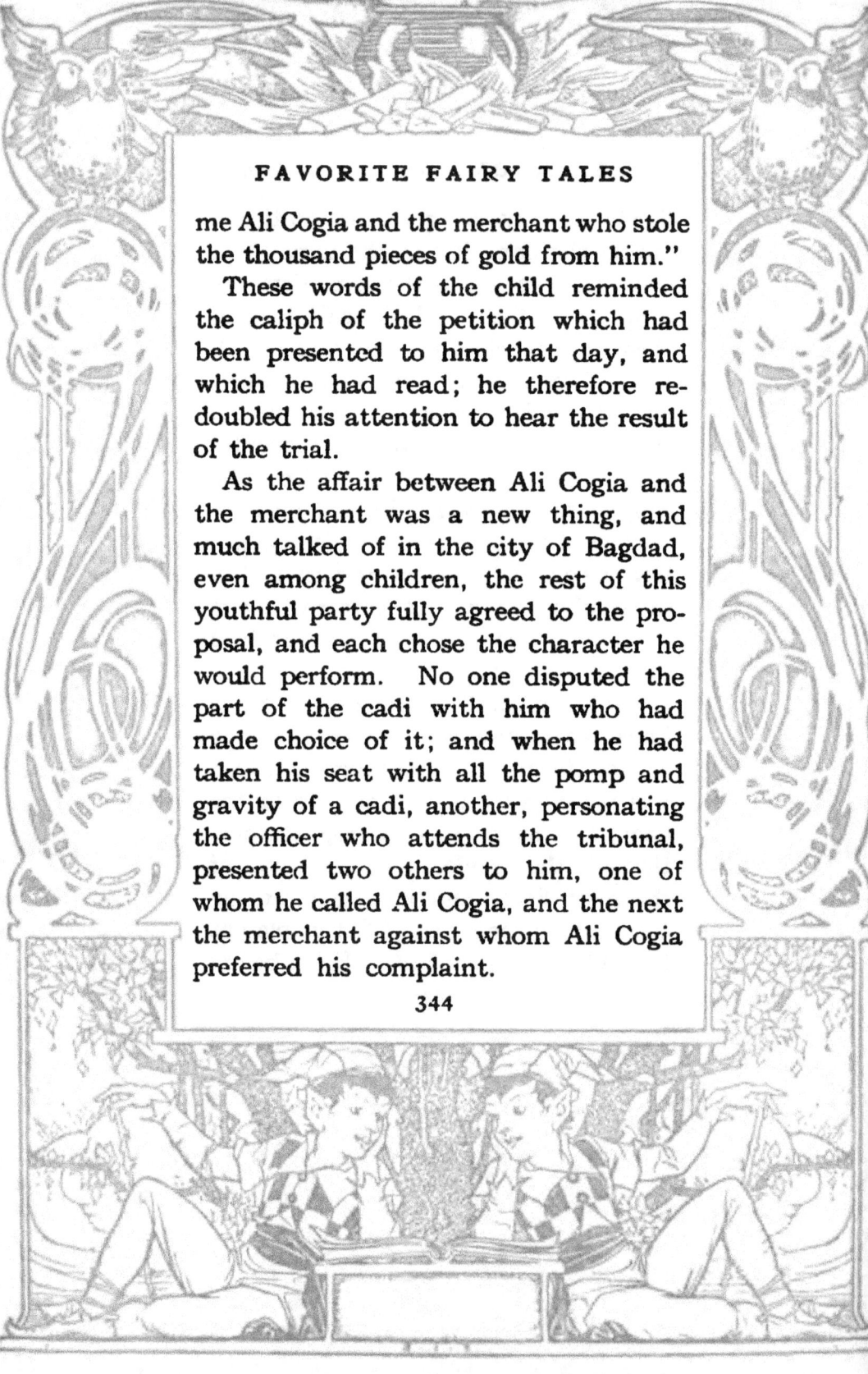

me Ali Cogia and the merchant who stole the thousand pieces of gold from him."

These words of the child reminded the caliph of the petition which had been presented to him that day, and which he had read; he therefore redoubled his attention to hear the result of the trial.

As the affair between Ali Cogia and the merchant was a new thing, and much talked of in the city of Bagdad, even among children, the rest of this youthful party fully agreed to the proposal, and each chose the character he would perform. No one disputed the part of the cadi with him who had made choice of it; and when he had taken his seat with all the pomp and gravity of a cadi, another, personating the officer who attends the tribunal, presented two others to him, one of whom he called Ali Cogia, and the next the merchant against whom Ali Cogia preferred his complaint.

344

The pretended cadi then addressed the feigned Ali Cogia. "Ali Cogia," said he, "what do you require of this merchant?" He who personated this character then made a low bow, and informed the cadi of the facts, and concluded by beseeching him to be pleased to interpose his authority to prevent his sustaining so considerable a loss. The feigned cadi, after having listened to Ali Cogia, turned to the merchant, and asked him why he did not return to Ali Cogia the sum he demanded of him. This young merchant made use of the same arguments which the real one had alleged before the cadi of Bagdad, and also in the same manner asked him to suffer him to swear that what he said was the truth.

"Not so fast," replied the pretended cadi; "before we come to swearing I should like to see the jar of olives. Ali Cogia," said he, addressing the boy who acted this part, "have you brought the

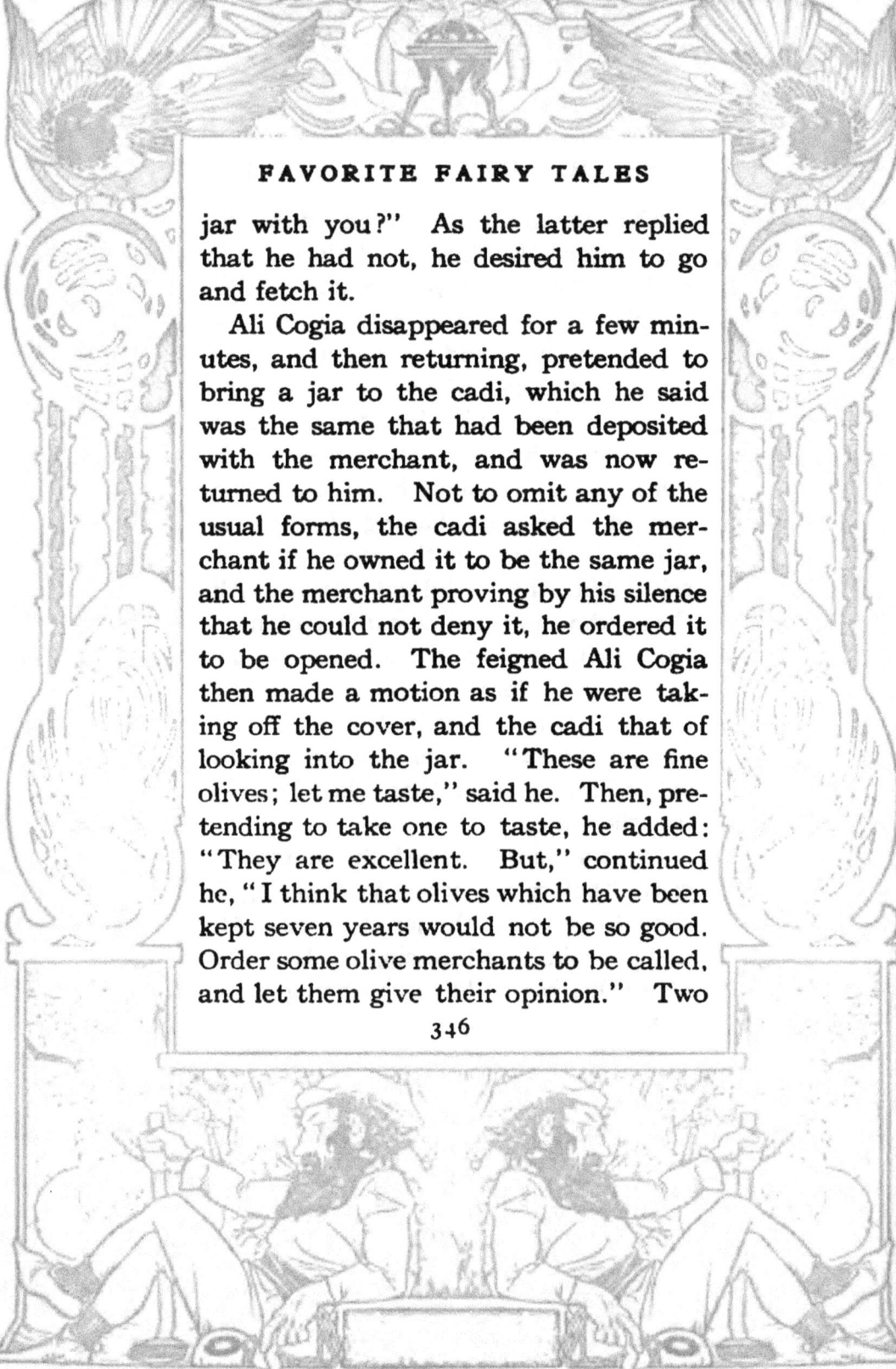

jar with you?" As the latter replied
that he had not, he desired him to go
and fetch it.

Ali Cogia disappeared for a few minutes, and then returning, pretended to
bring a jar to the cadi, which he said
was the same that had been deposited
with the merchant, and was now returned to him. Not to omit any of the
usual forms, the cadi asked the merchant if he owned it to be the same jar,
and the merchant proving by his silence
that he could not deny it, he ordered it
to be opened. The feigned Ali Cogia
then made a motion as if he were taking off the cover, and the cadi that of
looking into the jar. "These are fine
olives; let me taste," said he. Then, pretending to take one to taste, he added:
"They are excellent. But," continued
he, "I think that olives which have been
kept seven years would not be so good.
Order some olive merchants to be called,
and let them give their opinion." Two

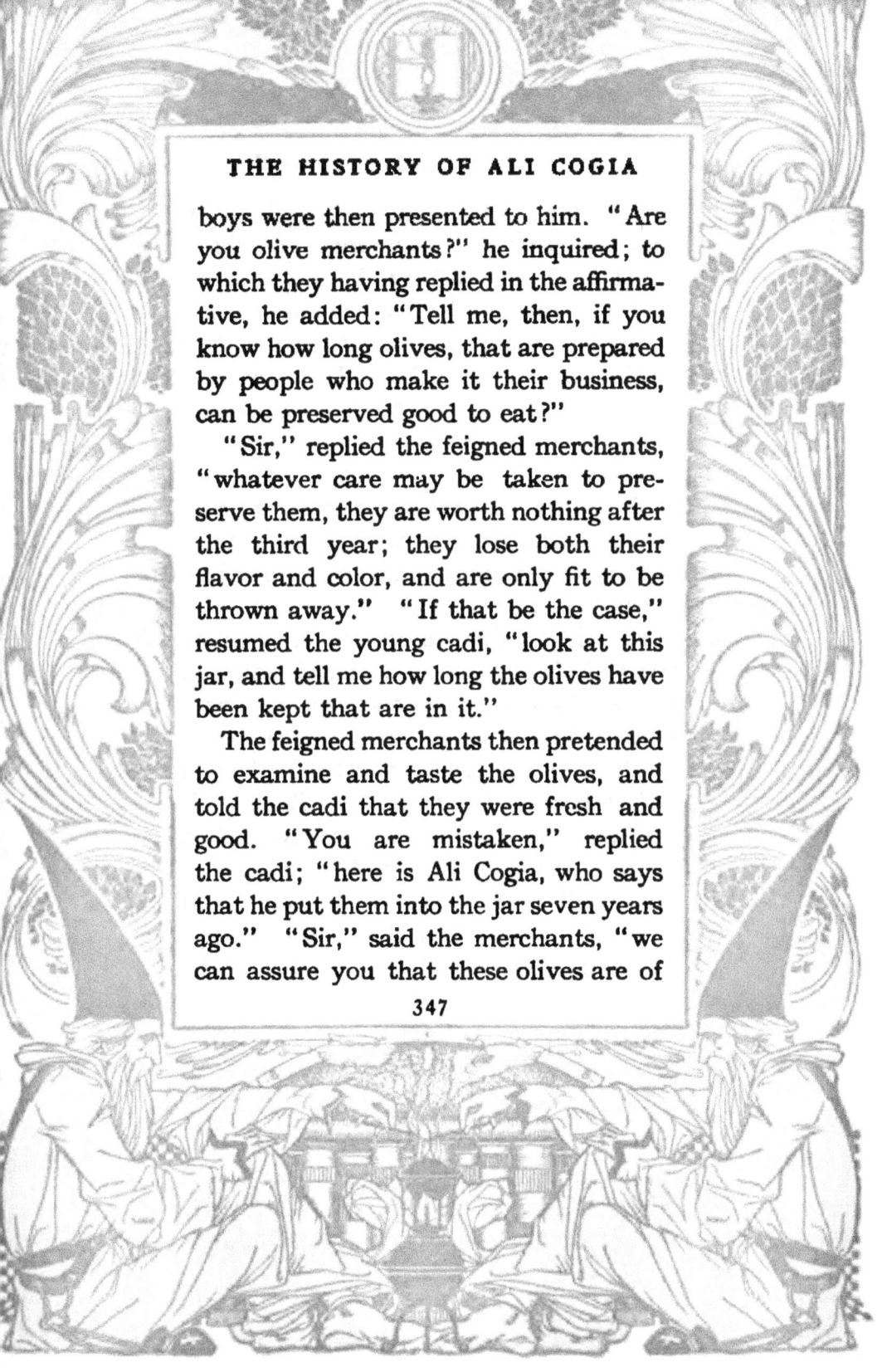

boys were then presented to him. "Are you olive merchants?" he inquired; to which they having replied in the affirmative, he added: "Tell me, then, if you know how long olives, that are prepared by people who make it their business, can be preserved good to eat?"

"Sir," replied the feigned merchants, "whatever care may be taken to preserve them, they are worth nothing after the third year; they lose both their flavor and color, and are only fit to be thrown away." "If that be the case," resumed the young cadi, "look at this jar, and tell me how long the olives have been kept that are in it."

The feigned merchants then pretended to examine and taste the olives, and told the cadi that they were fresh and good. "You are mistaken," replied the cadi; "here is Ali Cogia, who says that he put them into the jar seven years ago." "Sir," said the merchants, "we can assure you that these olives are of

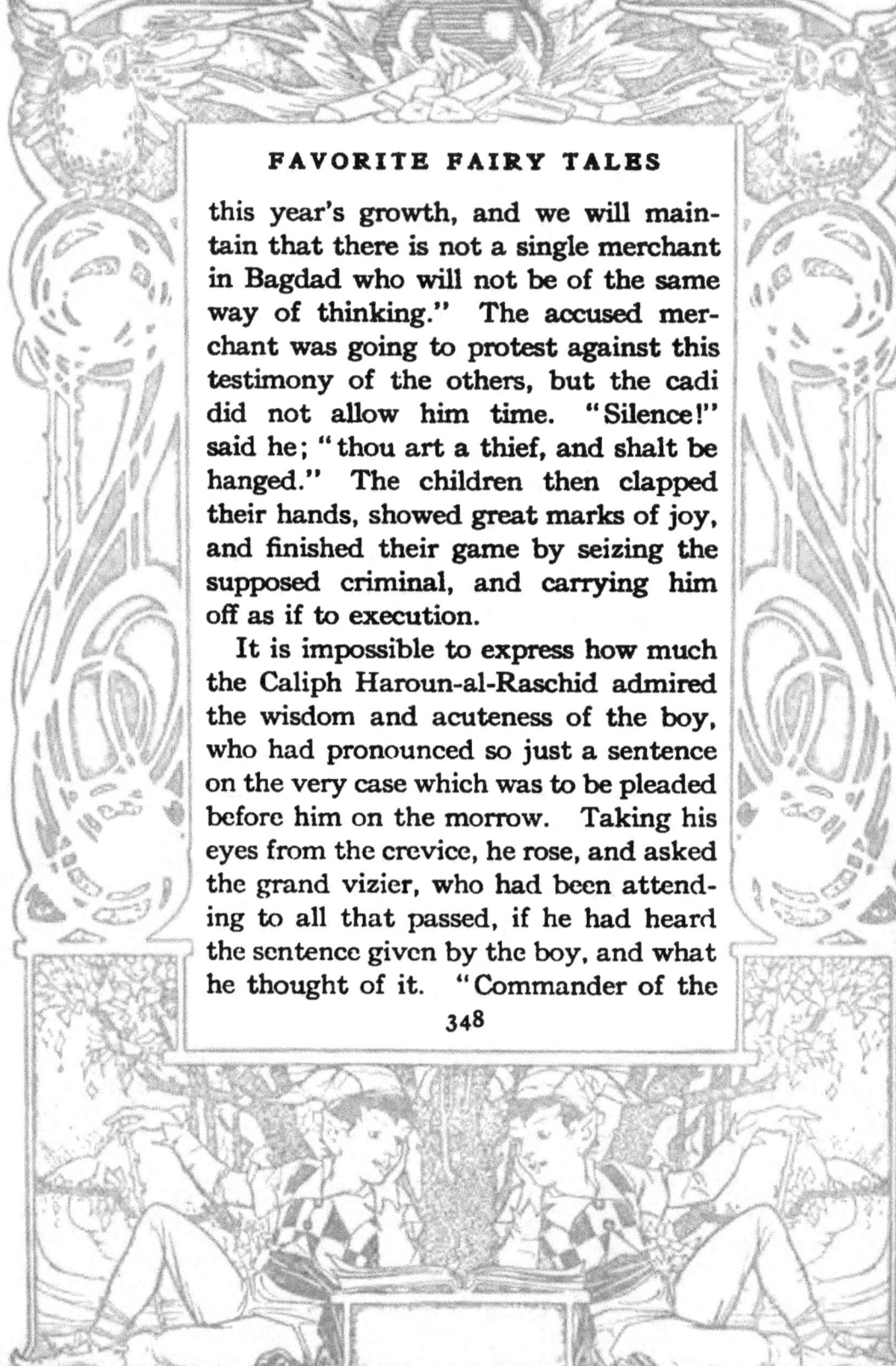

this year's growth, and we will maintain that there is not a single merchant in Bagdad who will not be of the same way of thinking." The accused merchant was going to protest against this testimony of the others, but the cadi did not allow him time. "Silence!" said he; "thou art a thief, and shalt be hanged." The children then clapped their hands, showed great marks of joy, and finished their game by seizing the supposed criminal, and carrying him off as if to execution.

It is impossible to express how much the Caliph Haroun-al-Raschid admired the wisdom and acuteness of the boy, who had pronounced so just a sentence on the very case which was to be pleaded before him on the morrow. Taking his eyes from the crevice, he rose, and asked the grand vizier, who had been attending to all that passed, if he had heard the sentence given by the boy, and what he thought of it. "Commander of the

Faithful," replied Giafar, "I am astonished at the wisdom evinced by this
boy at so early an age."

"But," resumed the caliph, "do you
know that to-morrow I am to give my
decision on this very affair, and that
the true Ali Cogia has this morning
presented a petition to me on the subject?"

"So I understand from your majesty,"
replied the grand vizier. "Do you
think," said the caliph, "that I can give
a juster sentence than that we have now
heard?" "If the affair be the same,"
returned the grand vizier, "it appears
to me that your majesty cannot proceed in a better manner, nor give any
other judgment." "Notice well this
house, then," said the caliph, "and
bring me the boy to-morrow, that he
may judge the same cause in my presence. Order the cadi, also, who acquitted the merchant, to be at the
palace, that he may learn his duty from

this child, and correct his deficiencies. I desire, too, that you will tell Ali Cogia to bring with him his jar of olives, and do you procure two olive merchants to be present at the audience." The caliph gave this order as he continued his walk, which he finished without meeting with anything else that deserved his attention.

On the morrow the grand vizier repaired to the house where the caliph had been witness to the game the children had played at, and he asked to speak to the master of it, but he being gone out, he was introduced to the mistress. He asked her if she had any children; she replied that she had three, whom she brought to him. "My children," said he to them, "which of you acted the cadi last night as you were playing together?" The eldest replied that it was he; and as he was ignorant of the reason for this question, he changed color. "My child," said the grand

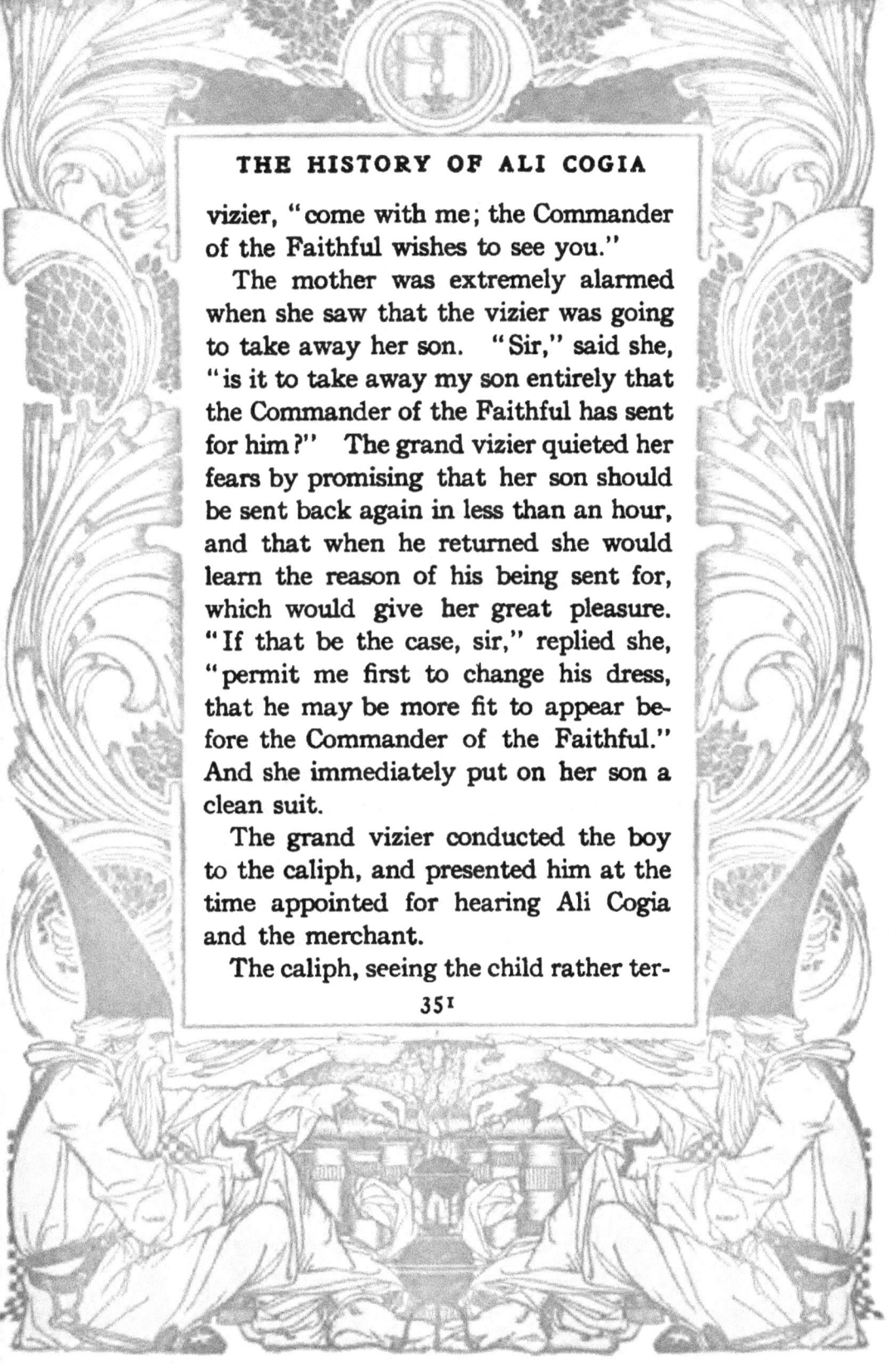

vizier, "come with me; the Commander of the Faithful wishes to see you."

The mother was extremely alarmed when she saw that the vizier was going to take away her son. "Sir," said she, "is it to take away my son entirely that the Commander of the Faithful has sent for him?" The grand vizier quieted her fears by promising that her son should be sent back again in less than an hour, and that when he returned she would learn the reason of his being sent for, which would give her great pleasure. "If that be the case, sir," replied she, "permit me first to change his dress, that he may be more fit to appear before the Commander of the Faithful." And she immediately put on her son a clean suit.

The grand vizier conducted the boy to the caliph, and presented him at the time appointed for hearing Ali Cogia and the merchant.

The caliph, seeing the child rather ter-

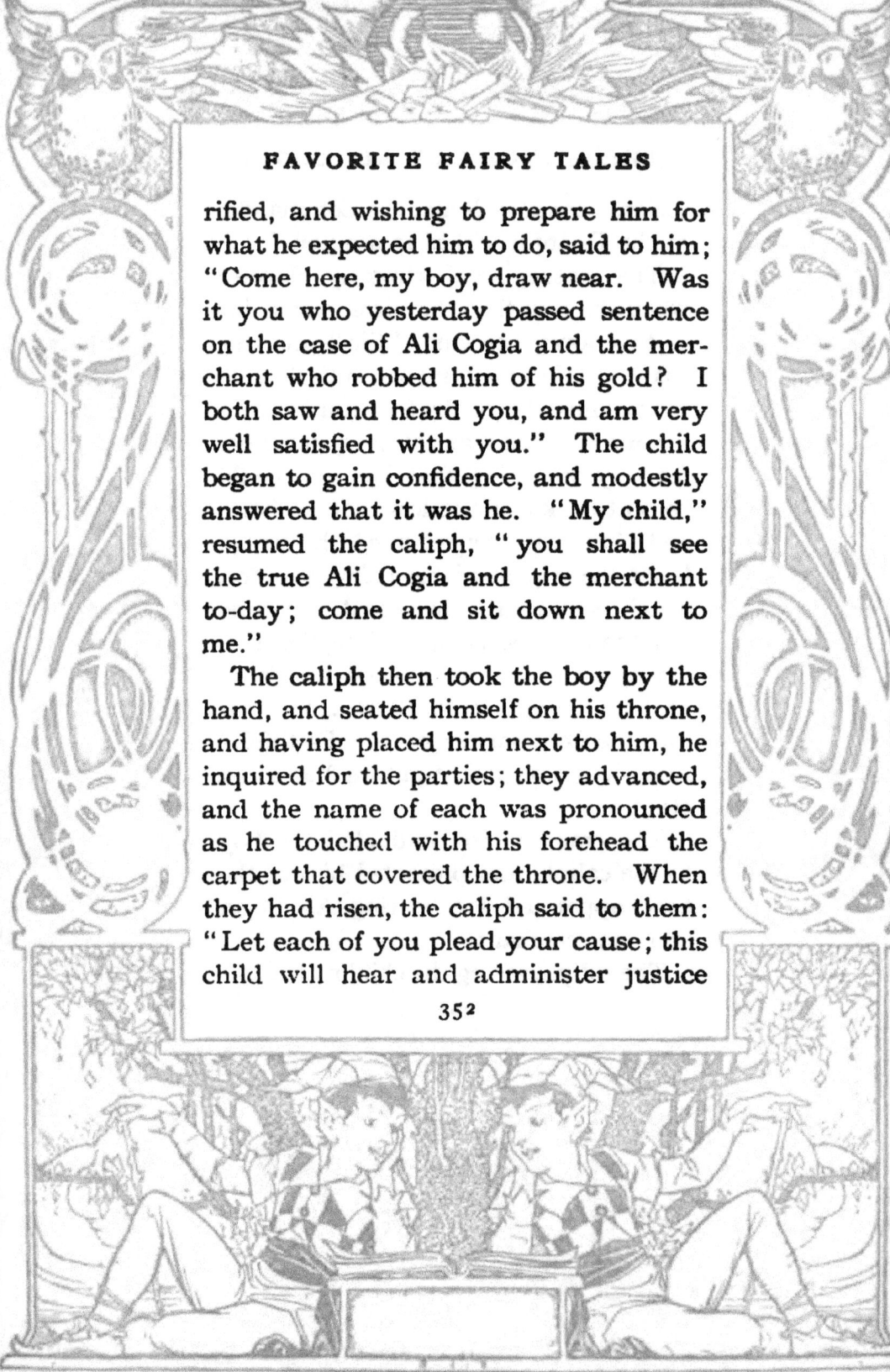

rified, and wishing to prepare him for
what he expected him to do, said to him;
"Come here, my boy, draw near. Was
it you who yesterday passed sentence
on the case of Ali Cogia and the merchant who robbed him of his gold? I
both saw and heard you, and am very
well satisfied with you." The child
began to gain confidence, and modestly
answered that it was he. "My child,"
resumed the caliph, "you shall see
the true Ali Cogia and the merchant
to-day; come and sit down next to
me."

The caliph then took the boy by the
hand, and seated himself on his throne,
and having placed him next to him, he
inquired for the parties; they advanced,
and the name of each was pronounced
as he touched with his forehead the
carpet that covered the throne. When
they had risen, the caliph said to them:
"Let each of you plead your cause; this
child will hear and administer justice

352

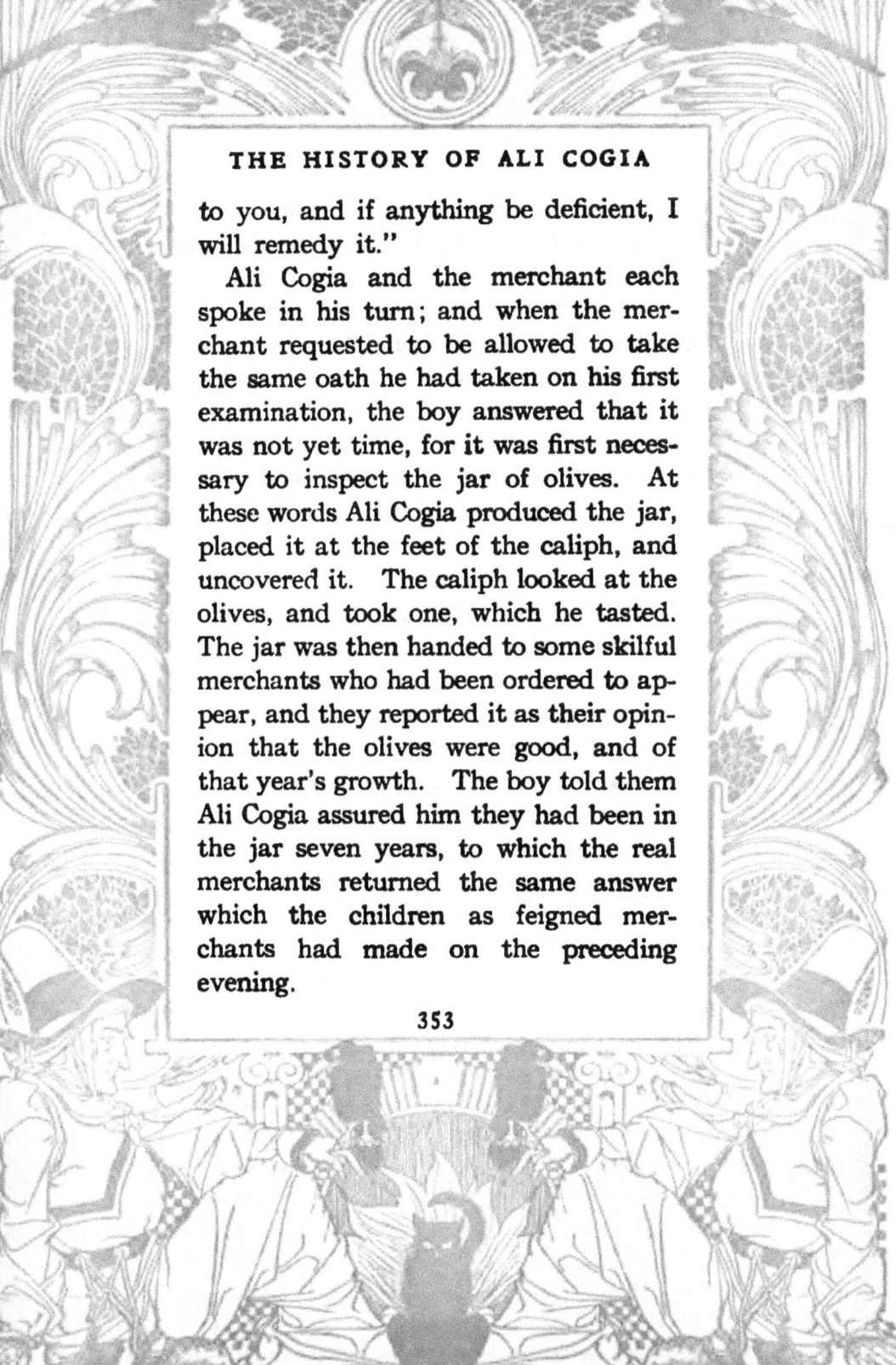

to you, and if anything be deficient, I will remedy it."

Ali Cogia and the merchant each spoke in his turn; and when the merchant requested to be allowed to take the same oath he had taken on his first examination, the boy answered that it was not yet time, for it was first necessary to inspect the jar of olives. At these words Ali Cogia produced the jar, placed it at the feet of the caliph, and uncovered it. The caliph looked at the olives, and took one, which he tasted. The jar was then handed to some skilful merchants who had been ordered to appear, and they reported it as their opinion that the olives were good, and of that year's growth. The boy told them Ali Cogia assured him they had been in the jar seven years, to which the real merchants returned the same answer which the children as feigned merchants had made on the preceding evening.

Although the accused merchant plainly saw that the two olive merchants had thus pronounced his condemnation, yet he nevertheless attempted to allege reasons in his justification; the boy, however, did not venture to pronounce sentence on him and send him to execution. "Commander of the Faithful," said he, "this is not a game; it is your majesty alone who can condemn to death seriously, and not I; I did it yesterday only in play."

The caliph, fully persuaded of the treachery of the merchant, gave him up to the ministers of justice to have him hung; and this sentence was executed after he had confessed where the thousand pieces of gold were concealed, which were then returned to Ali Cogia. This monarch, in short, so celebrated for his justice and equity, after having advised the cadi who had passed the first sentence, and who was present, to learn from a child to be more exact in

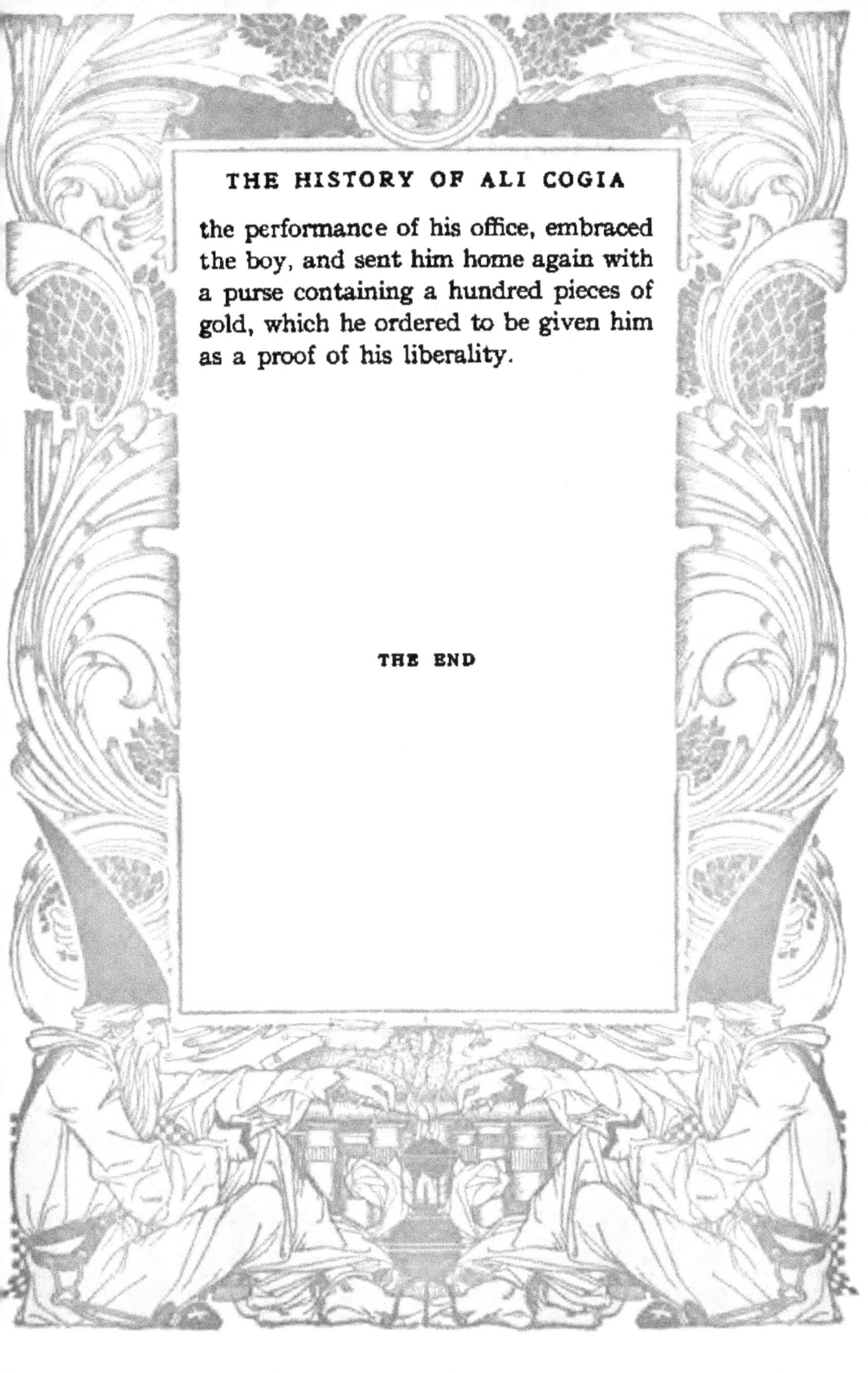

THE HISTORY OF ALI COGIA

the performance of his office, embraced the boy, and sent him home again with a purse containing a hundred pieces of gold, which he ordered to be given him as a proof of his liberality.

THE END

www.ingramcontent.com/pod-product-compliance
Lightning Source LLC
Chambersburg PA
CBHW060811030726
47503CB00002B/435